"Danger... drama... suspense... adventure... moral courage... these are the elements of legends and heroes, of daring men and sturdy women who stared adversity in the face and would not bow before it.

"In *Adele*, Elisha Wahlquist skillfully weaves these age-old threads into a grand tapestry using the backdrop of the French Revolution to create a story on an epic scale, providing a fresh perspective on this convoluted period in European history, and giving a subtle, sensitive commentary on the controversies of our own time.

"Against this framework, the main characters shine like stars against midnight, delivering unique points of reference and inspiring, godly role models for boys and girls alike who peruse the pages of this novel.

"In an age when so much good has been forgotten or forsaken, *Adele* will help rouse a new generation to take up their weapons and fight for godliness and goodness in a corrupt world."

— Karen Spangler, writer

"*Adele* is a great way to learn in depth about the French Revolution—not just what happened during the days of the guillotine, but what led up to and caused the horrific slaughters. It didn't happen without warning and the recital from a young ladies' viewpoint adds unique suspense to the history of this dangerous time. Woven in with the historical happenings is the story of family striving to do the right thing despite the difficulties."

— Elizabeth Ehlinger, homeschooler

"...a stirring tale, written in a classic manner, yet simple enough for the average reader.... I gained new insights into the people of the Revolution. There are strong lessons and the gospel message is woven in. Recommended for children (age 12 and above) and adults!"

— Melissa Merritt, blogger

Adele

Two Girls. Two Paths. One Revolution.

* * *

* * *

Adele

Two Girls. Two Paths. One Revolution.

by Elisha Ann Wahlquist

* * *

Adele: Two Girls. Two Paths. One Revolution.
Copyright 2014, Elisha Ann Wahlquist
www.untaintedbytheworld.com
First Printing, Summer 2014

Published by BookLocker.com, Inc., Bradenton, Florida.

ISBN: 978-1-63263-552-5

Description: Two cousins follow different paths as the French Revolution comes to a head, bringing destruction and death—which path is right?

Printed in the United States of America on acid-free paper.

* * *

TO MY MOTHER
AN INSPIRATION, ENCOURAGEMENT, EXAMPLE

* * *

***

Contents

***

* * *

"All circumstances taken together,
the French revolution is the most astonishing that has hitherto happened in the
world. The most [staggering] things are brought about,
in many instances by…the most ridiculous modes,
and apparently by the most contemptible instruments.
Everything seems out of nature in this strange chaos of levity and ferocity,
and of all sorts of crimes jumbled together with all sorts of follies.
In viewing this monstrous tragicomic scene,
the most opposite passions necessarily succeed and sometimes mix with each other
in the mind: alternate contempt and indignation,
alternate laughter and tears, alternate scorn and horror."
—Edmund Burke,
<u>Reflections on the Revolution in France,</u>
winter 1790

"I die on the day when the People have lost their reason;
ye will die when they recover it."
— Lasource, a Girondin deputy, to the Jacobins who condemned him to death

* * *

Flight at Midnight

...Half-climbing, half-lifting herself out of the hole, Adele realized how real the danger was. To her left, a bonfire shot a great glow of light over the ornate garden. She glimpsed sprawling, moving figures, hearing their uncouth songs and laughter. Some reeled along the walkways with brazen maids. *They are so awfully close — what if....* She refused to think of it.

Suddenly there was a shout. The hedge bulged and broke; her father burst through, an arm around Grandpapa de Duret.

"They've seen us — fly!" he panted, half-supporting the older man as he hurried into the darkness.

Adele slowed long enough to make sure Berthe had Paulette, then her feet winged their way over the smooth turf with the others, while from behind erupted an enraged cacophony of shouts. Almost carrying Grandpapa de Duret, her father was guiding them across the coverless silver lawn towards the dark fingers of ornate woods to the left.

The Le Merciers were running through the artfully-spaced trees now: Adele felt a stitch beginning in her side. She had not run since she was a little girl, and felt horribly out of practice. Stray wisps of hair lashed her face. As she turned her head to shake them out of her eyes she saw their pursuers, lanterns flashing erratically. Even as she looked, one tumbled on a hassock and lay prone, shouting drunkenly for his comrades: his lantern had gone out. Another, puffing unsteadily, stopped to help him, and Adele's heart grew light with desperate hope. *If it comes to a fight, the odds are more even now....* But an instant later she remembered, *The horses! They will have them out of the stables by now. Then all is truly lost!*

They ran on through the forest, their breath catching in their throats, their weary legs half-tripping over uneven ground and underbrush. Above, the trees made dark, monstrous shapes. Their pursuers were hidden by the brush, but Adele could still hear their shouts. Her skirt caught on a clump of brambles, and she was forced to stop, panting, to wrench it free. The pounding of her heart sounded like pursuing hoofbeats....

BOOK THE FIRST

The Storm Gathers Strength

Loss

1.

My grief is great; but oh! greater far
Because I know not the Morning Star.
I grasp at meaning, and find instead
Deep, dark air and vacant bed.
                    — Ianthe

With volcanic rumbles, France stirred in her sleep as Spring burst upon the year 1786. The endless ocean, playing in the English Channel and bathed in the newly hot sun, hissed and roared along the coastline, throwing itself against the pilings of the *ville basse*, the lower city of Le-Havre-de-Grace. Leaving the docks and advancing over a packed jumble of gray-tiled roofs and tottering chimneys, one came upon the smooth stone beauty of the Le Havre Cathedral. The upper city perched on the cliffs above, with its wider streets and the villas of the rich.

Passing into the higher countryside beyond and winding on a rutted dirt highway past bent laborers in pale green fields, a traveler's eyes would fall naturally upon a pleasant chateau in extensive, wooded grounds. Set in its quarried stone face, an elegant array of windows and steep slate roofs struck a harmonious balance. Two short, peaked turrets on the ends surveyed the countryside.

In the garden below this spacious country house, a peasant with a scythe tended the lawn that lay level and large amidst vibrant flowers. The clean salt-tinged air poured itself jubilantly along the walks, caressing the graceful, low lines of the chateau. The joy of new life sung from every mute tongue of nature was contagious. After a cautious cough and a glance upward at the mullioned windows, the peasant was so far moved as to attempt a mumbled folk song.

But in the chateau there was one who could not appreciate the glory of the spring morning. Teased waves of brown hair shaded the pale countenance of a twelve-year-old girl, whose square jaw was softened by the rounded neckline of her full-skirted sapphire blue gown. She gazed upon the garden with red and unseeing eyes. Her merry world had been shattered by something deeper and more bewildering than anything she had ever known.

"Why? Why? Where has she gone?" burst from her lips. Clasping her hands, she stared out the window, a tear trickling down her rosy cheek. Almost inaudibly, she went on, "She is gone—dear, dear, patient *gouvernante*....How many times I teased her, or hid my books!" More diamond tears followed down a face unaccustomed to crying.

A scene from that morning flashed in her mind: her father, curled wig tied with a ribbon, pulling on his hunting gloves and pausing to listen to her earnest question. A grave look flashed across his lean face. Then, patting her on the head, he had said cheerily, "We cannot know. We must light candles for her and pray to the saints, and...and hope she did enough good, Adele." She remembered swarthy Denis, her father's *valet-de-chambre*, standing nearby and saying with a wink, "Madame Adele, don't worry your pretty head about it—life is too short. Enjoy yourself now, while you can." *Why does he wink at me so?* she asked herself.

She thought of her father's words, and her youthful voice rose with a new tone, despair. "But how *can* I know? How can anyone know if they have done enough good? No one can tell me!"

A speckled brown song thrush fluttered close to the window, its flashing under-wings diverting her attention. She followed its erratic course over the lush garden until it landed on one of the surrounding hedges. Then her thoughts wheeled back to the subject wrenching her heart.

"We must try and try and *try* to be good," she murmured. "But...one must still go to that terrible place, Purgatory, to atone....Did not Father Lefebvre say so?" She shuddered. "But why—why would she be there? She was so *good*..."

She seemed to see the petite, upright figure of her *gouvernante* Marie, taking the daily stroll with the children. Adele remembered covertly trying to copy her elegant carriage. Her stiffly laced and boned blue gown made her kind blue eyes look even brighter. Adele's sister Olivie, her younger by two years, strolled nearby, her dress a green miniature of Adele's and the *gouvernante's*. Four-year-old Charles—nicknamed Charlot—pranced up the path ahead. He was still in the loose, long dress that babies wore—being not yet old enough to attain to a man's breeches and jacket. A manservant in their family's green-and-white livery brought up the rear of the small procession.

Coming around a bend in the tree-lined path, they encountered a haggard, thin peasant woman resting wearily in the shade of the high hedges lining the road. Her tanned, wrinkled face was cradled in roughened hands. Her elbows rested on her knees.

"How, now, you lazy serf! What are you doing on the marquis' grounds? A blighted beggar, I'll be bound!" the manservant exclaimed roughly, advancing upon the woman. She started up, fear giving strength to her feeble frame.

The children gathered around their *gouvernante* with wide eyes. She stepped forward with lovely compassion. "Jacques, she is doing no harm," she remonstrated gently. "She does not seem the usual importunate beggar. Can you see how weary she is? I am sure she but wandered off of the highway to rest in the shade." Her irresistible eyes were fixed on the manservant. He backed away, saying to the peasant woman in a subdued tone, "I suppose you may pause here for a moment—but then you must move along." The woman still cowered, and Adele remembered how Marie had bent forward, the sun shining on the powdered curls of her wig, and tucked some coins into the woman's gnarled hand.

Dear gouvernante…how I shall miss her! Adele's eyes filled again as the scene faded.

Anonymous

A slow step echoed in the hall without, and Adele drew back into the curtains. In a moment, a stout, elderly gentleman entered. The most noticeable features about his fleshy face were his receding chin and hard, twinkling eyes. His knee-length, plum velvet coat was adorned with large gold buttons, and he wore a plum cockade in the fusty hat topping his powdered wig. Adele rose with a curtsey.

"Ah! I thought I would find you here, *ma chérie*." He came over and sat down on a chair, richly carved with pomegranates and leaves. His eyes noticed the harp in the corner. "You are not practicing, eh?"

"No, Grandpapa des Cou."

"Ah—you do not have the heart for it, *n' est-ce pas* (isn't this true)?"

She looked into his eyes with an appealing directness. "How I miss dear *gouvernante*—practicing only makes it worse! Grandpapa, if only I could know what has become of her! She is gone; where is she?"

"Well, *chérie*," he shrugged, "'tis a deep question, and wiser heads than yours have wrestled with it." Seeing she was waiting for more of an answer, he continued, "I am sure your father and the priests would say you should pray to the Virgin Mary for her soul—your father has already commanded a special Mass to be said for her."

Her quick perception caught something indefinable behind his words. "You attend Mass, Grandpapa. Do you not believe what the priests say?"

"Oh," he replied hastily, "the Church is a bulwark of social respectability—never forget that, *ma chérie!* Do your duty, go to church; you must retain a good social standing." He laughed faintly, then said, "However, as for believing it all…well, Reason and Self-evident clarity are my criterion of truth. Has Felicienne—has your mother—introduced you to Descartes and Locke?"

"Yes, Grandpapa."

"Good, good. Yet I suppose there is no need for haste; you are only twelve years," he said, half to himself. Then he looked straight at her. "Now, remember this, *chérie*. You are Madame Adele Helene de Coquiel di le Mercier, a peeress in France. From your mother's side, a des Cou. *Data fata secutus*—follow the destiny allotted. Put your chin up, remember the world is yours to rule, and act worthy of your blue blood."

Self-satisfied, he patted her silk-covered shoulder, repeated "*Data fata secutus*," and arose, leaving Adele to new and strange reflections.

~*~*~

In her costly boudoir at the other end of the long chateau, a young woman of two-and-thirty fussed at her red-haired chambermaid. "Can you not you tie my laces more adroitly, Berthe?!"

Darting an irritated glance at her mistress' back, the maid murmured a subservient apology: "Pardon, Madame Félicienne de Coquiel di le Mercier." Arranging the white scarf in the low neckline of the flowered gown, she fastened the ends with a jeweled pin. As the finishing touch, she fixed a feathered chapeau atop the marquise's high, teased hairstyle.

"There—finally, you have finished!" her mistress exclaimed. Swishing quickly from the gold and white room, she paced down the lengthy hallway beyond. The stiff portraits and aureate statuary lining the hall merited nary a glance from her tempestuous eyes.

Usually hers was a warm and loving disposition, but the death of her daughters' *gouvernante* had ransacked the depths of her heart. She had found in the *gouvernante*, Marie, a sympathetic confidante, a friend to take the place of her sister Juliette, who had long since moved with her husband, Jean de Lobel, to Paris. Now Marie was gone—how sudden it had been! And not even time for the final rites! Félicienne could not find solace or comfort, and had taken to

storming her world with sorrow's wind and rain.

Passing by a half-open door, Félicienne beheld her eldest daughter inside. On impulse, she entered. The girl looked up from a book by Locke and curtseyed deeply.

"Adele, 'tis not your usual time for study."

The girl flushed. "No, Mother; but I asked Grandpapa about *gouvernante*—"

Her mother interrupted, "Oh, I wish I could believe she is..." then trailed off.

Adele turned questioning eyes on her mother's despairing face. Half to herself, Félicienne continued, "Father taught me Locke, Voltaire, and the others—if, as they say, something is true only if it is reasonable, then how could the hereafter be true? It is not self-evident or clear..." She paused, noting her daughter's agitation, and took Adele's hand. "Life is fleeting—I suppose we who can should enjoy it, for afterwards is nothingness, as far as I can tell. Live now; be gladsome today, Adele, for it is all we have."

As she turned away, Felicienne murmured to herself, in tones of agony, "Afterwards is nothingness—oh, Marie! can you be *nothing* now? You, who last week were living and enjoying life…now gone…*gone?*"

~*~*~

As the silent weeks dragged on, the thin crust of Time formed upon the wound, but mere distance did not bring true healing. Adele noticed that her mother grew more languid and withdrawn. She, who before would sit for hours in the garden with her children and *gouvernante*, and was always involved in the gaieties and parties of the aristocracy, now seemed distracted and tired. Adele fretted in childlike silence at these changes. Little things perplexed her, such as the fact that her mother did not lace up her conical bodice as tightly at the waist. Other things, too…

On one of these lackluster days, Adele, bright Olivie, and toddling Charles were passing through the spacious entryway with Berthe and their escorting manservant when their older brother entered from the opposite direction. Honore was a handsome, well-built youth of fourteen years, with deep brown hair under his tricorn and emerald eyes shining above his white *cravate* and ivy-green waistcoat. He was followed at a familiar distance by a servant-lad, Marcel Martin. Befitting his station, the latter's long figure was clothed in a plain brown jacket and knee breeches, while his tan waistcoat was without the elaborate embroidery of Honore's. He bowed as they approached the girls and Charlot.

"Going out for a stroll?" Honore inquired, with a lively glance. He was only two years older than Adele, but the younger ones thought him very old and important.

"Yes," Olivie answered, bestowing a bright smile upon Marcel. The son of a trusted retainer, he had almost gained a brotherly status despite the difference in rank.

Little Charles looked up at Honore. "Can you come, 'Ore?"

Shrugging, Honore turned to Marcel, who merely looked careless and inattentive. "I think that project can wait a bit," he said, half to himself, then looked at his expectant brother and said, "*Chaque chose en son temps*—each thing in its own time, as Benoit says; yes, I will come, Charlot."

The toddler clapped his chubby hands, Olivie gave a few skips despite Berthe's censoring eye, and even Adele's face brightened. Long-faced Marcel came along without being asked; he was Honore's languid shadow.

The sky was no brighter and the air no fresher, but a spirit of merriment and life fell upon the party. Olivie's brunette eyes sparkled.

8

Though she remembered to keep to a ladylike pace, her rosy mouth quite ran away with her, full of exclamations and odd little tid-bits of things that Charlot or her lap-dog Leon had done. Adele, sobered by her recent deep grief, was content merely to walk beside Honore and enjoy his unusually-pleasant mood. Of late he had spent much time with several other marquis' sons, and had become stiflingly supercilious around his siblings.

However, Olivie's sallies were too much to be borne with an indifferent face; "…so Leon went chasing after the mousie, but it popped right into a hole—and while he was sitting there, growling like he was a fierce lion, it popped out of another crack and raced right by his tail! He looked so offended, I almost burst! And then he went tearing off across the yard after it…." The whole group was aglow with smiles. Marcel even quickened his lazy gait to keep up with the darting Charlot. Berthe paid no attention to how far they had gone, and was as surprised as any of them when the gatehouse opening onto the highway loomed ahead.

"Can we walk a bit longer, please, Berthe?" Olivie pleaded. "It is such a pleasant day—"

"—and we finished our lessons betimes this morning," Adele added.

Berthe wavered. "Did not Master Honore say he had something to attend to?"

"A mere trifle," he replied. "Marcel and I will have time for it later." Turning to Charlot, he cried, "Forward—march!"

"March!" echoed Charlot loftily, strutting onward. The affected stiffness of his chubby legs made the other children laugh.

When they neared the little stone guardhouse they were still giggling. Then they noticed an older man, staff in hand, standing wearily in the road. The guard in charge of the gateway was briskly ordering him away; "Off with you! You say that you know the Marquis? *Ma foi!* [My faith!] You cannot pull the wool over my eyes, you tatterdemalion! On foot, and dressed like that, to say you are a friend of the Marquis!" He broke into a loud guffaw.

The older man, dressed in worn clothing that had seen better days, answered quietly, "*L'habit ne fait pas le moine*—the clothes do not make the man, my good fellow. Let me pass, and it will be as I say. If your master is indeed De Coquiel di le Mercier, I have reason to believe he will be glad—very glad—to see me, and wroth with you for preventing me."

"Bah!" the guardsman brandished his pike. "Like as not you have come looking to pinch a goblet or two, like the vermin who have overrun the country, calling themselves beggars! Away, I say—"

He was cut short by Honore. "What is this?" he asked, with as much disdain and the deepest voice that his fourteen years would allow.

"Ah, Master de Coquiel di le Mercier!" The guardsman struggled to keep from sneering at the pompous stripling. "I am shooing away this beggar who is trying to gain access to your worshipful father."

A gush of feeling overwhelmed Adele at the sight of the meek, frail man, who had laid a trembling hand on the stone coping. An unbidden picture of her dear *gouvernante* flooded her mind. Unconsciously she stepped to Honore's side, asking, "Is he really a beggar?"

"I am sure of it, Madame de Coquiel di le Mercier," the guard began.

"Yes, send him away," the manservant chimed in. He gave a knowing gesture, rubbing his fingers over imaginary *louis*. "He wants money, from the looks of him."

Honore hesitated; latent feelings of resentment arose as he remembered how his haughty friends chaffed him for his acquiescent "greenness" in dealing with servants. *Why are these mere canaille trying to give me, a De Coquiel di le Mercier, advice?* Setting his jaw, he addressed the man himself.

"Sirrah, what is your name? Are you a beggar? I heard you mention my father."

The traveler looked at the young man, and his weathered face wrinkled into a tired smile. "My name, young sir, is Francis Parrain de Duret." The young and old faces watching him looked blank, and he went on, speaking very slowly and fishing in his wallet for something, "Many — many years ago, when I was a young man, I went to the Paris University — you know, the Sorbonne — with a grand — grand fellow-student, Johan Antoine de Coquiel di le Mercier. And —"

Suddenly, he slumped to the ground, his large wallet falling from his back.

"A vagabond, as I said," began the guardsman in his gruff, hardened voice, "See, he has fainted from fatigue or hunger." But Marcel had already sprung to the man's side, and Honore was not far behind.

"Of a surety, we must bring him to the house," Honore said. "He may be telling the truth — he mentioned my grandfather's name."

The menservants looked surly enough, but one was turning back to the chateau for a cart when one rumbled in the gateway, driven by a rough peasant. They lifted the inert form into the dray, and Marcel placed his wallet beside him.

"Drive him carefully to the house, and have Marthe take care of him," Honore commanded. The peasant clucked to the carthorse and the little group turned to follow it down the avenue. All, that is, except one. Little Charlot ran to the spot where the man had fallen.

"Look! Look, Adele!" he cried. A gold object glinted from his upraised hand. The siblings turned—Marcel, Berthe, and the manservant stopped unwillingly.

"What is it, Charlot?" asked Adele.

"The man—he drop this!" The small boy toddled over to where they stood.

Adele stooped to look at the circular, smooth object. "A ring!"

"And—look—our crest!" cried Olivie, holding it to the light. "He must have dropped it when he fell."

"I did notice that he was trying to get something out of his wallet," Honore mentioned. "Mayhap this was it." He smiled down at the four-year-old looking eagerly up at them. "Good find, Charlot! We would have missed this if it hadn't been for your sharp eyes!" He threw a parting remark to the guard as they turned once more for the chateau: "So, Jules, this certainly sheds new light on *your beggar.*"

The manservant lingered behind for a moment at the guard hut. "Our fine little lord always manages to get in the last word," he grumbled.

"Ay, the swine—they lord it over us," the other snarled. "They say, 'Jules, keep vagabonds from entering the grounds,' and then—*voila!*—'Jules, how base of you to prevent this beggar from entering.' *Ma foi!*" He spat on the ground.

The manservant turned for the chateau. "Mayhap the tables will turn some day," he returned, "and then we shall see who is the better—the dogs!"

"Hist, man! Guard your tongue!" The men started, and their eyes fell on Denis, their master's valet, who had just ridden through the gate. He eyed them with mingled derision and humor. "'Tis quite fortunate for you that it was I instead of the marquis who heard those words." He savored their fearful expressions. Before spurring his steed down the avenue toward the chateau, he added, "Though there are haply more who share your opinions than you know."

Adele happened to glance back at that moment. Though she was halfway down the avenue and could not hear what was said, there was something about Denis' attitude that did not seem to fit his usual respectful manner. She tucked it away in the file of his other little inexplicable doings, to pull out and mull over later—*Perhaps with Honore; if his mood holds.*

~*~*~

The room was cool and shadowy. Deep and intricate plaster moldings ran around its doorframes and high ceiling, while gilded wooden furniture was placed artfully in the open space beside the high-posted bed. Adele and Olivie sat down circumspectly on a curved, elegant sofa. White upholstery contrasted with its dark carved cherry frame—the girls made a lovely picture on it with their green and rose embroidered gowns of stiffly shaped silk.

"There—we are dressed for dinner, and have a few moments to ourselves," Adele said, positioning herself. Her posture had a sort of rigid gracefulness—the fruit of many hours of balancing a book on her head, the accepted method to achieve the "proper" posture.

"I wonder how our poor traveler is faring," said Olivie, arranging the white scarf that lay across her shoulders and was pinned in front by a vibrant roseate posy which matched her dress.

"I am sure we will know before dinner," Adele answered. She stared off into space, then remarked, "Olivie—were you not surprised by Marcel? I never saw him move so quickly. He positively leapt to that man's side when he fell. Yet until that moment I had thought he was not interested—as usual."

"Yes; he did not seem to be paying the least bit of attention," Olivie confided, "until then…"

"Dinner, Mesdames," a servant said, rapping on the door. She curtseyed deeply as the girls stepped out into the wide corridor.

"How is the sick man, Marthe?" Olivie asked.

"The man? Ah! You mean the man who arrived today? He came to himself, but became mightily worried about some token—some ring—that he said he must have lost."

"Oh!" both girls cried. Adele added anxiously, "Did someone tell him Charles found his ring in the grass? Honore has it now."

"I certainly did not, Mesdames—I know nothing about such trifles." Then noting the girls' worried faces, she said kindly, "You must go to dinner, but I will ask Master Honore and give it to the man, if you wish."

~*~*~

The blues and grays of evening were falling, and the last rays of the expiring sun fell through a mullioned window on the seated marquise. The painted flowers on her cream silk dress glowed, but not as brightly as the ruby lips of the lady. In a moment, her husband entered and stood beside her settee. His tall, active frame was clad in an embroidered banyan, a loose robe of exotic colors. Replacing his usual wig was a brightly colored dressing cap. His face was handsome and young—he was but thirty-two—and his eyes were keen hazel.

Felicienne looked up with some interest in her youthful face. "Have you heard the children's story?"

"Yes, Felicienne." His brow furrowed with thought. "I spoke to the man this evening—Monsieur de Duret, he says his name is."

"It is a curious tale. The children seemed to have arrived just in time to prevent his being turned away by that blockhead Jules." She pursed her lips.

"I know. Yet I was also inclined at first to doubt his story. However, there is truth in his eyes and face." He turned and seated himself in a nearby armchair. "He says that he and my father attended the Paris university, *La Sorbonne*, together, and became fast friends. When they graduated, they were forced to part—he traveling southward to his family seat, while my father returned here, to his estate. At their last parting, my father gave him a ring with our family crest. He says he received a letter a few years later from my father, in which he mentioned that his wife had borne a son, which they had named Francis Johan de Coquiel di le Mercier—Francis after this De Duret, and Johan after my father. After that, he heard no more. The few letters he sent over the years were not answered, and he assumed their replies had been lost or damaged in the mails."

"The ring adds a real element of truth," Felicienne mused.

"Yes. The few facts I know about my father bear out his story. Father and Mother died soon after I was born, which explains why his letters were never answered. This man, De Duret, was rather broken up by the fact that my father is dead—he had hoped against hope that such was not the case."

"How is his health? He fainted at the gate, I heard."

"Marthe says he is merely worn out from his journey and lack of food. He was traveling by coach, but it was attacked by those beggars which swarm like flies over France. They killed the coachman when he resisted, and turned out the passengers after taking all their money. He was left alone to make his way the best he could on foot, penniless and friendless. It was almost too much for him."

"Ah—those beggars! Thieves, and worse, they are! They are the scourge of the nation." Felicienne's lips were thin with annoyance.

"Perhaps he will be able to tell you more about your father, whom you know so little about."

"Yes, I suppose so," he shrugged. Then he added, "I offered Monsieur de Duret our hospitality, and he accepted—it seems he is alone in the world, and I am pleased to offer a roof to an old friend of my father. I am sure you will make him feel at home, Felicienne."

There was a short silence. He fingered the loose cuff of his robe before mentioning, "Felicienne, I am going on a hunting trip tomorrow with Du Sauchoy, Du Chemin and some others, and shall not be back for several days."

"You and your hunting—I believe you are married to it, instead of to me," Felicienne jested. But her face revealed the deeper hurt beneath.

Sensing deep waters and trying to turn the conversation, Francis said, "I noticed that you have been instructing the girls since the death of Marie. Have you thought of a suitable replacement *gouvernante* for them, Felicienne?" She dropped her flushing face, and he instantly knew he had said the wrong thing. "My dearest..."

"I just cannot bear the thought, Francis! I know...I know I should..." her voice trailed off in tears, and she buried her face in her white hands.

His expression said, "*Ma foi!* These women!" but he answered hastily, "*Ma cherie*, banish the thought until you can bear it. You are quite capable to teach the girls—I only thought to relieve you." He placed a hand on her shoulder.

She looked up into his strong face and said simply, "Thank you, Francis."

He answered with a tender expression. However, when the door closed, she heard the mutter of Denis' voice in the hall leading to her husband's room. Francis answered, "Yes, Denis, all must be packed and ready. I am leaving early tomorrow." The valet said something indistinguishable, and her husband replied, his voice growing fainter as he went into his room, "Ay, wolves! It shall be fine sport, if Du Sauchoy manages it well; and he says his gamekeeper is one of the best. I cannot wait..."

The voices faded away, and Felicienne murmured bitterly, "It is all he cares for! I—I am nothing!—merely a pet to appease, a distraction from his all-consuming passion." Her lips set in a firm, hard line. "My confidante gone, my husband obsessed with his sport, my life a weariness....But I must make the best of it. As my father would say, '*Au point ou on en est, autant faire les choses jusqu'au bout*—considering our situation, we may as well go along to the end.' I cannot wait until I can once again join the parties—perhaps—perhaps they will lift this dark mood…" She bowed her face in her hands and wept.

A People Called Huguenots

2.

Blessed is the man, whose strength is in Thee, in whose heart are Thy wayes.
They going through the vale of Baca [weeping],
make welles therein: the raine also covereth the pooles.
They goe from strength to strength, till every one appeare before God in Zion.
— Psalm 84:5-7, Geneva Bible

"Hi, there! Rouse up, and take our horses!" bellowed a large, loose man, tending to corpulence. His ruddy, sweating face contrasted sharply with his carefully powdered wig. He was the marquis du Sauchoy, the owner of the hunting lodge and surrounding forests.

There was a bustle of feet. The gentlemen swung out of their saddles while lackeys grasped the bridles of their sweat-flecked mounts to lead them away and walk them down. It was a brightly-colored group; blue, gold, and green shone in the hot sunlight. It had been a merrier sight in the early morn, when they had set out at the martial cry of the hunting-horn; now their festive outfits were mud-spattered, their horses lathered, and their wigs awry.

The gentlemen — three men and a lad of fourteen years — lounged into the hunting lodge, where they soon changed to fresh garments and collected themselves in the rustic parlor. On the unvarnished wood walls hung mounted trophies and scattered paintings of hounds and huntsman; above the vast and rough fireplace hung a gilded hunting horn. Despite the attempts to be provincial, the extensively-ornate style of that period was prominent in the highly polished and carved chairs, the plush sofa, and the gilt frames of the paintings. It was the late Baroque age of French architecture.

"It was rare sport, today," began Du Sauchoy, lolling on a chair underneath the great head of a stag.

"*Certes*, it was," replied Francis absently. "I must extend my thanks again to you, Du Sauchoy, for the opportunity. 'Tis not often that the wolves are so plentiful—your beaters knew their work well."

"I agree," said the third man, his square face breaking into a genial smile. "Thank you, Du Sauchoy. When we came upon that pack in the narrow glen, 'twas a stiff fight." He and his son, who sat nearby, shared the same thoughtful, serious brown eyes, which, however, could sparkle like nothing else when something touched their ready fancy.

"No thanks necessary, my friends," Du Sauchoy's small eyes shone. "When my gamekeeper informed me of the den there, I knew it was the place to drive them to bay."

"I am glad the beaters managed to turn them," Francis answered. "At first, I thought the brutes would manage to break through and disappoint us of our sport."

"Yes, those were a dicey few minutes; though well repaid by the fierceness of the wolves' attack upon us when they were finally headed back into the hollow. The lead wolf leapt nearly upon us before you dispatched him with a sword-thrust, Francis." Du Chemin was interrupted by a rapping on the door. "*Entrez.*"

"Sir, a messenger has just arrived from Chateau di le Mercier," a domestic announced.

Francis de Coquiel di le Mercier was on his feet before he knew it. Ever since the sudden news of Marie's death had been announced to him via messenger, he had been tense about news from home. "Show him in."

The manservant entered, his livery stained from hard riding. He bowed deeply, hat in hand.

"What news, Jacques?" asked Francis.

"Sir, here is the message." He proffered it in his thickened fingers.

Francis read it, then smiled. "Nothing to worry about, gentlemen," he said. "A mere announcement that my wife has safely delivered our latest little one: a girl." He added to himself, "We shall call her Paulette—Paulette Constance."

"Congratulations, Francis!" Du Sauchoy said heartily. "I am glad to hear that nothing is amiss. 'T'would be too bad to break up our hunting party early. You know I expect you and Du Chemin to spend at least three more days here. The game will afford grand entertainment."

Francis remembered the still reserve of his wife of late. "I shall certainly stay," he answered, and the conversation dropped.

A little later, their host departed on some trifle, and Francis sat brooding for a short space. The maddening coolness of his wife, the futility of the *gouvernante's* death, the building tensions with the peasantry, the low volcanic rumbles of deep problems in France — even his favorite sport could not drive these troubles away. *Today's hunt was exhilarating,* he thought to himself. *The thrill was high, the wolves fought fiercely; I made a skillful death-wound to the pack-leader as he lunged for my throat — what more could I want?* He leaned back further in his chair, toying with the golden watch chain drooping from his emerald waistcoat pocket. *Yet — yet even amidst the thickest excitement — there was — there is — an emptiness.* A line from Cowper arose to his mind:

> *Ask what is human life — the sage replies,*
> *With disappointment low'ring in his eyes,*
> *'A painful passage o'er a restless flood,*
> *A vain pursuit of fugitive false good,*
> *A sense of fancied bliss and heartfelt care,*
> *Closing at last in darkness and despair.*

He shook himself. *No; it cannot be. It cannot be all emptiness.* He forced himself to think this, for he felt the hollow hunger too keenly for comfort. *I must merely be tired tonight.* He glanced at Du Chemin and his son, talking in low tones. He knew they shared his fatigue. He remembered Tristan's youthful hunting efforts throughout the day — how he had ridden bravely after a wolf that had broken away into the brush. Yet on their faces was a deeper content than anything a hunt or outward pleasure could bring. He had never really noticed it before. But now, he was at leisure to really *see* into his own soul — and it was void of that inner peace he saw in them.

He mentally ran through a list, looking for some explanatory fact, some excuse for the other's happiness. *His estates are mayhap as ample as mine, tho' a bit poorer...wife plain....He must bear with his wife's mother, who* (Francis made a face) *is renowned for her sharp tongue and querulousness....No, nothing there.* Then, faintly, he remembered something Du Chemin had told him years ago. *He is a Huguenot — of course a quiet one, for Protestantism is none too graciously tolerated here...*

Francis caught a few of Du Chemin's words. "...France is facing perilous financial difficulties, and the long-oppressed peasantry are rising. No man has been able to propose a solution yet; I fear there will be be hard days ahead."

Tristan Du Chemin smiled at his father, and it was like a light had flooded the heavens to see such an open, loving, filial look. "Christ says,

'Lo, I am with you always, even unto the end of the world.' Oh how many times you have told me that, Father…"

An envious moodiness came over Francis. If only his son could be like this man's son; if only he himself could have the contentment of this man!

~*~*~

Honore strayed silently through the rococo halls of the chateau, his feet sinking into the luxuriant carpets. Marcel paced behind him with the quiet tedium of a servant. Outside, a steady, slow rain dripped from a spiritless sky. Honore's usual pastimes were out-of-doors — riding, hunting, and the like — and rainy days typically meant boredom.

Honore stared aimlessly at a large and ornate family portrait. Looking out from the painting were three figures. The first, his paternal grandfather, sat in a serious attitude: a curled, powdered wig framing a youthful face and steady green eyes. Seated nearby was his sweet-faced wife, only sixteen years old, wearing a stunning blue dress with enormous hoops, her towering, powdered hairstyle decorated with roses and azure ribbons. A tiny baby in a beribboned, lacy white gown was held in her lap. Honore remembered the story. Francis was that baby; his parents had died of a contagious disease soon after the portrait was completed, leaving Francis to be raised by relatives, far away from Le Havre…. The voices of two maids wafted out from a half-open doorway ahead.

"…the cook told him to begone, but the ragged rascal insisted on speaking with Denis — Master's personal valet!"

"*Ma foi!*"

"And — think of this, Marthe — Denis *greeted* the churl, and talked to him outside for a long time!"

"Oh?" the other voice tittered. "*Un chien vivant vaut mieux qu'un lion mort* — a live dog is worth more than a dead lion, they say." The voices died down as the maids moved to another part of the room.

Honore drew his brows together. *Why would Denis and that man talk together? It could be nothing — but yet again, Adele has mentioned other strange incidents….* He turned to Marcel, and saw in his face that he also had overheard. "We shall go and find my sisters."

It did not take long to find Adele and Olivie — they were seated with prim grace on a divan in the library. Adele was pretending to read a book. Her eyes wore a tearful, far-off look; Honore guessed she was thinking of her *gouvernante*, Marie. Even Olivie's usual vivacity seemed dampened by the monotonous rain.

19

With the merest touch of condescension, Honore related what he had heard, but soon thawed as Adele related in turn several little idiosyncrasies she had noticed lately about Denis.

Olivie, who had been listening intently, piped up with bright eyes, "What if we all spied on Denis? Then we could see what he is up to."

"I don't know if we would find out anything interesting," Honore remarked, a bit miffed that she had made the suggestion. Olivie's face fell and he conceded, "—however, it would be an amusing pastime when we have nothing better to do. We could be like the king's *espions* [spies] Father mentioned."

"And Marcel can help us!" Olivie said.

Marcel agreed. "I can go places and hear things that you cannot."

"Oh, let's," cried Adele, losing the last vestige of listlessness. "And, oh—we should have some system, some motion, to let each other know when we have discovered something interesting. Like—at the ball last night, Mother raised an eyebrow, like this, when she wanted Father to come over."

"*Bon!* A good idea, Adele! But what shall we—" Honore trailed off, trying to replicate Adele's easy eyebrow motion, and grimacing with the effort.

Olivie giggled. "Not that! Honore cannot do it discreetly!" Her brown eyes danced.

Pursing her lips, Adele adjusted an errant curl, and then with a slight, gracious motion, placed her hand back in her lap.

"That's it, Adele!" Honore cried. When the others looked puzzled, he said, "How about this?" He copied the motion she had made as she put her hand back in her lap—touching his thumb to his index and middle fingers. "That would be easy to make, and who would notice it unless they were looking for it?"

Marcel nodded his approval, and the girls both agreed.

"Father is gone often, and Denis goes with him, but they are at home now," Adele said.

"We shall start—Marcel and I will see where he is at present." Honore rose to his feet.

The girls stayed in the library, but gone was their former indifference—Adele stared out the window at the falling rain with a thoughtful expression in her eyes, while Olivie sat practicing their secret gesture *ad infinitum*.

~*~*~

It all began so simply.

One bright and sunny afternoon, Adele and Olivie were walking demurely down the hallway, needlework in hand, when they came upon Charlot and his nurse. Olivie burst into giggles, for Charlot had wound his blanket around himself so that only his mischievous blue eyes peeked out. His nurse attempted to lay hold on the blanket and Charlot turned to run, falling forward in his tangled drapery. At the same moment, Monsieur de Duret emerged from his room. Stepping forward, he caught the child. The nurse started forward with frightened apologies—any other guest would have scolded her sharply—but M. de Duret looked down at Charlot and merely said, "Be more careful, Master Charles." Then, noting the child's wrappings, his eyes took on a faraway look.

Bending down, the nurse tried again to take off the boy's encumbering blanket, but Charlot resisted. He tensed his little frame, opening his red mouth as a prelude to what would certainly have become a scream if Monsieur de Duret's voice had not broken in.

"Charlot, have you ever heard of the baby whose parents wrapped him up as you are now?" he asked.

The big blue eyes looked up questioningly, and the little mouth composed itself into a quiet, "No."

"Could you tell us, Monsieur de Duret?" Olivie asked.

His wrinkled face looked up with a smile. "Ah, I have more of an audience than I thought. Perhaps we should go out into the garden?"

They passed down the hall, into the vaulted entryway, and then into the parlor. Its large French doors opened onto the back terrace. Stepping out, they traveled down the shallow stone steps to the lawn with its dancing fountain.

Flowers blazed in careful geometric designs around the fountain: white, low-growing candy-tuff, pink Sweet Williams, and purpled blue Cantebury Bells. A high, walled hedge enclosed the lawn. Artfully placed marble benches offered nooks to stop and regard the views.

The focal point of the garden was a white, circular "folly." Its pale, "gothic" stone columns, bedecked with climbing roses, arched to join each other, creating eight door-like openings, while the whole structure was crowned with castle-like crenellation. The children oftentimes played in it, pretending to be their medieval ancestors. Such buildings, called "follies," were very popular in France and England at that time.

The little group was soon seated in the folly. Luxurious climbing roses drooped their sweet blossoms invitingly overhead. M. de Duret adjusted his powdered wig and began his story. "Almost one hundred years ago in France, a father and mother needed to flee secretly to England, for their lives and that of their small baby were in danger."

"Why were they in danger?" a voice asked, and Honore appeared on the path, stepping through one of the clipped arches in the hedge.

The older man looked up. "Well, Master Honore, they were Huguenots, and the king had decreed that it was unlawful to be a Huguenot in France." Seeing the children's wondering faces, he explained, "A Huguenot believed the Catholics taught heresy. They sought to worship God in spirit and truth, without the unbiblical trappings of Popery. But the king decreed that Catholicism was the religion of France and tried to force the Huguenots to deny their faith. He also kept them from leaving France." Old sadness tinged his face.

"But the baby?" Charlot asked. "The baby and blankets?"

M. de Duret seemed to draw himself out of the mists of memory. "Ah yes—the story. The baby's parents realized they needed to flee, to protect themselves and especially their child. If they stayed, the priests would seize him and raise him up to believe heretical doctrine! They thought very hard. How could they escape? They could disguise themselves, but what about the baby? He would give them away, for they were already suspected and watched. After much prayer, the Lord gave them a solution. One dark evening, the wife gave her baby a sleeping draught and then wrapped it up firmly in a formless cloth bundle. She tightly tied a string with a loop on one end to a corner of the fabric. Carefully, after dusk, they placed the bundle in the street gutter—have you seen one?"

"I have," said Olivie. "In Le Havre, in the middle of the street runs a deep gutter—it carries refuse." She made a face.

"Quite correct," returned Monsieur de Duret. "They placed their precious bundle in the gutter, and with beating hearts walked forward a few paces to the gate. The gendarme opened the gate for them: 'They would never leave without their baby,' he thought, 'They will be back.' It seemed an eternity to the anxious parents before the gate was barred behind them and the man went back into the guard-room. Then the two turned with sickening apprehension. Hands trembling, the father stuck his hooked walking-stick in the gutter that ran under the gate. After a few minute's anxious fumbling the stick caught the loop of string, and the bundle slipped safely along the gutter, under the gate, and into the parent's waiting arms. Oh! How glad they were, and how they praised God for His mercies!"

"I am sure they went straight to a church and paid for many Masses of thanksgiving to be said," Olivie said thoughtfully. "Perhaps in our grand cathedral in Le Havre de Grace."

"No, no," Monsieur de Duret smiled. "For they were Huguenots, and believed that God was not pleased with such trumpery. Instead, they thanked God with their whole hearts, knowing that He hears the prayers of even His most humble followers. They escaped to England where they could worship Him and raise their child in peace and with a good conscience."

Adele repeated mentally, *Knowing that God hears the prayers of even His most humble followers? Not just the priests?* Then, looking up, she asked aloud, "Can you tell us more stories, Monsieur de Duret?"

"Every day?" added Olivie, with a hopeful look in her bright eyes.

"I would be pleased to do so," he answered, "but I must ask your mother."

And Felicienne, who had watched the scene apathetically through the diamond panes of her boudoir window, was quite forward in her approval. Their guest had made a favorable impression from the first, and had been a ray of sunshine in many small ways. She murmured, "It will keep them quiet and entertained, and the fresh air is good for them."

So it began—simply, quietly—and became the most treasured time of the children's day, something they were careful not to miss.

~*~*~

Several months later, summer was at its height. The sun shone heavy and hot, and the marquis de le Mercier sighed with relief as he turned his horse into the tree-lined avenue which swept up to the chateau di le Mercier.

The marquis' pale blue jacket was long, trimmed with gold braid like his large hat. Its pretentious gilded buttons were merely for show; fashion dictated that coats meet only at the neck, then slope sharply away to display the embellished waistcoat. His waistcoat was a golden yellow, while where tight blue breeches met high leather riding boots, there was a glimpse of saffron stockings. Though his lean face was shaded, nothing could hide the harassed look in his unnaturally bright eyes.

A few servants rode after him. They pulled up before the broad stone landing of the chateau, and the warm stillness was broken by several lackeys, hastening from the stables.

The master of the house was halfway up the steps when he seemed to change his mind, turned, and paced away along the trellised path leading to the gardens. He had been away from home so often; this last time for almost a month—on financial business in Paris. He had no desire to meet the chilly eyes in his wife's beautiful face.

"Master, what about your portmanteau?" asked Denis, stepping after him. The marquis continued on his way unheeding. Denis' shrewd glance followed him. Shrugging knowingly, Denis ordered the menservants to begin carrying in and unpacking the various bundles.

As Francis passed the windows that lined the side of the chateau, his eye fell upon a great bumblebee on the inside of the glass butting its black head with futile anger against the panes. It captured his predicament exactly, and he watched it with an almost fierce gladness.

Suddenly, the sweet, breathless voice of Olivie rose from beyond the living hedge-wall. "What happened next, Grandpapa? Did they get safely away from the wicked priests?"

Strange, he thought, *is not Felicienne's father in Paris with her sister at present? Though it suits him to be telling the children his skeptical views of the clergy.*

That skepticism has almost become mine, he thought bitterly. *Who can assure me that the painted Virgin hears? She has given no help.* He walked farther on, and struck at an unoffending hollyhock with his riding whip. *What was it that the Du Chemin lad said? Something about the Lord Christ....He will be with us – to the end of the world. With us? That assurance....* What came to him was a picture—a picture of the glowing peace of Tristan du Chemin.

A man's cracked voice broke through his thoughts; "...but he refused to recant. He said, 'To this truth will I cling; God help me.' So the priests tortured him. They led him to a cell with an iron floor, and heated it to an unbearable pitch." The voice broke, then continued, "But he would not deny his Lord. So they did it again, and again...the flesh on the soles of his feet was completely burnt off."

Francis shuddered in spite of the heat, and drew closer. The voice continued, "This crippled him for life. But cripple or sound, dead or alive, a staunch Huguenot he remained. 'You cannot separate my faith from my soul, do what you will with my body,' he told his cruel persecutors."[1]

"Oh, what wicked, wicked men!" cried Adele's voice, and through an arch in the bushes, her father's eyes lighted upon the storyteller and his listeners. *Ah – that explains it – 'tis M. de Duret!* Francis thought. Olivie and Adele were seated on the green sward like living flowers, while Charlot played on the path with a carved toy and Honore and Marcel lounged against the hedge. Madame Felicienne, in a pale, moss green ruffled dress, was half-reclining on a sofa, listening as her fingers flew on some delicate needlework. Francis' eyes traveled from her huge feathered hat, down her wealth of mounded dark curls, and then at last, half doubtfully, to her face. There was a glowing, peaceful look there. The change caught his wondering attention, and he felt his stiffness melting. He could not remember a time when she had not worn a slightly pinched look of cynicism.

M. de Duret was about to continue when, shifting his position, he happened to glance up. He rose to his feet and bowed pleasantly, saying, "Welcome home, marquis."

The girls hastened to their feet with curtseys. Honore and Marcel straightened up respectfully and bowed. "Welcome home, Papa!" the children cried. They, too, seemed to have an indefinable lightness hanging about them. *I must speak to Felicienne,* Francis told himself.

~*~*~

After their first greetings of their father, Adele caught Honore's eye and, pretending to push back her hair, touched her thumb to her first two fingers. Honore smiled knowingly and moved off in the direction of the house.

Denis, he found, was busy unpacking in his father's room. Inconspicuous loitering and listening from the room opposite failed to uncover anything. Not a servant came down the hall, and the only noises were the click of opening portmanteaus and the muffled movements of Denis as he put his master's things away. Honore was about to leave when he heard a manservant approaching. The man paused at the doorway to his master's rooms and knocked.

"Come in. What do you want?" Denis' voice asked.

"You asked me to hold anything that came for you," said the other.

"Yes? What do you have?"

"One letter, M. Denis—from Paris," replied the man.

"Ah! I thank you. You did well."

The man began to leave, and Honore moved forward to try to see the messenger, but realized in frustration that he could not do so without being seen himself.

When Denis left the room a few minutes later, Honore entered to see if there was any clue, but found nothing. *And it is not necessarily suspicious,* Honore had to admit. *Denis, his father and grandfather have all served our family, and having accompanied my father to Paris, he may have legitimate connections. But….*

~*~*~

It was evening before Francis found an opportunity to speak to his wife. There were various seigniorial duties to catch up on, and (unusually) so much the children wanted to show and tell him. But as the

'witching twilight sank into purple pomp and splendor,

he found her in her boudoir, her face reflected in a gilt mirror.

"Welcome home again, Francis." She turned to greet him, her green eyes frank and warm.

"I am glad to find you so well, *cherie,*" he answered. "You have not looked so in years."

"Nay—I think not," she blushed rosily.

"There is a difference in you, I think," he pressed.

She thought she saw a real and new interest in his normally preoccupied eyes. After a short pause, she said cautiously, "Francis, for some time now Monsieur de Duret has been telling the children tales from the past. They truly look forward to it. In fact, they have taken to calling him 'Grandpapa de Duret.' He has been such a blessing, a truly wise and kind man. I have never met a man so patient, so unselfish and caring of others."

"Yes?"

"The weather has been so pleasant of late, I joined their afternoon storytimes. Hearing the stirring tales, I have become more and more interested in those stalwart refugees, the...Huguenots." He neither winced nor flamed, and she continued, "The persecutions and perils the Huguenots met with were terrible, but—others in history have been hounded down, too—that is not what has spoken most to me. The *way they bore* those persecutions—*that* is the difference, Francis!" Her radiated conviction, and his sympathetic look encouraged her to go on. "Outwardly, I have had everything in life that should make one happy. My station is infinitely better than most of the unhappy people of France. And yet I have found it empty. But these Huguenots, Francis—even in the midst of their perils and trials, they had an inner strength, an inner peace, that is incomprehensible!" She looked out the window at the first star, shining like a forgotten jewel in the deepening blue sky. "I think they had something worth dying for," she said quietly. "Worth *living* for."

"I almost...I almost believe you are right, Felicienne."

For some time, the muffled ticking of a clock in the hall was the only thing breaking the pensive stillness. At last, Francis said, "By the by,

Felicienne, I have asked the Du Chemins to come for a visit soon. Goodnight, *cherie*."

Francis softly closed the door, and, flickering candle in hand, turned down the ornate hall. *I wonder…I wonder if M. de Duret is awake still?*

A few short, sumptuous passages, rich with figured wallpaper and candles set in brackets, brought him to his guest's room. He met a servant coming out with a silver basin of fair water. The man bowed upon seeing him.

"Is Monsieur de Duret accessible?"

"I think so, my lord."

"Tell him I request a few moments' conversation, if it is not inconvenient."

The servant soon reappeared. "He says it would be a pleasure, my lord."

As the marquis entered softly, M. de Duret stood up from an ornamented writing desk. It was a beautiful, intricately-carved piece of craftsmanship. "It is very kind of you to visit, marquis," he bowed.

"I am the one that must claim the pleasure," Francis replied. "I hope all has been favorable while I have been gone. You must inform me if the servants are not as attentive as they should be, or if you require anything."

"I have not lacked for anything, but I thank you for your solicitude, marquis."

After a few more pleasantries, Francis' quick eye caught the gilded title of a well-worn book on the writing desk: *Pseaumes de David, mis en Rime françoise, par Clément Marot et Théodore de Bèze.*

"I am afraid I have interrupted your studies," he said, with a courteous inclination of the head.

"Not at all, marquis; I was merely reading for pleasure—the Psalms of David, in verse." He smiled. "But pray be seated; I am sure you did not come to discuss the Psalms."

"No—and yes," Francis replied, seating himself in an upholstered chair. Now that he was there, he was not sure how to begin. He shifted in his seat. "I have come—well, I have come—I have felt the emptiness of the *state* religion; and the emptiness of *no* religion. Life seems without meaning or purpose. And yet—I have now met and heard of a people who seem to have…" he paused, searching gravely for words; "I have met people who seem to have peace—and I have noticed that they call themselves *Huguenots.*"

The deep, steady eyes of De Duret did not change, unless they grew brighter. "I suppose you know that *I* am a Huguenot," he said simply. "What you do not know is that *your father* was one, too."

In Francis' clear eyes leapt up a singular, surprised gleam.

"Yes, your father, my bosom friend, was a Huguenot," M. de Duret went on. "And he wished with all of his heart that his son would share his faith."

"My *father!*"

"I do not ask you to believe my bare word. But I have here a letter, the first and only missive I received from him." He pulled a timeworn and well-creased parchment out of the escritoire.

"My father—a *Huguenot?*" Francis' eager, trembling hand reached forward. As he took the foolscap, his eyes fell upon the wax impression of his father's ancestral seal; the very one Francis himself had used that afternoon on some documents. And the crabbed, distinctive handwriting, seen so many times on old rent deeds and seigniorial papers—how could it belong to anyone else?

My dear Francis,   *18 June 1754*

I feel our Seperation deeply; the Years have seem'd long since we last Parted.

You will remember my Mother: she passed away, full of Faith, this last Year. It has been a Cruel blow. Yet I have found Christ all-sufficient. Her relations are full of grief, and spend their time in Masses Candles and wild prayers for her soul. How great My joy is, knowng that she is in Heavn with Christ, not in Purgatory. It is not her Good Works; they are as worthless for Salvation as filthy rags: it is Christ's Sacrifice and His unmerited Grace.

The letter went on, and then he saw the line:

I have the Joy and Pleasure to tell you that Brigitte and I have been blessed by God with a man-child. We have call'd him Francis Johan, Francis after you, and linking that dear name with my own, Johan. How Brigitte and I pray over him that he will learn to follow our Lord Christ, and to press on in the Reformed and Huguenot faith. France is so Steep'd in Catholicism that it is Difficult to stand fast; I trust, Francis, that you will add your Prayers to ours for this Child. Lord, keep him true to your most holy and Precious Faith! Teach him Thy truth, so he may Pass it on for a Hundred Generations more.

Francis looked up, and his eyes were brimming with tears.

Dawn At Last

3.

Slow buds the pink dawn like a rose
From out of night's gray and cloudy sheath;
Softly and still it grows and grows,
Petal by petal, leaf by leaf.
— Susan Coolidge

T ime marched unheeding past the anniversary of Marie's death. The warm and long months of Summer had given way after a short skirmish to the blustery chill of Autumn. The year and a half had been filled with spiritual battles: darkness, light, struggles, painful victories, and relapses. But 'twas our Lord who said:

My grace is sufficient for thee: for My power is made perfect through weakenesse.

The fire flickered in the *cheminee*, glistening on the bronze cherubs adorning a mirror, and glowing on the stiffened lemon-and-cream silk dress of Adele. Her fair brow was furrowed with deep, strenuous concentration. In a moment, she picked up a quill pen and began to write in a clear though imperfect hand, pausing at times over difficult words;

> *My dear Stephanie,*   *September 3, 1787*
> *Mama tells me she is sending a letter to Your mother and I may include a Note to you. So I have set down to write. I Hope you are well there, here wee are all Well in Body and Speerit, as Papa said Yestereve.*
> *Wee have heard Rumors that the Paris* ~~Parleemant~~ *Parlement ws Exiled to Troyes the King punishing them for not Following His Wishes. Papa is Sure you know more Perticulars. There is much Foment here in Le Havre.*
> *I made a Peece of fancy-work this Summer.*

Pursing her cherry lips in thought, Adele paused. A letter was an important thing; what else should she say? "Tell her things that have happened," her mother had said. She wiped the quill and re-dipped it before putting it to the paper again.

> *The Du Chemins Stay'd here most of the Summer But are Gone now. They have no Girls but Honore is Glad to have a Friend his age, Tristan.* ("And he has joined us in *espionnage* against Denis," Adele mouthed with a smile, but did not write it down.) *Mme. du Chemin is very Nice and wee love her. They brought a Godly man with them who leads Services not Masses. Papa and Us are pleasd by his sermons Alot.*
>
> *Olivie sends her Love and Charlot gave me a Rose for you but it Wont fit in the letter Mama says. I Wish I could see you betimes. Give your Mamma and Papa my respects and also Grandpapa des Cou.*
>
> *I Am, your loving Cousin*
> *Adele Helene de Coquiel di le Mercier*
> *P.S. I forgot.* ~~Babby~~ *Baby Paulette is more than a Year old now. Olivie and I like to Play with Her. Shee hides in the curtains and we Search for her.*

She looked the letter over hard several times, then folded it with the utmost care and wrote on the outside;

> *To Madame Stephanie Aimee-Juliette de Lobel*

She smiled, and her mind wandered back to the delightful times the two had spent together before the De Lobels had moved to Paris several years before. *Madame letter, I wish I were going with you.*

~*~*~

The wind whipped down the noisy lanes, and, being in a lazy or disdainful mood, cut through the rider's cloaks instead of going around. The sun was shining—*But he seems to be hoarding his golden treasure of heat*, Honore thought. He wrapped his long cloak more tightly around himself. The metaphor appealed to him so much that he said aloud, "Look, Marcel—even the sun is having financial difficulties!" From his mount, Marcel's quiet eyes did not quicken much, but Honore knew his servitor, and continued, "Papa told us that France is in perilous economic straits; *Le Roi* Sun up in yonder sky looks like he is having a heat shortage, too, *n'est-ce pas?*"

Marcel's mild smile was all the reply that Honore expected, for that was Marcel—phlegmatic and perhaps a bit dull. Mayhap too languid for a servant; but his father and grandfather had been faithful servitors, and their son was humored for their sakes.

Ahead, the narrow street abruptly bulged open into a bustling market place. Brimming carts full of green cabbages, baskets of brown eggs, and gourds of striking colors were drawn up in lines across the square, and busy, haggling people swarmed among them. Halfway through the packed jumble, another mounted man, followed by a liveried manservant, hailed them. "Francis de Coquiel di le Mercier!"

"Du Sauchoy! I thought you were in Paris!" Francis pulled up his steed, and was soon exchanging pleasantries with the other, a large, florid man decked in the height of fashion.

"I have come straight from there. Have you heard the latest reports?"

"Heard what, Du Sauchoy?"

"Paris is a boiling pot. After cooling their heels in sleepy Troyes, the Paris *parlement* finally agreed to register the proposed loan—of some 485 million—with the condition that there will be an Estates-General. The King's new Controller-General, Cardinal Lomenie, was finally forced to assure them that one would take place in 1792."

"The Estates-General! I have heard talk of it, but nothing sure until now. It has not been assembled in almost two hundred years!"

"Yes," Du Sauchoy said grimly, "people say it is a sign of the King's weakness. Though he is as averse as ever to giving up any of his sovereignty, and upbraided his minister for that promise. But my sources say Lomenie replied, 'It was only an empty promise; it will not be carried out.' *Certes!* The Paris *parlement* assembled to register the loan, but then everything was overturned by their obstinacy, and by the duc d'Orleans (who has ever opposed his cousin the King, as you know). D'Orleans declared that *parlement* does not have the authority to confirm loans—only the Estates-General does. Of course, this brought upon him the wrath of the King: the next day (last day-week) came three *Letters-de-Cachet*, banishing Orleans to his chateau de Villers-Cotterets and the two other leaders to the Stronghold of Ham and Mont St. Michel. Now, the *Parlement* is in a foment—instead of cringing in fear, as might be expected, they are rearing under Lomenie's whip and beginning to headily question the legality of *Lettres-de-Cachet* in general! Paris is wild, and the provincial *parlements* are rising. No man knows where it will lead."

"We shall see. The King only called the Paris *parlement* because the Assembly of Notables showed themselves too autonomous—and yet the Paris *parlement* has also not shown the blind obedience he demands....God only knows what will happen! The King is in a fix. Legally he needs some governing body to approve this desperately-needed loan—and parlement is now reveling in the position of power this places them in. France's financial troubles have put the King's back to the wall. What with the debts incurred in supporting America's War for Independence, fiscal irresponsibility, and the extravagant spending of generations..."

The men continued discussing the issue while the lads sat back on their mounts and watched some filthy street gamins cavorting after a skeletal cat. Presently, a rough, ruddy English sailor pushed his way through the throng. Marcel swung down from the saddle and returned his salutation.

Marcel introduced him to Honore, "An acquaintance of mine—we met when your father arranged with the sloop Clemence to obtain Bibles he ordered." He spoke in English, for the benefit of the sailor. Living near Le Havre, all of the family had learned English.

"Ay, and the prettiest smuggler she is, with the daintiest foot—when not hired out lawfully," chuckled the tar. He moved back a few paces with Marcel, and their voices were lost in the throng.

Honore turned his attention back to the mart. Around him rose the clamor and bustle of crowded market-day—loud bawling of hawkers, shrill voices of wizened peasant women, sharp, animated bargaining of countless scores of housewives and servants....Occasionally, hoarse exclamations rose, when an urchin was caught stealing from a marketbasket. Of a sudden, Honore's horse was shoved aside by a beetle-browed peasant's cart.

"How now, sirrah!" he cried, reaching for his sword. But instantly his conscience remonstrated, and he was ashamed of his outburst. *Alas! And I had thought I had conquered that,* he thought, lowering his flashing eyes. *What was the verse that Grandpapa de Duret gave me? 'When He was reviled, He reviled not again.'* To the peasant he said aloud, "My pardon for speaking roughly, my good man—pass on your way." When he looked up, he saw that Du Sauchoy and his father had noticed the encounter.

"Never apologize to a menial, young man," Du Sauchoy boomed. "It lowers one's standing. The dogs need to learn to properly respect rank!" He added in a lower voice to Francis, "Have you heard the rumors? Too many of them are grumbling and discontented. The saying goes, 'If the King cannot control *Parlement*, why should he lord it over *us*?'"

Honore caught his father's approving eyes, and that was sufficient reward. He heard his father answer, "Yes, I have heard—the winds of revolt are stirring. I agree with you that respect is a good and needful thing, Du Sauchoy. But as a philosophical point, do you think the peasantry can truly respect our rank when we act as if they are less than human? The Lord Christ treated even the lowest with pity and ruth—and He gained true respect and love."

Du Sauchoy flushed, but then replied, "Ah, Francis—Religion, religion, of course, is quite a good thing, but one can perhaps have too much of it." He smiled benevolently.

The bell of the nearby Le Havre Cathedral tolled. *Dong! Dong! Dong! "Peste!"* he exclaimed. "Three o'clock?" He gathered up the reins of his white horse in one fleshy, gloved hand. "I ask you to excuse me, gentlemen—I must be at my Lord Mayor's in half-an-hour, to relate the news. If I can ever be of any service to you…"

"*Le temps, c'est de l'argent*—Time is money; I would not keep you. I am glad to have met, du Sauchoy, and my hearty thanks for the news you have conveyed. Will you be anywhere near Chateau di le Mercier? I urge you to avail yourself of my hospitality, and I know the marquise would add her gentle demands were she here."

"Alas, I am grieved to say that I shall be departing early on the morrow to see Michel, and will not have so much as a moment to spare on the way. Present my sincere regrets and compliments to your noble lady, and tell her that I hope to avail myself of the opportunity in the near future. Adieu!"

Both parties lifted their hats, and rode off at a walk in opposite directions. Honore scanned the throng. The seaman had gone.

~*~*~

In an airy room, a girl of some thirteen years pushed her brocaded shoe closer to the glowing fireplace—the room was a bit chilly. Her deep periwinkle gown brought memories of the clear and cold October skies that were past. Presently, a maid brought in a silver tray.

"Tea, Madame Stephanie?"

"Ah—yes." The girl looked up petulantly. Her large, stunning blue eyes were framed by luxuriant waves of golden hair. If anyone had been there beside the impassive maidservant, they might have caught their breath at her beauty. It was that of a china doll—almost too perfect.

The fair goddess dipped her quill in some ink, and began:

Dear dear Adele,   *December 5, 1787*
Mama says I have Chatterd and Scolded like a Magpie until Shee gave me leave to ~~Rite~~ Write to you. I was so Glad to receeve Your Letter.

I am Well I wish Brother Leuren was not as Well as hee is for hee is a Nuisance.

Paris is Regorge de Brochures [Flooded with Pamphlets]. Every One cries for the Estates-General. I have some Gossip for you tho' it is the Truth. Loumenie is worn out with Fighting Parlement he is sick and reduc'd to a milk Diet. Serve him right! Parlement still stands Gainst the King. We and most all of Paris are Cheering for It. Old D'Ormesson has sayd Messieurs, you will get States-General, and You will Repent it. Papa thinks hee is a Fool and I think hee is a Dunderhead. See I had News about the Parlement, didnt I?

I have Made a Peece of needle Work too it was a grand Bother. So I tryed being Stuborn like Parlement and it workd. Now Mama sayes I do not have to stitch Another. Shee is always busy Writing.

Wee have had many gay Parties this year yestereve saw Madame de LaFayette shee ask'd me to send her Love to your mother.

Kisses to you and I Wish I could see you soon. My respects to all your family Mama says you all must Come and visit. That would be Nice I know you agree.

> *Your dear friend and Cousin*
> *Stephanie Aimee-Juliette de Lobel*
> *P.S. The Baby sounds Nice. I wuld let the Nurse play with It.*

~*~*~

It was the sixth of May — May, whom Milton hailed with delight:

> *Now the bright morning Star, Day's harbinger,*
> *Comes dancing from the East, and leads with her*
> *The Flow'ry May, who from her green lap throws*
> *The Yellow Cowslip, and the pale Primrose.*

Pale pink and buttery-gold flowers carpeted the grassy meadows, and the trees lifted many-hued green hands to the clear blue sky. It had rained the day before, and everything was clean and fresh. All Nature beckoned busy mankind to enjoy the nectarous sights and smells. However, two figures on horseback had more pressing things at hand. Passing by the fields, where wizened peasants worked in weariness of mind and body, they swung in at a gateway and galloped up the long, poplar-lined driveway to the Chateau di le Mercier. Before its grand arched doorway they reined in their lathered bays.

A small herd of pert stableboys instantly raced out to take the horses, vying to be first, since those worthies would perchance get a *sou* or hear snatches of news. They were disappointed, for the travelers strode straight up the smooth steps and the manservant shut the door firmly behind.

"Shall I announce you, Master du Chemin?" the man asked, helping him take off his light outer cloak. "Or would you rather attend to your toilette first?"

Tristan du Chemin glanced wryly at his mud-splattered cloak, but a further look showed him that his other garments, being shielded, had escaped. "No. Present my compliments to the marquis, and tell him I come with tidings."

They were left to wait in the generous entry, with its elaborately-framed baroque paintings, high, detailed cornices, and deep plaster architraves. On one side of the room was an imposing suit of armor, worn in battle by some warring De Coquiel di le Mercier of the past. On the right and left, doorways opened to wide hallways, while straight ahead the grand staircase swept upstairs. To the side of the stair, a door led to the parlor, which in turn opened onto the garden behind the chateau.

In a moment, the servant returned and led Tristan to the parlor, while his manservant carried his master's things to a guest suite.

Bowed in by the servant, Tristan entered, expecting that the marquis was alone. But instead his deep brown eyes were met with a dazzling bouquet of color. The dark green dress of the marquise, with a small white-gowned little one in her lap. An intense rose-color with curling golden-brown hair, then a goldish green, and an almost saffron yellow with blue ribbons. *Adele, Honore, and Olivie,* he thought, as Charlot's small blue-smocked figure attached itself exuberantly to his leg in welcome.

Tristan bowed deeply to the marquis and M. de Duret and kissed the marquise's hand, bestowing a greeting on little Paulette. He received a warm, brotherly greeting from Honore, while the girls' modest eyes spoke their pleasure. Blue-smocked Charlot, not to be forgotten, pranced about, exuding delight.

"It is always a glad day when a Du Chemin enters our abode," the marquis said. "But pray be seated. We did not expect you so soon. What is your news? I trust that all is well at home?"

"All is well, Monsieur de Coquiel de le Mercier. My father would have come himself, but he has pressing business at hand, and so sent me with the latest news from Paris. He has written the details." He proffered a sealed packet.

"My sincere thanks, Tristan. I am grateful. Pray begin."

"You are aware, I am sure, marquis, that the Paris *parlement* has stubbornly refused to follow the King's demands, and the twelve other *parlements* have added their angry barks about the King's heels. But the country is gravely deficit—money is desperately needed. Things cannot remain at a standstill without dire developments."

"Yes; go on."

"A whisper of a rumor floated about last week, to the effect that the Intendants of Provinces had all been ordered to be at their posts a certain day. Even more quietly the murmur ran that there was incessant printing going on in the King's Chateau, under lock and key—even to the extent that the printers were not allowed to leave, but were handed in food. Scenting danger to the *parlement*, D'Espremenil himself, it is said, prowled around that printing-office, and, with five hundred *louis d'or*, managed to get his hands on what was being secretly printed."

The alert eyes of Olivie caught a shadow at the keyhole. With a deft movement of her thumb and forefingers, she caught Adele's attention and whispered with a twinkle, "I think one of the menservants is as curious for news as we are!"

Tristan continued, "Those proof-sheets revealed the King's plan to oust *Parlement* from its haughty platform of defiance: in one day a printed proclamation was to descend on the nation, announcing that the life-blood of the *parlements*, their lawsuits, were no longer their domain—they were now given over to new Minor Courts, called *Grand Bailliages*! Of course, D'Espremenil hasted back to Paris with this news and convoked an instantaneous Session of *Parlement*. *Parlement* listened astonished, then exploded in thunder. Led by D'Espremenil, they swore a patriotic oath and declared the rights of parlement, defying Lomenie and despotism. But in the gray of the next morning, May 4th, Lomenie launched *Lettres-de-Cachet* aimed at the two leaders, D'Espremenil and Goeslard. Rumor has it that they were warned by a friendly bird, for they both escaped the tipstaves and fled, disguised, over the roofs to the *Palais de Justice*—and in an hour, to the delighted roar of the populace, *Parlement* was assembled. It declared it would not give up its two 'martyrs,' and that the Session would be permanent until the pursuit of them was given up."

The marquis stirred sharply. "*Certes!*" he exclaimed. There was a long-drawn breath from the corner where Monsieur de Duret sat. Honore's narrowed eyes were fixed on his friend.

Tristan continued, "And so it lasted, for six-and-thirty hours—speeches, and more speeches—until the King sent Captain D'Agoust, a brave and hardy soldier, to seize the two leaders and turn *Parlement* out of the *Palais de Justice*. There was much protest, and some said, 'We are all D'Espremenils!' but the eye of D'Agoust—the eye that had once made Prince Conde give satisfaction and fight—was inexorable, and they were forced to disband. What will befall next is not certain, but *Parlement* is shorn, and my father and others think it shall not recover from this blow. But whether it means that the King's will shall now be followed is another matter. The provincial *parlements*, my father says, will not likely give up the lawsuits to the upstart *Grand Bailliages* without a fight."

Silence followed his words, and Adele noticed the shade had gone from the keyhole. Then her father spoke, shaking his head.

"These are news indeed. '*Les petits ruisseaux font les grandes rivieres*—the little streams make the big rivers.'" Straightening up, he said, "It is all in God's hands. We must do our duty, trust in God, and ask Him to have mercy on our poor country."

Soon the marquise was called away on a question about the dinner, while the marquis retired to read M. du Chemin's packet and write a reply for Tristan to take back. When the children were alone, Tristan asked, "Any new developments regarding Denis?" Adele laughed merrily, for they all viewed their *espionnage* in a half-comic, half-serious light.

Honore recounted a few incidents, such as Marcel's unobtrusive victories; "He sits around with that dull expression, and the other servants don't even pay attention to him. Through him we overheard that recently Denis has been seen around the kitchen more than his wont."

"Kitchen gossip is that he has an eye out for a scullery-maid, one Louise," Adele said ("And she is pretty," inserted Olivie), "but we wonder…"

"Hmmm," Tristan said. "I would be surprised if a man of Denis' standing would stoop to paying court to a kitchen maid, no matter how lovely her face."

"He doesn't seem to mind low company," Olivie said. "I saw him just the other day with a very grimy guttersnipe."

"Yes, but—" Honore began, but cut himself short as footsteps were heard in the hall.

"I have come to take Master Charles and Madame Paulette up to the nursery for dinner," the nursery-maid announced, picking up Paulette; and the group separated to change for dinner.

~*~*~

A great lightning-bolt sizzled, followed immediately by a colossal peal of thunder. Charlot started up from his seat at the window and ran straight into the arms of Adele, overturning her embroidery frame and knocking the needle from her hand.

Checking an irritated exclamation, Adele held the boy close. "We are safe, Charlot—it was only thunder."

"But it was so loud, Adele!"

"Yes, it was."

Dark clouds brooded over the summer landscape as gusts of fierce rain began to pelt the windows. *I do hope that Papa, Honore, and those in the fields are safe.* The front door burst open, and the wind flung open the parlor door violently, smacking it against the wall. With relief, Adele saw her father and Honore entering. Their clothes were soaked.

"We just barely beat the storm in," laughed Honore.

"Thanks be to God," her father answered. "I have not seen one so violent in some years." The two swung up the staircase towards their respective bedrooms, dripping as they went. But the storm did not end there. The sky deepened to violet, and suddenly a great and incessant rattle filled the air.

"Hail!" Olivie exclaimed, entering the parlor, where Adele was telling Charlot a story.

"Hail! Yes, it is," Adele answered.

Honore hastened in, wearing dry clothes. "Is this the favored spot for viewing the grand spectacle?" he queried playfully.

"I suppose it is now," Olivie answered, "since I have graced it with my presence." She went off into peals of merry laughter, joined by the others.

"Will you grace the Estates-General, too, this coming May?" asked Honore, in the same teasing strain.

"So it has been decided?" Adele broke in seriously.

"Yes, it has," he replied. "Lomenie announced that it shall take place this coming May—May the fourth, 1789."

"What is the Estates-General, Honore?" Olivie asked.

"It is made of three sections—three Estates. The First Estate is composed of representatives from the clergy. The Second Estate is the nobility, and the Third Estate the lower classes (merchants, commoners, and such like). Those who are too poor and pay no taxes have no representation—they cannot even join the Third Estate," Honore answered.

The hail continued in torrents outside, and Adele moved away from the window, worried that it might break under the barrage. Charlot did not mind the hail as much as the thunder, but to entertain him the three began to tell stories and sing *chansons* of days past. It was after a particularly lively one that Olivie looked out through the lessening hailstorm and cried, "The fields!"

"The fields?"

"Look—the hail has beaten them down!"

"And they were ripe unto harvest, too," Honore said.

Charlot looked uncomprehendingly at their sobered faces and asked for another song. "Nasty hail is going away," he said cheerfully.

It was only until the day after that they learned the full extent of the storm's destruction. For sixty leagues around Paris the crops, ready to be harvested, had been almost completely destroyed. Old men shook their heads; "'Twill be a scarce winter for many."

~*~*~

The sun had gone down in a weak halo of dull orange, and the short winter's twilight had almost faded into black. The night was sharp; the keen wind seemed to have invisible spears of ice in it. Amidst the deepening darkness, the chateau glowed like a late firefly with the sparkling light of a myriad candles. From inside wafted the strains of one of Haydn's minuets, and a rainbow of rich garments glittered—waistcoats, gowns, and hats brilliant with embellishment. It was one of the grand fetes of the season.

Two craggy dowagers, resplendent in fiery jewels, were seated to the side of the long room, watching the dancers and passing gossip and news.

"And Lomenie announced that Treasury payments shall henceforth be three-fifths cash, *two-fifths paper!*" one said with unutterable scorn.

"Serves him right to be dismissed," said the other. "Necker shall do much better, they say; at least he is the darling of the hour at present." Then her roving eye found a more interesting topic. "Ah, Lucile—who is that young gentleman there—"

"The one with the blue waistcoat?"

"No—" she pointed with her fan, "the one *there*, with the gold hose and green garters, speaking to Madame Felicienne."

"The son of the marquis du Sauchoy—Sebastien. You don't know him? He has been in Paris, attending the Sorbonne, they say. I wager a pair of gloves that he has taken a shine on…"

Unnoticed by the scintillate throng, one of the French doors opened and a lithe figure in a hooped gown slipped out into the darkness and stepped across the pavement to the garden. As the light from the house

behind her shone on her coiled brown hair, Adele raised her youthful face
to the stars.

> *She was not fair,*
> *Nor beautiful; — those words express her not.*
> *But, oh, her looks had something excellent,*
> *That wants a name!*

Ever since she had come to Christ a year before, a joyful light had
shone in her eyes, imparting a rare attractiveness to her otherwise
unexceptional countenance. The song in her heart overflowed often in
sweet, rich smiles.

The crystalline stars twinkled at her, beckoning. The light behind
impeded her view of their full glory, so, wrapping her luxurious Indian
shawl more closely about her shoulders, she stepped out of the pool of light
for a better look.

As she stood there in the shadow of a potted topiary, minding not
the cold in her starry absorption, a low, rapid voice intruded upon her
thoughts. She came back to earth with a jolt of bewilderment. *Who is out in
the garden?* She tried to pierce the blackness in front of her, but it was
absolute.

"…do your part, and I shall not fail in mine, my *garcon*…" a gust of
wind obliterated the rest of the words, and the only other thing she caught
was, "Adieu—I shall expect a report of your progress." She remained still,
and a darker figure separated itself from the blackness and came along the
path towards her. That certain slouch, the alert carriage of the head, was
familiar….

She saw he would pass right by, but she had no time to evade his
rapid steps. As he neared, one of the French doors of the house was thrown
open, letting an extra paean of light into the darkness. The figure almost
recoiled, and perturbation flashed upon his countenance; but just as swiftly
he smoothed his face and said, "Madame Adele! What are you doing out
here? You shall catch cold!"

Inwardly, she gasped, *Denis!* Outwardly, she said aloud, "Enjoying
the stars…as no doubt you were."

He flinched, and she saw he was studying her face. *Had she heard?*

"Adele? Mother is asking for you…." She turned and saw Honore
standing in the open French door.

Denis moved forward, bowing with honest relief to the youth. "She
is here, Master Honore—I have found her—looking at the stars, she says."

Adele smiled at how easily Denis had glided into the position of *her* discoverer rather than it being *her* who had discovered *him*. She refrained from saying anything, and took the arm her brother offered, sensing rather than seeing Denis' eyes upon her. It chilled her. Maybe this was no child's play.

Once Denis had bowed them inside and departed, she pressed Honore's arm, signaling with her fingers as she whispered, "Do see me afterwards, on some pretext."

The Two Faces of Denis

4.

Idle rumors were added to reasonable apprehensions.
— Lucan

*I*t was late January, 1789. Suspended in the thin strip of dark sky between the black houses of a narrow lane swung a dingy sign. The gray, lumpy animal figure on it looked like some prehistoric monster, though when a gust swung the creaking sign into the light from the bleary tavern windows, it revealed the faded words, "The Silver Salamander."

Inside the sordid tavern, smoke from greasy, guttering candles rose in the thick air, adding their sooty haze to the unsavory atmosphere and peeling walls. A varied mix of men clustered round the grimy tables. One, heady with alcohol, was singing a blundering rendition of a popular song to the drunken laughter and applause of his fellows. In one corner sat a few elderly *rentiers*, each quietly sipping his customary evening glass. A hollow-eyed woman with a ripped, stained dress pushed in. Stumbling out again with her purchase, she brushed against a grimy youth slumped on the floor against the doorframe, his blackened cap tilted over his face. In a farther corner three fellows huddled conspiratorially over their wine. As the waiter, an ill-favored lout, passed, they fell silent, beginning again once the coast was clear.

"You say you have had but indifferent success," said one, looking across the narrow board to a red-nosed, scraggy man, whose blood-stained apron proclaimed him a butcher.

The butcher returned his look sourly. "Yes—but I have done my best. I owe much to you, *capitane*—we shall try to do as you desire. But many mayhap have a question that needs an answer. Some ask why elect De Coquiel di le Mercier? *We* ask why you want your precious lord elected, as well."

"Ay, that's what the fellows I talk to say," piped up the third, a scrawny mouse of a man. "We all know he is better than most *seigneurs*. A few are eager to support him because of his many charities of late. But others ask, 'Why?' What should we tell them? Why do they—why does Jacques Martin, for instance—care to have the marquis de Coquiel di le Mercier go to the States-General? Our interest is in the Third Estate representatives: they are elected from among us; but why should we care a fig for the Second Estate, the nobles? Why?"

The first speaker gave them a long look, in which the scar across his cheek whitened. "Why? *Why?* Comrades, I shall lay my cards upon the table. Do I care about my master getting this appointment? *Ma foi!* I care not—he himself does not care; he knows not that I am pulling strings to elect him." His voice deepened in his earnestness. "But, comrades—*I must be there!* Paris is alive—Paris is beginning to shake off the fetters of the tyrants! She needs guidance; she needs able men to direct the flood: men who will ride the crest of the wave. You two know, better than most—" his pointed gaze pierced them, "you two know my influence in high places, even in the cases of two such worthies as your not-exactly-respectable selves."

The small man cowered against the grimy wall. "*Capitane,* you saved me—do not accuse me—do not accuse me!"

"Through some quiet maneuvers with my lord's papers, yes," Denis returned, his crooked dark eyes studying them both.

"We meant no disrespect, Denis," wheedled the other, picking up his glass with a grubby hand. "You know we are faithfully bound to you. We will find a way to do as you wish."

"Tell them the truth—the marquis de Coquiel di le Mercier will care for the poor and oppressed," Denis said. "No other marquis in this district will truly represent their cause in the Second Estate. He has a new compassion and care—he is not the same man he once was (it is strange; I understood him then). But he will be true and just and not seek his own. I know not why, but 'tis the truth."

The butcher laughed unmusically. "So our labors are to get our *capitane* to Paris, eh? We shall grease their palms, and tell them that the marquis will truly represent their cause. *Bon!* May you cause confusion to the King, and to all the enemies of the Third Estate! I propose a toast to our *capitane!*"

"*Merci,* comrade. So you will both continue your work?"

They nodded readily—"With vigor, *mon capitane!*"—and he slipped *louis* across the table to each.

"I knew I could count on you, my comrades. Let us drink a toast before we part." Denis turned easily towards the packed assembly beyond and, raising his voice, cried, "A toast! Let us toast the Third Estate! Long may it live!"

"Long live the Third Estate!" came the drunken and uproarious response.

~*~*~

As Denis and his ill-favored companions passed out the tavern door, the smaller man stumbled unsteadily against the dirty youth. With an oath, he kicked the figure, which merely slumped down still further.

"He's asleep, the beggar," the man muttered, and he followed the others out into the blustery night. They parted immediately; two slipping away on foot while Denis mounted a nearby horse and set off at a brisk trot through the darkness for Chateau di le Mercier.

A few minutes later, the bedraggled youth near the door shook himself. He yawned, stretching his patched, grubby garments, and, hat still low, wavered to his feet before stumbling out into the night. For several narrow dirt streets he pursued his slouching, uncertain pace, repeatedly pausing at doorways to shelter against the cold, whistling wind.

As the houses began to look more affluential and the street changed from packed, stony earth to cobblestones, he quickened his pace. Turning down a side lane, he glanced around, dropped to his knees, and wormed his way through a hole in a nearby hedge. When he emerged on the other side, his tattered apparel had been replaced by the sober green livery of the De Coquiel di le Merciers. His hat was crisp and peaked, and as he strode down the street with rapid steps and erect carriage, the moon shone full on his solid face and dark brown eyes and hair.

A few more streets led him to the stable of a lodging-house. Slipping inside, he nodded familiarly to the sleepy groom. Minutes later he led out his horse, mounted in one motion, and moved briskly off in the direction of the chateau di le Mercier. Through the silent outskirts of the city and into the countryside beyond he urged his steed. When the houses fell away and barren fields stretched on both sides, the pitiless wind increased in force and swept across the wastes, howling at lone cottages and clawing with icy fingers at the abodes of the rich—an apt picture of the human storm that was to tear France to shreds in a few short years.

Pressing his hat more firmly on his head, the rider squinted ahead at the silver line of the road. No one was in sight. He urged his willing mount to a faster pace.

Soon, the high hedges bordering the De Coquiel di le Merciers' estate rose on his left. In a few minutes a gap of deep blue-black sky in the hedgerow proclaimed the stone entranceway to the estate. A guardsman hailed, holding a lantern high. With barely a pause, the rider doffed his hat. As the yellow light struck his face, the guardsman nodded in recognition.

The rider started forward, then reined back his horse. "'Tis a cold night to be outside, Jacques," he said.

"Aye, Marcel," the man nodded. "But I must needs be up, for the party is going late tonight. It is not *my* desire to be out on a night such as this." He paused, then chuckled, "Some fools, like you and Denis, are out in this weather of your own choice, are you not?"

"*I* was sent by Master Honore," Marcel stated. "But Denis?"

"Aye, he was out—he passed in but a few minutes ago—it's a wonder you did not overtake him on the road," the guardsman said.

A rattle of hooves and carriage wheels came from the house, and casting a quick glance down the dark lane at the glowing chateau, Marcel said, "I must go—the party is ending. Jacques, I will tell the cook to have a hot drink for you in the kitchen when your shift ends."

"You are a good fellow, Marcel," Jacques said heartily. "I thank you."

Marcel shook the reins and proceeded at a smart pace down the avenue to the house. Its welcoming light spilled generously into the freezing darkness beyond. As he passed the front of the house to ride around to the stables, he caught a glimpse of Madame Felicienne framed in the door, bidding "*au revoir*" to her silk-garbed and fur-robed guests.

After stabling his horse, Marcel entered into the chateau through the tradesman's door in the kitchen, making sure to tell the cook about the hot drink for Jacques. He then made his way up the servant's stairs to Honore's room. Throwing himself luxuriantly into Honore's chair, he stirred up the fire and settled himself to wait. The party took some time to wind down—it was at least an hour later that Honore opened the door of his room and saw Marcel sprawled in the chair, basking in the fire's heat. With a somewhat shamefaced expression, Marcel sprang to his feet and bowed.

"Is Madame Adele coming?" he asked.

"Oh no, 'Madame Adele' is not coming," said a merry voice, and Adele entered, candle in hand. It glittered on her delicate gold necklace and the gleaming smooth silk of her hooped gown. Her hair was piled on her head in masses of lovely dark curls. She shut the door behind her and set the candle on a writing desk.

"What is your news, Marcel?" Honore asked.

"I followed Denis to 'The Silver Salamander,' where he was joined by two rascally townsmen. They talked for a good while—but in such low tones that I could not hear what they were saying."

"*Peste!*" Honore muttered.

"On finishing their discourse, though, he turned and saluted the company, crying, 'A toast! Let us toast the Third Estate—Long may it live!'"

Adele's eyebrows went up. "So he is in favor of the Third Estate."

"The frequenters of 'The Silver Salamander' are not well-to-do, my lady, despite the fancy name," Marcel smiled wryly.

"You are right, Marcel—he might have said that because he knew it would be popular there, not necessarily because that is his opinion," Honore said.

"Yes, but—"Adele began, then said, "Why would Denis have any reason to meet with such men? What means all this?"

Honore answered, with knotted brows, "We *must* keep watching. He is up to no good."

~*~*~

Some days afterwards, a carriage drove along the narrow, contorted street and passed the dark maw of the "Silver Salamander." The crowned salamander itself (the coat of arms of Le Havre de Grace) swung drunkenly overhead. A short distance up the street, the carriage ground to a halt in front of the smallest of a small and disreputable row of huts. Dirt and refuse lay in heaps everywhere, while a scrawny dog slunk away into a miniscule alley.

A footman, brave in livery, opened the coach door. Felicienne, Adele, and Olivie stepped out, well bundled against the cold, biting air. Leading the way to the hovel, with its crazily leaning walls and one tiny, begrimed window, the manservant knocked smartly on the discolored door.

A faint voice sounded from within. "Come in!"

The servant held the door open stiffly, and bowed as the ladies entered.

"Madame Felicienne! And Mesdames Adele and Olivie! Our sunshine has entered again!"

The marquise smiled. Ignoring the smells that rose from the refuse pile outside the door, she moved closer to the wizened figure which had risen stiffly to curtsy. A black, stained kettle hung in the miserable, glowering hearth, and the dirt floor was the least repulsive thing about the place. But despite the abject poverty, there were token attempts at cleanliness in the scrubbed, cobweb-free walls, which was more than could be said of most dwellings in that section of the city.

The marquise ducked gracefully to avoid knocking her head on the low, smoke-stained beams and spoke with a smile, gesturing towards the basket Adele held, "I have brought you a few things, Marie-Louise—I know you must have need of bread, and I had the cook make up some broth, as well. This winter has been very difficult for so many, and I knew you were not exempt."

Amidst her maze of wrinkles, the woman's beady black eyes lit up at the sight of the bread. "Ah, Madame—you are too kind! We have indeed suffered most grievously—the hail, and Marc here has been too weak to look for work…" A decrepit man smiled wanly from the rude corner pallet.

"I knew not until last week that bread was so scarce among the people," Felicienne's green eyes were lit with compassion. "I shall endeavor to come again. I am sorry to see you in such a state, Marc. You shall have my prayers."

"I shall be grateful indeed for them, my lady," the man said, pitifully eager. "Someone who is so good as to help feeble old bodies such as we are will certainly be heard by God."

"Oh, but it is not my goodness, you must know!" the marquise said. "All my righteousness is like filthy rags. My good works could never atone or save me, but Christ—Christ alone—has washed me from my sins. God hears me because of what His Son has done for me."

Her face glowed with such a peace that the old man, despite his Catholicism, was moved to say, "Ah—Madame Felicienne—haply you can tell us more another time. There is so little hope for us as can't do enough good…" Then he shifted the conversation. "You have heard the unrest among the people, Madame?"

"Yes, we have heard some reports. There seem to be many rumors afoot agitating the peasantry."

"More and more are rumbling against their lords, Madame," Marie-Louise put in. "Even in our neighborhood." Then she burst out in her cracked voice, "*We* love you, Madame Felicienne! You and yours have been so kind to us, not like some *seigneurs*—and we and a few of the others know that. But the younger ones…" her voice died, then rose again, "The rumors—they are music to their ears. We who have lived long and learned much are ignored."

"Even our own sons, Madame," Marc chipped in. "They have caught the madness." A small tatterdemalion of a boy slipped in, and Marc changed the subject, saying, "We have kept you, Madame, and mayhap bored your ears with our ailments. Thank you again for all you have done for us, and may the Virgin bless you!"

Curtseying, the marquise and the girls left amid sincere farewells, their manservant closing the door tightly after them against the chill blast of wind.

"The wind is trying to freeze our very marrow," Olivie remarked, as they tucked their bonnets closer round and entered the grateful protection of the carriage.

They had other cottages to visit that afternoon, and it was late when their carriage turned towards home. Leaning back into a pile of richly brocaded cushions, the marquise thought back to their chat with Marc and Marie-Louise. *They did not say much, but I think they were trying to warn us,* she mused. *Marie-Louise accented that they loved us...has it gone that far? Are most of the peasants ready to turn upon their lords?* She was still pondering the question when they pulled up in front of their elegant stone chateau. The manservant assisted them to alight. They expected the front door to be opened from within by a footman, but to their surprise, nothing happened as they approached.

"I pray nothing unusual has occurred." Felicienne quickened her step, sharing puzzled glances with the girls. Their accompanying manservant hastened up, and as he swung open the door, their eyes fell upon the nonattendent doorman. He was seated at the side wall reading a pamphlet, and a group of lounging menservants hung around him, staring at the leaflet and listening to him read aloud. His deep voice reached them as they stood just without the door:

"...What is the Third Estate? EVERYTHING. What has been the political order until now? NOTHING. What is it asking for? To become SOMETHING."

Composing her shocked face, Felicienne stepped in the door, cool and serene, and the group jumped guiltily. The doorman pushed forward as the others hastily separated down the halls. "My lady—ah—I must apologize—the door—"

Felicienne smiled, and Adele tucked that gracious, forgiving look away in her memory—it would stand her in good stead in days to come. "I forgive you for leaving your post. May I ask what you were reading?"

He looked up with eyes in which relief was conquering sullenness. "Surely, Madame."

She took the paper, looking at the front. "What is the Third Estate?" she read. Then she looked at the man. "If you have another copy, I would like this."

The man assured her that he could get another, as a second manservant, who had been hanging back furtively, came forward with a bow to Adele. "Madame, this letter came for you," he said, proffering a sealed note.

She took it, and scanned the uneven hand. "From Stephanie!"

At that moment, a booted stride was heard outside, and the doorman sprang to open the door. A tall young man in riding boots and jacket strode in, gloved and spurred, with a sword at his side and a green cockade in his dark hat. Honore was a youth of seventeen now, and his face had lost the roundness of boyhood. No longer strutting like a cock, he had grown in inner character, and his carriage spoke of true manhood. He bent his green eyes, like his mother's, on the group, and bowed. "News?"

"Perhaps," his mother answered. "At least, things to discuss, if my first glance of this pamphlet was aright."

He scanned it. "*That?* — it is the scourge of the countryside — it is everywhere!"

"Is that so?" Felicienne answered, tucking it in her reticule. Then she said, "Dinnertime nears, and we must ready ourselves. Afterwards, when we gather in the parlor, we will have opportunity to peruse this further — and Adele, would you bring your letter to fill us in on the news from Paris?"

"Yes, Mama."

~*~*~

So it was that the evening darkness and chill found most of the family gathered in the parlor around the necessary fireplace, while Adele read aloud:

My Dear Adele,   January 24, 1789
Your letter arrivd safe and was a Gladsome divershun from things Here.
The Seine is Frozen completely, wch makes it very Hard to get food into the city. Wheat is very Scarce the people Complain loudly. There are long Lines for bread.
Papa is busy. He delights in the Stir hee says France is shaking off the Chains and is a rising Giant. I hope so as I am Bored since there have been no grand Parties of late.

I must go, wee are going to the Theatre. Madame Claire Lacombe will be playing. Shee is Pretty and what You might call radical but I like her and she has become fast friends with Mama.
My respects and love to you and your family, etc.
Your friend
Stephanie Aimee-Juliette de Lobel

The fire popped and crackled, and the winter wind shrieked in the darkness outside the house, beating against the windows and clawing with chill talons at the doors. Charlot, now a sturdy boy of seven years, ceased his whittling long enough to move closer to the warmth of the blazing logs. With thirteen-year-old Olivie, he watched the sparks flying upward and dropping down, spent, into the cinders. Paulette was playing with a bright picture-book with rude woodcut illustrations. She was no longer a baby—she was almost three.

Time has flown on as it does, and the younger ones are growing up, Adele mused, watching them from under her long, dark lashes. She herself was blossoming into womanhood in a culture of early marriages and encouraged maturity—she was fifteen.

"Here is my bit of information, Francis," Felicienne said, bringing a pamphlet out of the folds of her skirt. "A real fire-brand."

"It is everywhere," Honore added. "It is eagerly read by almost everyone one meets." The marquis took it curiously, and read aloud:

"What is the Third Estate?
We have three questions to ask ourselves:
  1.What is the Third Estate? EVERYTHING.
  2.What has been the political order until now? NOTHING.
  3.What is it asking for? To become SOMETHING.
Who would dare to say that the Third Estate does not have in itself all that is needed to form a complete nation? It is a man who is strong and robust but still has one arm in chains. Take away the privileged order, and the nation would not be less, but more.

And so what is the Third Estate? It is EVERYTHING but an EVERYTHING shackled and oppressed. Without the privileged order, what would it be? EVERYTHING, and EVERYTHING flourishing and free. Nothing can go well without it; everything would go infinitely better without the others.

…The Third Estate, then, contains everything that makes up the nation; everything that is not part of the Third Estate cannot consider itself as belonging to the nation. What is the Third Estate? EVERYTHING.

What can the Third Estate do if it wants to gain its political rights in a way that will be beneficial to the nation?

The Third Estate must meet separately; it will not associate in any way with the clergy or nobility and will not vote with them either by order or by head.

But the Third Estate, it will be said, cannot form the Estates General. All the better! It shall compose a National Assembly."[1]

"What dangerous words!" Francis commented. "Children, this is deceitful on many fronts. True liberty is the freedom to do right, not license to do anything one desires. When this writer says that the Third Estate must refuse to vote with the others, and compose itself, on its own authority, as a 'National Assembly,' he is urging open rebellion and defiance to the governmental authority, saying that *power* equals *right*. In his eyes, the Third Estate *is* the nation—all the clergy and nobility are merely chains that must be broken and thrown away."

Wide and concerned eyes looked up at his face. The stillness was broken by the cracked voice of M. de Duret. "In times past such fanaticism was marginalized. But now the people are tinder, waiting breathlessly for any spark to set them ablaze. This, and other pamphlets I have seen, are certainly inflammatory enough. Honore, you reported that they are devouring these words. O Lord, have mercy on this nation!"

~*~*~

Honore held his mount down to a jolting trot as he rode beside his father's steed through the wide city thoroughfare. Behind came the rhythmic *one-two-three-four* of the horses of Marcel and another manservant. The inhospitable wind had abated, but the clear sky was a pale and frosty version of its summer turquoise. It had been one of the hardest winters in many years, and wasn't about to release its hold on shivering humanity.

"Do you have an idea of what will happen at the assembly, Father?"

His father answered through the *cravate* wrapped round his chin for warmth, "We shall see, Honore. I believe that Sieur Maurepas will be elected the deputy for this area."

"Indeed, Father."

A few more minutes of riding through the busy city street brought them in sight of a stately building. This was where the Second Estate deputy for their area would be chosen, and the nobility and lords would also write out a *cahir* (a list of grievances to send to the king).

A vast crowd of curious onlookers were assembled there—workmen, loungers, and merchants hawking their wares—eyeing the assembling notables and filling the air with rough voices. A large body of the crowd were of the very lowest class. Paying no taxes, they could not vote even in the Third Estate assemblies, but their woeful lot in life was affected by the proceedings, so they gathered longingly at all the convocations. Across the heads of the excited mass, Honore spied a lord—Sieur Maurepas—arriving from the opposite direction. He was the man Francis guessed would be voted as the deputy.

As Francis and Honore neared, a sort of rustle ran through the crowd, and several shouts went up.

"De Coquiel di le Mercier!"

"Vote for him, my hearties!" cried a broad sailor with loose, unshaven features.

"*Oui! Oui!* De Coquiel di le Mercier!" was caught up on many throats.

Then, as the popular deputy-candidate alighted from his horse and hasted impatiently through the press to the building, a disapproving rumble filled the air. And when he pushed a bystander out of his way, the rumble rose to vocal resentment.

Honore caught his father's eye. *What is this?* Swinging lightly off their prancing horses, they handed them to Marcel and the other manservant and advanced on foot through the crowd. It greeted them with loud shouts, moving aside to let them pass. Francis inclined his head in grave thanks.

Even when they had entered the building, the shouts of "De Coquiel di le Mercier!" still rang in the air. Francis was soon involved in discourse with other attendees, and Honore was left at leisure to study the gathering. It was a rich and varied one: ribbons, embroidery, and lace ruffles competed everywhere, with the most exquisite tailoring and vibrant colors that could be produced. All of the attendees wore powdered wigs—some large and curled all over, others with curls only along the sides, the straight back-hair tied in a ribboned queue.

Two men passed nearby, and Honore could not help but hear some of their conversation.

"De Coquiel di le Mercier must be popular among the lower classes," said a man with a scarlet waistcoat.

"The way events are shaping, I deem it wise to go along with the rabble as much as is possible—throw the dogs a bone," a florid man replied, twisting his gold-headed cane. "Yes, *mieux vaut plier que rompre*—it is better to bend than to break. Besides…"

They moved on. An old, bent gentleman hobbling to a seat was remarking to another, "…and De Coquiel di le Mercier is worthy—he is quite as good a representative as anyone else. We might do worse."

The other answered, "Besides, it's been made worth my while to vote for him." He laughed. "I think I can offer you assurance of reward as well, if you vote likewise…" Honore's eyes widened.

The meeting began with long formalities, and Honore's mind drifted back to the day before. Riding through a village, he and his father had passed a parish church. The peasants, rude and mostly illiterate, were gathered around outside, choosing *their* deputy and painstakingly drafting their *cahir*, their list of grievances and petitions. Vividly, he remembered the pitifully hopeful looks on their careworn faces.

His father and he had heard some of the *cahir* as they had ridden slowly by: '*…We would like the roads, which are extremely bad, to be repaired. We are very poor and we beg His Majesty to have pity on our farmland because of the hail we have had. The lord of the neighboring parish has given them great alms, but we can expect help from no one but His Majesty…*'

Alas, Honore thought with compassion, *they put too much stock in the Estates General! They have great and grievous problems, but they are looking to the government to save them—when, as father says, the government cannot be our God.*

He came back to the present. The proposed statements for the *cahir* were being gravely and decorously debated. He glanced out a diamond-paned window at the curious, noisy mass outside, hearing their intermittent cries of "De Coquiel di le Mercier!"

Someone, he thought, *must have rigged this—why would these men (especially that sailor; how would he know about or care a fig about my father?) why would these men shout for him? Why would they come to get a certain man elected?—I suppose, perhaps….That man with the lank black hair…where did he go?…ah! there he is, stirring up the crowd—he seems to be the ringleader.*

His eyes followed the man, hat pushed low and scarf muffling his face, he moved among the crowd. Suddenly, a small, excitable man flung his arms up in a fervent gesture, accidentally knocking up the hat of the mysterious "leader." Honore had a clear, unobstructed view of the man's face for the few startled seconds it took for the man to recover his hat and angrily shove it on again.

Denis!

There is no mistaking those eyes, and that scar....But why? Ah! What did Adele mention at the party last month.... His face lengthened, and he purposed, *I must tell Father.*

The cries from outside grew louder as the voting took place inside. Honore was almost not surprised when it was announced that Francis Johan de Coquiel di le Mercier had been chosen as the deputy—though by a close margin. Honore's thoughts were consumed with a valet named Denis.

~*~*~

A sparrow fluttered across the bare fields, cocking his head to watch for any grain or insect that might be hidden in the shallow furrows or amid the stubble. Above him the lavender blue firmament seemed colder because of its pale cloudlessness. Giving up its search for a moment, the bird flew upwards and made its way towards a cluster of high hedges in the distance. As he drew near he was joined by a small flock of his own kind, also searching greedily for food. Curving in an aerial ballet, they swept over the final hedges and into a garden nestled behind a stately chateau. The other birds flew straight in and landed on the lawn, immediately commencing to search for bugs, but the first sparrow alit cockily for an instant on a second-story windowsill.

A girl who had been leaning against the sill, her face almost to the glass, stifled an exclamation. Slowly she bent her head for a closer look, but the movement, slight as it was, startled the little brown bird. With a saucy flip of his tail, he flashed down to join his brethren on the grass below. The girl half-turned and called into the room, "Adele, did you see? A little sparrow landed right here!"

"Ah!" Adele answered, bending with intense concentration over some needlework. "How dear."

Olivie's face broke into a smile, and she waited to see if Adele would come out of her absorption. Then with a knowing shrug, she turned back to the window, shaking her curls. Leaning against the thick velvet curtain and resting her arms again on the sill, she peered down with interest at the busy songbirds with their little quarrels and little successes. She was so enraptured by the scene that she would in all probability have never noticed a figure behind the folly if it had not been for the birds. With a sudden movement, they scattered upward and disappeared beyond the garden walls. Olivie cast her dark eyes about, looking for what had disturbed her small "friends." Her eyes found nothing until she saw some movement at the very end of the garden, near the white stone folly.

"Adele!" she hissed. "Come here!"

Adele started at the urgency in Olivie's voice. Leaping up and overturning her sampler, she joined her sister. "What is it?"

"Too late," answered Olivie—indeed, there was nothing to be seen now. "I saw Denis over by the folly, and he was carrying a cloth bundle."

The girls stared at each other in bewilderment. "What—are you sure it was Denis?" Adele took control. "Olivie, you stay here, to watch for him. I shall go downstairs to see if he comes in the servant's door or the front door."

"I shall watch—he won't escape me!" Olivie stared with owlish seriousness through the glazed panes. Smiling broadly, Adele left the room, holding herself back to a staid, unconcerned walk. She made pretence of getting a book from the downstairs library, and then paced along the south wing to the kitchen, where she affected to have come with a query about a certain dish. She dawdled as long as she could, then left and began slowly walking down the hall, listening for the kitchen door to open.

She was almost at the parlor in the center of the chateau when she heard rapid, unmistakable footsteps behind her. Turning with all the outward nonchalance she could muster, she beheld brisk, debonair Denis. Adele managed a bored greeting, but once he had passed she couldn't help but look again. He had no bundle....*Though he could have laid that down somewhere,* she reminded herself. She was about to continue on when she heard light footsteps on the main staircase, and Olivie came into view. As soon as she saw Adele, she made their secret gesture, and they slipped into the nearby library.

When the door was closed, Olivie said, "I just saw Denis—he went past my door upstairs! But I know that he did *not* come out of behind the folly, where I had seen him!"

"Are you sure it was Denis you saw by the folly?"

Olivie looked bewildered. "I *know* it was Denis."

"Mayhap you saw someone else, someone that looked like him," Adele reiterated.

"I do not think so," Olivie said, hesitantly.

Asking guardedly in the kitchen did no good, for the cook said she'd been bending over a pot at the other end of the kitchen and so would not have seen anyone if they had come in the door.

Olivie was stumped, but Adele was sure there had to be an explanation. "Perhaps he did come in the kitchen door, and I merely didn't hear it," Adele said. By the time their father and Honore came home, she had almost convinced Olivie that she *couldn't* have seen Denis, that it must have been some other man by the folly. But Olivie still had her private doubts.

When they found a moment alone with Honore, they told him their news, and he in turn related what he had seen at the assembly. After some discussion, it was decided that Honore should tell their father what *he* had seen, but wait to tell him about the girl's puzzle. "We should investigate further," they agreed.

"It may be nothing—just an over-suspicious fancy," Adele concluded.

But Olivie murmured to herself, "But I didn't imagine it. I really thought it was—I really *think* it was Denis."

~*~*~

In the marquis' bedroom, as the evening died in red clouds and orange fire, stood two figures: the marquis, erect though disturbed and wearied with the long events of the day, and his valet, hovering about and aiding his master in undressing. The process took some time, for the garters, tight knee breeches, painstakingly knotted *cravate*, and multitude of fastening ties on waistcoat and breeches made a valet almost a necessity. It was not until all that had been removed by Denis' accustomed fingers, and the marquis was robed in his radiant silk banyan, the hot and scratchy wig removed and replaced with a flat dressing cap, that Francis spoke to his servant.

"Denis?"

"Yes, Master?"

"An odd thing took place today. At the assembly, there was the usual curious crowd—but many were not just onlookers, they were actively shouting my name, crying that I should be chosen as the deputy."

The valet turned a studiously casual face on his master. "Ah— really? How fortuitous."

"Not only that, but Honore saw a familiar face in the crowd, urging them on," the marquis continued. "It was muffled up well, but he says he can swear to the fact that it was—*you*, Denis."

A sudden look flashed across Denis' countenance, but he answered coolly, "Yes, Master?"

The marquis half-smiled. "Come, come, Denis. You know it was yourself. I suppose you did not tell me about your plans because you knew I would not approve of such methods."

His dark eyes inscrutable, the man answered, "Perhaps that was my thought, Master."

"I thank you for your zeal on my behalf, Denis, but I must make sure you understand to never employ any such tactics in the future, no matter how laudable your aims."

Denis bowed stiffly, replying with the familiarity his status as *valet-de-chambre* gave him, "But Master—you cannot be too conscientious! Everyone else is taking advantage of the situation—if you shun such methods, you will fall behind and become of no account."

Francis gazed at him with concern and misgivings he had never felt before. "My man, it may be your opinion that we must employ any method to gain success and influence. I, too have heard the common saying, '*qui veut la fin veut les moyens*—the end justifies the means.' I myself have said such things in the past. But I have come to realize over the last few years, as I have studied the Bible, that it is a false statement. Wrong never produces right. I must again emphasize that I want no servant of mine to employ underhanded methods."

"Yes, Master." There was a pause, and then the valet leaned forward, his eyes burning with secret knowledge. "But Master, I would have you know there are quite a few—among them very important figures—secretly *capitalizing on* and *spreading* the unrest and dissention throughout this nation. This is no small uprising, no scattered, impromptu series of events. That is what it seems. *But I know better.*"

The marquis did not go to bed until late that night. His solitary candle could be seen through the window of his bedroom, casting its quivering light on the form of a man on his knees.

~*~*~

It was an unusually brilliant morning in early April. The months before had been filled with an increasing rumble—layer upon layer of assemblies, consolidating *cahirs* and approving the deputies voted on at the lower meetings, while the Press unloosed pamphlets and opinions of a stirring, oft-times seditious sort and the excitement of the nation rose and swelled in loud waves. The king finally proclaimed that the Third Estate would be granted twice the amount of deputies as the other two—some 600 compared to the 300 of each other Estate—thus gaining the King immense popular adulation.

The De Coquiel di le Mercier children had not been idle, either. They had seized every possible opportunity to spy on Denis. Honore and Charles had gone over the garden near the folly several times, though they had not found any further clues. After Francis' words to him on the night of the election, Denis had behaved with (to the children) almost maddening circumspectness, and they could discover nothing suspicious in his steady schedule. Adele even wondered if he had become wise to the fact that little eyes were upon him—she remembered the near "slips" Olivie had made in youthful enthusiasm.

Francis Johan de Coquiel di le Mercier had been confirmed as a deputy for the Second Estate. He spent much time wrapping up his affairs, readying himself to attend the meeting of the Estates-General in Versailles in early May. He and his wife had decided that the entire family would travel to Paris.

"There is so much unrest among even the formerly quiet peasants of this area," he said. "Paris is volatile too, but I would like to have you all with me—I would worry to leave you here alone."

"I think that is wise, Francis. We have seen many warning signs of late here in the province, and the rumors of risings have acerbated the instability. Besides, my sister has been urging us to come for a visit, and it would be pleasant to see her again for some months."

Therefore, this sunny April day in 1789, Honore and Monsieur de Duret stood on the level stone landing in front of the château, surrounded by a gaily-colored group bidding them good-bye. What last injunctions, bits of quavering mirth, unheard comments, and loving glances were exchanged! "Remember, the house must have room for— ... We shall see you again, soon!—don't forget my letter to Stephanie ... say 'Bye bye,' Paulette! ... Make sure the wallpaper is nice! ... Who cares about the wallpaper!? We just want a house! ... Good-bye! Good-bye! ... We shall stop by the Du Chemins on the way—Good-bye, Paulette; Adieu, Adele, the parting won't be long, you all shall follow shortly ... God bless!"

Two mounted menservants rode up, bringing with them the mounts of M. de Duret and Honore. Marcel was not going—Honore wanted him home to help the girls with their *espionnage*, and had asked his father if Marcel might stay.

At last, Honore swung lightly into the saddle, a picture of ease and grace, while thick-set, bewigged Grandpapa de Duret mounted stiffly with the aid of a block. In the saddle, however, the older man looked hearty enough for a good day's ride at an easy pace. It would take some two days of riding to reach Paris.

The four set off down the tree-lined avenue in the bright sunshine. Honore turned in his saddle for a final look back. Waving, he shouted, "Adieu! We shall find the perfect house for rent in Paris—with nice wallpaper, too, Olivie!"

A Search

5.

Reputations are made by searching for things that can't be done and doing them.
— Frank Tyger

S tephanie de Lobel (Adele's cousin) stirred, rumpling her dress, then remembered herself and carefully smoothed the lavender gown into artistic folds. The fifteen-year-old made a pretty picture — and she knew it — against the muted wallpaper and richly-carved chairs. Her loose golden curls cascaded down the latest style of gown, with its more curving corset and open shawl. But a look at her petulant, bored face took some of the delight out of the picture.

She did not notice the sound of approaching horses — that was a frequent occurrence, in these busy streets — but she did hear them stop. *Probably a friend of Father's*, she thought languidly, then, *Mayhap it is the delivery of more pamphlets....I wonder...*

She leaned forward and looked into the street below. A frowsy woman in a tattered red dress walked by, calling out her wares in a raucous sing-song. Stephanie's eyes caught sight of two horses standing below, near the front door. A manservant on a chestnut horse held the bridle of a riderless blood red bay. Now *this* was something interesting, something out of the ordinary! *A lordly visitor for Father, perhaps?* The horse arched his black mane, flicked his dainty rufous ears, and stamped his back foot at the approach of several wiry street gamins, shouting and roughhousing. *What a splendid horse!* Stephanie admired its clean, strong lines. *I wonder who it belongs to....* She sat watching. When nothing happened, she leaned back in her chair and picked up a book with a white, languid hand.

She was startled out of her uninterested perusal of the novel by a hurried knock at the door. "Come in," she said.

The butler entered with a rushed manner. "Your father has requested your presence in the parlor," he said. Turning away, he muttered something about "...these grand ideas...doing without the proper number of servants…more work for us that are left…" but Stephanie paid him no attention. The De Lobels had laid off several servants recently because M. de Lobel, a zealous proponent of radical ideas, had the notion that as many as possible should be free from "the shackles of servitude."

Casting another glance at the horse below, Stephanie rose. The servant bustled on ahead, the red back of his coat disappearing from view. Stephanie followed him down the staircase in a more leisurely fashion. She had just entered a short hallway when, from the parlor ahead, came a shout. "Stephanie!" She scowled in annoyance: that impetuous voice could belong to no one else but her thirteen-year-old brother. A few more steps took her to the dark green parlor door, where she paused, adjusting her sheer scarf fastidiously, and then entered.

A quick, disappointed glance showed her only her father, a pale, square-faced man with radical hazel eyes, and her brother Leuren, who shared Stephanie's blue eyes and blond hair with the addition of an impudent nose.

Her father was dressed in a brown jacket with green facings and gold braid. He had just entered from the open door opposite, and his hat was in his hand, as if he had just greeted or bid farewell to a guest. In his hand he held a cream paper. "A letter for you, Stephanie."

She hurried forward, her eyes lighting with pleasure, but Leuren was quicker. "I'll take it," he cried, snatching it from his father's hand.

"Leuren!" she said, with heat. "Give it to me!"

"Ah—I'll just take a look at it myself," he teased.

She started forward, her eyes a boiling azure. He danced lightly out of the way, taunting her by holding the letter up, just beyond her reach. M. de Lobel shrugged his shoulders. A phrase of his wife's went through his mind: "They must be left to nature, free to express their emotions so they may grow up into proper citizens, unstunted by society's restraints." He sighed and glanced into the entry behind him.

By this time, Stephanie had made several unsuccessful runs at Leuren, who always managed to twist out of her way at the last moment. Her face was flushed, and she spoke as if she were cutting each word in half and spitting it at him. "Give—It—To—Me—*Now*,—*Leuren Andre de Lobel!*" She caught the lapel of his coat, and with her other hand grabbed for the letter as he strained away from her.

At that moment, she happened to glance up, and her blue eyes grew wide with mortified astonishment. A tall, well-built young man in immaculate riding attire was standing just within the doorway, watching their squabble. She released her hold on Leuren, shooting an accusing glance at her father. *How embarrassing to be caught in a family brawl!* she thought.

With an attractive toss of her head, she advanced forward—a lightning-quick change to sweetness. She opened her eyes wide for their full effect, saying in dulcet tones, "Father, would you give me the pleasure of introducing me to our visitor?"

Her father turned from the still insubordinate Leuren, saying with a short laugh, "What! You do not know him?" With a sardonic grin, he said with exaggerated punctiliousness, "Stephanie, I would like to introduce you to Honore Rene-Luc de Coquiel di le Mercier. Honore, my daughter, Stephanie Aimee-Juliette de Lobel."

The handsome young man bowed. "It is a pleasure to see my cousin after so many years. I must confess myself also surprised at how you have changed—you are no longer the capricious little girl who played in the gardens with Adele and I."

Stephanie studied his open face, trying to see if he was speaking pleasantries or making a pointed reference to the scene that had just occurred. She couldn't decide, and his face was so attractive that she said lightly, "You have changed as well, Honore—I can barely recognize the little boy who knocked over our doll's boudoir." Her eyebrows arched artfully. "But we did not know of this visit—"

"His father has been confirmed as a deputy to the Estates-General," her father broke in, "and Honore tells me that he has come to find a suitable house for the family."

Stephanie turned to the young man—a far more interesting person to talk to, in her eyes, than her father—and said, her big sky-blue eyes fixed on his verdant ones, "Will Adele be coming?"

"Yes—depending on the roads, my whole family will arrive in two weeks. I know Adele is looking forward to seeing you," Honore replied. "She entrusted me with a letter for you, which—" his eyes sought out and spoke mutely to mischievous Leuren, "—which I am sure Leuren will manfully present to you." Stephanie watched in amazement as her brother sullenly advanced and put the letter in her hand, to be rewarded by a warm smile from Honore, who then turned to her father. "M. de Lobel, I am sorry to say that I cannot stay now. I have much to do in the next few days."

"We shall not keep you—do look up M. de la Croix," M. de Lobel replied. "He should be able to aid you. Let me know of how I can assist further."

"I will certainly do so. My grateful thanks for your offer. Adieu."

Honore bowed to Stephanie and her brother, and then moved with their father through the parlor door, past the meretricious statue in the dark-paneled entry, and to the broad front door. It closed behind them, leaving Stephanie clutching the letter and staring into space.

Leuren, after casting amused glances at his sister's discomposed countenance, sneered, "And there you were, blundering about in a rage, as he looked on..." Snorting, he ran from the room, pursued by his sister's blazing eyes.

~*~*~

Adele sighed wearily, and a vexed look creased her usually pleasant face. The whole household was supremely busy, packing and doing the little important odds and ends, but everything seemed to be going wrong. Missing the maid needed to pack her clothes, she stepped into the hall and collided with a small white figure.

"Paulette!"

She caught the little one in her arms and glanced down the wide, airy hall. No one else was in sight. The hall was empty from where she stood to the open windows at the very end, letting in the living April breeze. She stared out at the waving green trees beyond. Paulette tugged, trying to free herself from Adele's grasp. Remembering the many duties of the moment, Adele strode down the hall, glancing into the open doors and holding her little sister's hand. *Where is your nurse?* she thought fretfully. *Letting you run around the house is most inconvenient....ah, if only Grandpapa de Duret was here — he was always glad to entertain the younger ones...but he is far away with Honore in Paris....* Suddenly her conscience smote her. *Grandpapa de Duret and Madame du Chemin are always cheerful and selfless, no matter how trying the circumstance...but I have let myself become flustered and overwhelmed — I am not being peaceful and patient, like Christ, my example! O, Father God, forgive me!* She had neared the windows at the end of the hall, and turned a sorrowful, yet resolved face to the yellow sunlight that danced in. *Dear Father God, help me to thank You for everything, to rest in Your guiding Providence and be a light and a joy to others! Help me to be faithful in the little things.*

With a lighter heart, she cast a last long look at the green fields. Some movement in the cobbled stableyard below caught her attention, and she noted a mounted figure — Denis — alighting at the stables. Then turning with Paulette, she walked back down the long hall to descend the main staircase. When she reached the bottom, the parlor and entryway were equally deserted. Hearing servant-voices from the kitchen, she turned in that direction, hoping to find Paulette's nurse or her own errant maid.

There was quite a little gathering of idle servants in the kitchen, as she had expected—though upon her entrance they seemed to find something to do, or flitted off with some murmured errand. The servants were less and less reliable as the flurry of revolutionary pamphlets increased. There she found Paulette's nurse, who took over her charge with a deep curtsy and equally deep apologies. Adele asked after her own maid, and found the general consensus was that she was "with the marquise and Berthe" upstairs. Adele turned to leave.

Opening the kitchen door leading onto the empty hallway—or what she assumed would be an empty hallway—Adele was startled to see Denis just passing the door, dressed still in his mud-splashed riding garb. *How did he get here? He could not have come in by the kitchen door—I was just there,* Adele thought, *and he could not have come in the parlor or front doors, because those are up ahead...and...he would not have had time to go in them and come all the way down the hall, to be coming back when I came out....* She paused, then remembered where she was going and walked steadily up the stairs, a puzzled expression creasing her face.

~*~*~

The sun was low and heavy in the sky that evening when a carriage clattered past the gatehouse and swept up the long, shadowed avenue to the château di le Mercier. A middle-aged lady in a strong yellow hooped dress alighted, aided by the footman, then a man in a mauve waistcoat and a tall youth with dark hair and eyes. A doorkeeper rapidly ushered the Du Chemins into the parlor, while various menservants aided the Du Chemins' servants in unloading the carriage and bearing the luggage to their apartments. The meeting in the parlor between the Du Chemins and the De Coquiel di le Merciers was very convivial.

"I hope all is well with your rooms," Francis said, after the first greetings were over.

"Quite fine, thank you," Christophe du Chemin answered, pulling a large embroidered handkerchief from his mauve waistcoat. "I had our luggage carried up, though we shall have to reload it all when we leave. When were you planning to depart for Paris? In two days, or three?"

Francis was about to answer when a maid appeared and announced dinner. They adjourned to the long, heavily wainscoted formal dining room. Its great and costly chandelier burned with shapely candles.

After a sumptuous evening meal of many courses, the fathers retired to Francis' study, while the mothers went upstairs to consult on which gowns should be packed. Charlot and Tristan went straight to the library, and Adele and Olivie followed momentarily. As the girls pushed open the heavy library door, Tristan looked up from a book Charles was showing him. "Our greetings are all said, but how have things been here? Any news from Honore?"

Adele replied with a frank smile, "Yes—we heard from him last day-week; he and Grandpapa de Duret have found suitable lodgings. He said it took some little time—with the coming flood of deputies, many houses had already been taken. I am sorry he is not here to greet you, but we shall all see him within a week, if all goes well."

"Yes, we shall—and that shall be a pleasant meeting. Has anything of note occurred here while he has been gone?"

"Packing, and packing, and packing," Olivie sighed extravagantly, seating herself on a plush ottoman.

"Yes, packing…and, well, today I did see something strange." Adele sat down in an armchair and related Denis' inexplicable appearance.

Tristan's manly face grew thoughtful as she spoke, and at last he said, "I wonder—does that have anything to do with Olivie's sighting of Denis near the folly, a month and half ago?"

"I don't know. I have wondered," Adele replied.

"Let's go!" Charles exclaimed, springing towards the door.

"Go where?" Olivie asked, while Tristan said, "Wait, Charlot!—we must lay our plans first."

Charles returned reluctantly, but brightened when Tristan continued, "But we shall go somewhere soon, never fear." He settled himself thoughtfully into an armchair and looked across at the girls, while Charlot stood on one leg nearby. "First; how I wish Honore was here!—but there's no use asking for what we cannot get," Tristan began. Chin in hand, he mused for a minute. "What we need to do is find out where Denis is now, and whether he will tarry there for a while. And—where is Marcel?" He half rose from his chair.

"Don't go," Adele said, "you don't have an excuse for loitering. I think Olivie is the best for that; she has a habit," she threw her sister a gentle, teasing smile, "a habit of going to the kitchen to ask for the next day's menu."

Olivie stood up with outward decorum, but trembling with excitement. "I should go right now, Tristan?"

"Yes," he said, then suddenly grinned. "But wipe your feelings off your face, or they may be noticed."

"Yes, my lord," Olivie replied. With a straight face and a proper curtsey she left.

Tristan glanced across at Adele. "She makes it a habit, you say?"

Adele's eyes smiled back. "She is of the strong opinion that she may learn some clue that way," she answered with a twinkle. "At least, it is a handy excuse tonight."

Olivie was back within ten minutes, and she closed the door carefully before replying, her face triumphant.

"Tell us, Olivie!" Charles said, hopping up and down in his seven-year-old glee.

Olivie answered soberly, "Breakfast is crepes, wild duck, rolls, and smoked venison. I may have forgotten a few particulars. The noon-day meal is—"

"*Olivie!*" Charles cried in agony.

A grin exploded over her face. "Papa has given most of the servants an evening off tonight, and they are mainly gathered in the kitchen. Denis is there—quite ensconced with your footmen, Tristan, and some of our menservants—drinking and talking. He did not even notice when I came in; he looks as though he will be there for several hours yet."

"Grand!" Tristan answered. "I thank you, Olivie. What about Marcel?"

"He is coming—I think," Olivie replied. "I made him our signal."

"*Bon!*"

A minute later, Marcel slid in with quiet grace, carrying a candle. "What is in the air?"

Tristan filled him in, concluding with, "I think the best plan would be to search the hallway and rooms right past the kitchen door where you say you saw Denis earlier, Adele."

"It is our best chance for that, Master Tristan—the servants shall be occupied for some time," Marcel said. "I have brought a candle, so we need not bother with a light in the dark rooms."

"What are we looking for? What shall we find?" Olivie asked.

"Frankly, I do not know, but I have my suspicions," Tristan replied. "Oh, and Charlot—"

"Yes?" Charles answered, his face alight.

"—if you would be on guard, 'playing' with a toy—just past the kitchen door, where I shall show you—that would be a great help."

"Yes sir!"

They slipped out into the hall. It was empty, as Olivie had said. Turning to the left, they could hear the chatter and conviviality from behind the closed kitchen door. They hastened down the hallway and past the door, but no one looked out. Charles settled on the floor nearby with a wooden toy, while the other four scanned the narrow hall ahead, doors set at intervals in the paneling.

Olivie tried the polished floor with a silken shoe, while Adele, bright in a green and crimson gown, touched the first door handle. It opened easily, displaying a plain servant's room. As she glanced in, the full hopelessness of their task hit her. *What are we looking for? A secret passage? But — but it could be anywhere — it could be so well hidden that no amount of our amateur sleuthing could ever find it! And what if there is no passage at all?* She paused irresolute and heard Tristan's lowered voice from behind her. Across the hall, on the same wall as the kitchen door, he was fingering a door knob. "What is in here?" he asked.

Before Adele or Marcel could answer, Olivie hurried up. "That is the pantry," she said, reaching to open it. The two slipped inside. Adele was about to join them, but then remembered her misgivings and turned to search farther on. She didn't want Tristan to see her doubt. As she left the pantry door, she heard Tristan ask, "And what is this? A door — and steps leading down!" She heard but part of Olivie's reply before moving out of earshot, "Oh, that? That's just the door to the wine cellar. No, 't leads nowhere else…"

She glanced back down the hall and saw Charles, busy and important, playing near the kitchen door. The sight brought a small smile back to her face. *This may prove fruitless…* she thought, *but…*

Tristan and Olivie emerged from the pantry with dust on their hands and faces, and the three moved further on down the hallway. Suddenly, Charles' voice came to them clearly, and they knew he was trying to warn them: "What you doin', Virginie?"

Adele glanced about, seized the nearest brass door handle and whispered, "In here!" Not until they tumbled into it did they realize it was a linen closet; they squeezed in among white sheets. Marcel swung the door shut softly, and a few moments later the servants' voices grew louder, passed, then faded down the hallway. Olivie breathed a great sigh of relief.

"'Twas a close one, I must admit," Tristan replied in an undertone. "Let us keep on."

But soon they had reached the hall's extremity, and turned to face each other, the same thought in each mind: *We've seen nothing suspicious; we have no clues whatever.*

Adele caught Tristan's look of baffled determination and noticed Olivie's patent disappointment. *I must think of a distraction to cheer her.* Aloud, Adele said, *"Paris ne s'est pas fait en un jour* — Paris wasn't made in a day. Why not show your new book to Tristan, Olivie?"

Marcel hung back, and Adele heard him mutter, "Oh, for Honore!"

Tristan shot him a keen glance, and stepped back a pace to stand beside him. "We must not give up, eh, Marcel?" he said. To the others he said, "I want to examine that pantry again — just a foolish hunch of mine."

They made their way at a steady pace down the hall and back in sight of Charlot, who was still plying his toy with diligence. He looked up, and Olivie replied, "Nothing."

"Nothing — nothing *yet,*" Tristan amended, entering the wide pantry. The other three followed. Adele cast her eyes about the deep, layered shelves, the cool marble slab with a brace of pheasants lying stiff upon it, the hanging onions, the bins which she knew stored the hardy fruits of last year's harvest.

"Stay in here to give us the alarm if anyone comes in, Olivie," Tristan directed. She nodded, the "adventurous" look coming back into her eyes.

On the farthest wall was an ancient, heavy oaken door — Tristan strode rapidly toward it. It opened easily enough, and he sprang down the stone steps, a vaulted stone ceiling growing above his head at each downward step. *This must have been where Tristan and Olivie got dusty,* Adele thought, brushing aside a cobweb.

Once down in the vault, Adele's eyes adjusted to the dark. It was a square room, with walls, ceiling, and floor dating from a couple of hundred years before. *And everything looks as it did then,* Adele thought, holding up the candle for the others. Running along the two side walls were racks and pigeonholes filled with dusty wine bottles and kegs of stronger brew, while for want of a better place, a few kegs were scattered against the otherwise empty farthest wall. On everything lay a feeling of permanence — as though the wine cellar had looked like this since it had been built, centuries ago.

Adele placed her free hand against the wall, and shivered at the coolness of the stones. "There seems to be nothing here," she almost said. It did seem hopeless; her spirits sank as she watched the others' careful searching.

A Discovery and a Rose

6.

Quand le vi nest tire, il faut le boire —
When the wine is drawn, one must drink it.
— French Proverb

*A*dele shifted position once more, holding the candle high. Tristan and Marcel had been examining the floor of the wine cellar for some time. Straightening, they glanced at each other, shaking their heads in the negative.

"It really would be the best place to find something queer, though," Tristan said to no one in particular. "Old places like this...." he moved to the farthest wall and ran his hands along it.

Adele watched the two tenacious youths. Suddenly, Marcel stiffened, with a stifled exclamation. Tristan was at his side in a moment, and Adele joined them seconds later, bringing the candle close. Marcel was feeling along the outlines of the irregular stones. "Here — knife," he muttered. The sharp, thin poniard in Tristan's belt was out in a moment, gleaming dully in the uncertain light. He tried its edge in one of the cracks between the stones, about shoulder height. The blade entered only an inch or two, and Adele bit her lip in disappointment. But as Tristan slid it upwards along the crack, it suddenly slipped in much deeper, and moved almost freely along.

"I think we're on to something," Tristan said, a thrill in his voice.

"And look — a slight discoloration along both edges of this long crack," Marcel said. "Mayhap someone else has done this, and has not been careful to keep the hilt away from the wall."

Tristan grunted, for the blade had come to a halt a little distance above his head. He took it out, and turning it on its side, slid it sideways at that point. It went easily along for about an arms'-width, then stopped. Adele caught her breath, her eyes bright with delighted wonder. Re-inserting the blade at the top of the vertical crack, Tristan slid it downwards. When it reached shoulder-height, where it had stuck before, it slid by easily enough, and—a stone door in the wall swung outwards.

Marcel and Tristan grinned triumphantly at each other. Adele could hardly believe it, and yet there it stood before them—a dark, gaping entryway.

"You pressed down the latch with the poinard," Marcel said, bending over the exposed edge of the door. "Now—shall we enter?"

"Yes—but first I shall check to make sure all is quiet and clear above." Tristan started upwards, then paused halfway up the steps and looked down on Adele and Marcel, still near the secret doorway. "If only Honore could have been here," he said, and disappeared into the pantry beyond.

He returned in a minute with Olivie and Charlot. Their eyes widened immeasurably at the gaping hole in the wall.

"It would be useless to have them on guard up there; if we venture in farther we couldn't hear their warning," Tristan said. "One of us must stay on guard here. If anyone came down, your presence would be least suspected, Marcel," he said reluctantly.

Marcel nodded with his usual imperturbility, settling down on one of the casks.

With bated breath, Adele followed Tristan, Olivie, and Charles into the opening. In the pools of candle-light, an arched stone roof and gray, rough-cut stone walls and floor were revealed, proceeding straight ahead into blackness. They went slowly, examining everything. Adele wondered that there was not more dust, since the passage seemed so old; then realized with a shock, *It is still in use!* She wondered to herself, *How did Denis know of this, and why not Father? For I remember him telling Honore and I once that he knew of no secret passages in our chateau—much to our youthful chagrin.*

Olivie uttered a short exclamation. Ahead the passage continued straight on; but an arched doorway and passage gaped on the left.

"Which one?" Charles asked.

"Straight first!" Olivie said.

Tristan shrugged. "I see no difference."

A few steps further led to a blank wall—a dead end. Olivie looked disappointed, but Tristan was already examining the wall. "Whereabouts would we be?" he queried, turning his face to Adele.

"Under the stables?" she guessed.

"That is what I am thinking," he replied. "It might be unwise to open this door at present. Let's go back to the other passage!"

Going back, they followed the new trail for some little time, when suddenly the monotony of the dank walls ended with a thick wood door. Tristan pushed it open. From the empty darkness, it seemed that they were in a wider chamber. Tristan held the candle up. The faint light disclosed a rectangular room, with a heavy chest and dusty mirror. Opposite was another solid door.

Olivie ran straight to the chest. "May I?"

"I suppose so," Tristan shrugged. "It may give a clue to what Denis is using this for."

In a twinkling Olivie had raised the lid and was rummaging about in the chest.

Adele glanced curiously into the mirror. It revealed her own face, rather dingy, with several cobwebs in her hair, and Tristan's even dustier countenance looking over her shoulder.

"Look here!" Olivie cried, lifting out a cloth bundle. Several other articles of clothing appeared in rapid succession: two limp, mean hats; several dirt-stained shirts and waistcoats; a ragged jacket; various faded colors of cravats and sashes—"A whole collection of disguises," Adele breathed.

"Yes; and this bundle looks just like the one I saw Denis carrying near the folly," Olivie said, motioning to the first bundle, tied with string. "And look—an empty bottle of one of Father's best wines!"

Tristan was onto something else. "Yes; the folly," he murmured. "Put things back how we found them; 'twould not do to have him suspect that anyone has discovered his secret."

After everything had been placed carefully back in the chest, they moved curiously to the hitherto unexplored door. It opened onto—what else—a straight stone passage, stretching into dead blackness.

"I feel sorry for Marcel," Adele said after a bit. "Should one of us go back to relieve him?" Just as she said that, the corridor turned at a right angle, and Tristan exclaimed with satisfaction. Adele peered ahead, looking for some change; but they went on for some little time before a short flight of steps appeared ahead, filling the entire passageway. The roof looked unbroken, but when Tristan half-climbed the steps, he could discern a trap-doorway, and a ring to push it up.

"This candle would give too much light," he grunted, "can't risk trying to open this yet—it's too dark outside, and the light might be noticed."

Adele had been pondering the distances and directions they had traveled underground. "We are under—or near—the folly, aren't we?" she asked, looking up at Tristan.

"Yes—I really think we are," he answered. "Well, Olivie—you were right! You did see Denis here."

"I must apologize for doubting you, Olivie," Adele said. "You were right all along."

"I forgive you." Olivie bubbled. "I'm glad we found this! What news we will have to tell Honore!"

"First we can tell Marcel!" Charles cried, darting off down the passage, back the way they had come. He slowed when he went beyond the lantern light, however, and waited until the others caught up to him. Then he and Olivie skipped on ahead, at the very farthest reach of the light, while Adele and Tristan followed a little more slowly.

"So Denis has been using this as a way to store peasant-clothes and get in and out of the house without suspicion," Adele voiced her thoughts aloud.

"Yes; and what a handy place!" Tristan answered. "Your father knows nothing of this passageway?"

"No; a few years ago, Honore and I had been reading tales of old and asked him particularly about any such passage or hiding place in our chateau," Adele said. "I cannot think how he would not have known, though, when Denis did."

Tristan's brow knit in thought, and it was some time before he spoke. "Correct me if I am wrong," he said finally, "but did not Denis' father and grandfather serve your grandfather and great-grandfather as their *valet-de-chambres*?"

"Yes; the men of his family have faithfully held that position for as far back as I know," Adele answered. They reached the first door, passed through the wide room, and went out the other door into the corridor beyond.

"And your grandfather died when your father was young?" Tristan broke the silence again.

"Yes," Adele replied. "He was a toddling little baby." She paused, then added, "I remember hearing that Denis' father died in a hunting accident when my father was eight years old or so."

"Denis took over his present duties then?"

"Yes. I know his father had trained him to fill that position. Denis was only a few years older than my father."

"So…what if Denis' father told him about the passage, but your father was never told? Your grandfather died too early to tell your father…"

"…and Denis never thought to tell him? I know not," Adele answered.

They reached a "T"—to the left branched the short hall leading to what they presumed was the stables; to the right, the one leading to the wine cellar and the secret door. As they entered the wine cellar, Marcel gave a subdued exclamation of satisfaction. "There you are—you have been gone quite a while," he said.

"There was a fair bit to explore," Tristan answered.

"Lots of hallways—and a room—and a chest—disguises!—Tristan says it goes to the folly!—and the stables!" Olivie and Charles breathlessly interrupted each other in their excitement. "Come see!" Olivie finished, while Charlot tugged on Marcel's coat.

"I can stay out here," Adele said quickly, seeing Tristan and Marcel exchange glances. "You go, both of you—and Olivie and Charles."

"We shall not be long," Marcel said. "You will have to clean up, Mesdames—and you too, Tristan—and quickly, before anyone sees you and wonders."

Adele glanced down at her begrimed hands—quite a novelty!—and then at the dusty and cobwebbed attire, faces, and hands of the others. "You are right," she laughed. "We are quite a sight!"

At first, after her companions had disappeared with the lantern into the gaping doorway, Adele forbore to sit down. But as the minutes slipped by, she grew tired of standing. Feeling for one of the kegs in the darkness, she daintily brushed off the top before seating herself with her usual care. She was full of thoughts: exultation and wonder at having found this secret passage; shadowed concern and puzzlement at all the implications involved. She was deep in musings about her grandfather and his early death when the sound of steps startled her. She sprung up, then realized in relief that the sounds were from the secret passage. A moment later, a splash of light against the farther wall, and Olivie's voice, reassured her further.

"A real find," Marcel greeted her, as he stepped into the wine-cellar, lantern in hand.

"And now, let us all hasten to clean our faces and hands; we shall meet in the library when we look presentable once more," Tristan said. He and Marcel slid the stone door shut and carefully moved the candle about to make sure they had disturbed nothing.

Adele hurried the younger ones upstairs, fearing at any moment that a servant would step out and see them. Charlot's hands were grimy from the walls, and a bold, sooty streak across his chubby countenance showed where he had wiped his face. Olivie was only a slight bit cleaner, and Tristan and Marcel were noticeably grubby. Marcel had turned off into his room downstairs, and once upstairs Tristan betook himself to his suite.

It took some scrubbing at the water basin to make Olivie and Charlot clean; "Our maid will wonder what we were doing with the water she set out for our bedtime," Olivie giggled.

"I will tell Marcel to refill them with fair water," Adele replied. "There, Charlot—you look almost as clean as before our adventure." She smiled, patted his face dry with a cloth, and addressed herself to her own toilette. "And do not speak of what we found to anyone, unless Tristan or I tell you," she warned.

"Hurry, Adele; they will be waiting for us in the library," Olivie urged. "We have taken so long." Adele cast one more glance into the small gilded mirror. *I look a bit tousled, but not remarkably so.* They hastened downstairs to the appointed rendezvous. However, they had to wait for more than a half hour in the library before Tristan showed himself, with Marcel right behind him.

"What took you so long?" Olivie demanded.

"We took a dark lantern out to the folly," said Tristan, "and managed after much blundering about to find the trapdoor from that end. Whoever built it, hid it well—if we had not known that there must be a trapdoor there, I doubt if we could've found it."

"It is artfully concealed by the folly and all the shrubs and rosebushes, and the turf covers it," Marcel agreed.

"But why does Denis only know of this?" Olivie asked.

"I am not sure—we may never know," Tristan said. "It seems as though he must have been told—perhaps by his father—but your father never was. Mayhap Denis thought 'twould prove useful someday to be the sole possessor of the secret of the passage. I do not know his reasons for not telling your father, but it has certainly been helpful to him these last few years."

"Yes; helpful to his sneaking plans—whatever they are," Marcel said. "How handy to store worn and dirty clothes there, where no maid could find them! To be able to slip outdoors and return again with no one suspecting anything: is he not in charge of the wines?"

"Yet he was seen around the kitchen often enough last year to give rise to servant-talk that he was enamored with the scullery-maid Louise,"

Adele reminded them. Then she burst out, "It is too bad that we have found this so late! We shall be leaving in just a few days, and it will do us no good. If we had found this some months ago…"

"Still, it is a victory, though a belated one," Tristan said.

"And in Paris, Denis won't have a secret hiding place for his disguises," Olivie said. "It will be easier to spy on him."

"I do not know about that," Adele answered. "He will probably be gone with Father most of the time."

"A great plan, that, to have exits into the stables, chateau, and the folly," Marcel mused aloud. "*Souris qui n'a qu'un trou est bientot prise*—a mouse that has only one hole is soon caught."

"I cannot wait to tell Honore," Tristan said. "What an exciting find!"

"And we will inform Father at the first opportunity," Adele said. "To think—he has been lord of this manor for so many years, and never knew of this! It was lying beneath our feet the whole time!"

~*~*~

A few short and hectic days later, Adele lingered on the garden lawn, gazing with intense hazel eyes at the flowering panorama before her. Behind her in the chateau, she heard hurrying feet and last-minute instructions—but her ear was strained to catch other noises. A bee buzzed by, a lark sang and soared high in the pale azure dome overhead, while the rippling music of the fountain underran all the sounds of nature. The scattered clouds were reflected in the pool before her, while the water in turn was reflected in her eyes. She was trying to capture the whole scene forever in her memory, as if she would never see this dearest of dear scenes again. She could not have told anyone why she felt that way—why she drank it all in as if she were never again to behold it in this life—but she felt it, nonetheless.

One of the French doors opened, and Charlot's boyish voice called, "Adele! The coaches are ready! Madame du Chemin told me!"

"I will be there," Adele answered, turning and smiling at his enthusiasm. He was so excited about this trip to Paris—it was an adventure for him. It would be doubly pleasurable since the Du Chemins were to journey with them. This was due to the widespread unrest and the fearful reports of the Brigands, fierce "beggars," whom popular report had swelled into gigantic bands of marauders. Looking back over the centuries, much of those reports were exaggerated—though it is true that the rascally

Brigands existed. But at the time, the wild overestimations seemed all too real and terrifying.

As Charlot disappeared into the house, Adele stepped quickly over the grass to a path. Passing the gazebo-like folly with a smiling, secretive glance, she went to the back right corner of the garden. There, in its full splendor, stood a lush rosebush, its profusion of deep rose-pink blooms cascading over the hedge on one side and leaning invitingly over the path on the other.

She stepped under the living arch, looking up at the strong, slender, thorned stalks, blue-green leaves, and roseate beauty of the masses of flowers, with the morning sun painting each with extra-vivid hues. This was her rose—the one the wizened gardener had planted when she was born. She felt as if she had stepped into a bower outside of time and trouble. A peace flowed over her as her father's favorite verse came to mind: "…lo, I am with you alway, even unto the end of the world."

She sensed she would never see it again. Suddenly a great desire came over her to pluck a coral-colored bloom and bring it with her. *T'will wilt on the road, but I will dry it—a memento of home…* she thought, choosing a generous, perfect blossom. The stem resisted her efforts, and she had to twist it with care in order to avoid being pricked by the sharp thorns. The struggle so absorbed her attention that she started when a voice said almost beside her, "Perhaps I can help?"

On the path, half-screened by the drooping rose branches, stood Tristan du Chemin. With him was Charlot, almost dancing with eagerness to be off.

"We were coming to tell you it is time to depart," Tristan said, with his free, brotherly smile. If he saw her brimming eyes, he did not comment, but drew a poinard, saying, "Which rose did you want?"

"It is Adele's own rosebush—mine is the white one there," Charlot piped in, his eyes darting along the shining steel with admiration.

Adele gestured toward the blossom she wanted. A swift motion of the sharp blade brought the gorgeous bloom into her hands.

"Thank you," she said, with a grateful look, tucking the rose in the clasp on her scarf as the three turned down the path and hastened to the chateau.

At the steps she paused and looked back. *Lord Christ, help me not to value earthly things more than Your plan for me,* she prayed silently, following the others through the parlor and then the entry for perhaps the last time. *I thank You for this dear place—and—and I thank You for the new adventure that lies before my family and me.* She was almost at the door of the second carriage now—Tristan and Charlot had entered the first—and a footman held open the door for her. *Lord Christ—help me to be a 'city set on a hill,' 'salt with savor,' in Paris.*

At a cry from the coachman, the horses started forward, their manes waving in the breeze as they trotted away under the tall trees lining the avenue. Adele watched until the chateau was lost among the trees. She only half-heard Madame du Chemin's talk to Paulette as they crested a hill near the river. Looking back, she caught her breath. There, running away from them in a descending wave lay fields of purple and gold, with clumps of trees and acres of forest rising above the billows. Sitting like a galleon riding the waves was their chateau, the eastern morning sun bathing it in almost luminescent light. It was so beautiful—smooth, carved stone rising in pillars, crowned with two flanking turrets. A glittering silver line lay far beyond the chateau: the ocean!—a dazzling backdrop. Adele felt as if she could have gazed at the scene for the rest of her life.

Just as the carriage began the downhill ascent a cloud slipped across the sun, throwing the chateau into a foreboding shadow. Then it was gone, and the wheels kept on, turning, turning on the south-eastern road to Paris.

~*~*~

Two days later, the setting sun cast its last beams across the parched landscape and found rest on two carriages lurching steadily east into the darkness beyond. Physical darkness, yes; and yet 'twas an apt symbol of the spiritual darkness of the city whose walls smudged the horizon:

> *Because that when they knewe God, they glorified him not as God,*
> *neither were thankefull, but became vaine in their thoughtes,*
> *and their foolish heart was full of darkenesse.*
> *When they professed themselves to be wise, they became fooles.*

As they drew near, the sun sank down behind them in streaks of vivid orange and scarlet, as if dying for the last time. As the city grew ahead, the blackness increased until it was almost palpable, broken only by the small pools of light thrown by the torches fastened to the carriages. The inhabitants were silent, wearied by the long days of travel and made sleepy by the darkness. Suddenly, they passed a far-flung tavern. The fierce yet welcoming blaze of its lights flashed by—giving a momentary glimpse of the white steed on its sign, a few hunched men inside, and a tall figure silhouetted in the door—then it was swept behind and they were in darkness once more. Madame Felicienne spoke. "I am glad Honore and M. de Duret have prepared our lodgings. With a little unpacking, our new home will be habitable."

"Yes—" Madame du Chemin answered, but cut herself short as a loud, rattling blast of sound came from ahead. "What is that?" she exclaimed.

Their maid, Berthe, gave a cry as a second sharp volley burst from the dark city ahead. They knew now it was the sound of large guns. The carriages came to a swaying halt. Paulette woke, crying. Adele drew the little one closer and smoothed her forehead. "Go back to sleep," she whispered. "We have not arrived." The toddler, awake but calm now, laid her head on Adele's aching shoulder and was silent, clasping her arms around Adele's smooth neck.

The women could hear the men in the first carriage talking, and several more retorts broke the otherwise silent countryside. After several suspenseful moments, the rumble of gunfire died away and did not resume. The subsequent silence pressed heavily on them. Then the dark shape of Francis' cocked hat appeared at their window. But before he could speak, the clatter of a galloping horse approached rapidly from behind. Francis' hat disappeared as he turned to face the rider. "Hail! Who goes there!" he cried.

"At last!" exclaimed a well-known voice, that of Honore.

"Honore! What are you doing here?"

"There is a disturbance in Paris—near the dwelling we procured," answered the heart-warming voice. "It started yesterday in front of Sieur de Reveillon's wallpaper factory. The crowd got ugly—but Paris has had disturbances before. M. de Duret and I were relatively unconcerned until they broke into and burned a workshop. They damaged Reveillon's house, too. Seizing two cart-loads of paving stones, they used them to resist the *Gardes Francaises*, who could do no more than keep Reveillon's paper warehouse from being destroyed. After receiving these reports, M. de Duret thought I should come out and wait at 'The White Horse,' to guide you around the unrest."

"A very wise plan, Honore; I thank you. Do you know what the firing was just now?"

"Before I left the city, I heard a rumor that the Swiss Guards were to be called out against the rioters. The Swiss Guards are a brave and resolute set, and were equipped with cannons. The firing has ceased—it may be the mob has been dispersed."

After this short delay, the carriages were on their way once more, with Honore in the lead on horseback. Some minutes later, an ancient city gate loomed ahead. After pausing at the barrier they rumbled through and down the dark streets. At intervals, lampposts shed hazy pools of light into the darkness. Dim figures scuttled by in the shadows. As they turned left into a narrow street, two scruffy men stumbled by. In the short moments they were illumined by the flickering carriage lights, Adele noticed that one was helping the other along; and that the latter, a lean man with a paper-white face, was clutching his side. His clothes were clotted with an ugly red liquid.

"Some of the rioters, no doubt," murmured Madame du Chemin, with pity. "Ah! The poor things—led astray by…"

Their carriage halted abruptly, and a footman swung down from above and opened the door, revealing the front façade of a house. Rows of lighted windows swept the eye upward to the scintillating stars in the black sky above. Then the front door opened, and light poured down the few steps as a tall servant advanced, holding a torch. Behind him came the stout figure of M. de Duret.

Adele was one of the first to alight, and found herself, still holding Paulette, at Honore's side. "'Tis so good to see you, Adele," he said warmly.

"Yes, Honore," she beamed up at him. Her hands were full, but she managed to deftly signal with one of her eyebrows. "What is it?" he queried, drawing her closer into the shadow, as the others bustled gratefully out of the carriages, stretching their cramped legs.

"Ah, Honore! Well met!" cried Tristan's voice, and the two greeted each other with a hearty handclasp. Then lowering his voice, he stepped closer. "Has Adele told you yet?"

"No; she was just about to," Honore answered.

Tristan glanced about, noting the servants and others who were moving about nearby. "Adele will tell you later," he said rapidly, "but we do have news, Honore."

"This go, sir?" a quick voice broke in, as a manservant bustled up, hefting a heavy portmanteau.

"No—it is my luggage," Tristan replied. Just then, Francis hastened up and questioned Honore as to the site of the disturbance, while the voice of the marquis du Chemin was heard, calling for Tristan.

"*Adieu*, Adele—I shall see you soon, I hope," Tristan bowed to Adele, then strode off to join his father. At the same moment Francis turned from Honore and spoke a few quick words to Denis, who disappeared into the blackness with a pleased expression.

There was a scurry as menservants carried in the last bundles and portmanteaus under the able direction of Grandpapa de Duret, and a bustle of last-minute good-byes to the Du Chemins, whose place of residence was down a couple more streets. "It was so pleasant to travel together .... Yes, we shall make sure to see you as soon as we're settled .... You shall be at the LaFayette's tomorrow night, shall you not? .... Yes .... Here, my man, do not forget this small chest .... Charlot, come this way, to the house .... Adieu, and God bless!"

When the flurry subsided, Adele found herself in an entryway that seemed narrow and cramped compared with their grand, spacious foyer at home. It was papered in pale gold, with white moldings and cornices around the white ceiling and doors. Straight ahead stretched a deep green hall hung with paintings, and with doors opening off of it. In the entry and to the right, a dark wood staircase climbed to the second story. To the left was a wide door, and Olivie was already turning the knob with curiosity. "Where does this lead, Honore?"

"To the parlor—it looks out onto the street," Honore answered. "Down the hall are the library, dining room, kitchen, and miscellaneous; that door at the end opens onto a small portico with a tiny strip of what they call a garden here."

"Honore, it even has nice wallpaper!" Olivie cried, fingering the slightly embossed pattern on the wall.

"I am glad you think so—I tried my hardest, Olivie," Honore grinned. He added half-seriously, "T'was probably made by some of the wretches that rioted today."

"Yes; tell us more," his father said.

"There are many reports flying about, but it seems that the disreputable ruffians who loiter in considerable numbers—*Brigands*, they are called—were the ones who incited (at least added extra fuel to) the riot. The mob seemed to be under the mistaken impression that Reveillon, the owner of the wallpaper factory, declared that the people could subsist on fifteen *sous* a day. They feared he would cut their wages to that slim amount. In reality, Reveillon merely stated out of kindness that the price of bread should be brought down to fifteen *sous*. But popular report twisted his words, and the workmen rose, with the enthusiastic aid of the *Brigands*. The streets were choked with men, the ascending smoke from the warehouse they eviscerated and set alight was even visible from here; musket-volleys were responded to by fierce yells and missiles of all kinds—tiles raining from roofs and windows; in fact, the situation was getting to be more than the *Gardes Francaises* could handle—"

"Where do I sleep, Papa?" Charlot cried, scampering about in excitement and falling with a crash over a forgotten portmanteau. He bounded up again with an eager disclaimer that he wasn't hurt—and assuredly was *not* tired!

"There are bedrooms for us upstairs," Honore answered, turning to his father. "I put his things in one of them—of course, we can change that later."

"Fine. At present, let us address ourselves to getting everyone to bed; it is late, and even those who are *not* tired—" this with a smiling glance at Charlot, "—even they need some rest."

Berthe put a hand on the boy's shoulder and led the way up the stairs; Adele followed behind with sleeping Paulette in her arms. However, as Adele reached the landing, the front door opened and Denis entered. She paused, looking down over the carved balustrade.

"Denis, what is your report?" her father asked. Denis' hair, usually tied neatly back in a dark queue, was disheveled, and his face keen with something—*Perhaps excitement,* Adele thought.

"I went down to Saint-Antoine—staying out of the way of the *Gardes*, of course—they mayhap could not distinguish me from a rioter," Denis' smile was crooked. "Most of the people were hastening discomfited back to their abodes, but a wounded man was willing to stop and tell his tale of woe. He said the *Gardes Suisses* appeared after dark with two or three pieces of artillery. They charged the group to depart, in the King's name, and when answered by cries of defiance, they loaded the cannon with grape-shot and commanded the group again to disperse. The answer, according to my informant, was slightly hesitant, but it was still defiant, and so they fired upon the contumacious mass."

"That is what we heard as we approached the city!" Francis said.

"Yes, master," Denis answered. "The noise did seem too loud to be mere musketry. 'Tis difficult to guess the number of dead—I heard everything from 'four to five hundred' (that from a frightened shrew of a street gamin) down to 'at least twenty-five.' I am inclined to think it was more close to the latter figure, but it was dark…"

"Madame Adele, the bed is ready for Madame Paulette," Berthe said. As she followed Berthe, Adele heard her father say, "*Quand le vi nest tire, il faut le boire*—When the wine is drawn, one must drink it."

She entered a cool and quiet room and heard no more, but gratefully laid the sleeping form down and rubbed her aching arms. She was not used to holding Paulette for such an extended period. *I must try to accustom my arms to it — here in Paris, we shall have fewer servants,* she mused inwardly. *Father says it is best to familiarize ourselves to that now, because we may find it needful later. Abroad, also, they often do not have as many servants.* Then she thought, *What a harbinger — we arrive in Paris on a day of riot and bloodshed!*

It was a greater prognostication than she could have foreseen. Blessed are we mortals, that Providence holds a curtain over the future!

All that Glitters is not Gold

7.

And still they dream that they shall still succeed,
And still are disappointed.
— Cowper

"*C*ertes! So you found a secret tunnel Denis was using! And it had three openings; the stables, folly, and wine cellar?" Honore asked quietly, beside Adele. Their carriage bumped and rattled over the cobblestones. Across the aisle their parents sat, absorbed in conversation.

"Yes," she replied with a deep smile. "I had planned to tell you before, but we have been busy ever since we arrived last night."

"How I wish I could have been there!" Honore replied. "To think that you found it!"

"It was Tristan—Marcel, too," Adele replied. "We would never have found it without their persistence."

"We must tell Father of this," Honore said. He glanced across at their parents, but they were deep in talk.

"Yes; though it may be difficult to find time," Adele answered, "So many things claim his attention." They fell silent, but she sensed his thrill over their find.

Presently, the carriage slowed and checked, recalling Adele to matters at hand. She quivered with a different excitement as she peered out the small glass pane of the carriage window into the darkness. The carriage halted. The door was opened by the footman, and she stepped out decorously, following the resplendent figures of her mother and father. A tall, ornate house loomed in the darkness overhead, and their footman rapped on the heavy door—it was the palatial Paris residence of the LaFayette's. Adele's eyes gleamed with breathless impatience. Tonight she would finally see her cousin Stephanie again!

There was a knot in her stomach, which did not mend matters. Of course, she had participated in the parties and fetes at home—but this was

Paris, and the attendees some of the most influential of the *ancienne noblesse* in the kingdom. And the LaFayette's—high society indeed. She glanced down once more at her delicate deep blue dress, and smoothed her pale scarf for the twentieth time.

The door opened instantly upon their footman's knock, and a glittering stream of light shot forward as a liveried doorman bowed profoundly and beckoned them into the spacious entry.

Overhead a large crystal chandelier, agleam with candles, shone a sparkling, dynamic light on the rich, cool blue of the walls and danced off the enormous gilded frame accenting one wall. A prim maid whisked the ladies off to an adjoining room to take off their wraps. Rejoining Honore and Francis in the entry, a manservant bowed them through the wide archway opposite.

A sumptuous room with elaborately framed paintings, scattered gilded chairs and richly carved low tables met Adele's eyes. At the far end, looking out the French windows into the darkening garden, was a perfectly polished area cleared for dancing. Mingling among the furniture were sleek and *soignée* figures. Even at the most fashionable Le Havre de Grace ball Adele had never seen such perfectly tailored and dandified accoutrements. Gold lace, detailed embroidery, gorgeous fabrics…a true feast for the eyes.

But she had not much time to take this all in—at the moment, it was merely a confused, swirling sensation of opulence. Nearest her a slender woman chatted with a short, stout man in uniform. The lady broke away with a gentle excuse and advanced. The encircling candlelight showed her mint gown with rose highlights to perfection, and her sweet oval face was framed by a wealth of light curls. She was thirty, but her face had an air of sweet youthfulness that made many of the fashionable crowd declare 'she could not be more than twenty.' This was Adrienne, marquise de LaFayette, the wife of the acclaimed soldier who had fought with George Washington in America. Sweeping up, their hostess exclaimed with delight, "Felicienne! At last!"

Adele's mother curtsied beautifully, answering with equal warmth, "Adrienne! How glad am I to see your dear face once again!"

"It has been too long, as you know, dear heart," Adrienne answered. She smiled at Francis. "You are welcome, and doubly so because you have brought your wife, marquis."

He bowed. "It is a deep pleasure to meet once more, marquise."

"I know Gilbert is looking forward to seeing you," she answered, casting a quick glance around the sparkling assembly. "At the moment he is speaking with M. Talleyrand…" she broke off with a silvery laugh, but remarked *sotto voce*, "Quite a waste of time!" Then she said aloud, "But you must introduce me to your children — they have grown so!"

"This is our eldest, Honore," answered Francis — Honore, in a suit of forest green which accentuated his dark-haired good looks, bowed — "and this is our eldest daughter, Adele." Adele curtsied, her hooped dress sweeping the ground in the approved fashion.

"It is a great pleasure to meet you both, I assure you. Now I simply must introduce you all to General—" she turned to the short man she had been conversing with before, and drew him in. The introductions quickly passed into pleasantries and light conversation.

A little time later, Adele found herself in a corner formed by a potted orange tree and two velvet couches. Here she was free to study the assembled gathering. Her eyes passed over the brilliant and now crowded scene. Across the room she watched her father and the Du Chemins talking to a thin man with an aquiline nose. He had been introduced to her earlier as her host, the marquis de LaFayette. A stout man with a mottled face joined them. Immense buttons bulged from his tight saffron jacket. His face was scarred by the deep pits of smallpox and grievously lined with the dissipation of a selfish life. Their conversation sparkled. But from a certain grave expression on her father's face Adele guessed that it was mere froth, not substance.

Near her were a coterie of satin and silk-garbed ladies. From their eyes, eyebrows, and tittering, Adele gathered that they were discussing some spicy bit of gossip. A pleasant-faced woman passed near the glittering group. Fluttering out of it, a short lady greeted her warmly and beckoned her to join.

"I have so missed the sight of your face, Madame Anne," the short woman bubbled, motioning with her painted fan. "What a gorgeous dress, too! It becomes you rarely!"

"Ah, yes," another gushed.

"Have you heard, Anne, of the latest…"

Adele's gaze wandered, and she paid no more attention to the group until Madame Anne was called away on some pretext a little later. Almost as soon as Anne was out of earshot, one of the other women (the younger, shorter one that had greeted her most warmly) remarked to the others, "Can you believe her impudence! Wearing that old gown, as if that is good enough here!"

"And smiling so sweetly! She's been ruined by all her foolish religious notions!" scoffed another.

The short woman added with an elegant shrug, "She thinks she can move in high society *and* be a saint. *Ma foi* (Indeed!)*! Il ne faut jamais courir deux lievres a la fois*—one should never run after two hares at the same time."

"And the way she misunderstood us and thought we were *praising* her..." a woman with a gold filigree fan simpered maliciously.

Turning with sad distaste, Adele's recognized a young man. *'Tis Sebastien du Sauchoy.* He was advancing through the crowd, engaged in animated conversation with a striking blond young lady whom Adele had noticed earlier but not met. Adele was embarrassed by the free, bold flirtation of the girl, who she guessed to be around her own age. Adele's parents had raised her to show respect and pleasantry to all, tempered with maidenly modesty. Looking about, she realized that quite a few others, young and old, were engaged in the same bold enticements. She blushed and glanced away.

The pair's course took them right past Adele. Spying her, Sebastien bowed deeply in recognition, to which Adele returned a cool curtsey.

"My dear Madame Adele! What a distinct delight to see you here!" Sebastien greeted her with warmth.

"The pleasure is mine," she returned, in the formal floweriness of the day. She eyed the girl beside Sebastien. *She looks so familiar....*

"Perhaps you have not been introduced yet?" Sebastien said. "Madame Adele, may I present Madame Stephanie Aimee-Juliette de Lobel. Madame Stephanie—" he cut himself short with utter astonishment as the girls' polite faces lit up with genuine emotion.

"Adele!"

"Stephanie!"

Both girls checked the impulse to rush into each other's arms as they would have done years ago as little girls, but their faces spoke eloquently of their delight.

Seeing Sebastien's puzzled look, Stephanie laughed at him archly, "Fancy you making such a mistake as that, student of the Sorbonne! Adele and I are cousins!"

Sebastien recovered self-possession quickly, and met Stephanie's dancing blue eyes with affected dismay.

"Nevertheless we are so grateful—aren't we, Adele?—for your gallant introduction," Stephanie said. "This place is so crowded; who knows if we would have otherwise found each other...." She shook her golden curls in artificial lamentation, and smiled brilliantly. Then, withdrawing her arm from his, she looked up at him and said, "I hate to impose on you, Sebastien, but would you have the goodness—I left my reticule over there—" She gestured to the far corner, and Sebastien answered, "With pleasure, Stephanie. I shall return, ladies." He bowed and left, moving with poise through the cosmopolitan crowd.

Stephanie watched him go, then turned to Adele and drew her arm through hers. "This is the perfect little quiet spot—how charming that you discovered it so quickly! I must tell you all about…"

Adele found her cousin a veritable chattering magpie, full of talk about clothes, jewelry, and the latest hairstyles, as well as piquant tidbits of gossip—the latter Adele did not enjoy. "And look over there—the man with the ugly pocked face, who has been talking forever with the marquis and your father—he is the comte de Mirabeau. He has been imprisoned various times by his family for his loose dealings with women, and has written books, some of which are deemed scandalous…"

"Then why is he here?" asked Adele, horror written all over her face.

Stephanie shrugged with amusement at her cousin's face. "He is a powerful man, and the people love him. They could care less about his failings—what you might call his *sins*." Seeing Adele's continued aversion, she added, "Besides, as long as he is following his heart, is it not right? The cold, logical Reason of the past that Grandpapa des Cou dotes on would perhaps condemn some of the things the comte de Mirabeau does, but the new writers say our heart is the only true guide. And a far more pleasant one, I must admit," she finished, with a toss of her golden curls. Then, noting Adele was about to reply, she said, "Do you see that lady over there—the one with the silver fan?"

"Yes, I see her—the one talking to the man you told me was Talleyrand, the Bishop of Atun."

"You are a sharp learner, Adele!" her cousin cried with delight. "I had forgotten your keen memory. Yes, that is the one. She is Madame Necker (the wife of France's new finance minister, you know). Have you ever seen anything like the dress she is wearing? I bet you cannot guess what it is made of! Such rich and vibrant colors on that pale cream background!"

"Those flowers certainly are brilliant," Adele agreed. "I should say it was painted Indian silk."

"It *is* handpainted Indian silk, and is rumored to have cost quite a sum," Stephanie said. She was inwardly piqued that she had not remembered that her cousin, coming from a port town, would have seen many imported goods and would thus not be as easily impressed as, say, the Fournier sisters, who had just moved to Paris from land-locked Dijon.

"Ah—here comes Sebastien," Stephanie remarked. "To think, Adele—" she linked her arm in Adele's and gave it a little laughing squeeze, "—to think that he would introduce us to each other!"

Adele heard in the background the sound of strings, and saw the musicians tuning up. A thought slipped into her mind—a quick prayer that someone would come and take Stephanie off to dance, so Adele would be free of her conversation. But a moment later she reproved herself inwardly: *'Tis an uncharitable wish...* And in her heart of hearts she knew she still loved Stephanie—the old Stephanie, the one she had known and played with years before.

Stephanie continued on about Sebastien—his height, the deep brown of his eyes, the "irresistible" cut of his coat—but had to cut short as she noticed him nearing. With him was Honore. The young men bowed as they came up, and the girls curtseyed in reply. Stephanie addressed herself showily to Honore, with barely a glance at Sebastien.

Seeing himself ignored, the latter turned to Adele and was about to speak when Adele heard Honore say "'Tis not possible, cousin; I was charged to tell Adele that we must make our farewells..." At the same moment Adele noticed Stephanie's eyes glance on her and Sebastien, and heard Sebastien asking if Adele would "do him the favor" of dancing with him. Adele would have answered in the negative, but she did not even have to speak. Instantly, Stephanie was there, smiling her brightest. "Unfortunately, no, Sebastien," she purred. "Honore has just informed me that they must leave—now, before the fun begins! But surely you would not abandon me?" She smiled up into his face, and Sebastien acquiesced with only the slightest hesitation.

Adele turned with relief and noticed her brother's eyes smiling down on her. "You stepped neatly out of that," he remarked.

"Did I?" she replied dazedly. "It was Stephanie."

"Yes, for her own purposes—but it served you just as well," he answered with another sparkle in his eyes. Then he turned and began leading the way through the merrymaking crowd. Many were making their way in twos to the dancing floor, and various times the brother and sister had to step aside to wait. Adele couldn't help overhearing a large and powdered dowager nearby, speaking to Talleyrand, the dissolute and disingenuous Bishop of Atun.

"...some others, yes. But the Abbe Sieyes! He is such a *profound* man!" the woman gushed.

"Profound! Yes—he is a perfect cavity," Talleyrand replied, a venomous wit lurking in the depths of his small eyes.

~*~*~

Dawn was breaking over Paris, and the pale lemon light of early morning filtered through the rooftops and entered at last into the front upper room of the house where the Le Merciers were staying.

Adele rose, deep in thought, from the chair in front of her dressing table. The table's carved walnut back framed an oval mirror, while below the flat desk several drawers for toilet articles surmounted four gently curved legs. She had left her long, carefully curled hair down this morning, merely securing it back with a smooth green silk ribbon. Ten short years before, only a full "updo" would have been permissible, but fashion was transitioning and tending toward loose and flowing styles. Fashions for clothes were also changing; her conical bodice was shorter and more curving in shape, being filled in with a longer, puffier scarf. Around her waist, she absently tied a wide green ribbon, matching the one in her hair.

She walked over to the window, thinking what a contrast the muted light was to the strong living radiance that had streamed in her windows at the chateau in Le Havre. She looked down, and her whole soul longed for the sweet, intense green of the trees and fields of home. For what met her eyes was something entirely different.

The streets were full of life, true. It is said that Parisians live and eat and die in the streets; that the streets are more their home than anywhere else. Adele surveyed the stream of humanity tramping below across the dusty grayish-brown cobbles, framed by the dusty grayish-brown houses. The people's movements were for the most part lively; but there was an eternal pinched weariness on many faces and bitter resentment on others. Just below passed a ribald knot of men with long, lank hair and sallow faces. Conspicuous in their belts or brandished with a swagger were thick, brutal-looking sticks. "The Brigands," Adele whispered. More swarmed by; wild, uncouth figures who seemed to care not for God or man—and certainly not for the king.

She looked away, horrified, and noticed a bent woman hobbling by, balancing a heavy load on her back. Darting in and out of the figures below were numerous street Arabs, busy on honest or mayhap dishonest business. Then a bright carriage pushed its way through. A ragged girl, toiling along with a market basket, happened to be in the way, and the driver flicked his whip at her. She cried out, ducking into a doorway, her shrunken face (though she was young) filled with fear. A gaunt woman passed, trying drearily to sell some bright flowers; a little old man shuffled by, hooted at by errand boys and shoved aside by Brigands....

As she gazed, the figures below all seemed to run together, and she once more seemed to see the blazing candles, luxurious surroundings, and effulgent figures at the LaFayette's glamorous fete. There, the faces had at least seemed happy. But as she thought back, she glimpsed emptiness behind those brilliant faces—an emptiness perhaps deeper than that of the poor man, because it was concealed with money and outward success. Behind the laughter lay bleakness. Behind the flattery lay a desire to use the complimented for some purpose—perhaps to rise still higher in the giddy spiral of intrigue and power-grabbing. Little things came back to her mind like living strokes of lightning: the false laughter of the mocking group of ladies—the look in the eyes of Bishop Talleyrand—the fat, selfish face of the Comte de Mirabeau—the falseness and gossip and scintillating emptiness. Under-girding it all was the bittersweet memory of seeing her cousin again.

Adele looked up at the strip of sky above the housetops, sick at heart. "So this is Paris," she said aloud. The sky was a blank blue, and did nothing to raise her spirits. *They are all—from the nobles to the lowest street gamin—trapped under the burden of falsehood.* She pressed her lips together in intense concentration. *Some under the leaden weight of Popish superstition; many more bound by the cynical cords of atheism. They are trapped—trapped in a web of hopelessness. They are all astray, blind, suppressing the truth in unrighteousness....*

"Adele!"

"Coming," Adele answered. She turned from the window and passed through the silent room to the stairway, a voiceless gloom settling over her. Olivie came down the hall, laughing, and joined her as she went down the stairs, but Adele hardly noticed. Her heart was filled with an ache for the bright and dismal people of Paris.

~*~*~

Three days passed drearily for Adele. This was unusual, and she resented the feeling of bewildered pity for the teeming hopeless masses and for the hollowness of the rich. Outwardly she kept a calm and blithe demeanor, but it was a talk with her mother that resolved her inner turmoil.

A little while after dinner, Adele left the garden and entered the main hallway. Down the hall, candles flared in evenly-spaced brackets; her eye followed their pleasing line to the entranceway at the end. She caught sight of Olivie's dainty form there, skipping about with her little white lapdog and urging him to come up the stairs. In a moment, seeing the dog had his own ideas, Olivie scooped him up and disappeared up the stairway, with Leon squirming in her arms and licking her face with his rough little tongue.

Adele saw a stream of light coming from the library door ahead, and remembering a book she desired, she went in. Her mother was seated on a divan between two of the bookcases, and she looked up, book in hand, and smiled. She was dressed in a sunny yellow gown— a *robe a l'anglaise*— of striped silk, the bodice and skirt curving away to display the quilted cream underbodice and petticoat.

"Adele—what has been in your thoughts of late?" her mother asked, moving over to make room on the blue velvet settee.

Something about the question, and her mother's smile, broke Adele's restraint. Before she even knew it, breathless words were pouring from her lips. Her mother said nothing at first, but merely looked into her daughter's face with understanding in her green eyes. When at last Adele's flow of words ran dry, her mother answered with simple, loving directness—words Adele mulled over and cherished—words she would remember the rest of her life. Finally, as the candle flickered and threatened to go out, they brought their converse to a close and parted for the night, a special sense of sweetness and communion lingering between them. Later, as Adele readied herself for bed in the half-light of her room, one sentence came back with overwhelming distinctness:

"You are troubled, Adele—and rightly so—to see the inner hopelessness of the rich and poor alike. St. Augustine answers the question thus: 'Thou hast made us for Thyself, O Lord, and our hearts are restless until they find their rest in Thee.' The people you see in Paris have not found Christ, and so their hearts are restless and disturbed. They need the truth—they need to hear the freeing news of how God has saved us from our sins—how we can be free, through the death and resurrection of His Son Jesus. That alone can give meaning and blessedness to rich and poor alike."

~*~*~

The Estates-General began in Versailles with a grand procession of all the delegates and a gaudy display of pomp, cheered wildly by upper class and commoner alike. Versailles, some little distance from Paris itself, held the King's sumptuous palace and the pleasure-houses of the queen.

Since the convening of the Estates-General, the number of gazettes had exploded. It seemed as if everyone in Paris—from the highest lord to the lowest serving-girl—was reading the newly-uncensored newspapers and pamphlets. They were being printed by the score, spewing forth all sorts of revolutionary and reactionary content.

Monsieur des Cou himself mentioned the newspapers, as, standing in the door to her gilded parlor, he bid farewell to his daughter. "I shall come and visit again soon, Felicienne. By the by, my dear," he waved a hand nearly hidden by ruffles, "have you read some of the latest pamphlets? Stirring, very stirring!"

Felicienne smiled, "I have not read many, Father, though I do hear that they are quite...*volatile*."

"Volatile—yes, I think that is a good description, Felicienne." He crinkled his fleshy face judiciously, his receding chin looking remarkably out of place. "Between ourselves, I think some of them are getting a little out of hand. My contemporaries and I (by this he meant himself and his favorite Enlightenment authors, though most were dead) have not yet given the final verdict on this new movement. We work from sound, logical principles—" His daughter hid a smile at that false generalization, but he failed to notice, "—as I was saying, we think in sound, cold logic and reach proper conclusions. Everything can be rationally discussed, and truth is only what is reasonable. I taught you to think logically, Felicienne. But this new generation..." he shook his head sagely. "Even your sister Juliette was this very morning propounding to me the infamous idea that what *feels* right *is* right. Reason, she says, is not good enough—it is too cold and hard. That is mere foolishness—everyone knows how changeable and baseless emotions are!"

Berthe appeared that moment, and M. des Cou paused while Felicienne instructed her to fetch her hat and equipment. He then said, "I must not keep you, Felicienne—you have calls to make this afternoon. Farewell for the present, my daughter!"

"I shall look forward to seeing you again, Father. We shall be at Juliette's next day-week, and will see you then, I hope," Felicienne answered, curtsying goodbye as she accompanied him to the front door to see him off.

As the manservant shut the door, she mused with a humorous smile, *Ah, Father, how inconsistent your thinkers are! Your 'friends'* — her smile deepened, and she sat down on a cushioned sofa—*held that* man's reason *can on its own decide truth. The present generation has not rejected your ideas— they have merely taken them further, and decided that* man's heart *can decide right and wrong and what is truth. They have taken your ideas to their logical conclusion; for a man's mind is entwined with his heart and feelings. You both cut loose the bonds of truth – you both wrongly proclaim man's sovereignty over God. Father, you criticize the new ideas because man's emotions are changeable and depend upon the situation. But the same could be brought against your cherished theories. For even our 'cold, logical minds' are dependant on outward, physical things like mere meat and drink. But the largest objection is that we are created beings. The great Creator of all things arbitrates what is right. We are accountable to Him. In Adam's fall, we all fell. No man can set his own mind as the arbiter of Truth, because we are all sinners, under the curse. Because we are changeable created beings,* **that** *is why we must have something outside of us – God's Word – to shape ourselves by; a firm rock of Truth to build upon. And there are some things – what does the verse say? – that are not logically discerned. Ah, yes: 'But the naturall man perceiveth not the things of the Spirit of God: for they are foolishnesse unto him: neither can hee knowe them, because they are spiritually discerned.'*

Glancing up into a baroque mirror on the wall, she remembered her afternoon errands. *Where is Berthe? I hope she remembers my handiwork when she gets my hat.*

After a few more minutes of musing, she started up. *Where is she? I must be gone – I have such a list of people to call on after the last party!* With quick, graceful steps, her hooped skirt swishing elegantly just above the tops of her small shoes, she ascended the staircase. Passing Charlot's room, she glimpsed Adele's bright face and heard the children's bubbly laughter. Advancing past the closed door of the next room (it was her husband's), her thoughts flew to Francis. The room was empty, for, like the other delegates to the Estates-General, Francis must stay in Versailles. *He says he will be able to come visit us weekly,* she consoled herself. Then she remembered, with a sudden rush of girlish delight, *That means – tomorrow!*

The next room was her own. Entering softly, her eyes fell on her maid Berthe. The latter was leaning against the wall reading a newspaper, her face aglow with interest. Dangling from her free hand was her mistress' newest hat and silk reticule.

"Berthe?"

The maid started, trying hastily to hide the paper in the folds of her dress, making a pretense of being busy gathering her mistresses' things. Felicienne smiled.

"What were you reading, Berthe?"

Berthe handed over the paper. "It wasn't me that bought it, truly, marquise. One of the scullery girls lent it me."

The marquise's fair face sobered with concentration as she glanced through the pamphlet. Her ruby lips formed the newspaper's title without thinking. "*Lettres a ses Commettants.*" She remembered M. de Duret's remark that it had been published by the infamous comte de Mirabeau as "*Estates Generaux,*" but had been barred by the government for its content. The newly-loosened government censorship still allowed other radical pamphlets, but the government felt that Mirabeau's was *too* subversive, and so had forbidden it. But the wily Mirabeau got around that by calling it "*Lettres a ses Commettants*—Letters to Constituents." This insinuated that the government was forbidding a member of the Estates-General to inform his constituents of what was going on—and that looked bad. Thus, though the paper's contents were just as rabid, the government was forced to back down—and the paper continued its poisonous course unchecked. Felicienne furrowed her pretty brows, trying to decide what to say to her maid. Finally she spoke.

"These ideas—they are dangerous, Berthe." Noting the latent idealism in Berthe's oval face, she realized she had to choose her words discreetly. She tried again: "Berthe, do you know that the author of this is an utterly unscrupulous rascal? Adultery is just one of the crimes he has been convicted of. He is a filthy, vile man—not fit to lead; and certainly not leading in the right direction. You heard the verse M. de Duret read to us in devotions this morning...." She pulled a small bound book from one of the inner drawers of her bureau. "Here it is, in the gospel of Matthew, chapter seven." Berthe shifted position, outwardly respectful, inwardly wincing. Ignoring the nagging sense that no amount of words would break through to her maid, Felicienne read the passage in her clear, modulated voice:

"*Beware of false prophets, which come to you, in sheep's clothing, but inwardly they are ravening wolves. Ye shall know them by their fruits. Do men gather grapes of thorns? Or figs of thistles? So every good tree bringeth forth good fruit, & a corrupt tree bringeth forth evil fruit. A good tree can not bring forth evil fruit: neither can a corrupt tree bring forth good fruit. Every tree that bringeth not forth good fruit is hewn down and cast into the fire. Therefore by their fruits ye shall know them.*"

She closed the Bible and looked straight into her maid's gray eyes. "Can you see, Berthe? We need to be careful to discern the fruits of people's lives before we listen to what they say. The words in that paper may seem attractive, but we need to test them by the fruits of the author's life and by the clear guide of Scripture."

Felicienne perceived she was getting nowhere, and remained in sorrowful thought for some time after Berthe had been dismissed to finish gathering her mistresses' things. *I have not spent enough time discipling the servants. 'Tis my duty as a Christian woman to help them....And how miserably I have failed, it seems!*

At last she rose, reproaching herself for wasting time. A whole afternoon of social calls lay ahead of her, and she was getting a late start.

~*~*~

Time winged by like a bird: now fluttering, now beating steadily; but ever onward to its final resting place. Two weeks later, four figures rode briskly into Paris from Versailles, the western sun setting in rich golden hues behind them. Two of the riders—Francis de Coquiel di le Mercier and his brother-in-law Jean de Lobel—rode abreast. The last, ebbing rays of the sun highlighted M. de Lobel's plain black mantle, white cravat, and dark *chapean rabattu* (hat) with dull crimson, while it sparkled on the gold-worked, bright velvet cloak of Francis and danced off his nodding plumes. Usually the two would have dressed with equal richness.

Jean de Lobel was the third son of a lesser son of a noble family. But he had managed (like the also-nobly-born comte de Mirabeau), to get himself elected as a deputy of the Third Estate, representing the commoners. Francis, meanwhile, had been elected to the Second Estate. Francis, therefore, was wearing the assigned dress of the Second Estate deputies, while Jean de Lobel wore the costume of the Third Estate representatives. Both were going home—Jean with indifference, Francis with manifest anticipation and delight. Behind them hovered the inscrutable face of Denis and the pudgy one of Jean's manservant.

The party slowed their pace as they traversed the narrow streets of the city, speaking little. Francis had tried to converse with his brother-in-law, but his attempts merely uncovered that Jean was vehemently in support of the reactionary opinions of the time. Since Francis, as a Christian, entertained far different ideas, their weekly rides home from the Estates-General were usually made in fairly amiable silence or small-talk, punctuated at times by intense, animated discussion. For no dull cloak or heavy, square face could hide the ardent zeal that lit up Jean de Lobel's light brown eyes from within—while in turn the frippery of Francis' ornate attire could not disguise the keen, serious adherence to truth which shone from his lean, handsome countenance.

It seemed a long time to Francis before they pulled up their horses in front of his abode's tall façade. "Will you come in, M. de Lobel? It has been a long ride," he said, swinging deftly off his steed and already advancing to the door.

"I thank you, but I shall be on my way," M. de Lobel answered.

Francis, handing his horse to Denis, answered, "Then I shall meet you tomorrow night, to travel back to Versailles."

Jean never knew why he lingered, but he paused idly to watch Francis enter his front door. As the portal opened, there was a stream of light, a rush of joyful noise, and eager little hands gleefully pulled Francis through the door. The little De Coquiel di le Merciers knew it would not do to make a scene in the street, and so had waited, almost bursting, to get their father inside and shower upon him their happy hugs and kisses. The door shut abruptly, leaving the street darker and more lonely than before. Jean de Lobel turned in his saddle and started his horse off at a walk for his home, his head bowed in contemplation.

As he passed slowly through the streets, he was greeted with shouts of acclaim by the common people. For was he not one of their own deputies, working in the Estates-General for their good? Several bedraggled street arabs even went so far as to follow him, almost as a little entourage, throwing their hats in the air and making what they supposed were encouraging noises. Jean de Lobel absently nodded in acknowledgement—he was used to such things. The Third Estate representatives were the established favorites of "the people."

Soon he reached his dwelling, having first left his horse at a nearby livery stable. A footman opened the door, illuminating the fast-darkening street. The servant looked wooden and deferential, and solemnly turned away to attend to his duties. No laughing welcome met M. de Lobel—only a silent entry stretched before him. He had expected it, but somehow it seemed the more bleak after seeing Francis' welcome. His shoulders sagged a little, and he started up the staircase for his room. Reaching the landing, he met his daughter Stephanie.

"*Bonjour*, Stephanie," he said, with an attempt at heartiness.

"Oh—it's you, Father. *Bonjour*," she answered absently. "Mother is in her room." She almost turned to leave, but some vague feeling stopped her; and she added, "I wouldn't go see her yet, if I were you."

"Oh?"

She made a slight gesture. Then, mimicking her mother's voice when she was irritated, she said, "Children, no more of that! I am writing, and I must have no noise or interruptions! I won't warn you again!" That said, Stephanie turned again to go. Suddenly, an almost overpowering flood of emotion seized her. She saw for the first time the sad and weary expression in her father's face, the droop in his shoulders. She saw, almost from his eyes, the preoccupied uninterestedness of her mother and her own aloofness.

A memory flashed to the forefront of her mind: the glad expression in Adele's eyes when, the day before, Adele had mentioned *her* father. It had piqued and surprised Stephanie at the time, but now it stood out in convicting sharpness. Stephanie wouldn't admit that she was wrong to be cool and disdainful, but she felt a need to assuage her conscience. Swerving round, she said with an unusually warm smile, "Father, it is a pleasure to see you again. I am sure you desire to change clothes, but I shall be in the parlor, if you would like to visit before dinner."

A look of surprise flickered in her father's eyes, but he bowed in response to her curtsey, and they parted — he to his room, she to the parlor.

Unfortunately for Stephanie's good intentions, when she went into the spacious, picturesque parlor with its carved walnut furniture, velvet cushions, and bookcases, she found Leuren reading one of her "very own" books. In the squabble that ensued she forgot about her ideas to be kind to her father. She only dimly noticed his weary face trying to bring some peace to the situation, and then her mother's furious entrance, because her writing had been disturbed.

Dinner at the De Lobel's that night was a sullen affair, with the master of the house a point of interest only because he carried up-to-date news of the Estates-General.

The *Palais Royale*

8.

No National Assembly ever threatened to be so stormy
as that which will decide the fate
of the monarchy, and which is gathering in such haste
and with so much mutual distrust.
— comte de Mirabeau

*L*ater that evening, after the children were in bed, Francis and
Felicienne went out the many-paned door into the small back
garden and stood together among the climbing foliage. The sun
had almost set—a pale pink cloud hovered above the horizon. The higher
clouds had tarnished to a dark gray-blue, and above swept the great indigo
vault, pierced by the first few stars, mere pinpricks of white brilliance.

A portly maid in a striped brown housedress stepped out, placed a
lantern in a bracket, and left with a curtsey. The lantern illumined bushes
and flowering plants, growing in orderly patterns along the wooden fence
and framing a stone seat. Beyond, wide-awake Paris hummed and
buzzed—but this was a little haven of rest in the midst of the vast, never-
sleeping metropolis. Felicienne slipped her arm through her husband's as
they seated themselves.

"'Tis not to be compared to our estate back home, but it is a garden,
I suppose," he said, breaking the pleasant reverie.

Felicienne answered, "Yes, Francis: and truly I have been grateful
for this bit of green." Turning her face to the darkening sky, she continued,
"And—even in this brown city—the stars are still the same."

Another pause, and Francis mused aloud, "The same stars have
looked down upon thousands of years of the strivings of man...have stood
in the sky above all sorts of utter cruelty, and stared down without
changing upon bloodshed, strife, and evil. I think, Felicienne, that they will
see much more of the violent dealings of mankind before even a few years
have passed. Oh, these people—how I yearn for them to find freedom in
Christ! Instead, I am afraid that their actions are crying out for God's just

punishment. True, much injustice has taken place, and the people have many real grievances that must be addressed. The terrible abuses of power and unChristian oppression must be righted. At present, men have unequal worth in the eyes of the law — a peasant's life is not of equal merit as a noble's. This is not right. As I read the Bible, Felicienne, I see that each person — even an unborn child — was counted as precious and important by the God Who created them. We know that men are not equal in abilities or even position — but must receive equal weight and consideration before the Law. The radicals say this is what they are demanding — that they are righting wrongs and destroying oppression. Even LaFayette hopes that this insurgence will be like the glorious American revolution he played such a part in. But..." he trailed off amid graver thoughts.

Chin in hand, he continued, "I cannot see how this unrest is like that revolution at all. Those people, the Americans, were fighting to hold King George to his own precepts and charters — to hold him accountable to his own laws. But the people of France are trying to tear down the framework of law and society. They hope to raise up a new and different society altogether, with new morals and new standards." He looked off unseeing into the darkness, murmuring, "They are very different, these two revolutions."

Felicienne looked gravely into his face, "What of the Estates-General? I have tried to keep abreast of developments through the papers, but that seems impossible. By the time things are printed, they are so rabidly partisan it is difficult to tell what is fact and what is 'editorial license.'"

"The progress — or rather the non-progress — of the Estates-General: *that* concerns me, *chérie*. We are making no forward movement. As the marquis de Ferrieres remarked to me: 'We spend the whole day in useless chatter and shouting, with no one listening to anyone else.' Four weeks of session now, from nine o'clock to half-past four: the clergy in their room, we of the Second Estate in ours, and the Third Estate in the main room, as Estates-General precedent dictates. We and the clergy proceeded straightway to verify and constitute ourselves apart. But the Third Estate does nothing but adroit formalities, saying they are waiting for the other two Estates to join them collectively and 'verify the powers in common.' They want us to break former law and instead vote as individuals, instead of by estates."

"But Francis, if that happened they would be in control! The two combined votes of clergy and nobles are equal to their one vote, which is, I suppose, why they object to it. But if the Estates-General voted by head, the

Third Estate (with their double quota of delegates) would have the majority."

"You are utterly right, *ma chérie.*" He smiled into her expressive face. "We of the Second Estate have refused to agree to that breach of precedent. We have insisted on following the time-tested way ordained by the king. This has brought on an impasse. They will not acquiesce, but instead —" He uttered a short, mirthless laugh. "This is really the most laughable thing about the whole business. The deputies of the Third Estate spend their time making longwinded and senseless speeches. They declare, with ludicrous sorrow, that they cannot become organized (which is, they say, because we will not join them); they utter long patriotic lamentations, bemoaning the fact that they are, because of us, a mere inorganic body, which longs — oh so passionately! — to become organic, so it can begin helping the people. But alas and alack! The stubborn nobles and clergymen are preventing all their most laudable aims..." he sighed. "We cannot give in to them or play their foolish game, but their cunning tactics are winning at present, Felicienne. The people believe what they say, and wholeheartedly support them."

"What can you do, Francis? It seems hopeless."

"I am bound to stay and represent truth and justice. Some of my co-deputies are secretly discussing flight to another country — if the Third Estate succeeds in gaining control, they say that the best thing for France and their honor is to flee, working abroad to bring France back to her senses. Others are merely waiting to see what turn events will take, not committing themselves to support or oppose the Third Estate. But as you know, *qui ne dit mot consent* — he who says nothing consents. I must speak the truth."

"Yes, Francis — never give up. I will be praying for you. How I wish I could do more to support you, dearest."

"Overseeing the household in my absence helps me more than you think, Felicienne; I am glad I can leave it all without a worry in your capable hands. What are the political opinions of our servants? I am concerned to see how the lies so easily spread and are believed."

Her face took on a pensive look. "M. de Duret has been of great assistance, but I do not know how much we have accomplished. The servants would not contradict their mistress or M. de Duret. Yet our words do not seem to be reaching their hearts."

"Do not grow weary in well doing, Felicienne. What saith the Scripture? 'In due season we shall reap, if we faint not.'"

"I know. I encourage myself with the remembrance that once I, too, was deceived with such falsehoods and 'tossed about with every wind.' God alone can work in their hearts, as M. de Duret reminds me."

Francis nodded. "Denis is, I know, wholeheartedly in support of the Third Estate—I suspect he favors the most rabid pamphleteers. Speaking to him has done no good. Yet I hesitate to dismiss him, Felicienne." He fingered the ruffles at his hands unconsciously. "He has been a good servant. And what would he do if I discharged him? Turn instantly into a free-agent firebrand?" He shook his head, and his grave face caught the light. Felicienne noticed the shadows that had gathered in his countenance since their arrival in Paris. She longed to magically smooth those cares away.

After a moment's silence, Francis turned to his wife. "I hate to leave you, Felicienne; the Brigands have multiplied; even the common people of Paris are more threatening and temperamental."

Felicienne's winsome face, framed by her dark curls—powder was out of fashion now—glowed in the yellow radiance of the lantern, while all else was thrown into blackness. It seemed to Francis a symbol of hope—a reminder of how God's peace and beautiful light can live, yea even flourish, in the midst of the most hateful and powerful darkness that Satan can bring. What peace—yea, and love—were in her fair face and shining out of her rich green eyes!

What a contrast this open, loving face was to the cool, cynical expression it wore before the light of the glorious gospel of Christ had come to her heart—and his too. How he himself had been transformed with a new hope by the convicting light of Truth—how his heart had been turned *towards* his wife and children. The memories, and the contemplation of God's utterly unmerited grace to him, took his breath away. When at last he spoke, in a lower, deeper tone, he put his arm around her slender form.

"Dearest, five years ago, I am ashamed to say, I looked for every opportunity to leave home. But now…"

"But now?" Felicienne asked shyly, looking up into the face bent down near hers.

"Now—it pains me to leave you even for a day," he answered huskily, drawing her to him. She laid her head on his shoulder, where it belonged.

~*~*~

On a hot, breezy summer morning—the 4th of June, 1789—Adele, Stephanie, and Olivie were ensconced in a shaded nook of the de Lobel's small garden, ostensibly inspecting the flowers. Smoothing her blue-striped gown, Stephanie declared she "cared for none but roses."

Just inside the open French windows a patch of moving green scooted about—three-year-old Paulette. Seated gracefully nearby on ornate chairs were the two mothers. A verdant silk gown with billowy white at the neck and sleeves provided a pleasing contrast to the dark brown hair and rosy cheeks of Felicienne de Coquiel di le Mercier, while her sister Juliette de Lobel wore a summer blue dress, cut fashionably low and filled in with a thin muslin scarf. A blue ribbon was twined among the mellow gold of her hair. She had just re-seated herself after saying good-bye to a few afternoon callers.

The sister's faces were alike in some ways, but if we listen in on the conversation of the recently-departed visitors, it may be revealing. One, a heavy, high-colored gentleman remarked, "Beautiful women, both of them. 'Tis pleasant to see two sisters so fair."

His shorter companion settled his tricorn as he answered, "Superb women, yes. But if I did not know that Madame de Lobel was the younger, I would assume she was the *elder* sister."

"Ah—yes. 'Tis rare in Paris to see such serene beauty as the Madame de Coquiel di le Mercier. She seems to glow from within; whereas Madame de Lobel has more the icy sparkle of the diamond." He settled his corpulence into the carriage seat and signaled to the driver.

If we leave the gentlemen to rattle on through the narrow streets and we return to the De Lobel's, we would see the cousins examining a scarlet rose. A moment later several young men and boys strolled into the garden—tall Honore, shorter thirteen-year-old Leuren and seven-year-old Charlot. Marcel Martin followed. The uncombed blond hair hanging down from under Leuren's hat and his insubordinate expression made him stand out from the others.

As Adele looked up, her sympathetic glance was caught by Honore's sharp green eyes. He smiled a bit wearily. Adele knew what that meant. Leuren, willful and spoiled, made the long afternoons quite a trial for Honore, even though the latter was the elder by four years. Adele felt a swell of pride as she thought how her older brother had borne the situation without a single complaint.

She turned back to her companions, and found Stephanie yawning affectedly behind her fan. Fussing with her absurdly poufy scarf, Stephanie remarked, "I declare, Adele, I am quite done with these flowers! But what shall we do…" Then her face lit up, and she pushed back her golden hair. "I know—we can go to the *Jardin du Palais-Royal*! You simply must see it!

'Tis quite the place to be nowadays—how can I have forgotten it?" With these and other expressions, she hastened to the young men. Upon receiving their consent, she turned back to Adele. "It's decided—let us go!" she bubbled, as if she held a new toy. "We will set out now—it is only a short walk."

"I shall ask Mother," Adele answered more calmly, though the idea of having something to do was delightfully appealing.

"Oh! Mother? Boh! I don't have to ask Mother—she lets me do whatever I like!" Stephanie cried. She waited impatiently while her cousins asked their mother's permission.

Felicienne glanced at her sister Juliette. "Is it safe and fitting? I have not been there myself, though I have heard of it. Is it not the center of all the pamphlets and tumult?"

Her sister smiled with a touch of scorn at what she considered Felicienne's fussy carefulness. "We go there often, to attend plays at the *Comédie Française*. Leuren has gone by himself before."

Felicienne did not look very impressed, but if Honore and Marcel would be with the group…. Turning to the children, she announced, "You may certainly go—but do stay together, children. And Honore, you are responsible for the girls and younger ones."

So it was that the little group set out, smiling and laughing, and in a few minutes found themselves entering the arched stone gateways of the *Palais-Royal*. Towering overhead, the walls were ornamented with intricate stone carvings of people and other figures. Through the gates passed a stream of people, some entering, others leaving. They were composed of all classes and stations—though, Honore noted, quite a large majority were Brigands and the lower classes.

"The gates are open at every hour—day or night," Stephanie informed them.

"But is not the *Palais-Royal* owned by the king's cousin, Philippe d'Orleans?" Olivie questioned.

"Ah, yes—Philippe d'Orleans owns it, but he opens it to the public. It has made him a great favorite," Stephanie answered. She added with a deep smile, "There are advantages to distributing pamphlets and making your speeches here—d'Orleans has forbidden the police to enter."

Adele did not answer—she was wholly occupied in *seeing*. A large rectangular courtyard stretched out before her, framed on three sides by the Palais-Royal building, a grand and florid palace of light gray stone. Arcaded facades framed those three sides, under them rows and rows of shops. But Adele was not free to linger, for Charlot was already calling her attention to a performing bear which was bobbing up and down some distance ahead, almost hidden by the crowd.

"Look, look, Adele!" he pointed. "A bear! I want to see the bear!"

Following Charles' desire, Leuren, familiar with the place, took the lead. Over the multitude of conversations rose the shrill cries of newsboys announcing new pamphlets and the strident shouting of rough-and-ready speakers, while their open-mouthed hearers filled the air with

thunders of applause for every sentiment of more than common hardiness.

Quite a crowd had gathered around the bear, but Adele and the others managed to find an opening due to Marcel's quiet efforts. Charles was fascinated—he had never seen a bear before; certainly not one so grand and big!

Adele also watched with interest until a few words spoken nearby attracted her attention, for they were not in French. She turned and beheld a family—father, mother, and two children; from the conservative cut of their clothing, unmistakably from England. They were sightseeing. Hearing their solid English pronunciation brought a wave of strange homesickness to Adele—for Le Havre de Grace was a busy port, and English voices were often heard there. Now she wished with all her heart even for a glimpse of that familiar sea, where she had so many times heard the deep voices of the sailors singing their English chanteys.

Stephanie soon tired of the bear's antics and suggested they look at the shops. Acquiescing, they turned their steps toward the arcades. But as they crossed the crowded square, a voice hailed from behind. "Andre!" Most of their group assumed the call was directed beyond them, but Leuren wheeled round sharply and answered with hearty recognition, "Gaston!"

By this time everyone in their party had turned, and they beheld three scruffy youths of roughly sixteen to eighteen approaching. One was short, with a swarthy cast to his sharp face. Another was lanky and angular, with stringy hair falling round an ungainly countenance. The third had an audacious, handsome face and dark hair. Though they were of a tolerably high class, they were dressed in the rough negligence that was the height of fashion among the supporters of the Third Estate—long hair fell from under their *chapean rabattu*, while they brandished knotted sticks like the *Brigands*.

They greeted Leuren freely, slapping him on the back and exchanging laughing banter. Little puzzle pieces suddenly fell together in

Adele's mind. *Leuren's hairstyle, his defiant expression, his unkempt clothes...all are attempts to fit in with this crowd!* She wondered if his parents knew his leanings; then remembered they themselves supported the Third Estate's goals. She quailed inwardly, looking with gratefulness at her own brothers.

But now one of the youths—the one with the dashing face, named Gaston—was speaking to Leuren. "Andre, introduce us to these beautiful *Madames.*"

There's no mistaking it that time, thought Adele. *He called Leuren 'Andre.'*

Leuren introduced his sister and cousins, and the young men bowed and smiled with unruly gallantry. Stephanie lapped up the attention. Adele was polite but reserved; Olivie followed her example. Adele hoped the rowdies would soon leave, but instead the youths joined them with easy familiarity and moved along, conversing freely. The group composed of the De Coquiel di le Merciers and De Lobels, and now including these disorderly friends of Leuren's, ambled towards the arcades.

Promenade in the Palais Royale, by Philibert Debucourt, 1798

Boutiques carrying every sort of imaginable product pressed close beside cafes with sprawling tables, while gaming places were prolific and added their own peculiar din. Bookshops, hair salons, and refreshment kiosks abounded. It seemed that every café had at least one orator, standing on a table and haranguing an impromptu crowd of sympathetic listeners. They passed one pamphlet shop with the name *M. Dessein* on it—the crowd so thick that anyone wanting to get to the counter could not do so without vigorous elbowing and shoving. The young men and Leuren seemed to have many friends—they were repeatedly hailed by equally impertinent people swaggering forth from the shops and cafes.

"Thirteen pamphlets came out today, sixteen yesterday, and ninety-two last week," Gaston informed them, smiling his bold shark-grin at Stephanie. "Tyranny will not be able to stand against an informed populace."

Sharply, a loud, explosive *boom* echoed. The girls and Charles started, but no one else seemed to even notice it.

"That was the noon cannon," Leuren said scornfully.

The lanky young man with the ungainly movements added, "The cannon was set up by a scientist, on the prime meridian. It is so aimed that at exactly noon, the sun's rays pass through a lens, and the ensuing heat sets off the fuse, firing the cannon. These advances will grow and flourish as we shake off the shackles of conventionality—science and free thought will blossom," he explained, with vigorous gesticulation. "Like the first buds, now that the frost of convention is breaking, they will unfurl..."

At that moment a small, spare man bustled towards them. After a moment's rapid conversation punctuated by exclamations, he scampered off, and the young men announced with regret that they had urgent business elsewhere.

"The news is that the sickly dauphin has died," Gaston said.

"The king's son!" cried Olivie.

"He has been ailing for quite a while," Honore remarked. "Still, what a blow!"

"A blow for us, you mean, yes," Gaston said, twisting Honore's remark, "as it entails leaving these delightful ladies. I hope to again have the pleasure of seeing your lovely faces, Mesdames," he added, with an impertinent bow.

The others bowed and added their adieus. As they turned away with an excited air, Adele caught the words "Breton Club" and "What luck!" Glad to be rid of their company, she turned to Leuren. "Why 'Andre?'" she queried, raising her eyebrows.

Leuren bristled, muttering, "It suits me."

"But you were named *Leuren* after Grandpapa des Cou," Honore remarked.

"Um-hum," Leuren grunted, then a questioning look from Honore seemed to call forth more of an explanation, for he burst out, "I hate that name! What an old fogey! Why do I have to be shackled to that fusty old name!"

Even Stephanie seemed taken aback by his vehemence, for she hissed sharply, *"Leuren!"* in a tone that gave Adele another insight into why Leuren might not care for his name—*At least I wouldn't, if it were pronounced in such tones,* she thought.

Leuren shoved his hands into his pockets and turned away, and Adele took the hint and inspected the nearest shop with interest. Stephanie joined her in a moment or two with the air of having given Leuren up as a "bad job."

The shop displayed a wide variety of objects but Stephanie soon tired of it—a *boutique* a few stalls down had caught her eye, and she flitted delightedly over. When Adele and Olivie joined her, they found it was a jeweler's. The girls gazed at the scintillating brooches and sparkling necklaces. Their brothers, however, had not noticed the girls' departure, lingering intent at the miscellaneous *magasin* some twenty yards away. Its broad window held an attractive display of daggers and metal objects. Leuren lounged against a pillar nearby, hands in pockets.

But Stephanie soon had exhausted the capacity of the *boutique,* and caught Adele's arm. "Come this way—it's only a little further to my favorite jewelry shop," she said, her eyes sparkling.

"Well, I suppose, since it's not far," Adele answered, with a glance back at where the young men were wrapped in deep contemplation of a poniard.

"Oh, don't worry about them—it's just a short bit away," Stephanie said.

Either Stephanie was a poor judge of distance or she had misrepresented the nearness of the shop, for when they reached it and Adele glanced back, she could only catch glimpses of her brothers through the crowds. But she had hardly time to think about the uncomfortableness of the situation, for Stephanie was calling her to look at emerald-studded earrings.

As she bent over a particularly dainty wristlet, Adele's attention was attracted by noises from the bustling café beside them. She glanced over with innocent interest. Groups of rowdy young men lounged at the tables, along with mixed passersby. Curiously watching, she unintentionally looked directly into the eyes of one of the young men. She blushed, turning back to the wares in front of her.

"Look here, Adele—have you ever seen such delicate gold work?" Stephanie asked.

Olivie moved close to see. Adele walked to Stephanie's other side, absently pushing her ivory fan in her reticule. Slightly unnerved, she did not notice that it lodged only halfway in her purse.

While admiring the frail, lace-like gold-work on the bracelet with the other two, she cast a furtive glance over at the nearby café. Her unease grew as she saw the young man still staring insolently at her.

"It is lovely—but Stephanie, don't you think we should join our brothers?"

"Whatever you say," Stephanie said, tossing her head.

"It would be nicer—we can always come back here with them," Adele answered. "Let us join the others, Olivie." She turned, and Olivie joined her. Stephanie lagged behind.

At the café beside them, a rough orator had leapt onto a table and was in full cry. "...Your families are hungry! The Third Estate would do something about that, if it only could act! But the king!—and the nobles!— ah, my comrades, shall we not shout, 'Down with the king and the cursed aristocrats!'? With rapacious hands they—"

A listening crowd had gathered, blocking the path to their brothers. Adele and Olivie began to hurry around the growing throng. Glancing back, she saw that Stephanie was taking her time, apparently liking the noise and press of the assemblage. Stephanie viewed a large group of strangers as merely a bigger audience; she loved being the center of attention. But to Adele, a group—especially one like this—meant staring eyes, perhaps accompanied by unpredictable actions. She moved on as quickly as maidenly decorum permitted.

At one point, the press of rough folk flocking to hear the speaker began to surround them, and the girls were forced to stop and wait for a clear path to open up. The strident, hoarse voice of the rabble-rouser, calling for "freedom from the tyranny of centuries!" did not add any comfort to the situation.

"Here is a way, Adele," Olivie said in her small, sweet voice, and Adele saw with relief an opening in the throng.

"Thank you, Olivie—we shall be with Honore and the others in just a moment."

She turned gratefully in the direction indicated, and squeezed through the aisle. But—advancing there was the same young man from the café who had met her unmeaning glance before: a few companions lounged at his side. Trying to quell the nameless alarm rising within, Adele looked down, outwardly composed, into Olivie's face and said, "I think we shall have to go another way." Before Adele could say more, the young man was bowing before her. His mane of blond hair hung about a handsome lean countenance that was singularly strong, with an aquiline nose and burning blue eyes. "If I may take the liberty of introducing myself, Madame—"

One of his companions, a red-faced, slovenly fellow with a dirty cravat, interrupted him in mock courteousness. "It is rather a large liberty, Jules—but if *I* introduce you both properly, 'twill not be—" He winked, extending a thick hand. "Madame, may I introduce to you Jules Durand; Jules, this is Madame—"

Adele, in an attempt to ignore them, was examining a nearby statue while glancing about for a way through the oppressive, jostling crowd. However, the last words of the "introduction" were spoken in such a loud tone as could not be believably ignored—and besides, she saw Stephanie coming up. Facing them with all the courage and self-command she could muster, she said firmly, "My name is none of your business; pray let us pass." She made a commanding gesture forward, privately relieved that Olivie had caught on and was supporting her reserved demeanor.

The young men made no motion to move out of the way, and Jules replied, "Now really, Madame *Belle* [beautiful]—" He leered into Adele's face, to be met by a pair of frosty eyes.

Stephanie arrived at the moment with her most attractive smile. "I see you have met some friends, Adele; how charming! Would you introduce—"

Suddenly another voice broke into the scene; a deep, pleasant masculine voice. "Excuse me, Madame—"Adele turned from Stephanie and the young men to face this new situation, praying inwardly. However she was reassured slightly on seeing the man who spoke. His frank face looked about thirty years old, and he was dressed in the dark blue and red uniform of the *Gardes Suisses* (the Swiss Guards), a bearskin headdress on his crisp locks.

"Excuse me, Madame," he said again, "I hope I am not intruding myself upon you, but you dropped this a few minutes ago." In his hand was her ivory fan—a priceless family heirloom, presented to her grandmother many years ago by the late queen.

Adele thanked him, and he would have withdrawn, but she added, "Would you do me the favor of escorting us to my brother? I am sure he desires to thank you, as well."

He acquiesced with a bow, and she turned back to Stephanie and the "gallants." The sight of the brawny figure of the Swiss Guard behind

Adele must have disconcerted those worthies, for they were slipping off into the crowd. The little group met with no other hindrance.

Reaching her brothers, Adele signed with relief. She introduced the Swiss Guard and told Honore how he returned her fan. Honore added his thanks, and soon was involved in an interesting conversation with the man, an officer named Hans Diesbach. He was off duty, and had come to the *Palais-Royal* to see for himself the pamphlets and crowds—he was a guard at the King's Versailles palace.

"My father is a representative of the Second Estate, and I know he would desire you to visit his quarters in Versailles," Honore said. He tore off the corner of a political pamphlet he had bought earlier, and wrote down his father's Versailles address. "Now don't forget to call on him—I shall let him know of the service you have rendered, and he shall certainly be expecting you," Honore added.

"I shall do so, Monsieur de Coquiel di le Mercier," *Officier* Diesbach said. With a respectful bow, he moved off through the crowd.

"It is time we return to the De Lobel's," Honore said, glancing at the sun. "This is certainly the place where things are happening—thank you, Stephanie, for thinking of it." Aside to Adele, as the little party turned towards the grand stone gateway, he said, "It was certainly unlooked-for to meet that officer—I wonder if it will prove useful in the future."

Behind the Scenes

9.

Quand les fevers sont en fleur,
Les fous sont en vigeur.
When beans are in flower,
Fools are in power.
— French Proverb

I n the green-papered dining-room of the De Coquiel di le Mercier's Paris residence, a maid moved about with care. She approached each silver candlestick, taper in hand, and soon even the darkest corners were filled with mellow light. Sounds of soft laughter came faintly from the parlor down the hall. The maid cast one last glance round. The fine white china with its blue designs; damask tablecloth and matching napkins; newly-polished silver utensils; fluted glassware—yes, everything was right. She sighed, silently pushing open the door to enter the hallway. Near the door leading to the garden she saw two figures standing close together in conversation, and the curiosity of a servant caused her to retreat back into her doorway.

Half-hidden by a potted orange tree stood Denis, her master's valet, and Berthe, her mistresses' *femme-de-chambre*. He was speaking rapidly but in such a low voice that the eavesdropping maid could barely hear a murmur. Berthe seemed to be listening with half-coy assent, but a moment later an undecipherable expression stole across her face and she answered in a few short, reluctant words, shaking her head. The noise of approaching footsteps broke up their *tête-à-tête*, and they quickly parted.

With the mischief of gossip in her eyes, the maid moved towards the parlor, passing the servant-boy Marcel in the hall. She chuckled to herself. *What a tidbit to relay in the kitchen! Or mayhap to save and profit from later....*

In the parlor, her mistress was talking to a pleasant-looking woman, Madame du Chemin. The lady's deep brown eyes were lively, but there was a paleness in her oval face which bespoke ill-health. At a pause,

111

the maid approached. "Madame, dinner is ready," she murmured, curtseying.

Felicienne smiled in answer and told Francis, who rose and proffered his arm. Madame and Monsieur du Chemin followed suit, and the older children walking decorously behind. The younger ones, Charles and Paulette, were upstairs having dinner with their nurse.

As they broke pieces off the fine white rolls and dipped them in clear golden leek soup, Madame du Chemin remarked, "Where did you get these rolls, Felicienne? What with the lines at the bakeries, my Marthe has had quite a struggle."

"There is a little shop, Bertrand's, on a small cross street near here; *rue Vertier*," Felicienne answered, looking across the table. "But I must send the cook there directly in the morning." She smiled. "Though actually, she was delayed this morning, and the proprietor had set aside bread for her—I think he favors us because our bread is given to the needy."

"I particularly noticed the lines this evening, on my journey here from Versailles," Francis remarked. His large white napkin, like the other men, was tied round his neck to protect the ruffles and lace of his shirt. "There have been lines for bread at the bakeries all year, but they have grown *much* longer in the last weeks."

"With last year's bad crop, and then the hail of last July—almost a year ago now—the shortage of wheat, and thus bread, has been severe," Christophe du Chemin agreed. "From reports I hear among my contacts in the countryside, this year's crop is looking poorly and will not assuage the pressing need."

"Though the famine has nothing to do with the King, the people add it to their list of grievances. Hunger stirs their unrest and rebellion," Francis said.

"The orators are not averse to using it, either," Madame du Chemin answered. "Tristan and I were at the *Palais-Royal* today, and some were saying that if the Estates-General would consolidate and vote by head (as the Third Estate desires), there would be bread aplenty. Was it not so, Tristan?"

"Yes, mother. One, a *Brigand*, was shouting, 'Down with the aristocrats! Down with the King! Then we shall have bread and freedom for all!'" Tristan's green eyes were sober. "There was quite an approving crowd, soaking in his words."

"Things must come to a head, sometime." Francis put his glass down with a weary gesture. "It has been almost *six weeks* of stalemate between the Third Estate, our Second Estate, and the First Estate. Many in the opposing two Estates are being worn down by the deadlock and the people's ecstatic support of the Third Estate. Most of the First Estate are now vehemently in favor of the Third Estate's actions. At least one hundred and forty-nine of the clergy wish to join the Third Estate outright—they are only held back by his Grace of Paris, Archbishop Antoine-Éléonor-Léon Leclerc de Juigné. Even some of my comrades in the Second Estate are weakening."

Adele exchanged a portent glance with Honore across the table. Things not only *could* get worse, but it seemed likely they *would* do so—and soon.

~*~*~

A week and a day later—Sunday, June 14th, 1789—various aristocrats gathered in the Du Chemin's large parlor. Around the top of the yellow-gold walls ran a painted border of gold and deep orange, while the sober orange floor had cream highlights to match the off-white moldings of doors and windows.

A Huguenot pastor was staying at present with the Du Chemins, and so a few Huguenot families met quietly for worship on Sundays. Others arrived; waxen, thin-lipped Madame Necker (wife of the king's finance minister) brilliant in a full, lavender-colored silk dress—she hardly came at all, though she professed to be a Protestant. Adele thought that mayhap with the rumors and mounting tension of the last few weeks she had come to especially pray for Divine help. Necker was losing favor with the King.

Of course dear "Grandpapa de Duret" was there. Adele smiled as she watched him draw a carved jack-man out of a capacious pocket to show a rapt Charles and little Paulette. One or two families of small social standing entered; Adele wondered if they came merely to gain graces with her father or Madame Necker.

The parlor door opened, and a liveried butler announced, "The marquis la Motte." A man of medium height stepped in. Above his long face and lively brown eyes, his black hair curled back into a queue, his ensemble shades of green. He was a court official in Versailles, with access to the King. With a flutter of creamy blue ruffles, his wife came next; her plump, round face made radiant by cheerful bright blue eyes. Seven-year-old Christelle, a miniature of her mother, flitted over to join Paulette and Olivie. Adele's special friend entered next—petite, pleasant Elisabeth la Motte.

Rising, Adele thought back to the *fete* when her father had asked her to make sure to greet a new girl whose father he'd met in Versailles. How Adele's rapid imagination conjured up all sorts of pictures of the girl—older than she, stately and tall; or perhaps pale, wispy, and childish; or maybe boisterous, with golden curls like her cousin…but certainly much older or quite a bit younger than herself, she had thought. She smiled as she looked at her friend—for Elisabeth was her own age.

Rich black curls framed Elisabeth's wide, open forehead, while her serious yet merry blue eyes were like jewels. Her scintillate yellow dress with its wide stripes complemented her small, well-formed figure, while her impish, shy demeanor was entrancing. *Elisabeth's quiet, sunny directness is so uniquely warm and special.*…But Adele had not much time to ponder, for Elisabeth was saying, "…My father reports that the king and queen are distracted and depressed by the death of their son. They seem unable to rouse themselves to combat the mounting pressure of the Estates-General deadlock. They seem to think that events will calm of their own accord. What think you?"

"My grandfather shrugs and says, '*Quand les fevers sont en fleur, les fous sont en vigeur*' —When beans are in flower, fools are in power," Adele said. "But I—I tremble, for *something* must happen; the pressure, as you say, must either burst the vessel or find a vent somehow."

Elisabeth nodded slowly, her brow contracted. "Yes. Last Wednesday, the abbe Sieyes declared that the Third Estate should move ahead and formally verify its powers, inviting the other two estates to join them. The Third Estate agreed, stating that if the others do not join them, they will begin to act without them."

"And they really mean it, I have no doubt," Adele answered. "Will the King be ever prodded into action?"

Elisabeth seemed about to answer, but a stir in the room made them look round. The pastor was standing up to start the service. With murmured adieus they parted to find seats.

Adele noticed that as Elisabeth's mother passed Madame Necker she murmured as she curtseyed, "Your husband is in my prayers, Madame Necker."

A startlingly taut face turned to Madame la Motte and answered, "Ah! He is a falling star—but I thank you."

Adele remembered how her father had said that Necker, the finance minister, was doing his best, but the national deficit was too great. And the queen's dislike of him and her efforts to influence the king against him hindered all his efforts. Now there were quiet rumors afloat foretelling his downfall.

The pastor, an elderly man with an emaciated face and prominent, kindly brown eyes led in the first song: Psalm 1 in the Geneva Psalter. Old and young, bass and soprano, joined their voices together in reverent song:

> "How blest the man who keeps from evil ways,
> who heeds not sinful counsel all his days,
> nor seeks the company of wicked scoffers,
> but takes delight in all the LORD God offers
> within the statutes of his holy Law:
> both day and night he ponders it with awe.
>
> He's like a tree that grows beside the stream,
> whose fruitful limbs with ripened bounty teem,
> whose verdant leaves will fade and wither never;
> all that he undertakes in faith will ever
> be blessed by God with great prosperity.
> But wicked ones a different lot shall see.
>
> For they, like chaff, before the wind are blown
> and will not last before the judgement throne,
> nor will they stand in council of the holy.
> But GOD protects all those who follow solely
> the paths of virtue and of righteousness,
> while death shall stalk the ways of wickedness."

After the psalm and a prayer, the pastor said in his strong, cracked voice, "My sermon today is on Proverbs sixteen, verse twenty-five. *'There is a way that seemeth right unto a man, but the end thereof are the ways of death.'*" After illuminating the text and bringing home the need of each person to repent of their own iniquity (doing their own will), he began to explain how these words also related to broader groups.

"The Third Estate," he said, "is doing what is right in their own eyes, but they are doing wrong: for they are defying authority. They are not acknowledging the laws and principles of their Creator. The end of their ways — though it may come slowly, as God is merciful even to the wicked — will be destruction."

To many at the time in France, such words were foolishness. The common people would have almost torn apart the speaker in rage had they heard, for they saw in the rebellious actions of the Third Estate their rising savior from every ill. Far away in America, where a love for their Revolutionary War allies still burned, a newspaper calling itself *"The Christian's, Scholar's, and Farmer's Magazine"* reported naively in its May issue, "Pamphlets and handbills without number circulate as they did in America; and breathe the same spirit. The assembly of the Estates General, will be the epoch of the glory of [France], by uniting the majesty of the king with the greater majesty of the people, that union will be produced which will render [France] the most powerful nation in Europe." As Grandpapa des Cou said, "'Twill be a move to a more balanced power, like that of the American Revolution; 'twill show the King that he is not all-powerful."

And even though the aristocracy viewed the actions of the Third Estate with mistrust, many still hoped to use the upheaval and negotiations to secure more power and privileges for themselves.

But Adele and the others leaned forward and listened to the sermon with eager interest.

~*~*~

The news flew like a trumpet-blast through Paris only a few days later. Stephanie first heard it as she accompanied her mother to a play at the *Comédie Française.* "The *Palais-Royal* is especially crowded and agitated this evening," she thought, watching the wild and boisterous crowds with bright eyes as the sun set in the western sky.

Once in the ornate, plush theater foyer, Madame Juliette de Lobel handed her daughter a ticket. "I shall meet you at our seats; I am going to the dressing rooms to talk with Claire Lacombe..." She moved off, a striking figure: her wide hat perched coquettishly on her perfectly-coiffured locks of golden-brown hair, her brilliant saffron-colored gown commanding attention with its low neckline and the wide russet ribbon around her small, corseted waist.

Stephanie lingered in the foyer. She liked seeing and being seen, and this was a radiant and fashionable crowd. She presently spied tall, handsome Sebastien du Sauchoy moving among the press. He was wearing a tailored dark double-breasted coat with long tails, and the tight, pale-colored breeches that were becoming more and more popular. By adroit maneuvers with her fan, she managed to catch his eye. Stuffing a miscellany of pamphlets in a pocket of his brown coat, he advanced to meet her, gloves and stick in hand.

"My dear Madame Stephanie! What a pleasure to see you," he said, bending over her hand.

"The sight of your face is always welcome to me," she replied.

"Are you here for the premiere?" he asked, motioning to a large placard pasted on a nearby wall.

"Yes; are you?"

"Well, perhaps—if you would let me have the pleasure of your company."

Stephanie showed the full brilliance of her smile as she answered, "That would be lovely!" They drew aside a little out of the crowd, and she asked, "The *Palais-Royal* is especially animated today, *n' est-ce pas*?"

"Yes, and for a reason. I have just been buying the papers, and they are all talking about it—the Third Estate is no more!"

Stephanie's blue eyes opened to their full extent. *"Non!"*

Sebastien's brown eyes sparkled from under his wide hat-brim. "Well—'tis not the literal truth. In reality, they have declared themselves to be no longer the Third Estate. Now they declare themselves to be the 'National Assembly,' an assembly not of the Estates but of the People. They have invited the other two Estates to join them, but have made it clear that they shall proceed to govern and act in any case. Listen here to what the *Moniteur* says they have decreed." Pulling out one of the pamphlets from his pocket, he read, "'...It is clearly evident that it is the duty of this assembly, and of this assembly alone, to interpret and present the general will of the nation: between the throne and this assembly there can be no veto, no power of prohibition.'" He looked up from the paper and down into Stephanie's brilliant eyes as he added, "Versailles is in a tumult; the King, according to reports, is beside himself. The National Assembly fears him not, as is evident by their declaration that they will not allow him to veto their decisions."

"The *National Assembly*—I like it," Stephanie said, savoring the new title. "The King is but a weak dish-rag. I am glad someone is finally putting him in his place." She sniffed in disgust.

The crowd began moving into the theater—the play was about to begin. Sebastien offered his arm, and Stephanie smiled up at him as they moved towards their seats. *This,* she thought, *is the life*—stirring events, a handsome young man attentive at her side....Glancing back in a glow of satisfaction, her eye caught a glimpse of a young man moving rapidly through the crowds. In a moment he was gone, but Stephanie's heart stumbled a bit, and she half-turned. It was the dashing face and careless long locks of her brother's friend from the *Palais-Royal*, Gaston Xavier de la Roche.

~*~*~

The streets were gloomy and dull; a slow Autumn rain made Jean Gabriel de Lobel tuck his head down in an attempt to avoid the miserable drizzle. Despite the inclement weather, he was happy as he traversed the muddy, ill-paved street, the wet houses dripping gloomily on each side. Just a few short days ago, the Third Estate had finally made the bold move he craved! And in the short days since declaring itself the "National Assembly," five standing committees had been formed; one a "committee of subsistence," much to the joy of the famishing populace.

It was Saturday. Jean quickened his steps as he approached the *Salle des Menus*, the usual assembling-place. Black-garbed deputies splashed through the mud alongside. Up ahead a thickening crowd of deputies sloshed forward, led by Bailly their president. From the head of the street, almost in President Bailly's face, a shrill herald cried out, "By the order of the King: A *Séance Royale* [Royal Meeting] will be held Monday; there shall be no meeting of the Estates-General until then." Bailly walked past as if he had not heard the man, though from various other parts of Versailles, heralds could be heard, repeating the edict. With supreme indifference, the Third Estate deputies pushed past the herald, continuing on to the *Salle des Menus* as if the summoner was but a creaking door, noisy but meaningless. Jean's square face split with a smile at the herald's consternation.

Up ahead, the deputies slowed, pressed forward, then stopped at the door of their accustomed building. Jean de Lobel tiptoed to see above the six-hundred-odd black slouch-hats. The wind picked up, driving the drizzling rain into their faces. *What is the hold-up?*

From a window in the row of houses above Jean heard a rustle, and glanced up despite the rain. From several fashionable windows, courtiers and ladies of the court peeped out, amused at the confused and sodden state of the men who had declared themselves the masters of France. A lovely face pressed closer to the window, and Jean could almost hear the mocking laughter that parted her pretty red lips. A flame surged up in him; he pushed his way to the door of *Salle des Menus* with violent energy. *We shall show them that we shall not be foiled!* he thought angrily. But that was more difficult than he had realized. At the door, President Bailly was remonstrating with an apologetic but firm Captain of the *Gardes Francaises*; armed soldiers stood on guard nearby. The captain was speaking; behind him issued the sharp and energetic sounds of sawing and hammering.

"I am grieved to say, Monsieur, but workmen are building here, setting up the platform for His Majesty the King's *Séance*; no, Monsieur, unfortunately, no admission." Here the Captain paused and seemed to have a bright idea. "But, Monsieur, the joiners might destroy your papers; if you and the Secretaries desire, I can allow a few of you in to take away your documents."

President Bailly and the Secretaries entered. Jean stood outside with the other grumbling deputies. The raw gray skies did nothing to brighten the scene. Jean could see little in their crestfallen faces of the "heroes" who had been so bold the preceding days, and his heart quailed. Would this setback cool their ardor? *Not if I can help it,* Jean resolved, a zealous light in his hazel eyes. He seized upon a gruff-looking but powerful man close by and addressed him in a loud voice calculated to gain attention, "What say you, Comrade? We shall not let this weak maneuver arrest our good progress! Where shall we meet today?"

"Well—now, let's see…" The man replied hesitantly; but Jean's idea had been heard. Soon the wildest counsels were being put forth with angry gesticulation, applauded by the gathering bystanders. A pale wisp of a man nearby cried, "The outdoor staircase at Marly! We should convene there, under the King's very windows!" A large group of deputies were rallying around the idea of going to the *Place d'Armes* (Chateau Forecourt).

Jean joined President Bailly and a few others as they departed to search for a meeting-place. Hastening down the street, Jean found himself beside a lean, long-faced man with strong brows and cold eyes—M. Guillotin, a doctor. Though at present an obscure "National Assembly" deputy, he was destined to have his name remembered till time immemorial by a brainchild that would be fondly called *La Guillotine*.

The doctor and he pushed forward along the muddy streets, being joined by one of the bystanders, a man with long dark hair and a scar on his cheek. Presently, the dark-haired man exclaimed, "Here!—this will be the very place!" The men opened the doors and found themselves in a large, bare-walled tennis court.

Once President Bailly had approved the building and sent messengers back to bring the deputies, Jean had a moment to spare to address the man who had aided M. Guillotin and himself. "I am indeed grateful, Denis, that you suggested this room—'tis perfect for our needs. 'Twould not have done to let the King's maneuvers succeed."

"Most certainly not," Denis' dark eyes kindled.

"I am also indebted to your report the other night," Jean de Lobel said warmly. "Your information on the Second Estate was invaluable in turning the tide."

"I knew it was of no use to my master," Denis' mouth quirked, "but that an able, clear-headed man like you would use it to advantage."

"I must say that it is a surprise to see you here, Denis, nonetheless," Jean said.

"You know where my heart is, M. de Lobel," he answered. "But you do not mean that, I know—you wonder how I have the time off. 'Tis this way: because the Estates-General were given a holiday, my master set off at once for his house in Paris, leaving me behind to wrap up his affairs here." He shrugged expressively. "But there are more important things to attend to; and as long as I arrive in Paris sometime today, he will not inquire too closely." A sneer of something like derision crossed his features. Seeing Jean did not speak, he moved away and climbed into the overflowing galleries, for the rumpled "National Assembly" deputies were entering in a steaming flood.

The Tennis Court Oath, by Jacques-Louis David

All was flummoxed disorder for some moments; from every vantage-point—wall-top, chimney, gallery, nearby roofs—clustered eager and vehement spectators. A table was found for the President; most of the National Assembly had to be content to stand. Experienced M. Mounier stepped forward, and in the words of a witness, "*suggested, in moving tones, that no doubt the king had been motivated only by good intentions in his desire to hold a* séance royale, *but that the way in which the session had been announced was entirely unacceptable."*

Then Mounier's voice rose in even more passionate tones. "Let us all swear," he cried, "let us swear to God and our country that we will not disperse until we have established a sound and just constitution, as instructed by those who nominated us!"

The assembled deputies erupted in energetic acclaim; Jean saw tears running down the cheeks of many of his fellow-deputies, while others broke apart into little groups, embracing each other or striking noble attitudes. Several, in the excess of their enthusiasm, swore wildly that they would not return home to their wife and children until they had proved themselves more worthy of their loved ones by creating a constitution— "their patriotic duty." The atmosphere vibrated with passion.

An official oath was written out. Standing up impressively on the table, President Bailly was the first to swear it, in such sonorous tones that even the spectators outside could hear, and shouted their approval. All solemnly and sacredly took the oath after him, holding their right-hands high. All? It seemed so at first, but as Jean stepped away from the table after signing, he heard an obscure deputy, M. Martin d'Auch, telling the President and secretaries, "I shall not sign; I will not swear that oath." Jean turned back to the table, his eyebrows contracted and fist clenched. But as he came closer, he remembered Francis de Coquiel di le Mercier, and somehow the thought of that sincere, though (Jean thought) utterly mistaken man choked the tense, angry words in his throat.

Instead, thinking the crowd would tear to pieces such an "unfaithful deserter," Jean went so far as to spread rumors that d'Auch was "deranged in the head." As he remarked under his breath to M. Guillotin, "'Tis the kindest thing to do, to excuse him so." M. Guillotin replied politely, "Yes, one doubts the sanity of a man who turns down such a glorious venture." Jean did not reply; the image of Francis and his clear sanity flashed through his mind.

Finally the session came to a close at four-o-clock that afternoon, with the decision to convene next on Monday, an hour before the *Séance Royale.* Jean de Lobel adjourned to dinner with a glowing heart. "*Quand on veut on peut*—When one wants, one can do it. And we are *doing* it!'" he cried, exultation in his voice and an extra briskness in his step.

~*~*~

Perhaps to gain time after this unexpected event, the King changed the date of the *Séance Royale* to Tuesday. Whatever his reason, all it did was give his enemies more time. The night before the *Séance*, a close and conspiratorial group of twelve or so met at the Breton Club. Though composed of only deputies, they were not all deputies of the former Third Estate. At least one abbe was there, one of the most radical members of the First Estate.

For some little time, one man had been reading off various resolutions and measures in a low, monotonous tone. With a sudden, vigorous movement, a man who had been sitting back in the shadows leaned forward. The light fell full on his square, zealous face, though his eyes were lit from within. "We cannot let the king's *séance* tomorrow dampen the forward momentum we have gained! Several of the reform measures the king will announce tomorrow would have gained universal approval if they had been announced two months ago. Even now, they will be welcomed by some. This we *cannot* allow to happen. We must reject them all. We see better horizons opening before us." His voice shook with passion.

"I agree wholly, M. de Lobel," the abbe Gregoire answered from a dark corner, while others nodded approval. "And yet the question is how to nullify the potential power of these conciliatory, compromising measures. First, we must all remain in our usual chamber after the *séance royale —*"

"—even if the King forbids it," broke in another deputy, a fair young man with a jutting chin.

"*Even* if the king forbids it," said the shadowed mouth of the abbe Gregoire — the others could see only his steady eyes, glittering in the lamplight.

"We must go among all of our colleagues, to let them know what is about to happen and inform them of our plans," remarked another, his long face tense.

There was a general assent to this, when one said, "But how can the wishes of twelve or fifteen people —" he looked around the close chamber " —how can the decision of so few determine the actions of twelve hundred deputies?"

Jean de Lobel remembered not afterwards who answered, but the soft-spoken reply always carried a sinister, secret thrill in his memory afterwards.

"How? We shall use the magic word 'they.' We will say, 'This is what the court is about to do, and as for the patriots, 'they' have agreed on such and such measures.' 'They' can mean four hundred people just as easily as it can mean ten."[1]

The meeting broke up soon after, and Jean and the other deputies hastened off in various directions to carry out their mission of sedition.

An Old Rival Reappears

10.

'Tis too strong for such a king; foment breeds rebellion,
As the gaunt populace raises voices and arms;
Ah! For a King like the Kings gone by! But
Generations of degeneracy have whelped a weakling,
Good for nothing but a quiet round of pleasure.
— Ianthe

*T*he next morning the cities of Versailles and Paris awoke with a heightened sense of anticipation. Some viewed the morn with dread; some with delight; to others, it held last glimmers of hope for stability by foiling the swollen Third Estate; while others gritted their teeth and prepared for the battle of wills that was to take place. The sun refused to give any message of hope as it sulked behind leaden clouds. The clouds in turn deepened the atmospheric gloom by discharging a steady, miserable rain over Versailles.

Pressing against the damp wall of a house, trying to benefit from the slight shelter it afforded, Jean de Lobel grumbled audibly as he removed his hat for the fifteenth time to dump off the rain accumulating on the curved brim. He and the other deputies of the "National Assembly" huddled under porches and in meager doorways from the bitter rain, waiting while the Court and members of the First and Second Estates paraded in through the front door.

A man in the Second Estate's rich attire walked rapidly along the street. Jean recognized Francis de Coquiel di le Mercier. Francis' lean face seemed even more lined, and there was something in his glance at the waiting "National Assembly" deputies that was almost too sad for words. Even antagonistic eyes saw here was a man who, foreseeing failure, still goes on, determined to do his duty. A deputy standing near to Jean muttered, "They may dislike our doings, but some of them still are *men*."

As for Francis, his heart was full of prayer—strength for the weak King, repentance and acquiescence from the recaltriant deputies. Again and again through his mind ran the words of M. la Motte, spoken over the breakfast-table this morning: "Alas for our country! Would God we had King Louis the Just to face these deputies!"

At long last the other two estates were assembled, and the Third Estate deputies—the self-styled "National Assembly"—were allowed by his most gracious Majesty to enter. They filed in, sullen, sodden, and sulky. But they rose and removed their hats with the other two orders as the King began to speak.

Painting by Auguste Couder

A heavy spirit seemed to settle over the assembly, and was in no way lessened as the King continued, his voice trembling at times. When he finished, the silence was palpable. He gave permission to the deputies to be seated and replace their hats while a declaration of the King was read—one of the principal statements being that the King annulled all declarations of the so-called National Assembly and confirmed that the three orders were to meet separately. Francis noted the displeasure of many at these words. *Where is Necker? This bodes not well,* Francis thought. *He should have appeared with the King to add weight.* Meanwhile on the other side of the hall, the Third Estate deputies had raised Necker to a hero's status, inferring from his absence that he was against the King's measures.

Francis focused on the King. A man of medium height, dressed in royal regalia, with a fleshy, broad-jawed face and wide lips met his eyes.

The king was almost thirty-five, and tending to corpulence. His eyes were pale, his nose long and straight. Despite his rich garments, he had none of the magnetizing, commanding kingliness of past French monarchs; he seemed an anticlimax; a weak, plain man. But today he was firm enough as he lengthened his discourse, especially as shouts of "*Vive le Roi!*" rose from the ranks of the second estate as he mentioned various concessions. As his speech went on, it was clear that he planned to grant France considerable constitutional privileges—a positive change. Francis rejoiced at the strength in the King's voice as he stated, "The three orders *shall* vote separately."

The *Gardes-des-Sceaux*—Keeper of the King's Seals—then read out the King's five-and-thirty articles. He annulled all limited powers, desired that all property rights should be observed, such as tithes, seigneurial dues, feudal rights, etc., and abolished the *lettres de cachet*, though reserving certain general rights to his discretion. *He has drawn up the Constitution himself,* thought Francis. *Alas! If only these articles had come a few months ago! What general rejoicing and quietness they would have brought! But now it is too late; the Third Estate has drunk the heady draught of power.*

Once the *Gardes-des-Sceaux* finished reading, the King rose again and made a third speech. His tone held less assurance than before, though he was making an obvious effort to be firm. At times during the reading of the articles, members of the first or second estates hailed favorable points with exclamations of, "*Vive le roi!*" but the third estate sat glowering, and it could not but tell upon the King. And now, during this last speech, all of the assembly held their tongues. "If the Three Orders cannot agree to effect these articles," the King said in his final address, "I myself shall effect them."

The hint was broad and pointed. "If," Louis was saying, "you Estates do not do as I wish, I shall disperse you, and I shall be the hero and rescuer of the people."

The King stood up, looking briefly at the silent assembly. What bitter or sad thoughts passed through his mind none can tell, but he left the room in equal silence, followed by his retinue. The Séance-Royale was now at an end; the First and Second Estates followed with propriety. However, the Third Estate deputies remained—as those few in that dark room had directed. Yet they were vacillating and unsure—a mere touch could have scattered them. Knowing that the King had commanded that no one should meet until the next day, many looked fearful, and some began to move towards the door.

Jean de Lobel was beginning to fear as to the result when the comte de Mirabeau stood and spoke. Jean watched with eagerness his confident, bold manner. Resolve began to creep back into the faces of the deputies. Many even among the Third Estate had shunned Mirabeau because of his debased reputation; yet in this hour of distress, they followed even such a dissolute man. Mirabeau, having, in his own words, "for forty years struggled against despotism" (chiefly by defying God's law and man's convention) had "made away with all formulas" and become the spokesman of a nation desiring to do the same.

Mirabeau had barely begun when there was a disturbance at the door, and the marquis de Breze (the king's Master of Ceremonial) approached, as a timid man approaches a half-wild beast. He began to speak, but in such a low voice that only those nearest could hear.

"Louder!" cried several voices from the back.

"Messieurs," he said, raising his hesitant voice, "you have heard the king's instructions [to disperse]."

Jean rejoiced inwardly that the Master of Ceremonial was such a weakling—*What damage a strong and valiant man could have done! But he, even the most vacillating can despise.*

"Yes, Monsieur," Mirabeau answered the marquis de Breze, "we have heard what the King was advised to say: and you, who cannot be the interpreter of his orders to the States-General; you, who have no seat here, no right of speech; *you* are not the man to remind us of his words." Mirabeau paused in his cutting dialogue, his voice gaining power, "However, to avoid any misunderstanding or delay—Go, Monsieur, tell those who sent you that we are here by the will of the People, and that nothing but the force of bayonets shall dislodge us!"

The assembled deputies erupted with applause, crying, "Hear, hear!" De Breze, that faithful but fainthearted man, slipped out.

Meanwhile, tumult was waxing outside. Rumors flew. The people shouted in favor of Necker and the Third Estate. The king and his courtiers were thrown into corresponding agitation. As a riot swelled the French Guards were called out—but the two companies refused to fire when ordered!

His Grace of Paris, the conservative leader of the First Estate, who had done much to keep the clergy from joining the Third Estate, was mobbed. His coach-panels were broken, and he only escaped alive due to his coachman's furious driving. But Necker was called for and carried home in triumph—for he had *not* been at the *Séance*, and there were rumors that the King planned to dismiss him; the latter suggestion rousing the populace's wrath. All was tumult; all was confusion; the King and his supporters made themselves scarce and did nothing to oppose the rebellious Third Estate.

To add to the people's delight, all of the First Estate (the clergy) joined the National Assembly, and forty-eight of the Second Estate as well! Meanwhile the National Assembly grew in daring. It decreed, "Infamous, traitorous toward the nation, and guilty of capital crime, is any person, body-corporate, tribunal, court or commission, that now or henceforth, during the present session or after it, shall dare to pursue, interrogate, arrest, or cause to be arrested, detain or cause to be detained any [member of the National Assembly] on *whose part soever* the same be commanded."

Fanaticism glowing even brighter in his eyes, Jean de Lobel added his voice to the general acclamation. As for Francis de Coquiel di le Mercier, he paced his room. He had received news that his friend the marquis de LaFayette had been one of those who joined the National Assembly. LaFayette fervently believed that this would bring freedom to France, as the War for American Independence had done. He had known LaFayette's leanings; but it was still a blow.

He was alone, accompanied only by sad and gloomy thoughts: for Denis was away, Francis knew not where. He suspected that wherever the tumult was the wildest, there was Denis. And his heart grew sadder than ever at the thought of what his boyhood servant-playmate had become.

~*~*~

"Ah, Felicienne! A timely arrival," Juliette de Lobel exclaimed, greeting her sister with an embrace.

"I have merely stopped by on my way home," Felicienne smiled in reply.

"Oh, you must spare some time to go to Madame LaFayette's salon with me: here, freshen yourself, and I will fasten a ribbon in your hair....do you prefer burgundy or this deep green one? ...Ah, the burgundy goes best with your coral dress, and brings out the color of your lips." So chattered Juliette, and Felicienne submitted good-humouredly, though wondering at her sister's unusually bright spirits. Juliette herself was arrayed in a faultless lavender silk which made her pale features and hair even more fairy-like. "Come in my carriage, and I will take you home afterwards—I shall tell Pierre to dismiss yours," Juliette said, as they stepped out into the clear, fair air.

The marquise de LaFayette's brilliant salon was full of chattering groups of gorgeously-dressed *noblesse*. All the salons and gathering places were buzzing since the failed *Séance Royal* and the National Assembly's actions. Yesterday, the day after the *Séance*, ten thousand people had gathered in the *Palais-Royal* alone.

In a half-circle of chairs near the doorway a lively conversation was taking place, and Felicienne and Juliette were soon drawn into it. The marquis du Sauchoy was talking, but Felicienne had barely caught the gist of his talk before a tall, suave gentleman approached their circle. His attire and powdered wig were so faultless as to direct attention from themselves to his slim figure, lean yet striking face, and deep blue eyes. He bowed to all, then directed himself specifically to Felicienne, who returned his gaze with puzzled interest. Out of the corner of her eye, she noticed that her sister was intently watching her reaction.

"My dear marquise," the newcomer said with an especially-deep bow, "how this brings me back to the days of my youth! Though, indeed, you have not aged a day — "

"Philip de la Noye!" Felicienne cried, rising with a graceful curtsy. He took her hand with equal grace, but more warmth.

"How could I not have recognized you, even for a moment!" she said, resuming her seat.

He smiled as he took one nearby, remarking, "It has been many years, Felicienne; that is excuse enough, especially since Father Time has not been as good to me as to you. Indeed, I feel that He has forgotten you altogether."

Felicienne blushed, which obviously pleased De la Noye; most Parisian ladies had either forgotten how (or trained themselves not) to blush. "I have been very blessed," she murmured. "But where have you been, these years?"

"Abroad, on missions for the King," he replied. "But where have *you* been? Hidden away on your husband's estate? *My* wife would not have been tucked away thus."

Felicienne crimsoned, but without embarrassment this time, and Juliette thought it was high time to make a diversion. She knew that years before Philip de la Noye had been a suitor for her sister's hand, but her parents had decided in favor of Francis de Coquiel di le Mercier. Juliette was not quick enough, though, to prevent Felicienne answering with quiet joy, "I would not mind being hidden away anywhere, as long as I was with my husband."

"Talk about being hidden away, De la Noye," Juliette broke in with an irresistibly sparkling manner, "have you heard of the supposedly hidden maneuvers of the troops?"

"I have only just arrived in Paris, my lady—I am sure you know more particulars than I," he answered somewhat absently, casting a covert glance at Felicienne. She had changed since he had seen her last—he marveled at her simple, uncynical grace and the way she spoke of her husband.

"'Tis difficult to sort through the rumors, but the King is most definitely gathering troops around Paris," Juliette replied.

"He fears the National Assembly," a pudgy dowager said.

"He has reason to," another lady said, fanning herself with slow content. "They must be squelched."

"Arresting them would solve his difficulties—he thinks."

"The poor are angered by the mustering soldiers, are they not, marquise de Coquiel di le Mercier?" Du Sauchoy asked.

"Yes," Felicienne answered frankly. "They have—mistakenly, I think—set their hopes upon the National Assembly. The news of the troops the King is collecting enrages and affrights them—they know all too well what the King means to do: end their wild hopes."

"How come you to be the authority on the opinions of the poor, Madame Felicienne?" De la Noye asked, turning to her.

Juliette cut in with a merry laugh and an arch smile. "If it wasn't for the fact that she has a husband, De la Noye, I would think she would become a nun, for all the time she spends in charity to the poor."

"Truth, Felicienne?" questioned De la Noye, turning from her sister.

"I have no intention of becoming a nun—far from it, sister!" Felicienne's amused glance softened her words. "I know I can do far more as a wife and mother. But I am blessed with resources; and should I not use them? Have you seen the bread lines? How many workmen stand in them all day for a scant black morsel, only to find it snatched by those who are stronger or more famished? Oh, how many are starving and dying for want of bread! The 'masses' should not rise in violence—but have you ever considered how they might have been provoked into desperation, the way they are slighted and abused?" Her voice had not gained in volume, but rather in pathos, and she stopped with a most appealing look of heartfelt compassion in her lovely face.

"But, truly, Madame Felicienne," sniffed the lady with the fan, "you judge us harshly. I know I always give my due to the priest to distribute to the poor."

"I judge no one," Felicienne replied, "How many years did I myself give a pittance—enough to salve my conscience—to the poor of my estate on holy days, and yet was wholly neglecting and oppressing them daily?" She looked from face to face, but most of the powdered and polished faces were unmoved or bore sneers. She was fain to stop there, but an indescribable look of question on De la Noye's handsome face led her to add, "It says in the Holy Bible, in Exodus, 'The people of the land have used oppression, and exercised robbery, and have vexed the poor and needy: yea, they have oppressed the stranger wrongfully. And I sought for a man among them, that should make up the hedge, and stand in the gap before me for the land, that I should not destroy it: but I found none. Therefore have I poured out mine indignation upon them; I have consumed them with the fire of my wrath: their own way have I recompensed upon their heads, saith the Lord GOD.'"

There was a silence, then one of the ladies effected a diversion by dropping her fan, and skillfully introduced another topic. Soon after, Felicienne and Juliette took their leave. Making an excuse, Philip de la Noye accompanied them to the carriage, handing Felicienne in with consummate grace.

Once hastening through the streets, Juliette threw herself a bit wearily among the cushions. After a pause, she addressed her sister with a thin smile. "You talk so strangely, Felicienne."

"Do I?" Felicienne asked.

"I cannot understand your religious fervor….It does you no good, only harm—you, who used to be the brightest and merriest belle of Parisian society."

Felicienne's eyes framed her question, though her lips formed the words, "Does me *harm*?"

"You are still one of the most beautiful ladies in Paris—why then do you bring up such awkward subjects as religion, and speak as if you believed what you said! Philip de la Noye is a man of much influence at Court."

"I care not for the opinion of De la Noye," Felicienne said.

Juliette shot her a questioning glance. "You could do so much more for *your husband* if you spoke with more discretion," she returned, smugly taking up an unassailable position. "Your looks and your manner could win him favors and positions—you must stay away from religious babble."

The words hurt, and but more painful than the words or the thought of what the fashionable crowd might think of her was the contemplation of the scheming, cool calculation existing in such circles, of which her sister was an illustration. Felicienne thought, *What a small and stunted realm of topics, if one cannot speak of things that are meaningful* – but her lips said, "But—"

"Put some doubt, some cynicism, into your tone," her sister continued, "if you must talk of such matters."

"Would you have me act a lie?" Felicienne asked in a low voice.

"A lie? How you could be so deluded as to be in earnest about religion, I cannot tell," Juliette replied.

Felicienne was about to answer when the carriage stopped and the footman opened the door to assist her out. Giving him her hand, she turned back one instant to Juliette, saying, "I was lost, and now I am found."

> *O fools (said I) thus to prefer dark night*
> *Before true light,*
> *To live in grots, and caves, and hate the day*
> *Because it shews the way,*
> *The way which from this dead and dark abode*
> *Leads up to God,*
> *A way where you might tread the Sun, and be*
> *More bright than he.*

~*~*~

In a small gilded room on Saturday morning the 27th, the marquis la Motte and Francis de Coquiel di le Mercier were seated at a table. Concern filled their faces.

"I can offer you no hope from that quarter, Francis," La Motte's lengthy face looked even longer than usual, though there was a certain peace in the black eyes beneath his thick black hair. "The King has decided that he will give in to the National Assembly—I expect any minute to hear the news of his proclamation, *ordering* all those who have not joined to unite with that juggernaut."

"Is there no way out? I would not join the National Assembly of my own free will—it is a runaway horse."

"And he is letting it take the bit in its teeth," La Motte answered. He added, "Though I know not what else he could do. It has been represented to him—not by me—that the want of bread in France is so severe that there is no extremity to which the people might not be driven; that Paris and Versailles will be burnt; in short, that all sorts of mischief, misery, and bloodshed will follow unless he gives in to the National Assembly."

The street-noises had been a murmuring backdrop all the while, but in the short silence that followed they could hear a herald coming down the street outside, shouting out a proclamation in strident tones. "By the order of the King: All deputies must join the National Assembly…"

"It is done," Francis said to himself. Then he broke into prayer. "Lord, we put not our trust in man, but in Thee…"

"*Amen*," La Motte concluded.

"I must send an answer to Du Sauchoy," Francis said after a moment. He struck a bell, and called, "Denis?"

The door opened and Denis appeared, noting his master's somber expression. "Yes, master?"

"Deliver this to Du Sauchoy, Denis — he resides at present at —"

"I know where he is, master. I shall be back." Denis bowed, taking the sealed letter. He stepped into the foyer, settled his hat on his head, and had placed his hand on the doorknob when there was a rap on it from without. He opened the front door. A handsome, immaculately-dressed gentleman stood on the steps.

"Present this to your master, my man." With a flourish of his deep yellow sleeve the newcomer held out a calling card. Denis' eye only had time to read the words, 'Philip Emile de la Noye, marquis…' before the man said, "I request an audience."

"An audience? — sir, my master is the marquis de Coquiel di le Mercier."

"I am mistaken?" the man's brow knit into a frown. "I was directed here on good authority, as being the residence of the marquis la Motte —"

"It is indeed, my lord," Denis replied. "I am not a servant of this house."

"Well, then — let me in to see one!" the man cried, with a somewhat forgivable expression of ill-humor. Then he paused. "I gather your master does not favor the National Assembly. Do such opinions please you?"

Denis studied the lean, inscrutable, handsome face of the marquis. "They do not, my lord."

"If there be any occasion for you to quit his service, come to me — I can give you a position."

Leaving Denis in a state of astonishment, the marquis de la Noye entered the house.

~*~*~

It was a sweet evening in early July; the sun was beginning to dip closer to the horizon, preparing to turn the scattered clouds into purple and gold banners. Adele was reading a book in the parlor, and giving little heed to the antics of Olivie and her lap-dog. The latter frisked about, chasing the twitching end of a ribbon.

"Look at Leon, Adele! Oh—he's almost got it!—" cried Charlot, dancing about in delight.

Smiling, Adele turned, and met the eyes of the entering Honore.

"What shall we do this evening, Adele?" he asked. "Mother and Father are gone to the party at the Fourniers."

"Yes; I know."

A soft knock at the door announced Berthe. "Time for Master Charles to go to bed; Nurse awaits upstairs," she announced. Charlot's face fell and he cast a beseeching glance at Adele.

"No—you must go to bed," Adele replied to his look. "Honore— mayhap we should—"

There was a knock on the street door, and they heard Marcel's languid answer, "I shall present it."

A moment later Marcel entered the parlor, handing a card to Honore. Berthe moved to the window and snuck a look through the thin curtains, glimpsing a lean face with blue eyes and an aquiline nose. It reminded her of a face she had seen long before.

"He said he was calling on your Mother," Marcel said.

"You may tell him—and truthfully—that she is not at home," Honore answered. "I shall let them know, so they may return the call."

Marcel disappeared with a phlegmatic air, and Honore tossed the card to Adele. "Does that name look familiar?" he asked, carelessly seating himself.

"Philip Emile de la Noye—no, most assuredly not," Adele answered. "Mayhap he arrived recently in Paris."

Berthe shepherded Master Charles out, but as she ascended the steps she muttered, "De la Noye? That 'minds me of that gentleman I saw once or twice with sister Camille—but that was years and years ago. It could be another altogether—*she* would know." She shrugged and put out her hand to guide Charlot to his room.

BOOK THE SECOND

Explosion

The Mob Rises

1.

There can be no such thing, in law or in morality,
as actions forbidden to an individual, but permitted to a mob.
— Ayn Rand

T rying to tuck stray hairs into her elaborate up-do, Adele surveyed the result in her oval dressing-table mirror. A frown creased her face — she was fretting. *Where is Olivie? She's always leaving just when I need her....such a gad-about....*

Olivie burst in the door, hands overflowing with flowers. "I've been out in the garden," she said. A simple white frock shielded her sunny yellow gown. "Roses make such lovely ornaments for hair — and are perfect for church." She placed the blossoms on the dressing table, then, looking critically at Adele, selected a few. "You will want these *pêche* ones; they complement the peachy tones of your dress — here, I will fasten them —"

Shame tinted Adele's cheeks. *How could I have been so selfish?* As Olivie deftly inserted flowers into her rich waves of golden-brown hair, Adele prayed silently for God's forgiveness. "As for you, sit here," she murmured to her sister. "I will arrange your hair."

Seating herself, Olivie remarked, "'Tis odd to do our own hair, is it not, Adele? At the chateau there was a maid for that."

"I do not mind," began Adele — then, as a willful lock of Olivie's hair refused to behave, she added, "Except when the hair is rebellious and refuses to cooperate." Olivie giggled.

"Stop!" Adele scolded playfully, "you'll disarrange your hair!"

"Most of the time I like having fewer servants," Olivie said, barely restraining her mirth. "One can do more things — can you imagine the scolding dear Marthe would have given me for going into the garden too early?"

Adele smiled. "But Mother never minded."

"No, but Marthe always did."

For a few minutes the girls were silent. Adele was abstractedly tucking pale cream roses into Olivie's piled curls when a hoarse shout from the unusually- quiet street below attracted their attention. *Was it a herald?* But Olivie's hair was in a perilous not-securely-fastened state; Adele had to keep her hands in it to hold it together. Despite her hasty pinning, the voice faded away before they could look out. They did notice a sullen knot of people in the street, gathering round a large placard.

There was a rap on the door, and the girls both cried, "Come in."

"A letter for you, Madame Adele," Denis said, entering. He turned to leave but Adele's voice stopped him.

"A letter! But no messenger has come this morning!"

Denis clasped his hands uncomfortably, but his voice was carefully composed. "Certes, Madame Adele, but… let us say that in the excess of my duty, I was not able to deliver it 'til now." He cringed inwardly as she broke the seal, read the date, and looked up with puzzled eyes.

"This is dated the 8th of July, and today is the 12th! What on earth?" she cried.

"I have been occupied," he muttered, before slipping out.

With your own business and not Father's, Adele thought. As Olivie slipped out the door, Adele settled herself and began to read.

Dearest Adele,   *Wednesday July 8th, 1789*
    I knew I wuld not See you for some days but am Bursting to tell you so I am Writing have you Heard of the Prisoners who were ~~Resku'd~~ Rescu'd from the Abbaye?

Adele remembered it well. *It began because the Gardes Francaises disobediently made a secret pact to not act against the National Assembly. The King knew something must be done, so he threw the eleven ringleaders into the Abbaye Prison. This enraged the people….* She kept reading:

    Papa is Verry Proud and seys there were Four Thousand Youths who storm'd the Prison. They Rescu'd the Eleven and Some Others and Feast'd them in Palais-Royal. Our faible king does Nothing what a Despicable wretch Hee is.
    But you know That as well as I. My News is different. Dont tell but Leuren was part of the Rescue of the imprisoned Gardes Francaises my Parents dont Know but I caught Him coming in Late that ~~Gloreeus~~ Glorious Night. Keep this a Seecret for your Stephanie's sake as tho' they are Proud I doubt my Parents wuld be Happy to hear about Leuren tak'g Part.
    Shall I see You on the Twentyfifth? You must come. I Miss You,
    Your cousin,

Stephanie Aimee-Juliette de Lobel
P. S. I remember now You told me you do Not keep Secrets from Your parents. I allow you to Tell them since I Know you wuld Anyway. Just Not mine.
P. P. S. I Condescend to have Honore know Too.

Adele was pondering the note when she caught sight of Honore's blue silk jacket passing her half-open door. "Honore!" she called softly. As he turned back, she placed her thumb and forefinger together lightly.

"What is it?"

In reply, she placed the letter in his hand. He read it and gave a low whistle. "He is young to mix himself up in such work."

"Remember what friends he has," Adele answered.

At first, Honore was puzzled, then his brow cleared. "Oh! The ones we met at the *Palais-Royal*? Yes, I see what you mean. Yet I think cousin Stephanie's fears are groundless—I think uncle would not mind to hear Leuren's part, though I wish he would!" Honore handed the letter back, smiling wryly. "On a different vein, Adele—have you heard about the King's proclamation? It is written on a monstrous placard in the street."

"I saw the sign, but could not read it from the window."

"Well, I'm sorry for all your lovely preparations—the roses look so pretty—"

"What do you mean, Honore?"

"I mean this," he said, drawing his eyebrows together, mystified. "It is a proclamation of the King's, 'inviting all peaceable citizens to remain within doors,' to refrain from gathering, but to feel no alarm. I am afraid it means we will, in obedience, refrain from assembling for corporate worship this morning. But what it really means I have no idea. What is the King hatching now?"

"Everyone is being asked not to assemble? I wonder if Father knows why."

"Yes, he does," came a rich voice from the doorway, and their father entered. "This is the King's effort to soften the news that must soon leak out—Necker has been dismissed and ordered to secretly leave town." Their father frowned thoughtfully. "The duc de Broglie has been deploying soldiers—there goes a company now," he said, glancing out the window into the street below.

From some quarter beyond came a muffled roar of many voices, and Francis shook his head. "They know."

~*~*~

Later that morning, Leuren Andre Gabriel de Lobel stretched and yawned as he sat up in bed. The sun was high, but the house was silent; his family usually slept in on Sunday mornings, and today was no exception. "Good," he muttered. Dragging himself to the washbasin, he rearranged his long blond locks to make them look more disorderly. Dressing with equal care, he rumpled his shirt and left the jacket unbuttoned to produce an effect of careless negligence. He stepped back to view the result. A sturdy, sullen thirteen-year-old looked back at him from the mirror, dressed in a dark jacket, tight tan breeches fastened just below the knees, and an insolently-tied white cravat. Hefting a stout stick, he gave an approving nod to the mirror before leaving his room.

He slipped into the kitchen, where the cook was bending over the hearth, trying to blow up a fire. He picked up a few rolls and stuffed them into an inner pocket before letting himself out into the side street.

Halfway down the street, a large placard caught his eye. He read it with scorn. "Well, here I am, sir King—and I am going to join a group of people, just to spite you!" he muttered, hastening his steps. As he neared the *Palais-Royal*, someone slapped him familiarly on the back. "Andre! There you are!" cried Gaston.

"Ah—I was looking for you, Gaston," Leuren Andre replied. "Anton—Anton Petit!" Leuren grasped the lank hand of Gaston's companion.

"Yes, and the tyrants shall find a bite to the sleeping lion they have dared to insult," Anton said, vigorously shaking his fist. His stringy yellow hair looked even longer and more unkempt than usual. "The champion of the people, Necker, cannot be expelled with impunity—"

Interrupting Anton's soliloquy, Gaston spoke to Leuren. "Come—there is work to do at the *Palais-Royal*."

~*~*~

The noon-cannon had gone off several hours before. Denis, ensconced in one of the cafes straggling along the sides of the *Palais-Royal*, studied the crowd with inscrutable eyes. It whirled and thickened, tossed about by fear, anger, and agitation, but was as yet headless. The news of Necker's dismissal and the gathering troops was known city-wide now, and more people were flooding into the gardens and milling around the central wooden tent. Denis took a sip of wine. "Not yet—not yet," he murmured to himself. "To speak now might play upon the wrong notes—"

Half an hour later, Denis noted a young man of his acquaintance, Camille Desmoulins, at some distance. Occasionally he could catch his earnest words, deploring the people's lack of courage. *But more is needed,* thought Denis. He was draining his glass when three youths came through the indignant, chattering multitudes. Holding hands, they shouted, "Aux armes! Aux armes!" Setting his wine glass down, Denis scrambled to his feet. He hardly noticed the way the people were galvanized by the sight; he was staring at the three. *Leuren, that little rat!....I have seen the other two before....* As he saw the ecstatic reaction of the crowd he thought, *That was the spark this tinder needed!*

A moment later, he noticed that Camille Desmoulins had leaped upon a table and was in full cry now. "*Aux armes!*" Camille cried, losing his habitual stutter in the heat of the moment; "Friends! Shall we die like hunted hares? Like sheep hounded into their pinfold; bleating for mercy, where there is no mercy, but only a whetted knife? The hour is come; the supreme hour of the Frenchmen and Man; when oppressors are to try conclusion with oppressed; and the word is, swift death, or deliverance for ever! Let such an hour be *well*-come! Us, meseems, only one cry befits: *Aux armes*! To arms! Let us all wear cockades. *Aux armes!*"[1]

Denis alone seemed to be still sane at the end of this passionate discourse. *Splendid! He knows how to fan the flames! Of course we aren't going to die like hunted hares — but 'twas just the thing. Look — the people are electrified! Splendid!*

Camille Desmoulins reached out, snatching a green ribbon and pinning it to his hat. "Green—the color of hope!" The cheering crowd grabbed for green emblems, pinning them to their hats. Trees were stripped of their leaves; Denis had the fortune to find a ribbon from his green livery in his pocket, for all the shops nearby were instantly despoiled of their green finery and trinkets. Everyone seemed mad with the impulse of the moment; men, women, and children. Desmoulins was mobbed; everyone tried to hug him; many faces were weeping—with joy, or perhaps with madness.

The tumult swelled and spread through the streets. The prince Lambesc, with soldiers, arrived to disperse the mob. But alas for him! Several charges through the crowds in the Tuileries gardens, using only the flats of their swords, only succeeded in knocking down a poor old schoolmaster who had meant no harm. His rushes to clear the streets were even more ineffectual; his men struck down a *Garde Francaise*, whose corpse was borne to the barracks of the *Gardes*—this did not improve the *Gardes'* humor towards the King or his cause. Despite his good intentions, Lambesc only encouraged the unreasonable fervor of the mob.

Denis assisted in throwing bottles at Lambesc and his troops, who were forced to withdraw. As the troop's horses wheeled and galloped off, Denis turned to find Leuren, Gaston, and Anton at his elbow. Leuren had a rapidly-forming bruise on his cheek from the flat of a sword — the other two looked more disheveled than even their regular toilet permitted.

"Introduce me to these two heroes, Master Leuren," Denis said.

"I go by Andre here, Denis," Leuren replied. "This is Gaston de la Roche; Gaston, this is Denis Moreau. Denis, this is Anton Petit; Anton, Denis Moreau."

They exchanged bows and smiles, then Denis asked Leuren, "What will you do about that mark, Andre?" He pointed to the darkening weal on Andre's cheek.

Andre shrugged in an unsuccessful attempt to look unconcerned.

"You must not alarm your parents," Denis continued. "They might not let you leave the house again tomorrow — and there will be great need for patriot hearts and arms." He paused for a moment, then said, "I know a milliner and cosmetic-dealer; here, come with me, and then home we must go to keep up appearances. *Ma foi!* It is intolerable!"

Leuren felt a close bond — the terrible bond of shared secrecy — twining himself to this mere *valet-de-chambre. Gaston and Anton are all right in their way,* Leuren thought, *but Denis is a man who understands me. Ah! Foolish boy!*

Denis turned aside and spoke a few rapid sentences to the other two. "Inform me of developments — I can be reached by asking at the servant's door of the De Coquiel di le Merciers' — or Leuren (I mean, Andre) can reach me." He took Andre's arm. "The place is near," he assured him, "and Mademoiselle Camille Martin will be able to give us some face powder to disguise that mark — now mind, do not get too close to the light."

"The troops are leaving the city — all of them!" cried one man, who seemed to have some authority. A roar answered him. Demonstrations of fierce, long-suppressed feeling erupted. As darkness fell, groups hastened to attack and burn the customs' barriers at the entrances to the city.

"Now let the King see what the people he has trampled on can do, even as a trodden snake raises its head to strike!" A sneer that was almost a smile crossed Denis' face.

When Leuren slipped home that evening, he found his family gathered around a middle-aged friend of his father's who was retelling the events of the day. His father was bemoaning the fact that as a deputy he would have to leave for Versailles and miss the events that were sure to come in the next few days. Leuren's arrival was hardly noticed, and he stayed in the shadows, his bruise undiscovered. No one paid him any attention, as usual.

Before making his way back home, Denis sidetracked, finding in the *Palais-Royal* the person he sought.

"Jules—Jules Durand!" he said, pushing his way through the swarming crowd around a pamphlet-shop. A youth looked up. Blond hair fell away from a commanding, lean face, framing large blue eyes and aquiline nose. As many others had noted, the boy's face was surprisingly noble—but Denis knew he was the son of a poor, middle class milliner.

"Ah—Denis!" Jules advanced rapidly to meet him, and they slid into seats at a café nearby.

"Your mother told me you would be here," Denis said. "I have something I need you to do for me this eve…"

"I am yours to command," Jules leaned forward. Denis drew out a coarse scrap of paper and began to explain.

~*~*~

The day had been a long, anxious experience for the De Coquiel di le Merciers. All troops had withdrawn from the city, leaving Paris utterly to itself. On Sundays, Francis usually gave the servants leave (hoping they would make it a day of rest), but today almost all of them were out in the streets. The family was in the parlor when Denis arrived home. He spoke lightly of the day's events, downplaying them as much as he dared, before excusing himself to pack his master's things—that evening Francis must travel to Versailles. As usual, the National Assembly (now re-named the National Constituent Assembly) would convene the next morning.

Francis gathered his family for a time of family devotions before leaving. "I shall read Psalms 27 tonight. Children, I want you to think of it throughout the week while I am gone." Then his low, even voice read,

"A Psalme of David. The Lord is my light & my salvation, whom shall I feare? the Lorde is the strength of my life, of whome shall I be afraide? When the wicked, even mine enemies and my foes came upon mee to eate up my flesh; they stumbled and fell. Though an hoste pitched against me, mine heart should not be afraid: though warre be raised against me, I will trust in this…"

A knock on the street door echoed. Marcel rose quietly and went out into the foyer. A few moments later he returned with a folded paper. "It is a message for Denis. Shall I give it to him?"

"Certainly," Francis said. Glancing down, he continued where he had left off, "One thing have I desired of the Lorde, that I will require, even that I may dwell in the house of the Lorde all the dayes of my life, to beholde the beautie of the Lorde, and to visite his Temple. For in the time of trouble hee shall hide mee in his Tabernacle: in the secrete place of his pavillion shall he hide me, and set me up upon a rocke. And nowe shall hee lift up mine head above mine enemies rounde about mee..."

There was a tap at the door. Denis entered, the paper in his hand. "Master—" he began, a cloud on his brow.

"Yes, Denis?"

"It will be a great inconvenience for you—but I have received news—"

"What is it, Denis? Speak out, my man."

"I have received news that my mother is dangerously ill; she desires me to come as soon as I can." He passed the paper to the marquis, who glanced at it critically before showing it to Felicienne, who was seated close at his side. Crinkling her forehead, she glanced up at him. "The writing reminds me of someone—but if it is true we cannot refuse him," she whispered. He nodded and turned to Denis, rising from his seat. "You must certainly go if indeed your mother is gravely ill," he answered. "May I see the messenger?"

Jules stood in the hallway, and met Francis' eyes with a clear glance of his own. *Surely,* Francis thought, *he does not have the air of a scoundrel.* Partially satisfied, he gave his permission for Denis to go.

"I shall be back in a day or two, if possible, my lord; thank you," Denis said, relief and gladness flooding his face. "I shall always remember your kind heart..."

Francis dismissed him to pack up his few things. Returning to the parlor, he spoke first to Marcel. "My boy, gather your things; I must take you with me to Versailles. The other menservants are out, and I must leave soon." Turning to Felicienne, he spoke with a tired sadness. "I fear me that this letter may have been concocted—but I cannot bear to refuse him if it is true." He seated himself with a weary air.

"Yes, Francis," Felicienne replied, "You acted justly." She put into those words such understanding and love that his face looked a little less care-worn. He read on:

"...Teache mee thy way, O Lorde, and leade me in a right path, because of mine enemies. Give me not unto the lust of mine adversaries: for there are false witnesses risen up against me, and such as speake cruelly. I should have fainted, except I had beleeved to see the goodnes of the Lord in the land of the living. Hope in the Lord: be strong, and he shall comfort thine heart, and trust in the Lord."

The street door opened and closed, and they knew Denis had gone. But there was a peace dwelling in that parlor that mere outward circumstances could not disperse, and which lasted in the heart of Francis even as he began the arduous night journey through barriers, unruly crowds, roadblocks, and more.

~*~*~

Though his comrades urged him to join in destroying and pillaging the customs barriers, Denis abstained. With his master taking those roads to Versailles, he feared he might be seen. Instead, he gathered with others in odd, unsavory nooks and corners, planning and plotting how best to thwart the royalists and ride and direct the rising tide of emotion.

The next day was the 13th. While the National Assembly in Versailles was voting in the marquis de LaFayette as their vice president, Denis, armed with a heavy two-edged chivalric sword from the ransacked *Garde-Meuble* (the King's Repository of ancient arms), was rushing and shouting in Paris with a heated crowd towards the Debtor's Prison of La Force; "Down with the aristocrats!"

Once the mob gained unstoppable momentum, Denis fell back and looked around to discern if his influence was needed elsewhere. On the *Rue Antoine* he saw a great carriage, piled with things, being "escorted" westward by several ragged fellows to the *Hotel-de-Ville* (the Town Hall). Denis' grim, satisfied smile highlighted the old scar on his cheek. "The guards we posted at the city gates are doing good work," he muttered, advancing and greeting the slipshod fellows with rough familiarity.

"T'were tryin' to take themselves and their things out of Paris," one answered him, motioning with a rough hand to the pale aristocrats within the coach. "But they didn't know—ha, ha!—that we've orders to take all comers to the *Hotel-de-Ville* for searching." The man gave another caustic laugh and kept on his way.

A street gamin, cavorting after them in scanty rags, cried eagerly, "There's already a great pile o' things there!"

"We broke the *Maison de Saint-Lazare* open," cried another scrawny urchin, brandishing a stolen pike, "and took the corn those gluttons stored there for themselves!"

The year before on this very day, a disastrous hail fell, ruining the crops; today, a tempest of another kind brews, wreaking greater havoc.

By afternoon, Denis had left the *Place de Greve*. Hurrying northward along the *Rue Denis*, he turned into *Rue Honore*, heading westward to the *Palais-Royal*. He almost ran into a sweaty but triumphant Leuren Andre de Lobel.

"Have you heard?" the boy cried, turning and falling in beside him. His countenance was flushed.

"Heard what, Andre?" Denis scrutinized the youth's face. "Your face powder is coming off—"

"I have come from the *Palais-Royal*," Andre panted. "The *Gardes Francaises* were ordered by the King to leave their barracks and go to Saint-Denis, and instead they have all—all three thousand of them—thrown in their lot with us!"

"*Bon!* They have decided that *il vaut mieux etre marteau qu'enclume*—it's better to be the hammer than the anvil!" Denis flourished his sword.

~*~*~

Past midnight in the assembly-room of the National Constituent Assembly, pale tapers burned; a hundred deputies lounged about in various stages of sleepiness and grumpy distraction. At the head table, the marquis de Lafayette slouched wearily in his chair, waiting for news. Due to the tumult in Paris, the members of the National Constituent Assembly had voted to continue in constant session until the crisis was over. Francis had been studying the awkward postures of the slumbering delegates in an effort to stay awake, but at last he shook himself and rose. With a slow step he made his way outside door. The sky was that state of pitch-blackness that exists in the wan, heartless hours before dawn; the stars, though beautiful, seemed inaccessible.

Francis looked again at the stars. *I wonder if Felicienne is looking at them now, too?* he wondered. He knew that most people in Paris would not be sleeping, if only half the reports were true. Leaving them alone all week, with such unrest in Paris! He wished with all his heart he could be with them. What might the mob take it in their heads to do—sack the aristocrats' houses, attack those in the streets? But his duty lay in Versailles for now, at the Assembly, and he bowed his head as he committed his loved ones to the watchful care of his Heavenly Father.

In the darkness of the street, muffled soldier-footsteps thudded past. The King had placed soldiers and cannon around the National Constituent Assembly—to protect them or perhaps as a veiled threat of his power.

Francis closed the door. He had remained to be a conservative voice and vote, but he knew he needed rest if he was to be of any use later on, when the full 1200 delegates assembled. A figure approached through the gloom, and a nearby candle in a wall-bracket illuminated the square face of Jean de Lobel.

"You look fagged, Francis," Jean spoke kindly enough. "Here—get some rest, and I'll wake you if anything occurs."

"I would be grateful for a few hour's repose," Francis said. "I thank you."

"Tomorrow—or rather, today, when it becomes light—there shall be a real need to be alert," Jean replied.

Francis would have asked how Jean knew this, but Jean's pale eyes were enigmatical, and Jean passed on.

~*~*~

In Paris some hours later, the rising sun illuminated great hurryings to-and-fro. The *Hotel des Invalides* was assaulted and despoiled of its stored guns, and the stormy masses of people flowed on to the Bastille.

Among a rough group of Brigands and townsmen rushing across the *Pont Neuf* (the bridge over the Seine river) bobbed the blond, straggling locks of Leuren Andre. He was clutching a gun ("reappropriated" from the *Hotel des Invalides*) in a grimy hand, and waving and shouting with the rest. They passed the *Hotel de Ville* with a roar, breaking into smaller streamlets in the narrow streets beyond—then coalescing with greater force in the wide *Rue Antoine* and joining the angry mob already before the Bastille.

When its tall round towers and crenellated battlements came into sight, Leuren paused to stare, his thoughts a torrent. This was the Bastille, so closely connected with the hated *lettres-de-cachet*! The jail for important and aristocratic prisoners, its name inseparably linked with injustice! Had not Voltaire, and later, Mirabeau been imprisoned here—and earlier than even they, the Man of the Iron Mask, whose face no living being was allowed to see? Popular tradition had turned the fortress into a symbol of oppression, the epitome of all the aristocratic might which crushed the populace! Yet it stood stoically in the glittering sunlight.

"The walls are thick," grumbled a wan shoemaker.

"The walls must needs be thick—the guards are a mere hundred old war veterans: useless *Invalides*," a hollow-faced man answered, with a desperate laugh. "We'll make them wish they were anywhere else before we're finished." He made the motions of firing a silver-mounted cannon—a gift from the King of Siam to King Louis XIV in years gone by. How would the Siamese be astonished to hear of its use now!

Andre had paused to survey the fortress, its serene stones looking braver than its scattered defenders. Now he looked up at the tops of the houses around him, noting how thickly they swarmed with gesticulating figures, dark against the sky. Suddenly, one of those black outlines altered, and a voice hailed him from above.

"Andre! Up here!" The voice was unmistakably Gaston's.

When Andre joined his friend on the housetops, what a sight met his eyes! From below, the scene had looked tumultuous and wild enough; from up here, he had a birds'-eye view: whole streets choked with men; feral, angry men, ever-converging and rallying toward the Bastille. Leuren took an eager breath, eyes widening with delight and something like fear.

"Lovely, is it not?" came a voice from his shoulder.

Andre turned with a puzzled exclamation. "Denis! But—you should be with my uncle Francis in Versailles!"

"Yes, I always accompany my dear Master there," Denis answered carelessly. "But you see, my dear mother is very ill—sick to death—and I received permission to visit her."

Andre glanced round for an old lady, and Denis and Gaston burst into hearty laughter. Andre's cheeks burned. Gaston's praise of Denis' inventive powers left dangerous seeds in Andre's mind—turning him more towards that perilous point where men call evil good, and good evil.

"Look!" one cried, pointing below, "the Governor of the accursed fortress is letting in a third deputation from the people for an audience with him!"

All eyes strained to see the result, but the drawbridge was closed after the deputation passed in. Leuren Andre pressed close to the edge of the roof.

A crackle of muskets—a loud shriek! Breathless suspense—then a cry of fury, which was echoed and re-echoed by thousands of angry throats as it became known that the governor's men had fired upon the refractory deputation! Instantly, the swearing besiegers began firing—doing no damage to the nine-foot-thick walls, but relieving pent-up "patriot" emotions. Denis alone thought, *When the 'deputation' was as unreasonable and violent as that one, what other course could old De Launay take?* He leveled his gun and fired at the soldiers standing motionless (and at present, unresisting) on the wall.

"Look! They are hewing down the drawbridge!" Andre cried.

"That is a point gained," grunted Gaston.

148

"He still has the eight towers full of cannon, the wide ditch, and that massive wall," Denis said, firing again and again.

The long face and stoop-neck of Anton Petit appeared as he thrust himself up onto the roof. "If De Launay is true to his word and detonates the gunpowder stored there—"

"—phew!—that will be the end of him, his prisoners, his fortress, and a goodly portion of the besiegers," Gaston finished. "If I were religious, I would pray to my saint that she would keep him from such a course."

A few minutes later Denis said, with a curse, "*Ma foi!* Those old soldiers, the *Invalides*, are not fools!"

The defending *Invalides* had lain down behind their battlements, and sheltered from the hail of bullets, were returning fire—while of their attackers, one and another fell dead as they aimed.

What the Mob Did

2.

Tomber de mal en pis –
To go from bad to worse.
– French Proverb

G aston had to shout over the yelling, the firing of guns, and the shrieking of the wounded. "Is that what I think it is?" he bellowed at Andre de Lobel, pointing to a small speck alone on a rooftop some distance off.

"A man—with a spyglass, I think," Andre cried back.

"What is he doing?—amusing himself by studying our faces?" Denis grumbled, but his voice was drowned in the din. The man certainly had a spyglass and was scanning the mob.

But that was forgotten in the rush of events that followed. Three cart-loads of straw were drawn up and set aflame—perhaps with some idea to smoke out the defenders. As it was, the smoke equally annoyed the besiegers.

Behind the swarming masses stood silent ranks of *Gardes Francaises*. There was a restrained power in their movements as they readied their cannon and primed their guns. Though at present they were inactive, their presence emboldened the rabble—for these professional soldiers were siding with them against the government.

"They might as well save themselves the trouble," Denis snorted, pointing to several groups of firemen who were directing their hoses at the walls and sending great clouds of spray into the air, vainly attempting to wet the touchholes of the Bastille's cannons.

"It makes a grand scene," Andre answered, aiming his borrowed gun.

" —and keeps De Launay from hearing the deputations, if he did want to answer them, the wretched, doddering fool," Gaston continued Andre's remark. "So far two, asking him to surrender, have come from the Town Hall—"

A coarse, heavy man standing nearby fell with a shriek, his body reeling against a chimney-pot. Gaston shook his fist at the smoke-and-spray-shrouded building before them and took steady aim.

Between this and that, De Launay could not make the decision to carry out his threat and blow up his fortress and the attackers. As he hesitated, the opportunity to carry it out slipped forever through his fingers.

Une minute d'hesitation peut couter cher — He who hesitates is lost.

~*~*~

Madame Felicienne smoothed down Paulette's baby curls and nodded to Adele. "What a sweet idea to play with the little ones upstairs — they have been read to long enough. Thank you, daughter."

Adele answered with a bright smile. Taking Paulette by the hand she left the library, with Charlot dancing after her slim figure.

Felicienne settled back into the upholstered seat, fingertips together. She had heard no fresh news since 1:00, and that seemed ages ago. She knew only that an assault, thousands strong, had been made against the Bastille, but how such an enterprise had fared, she knew not. Feeling restless, she rose and went to the parlor to check the hour — it was 4:30. *Why is it that time progresses like a snail when one waits for urgent news?* She fell into a reverie, hardly noticing the shadow of a coach that slowed to a stop outside.

"A gentleman wishes to see you, my lady," a footman said, handing her a card.

When she read the name, Felicienne's spirit plummeted down to the toes of her silk shoes. *Why,* she wondered, *would God send this man to my door when I am already worn down by the anxiety of today?* She longed to order the servant to tell her visitor that she was absent, but this would be a lie. Swallowing tears of frustration, she took a deep breath to compose herself. "Show him in," she said to the servant, "but first tell Honore that I desire his presence."

Honore arrived seconds before the marquis de la Noye was ushered into the parlor. Felicienne briefly met her boy's discerning gaze before turning to welcome the suave marquis into her presence.

"My dear Madame Felicienne — I happened to be passing by, and the thought of the fairest face in Paris was too strong for me to ignore — " the marquis said, advancing and taking her hand with bold, winning grace.

Felicienne replied with a gracious but cold restraint, "I thank you for thinking of me, marquis. May I present to you my son, Honore Rene-Luc?"

"Ah—he has your *matchless* eyes, Felicienne—" Philip de la Noye bowed.

"And *my husband's* handsome chin," Felicienne answered with a small smile. *Two can play* ***that*** *game, marquis.* Aloud, she added, "Pray be seated, marquis—have you any news?"

Seating himself on a divan, De la Noye assumed the air of a brilliant chess player. "I have heard that the marquis is a conservative in the National Assembly—but I am glad to find there is a more reasonable spirit in your fair heart."

Felicienne's green eyes met his with a questioning glance.

"I saw your representative, even if your husband's stance shackles open encouragement on your part," he said with an easy smile.

"I do not understand you, marquis—pray make yourself clear."

"The clearest I can put it is this—I have been over to the battle raging round the Bastille; with this little friend," he drew out a spyglass, "I saw your man Denis, firing away with the best of those ragged besiegers. Of course, it made me glad to see you were thus in support of liberty."

"Denis was there?" Honore blurted.

Felicienne's heart dropped further, and she had to look away to compose herself. *How disappointed Francis will be! How painful it will be to tell him!* Controlling her feelings of disappointment, she looked steadily up at the man opposite her.

"I thank you for the information," she said, "but that is none of my doing. Denis went away on a false excuse and is acting on his own, and—" she continued with a meaning emphasis, "—*against the wishes* of my husband *and myself.*"

De la Noye answered with an embarrassed gesture, "A thousand pardons, Felicienne. I must confess I was merely testing you; 'tis a rare thing here to see a woman with such...ah, fidelity...to her husband." He smiled frankly enough. "I must pray that you would pardon my impertinent jest—I am a Royalist myself, my lady; as you well know. Tho' I must admit the fire in your lovely eyes well repaid me."

After further pleasantries, De la Noye took his leave with a profound bow. As soon as the door closed behind him, Felicienne dismissed Honore—who had the good sense not to say anything—and went upstairs, heartsick. The news about Denis seemed far worse to her than the populace being in an uproar. Denis had lied! Francis' servant for many years, and his boyhood playmate...had lied to them! *Why? What action did we commit to turn him away?* A shudder wracked her frame. *He lied to us! Oh, how Francis will feel this when he learns! Denis was so close to him when they were young—'twill be like receiving a white hot knife to the heart; nothing in my power can assuage that sting.*

She paused in front of the gilded mirror in her room. Her mind replayed De la Noye's flattering insinuations about her being hidden away from society. Repulsion at De la Noye's presumption upon the past vied with weariness at the frivolities and dissipation of Parisian society, which winked at and took pleasure in the flirtations of even married people.... Added was the bitter realization of a traitor in their midst.

She had unlocked a compartment of her bureau, unconsciously picking up one trinket after another. A single tear rolled down her cheek and dropped onto the piece she was holding. Seeing the little wristlet in her fingers—thin, twining links of gold, set with tiny emeralds—her heart surged within her. It was the bracelet that the youth Francis Johan de Coquiel di le Mercier had given her, Felicienne Renee-Susanne des Cou, at their formal betrothal so many years before. Her hand tightened convulsively on it.

"Oh, Francis," she whispered, "duty calls us here; but oh how I wish we *could* be hidden away together—somewhere quiet and peaceful and far from Paris!"

There was a long and deep silence, broken at last by rooks cawing in the garden outside. Felicienne leaned her lithe body against the bureau, her head bowed in emotion. Still holding the bracelet, she said in a quieter voice, "Thou hast called us here, Lord God, and—and I know that thus this must be the place we can best serve Thee right now. But oh, our flesh is weak—give us strength as we struggle on in Thy Name; give us wisdom as to how we should deal with the World we find all around us and even within ourselves."

Then a seemingly irrelevant thought crept in, and she rose, taking the bracelet. *I shall have a jeweler add a few links—and shall wear it, as a reminder.*

~*~*~

"They surrender! They surrender!" The half-hysterical cries reverberated through the streets.

"Have they?" Andre asked, peering through the commotion to the portcullis of the fortress. Denis disdained to answer. He plunged down the stairway, through the house, and out into the streets below, Gaston at his heels. Anton and Andre paused until they could see the Bastille's gates opening; then they too hastened down. The fierce rush crushed them back against the doorway of the house. Yelling and half-mad with victory, the besiegers poured past, pressing towards the calm stone walls of the "building of oppression." They swarmed rapidly through the prison. Several patriots reached the towers. Wild shots broke out.

"They are firing upon *us!*" cried Andre in shock, as he ducked.

Anton answered with studious patience, crouching behind a pillar, "The wine of victory — not that any of these have been drinking, but you understand, my friend — the wine of victory is very potent; and, as these heroes have been denied it for so many hours, the results can manifest themselves in a temporary — ah — derangement or — "

Another bullet whistled past, from a victorious "patriot" on the walls of the Bastille. With a cry, Andre leapt backwards into the house. Peering out, he saw that the living torrent had slowed and begun to swirl. An angry throng pressed out of the captured fortress, dragging the governor and several soldiers whom the capricious will of the mob had selected as special objects of hate.

The governor, De Launay, a quivering, grey-haired man of about fifty, was in the grip of seething, shouting, ragged figures. "They surrendered on condition that their lives would be spared," growled a dissatisfied bystander. The crowd gathered close to the little group, kicking and menacing the prisoners.

There are few things more terrible than a mob, and that is because no one knows exactly what is going to happen. Under the influence of strong emotions, people throng together to do whatever strikes the mad fancy of the boldest or wildest. But despite the fact that as a group they do things they would not have done as mere individuals, they are still held responsible by God for their actions. So it is that God in His loving-kindness commands,

Thou shalt not follow a multitude to do evil.

The little knot of prisoners and the dancing, shouting horde moved out of Andre's sight into a side street, and he and Anton, leaving the brown doorway, managed to push their way towards the Bastille. When they reached the gateway, the noise from the street where de Launay had been dragged swelled from angry voices to a triumphant roar. Even Andre knew what that bestial noise meant, and he felt a twinge of pity for the trembling man he had seen, who was now dead to all emotions.

Prise de Bastille, Anonymous

As Anton and Andre entered the Bastille the sharp sounds of hammering fell on their ears. At one of the towers they found a small group of wild figures hacking away at a cell door.

"This is the last cell," grunted one, a hefty baker.

"How many other prisoners have been freed?" Andre asked eagerly.

"Six—a noble, four counterfeiters, and a madman," a scrawny tailor answered shortly, shaking back his long greasy locks.

A few more blows burst open the iron-bound door, and a huddled figure disclosed itself to the light.

"You are free, man! We have rescued you!" the baker cried, advancing towards the figure.

Out of the shadows came a strange old man. His grizzled beard fell past his waist, and he stared at them with vacuous eyes. "Go away," he said. "Leave me alone." Then he turned his back on them and began gabbling incoherently to himself.

"Another madman," the tailor muttered.

Andre looked, dismayed, at the others. Was this the glorious event he had thought it was? But when they left the tower and Anton slapped him on the back, calling him "a most handy fellow to have in a fight!" Andre let that unpleasant thought slip, and imitated the rough rejoicing and swaggering manner of his chosen comrades.

~*~*~

Francis stepped out under a leaden sky. Other delegates gossiped and talked around him; the National Assembly was adjoining for lunch. Down the street, with loud laughter and a brazen following Danton strode, a leader of the fiery, left-wing delegates. Outwardly, Danton was a stark contrast to mild, lavender-suited Robespierre, walking quietly alone—but Robespierre was the more dangerous. His daintiness and polite bows hid a ruthless, cold brain. Francis' eyes followed him with foreboding.

He came to himself with a start, and turned weary steps to a nearby eating-shop. "Francis!" someone called from behind.

Francis turned back against the flow of jacketed and behatted figures, and a man in a royal blue waistcoat waved and came forward. "May I join you, Francis?"

"With pleasure, marquis."

Francis and the marquis de LaFayette paced a few streets in silence, like the old friends that they were. The freshly-painted door of an eatery arrested their steps, and they found a semi-secluded table against the scrubbed wall outside. Francis broke the silence only after they had ordered.

"I am glad you have been made the commander of the new National Guard. Someone with a clearer head and more truly devoted to France would be hard to find."

LaFayette smiled knowingly. "But yet you wish it had not been formed."

Francis paused to swallow his *consumme*. "I am glad that there will be a force to keep the mobs in check, since the King will not use troops for that purpose," he answered. "I mistrust—this new 'National Guard' is given its power by the National Assembly, and as such may easily act against the King. Not with you in charge, of course, but if another is appointed...."

"You see it as a potential force against the regular troops?" LaFayette asked.

"Possibly—who knows? What concerns me is the fact that now we—the National Constituent Assembly—are the government. We were supposed to act as merely a constitution-making body, dissolving once a constitution was made. But now we have law-making powers and troops of our own—what government has more?" Francis looked narrowly at his friend. "You smile, Gilbert, at my views of the Assembly—you hope that there shall be a joint government between the King and the Assembly. But the Assembly has the bit in its teeth."

"I agree as to that, Francis. The people themselves have tasted power and are ravenous for more. But—" Gilbert took a long sip from his glass and looked out into the gray street. "The Americans have set up a model government with a 'President' and a bi-cameral assembly. I hope that with the new troops under my hand, we can use this victory of the Bastille to bring in a similar balanced government—a happy reunion between the people and their father the King; a change from the despotism of kingship to something better and more suited for our times. You were not there on the 15th to see the rejoicing of the people as they welcomed us into Paris and elected Bailly as Mayor. But even that was surpassed by the events of yesterday, when the King himself went to Paris. What shoutings of *Vive le Roi* and *Vive le Nation*! And when the King accepted the tricolor cockade from my hands and placed it in his hat, all was jubilation and good-will. The people have not been so warmhearted towards their Sovereign for a long time. I hope things shall now settle themselves, and we of the Assembly can proceed to make a Constitution for France. This, to my mind, is the crowning end of the revolution; we shall rise on the broken Bastille to an era of peace and freedom for France."

"I admit," Francis answered, "that despotism has harmed France. Much needs to be changed; the condition of the poor and the crushing weight of taxes needs to be addressed, as well as much else. I even admit that France might do better without a King; as the Americans with their Constitutional framework. But—Gilbert—my problem is not with that. What I wrestle with is the *method* by which this is being done. Rebellion has been rife—rebellion by the Third Estate, rebellion by the people." He, too, stared off into the gray, featureless street before continuing, "I fear, however, that even had our country gone about reform correctly, we would still face our most elemental problem—the godless degeneration that is due in part to France's slaughter of the Huguenots and its embrace of Deistic and atheistic philosophies. When humanity puts itself in charge, instead of God, the result will always end in destruction." He sighed. "When the King visited Paris yesterday, Bailly greeted him with, 'In Henri Quatre's case, the King had to make conquest of his people; but in this happier case, the people makes conquest of its King.' Bailly meant well; but I take it as a warning sign." He looked straight at LaFayette. "Your American friends were holding a King accountable to his words and charters. But France is throwing off a King *and* his charters."

A silence fell between the two. "You are a good man, Francis," LaFayette said at last, admiration in his dark eyes. "I hope to profit from your opinions, even when we disagree on points like this."

Francis smiled and extended his hand. "I must repeat, I am glad that *you* were chosen to lead the National Guard. I will pray for your success."

They clasped hands warmly, then rose and started down the street together for the National Assembly hall.

~*~*~

The sun had gone down. Seated in his Versailles apartments, Francis read a letter from his wife. He bowed his head in his hands, his stomach churning with emotion. Betrayed! Lied to, by someone who had meant all the more to him since he hadn't had a father!

Behind him, Marcel quietly laid out his master's brightly-colored silken nightclothes, pausing when a knock at the door interrupted the silence of the rooms. "Denis, master," he said when he returned.

"Show him in," Francis said. He laid aside the letter with trembling fingers, sweat breaking on his brow at the thought of what he had to do. Passing his hand over his forehead, he closed his eyes and leaned on the armrest of his chair. *Felicienne said she would say nothing to Denis, but send him to me when he came home,* he thought. When the door opened, he removed his hand to cast a heart-breaking glance at his boyhood companion. Denis stopped short. Alarm and guilt flashed in his eyes before he directed his gaze to the carpet. He shuffled his weight from foot to foot.

"Denis... Denis... *Why?*"

Denis looked up unwillingly and remained silent—besides, how could he gather the jauntiness to reply with a laughing excuse, as he'd planned, when pierced by those eyes?

"I gave you leave, trusting you. Do you have anything to say?"

Denis licked his dry lips and said, looking at the floor, "I—that is, master—" Now that he was again looking at the red throw rug, his tone gained a familiar strength. "I went to see my mother, but circumstances proved too much for me." He snuck a glance at Francis' face to see how much was believed—and dropped his gaze as if he had seen an apparition. *He knows all!*

"Are you at all penitent of what you have done? Not only are you in rebellion, you have incited others as well," Francis said. Then his voice broke and steadied itself with a control that was more heart-wrenching than a breakdown. "For the memory of your faithful sire and grandsire— for the youth you once were—the rambles we took part in together... I desire with all my heart to keep you. But Denis, I must have faithful men. Will you turn from these pursuits? Are you repentant for your actions?"

Denis' face was hard. As Francis spoke of former days, the scar whitening across Denis' cheek was the only outward sign of emotion. But at the word "repentance," all the wild elements (which he had given free reign the last few days) surged to the front.

"Turn back? Repentance?—*Never!*" He met Francis' eyes, but again had to drop his own blazing ones.

Francis reached for his escritoire and drew out a heavy sack. Counting out a goodly pile of coins, he glanced about for a bag to put them in. Nothing met his gaze except the bright silk nightcap Marcel had laid out. He snatched it with an abstracted air. Scooping the coins into it, he held the scarlet and gold parcel out to Denis. "Then I must discharge you," he said sadly. "Take this to support yourself as you seek another situation."

With a gesture of disgust, Denis pushed it away. "I scorn you!" he cried, his smoldering wrath finally breaking loose. "You and your gilded fetters of religion! Why I did not leave you at once after reaching Paris, I know not—"

"Yes, you do know why, Denis," Francis said. Denis stopped mid-flow, his guilty expression acknowledging the truth of that remark.

"I shall pray for you, Denis—I have no hard words for you."

Clenching his fists, Denis once more thrust aside the bulging nightcap and rushed out through the passage into the street. It was dark, but he minded not—so long as he could get away from that meek, forgiving man and the guilt he inspired. He had plunged along several streets, slipping on the foul, muddy cobbles and cursing everything, when someone lightly touched his arm from behind.

"Something for you." A dark, slim figure thrust a heavy bag into his hands and instantly fled down the alley and around a corner.

Denis stopped under a bleary streetlamp. As he did so, he recognized the gaudy package. "His nightcap!" he growled. But its mere touch—the touch of the *thing* he had placed on his master's head for most of his life—kept him from instantly throwing it into the mud. It gaped open as he shifted it in his hands and a slip of paper stuck up white against the gleam of coins. He pulled it out and peered at the familiar handwriting.

Evil never satisfies. When you realize that with repentance, come to me. I will take you back.
   Francis de Coquiel di le Mercier

"Repent? I shall *never* repent!" Denis cried. A stray mongrel ran cowering into a nearby alley.

He stuffed the paper and heavy nightcap into a pocket, but as he did so he felt his vision blurring. Putting up a hand to rub his eyes, he found his face wet with salty, bitter tears. The curses on his lips as he stumbled on through the dark street seemed to have frozen in his heart.

~*~*~

There were no traces of any emotion other than smug triumph on Denis' face the next afternoon, as he rode to a familiar quarter of Paris. *De la Noye is a good master,* he thought with a smirk, *the kind of man who knows that strings must be pulled, and sets about to pull them. No twinges of conscience to hinder his plans....and now, instead of waiting on a man with a bleeding heart, always apologizing for his humanity, I am entrusted with a mission after my own heart!*

His mind replayed his interview with M. de la Noye that morning in the latter's gilded morning-room.

"My friends from the Assembly and I," De la Noye had said, "want to create a network all over France composed of the new National Guard. Our plan is to send messengers throughout the country, spreading rumors and panic. Then, with proper coaching, the cities will send messages to the National Assembly, asking for authorization to form their own body of National Guards. The assembly, of course, will be flattered and will grant such a request. I have already sent out some trusted men on this mission. I need *you* to go through these cities—" his pale, aristocratic finger traced a route on the map that lay on the small, graceful table, "—and spread fear. Say the Brigands are about to sack the city; say anything you like. Only I want the people to panic enough to ask permission from the Constituent Assembly to form their own militia—" He lifted his dark head, his blue eyes took on a far away look, and he spoke half to himself, "Fingers of the National Guard all over France—a confederation, a militia that owes allegiance to the people and the Assembly...*then* we will take control." He smiled up at Denis. "I have noticed your usefulness as a 'mover and shaker' before..."

Denis came out of his reverie with a start. "Jules! Just the man!"

The youth hastened up to the side of his steed. "What is it? That is not the horse you normally—"

"I know; that one belonged to my former master. But I must be off, and I have no time—can you pass a quiet message to Berthe, the *maid-de-chambe* of Madame de Coquiel di le Mercier?"

"I can do anything you desire, Denis—but you will be back?"

"*Certes*, yes—in a week or a little more. Tell that to Berthe, and say that her devoted servant desires a *tête-à-tête* at your mother's house."

"That's an easy commission," laughed the youth. He snuck a sly glance up at Denis. "Shall I add a declaration of your undying love, and comment on her bewitching brown eyes?"

Denis flushed. "They're green," he growled, aiming a jesting blow at Jules with his short whip. Then he said, "*You* shall have my undying gratitude, Jules, if you deliver it. I cannot linger any longer—*Au revoir*!"

Camille's Secret

3.

O stormy people, unsad and ever untrue,
And undiscreet, and changing as a vane,
Delighting ever in the rumble that is new,
For like the moon aye ye wax and wane!
— Chaucer, <u>The Clerk's Tale</u>

*T*he hot sun pressed down on Leuren Andre's hat as he pushed through the crowded *Place de Greve*. Cresting the heavens above was the rich and elaborately ornate face of the *Hotel de Ville* (the Town Hall). Two square, symmetrical towers on the ends led the eye upward. Taller yet, an elaborate clock tower rose above equally-spaced second-floor windows. Niches along the entire face were filled with stone statues.

But Leuren had no eye for such things. A flood of brutal faces swarmed around him. Pressing towards the building, the crowd thickened, forcing him to a standstill. Seeing a gap between a thin, blue-bloused man and a heavy-set workman, Andre wormed forward.

"*Ohé*—what do you think you're doing?" the sharp-faced mason shoved him back.

"I must see what is going on," Andre insisted hotly.

"So must we, you whippersnapper," grumbled the man. "I aren't going to give my place to the likes of you!" He glared menacingly. Andre stopped shoving, but inwardly fumed.

Edging away from the mason, Andre asked a rough-elbowed washerwoman, "What is going on, anyway?" A patched shawl wrapped over her shoulders and crossed in front, tucking into her waistband—a common style.

"They're trying the scoundrel Foulon; the wretch who said, 'If those rascals have no bread, then let them eat hay!'" Her dark eyes blazed. "We've already given him some grass to eat, himself!" Her laugh set Andre's teeth on edge.

"His own peasants found him hidden on his friend's estate! *Certes,* boy—you should have seen him as we led him into Paris!" A tailor turned round with a friendly leer. "Barefoot and bareheaded, with grass in his mouth and nettles hung around his neck—!"

"But that was hours ago," griped a large man. "I'm getting tired of all this waiting! We've been out in this blasted sun for hours on end, while those legal fools talk on and on…"

"Why, the case is clear enough!" bridled the washerwoman. "Just hang him!"

"A rope over a lamppost—that's my idea," replied the mason, brandishing a rude pike. "Just give *us* a few minutes with him!"

As the washerwoman began to tell him all the details of her sister's family, and what her father always said at executions, Andre decided it was high time to move. He slipped off to the left, and his eyes lit up. There was Gaston, whom he'd come to meet! Gaston waved. Joining up, they tried to slip forward through the throng. This they were unable to do—the square was so packed.

Attaque de la maison commune de Paris, by Pierre Gabriel Berthault

But then there was movement in the crowd behind, and cries of "LaFayette!" The youths turned. A slight man in a green silk suit was advancing through the crowd. Pressing behind LaFayette as the crowd parted, Gaston and Leuren managed to make their way into the great hall of the building where the trial was being held. Squeezing in, they caught sight of a fair youth with long blond hair—Jules Durand. Gaston had arranged to meet him here, too. Jules hastily returned their nod.

Mayor Bailly's face was a picture of weariness—he had been trying for hours to delay matters.

"He hopes the issue will die on its own if given time," Gaston whispered in Andre's ear, as they stood on the outskirts of the packed, sweaty room. Andre got his first glimpse of the accused—an elderly man with white hair, the picture of exhaustion and terror.

LaFayette was speaking: "...This Foulon, a known man, is guilty beyond doubt; but may he not have accomplices? He should be taken to the Abbaye Prison, where we will question him."

Andre joined the enthusiastic clapping of the spectators, but Gaston growled, "He, too, is just stalling for time."

Foulon, confused and exhausted, clapped his hands with the others. It was a mere reaction—but the crowd interpreted this as a sign that he and LaFayette were in cahoots.

"See—they understand each other!" cried a wild figure. Instantly the clapping changed to howls of rage.

"A plot!" Jules' voice was a mere hiss.

"A device to deprive us of our victim!" growled an uncouth fellow at Gaston's elbow.

A man near Andre stepped forward. He was dressed soberly and neatly, but his face was aflame. "Friends!" he cried, "what is the use of judging this man? Has he not been judged these thirty years?"

The room erupted. Vainly, Bailly and LaFayette raised their voices in protest. The crowd rushed forward. A hundred hands seized the wretched old man and bore him outside to the thirsty masses in the *Place de Greve*. Andre and Gaston were swept along with the foremost, very near to Foulon—near enough to hear his helpless pleas and cries. "*Pitie! Pitie!*" he begged, but the screaming, howling mob bore him relentlessly towards a lamp-post at the corner of the *Rue de la Vannerie*.

Andre watched as a rope was fastened between the heavy iron post and the wrinkled neck of the begging, crying old man. He found himself liking this idea of vengeance less than he had thought, but he steeled himself as the rope rose. *Snap!* With a thud, Foulon fell, still living, to the ground.

"The rope has broken! Blockheads!" growled Gaston, pressing forward. "Make sure of him this time!"

But again, the rope broke. Andre felt he could not stand much more of this—he felt small and terrified inside. He had never seen a man die like this before—it was *not pleasant*. It was not at all like fighting at the Bastille.

The third rope held, and then a brawny fellow was called forward. Andre felt sick and turned away as the man beheaded the corpse and stuck the head on a pike, while the crowd yelled fiendishly. The enormity of what had been done rose in Andre's young mind in terrible colors: they had sent a man out of this world.

But just then he caught sight of Gaston's face, flushed with a high and savage joy. "So perish all our enemies!" someone cried, and Andre more than half fancied that it was Gaston. As Gaston and Jules moved in Andre's direction, Andre knew they would be quick to see his lingering horror. His decision was made before he even knew it—with a conscious effort, he met Gaston's look with sneering triumph.

"One less tyrant, Andre—may all others learn from his example!" Gaston's face was fierce.

"He got what he deserved," said Andre, "the rascal!"

His guilty horror passed away in knowing looks and sneering laughter, but Andre was never exactly the same again. A hardened place had formed, where he had crushed down and trampled on his conscience.

~*~*~

The clear hours of afternoon sun turned the De Coquiel di le Merciers' small garden into a rich and verdant jewel-box. Nestled against the small spot of trimmed lawn were Charles and Paulette. Charles was dressed in dark jacket and beige pants, with a pleated white frill around his neck, while Paulette had on a simple, gathered white dress. The seven-year-old was trying his best to entertain his wayward three-year-old sister, with varying success.

"Don't get off the grass, Paulette," he remonstrated, rising and rushing after her as she toddled onto the patio-stones. "Olivie will be done with her lessons soon—she will play—"

Even as he spoke, Olivie appeared through the open French doors, repeating some of her morning's lesson in her clear, sweet voice:

"King Marsile layed at Sarraguce,
Went he his way into an orchard cool;
There on a throne he sat, of marble blue,
Round him his men, full twenty thousand, stood."

On the top step she paused, her hand resting on the doorframe:

"Called he forth then his counts, also his dukes:
"My lords, give ear to our impending doom:
That Emperor, Charles of France the Douce,
Into this land is come, us to confuse.
I have no host in battle him to prove,
Nor have I strength his forces to undo.
Counsel me then, ye that are wise and true;
Can ye ward off this present death and dule?"
What word to say no pagan of them knew,
Save Blancandrin, of th' Castle of Val Funde."

She repeated the last lines with energy, savoring the syllables:
"What word to say no pagan of them knew, Save Blancandrin, of th' Castle
of Val Funde."

Charles was staring up at her, listening intently—heedless of his
charge, who was toddling away over the terrace, hands outstretched
towards a tempting rose-bush.

"Here I am!" Springing down the steps, Olivie caught Paulette in
her arms and swung her into the air. Paulette squealed with delight.

"What were you saying, Olivie?" Charles asked, drawing himself
onto the stone step at her feet.

"Is it not lovely? Mother is having me read 'The Song of Roland.'"
Sitting down on the last step, she drew Paulette onto her lap. "It is a very
old story, Mother says, all about a brave knight—but I have not reached
that part yet." She began chanting again,

"King Marsile layed at Sarraguce,
Went he his way into an orchard cool;
There on a throne he sat, of marble blue,
Round him his men, full twenty thousand, stood."

"Let us pretend this is our 'orchard cool,'" she said, her eyes
lighting. "You can be King Marsile, and Paulette will be your twenty
thousand men—"

"What would you be?" Charles asked. Glancing round and seeing Adele, he continued, "—and Adele?"

"Adele cannot," Olivie said sadly. Half-turning, she asked Adele, "Must not you be readying yourself for the party at our cousin's?"

"I can spare time to play," Adele answered. "My toilette is less important than you three."

"Oh—you are wonderful, Adele!" Olivie cried. "Adele can be Blancandrin, of th' Castle of Val Funde," she said merrily to Charles.

"But Blancandrin was a man," Adele smiled.

"We can pretend he wasn't," Olivie said, "and I can be your queen, Charles, who sits beside your great blue throne." She rose from the seat.

"Here is the throne—this stone bench," Adele said, going past them into the garden. "May I help you to your throne, O King?" She advanced with a soft, rolling step towards Charles, bowing most profoundly.

"You sit here, Paulette," Olivie said, placing the toddler beside the throne. "You are the great and terrible men of the mighty King Marsile!" Paulette laughed, clapping her baby hands.

"Make way for the illustrious King Marsile," Adele said from behind her, and Olivie turned with a low obeisance.

"Now King, say your piece—look grave and distressed," Olivie said. "You know, the part about your impending doom—"

~*~*~

Meanwhile, Stephanie fussed in front of her mirror. It always made her irritable, the process of taking the rags out of her hair. She bit her lip as one snarled, then pouted as the lock bounced free, half-uncurling. "Be more careful, Laure!" she snapped at the maid.

At that moment, her mother stuck a perfectly-coiffured head in the door. Her puffed, curled golden hair rested in lovely waves about her pale face and tinted lips. "I wish you to wear your rose-and-cream dress this evening," she said.

"Oh, Mother—" Stephanie answered, "I was going to wear my golden yellow."

Her mother swished into the room. "Your rose is what I desire you to wear, my dear."

"Why do *you* have to tell me what to wear?" Stephanie fumed. "The gold is much nicer."

Her mother's eyebrows contracted. "I *command* you to wear the rose."

Rising to face her mother, Stephanie flung a cream-colored ribbon to the floor. "I have already planned it out; what shoes, what ribbons—" she vented. Seeing a glint in her mother's eyes, she changed to a more conciliatory tone. "I am sure you have forgotten, Mother, but I wore my rose gown to the last ball—" Suddenly she noticed her mother's golden dress with its cream highlights, and a light went on in her head. "Let me wear the gold, and I will wear bronze ribbons, not cream."

Juliette wavered. She realized she did not have much chance of winning this battle, and a compromise was better than a complete failure. "As you wish," she said, casting a vexed look at her daughter and quitting the room.

Stephanie sat down on her dressing-stool and made a face into the mirror. "As if anyone would confuse us!" she said scornfully. "It is not like you look that young anymore, Mother." She tossed her head.

Her eyebrows knitted resentfully as the maid took out the last curls. As the woman began the tedious process of pinning some ringlets up, while letting others hang down bewitchingly, Stephanie's impatient fidgeting made the process longer.

When all was complete, Stephanie stood back and cast a triumphant glance in her mirror. The dress was certainly stunning. The gathered skirt ended in a double row of ruffles, while along the left side, part of the skirt had been ruched with auburn ribbons at intervals, adding interest. It swept back in a large bustle behind. The bodice was smooth and fitted, with quarter-length sleeves ending in wide, many-pleated ruffles draping beautifully from her smooth arms. A pleated collar tilted up high behind her head, then swept round in a half-circle on each side, leaving a "V" neckline partially filled with gauzy white. A large hat of the same color, with a sweeping brim and puffed fabric crown, crowned her piled hairdo.

Mother shall not dictate to me *what I will do,* she thought with a delighted smirk.

~*~*~

Some hours later, the De Lobel's house gleamed and glittered; already filling with guests.

One slim young figure strolled with lovely grace through the chattering groups, as if looking for someone. Adele's simple, gracious movements reflected her lack of self-focus—imparting a rare attractiveness to her composed face. The skirt of her spring green dress fell in soft folds, brushing the floor gracefully. Several inches above the hem, a gathered white flounce echoed the white ruffles of her fitted elbow-length sleeves. A dark green ribbon was tied round her small, corseted waist. Her face was sweet but not striking. Thin brows curved over bright hazel eyes, while high cheekbones lent a softening grace to her firm, square chin.

How different this assemblage was from the aristocratic, Royalist salons and parties Adele had attended thus far! Here, many were left-wing friends of the De Lobels. As she passed one group, a youth disengaged himself and bowed before her.

"Madame Adele! This is a pleasure I have looked forward to," Gaston said. His dark locks were more controlled than usual, and his attire today consummate.

"It is charming to see you here," Adele's dress swished as she curtseyed.

At that moment, Leuren Andre slid past. Gaston flung out a welcoming hand, catching him by the shoulder. "Andre! Is that how you greet a friend?" he queried in mock indignation.

Andre flung his head up and answered warmly, grasping his friend's hand with rough familiarity. Then, somewhat abashed, he bowed to Adele, excusing himself with an embarrassed air. Adele was conscious that her cousin had scrupulously avoided her eyes, and misgiving grew in her heart.

"A conqueror of the Bastille need not be ashamed," Gaston laughed to Adele.

"Was it such a noble thing?" asked Adele quietly, her hazel eyes wide and interested.

"Of course!—That great monstrous symbol of oppression? Think of the prisoners that languished in those evil cells for years!" Gaston replied.

"But there were only six there," Adele replied, "and they were ones you doubtless thought were a waste to save. Madmen? A wicked noble?"

Gaston looked at her with a different, keener glance. "That is beside the point."

"Then why did you mention it?" Adele replied, looking so sweetly guileless that Gaston could not take offence.

He began again more warily, "The taking of the Bastille has been quite advantageous for France. The King has come to Paris, professing himself a friend of the people—no longer a despotic master!"

"There is a way which seemeth right unto a man, but the end thereof are the ways of death," Adele said thoughtfully.

Gaston seemed to choke, and was about to answer when two figures emerged from the dim garden twilight. A golden-haired, golden-gowned girl was holding the arm of a tall youth in muted sea-green. On seeing Adele—or rather, it seemed to Adele, on seeing Gaston—Stephanie slipped her arm out of Sebastien's and stepped quickly forward, her face alight and rosy lips parted.

"Oh, Adele, dearest!" she cried, folding her in her arms. Then, her arm still around Adele's waist, she looked up at Gaston out of the corner of her eye. Her blond hair and blue eyes were set off by Adele's darker coloring.

He drew closer and bowed. "My dear Madame Stephanie—what a distinct delight! Since I received the invitation, I have counted the days till seeing your fairy face again."

Stephanie tossed her curls back with a winning smile. "I am simply *charmed* to meet you again," she declared. "We were coming indoors to sit—"

"There are chairs enough here," Gaston answered. Sebastien moved forward to hand Stephanie into one of the plush rosewood chairs, but Gaston was faster, and not only seated Stephanie, but seated himself in the chair closest to her.

Adele cast about for a good excuse to slip off, but Stephanie was beaming up at her and saying in the most dulcet tones, "Adele, dear, you must join us! Sit here—"

Adele allowed Sebastien to seat her, but resolved to turn the conversation to a possibly-worthwhile topic. "Have you heard about the deaths of Foulon and his son-in-law, Berthier?"

"With all due apology to the ladies, I would say, 'Good riddance,'" Gaston said.

"I agree," Stephanie flushed with enthusiasm. Adele wondered at her sudden political fervor.

"What a list of crimes was made against Berthier," said Sebastien. "I saw the placards: 'He robbed the King and France. He was the slave of the rich, and the tyrant of the poor. He drank the blood of the widow and orphan. He betrayed his country.'"

"To protest the murders, LaFayette and Mayor Bailly turned in their commissions," Adele said. Her brow was calm and eyes mild, but her chin betrayed an inner firmness.

"Yes. But Bailly and LaFayette have resumed their commissions now," Stephanie answered.

"True; but only after much coaxing and a show of contrition on the part of the people," Adele replied. "Yet I doubt the sincerity of the people's apologies."

"'Tis a good thing that LaFayette and Bailly yielded to the people," Sebastien chimed in, glancing at Stephanie. "They have the cool heads France needs. Was not that a politic move of LaFayette's to present the King a tricolor cockade?"

"Those two are good enough, in their own way," Gaston began smoothly, "but rather old-fashioned in their ideas, *n'est-ce pas*? When France expands her soul and reaches for the skies, will not such men hinder rather than help?"

Stephanie's blue eyes flashed to Adele's face, and perhaps something she saw there made her say, "Do you have an ear for music, Gaston?"

Gaston turned his strong gray eyes in her direction. "I know I have an eye for the music of beautiful faces."

Stephanie looked coquettishly up at him through her lashes. "There is a new piece by M. d'Alayrac that I would like critiqued," she said. "Come to the harpsichord." She rose with Gaston, then half-turned to Sebastien. "I know you too are a music critic," she beckoned. "Do join us; and you, Adele."

"I must ask leave to excuse myself," Adele said, rising with a smile. With a curtsey to the bows of the gentlemen, she turned towards the garden and paced down the wide stone steps into the gray-green twilight.

Behind a screen of blooming rosebushes she recognized her grandfather's cracked tones. As she neared, she realized that his voice always inflected downwards at the end of each sentence. She had never thought before how that created an impression of gravity. *What was he saying?*

"…and as such we concur. For indeed, Reason declares that—" Her grandfather stopped mid-sentence as Adele's light figure came around the bushes. "*Ma chérie*, it is good to see your lovely face," he greeted her. "Adele, let me introduce you to Jules Durand. Jules, this is my granddaughter, Adele Helene de Coquiel di le Mercier."

Adele had hardly glanced at the man, but as her grandfather introduced them a wave of rich color swept her face. That blond hair, striking blue eyes, and sensitive, noble face—it was the gallant who had caught her eye at the *Palais-Royal* those many weeks ago!

"*Mil* pardons, Madame Adele, for any impertinence in my manner when we met before," Jules bowed low, advancing to take her hand. "My only excuse is the loveliness of your face."

Adele answered with simple modesty, "You are forgiven, Monsieur Durand."

"If ever I can be of any service to you, Madame Adele, I place myself humbly at your feet," Jules said, with all the warmth of his nature.

Adele curtsied. "I thank you." Then she turned to her grandfather.

"We were discussing the proposition of *vox popli, vox dei* — the voice of the people is the voice of God," her grandfather said. "Jules argues most convincingly in its favor, while I, agreeing in part, hold with Socrates that there must be a group of wiser sages ruling above the populace to weigh Logic and Reason and discover the truth."

"I am sure you see it yourself, Madame Adele," the youth urged, piercing her with his clear blue eyes. "*Vox popli, vox dei* — it is so self-evident!"

"I think that phrase is used slightly out of context, if you are quoting from its earliest reference," Adele said. "The first mention of it is in a letter from Alcuin to Charlemagne."

Grandpapa des Cou turned with a humorous face to Jules. "My pardon, Durand," he said, "When I opened the treasure-stores of the past to her mother, I should have known that such learning would not stop with her." Then he cast a sly glance into the youth's face, saying, "But I think women are more attractive with learning, *n'est-ce pas?*" Jules bowed, and her grandfather looked towards Adele with a smile. "Pray continue, *ma chérie* — enlighten us on the context."

"Alcuin says," Adele pursed her lips for a second, remembering the words. "He says, '*Nec audiendi qui solent dicere, Vox populi, vox Dei, quum tumultuositas vulgi semper insaniae proxima sit.* — *And those people should not be listened to who keep saying the voice of the people is the voice of God, since the riotousness of the crowd is always very close to madness.*' So the earliest mention of it is actually coupled with a very astute critique," Adele concluded.

Her grandfather chuckled wryly at the youth's surprised face, saying, "Defeated! Out-maneuvered, by a mere girl!"

"It could not have come from more pleasant lips," Jules said. "Though I hardly think, Madame Adele, that —"

The sound of strings came filtering through the garden; the musicians were tuning up to start the first waltz.

"May I have the pleasure of —" Jules began to Adele, but her grandfather cut him short.

"No, I must claim the first dance," the elderly man grinned.

Relieved, Adele placed her hand on her grandfather's arm and they moved towards the brilliantly lighted house. She did not mind dancing with her grandfather, but this bold youth, with flattery on his lips...she was glad she did not have to refuse him outright.

As they positioned themselves among the other dancers, she whispered, "Thank you, Grandpapa."

He smiled back at her. "Those young blades must be taken down a peg."

The waltz was soon over, and Grandpapa des Cou led his granddaughter off the dance floor and to a quiet part of the room. "I must leave you here, *ma chérie*," he said, with a squeeze of her hand and a gallant bow.

Left to herself, Adele glanced around the room. She saw Jules, but his back was towards her—he was scanning another part of the glittering crowd. The sweet, soft air drifting from the garden beckoned her, and she again slipped out into the fast-darkening twilight. The moon and candlelight mingled to shed a dancing glow on the garden.

She had taken barely five steps out on the springy lawn when she heard a stifled sob, and saw a girlish figure on a stone bench, one pale hand across her face.

Adele hesitated delicately, then stepped softly forward. "I hope I am not intruding," she said, drawing near and laying a light hand on the girl's shoulder, "but if I could be of any help—"

The figure drew her hand from her face and looked up. The young lady was about sixteen, with pale brown hair and red-rimmed gray eyes. "Oh—it's nothing," she said in a light tone, but her pained eyes made her words ring false. She burst out, "I am sure you noticed already—it cannot hurt to tell what is already known." She moved aside on the bench. Adele took the hint and sat down beside her.

A tear trickled down the girl's cheek unbidden as she said, "'Tis— 'tis—I am so plain and ugly—and—" her voice trembled, "—no one ever asks to dance with me!" Pulling out an already wet handkerchief, she busied herself for several minutes by sobbing into it and wringing it out. Adele sat still, thinking and praying silently.

At last the girl roused a little and turned her pale, tear-stained face towards Adele. "Why are you out here?" she asked. "*You* could be dancing."

"I would rather not dance," Adele said.

The girl's eyes widened in utter disbelief. "What? Why?" she gasped.

"What is the purpose of dancing?" Adele asked in her turn.

"To enjoy oneself—a young man, with his strong arm about you, whispering and looking down into your eyes—" The girl shed a few more tears at this unrealized picture.

"But is that the kind of enjoyment we should indulge in?" Adele said. "You see, Madame—oh, I do not recollect your name—"

"Gabrielle Fournier."

"You see, Gabrielle, I would rather not spend my maiden years in the arms of a succession of young men, flirting with each. How will I break that habit of loose delight once I am married? I want to—" Adele paused, seeking for a way to explain herself. "Gabrielle, I desire to be able to fully love and care for the man I marry. Would not all those heart-scars from the past prevent me from giving my whole and undivided affection to my husband?"

Gabrielle gazed at her with something of the air of an ethnologist looking at a newly-discovered creature.

Adele had never thought of herself as beautiful, and indeed had been more plain than otherwise as a girl. But Gabrielle's eyes could see what Adele herself did not realize—that Adele had blossomed into a young woman whose pure, open expression was most attractive. "But—but you could have it all—enjoy the attentions of young men!" she cried. "And you do not?"

Adele's lips parted in a quick smile that lit her entire face. "Have you ever seen a botanist's collection of butterflies or insects? All stuck on pieces of board, with names written under?" she asked. "I think I enjoy young men all the more because I have not pinned them on a card marked 'admirer.'"

"I did notice your interactions with M. de la Roche and M. du Sauchoy," the girl remarked, half to herself.

"I count many youths among my friends and acquaintances," Adele said simply. "However, I seek to treat them as I do my brothers, not as if they were potential lovers to be snared."

Her companion moved restlessly on the seat, staring at Adele. Her lips framed several sentences, but she could not manage to get them out. Then she rose and paced up and down the garden; Adele followed without speaking. Light and laughter and music spilled from the open doors of the parlor.

The girl glanced inside. A whirling waltz was in full progress, and the bewitching, beautiful face of Stephanie flashed into view for a moment. Her partner's face was unmistakable—strong, proud, handsome Gaston de la Roche.

Gabrielle gave a cry and buried her face in her hands. "Think of what I am denied! No youth has ever looked at *me* like that!" she cried, in her weak way. "And you would have me give it up of my own free will?"

Adele's answer was quiet, but her voice was strong. "Is it not better to give something up than to not have it and be forever breaking one's heart longing for it?"

Gabrielle merely moaned in reply, her face in her hands.

"But I can give you what you wish, this once," Adele said. "Mayhap it will ease your despondency, though I hope someday you will see why I chose a different path."

Gabrielle's eyes were full of questions as Adele continued, "Dry your face, and come to the house."

Leaving Gabrielle in the doorway, Adele went up the steps into the chattering hubbub. Adele's eyes at last found the person she was looking for: in a moment she was curtseying to Jules Durand.

"My dear Madame Adele," Jules smiled brightly. "Have you come to give me the pleasure of dancing with you? One is just about to begin."

"You remember you offered your services?" Adele said.

"Yes, most assuredly, Madame Adele," Jules answered. "For anything you desire."

"Then — would you, as a favor to me, offer to dance with a young lady? — the one by the garden doors there, in the pink dress?" Adele half-turned to gesture across the room. Turning back to Jules, she queried, "Yes?"

"Y — yes," Jules said, surprised. "Of course."

Adele warmly smiled her thanks. "I will introduce you," she said, swishing back to Gabrielle.

Moments later, Adele was saying, "Gabrielle, may I introduce you to Jules Durand. Jules, this is Gabrielle Fournier — "

Jules took a step forward and bowed. "May I have this dance?" he asked Gabrielle, his eyes half on Adele's face.

Flushing, Gabrielle answered eagerly, "Oh, yes!"

As he turned with Gabrielle toward the dance floor, Jules shot a final puzzled glance at Adele. *She is such an intriguing young woman! What does she mean by all this?*

As for Adele, she was resting a hand on a nearby chair back and praying inwardly. *Have I done the right thing? Maybe I have not....Will she learn that her idealized pleasures are not worth it?....Perhaps...and yet perhaps not....O Lord, use this for Thy glory and Thy good in Gabrielle's life!*

She stood still and intense, but a few minutes later her thoughtful mood was pierced by gratefulness. *How free I am in Christ!*

~*~*~

It was a blustery Sunday afternoon a week later. Buxom Berthe hurried along a narrow street. Beside her towered six-to-seven-story tenements, with peeling paint or no paint at all on their naked, weathered timbers. A few squalid children with pinched faces, dressed in the remnants of clothes, tumbled about in the crooked alleys or sat listlessly on the filthy doorsteps.

Drawing her checked shawl closer, Berthe tucked it firmly in the neckline of her blue dress and smoothed her padded bustle. Busy with these adjustments, she almost passed her destination. A wider street crossed the one she was on, and on the corner stood a small shop, shoved into the streets by the last tenement. Pale milliner's-forms stared lifelessly out of the streaked shop windows, crowned in faded feathered hats; below them were various bottles and containers of creams and face-powders. Berthe turned the corner and advanced up two steps to the door. A peeling, achromatic sign nailed above the door looked wearily down at her as she knocked.

"Come in," a thin voice called. "How may I help—*Berthe!* What a pleasant surprise!" A pale woman with faded blond hair hastened forward, throwing slender arms around her more substantial sister.

"I have the afternoon off, so here I am, Camille," Berthe answered, taking off her hat. "I have missed you!"

"You have not been here for some time," Camille remarked.

"What with one thing or another, I have been so provokingly busy!" Berthe replied. "Never become a lady's maid, Camille! Especially not in a conservative household—'Berthe, you shall be late for family devotions,' 'Berthe, we must do double work on Saturday to rest on Sunday;' social engagements by the score, so many children! Olivie ripped her frock today, and—well, they do spend much time aiding the needy," she relented a bit in her tirade.

"I can see how it would be a trial—Denis has got quit of all that: I hear he is very glad. I know you have come to see if Denis is back from the provinces; he is, and may stop by this afternoon," Camille said. "But come, sit down."

The sisters seated themselves among the milliner's goods—bright hats hung on the walls, while ribbons and feathers peeped from drawers and baskets. At length, Berthe asked, "Is Jules home?"

"No—he is hardly home at all anymore," Camille replied. "He is busy, he says. And I grudge him nothing if he aids in throwing off the shackles the aristocrats have bound us with." Her narrow face, which looked as though it had once been unusually pretty, flushed with emotion.

"He is fighting for a just cause." Berthe's eyes kindled with agreement. "Speaking of aristocrats—I saw a gentleman recently; someone I knew long ago.…soon after acquiring the position of lady's maid to Mme. Felicienne. That must have been almost twenty years ago! I thought you might perhaps remember him—I know he was at the house a few times when you came to visit me."

"What was he like?"

"He is tall, good-looking, with dark hair and an aquiline nose," Berthe said. Glancing at her sister's face, she saw it tense with interest. "His name: Philip de la Noye."

Camille did not move a muscle, but all the color drained from her face in an instant. Berthe leaned forward. "Are you well, Camille?"

"It is nothing," Camille gasped, with a weak laugh, but her color did not return. "Just a surprise to hear the name of someone from old times—" Her voice, though light, seemed choked.

Berthe shot her a narrowed look and was about to say something when there was a firm knock at the door.

Camille started up. "Denis!" she cried in relief. "And here is Berthe, waiting for you…" She bustled about with housewifely zeal. Setting two dusty chairs in the farthest corner, half-screened by two pasty models, she shooed Denis and Berthe into the niche. As soon as they needed no more attention she turned away, and her animated mask collapsed. Hidden in the opposite corner by a standing mirror, she sank into a chair, her face working with emotion.

Meanwhile, the black head of Denis and the red-brown one of Berthe bent close in conversation.

"… so I went from city to city, bursting on each one with news of coming Brigands; almost every one panicked and sent a deputation to the National Assembly, imploring permission to create a chapter of the National Guard in their city to protect themselves. I succeeded beyond my wildest expectations," Denis said. "All over France, towns are forming their own divisions of the National Guard! The Constituent Assembly pretends they are merely giving in to earnest pleas by thus allowing the National Guard to spread its tentacles all over France—but I know that some of the members of Assembly have been, like my master, secretly working towards that end."

Then he looked keenly at her with his intense dark eyes. "Your lovely face has been the one that appeared before me in all of my travels, dear Berthe," he said. "Now, darling, have you agreed yet to—"

Over in her corner, screened by the mirror, Camille twisted her hands together with fierce passion. *So you are here, again, you —* Her tortured eyes brimmed with the bitterest of memories. *You, who made me think you loved me, and who promised to marry me — who then basely cast me aside upon the cruel world! No remorse even for my condition: no employer would take a pregnant girl!....oh, I hate you, I hate you, Philip!*

She shook a clenched fist, as if she saw his face in the back of the mirror. *And then Jules...having only a mother, mocked as illegitimate all his life — I have barely been able to scrape together a living for us, when if that wretch — Jules should have the riches of a De la Noye! If Philip would only — I can but ask him!....oh, my son!....But as for you, Philip — You have been gone for these eighteen years, but now that you are back — I shall have my revenge!* Her face was full of concentrated hate. *You must acknowledge our son; if you will not, do not scorn the abilities of even a weak woman! I shall be revenged for your falseness!*

The National Assembly's Futility

4.

For they know not to do right, sayeth the Lord,
they store up violence and robberie in their palaces.
Therefore thus sayeth the Lord God,
An adversarie shall come even round about the countrey,
and shall bring downe thy strength from thee, and thy palaces shall be spoiled.
…in the day that I shall visite the transgressions of Israel upon him…
I will smite the winter house with the summer house,
and the houses of ivory shall perishe,
and the great houses shall be consumed, saith the Lord.
— Amos 3:10-11, 14a-15, Bishop's Bible

F or a brief moment, Francis wished he could close his ears like he could close his eyes. In the middle of the room thronged eighty deputies, jostling and shouting to be heard over each other. If one said anything in favor of "the people" loud enough, hearty cries of approval and boisterous clapping reverberated from the spectator galleries, adding to the din. As the beginnings of a headache wrinkled in the back of his head, Francis wondered why chaos typified a normal day in the Constituent Assembly. His tired mind longed for peace and order.

He was seated on the far side of the room, on the *Cote Droit* (Right Side) with the other royalists. Next to them, and across from the president, sat the intermediate faction—those who supported a two-chamber royalism. Opposite the *Cote Droit* sat those of the *Cote Gauche* (Left Side), sometimes called the D'Orleans party, or—in derision—the *Palais-Royal* side. They supported the most reactionary opinions. Things, however, were so confused that Francis was not at all sure if D'Orleans even belonged to the side called after him. Francis' eyes alit on quiet, precise Robespierre, and remembered what he had overheard Mirabeau saying of him. "That man," Mirabeau had said, "will do somewhat; he believes every word he says."

Along the row of deputies near Francis a slip of paper was passed. All across the room, little papers moved likewise, slipping from deputy to deputy. Many had figured out by now that trying to out-shout other orators was not the best way to get things done in this confused madhouse. Papers were much better to "feel out" the opinions of others and gather supporters before making the grand plunge into the central whirlpool, there to try to pass one's ideas into law.

Nearby, several deputies laughed carelessly over a bit of gossip. Hardly anyone paid attention to the orators—except perhaps those in the galleries.

Francis adjusted his blue-gray jacket, fingering the large, silk-covered buttons that ran in a decorative line along the right side of his coat—their corresponding (and equally useless) row of embroidered buttonholes lining the left side. A paper in an inner pocket rustled. Remembering that a letter arrived that morning, he pulled it out and broke open the seal.

Far away in front the speakers still shouted—Francis noted that several had dropped out, their places filled by others, who, heads bent over their papers, were yelling their speeches in various tones ranging from nasal monotone to deep growling bass. He shook his head in disbelief. *And we think that this is like the revolution of America, that this mirrors the Congress that met to create their Declaration of Independence?* He turned his attention to the letter from the steward of his estate.

Le-Havre-de-Grace, 1 August 1789.

Sir, in order to avoid Alarming you, I have not until now mentioned the Fears whch have been distressing me for too long; but now I think it would be Unwise to leave you any longer in ignorance of them. There is Brigandry and Pillage on all sides. The Populace blames the Nobility of the kingdom for the high cost of Grain and is Enraged against them.

Reasoning is of no avail: this unrestrain'd Populace is Deaf to all but its anger; the peasntry of all the area seems ready to commit any Crime.

You will realize, Sir, that in such circumstances I am taking all possible Care.

As I was about to end my letter I learned that a Hundred Brigands, together with the vassals of the neighboring estates, have marched upon a neighboring manor, have taken away the deeds of taxes and rents and Destroyed them, also demolishing a Dovecote; they then gave them a Recipt of removal signed in the name of the Nation.

I am, yours faithfully dear Sir,
Benoit Roux[1]

Francis stared at the foolscap sheet for some time. *I have heard the same — nay, much worse — tales of the peasantry — burning manors, threatening their lords….Even the most sanguine among us realizes something must be done.* He shook his head with a wry, sad smile. *I wonder what the Breton Club will devise this time? They are adept at turning any disturbance to their profit.*

He roused himself from his thoughts. As happens sometimes in a tumult of noise, two subdued voices stood out crystal clear: they were from some deputies behind Francis.

"…t'was as dull as this day's assembly," one of them said.

"Why specify a day?" sneered the other. "They are all alike."

~*~*~

The very next evening as the eight o'clock session opened, a subdued fervor among the *Cote Gauche* (the Left) charged the assembly with tension. The radical Breton Club had decided its course and was ready to act. A proclamation calling for the restoration of public order was read, and immediately the duc de Noailles sprang to his feet. His clear voice rang throughout the building.

"…Order shall only be obtained," he said, "if the people have an interest in maintaining it!"

Francis listened intently as Noailles went on to urge that the assembly pass a proclamation declaring (among other things) that *everyone* was now liable to taxation, that it should be in proportion to income, and that feudal servitude should be abolished.

The duc d'Aiguillon spoke next. Then more and more deputies sprang to their feet, announcing more feudal rights or dues they would give up. The approval and enthusiasm burgeoned as the night grew older. Subtly, however, the tone began to change, and soon deputies were rising and suggesting various rights and privileges of *others* that should be abolished. These ideas were acclaimed with joy by the excited delegates and in turn inspired more and more radical renunciations. The frenzy built.

As hours passed and the impetuous excitement surged higher, a note was passed to Francis. He opened it and read the words:

To Le Chapelier, President
They have all lost control, close the session.
Lally-Tolendal[2]

181

Francis added his signature in agreement, then passed it on to be delivered to the president. But the note was either ignored or not seen. The tumult grew.

In the blackness outside, a bell tolled one o'clock.

~*~*~

The morning was yet new; it was three o'clock a.m., and the stars still held their distant, bewitching sway over the recumbent earth. Francis stood in the dimly-lighted parlor of the marquis la Motte.

"'Tis from the marquis de Ferrieres. I said I was passing your way, and would deliver it." Francis' handsome face was haggard with anxiety and fatigue. "I was surprised to see you awake."

"I knew that something of import was transpiring in the Assembly, and did not sleep well," Arnoul la Motte answered. "When you knocked, I had just decided to rise and go over to the *Salle des Menus*." Even as he talked, his fingers broke the seal of the letter Francis had brought.

"He wrote this there?" he asked, looking up at Francis.

"No: we went to his apartments discussing the matter," Francis replied. Then he bowed. "I shall leave you to peruse it at your leisure."

"No, no, Francis—I have called for tea, and you must wait to refresh yourself before going," La Motte insisted.

At that moment the door opened, and petite Elisabeth la Motte appeared. Behind her a maid bore a spotless silver tray.

"You, up this early, Elisabeth?" her father asked in surprise.

She answered him with a soft light in her blue eyes, "I was restless last night, and when I heard you rise early, I thought I would order a light breakfast for you to take before you went."

"Ah, Elisabeth—what a precious daughter you are! I wager you were restless only because you saw my concern over the Assembly last night." Her father looked at her with warm appreciation.

She blushed and turned to Francis with a curtsey, her starched white morning dress flowing gracefully. "I shall do the duties of hostess if you will permit me, marquis."

Francis smiled and lifted a fragile tea cup to be filled, while Arnoul began reading his letter.

"Listen to this, Francis! Ah—listen, Elisabeth!" her father suddenly cried.

"*...The deputies were all standing, all mingled together, in the center of the Chamber, agitating and talking all at once. Those of the former Third Estate*

182

tried, by Feigned enthusiasm and thunderous applause at evry new Sacrifice, to maintain the excitement. The assembly looked like a gang of Drunken men in a shop full of delicate Furniture, breaking and smashing at will everything that came to hand…

…a Multitude of voices cried out that since Individuals had given up their Rights and Privileges, justice required Provinces and Cities to make equal sacrifice of the Privileges and Rights which Weighed on the greater portion of the Kingdom…"

Arnoul glanced at Francis. "Can you confirm this?"

"It is truly what happened," Francis replied. "It began innocently enough with individuals renouncing their own privileges, and quickly became people repudiating the privileges of others. The latter is what is reprehensible; they have no lawful right to negate the prerogatives of others. All feudal servitude, rights, and dues are abolished—all religious or other tithes—hunting rights, priorities for advancement due to rank, any positions which were only for certain ranks, are now thrown aside." He paused. "I wish it could have been done differently," he said, resting his chin on his hand. "You and I have talked before, Arnoul, about the advisability of relinquishing feudal rights such as hunting and servitude. Now, *that* has been effected—but not, for some, out of love for the people. They saw that their rights were going to be taken away in any case—and so by relinquishing them they receive acclaim."

Francis' eyes had been far away as he spoke, but suddenly he turned them to La Motte. "Mayhap I am being too hard on the deputies, Arnoul, after the maelstrom I have just been through," he said. "I hope I am. But how could they even think they have a right to abolish such things as the king's hunting privileges, as if they were above him?"

~*~*~

Paris was jubilant. The abolishment of feudal privileges was hailed as a great victory. Camille noted the elation in the thin faces in the crowded avenue. She turned into a broad tree-lined street with pleasant large houses on both sides. A little waif scurried along, mayhap dreaming of living in one of the palatial dwellings instead of being huddled in odd corners of stables or outbuildings.

A liveried footman exited one of the houses and came towards her. Camille glanced down at her carmine dress, noting proudly how her careful pressing and re-trimming had masked the faded lines. It looked quite a new dress. She was about to speak to the footman when he turned aside to join a crowd gathering round a placard.

"What is it?" he asked of the crowd.

"Hush!" a fish-girl answered. "It is a decree of the National Assembly, posted today the 11th."

Anxious to ask the footman a question, Camille turned aside, listening idly while keeping a sharp eye out for an opportunity to speak to him.

"...the exclusive right of hunting and open warrens is likewise abolished. All hunting rights, even royal, and all private hunting restrictions, under whatever regulation, are also abolished.

All seigneurial justice is suppressed without indemnity.

Tithes of all kinds, and dues which may be in place of tithes, in the possession of secular and religious institutions, and other religious and military bodies, are abolished.

The purchase of judicial and municipal office is suppressed as from this moment. Justice will be rendered without payment.

Fiscal privileges are permanently abolished. Payments will be made by all citizens and on all property in the same manner and by the same method.

All special privileges of provinces, principalities, regions, cities, and communities are irrevocably abolished..."

The speaker droned on, but the footman turned away and shouldered through the crowd, bright in his white and red livery. As he neared Camille, she stepped out to meet him.

"Pardon me," she said, "but could you direct me to the house of M. de la Noye?"

The man stared reflectively, rubbing his chin. "New feller, is he? I cannot place him."

"I believe he moved to Paris recently from abroad," Camille said.

"I am sorry then, Mademoiselle," the man said [At that period, regardless of marital status, Mademoiselle was used for lower-class women, Madame for the upper-class]. Noting a movement at the window of the house he had exited, he said hurriedly, "I must be about my business." Camille moved aside, disappointed, as he hustled past.

Camille continued down the street, directing an attentive gaze to each house, though now she feared that this was the wrong street altogether. Presently she turned down a side street leading to another wide thoroughfare. A red-faced maid was standing at a side servant's entrance dumping out a pail. Camille approached, stepping carefully round the muddy pool.

"Do you want something, Mademoiselle?" the girl asked, setting down the bucket and adjusting a gathered cream mob cap.

"I am looking for the abode of the gentleman M. de la Noye," Camille asked.

The girl rubbed her nose thoughtfully. "New to town, is he?" she asked, and Camille felt a sinking feeling. Her feet, unused to stirring much beyond her milliner's shop, were aching in her fancy silk shoes. Just then the side door of the elegant house across the street opened, and a portly girl with a sallow complexion stepped out with a feather duster.

"*Ohé*, Laure," Camille's red-faced informant called shrilly. "Do you know where a gentleman called De la Noye lives? He's new to Paris."

Laure put down her duster and stepped across the street. "De la Noye…" Then she clapped her pudgy hands, saying, "Yes, I do—he has a very handsome horse-boy. You haven't seen him yet, Valerie? All the better for me—at present, I think he is rather partial to me." She grinned, showing a few gaps in an otherwise pleasant smile.

"But where does M. de la Noye live?" asked Camille.

"See the street up ahead?" the stout girl asked. Camille nodded. "Go to the next street after that, turn—ah—right, then count six houses down. It has a yellow door."

"Thank you very much." Camille pulled out a small coin and handed it to the girl. "Buy a new ribbon for your hat," she said. The girl's face broadened into another grin and she tucked it carefully into her sash. As Camille went on, she heard her telling the other all about the groom of De la Noye's.

It took her a little time to find the address, but once there, the mustard yellow door was unmistakable. Gathering her courage and trying to walk as if her feet did not hurt, Camille approached the door and knocked. It swung open only partially, and a footman looked out. "Yes, Mademoiselle?" he said, scanning her dark red dress, which despite all her care now had several mud splatters.

"I am calling on the marquis," Camille said.

"Your card?" The man looked at her skeptically.

"Tell your master that a lady is calling upon him," Camille answered haughtily. "A card is not necessary." She had a card, but she did not want De la Noye to see her name.

With one last dubious glance at her dress, the man showed her into the ornate entry and departed. Camille glanced around the room at the lovely furnishings, gilt-framed paintings, polished wood floors—and felt a great anger rising in her. Her son was entitled to all of this! She swallowed her feelings and composed her face as the footman returned down the hall.

"Regretfully, my master is not at home," he said with a wooden visage, already moving to let her out the door.

Camille was out in the street once more before she knew it. She half-turned back, but the dark yellow door was already closed. She paused on the doorstep, frustration and disappointment clouding her thin face. She bit her lip, and her dark gray eyes flashed. *He most plausibly is at home,* she fumed inwardly, *and figures that any lady he knew would present her card. Or, that rascal footman may have described me —* She clenched her fists as she moved slowly and rigidly away from the house. *I shall find a way to see him — I shall, or else!*

For some time she stumbled on in her pinching shoes until she came to a narrow street lined with bakeries and cheap cafes. She sank onto the nearest chair and buried her face in her hands. Out of physical weariness, yes—but more exhausting was the bitterness and hate that filled her heart.

~*~*~

The Du Chemins' parlor sent a cheerful glow into the street, but even merrier and more pleasant was the small group gathered in it.

Seated near a pastoral painting, Adele plied her needle industriously, occasionally casting her eye on her companions. Olivie, sitting to Adele's right, was paying rapt attention to the lively conversation between Honore and Tristan, while Marcel lingered unobtrusively over the backs of their chairs. A bit apart, her mother and Madame Du Chemin conversed in softer tones. The latter's graying hair was drawn back in soft waves from her wan, sweet face—a contrast to the rich, youthful beauty of Adele's mother. At their feet, Charles and Paulette amused themselves with rough wooden blocks. To Adele's left, her father and M. du Chemin discussed current events, while M. de Duret occasionally injected a wise word or two as he sat resting his hands on his cane.

Adele's position was strategic – she could listen for a few minutes to the highly educated discourse of the men, and in turn switch her attention to the spirited exchange among the younger members of the gathering....Adele smiled happily. It was so peaceful to be among dear friends who seemed somehow more like family than even her relatives. She let her mind wander back over the visits with the Du Chemins soon after her parent's conversion; those carefree, joyful weeks were linked inextricably with the freedom and wonder of being the Lord's children. There, away from the constraints of Parisian high society, she, Honore, Marcel, Tristan, and Olivie had employed their youthful *esprit*. *What games we played! What adventures we had! Exploring the brook that led to the sea, discovering Denis' tunnel....But now, we are adults, and in Paris....* She became slowly aware of a conversation beside her.

"...but it is all useless, now," Olivie said mournfully, looking at Honore and Tristan.

"Why so?" Tristan asked, with a quick glance of his hazel eyes into her usually bright face.

"There is no Denis to spy on any more," Olivie said, "so our secret sign is quite..." She trailed off, too disheartened to finish her sentence.

"True, Denis is gone," Honore said. "But there are intrigues and dangers that require our eyes and ears all the same."

Olivie's drooping face lit up with interest.

"Even without political issues and news, this city offers quite enough scope for that. We all need to be on the watch," Tristan agreed, nodding his dark head. "I should say that it would be advantageous to retain our sign."

"I am so glad," Olivie bubbled.

Adele felt a warm surge of agreement. "Do you remember when we discovered that secret tunnel?" she remarked, thinking fondly of their delightsome old life.

"I wish I could have been there," Honore sighed.

"That was the only wish we had, once we had found it." Tristan's whole countenance lighted with his free, full smile.

"Denis will doubtless never have a chance to use it again," Marcel commented, quiet amusement in his eyes.

There was a pause. Honore was about to say something when their fathers' conversation caught their attention.

"...yes, the upheaval is very serious, especially in the South-East," said Tristan's father. His gray-brown hair was tied back with a teal ribbon, and his face was unusually serious.

"Yes," Francis replied. "The deputies whose estates are unfortunately situated there all report dire revolts."

Christophe du Chemin looked across to Grandpapa de Duret. "M. de Duret, I was talking to an administrative official here—Perigny—and he said he had news of the estates neighboring your old one. He said the gentry from the area still regret your departure—indeed, most of them now blame your usurping nephew: there are many now who suspect that he managed to confiscate your estate (as was indeed the case). Perigny started to tell me more about recent events there, but he was called off on urgent business. Snatching up a copy of a letter he had been writing, he handed it to me, saying, 'This will give you a taste (albeit bitter) of the events there.' Here, let me read it:

"Paris, 13 August 1789. Sir, the flames are sweeping through Anjou and Maine. The comte de Laurencin read out to us yesterday the terrible events suffered by Madame his sister at two chateaux in Dauphine: papers burnt, the chateaux pillaged, and roofs removed if they were not burnt. They were not even left with the means of gathering and securing their harvest.

"At the end of her letter, M. de Laurencin's sister says that she is in despair because she was not killed by the first shot which reached her room; she has been hounded through two chateaux and then to a friend's house, and with her was her young and beautiful unmarried daughter. The two of them, with her husband, were pursued for thirty-five hours without respite."

Du Chemin paused, and there were murmurs of compassion and disbelief from around the room. Felicienne gazed across at Adele and Olivie, thinking of the terrible events De Laurencin's sister had gone through. Tristan's usually smooth brow was knotted, his chin set in a firm line.

"Is there not something that can be done?" Honore burst forth.

"The townsfolk of Cluny found something to do," M. du Chemin replied. "Perigny writes;"

"The monks at Cluny were more clever and more fortunate. The inhabitants of that small town have become attached to them, through their good deeds and the renunciation of their rights and dues, [so] that, under the leadership of one of the monks, the townsfolk wiped out the whole gang of marauders.

"The citizens of Cluny hid themselves, well armed, in the abbey, they concealed two cannon in a shed facing the main road into the town. The brigands had thought to take the abbey and the townsfolk by surprise; the inhabitants let them all come in, closed the gates of the town while at the same instant they uncovered the two cannon loaded with shot, and all fired at the same time. Not a single outlaw escaped. They were all killed or taken off to the royal prisons.

"They were found to be carrying printed papers 'On the king's orders'. These documents encouraged the burning of abbeys and chateaux, on the pretence that the nobles and abbots hoarded supplies of grain and poisoned wells, and intended to reduce the people, the king's subjects, to the direst misery.

"In Alsace the inhabitants destroyed the superb forests at Biché and Hagueneau, destroyed the fine glass-making establishments at Baccarat, and the king's own magnificent ironworks. They are at work now in the forest of St-Germain, cutting down the finest trees.

"It is impossible to be sure now, and for the immediate future, where to live in France, or who can preserve their wealth.

"The king is in a state of despondency and in reply to complaints, says there is nothing he can do.

"I remain yours most sincerely, Perigny"[3]

"Wild with their new hunting rights, the peasants have swarmed the carefully-managed forests, shooting everything, killing more than they can use, just for the sheer delight of doing so." Francis said sadly. "Wild animals in France are being hunted to extinction. The forests are being cut down, as well." His face relaxed for an instant into a smile as he said, "One man told me even his coach had been peppered by the peasants' stray bullets — they are not good shots, it seems."

There was a short pause, then Grandpapa de Duret lifted his wrinkled face. "I have been reading in Amos of late," he said, "and I see several things that apply to France. *'For they knowe not to doe right, sayth the Lorde: they store up violence, and robbery in their palaces.'* We aristocrats have been given much; therefore much was required of us. And yet as a whole we used our power and wealth selfishly. Violence and robbery towards the poor have been shamefully common for centuries. The Scripture continues, *'Therefore thus saith the Lord God, An adversary shall come even rounde about the countrey, and shall bring downe thy strength from thee, and thy palaces shalbe spoyled.'* Is not that what is happening? Though France's adversary is from within. It goes on, *'…Surely in the day that I shal visit the transgressions of Israel upon him, I wil also visite the altars of Beth-el, and the hornes of the altar shal be broken off, and fall to the ground. And I wil smite the winter house with the summer house, and the houses of ivorie shal perish, and the great houses shalbe consumed, sayth the Lord.'* The winter and summer houses of the rich are now being burned. I do not condone the unlawful, wrong actions of the peasantry; but I think that God is using them to judge the nobility for not following His ways."

"This nation is being judged for her apostasy," Christophe du Chemin agreed. "Lord, have mercy on Thy faithful remnant!"

Passion vs. Insouciance

5.

Un clou chasse l'autre –
Life goes on: one nail chases another
– French Proverb

*A*ugust had almost gone—the time of harvest, the time when all nature begins storing up. Chill breezes carried with them hints of urgency as Winter knocked at the threshold. Though in Paris, all seasons were alike in the rage of revolution.

As she stepped from her coach, Felicienne thought of what their estate would look like now. The image of reapers came to mind—and with a sudden pang, she could almost smell the rich, loamy soil, the dried grass, herbs, and lavender.... She came out of her reverie as her servant ushered her inside an ornate dwelling. The occasion was a *salon*, a sort of open-house common in Paris in those days, where people met to discuss the issues of the day. Felicienne curtsied deeply to the hostess, then advanced towards an empty seat.

As she did so, slim Adrienne de LaFayette started forward, her olive green dress rustling as she curtseyed. "Felicienne!" she said, in a hearty but quiet tone, "Dear heart, there's a quiet corner here—I have wanted to talk with you." She drew Felicienne into a seat removed from the lively repartee.

"It is a pleasure to see you, Adrienne," Felicienne said with sincere warmth.

"I am even more delighted, Felicienne," the marquise de LaFayette replied. "Usually when we meet—you know how it is." She shrugged almost imperceptibly, a wry smile on her lips. Then she leaned forward a bit. "This 'veto' business, Felicienne—it is rather alarming!"

Felicienne nodded, moving her fan slowly. "It began merely as part of the process of making the Constitution," she said, "but whether the king should have vetoing power or not certainly has agitated the populace."

"It is ridiculous to me," said Adrienne, "to think that we would not give the king some sort of limited power of veto. So far the Constituent Assembly has taken all other powers to itself."

They both spoke lightly to avoid notice, and no one paid them more than a cursory glance. A new and immensely popular gentleman had arrived, and everyone sought to gain his attention and hear what he had to say.

"Gilbert has had all he can do to just keep things fairly quiet," Adrienne said, "even with the help of the National Guard and his power of censorship. I hear that members of the Constituent Assembly who are *for* giving the king vetoing powers have been threatened."

"It is true. I received a note from Francis a few days ago," Felicienne said. Her face a shade paler, she spoke with quiet control, "He says he received an anonymous threatening letter: if he does not change his position on the veto, 'fifteen thousand will march to illuminate him.'"

Adrienne shook her head, laying a hand on her friend's arm. "Gilbert should be able to prevent that," she said. "He has set up blockades, and has patrols out watching for disorder; they are using force to suppress any unrest." Then she added, "Though it seems that all the new laws to enforce peace are merely driving the rebelliousness underground to smolder there. Mayor Bailly cannot help much to calm things, though he tries: he and the new three hundred members of the Town Hall must concentrate most of their attention on procuring grain to keep the people happy and fed."

"And for some reason, I hear, they cannot find enough," Felicienne replied. "We heard from our steward that the crop has been good this year: I cannot understand why there is scarcity, unless it is fabricated."

"I fear that is the correct assumption," Mme. de LaFayette answered. "I wish we could discover who is working such evil! At least, more than seventeen thousand of the poor are being employed by the city, digging, so they can buy bread."

"Should the government provide for its people? But at least they are working for it," Felicienne wondered. "Besides, Paris has no money, so this is plunging the city into deeper financial trouble."

"Too true; and yet *something* must be done to keep the people content." After a slight interlude, Adrienne spoke again. "Felicienne," she leaned forward, dropping her voice even lower, "I have a secret for your ears alone." Holding her outspread fan between them, she whispered, "Several in high places are hinting that perhaps the king might fly to Metz or somewhere, then march on Paris with an army of thirty to sixty thousand aristocrats and followers. He could quell the seditious people and take his proper place as an equal power with the Assembly. But this must be kept a profound secret."

"I shall tell no one but Francis, of course," Felicienne said. "I wonder you have the courage to even whisper such news—for if the slightest intimation of this reached the common people...."

Mme. de LaFayette nodded her agreement, then glanced round. "I would love to talk longer, but..." she smiled knowingly at Felicienne. Turning to an elderly matron several chairs off, she struck up a conversation about the latest fashion in hats.

Felicienne soon involved herself in an animated discussion on the subject of the proper etiquette for making calls, and how 'young people nowadays' seemed woefully lacking in that vital social quality; though she smiled inwardly at their view of its utter importance. Bigger things loomed on the horizon than mere etiquette—it seemed a waste of time to fuss over the finer points of presenting a card, the most correct entrance, etc.. *These things have significance,* she thought, *but* must not *eclipse charity and duty*....

~*~*~

A fortnight later, a carriage rolled to a gentle halt in front of the Tuleries gardens. Opening the door, a servant in green-and-white livery assisted two figures to alight.

"I wonder where Stephanie is situated?" Adele asked Honore.

Their mother and Marcel joined them. Francis had procured another valet since firing Denis, so Marcel was in Paris again. The four made their way across the cobbles toward the gardens. As they passed the double lines of symmetrical trees in raised beds forming the entrance, a couple approached, and Adele saw it was Stephanie de Lobel and Sebastien du Sauchoy. Behind Stephanie and Sebastien, rows of small shrubs curved towards each other, forming what could be termed an entrance hall, then the path went its regulated way through the extensive and ordered gardens.

"I am so glad you could come," Stephanie said, curtseying as they came up, while Sebastien bowed; "Mother and the viands are ensconced over this way."

She turned with Sebastien and led the way, passing the great octagon pool with its tall stone fountain and turning off to the left among a precisely-structured layout of well-groomed trees. In a small open space among this stiffly artificial grove a blanket had been spread, and Juliette de Lobel was seated on a stone seat. A maid was setting out an array of light dishes on the blanket. Juliette rose to welcome them, and in a twinkling had drawn Adele's mother to the seat and was engrossed in conversation. "…it was Stephanie's idea, but I thought that we two could enjoy ourselves, as well…" she was saying.

"It is pleasant to do something outdoors, before the weather grows cold," Honore remarked to Sebastien, while Adele was saying to Stephanie, "Do you expect anyone else?"

"The Fournier sisters should be here shortly," Stephanie said. "I invited Gaston, but—"

At that moment, the pale Fournier sisters, their stout mother, and a manservant could be seen through the carefully trimmed gaps in the verdure. Stephanie advanced to meet them, still on Sebastien's arm.

The young people soon seated themselves with perfect poise and began to partake of the light repast. Adele found that the duty of entertaining the Fournier sisters devolved upon herself, for Stephanie seemed to be enraptured with Sebastien, who reciprocated her single-minded interest. Honore aided Adele as much as he could, while Marcel remained in the background with the other servants.

The luncheon was almost over when a quick step was heard on the path, and the defiant, self-assured face of Gaston de la Roche came into sight over some low hedges. A few more steps brought him into the clearing. He bowed, long locks falling about his face.

Stephanie rose instantly with a cry of pleasure, advancing lightly to meet him. The others rose also—Adele noticed Sebastien's antipathy.

"…my apologies for being late," Gaston said, looking only at Stephanie.

"I am merely glad that you could come at all," she smiled winningly into his bold face.

After the introductions were made, Mme. Fournier, with a designing glance at her daughters and the young men, proposed that the young people take a turn about the gardens.

No one was more astonished than Adele when instantly Sebastien turned towards her. "I shall take Madame Adele," he said, offering his arm. Adele, in her amazement, looked at Stephanie—thus missing the fact that Sebastien's eyes were on her cousin, too.

"And *I* shall take Stephanie," Gaston swept her arm into his with a flourish.

Honore was bound, out of kindness, to escort Gabrielle and Anastasie, the Fournier sisters—and Adele, while assaying to join them, found herself, when the confusion settled, walking side by side with

Sebastien along the path, Gaston and Stephanie laughing and chatting ahead.

Sebastien was talking lightly about something; Adele forced herself to pay attention. "...have you seen the newest play? They say it has some quite witty jabs at the king."

"No, I have not seen it. However, 'a witty saying proves nothing,'" Adele quoted.

"Voltaire, of course," Sebastien said, with a nod of his wavy brown locks. "Your grandfather is rather mad on him, is he not?"

"He holds him in high esteem," Adele replied, "far more than I do...."

Up ahead, Stephanie and Gaston had slowed, pausing at one of the towering statues near the fountain, and Adele and Sebastien soon drew near. Adele cast a curious glance up into Sebastien's face, but he seemed oblivious to their presence, and passed by rapt in conversation with her.

"...Indeed, Adele," Sebastien said with easy laughter, "I am glad you differ with such an antiquated character; rather *passé*, no? There is much more to life, *n'est-ce pas?*"

She glanced away to avoid his eyes. Seeing Honore and the two Fournier girls in the distance, near a row of small trees, she subtly steered their course in that direction.

"What a pleasant garden," Adele said, "though—"

"What is your reservation, Adele?" Sebastien asked.

"I was thinking of the garden at home in Le Havre," she said, glad to have effected a diversion. "Here the ground is covered with tiles; only small holes let the plants through; it looks rather sterile and forced. There, things were trimmed and guided, but it was a living profusion of fruitful beauty." Her eyes brightened at the very memory.

"Turning that idea into a philosophical allegory, what think you of this quote from a contemporary of Voltaire's?" Sebastien asked. "I heard it used recently to excuse the uprisings of the people: 'It is not human nature we should accuse but the despicable conventions that pervert it.'"

"M. Diderot," Adele said, with a flash of her eyes. "The Bible is clear about the evil nature of man: all *will* go astray; we are only held back by the grace of God. Poverty or outward circumstances cannot excuse evil." She shook her head. "M. Diderot's wrong philosophies were revealed by the fruit of his life: he was an irreligious, materialistic, immoral man. Do we then trust and quote the bare word of such a man to excuse rebellious actions of destruction or murder?" Then she smiled and her face softened. "Excuse my heat; I have heard that sort of folly quite often of late."

"So you are quite the philosopher, Adele?" Sebastien said with an unruffled smile. "But back to gardens, I must confess that I, too, prefer the style of yours. Though this one is very pleasant to me right now," he said, looking down at her.

Adele kept her eyes gazing ahead. They had almost reached Honore and the Fourniers, and she was glad.

~*~*~

Across the wide street from Philip de la Noye's dark yellow door a woman lingered, well wrapped up in an expensive deep blue cloak. Long feathers accented her large blue hat. Presently, a carriage drew up and a short fleshy gentleman emerged. His footman knocked at the yellow door, and the man was admitted by a respectful doorman.

Camille waited a few moments, then glanced one more time at her blue dress before swishing across the street and knocking on the door. The young servant who opened it was not the one she had encountered before, and he ushered her into the hallway without question. Lanky and unsure of himself, he rubbed his hands together deferentially. Camille read him like a book.

"Inform your master that a lady wishes to see him," Camille said imperiously.

Bowing ingratiatingly, the youth hastened off. Reaching his master's study, he knocked and entered. Seated at a desk with his rotund visitor, De la Noye drew his dark brows together. "What do you want?"

"A lady to see you, my lord," the servant bent his long neck forward abjectly.

"Tell her I shall see her shortly. I have some business to dispatch," De la Noye answered distractedly, waving him off. "Where is Jacques today?" he muttered. Before the youth disappeared he added, "Offer her refreshments while she waits."

Camille sat down in a chair with something bordering satisfaction. *I have made it this far,* she thought. *I was right to think that with another visitor, he would be too busy to inquire….* she smirked.

"Is there any—anything I can do for you, Madame?" the youth asked uneasily.

"No," she said shortly, resuming her inward reflections.

It was perhaps twenty minutes later that the short man bustled out, pulling on his gloves and looking rather hot and bothered. After showing him to the door, the young manservant retreated towards his master's study to inquire if he was "available to receive the lady he had promised to see."

"Show her in," De la Noye grunted. He was satisfied with the interview—*I have the man where I want him*, he reflected smugly. His servant was out the door and on his errand before De la Noye remembered that he didn't know who the lady was. He shrugged. Scooping up the papers the short man had given him, he pressed a secret switch on his bureau. A hidden aperture slid open, and he placed them in it. Touching the same wooden button, it slipped shut with a soft click. Footsteps sounded on the polished wood floor outside. He stood with handsome grace and a polite smile.

As she stepped in, Camille kept her head tilted down, her wide hat concealing her face. Only when the door gently closed did she look up abruptly. Her face looked more beautiful and less pinched and faded than it had for many years—due to artful rouge and powder. A hard smile shone from her dark gray eyes and graced her pale lips.

De la Noye did not recoil, but the smile was dashed instantly from his smooth face.

"You did not expect me, Philip," she said crisply.

"Mademoiselle Camille Durand, I believe;—now, what brings you here?" he asked, carelessly.

"Do not play that game with me," she said with ominous control. "You kept away from France for many years, but now I have come to claim what is due."

"What is due? *Certes!*" cried the marquis. "Is there an account due? What is your occupation of late, Mademoiselle?"

"I am a milliner," Camille ground. "But—"

"I don't see how I could have run up an account there," Philip half-smiled, shrugging expansively. "How is sister Berthe?" he asked in a smooth tone, as if they were old friends reminiscing.

Camille flushed with anger, and high color showed through her powder. "I shall not let you wave this off, Philip." Her voice rose. "You false man! You deceiver! You heartless, base wretch, who shrugged and smiled—just as you do now—and left a girl with child to face the hard world alone! Look here!" she cried, thrusting a small, oval frame towards him. "Look at *your child!*"

Philip de la Noye took the miniature and looked with careless interest at the blue eyes, thin lips, fair hair, and serious, sensitive face of Jules Durand.

"What a handsome son you have, Mademoiselle Durand," he said, returning it to her thin fingers. "He must be a great aid and delight to you, I am sure." Then, partly dropping his nonchalant manner, he said, "Remember your place. You shall only hurt yourself, Mademoiselle Durand."

"You will not threaten me," Camille quavered, with strong emotion. She had not calculated on the strain of seeing *him* face to face. She forced her unsteady voice into a supplicating tone. "I came to ask you to give *our son* the inheritance he deserves; to instate him, or at *least* to provide for him."

"Come, come, Mademoiselle Durand," Philip waved a hand with careless remonstrance, "you are greatly mistaken. There is no connection between your handsome son and one such as myself. I cannot give handouts to every needy youth, and I will not."

"Will you not?" Camille's tone was still one of entreaty but her eyes flashed. She thrust out the miniature. "You will not acknowledge *your* son, and give him his due? You utterly refuse him? Nothing, not even enough for him to subsist on?" Her voice grew wilder and more pitiful with each sentence.

Philip de la Noye gazed at her, a serene expression on his handsome face. "*C'est la vie* — such is life, Mademoiselle Durand. Remember we were both young; we are more astute now," he shrugged with equanimity. "No, I shall not give your son even a *sou*."

Her voice steadied and grew hard. "Eighteen years ago you shrugged your shoulders — all duty gone!" She clenched her hands. "You *shall not* shrug me off this time, Philip! I *shall* revenge myself on you, though it take me years to accomplish it!"

Philip remained outwardly cool, but even he felt a slight tingle at the back of his neck. "Now, now, Mademoiselle. You are a milliner? If you keep your tongue, I will recommend your name to the ladies of my acquaintance."

"I shall not be bribed! I came for my son, not for myself!" Camille cried, stung. "I tell you to your face: I hate you, Philip! I hate you! I hate you! Hate you!" Her voice had risen to something near a scream.

"Consider your tone, Mademoiselle Durand — a lady would not want the servants to come running," Philip remarked, his dark eyebrows raised ever so slightly. "I wish you good day." With a minute bow, he crossed the room and held the door open.

Camille looked him straight in the eyes with a level, murderous look. His blue eyes dropped only slightly. She swept out with a scornful, proud face, head held high, mouth tight but quivering with emotion.

As she passed the staircase on her way out, a man in livery was stepping into the hall, and she cast a resentful glance in his direction. Then her face altered with a new emotion—astonishment. *Denis, in De la Noye's livery!* She proceeded smoothly on in case De la Noye was watching, but smiled, a thin smile that was not pleasant. *I already know someone who is in your very household, Philip!* she thought triumphantly. *All the easier to undo you!*

Meanwhile, Philip de la Noye took a turn or two about the room to settle himself. "Dear me," he drawled, "what a spiteful creature! And thinks she shall bring me down in some way!" He shrugged expressively.

But even he could not keep his mind from wandering back nineteen years—when the sixteen-year-old beauty Felicienne des Cou had married his rival, Francis de Coquiel di le Mercier. It brought him not a mere touch of pain. And then the foolish entanglement with Camille.... "She was quite pretty, then, and sweet," he muttered, seating himself in a chair. "What an inconvenient, hard woman she has become!...I shall watch out for her; but she cannot ruin me even if she does talk. She knows that, or she would have tried to blackmail me—ah, such is life! Every gentleman has had his youthful peccadilloes. If it does become public...Paris understands." He yawned, and lay back luxuriously in his chair. "*On ne fait pas d'omelette sans casser des œufs*—you can't make an omelette without breaking eggs."

Denis Appropriates a Tool

6.

Wine, drunkenness, heated hearts:
Foolish things are done:
In the end the serpent bites,
Alas! Down goes the sun.
— Ianthe

*I*t was several days before Camille recovered from the nervous effects of her interview with De la Noye. Hers was a highly-strung disposition, and for a time she seemed in a whirl, in which the only constant thing was her hatred of Philip, fueled by the knowledge that he had spurned their son.

But on the third evening she had finally come to a decision, and rose with partly-controlled agitation at the sound of a key turning in the lock. Her son Jules entered, his lean, stylishly disheveled outline framed against the darkness of the street.

"Is there something to eat?" he asked curtly.

"I have soup ready," she said, picking up the solitary candle and preceding him into the small, shadowed room beyond. The light flickered on rough, peeling walls. Jules threw himself onto a frail chair, which creaked dismally in protest, while his mother went to a stunted cupboard in the opposite corner and drew out a hunk of yellowish bread.

"It is the best I could get at the baker's," she said as he looked askance at the unsavory loaf. "As the lines grow longer each day, the quality gets poorer and poorer."

"I know," he grunted, "that is why I brought this." He pulled a light, white loaf from a capacious coat pocket.

"Where did you get that?" she asked in wonder.

Jules gave a short laugh. "I was at one of the cafés in the *Palais-Royal*, reading a pamphlet—a maid of some accursed aristocrat came by, a large basket on her arm." He smirked as he continued, "She was shoving through the crowd when *this* fell out of her basket right into my lap. I drew my paper over it. She turned around saying she had lost something. I, however, was absorbed in my paper....and here we are." Then the smile died from his blue eyes. "Those aristocrats—eating of the finest, while we starve on moldy, inedible pig food!" He kicked the dense yellow loaf into the corner.

Camille, mindful of future want, retrieved and dusted it off before returning it to the cupboard. She turned to her son, distress in her pale eyes. "Jules, Jules, have I not taught you to remain honest, though we are poor?"

Jules shifted on the seat. "Surely, Mother," he began, "I know you have; but this loaf came right to me."

"I know, my son, and I know the temptation." Her face twisted with former memories. "But I have always tried to be honest, no matter how needy; and I should hope that you, my son, will do the same. We must not stoop to stealing."

"Yes, Mother," Jules answered at length. "It is hard to watch them eat of the finest while we starve on what is barely food. But yes; I will."

The conversation ended. Camille dipped a bowl of soup and placed it on the table before him. She waited until he was eating, dipping hunks of bread in the thin soup, before addressing the subject near her heart.

"Jules, I have something to tell you," she said, drawing her thin brows together. "You know I never spoke of your father."

Jules stopped eating and looked up, his eyes taking in the emotion in her face. "You never would tell me."

"He was—is—a gentleman, a marquis," she said, speaking slowly and with effort. "He has come back to Paris. I had hoped, all these years...that he would do what is right, that he would have pity, for old times' sake....I saw him a few days ago, and urged him to instate you. But he—" the words stumbled out, then poured forth in a passionate torrent, as she told of her meeting with his father. At last she broke into perfervid sobbing. Jules' broad brow, blue eyes, and thin mouth were working silently, while his breath came quick and uneven. When Camille's angry tears ceased and she drew her hands from her thin face, Jules spoke.

"Those aristocrats!" he burst out. "Before, I bore them a grudge. Now, I *hate* them! The foul, destructive *beasts*! How could he be so selfish and uncaring?" His eyes, which before had been merely troubled and hostile, took on his mother's hard look of bitterness.

"What is his name?" he finally choked.

"His name is Philip—Philip Emile de la Noye."

"De la Noye!" The chair fell over as Jules started to his feet.

His mother's eyes widened. "You know him?"

"No—but Denis Moreau is his servant," Jules said.

"I know," she said, "and I think if you talk to him, he may be able to help us…"

Jules bent forward, his face clouded and malice-ridden, adding in eager comments as his mother laid out her plan.

~*~*~

The late September sky was a pale blue; gray, puffy clouds striped the sky. Higher in the atmosphere, feathery white clouds rested in patches on the blue firmament. If anyone in Versailles had peeked over the high hedges of the La Motte's sprawling back-garden, they would have beheld many bright, opulently-dressed ladies and gentlemen on the rich green lawn and wandering among the miniature glades. Despite the unrest, parties and *fetes* continued unabated.

Adele, holding Paulette's hand, was one of those enjoying the garden expanses after the claustrophobic confines of Paris. Coming round a clump of rosebushes to rejoin the main group on the lawn, she gave a subdued cry of delight. "M. Diesbach!"

The tall, pleasant-faced soldier turned from his conversation with her father. "Ah, it is my acquaintance from the *Palais-Royal*," he bowed. "Your father told me I would meet your family here."

"M. Diesbach and I have met over dinner several times," Adele's father told her, "but he has not had an opportunity to visit Paris again—the king is keeping his *Gardes Suisses* close to him in Versailles."

They chatted for some minutes, then Adele excused herself; Paulette was tired of standing still. As she moved off through the crowd, curtseying to friends, a small, poised figure with black curls caught her eye.

Adele smiled into the blue eyes of Elisabeth la Motte. "Elisabeth! I have been looking for you!"

Elisabeth's face glowed with one of her quiet, lovely smiles. "Adele! It is always such a pleasure to see you." Being brought up among the Court, she was more outwardly reserved than Adele. Yet she quickly warmed to others, and with close friends like the De Coquiel di le Merciers her true nature unfurled in vivacious cordiality.

"We can sit here," Adele motioned to a carved stone bench. "Maybe this time we shall have time for a good talk! Paulette, can you arrange these pebbles?" She seated herself with grace, keeping her back fashionably ramrod-stiff. The very motion reminded her with a sweet pang of her dear departed gouvernante, Marie. *How gouvernante worked on my posture....If only she could see how I have benefited from her patient lessons!*

"It does seem that we often do not have enough time to really converse," Elisabeth agreed, joining her decorously on the seat. By the exchanges already flying between Adele's vivacious brown eyes and Elisabeth's luminous blue ones, an established friendship was clear.

Adele felt a satisfying sense of restfulness sweep over her. *What a dear pleasure Elisabeth is!* she thought. *With her, I know I am with someone who can be trusted — who is an example for me to follow....* Her eyes moved to the silk-garbed figures on the lawn. They were also friends and fellow-Christians — she saw pale Mme. and stout M. du Chemin seated with a couple from church; Adele's mother and bubbling Mme. la Motte were conversing with Tristan du Chemin, while Honore was stooping down to show something to a laughing group composed of Olivie, Charles, and Elisabeth's younger sister Christelle.... There were other familiar faces there, too. *What a refreshing thing to attend a party composed of friends of like mind, for once!* Adele thought.

After sweet converse, leaping from topics such as Necker's triumphal return, to the delight of younger siblings, to admiration of the glorious and wild sky, Elisabeth was called away to meet a new guest.

Paulette had left her rocks and meandered across the lawn, stopping here and there to examine the grass, with Adele's watchful eyes upon her. Seriously contemplating a small flower, the three-year-old stepped back and tumbled against Tristan du Chemin. He looked down with some surprise, then laughingly set her on her feet again. Seeing Adele's eyes on the toddler, he advanced across the lawn to her, drawing Paulette gently after him by one of her chubby little hands.

"Here is your escapee, Adele," he said, hazel eyes sparkling from under his straight brows.

Adele smiled back. Taking Paulette's hand, she drew her onto the seat. Slipping a silk ribbon from her hanging reticule, she twisted it into a knot and presented it to Paulette with a twinkling smile. "See if this can keep you busy."

Tristan drew up an adjacent garden chair and seated himself, fumbling in the inner pocket of his slate-blue jacket. At last he drew something out and handed it to Paulette. Her face lit up. Dropping the knot of ribbon on the ground, she grasped the small toy with eager fingers. Adele bent over her. "What do you say, Paulette?" she whispered.

"*Remercier beaucoup* — thank you *very* much," Paulette lisped, lifting her large eyes momentarily from the brightly-painted doll.

"I saw it in a shop yesterday," Tristan said to Adele, "and thought it might catch her fancy." He stooped. Picking up the fallen ribbon, he returned it to Adele's fingers.

She glanced down again at Paulette, who was turning the doll over and over, gently caressing its wooden features. "You were right," Adele smiled. "A shop? Where?"

"I was at the *Palais-Royal*," he answered, "to see what the papers were saying, and —"

The tall, slim figure of Honore passed nearby, and Tristan cut himself short. Catching Honore's eye, he drew his forefinger and two adjacent fingers together in a light, rapid gesture. Altering his course, Honore pulled up a chair and joined them.

"I was telling Adele that I was at the Palais-Royal yesterday," Tristan said, "and by merest accident I came across your father's former *valet-de-chambre*."

Honore gave an exclamation of interest.

"I suppose it makes sense that Denis would be there," Adele said.

"I think he was surprised to see me," Tristan answered. "He told me that he is now employed by M. de la Noye."

Adele met his eyes with a small explosion of recognition in her own. "De la Noye! I have met him; but he is a Royalist! Why would he take on a man like Denis?"

"From our small researches and discoveries into Denis' character," Tristan's mouth twitched upward at one corner, "we know Denis is an intriguer, one who manipulates events. Who knows? M. de la Noye may have noted that as well."

"It does seem that, like the commoners, many aristocrats are trying to twist events to their advantage," Adele said seriously.

"M. la Motte told me today that influential people were endeavoring, behind the scenes, to foment the unrest even before the Estates-General convened," Honore remarked. "They hope to gain control."

"These shortages of bread are especially troubling," Tristan said. "One gets the impression that manipulators are trying to cause a revolt. I have heard reports that the harvest has not been bad, but that farmers are being secretly paid not to harvest grain and bakers bribed not to grind it. If these rumors are true, it is infamous! What we can do in response seems unclear, but we must stand up for the truth. If we knew who was responsible...."

It was only when a portly servant trod heavily by in the fast-darkening twilight, lighting the lanterns and tapers placed about the garden, that Adele realized they had been talking for quite some time. The formerly pale blue firmament had darkened to a deep cerulean, and wisps of soft roseate clouds curled about the western horizon. In the soft yellow pools of light cast by the *falots* moved various figures, laughing and chatting.

Adele glanced down at Paulette and noticed that the child was asleep, her little head pillowed on a fold of Adele's primrose gown. Clutched in her chubby hands was the miniature doll Tristan had given her.

~*~*~

The ordered verdure of the Tuileries garden had changed to soft autumnal colors: it was the last week of September. Scattered among the trimmed hedges and trees were small strolling groups. Open to all, the gardens were a favorite promenade ground.

Among the thicker trees sauntered a man in livery and an upper-class servant-woman, arm in arm. Seen from afar, the man looked unremarkable—the usual manservant. But close-up, his troubled dark brown eyes and taut face seemed subversive and defiant. A half-concealed scar on his left cheek did nothing to diminish the effect. The face of his companion, under her waves of reddish-brown hair, was sincere and enamored. The man was talking volubly, but in a restrained, quiet voice.

"So you agree, dear Berthe?" Denis was saying, looking down eagerly at her. "It is a simple matter, but we must act quickly. M. de Coquiel di le Mercier keeps his hard currency in the safe in his room. He has been collecting it to send overseas for safe-keeping. Why should he profit from money that could be of use to the cause of freedom? Besides, it was earned by the peasants' toil, so rightly it belongs to them! You, Berthe, merely need to access the safe using this key—when the household is asleep—" he pulled out a shining gray object. "I will be waiting for you at the street corner. We will go straight to a priest. By the time they realize what has happened, you will be snugly secreted away as Mrs. Moreau, in my new lodgings—and no search will find you there."

Dropping her eyes and blushing, Berthe took the key from his fingers and slipped it into her reticule. Denis drew his arm around her.

"When can you carry out our plan, my sweetest Berthe?" he asked. "It must be as soon as possible, before he sends it overseas beyond our reach."

Berthe considered. "Next day-week would be the soonest I could be sure of."

"But that will be the fourth of October—must it be so long from now?" Denis remonstrated.

"I cannot try sooner," Berthe said with decision. "Master is here now, there is a party in two days, the Du Chemins are coming over one of the evenings after that, then there is a big fete—the night of the fourth would certainly be best."

"I trust your good judgment, Berthe," Denis said. "I shall be waiting for you the evening of the fourth, then. Your master will leave for Versailles that evening—his rooms will be vacant. You should have no difficulty." He smiled reassuringly. "I am only impatient to have you as my own, dearest."

A far-off bell tolled the time. Berthe drew herself from his grasp and turned to go, rearranging her cream scarf. She had gone a few paces when she came back and asked, with searching green eyes, "This money will be used for the patriot cause, will it not, Denis?"

He drew her to him. "Of course, dearest, do not distress yourself," he reassured her. "We shall be striking a blow against the accursed aristocrats, and aiding freedom and liberty."

She nodded and walked away, contented, clutching the fiery gazettes he had given her.

Denis watched her go with inscrutable eyes—eyes that no longer seemed lover-like at all.

~*~*~

"I fear nothing good shall come from this, M. de Coquiel di le Mercier." The usually clear brow of Hans Diesbach was lined.

"I agree," Francis said, putting his fingers together. "I knew last night that there was a party for various officers—those of the Swiss, the newly-arrived Flanders regiment, and the Versailles National Guard. But from the angry unrest this morning, I guessed that something must have occurred there to incite the wrath of the populace."

"Yes. It was to be a welcoming banquet for the *Regiment de Flandre*," Hans said. "The idea was good—I helped arrange for it to be held in his Majesty's spacious opera apartment. The fete started well. After the meal, there were toasts—the King and Queen were toasted enthusiastically. A toast to 'the Nation' was significantly (at least, in the people's eyes) neglected. But these men are soldiers, sworn to be true to the King—what would the people have them do? Toast the power that is bringing the King to his knees?" His eyes were gloomy and he sighed as he continued, "The people are mightily offended, for all that. Back to the evening's tale. The wine began to take effect; many of the louder and wilder spirits expanded under its influence. The King and Queen entered, their young son in her arms! At their entrance, the band began to play "O Richard, O my King" — " his voice trailed off, and the soldier turned and looked out into the street.

Francis murmured the words under his breath:

"O Richard! O my king!
The Universe abandons you!
On earth, it is only me
Who is interested in you!
Alone in the universe
I would break the chains
when everyone else deserted you!"

"The song which has become the Royalist anthem in these troubled times," Francis said. "Such a stirring tune, such rousing words....Plato understood music's importance, saying, 'Let me write the music of the people, and I care not who writes the laws.'"

Hans turned from the window and came back to the table, leaning his hands upon it. "Yes, music has power," he said, "and over a group of wine-heated men — " he broke off, shaking his sandy blond head. "Pleased, the Queen bore herself with a graceful daring that could not be resisted, passing out white cockades to the officers. They erupted in ardent acclamation, pinning them to their hats — those wearing tricolor cockades tore them off and trampled them. That fact alone — and the large white cockades the officers and men are all flaunting today — has stirred the populace more than can be imagined." His honest face was filled with pain as he continued, "*Ma foi!* Must we not be loyal to our Sovereigns? What if we wear the Queen's colors? Is that cause to hate us?"

Then he looked straight at Francis and answered himself in a quiet voice, "Yes, it is. Because the people in France hate their government. They wish to destroy the King and Queen and all relics of the former state of things. They take offence when anyone affirms loyalty to those they are trying to depose."

"Yes, that is why," Francis said, meeting his clear eyes. "I thank you for the news, M. *le Capitaine*. From the unrest I have seen today, I am afraid this small event will have greater consequences than it should ever deserve." He glanced down at the officer's hat on the table. "But you do not wear the white cockade, I notice."

M. Diesbach sighed. "I cannot bring myself to do so. Our sovereigns are selfish and weak—I do not love their excesses and unconcern for the oppressed populace. But we soldiers are still sworn to protect and serve them. And I shall do my duty and fulfill my word, as a true Christian."

"You are doing what is right." Francis met those clear, determined eyes with his earnest hazel ones. Rising, he grasped M. Diesbach's hand in a firm handclasp which said more than words could.

~*~*~

The dreary afternoon sun slanted through gray clouds, down a narrow street, and into a dingy second-story chamber in a close-packed row of houses. The room's dulled wallpaper and broken plaster moldings spoke of former richness. A heavy, stained dresser stood against the wall opposite the window, an old wooden chest beside it. On the left-hand wall there was a closed door and a table with a chair: the other chair was left indifferently in the center of the room. An oval mirror hung beside the open door of another room. Nothing was too dusty, nor was it clean or well-ordered, giving the impression of a recent move.

There was a muffled sound from the next room, then footsteps. A moment later Denis pushed the door wide and entered, a heavy glass vase in his hand. He placed it on the table. "That will be for flowers—women always like flowers, they say." He chuckled dryly.

Throwing himself into in the central chair, he gazed off into space. *Now, if only she can get that money, I shall prove a nice husband, I suppose....If she fails, then – she will realize where my interest lies, that's all.* He leaned back in his chair. *Even with my pay, my pockets are thinly lined at present...it is fortunate for me that she is filled with patriotic zeal – of course, my judiciously-given pamphlets helped.* He stuffed his hands in his pockets and tipped back further still. *And it will hurt my former master Francis – that makes it doubly sweet! The sanctimonious fool.... Today is the third – tomorrow evening....Oh, he* can't *transfer the money before then! If he does –*

He was startled from his thoughts by a rap on the door. Rising and moving to the left-hand door, he tugged it open. Jules' fair but embittered face was framed in the doorway, a dingy staircase behind him.

"Jules! Enter!" Denis clapped him on the back, his face jovial. Only in Denis' eyes lingered the selfishness which ran his life. Like many, his soul was driven by what he hoped the Revolution would bring to him.

After preliminary banter, Denis said abruptly, "You seem distraught, comrade."

Jules looked up, startled. "Yes; I want to talk, Denis." His youthful face tightened further. "What do you think of your master, De la Noye?"

"He is a fine gentleman, but—"

"But?—" Jules asked, with an eagerness he could not conceal.

"At first when I took service under him," Denis mused, "I believed him to be a supporter of the patriotic cause. He employed me in many jobs to my liking—rumor-stirring and the like. What a ride I and others had, spreading the Brigand fears and thus causing the country-wide expansion of the National Guard! But subsequent events have revealed his true colors. He is a Royalist underneath it all. His efforts, ostensibly for the people, are in reality serving his own selfish interests. Mayhap he has forgotten the proverb, *On ne peut pas avoir le beurre et l'argent du beurre* — You can't have butter and the money from selling the butter." He laughed shortly, then paused. "He is a tolerable master—but I long to be of use to our country."

"So he is a fair master, but is not worth supporting wholeheartedly?" Jules asked. Denis nodded pithily.

Jules broke out, "I have always hated those smug aristocrats, but now—! My mother would never reveal who my father was—although you and a few others knew she was cast off heartlessly. She has now told me he is an aristocrat."

"All too common among the beastly, self-serving nobility," Denis grated.

"And his name: Philip de la Noye," Jules hissed, passion lighting his face.

A lightning-stroke passed across Denis's face. Memories flashed through his mind, connecting like puzzle pieces. "I should have known!" he cried. "Only—And your face bears it out," he said, gazing at Jules' handsome countenance. "You have his blue eyes, that aquiline Roman nose..."

"I did not come to find out how much I look like the scoundrel," Jules grumbled, "but because I know that you have influence, being in his very household."

"Influence?" Denis said, "—not yet. But I could do a few things, in a small way—What do you want?" he asked, turning suddenly.

"Surely a perspicacious, resourceful fellow like you could do quite a bit of real damage without it ever coming to light," Jules flattered. Denis looked pleased, and Jules continued, "A keen person might easily pick up incriminating information...."

"We shall see," Denis said. "It would give me more pleasure than you think to thwart his royalist schemes....The villain! I remember how beautiful your mother was, long ago—you can tell her that I will certainly set my wits to work and keep my ears open—though, mind, opportunity may not arise."

"I appreciate it, Denis—*remercier beaucoup*! I also stand ready to aid you, comrade," Jules said, his blue eyes warm. "A thousand thanks."

The room darkened as they spoke. Monstrous, leaden clouds closed over the sun.

Berthe's March

7.

A mile around the city,
The throng stopped up the ways;
A fearful sight it was to see
Through two long nights and days.
— Thomas Macaulay

O n the floor of the small but neat room she shared with Virginie, Berthe bent over a basket, busy folding a blue dress. There was no window, but she knew it was a little past noon.

Muffled footsteps echoed outside in the hall. Starting up, she thrust the basket under her bed and stood listening warily. They passed her door and grew fainter—she let out her breath.

"Tonight—is the night;—tonight—is the night," her pounding heart seemed to say. She remained stiff for several more minutes before drawing the basket out and continuing her preparations.

A quarter of an hour slipped by. Footsteps again!—but the *click-clack* told of unusual haste. Berthe had nervously pushed the basket under the bed as soon as the noise began; now she opened her door and looked out. She was just in time to see a hasty swirl of dark brown skirts as the maid entered her master's room.

Berthe cast one glance back to make sure all looked innocent—then stepped across the paneled hall. Entering the half-open door of her master's room, she asked, "Why such haste, Virginie?"

Virginie favored her with a hurried look before continuing to remove the sheets with flying fingers. Thrusting a whole bundle of them into Berthe's arms, she flew out into the corridor—but was back in a moment with a folded stack of bedclothes, which she arranged on the bed with deft celerity.

"Why such haste?" Berthe asked again, with inward misgivings, mechanically holding the rumpled pile of sheets.

"Guests—need enough room—just arrived," Virginie replied, in bursts, her hands still promptly dispatching her duties.

To Berthe, this was maddening— *Virginie has always been so uppity,* she thought with inward disgust. *It will be good to be gone. Always giving me the cold shoulder, as if she were so important. She's only a maid-of-all-work.* She thrust the sheets angrily back at Virginie, turned haughtily, and left the room.

When she reached the top of the winding servant's stairs, an unfamiliar manservant stepped out into the hall, carrying a portmanteau on his shoulders. His burly figure was followed closely by one of the De Coquiel di le Merciers' maids.

"This way," the maid said, leading the way to a guest room. She called over her shoulder to Berthe, "Mistress wants you downstairs."

Berthe hastened to the stairs. Halfway down she met a strange valet. His bow was rather impeded by the bundles he was carrying.

The downstairs hall was abuzz—Berthe met her mistress as the latter, glorious in a rich painted silk gown, stepped from the kitchen. She no doubt had been giving instructions to the cook.

"We have unexpected guests, Berthe—did not Julie tell you? We met them at the Du Chemins during church service." Felicienne drew her aside. "I want you to ensure that the guest rooms are presentable and ready. Your master's room, as well—for they are quite a large group. That will give us enough beds." She smiled, adding half to herself, "At the chateau we had room for four times this number, without any inconvenience—but this will do." Then she looked directly at Berthe. "I count on you to guarantee that the rooms are prepared. The maids can be forgetful when hurried."

Then, with a lovely rustle of skirts, Felicienne paced swiftly down the hall and entered the parlor.

Berthe felt weak. *What shall I do?* Her mind reeled; she slipped into the empty dining room to think. *Tonight master's room will be occupied! I was to get — **that** — and meet Denis....Now what will I do?....Would there not be some time before the rooms are occupied? But no...* She put a hand to her head, closing her green eyes. But thinking did not help: and time was slipping away.

She did not notice a girlish, silk-gowned figure passing the dining room door and pausing to look quietly in, with a puzzled countenance, before stealing softly down the hall.

At length Berthe drew her hands from her face. Putting aside her despairing, profitless thoughts, she hastened upstairs to do as she had been told. But she could not keep herself from thinking, as she smoothed a comforter or pointed out an empty pitcher, *What shall I do?* The other maids found Berthe especially tart and fault-finding that afternoon.

~*~*~

The evening arrived. Gathered in the kitchen, the servants chattered among themselves, making merry with the newcomers' servants.

"Just arrived in Paris, eh?" remarked a coachman in the Le Mercier's green and white livery.

"Yes—came in this morning," said the *valet-de-chambe* Berthe had passed on the stairs that afternoon. "Haven't even had a chance to see the city, and the master says we move on tomorrow. Rotten luck!"

"You are missing much, let me tell you," rejoined the coachman. "Paris is the very hub of freedom—soon we shall rise, unfettered by the shackles of the aristocracy and king!"

Berthe glanced across at Marcel. As usual, he sat quiet and dull-faced. *He could be be asleep, for all the attention he pays,* she thought.

Virginie, next to one of the visitors' maids, ignored the coachman's words and asked, "You are leaving Paris tomorrow? Where are you going?"

"Ah!" the man hissed sharply. "*Ne reveillez pas le chat qui dort!*—let sleeping cats lie!"

The maid beside Virginie laughed at him. "It is his sore spot," she said, turning dancing eyes to the others. "He does not want to leave France, and yet will not leave Master. So he is being dragged—by his own inclination, mind—out of the country."

"Coblenz," the valet muttered. "*Germany!*"

"All of your party going?" queried the coachman.

"Yes; our master and his family, and the three gentlemen with us," said the maid.

"Don't feel too bad—you won't be alone," Virginie said. "They say a goodly portion of the emigrating aristocrats choose Coblenz. It is rumored they are gathering forces to come back to France—with an army."

"*Certes,*" the valet admitted. "But come, tell of the news here..."

Berthe rose with weary impatience. Talking had afforded her no distraction from her perplexing thoughts, nor from her increasing feelings of doubt. *Why did they have to come tonight, of all nights? Any other night...* Her feet dragged heavily upstairs as she went upstairs to her room to try to think. One thing was clear—she must contact Denis.

She passed a restless, uncomfortable evening until her master left for Versailles and the guests retired to their chambers. After an hour or so, the overflowing household composed itself and a peaceful calm settled over the dim rooms. At last, peeking out of her door, Berthe deemed it safe to emerge. Over her arm was the big basket she had surreptitiously packed earlier—she had decided to bring it, to have less to carry later on.

The servant's stairs were deserted and dark—she felt her way carefully down and out the servant's exit on the side of the house.

The narrow alley, full of shadows, had never seemed so unfriendly—the faint moonlight could not penetrate its dark folds. Berthe drew her shawl closer round and shivered, not wholly because the cold. *Will Denis still be waiting?*

There was a light in the street beyond, but Berthe shrank from it as well, and hardly breathed until she turned into another thin sidestreet and came face to face with Denis.

His eyes shone—they darted to the basket she held. He reached for it. As she handed it across, a surprised expression surged across his face.

"It is light," he whispered.

"I could not get the money—yet," Berthe said quickly. She poured out the whole story of their thwarted plan.

His face darkened. "You must go back!" he said. "You shall wait until these inconvenient guests have departed—" He clenched his teeth before continuing, "I cannot linger. Here, I will give you directions to my lodging. I will meet you there. Take heart—all is not lost; we shall succeed!" Almost as an afterthought, he hastened to add, "You are so brave and beautiful, my darling Berthe—I cannot wait until you are mine forever."

Taking the basket, he smiled at her and slipped away into the darkness of the alley. Berthe made her way back fleetly to the side door, relieved when it closed noiselessly behind her. Ascending the stairs, she spent a restless night. Even the thought of the good she would be doing for "the patriotic cause" failed to wholly quell her growing, nagging guilt. And Denis' absent-minded words of love had stirred teeny, nagging doubts....

~*~*~

The sun came up the next morning—the fifth of October—but only a few saw him, for rain clouds threatened both Paris and Versailles.

After an early breakfast, a repetition of the hustle and bustle of the afternoon before took place. The servants rushed about packing and carrying bundles and baggage to the guest's coaches. It was not until some time after the last farewells had been said that Berthe could find time to talk to her mistress.

"There you are, Berthe," Felicienne exclaimed.

"Yes, mistress," Berthe answered, "Shall I go fetch your new hat from the milliner's this morning, Madame?"

"I have reports of rioting among the lower classes of women—but it is in the *Saint Antoine* district," Felicienne replied dubiously. "I wonder if you should go—the hat can wait."

"It is nothing," Berthe replied tersely, compressing her lips. "And do not trouble the cook to get bread—I will stop at the baker's on my way; 'twill save a trip."

Felicienne went to the window and looked out into the thinly-populated street before coming back to her maid. Berthe had already put on her gloves and wide-brimmed hat. "You may go, Berthe—but do not tarry."

Berthe's face lit up. "Thank you," she said a little too loudly, leaving with rapid steps. Moving down the hall, she paused outside the door of her room and pushed it open. Empty. She breathed a sigh of silent relief. Reaching under her bed, she hauled out a large sturdy basket lined with blue checked cloth. She braced herself when lifting; it was unusually heavy. Several cloth bundles peeked out. She drew the corners of the lining together, tying them closed with a ribbon. Carrying it with affected lightness, she opened the door and slipped softly down the hall and out the servant's door.

It had begun to rain—slowly and despondently. She was grateful for the pattens she was wearing, though their height made quick walking difficult, and the metal rang noisily on the wet cobbles. As long as the house was in sight, she walked warily, repressing the impulse to glance back, but once she had taken several side streets she relaxed a little.

Oh, how glad I am to get away! I thought I would never succeed! She remembered the unexpected development of the day before that had threatened to ruin their plans. How distraught she had been! *I gave him most of my things last night,* she thought; *which is nice; I have less to carry this morning.* In her basket now were a few last-minute clothing items and the cloth-covered bundles of her master's money, tightly bound so the gold *louis* would not rattle or clink. *There was more there than I expected,* she thought, *and so heavy!* She shifted the basket on her arm.

After several minute's walking, she pulled out the slip of paper Denis had given her and continued on, puzzling over his hastily-scrawled handwriting. In her absorption she did not heed the increasing commotion headed her way until it was too late.

The noise grew louder. Berthe looked up. Her eyes widened. A mass of seething, shrill women surged precipitously down the street towards her. Monsieur Malliard, one of the "heroes" of the Bastille, was at their head. The mob's faces were fierce and gaunt—more terrifying because they were women. Some brandished guns or rude pikes, while others dragged along a cannon.

The March of Women, Anonymous

Hastily, Berthe moved out of their way, into the shelter of a doorway. She had no time for anything else before they were streaming past with cries and uplifted arms, shouting, "To Versailles! To the Assembly!"

But Berthe was not allowed to shrink against the doorpost for long. An eddy of hoydenish women rippled towards her through the vast current, eyeing her opportunistically. Seizing Berthe roughly, the disheveled Amazons dragged her in among the marching ranks. Once in the current, there was no going back.

"I am on business—let me go!" Berthe cried.

But the debased women paid no heed to her cries and kept her forcibly among them, shoving and pulling. Indeed, she realized, they were seizing every woman they saw. Hugging her basket close, Berthe glanced about at the distorted faces. A large proportion were harlots and women of otherwise ill repute—they seemed to be coercing regular women and maidservants in order to gain respectability. The mob was representing itself as a crowd of famished mothers demanding bread for their little ones. Many (even those she doubted had little ones) cried, "Bread! Bread for our famished children!"

Berthe's roving glance of despair caught the face of one woman. *She is a man!* Berthe thought, astonished. A closer examination of several other "ladies" disclosed other men in dresses, too, masquerading as women. Berthe was confused. *Could this be false; could it be engineered?* she thought, *Like the uprisings Denis told me he so gallantly arranged and fomented?*

The thought of Denis reminded her of her "patriotic" ideas, and she tried to enter into the spirit of the swelling, bellowing horde. *Mayhap we can cause the Assembly to grant bread! If it weren't for these coins, I would join them gladly,* she told herself. *But I must get them to Denis…anything could happen in a crowd like this!* She looked for a way to slip out of the shouting column, the weight of her basket reminding her of her purpose.

The women who had compelled her had all scattered in search of other prey. Slowly, Berthe began edging out. Ahead, she could see the tree-lined avenue and corresponding parkland of the *Champs-Elysees*.

She was almost out of the moving line of women when they reached the Elysian Fields. There, inexplicably, the line slowed, then stopped. Others from behind crowded round her. *What now?* Berthe wondered, clutching her basket close.

In a few minutes, she saw that M. Malliard was arranging the straggling mass into semi-ordered ranks, appointing "generalesses" over tens and fifties. Berthe found to her horror that she was now under the direction and care of a tall, hard-looking woman in a grimy dress which may have once been blue. This unwomanly creature instantly marshaled Berthe and the nine others who were unfortunate enough to fall under her control. Berthe realized with a sinking heart that for now, at least, escape was impossible. What would the mob do to someone so "unpatriotic" as to attempt escape?

The rain dripped steadily—sodden skirts slumped and dragged, and all the white scarves in the bosoms of their dresses clung clammily. Her wet apparel further weighed down Berthe's body and spirit.

After plodding on for some time, they left the walls of Paris behind and marched on, still seizing any woman who had the misfortune to be out. Once out of the city, Berthe realized how large the mob really was. Behind, it stretched almost as far as she could see, and ahead of her as well—some eight thousand women and disguised men in all. At the head of the line, Malliard marched, still beating a drum, its sharp accents rallying and urging them on.

A mile passed, then another, and Berthe was beginning to droop with fatigue. Her basket was so heavy! She had been shifting it from arm to arm for some time past. Her shoulders slumped, and she half-closed her eyes. "How much longer to Versailles?" she asked the slender girl next to her—obviously a milliner's apprentice. Her voice was a little above a whisper.

"Two miles, I think someone said," the girl replied in an undertone.

The gaunt, fierce figure of their "captain" loomed over them. "Not tired, are you?" she grated, "with such a little burden? Why, I could carry it with a finger!" Her scornful stare at Berthe's basket stiffened Berthe with fear.

I must not— Berthe thought desperately, *I must not let her suspect me of tiredness—she will take my basket, and then—!* She knew its unusual weight would lead to its being opened and rifled.

Fear strengthened Berthe's sagging frame and squared her shoulders. She managed to carry her burden more lightly. But her heart could not keep from misgivings. *How can I keep this up for several more miles?*

A gilded carriage, moving toward Paris, was passing the column. Only its male coachman could be seen at first, so it passed the first ranks of the women without molestation—but as it slowly wheeled past Berthe's section, a woman's face looked out.

Instantly Berthe's "captain" sprang at the coach. Grabbing the reins, she forced the astonished coachmen to stop. Another hag wrenched open the coach door, and a moment later dragged out the lady occupant.

"My shoes!" the lady was saying, "I must not stand in the mud!—" Indeed, she was wearing beautiful thin silk shoes—any wet would not only irreparably damage the silk, but also cause the cardboard stiffeners to "melt," utterly ruining them.

Her disheveled captor replied with a bitter laugh, looking down at her own sodden and muddy garments, "More than your dear shoes will be ruined before you're done, Madame. You are coming with us."

The coachman sprung half-down, expostulating vigorously, but was driven back by a fierce rush of pikes. His mistress gestured up at him from the midst of the wild mass. He clambered down again, at risk to himself. She spoke a few rapid words in a low, self-possessed tone. He nodded quickly, sprang up onto the coach again, brought the horses round and set off for Versailles.

"She's in my group," shrilly cried Berthe's general, while the other woman protested vehemently.

"I got her out!"

"*I* noticed her first—and *I* stopped the horses!"

"*I* saw her first!—"

Berthe hardly noticed their heated argument, for she was staring at the lady they had "captured." When the coach pulled up, the gilded coat of arms on its shining door had caught her eye, and thus she had hardly been surprised, though she was pained, to see the round face and graying black locks of the marquise la Motte. That they would force such a lady to accompany them! It almost took her breath away. Berthe herself had been very grateful for her pattens already—it would be torture for Mme. la Motte to walk in high heeled shoes whose sides were dissolving in the wet.

Her thoughts were broken into by her captain, who had won the battle of words and pushed Mme. la Motte into her group.

Madame la Motte's bright blue eyes widened with surprise upon seeing Berthe. "Why, the *maid-de-chambe* of my dear friend the marquise de Coquiel di le Mercier!"

Their "captainess" said to the marquise, "As you two seem to be acquainted, you, little lady, will help this 'supporter of our cause.'" With harsh scorn she motioned to Berthe and turned away.

Berthe reddened at the mention of her mistress, but Mme. la Motte attributed her blush to modesty. "I am sorry to see they forced you to accompany us, Madame la Motte," Berthe said.

"*Us?*" Mme. la Motte asked. She raised her eyebrows slightly, but remembered how many servants inclined favorably towards the revolution.

Berthe flushed again. She wasn't sure of the answer. *I did not join them willingly....* she thought, *— but I do support what they are doing, do I not?* In her uncertainly she refrained from answering and glanced down, noticing when she did so that her companion's silk shoes were already fully clotted with mud. She found her thoughts running on again, *— or do I? These — nasty — women — and men too, shameful!....but we are marching with a glorious goal: bread for the people of Paris...*

"Your shoes, Madame," Berthe said with a surge of pity, "would you desire to wear my pattens?" Even as she said so, Berthe stumbled out of weariness, and her arms slackened.

"How very kind of you," Mme. la Motte smiled. "However they will not fit me—But you are tired, Berthe! Here, lean on my arm..."

To her utter astonishment, Berthe found the arm of this aristocratic lady around her, helping to support the basket. Berthe was a mere maid— far below such exalted members of the *ancienne noblesse*—most would not even *imagine* physically helping a servant! Berthe tried to draw away, partly in fear that her basket's contents would be discovered, and partly from amazement, but Mme. la Motte was not to be denied.

"My dear, you are worn out—let me help you." Her face radiated kindly concern. She seemed to forget her own bedraggled gown and chafing, wet shoes.

Berthe could only stare in astonishment. Somehow an undefined emotion found a chink in the hardness and hate which Denis had inculcated in her heart towards all aristocrats.

They struggled on towards Versailles: the long, marching column an angry wave, swirling on and on. What would happen when it broke on the sands of Versailles?

~*~*~

The household of the De Coquiel di le Merciers was a busy one, and between one thing and another it was almost midday before Felicienne gave a thought to Bethe's prolonged absence. She was in the parlor with Adele and Olivie, having finished the girl's lessons. Honore and Tristan du Chemin had been out practicing swordsmanship at a *maitre d'armes*, but had come in a few minutes before.

"Berthe should have been back long before this." Worry creased Felicienne's fair face.

"The streets were very agitated earlier in the morning," Honore commented. "On my way to fencing practice, things were so thick around the *Hotel-de-Ville* that I turned back and went to the *maitre d'armes* by a different route."

"Thousands of women swarmed the *Hotel-de-Ville*, tried to hang the Abbe Lefevre, and seized the guns and cannons there," Tristan said. "Then they marched out towards Versailles—could she have fallen in with them?"

"One would think she would have noticed the noise and slipped out of the way," Honore said.

Adele looked up with a steady expression. "She has been more distracted than usual in the last week," she mentioned.

"She was in the dining room yesterday, covering her face with her hands," Olivie piped up. "It was after our unexpected guests arrived."

Adele smiled at her younger sister. *Hardly anything escapes her.*

"That may have nothing to do with this," their mother said, "though I, too, have noticed a difference in her manner. She was certainly keen on leaving on those errands."

"If she got swept up in the crowd, there is nothing we can do," Honore said, "but I will go to the milliner's and look for her along the way. She may be detained on business."

"I shall come with you," Tristan said, rising with alacrity.

But when they returned an hour later, they were only able to report that Berthe had never made it to either the baker's or the milliner's.

"The mob was coercing women to go with them," Honore added.

"So she could be with the mob—oh, my Berthe!" Felicienne cried. "I hope she is not in danger!"

She pictured her near Versailles in a vast throng of women. None of them imagined that at the moment, their friend Mme. la Motte, herself almost worn out, was half-supporting the stumbling, exhausted Berthe.

The True Colors of the Revolution

8.

An angry man opens his mouth and shuts his eyes.
— Cato

"Death to the Austrian!" shrieked a coarse fish-wife. The call was repeated along the line with equal vehemence.

Berthe had heard that cry many times during their weary march, but it still startled her. The reality of the vague "patriotic" ideas now began to strike. They meant what they said! They meant bloodshed and the overturn of all society!

"The Austrian" was the queen, Marie-Antoinette. Even before the diamond necklace scandal in 1785 (in which the queen, though wholly innocent, was smeared), the people had despised her. Her extravagance and selfish preoccupation did nothing to dispel the rumors. Now it had become open hate, and killing her was mentioned casually.

Berthe shifted her basket. Despite her tiredness, she had refused to let Mme. la Motte carry it, knowing its disproportionate weight. But she did lean willingly on the stout arm that was still round her.

Spread out in the drizzling haze before them was the city of Versailles, surrounded by dim green forests and muted verdurous meadows. The column slowed to a stop. Malliard arranged the women into four rough columns, putting all the cannon in the rear, "as befitting a peaceable deputation." Then they set forth through the row of dripping elms. At crafty Malliard's request, they struck up the national anthem, "Henri Quatre:"

> "Long live Henry IV
> Long live this valiant king
> This fourfold devil
> With the three talents
> Of drinking, fighting
> And womanizing

Let us sing the refrain
That we will sing in a thousand years:
May God maintain
His descendants in peace
Until we take the moon with our teeth

Long live France
Long live king Henry
To Reims we dance
Singing as they do in Paris
Long live France
Long live king Henry!"

Berthe sensed the singers' ironical tone — *'Down with the King' is what they are really saying!* From all sides the lower classes of Versailles thronged the columns, cheering the vast concourse of Parisian women.

As they approached the *Salle des Menus* (the meeting place of the Constituent Assembly), they could see the palace and pleasure-houses of the royal family and the rows of drenched guards.

Mme. la Motte put her lips close to Berthe's ear. "My carriage is waiting on a side-street near the Assembly room," she whispered. "Slip out of the crowd with me when there is a chance."

The vast multitude of bedraggled, sodden women beset the *Salle des Menus*. The tall "captain" over Berthe and Madame la Motte left them and pushed forward towards the door.

"Now!" whispered Mme. la Motte. Letting go of Berthe's arm, she picked up her muddy, trailing silk skirts and slipped through the crowd. When the marquise glanced back, Berthe, chestnut hair streaking her face, was right on her heels, hope giving wings to her bruised, tired feet and lighting her green eyes.

The mass of women, their loose formation breaking apart, pushed forward, each striving to enter the Constituent Assembly. Malliard and a few others held them back, causing the whole mob to swirl back and forth. Mme. la Motte heard the voices of Monsieur Malliard and a few women at the doors, shouting directions and trying to select a small deputation among the thousands to present their petition to the Assembly. She tucked her skirts more firmly over her arm and darted through a fleeting gap, sodden shoes flopping painfully with each step.

She did not notice the gap close behind her. Berthe was trapped in the great throng of shoving, shouting humanity.

The side street Mme. la Motte turned into was equally choked, but she managed at last to break through. Down a quiet little alley, she glimpsed her coach. Now that the immediate danger was over, she stumbled with fatigue. Her carefully-coiffured mound of dark curls had undone, and soppy locks fell about her face. "Oh dear—of all things—what a—"

Seeing his mistress, the coachman jumped off his box and hastened forward. His face was a picture—he had never seen his mistress like this: never, in all his years as servitor! From the way she clung to his arm he knew she was about to faint.

Mme. la Motte put a brown, misshapen shoe on the step, then paused to look back. "Where is my companion?" Worry creased her face.

"Your companion, Madame?" The man lifted her into the dry and inviting interior.

Mme. la Motte turned as if to get out again. "She is not here!" she exclaimed in blank dismay. "She is caught in the crowd—oh, me!"

"Your companion, Madame?" the coachman asked again, making no move to let her out of the coach. *Has this adventure slightly unhinged her reason?* he wondered.

"Berthe, the De Coquiel di le Mercier's *maid-de-chambe,*" Madame la Motte said, "She was to follow me here—oh, we must find her! She was so exhausted—"

"If you go back, you might be seized again, Madame," the coachman protested. "Let me take you home and then I shall come back for her, if you desire—"

"She may be coming—drive as close as you dare now, Gilles," his mistress commanded.

The man would have remonstrated, but her determined look stopped his mouth. He quickly drew the red velvet curtains and shut the gilded door. The carriage began to move.

Mme. la Motte collapsed into the cushioned seats. She felt bitterly sorry that she had not double-checked Berthe's progress. *She may not have seen me turn into the side street,* she thought, *and so probably does not know where to go, after losing sight of me....poor thing! I must rescue her....*

Several different approaches to the milling swarm of wild women failed to disclose any sign of Berthe. When those on the fringes began to cast dark glances at the coach and shake their weapons, Mme. la Motte was forced to admit that they must turn for home. "But you shall come back to look for her!"

Fifteen minutes later found the marquise swathed in a loose warm robe in her room. Despite the attempts of her maid to dry her at the fire, rub her cold feet, and get her a cup of hot tea, Madame la Motte insisted on writing a missive before doing anything else. Her quill moved quickly over the paper.

Dear Felicienne,　　　　　　　　　　　*late afternoon 5 October 1789*
　　I am writing just a few Lines to tell you that your maid Berthe was Accompanying the mob of women, Possibly against her Will. They are here in Versailles now at the National Constituent Assembly. I was seperat'd from her unhappily but have sent Gilles back to Look for her; I fear it may be Impossible for there are something like Seven or Eight Thousand women there. What they shall do I know not – I pray for the safety of the King and Queen.
　　I shall Write when I receive News of her; God be pleased to allow us to find her.
　　I am, yours faithfully,
　　Susanne la Motte

Folding and sealing the note, she refused even Elisabeth's ministrations until the missive had been dispatched by messenger to Paris, with all possible speed. Then she sank back in the depths of a large stuffed chair.

When the manservant returned almost an hour later, he had no news of Berthe. He had even approached on foot, thinking to get closer that way, but had not caught even a glimpse of a maid with red-brown hair. "The guards are threatening the demonstrators, and riding through them to get them to disperse, but they merely close up again and cry 'Bread! Bread!' and such like," he finished.

"Oh, we must do something!" Madame la Motte said earnestly. "She was utterly spent!...We must keep a watch out for her..."

~*~*~

Just as Madame la Motte darted through the gap in the crowd, Berthe was jostled back by a sturdy Amazon and, unbalanced by the basket, fell. By the time she regained her feet the marquise's dark brown hat was the only thing she could see above the tossing heads and waving arms. She pressed after it with a haste born of desperation. *If I lose her, I shan't escape!*

But she could hardly make headway and found herself being swept along towards the doors by the women around her. In vain she pushed, trying again and again to break out after that now invisible brown hat.

Several minutes later she recognized a few faces, and realized she was back among her "regiment"—somehow she must have swerved back that way in the confusion, or they had been swept towards her. A wall loomed behind them, gray and dripping in the sullen drizzling rain. She was close to tears of frustration and exhaustion when her shoulder was suddenly seized, as if by talons. Berthe hardly needed to look up to know who it was—her tall "captain."

"Marshal together, wenches," the woman grated, "we must stay together—then we shall teach the Austrian a lesson, and gain bread for our families! You," she said, looking particularly at Berthe, "keep near me!" She glanced about. "Where is the other one—Madame high and mighty?"

Berthe kept silent, but thought sinkingly, *I only wish I knew!*

"Ah, well," the woman said. "I shall keep doubly sure of the rest of you!"

Berthe leaned against the wall, eyes closed, letting her whole body slump. But her fingers kept their convulsive grip on her basket.

"When will our Deputation return from the king?" asked a high, nasal voice.

"How can I tell?" was the hoarse answer. "May they come back soon, with a good answer—or else! I am not very patient."

"Neither am I," cackled the other.

Some time later, the twelve women of the deputation returned. "Life to the king and his House!" they shouted as they drew near the sodden mass of women. They told of their audience with the king, and the news passed from mouth to mouth throughout the throng.

"The king was gracious, and said he would ensure that provision will be sent to Paris, if possible, and that grain shall circulate freely," an excited women cried to Berthe and the women near her. "And when our spokesperson, Louison Chambray, was about to faint in the king's presence, he caught her in his arms—how well-disposed he is to us!"

Others, however, did not share such positive views.

"What are such promises of bread beyond mere words!" a lean-faced fishwife shouted. "I see no bread for my little ones!" She shook a thin arm, her wet sleeve flopping.

"*In his arms!* Shameless minx!" cried a broad-shouldered hussy in a faded red dress. "Is this the envoy we sent to represent us!"

"The traitress!" cried another. "Look at her fair, soft skin, while ours is rough with toil! To *la Lanterne!*"

The words were caught and repeated, in a kind of frenzy: "Traitress! Hang her!"

Berthe opened her eyes, and in horror beheld the crowd of women seizing the slim, fair figure of seventeen-year-old Louison. They dragged her, screaming and begging, to the nearest *Lanterne* (lamppost). A garter was drawn around her neck and fastened to the lamppost—Berthe turned away, aghast. *She did nothing wrong!* Berthe thought. *This is senseless, brutal....What kind of women are these? This cause, can it be right?*

A sudden clatter of hoofbeats and angry cries caused Berthe, huddled against the dripping wall, to look up again. Two mounted Bodyguards were galloping through the crowd. They swept up with incensed faces to where the women were about hang Louison. Cutting the rope with flashing swords, they drew her out of the indignant multitude—saving her from certain death.

She is saved! Berthe thought; *But by those whom I was told were our oppressors!* She closed her eyes again, still leaning against the wall, but her thoughts had taken a new turn towards those who, in the pamphlets, were painted in evil colors. And where did this late scene place the masses, whom before looked she had so favored? And what of Mme. la Motte, who had bravely helped her, though weak and exhausted herself?

She felt the weight of the gold *louis: To further these horrifying events? Non!*

~*~*~

Hours later, past eight-o'-clock that evening, Francis de Coquiel di le Mercier welcomed the adjournment of the session. Ever since the women arrived and Mounier (the president of the Constituent Assembly) left to go to the King with the deputation of twelve women, things had degenerated into chaos. The twelve women had returned hours before; but still Mounier did not return. The Vice-President, and even Mirabeau, failed to suppress the throngs of women and men which pressed into the *Salle-des-Menus*, loudly demanding bread.

They even forced the Assembly to decree that the price of bread would be fixed at eight *sous* for a half-quartern, and meat at six *sous* per pound. Francis shook his head. *Fixing the price will not solve our problem*, he thought. *If anything, it will acerbate it.*

Night was falling, Mounier had not yet come back, and no work could be done amidst the mob's cries for bread, so the delegates agreed to adjourn for the evening. Francis rose with most of the other delegates and began to file out, yawning and weary. Some deputies lingered, flirting shamelessly with the brazen women mingling among them.

Berthe's "captain" pushed, prodded, and by main force achieved her goal of entering the building with her charges. Pressed by the horde against a wall, Berthe gazed dully on the scene. Suddenly her pulse quickened. Over the heads in front she glimpsed a familiar face. Frozen, she looked again. Yes, it was her master, Francis! Her stomach lurched. *The basket! His money!* She shrank back among the unyielding women.

The exiting deputies were squeezing through a narrow path between the packed ranks of women. Suddenly one woman sank down, fainting, in front of a departing deputy. She was not a pretty sight— smeared with grime, with coarse graying hair falling loose over her gaunt shoulders. He stepped around her with a look of disgust, holding up his satin jacket skirts to prevent them from touching her.

There is my master, drawing near the woman.... Berthe could not help watching, fascinated. Francis bent down. Lifting the fallen woman gently, he glanced around for a protected area. In the press she would be trampled.

"Bring her here, Monsieur—there is room here," a woman called from the foot of the galleries. Francis carried over the still-insensible form, mud smearing his beautifully-embroidered silk waistcoat and jacket. *I doubt if it will come out,* Berthe thought. *One of his best coats! Ruined, yet he cares more for a shrunken old woman, one who supports all he stands against....*

Reaching the foot of the viewing-galleries, he laid her carefully down. Assisted by several rough Amazons, the old woman soon revived. Berthe could not hear what was said, but Francis pulled several coins out of his pocket and placed them in the woman's calloused palm. Her hand closed convulsively on them, her ill-favored, formerly hostile face melting into a look of amazed gratitude. With a bow as if to a lady, Francis turned and retraced his steps to the exit.

Berthe stared after him, new emotions heaving in her breast.

As Francis and the majority of deputies exited, more and more women crowded assertively into the chamber. Francis cast one glance back before stepping out into the wet darkness—the women were enacting a mocking parody of the Constituent Assembly.

~*~*~

Past midnight, the National Guard marched into Versailles from Paris. LaFayette accompanied them, their commander in title only. For hearing about the marching women, the National Guard had begun to breathe

227

threatenings against the king, demanding that LaFayette take them to aid the women. LaFayette refused, but they finally forced him to take them to Versailles.

In the palace, the marquis la Motte stood among the ministers and scattered courtiers who, with the king, awaited LaFayette's coming. *There is not a hopeful face among us,* Arnoul la Motte thought, *– if only the king could decide something! Decide to fly to Metz, or decide not to: but decide something, and show firmness of purpose! I know it is difficult; however...*

Three people were announced by the Usher, entering the room with respectful bows. LaFayette was first, with an expression of valorous sorrow. He advanced to the king. "I am come," he said, "to offer my head for the safety of his Majesty's."

Next spoke the two Municipals who accompanied him to state the wishes of Paris. They had four demands:

"First, that the honor of guarding the king's sacred person be conferred to the National Guards. Second, that provisions be got, if possible. Third, that the prisons, which are crowded with political delinquents, should have judges sent them."

The king nodded assent to all these—*What else can he do?* thought Arnoul la Motte—but his face changed slightly when he heard their fourth request.

"Fourth, *that it would please his Majesty to come and live in Paris.*"

The king hesitated, asking time for deliberation. This was granted, and the deputation retired.

Between arranging his recalcitrant troops and consulting with his officers, LaFayette was to get no sleep that night; and most of Versailles would have but broken slumbers, if they slept at all.

~*~*~

Berthe hardly heeded the news of the arrival of the National Guard; and even when LaFayette's deputation returned she was too tired to care. She had never been as wretched and exhausted in her entire sheltered life. Memories came, unbidden, of the many thoughtful kindnesses bestowed on her and the other servants by the De Coquiel di le Merciers. These new thoughts made her more miserable—was she not carrying money she had stolen from them?

Around her torches swirled in the deep blackness, shining on snatches of wet and ragged garments. People splashed through the muddy streets, their faces sullen and sinister in the orange, flickering glare. The brandished weapons—billhooks, pistols, knives on sticks, cudgels—did nothing to comfort her.

It was nearly three-o'-clock in the morning when the vast concourse of rabble began to disperse, seeking places to sleep. Berthe sloshed through the muddy dark after her "captain." She had a confused impression of a gothic tower and gray stone arches before sinking wordlessly into a corner of the church nave.

Pillowing her head on her precious basket, she was asleep almost immediately, despite her drenched, chilled clothes and the unyielding stone floor.

~*~*~

But sleep was a rare commodity that night. Only a few hours later—a little past five in the morning—Berthe found herself being shaken. Her sleep-heavy eyes opened to see her tall "captain" standing over her.

"Up, you slugabeds," she grated. "To the palace!"

Berthe groaned. "Up, I said," the woman shrilled. Releasing Berthe's arm, she reached to shove the basket from under Berthe's head.

Berthe was instantly awake. All her fears about the basket came back. She sat up jerkily, lifting the basket and setting it in her lap with amazing lightness. The other women were standing up around her, grumbling in tired voices and rubbing stiff limbs. She forced herself to rise and join them.

Berthe found herself tramping along through the bleak, cloudy morning gloom towards the palace. Her head ached from lack of sleep.

When they neared the palace, a large crowd of women and the dregs of Versailles and Paris were already gathered at the palace gates. They were in no good mood. Most garments were wrinkled, semi-damp, and shrunken from yesterday's wetting. Other than a few sausages and bread provided the night before by the Assembly's president Mounier, they had eaten nothing.

Even as Berthe and her group approached, the metal gate-fastenings gave way under the shaking of the multitude. With a great cry of victory, the mob surged forward into the Grand Court. Screaming in triumph, they shook their weapons menacingly at the few guards who showed themselves at the windows.

Berthe's "captain" hurried her group as close to the palace as she could. Right ahead of them was the bolted door leading to the innermost Court, the Court of Marble. Berthe longed to lean against the wall—her head was hurting, and her basket no lighter than yesterday. But she was given no time to rest. The multitude became more threatening, yelling curses and insults at the few visible Bodyguards.

Afraid for their lives, several Bodyguards fired. A man's arm was shattered: but worse, a youth, member of the Paris National Guard, was shot. He fell instantly, scattering the pavement with his brains. A howl arose from the mob.

"Here!" cried Berthe's "captain," motioning vengefully toward a nearby palace door. The rabid swarm rushed impetuously on it.

Within moments, the grate was forced open, and the living torrent swept in. The two sentries were trampled by the mad rush, then dispatched with a hundred pikes.

Berthe, to her horror, found herself swept along with the foremost. Past the gilded riches of the royalty, up the Grand Staircase.... Halfway up the stairs, she glanced down at the mob pouring in from below. Several other entrances had been forced. She hardly knew what she was doing— only her bruised fingers kept their fierce grip on her basket.

At the top of the stairs stood one of the Bodyguards— Miomandre de Sainte-Marie. Though the first pike-waving ranks had almost reached him, he stood immovable. Strong and unwavering, he pled with the angry press to disperse, even descending several steps towards the raging inferno. The shrill women rushed him, weapons upraised. Seizing his coat and belt and hauling him up bodily, his fellow-soldiers snatched him from instant death. Then they leapt into the room beyond and slammed and fastened the door—just in time.

But the mob was right behind them. The door held only moments before breaking open under their enraged blows. The Bodyguards fled once more—on through room after elegant room, each barricaded door only slightly slowing their ravenous, ragged pursuers. Berthe noticed how the rampaging women trampled everything in their path, no matter how costly or beautiful. What a sight—these wolf-like women on the heels of the well-trained male soldiers! But the Bodyguards seemed stricken with utter terror. What can a few do against so many?

Courageous Miomandre showed that even with such long odds, one brave man may do much. As his comrades fled apace and the onrushing flood roared towards the Queen's apartments, he turned back. Stationing himself before the Queen's door, he cried, "Save the Queen!" His alarm was just in time. Without that warning, the Queen would have been caught in her room and most likely slaughtered by the merciless she-beasts.

Berthe knew not how he appeared, but there he was, manful, resolute, and alone, guarding the Queen's door. Bethe could hardly believe such gallant dauntlessness. She screamed as the foremost women attacked him, but no one heard.

Already unnerved, the sight of his blood completely undid Berthe. The ferocious, maniacal faces swam before her eyes, and she fainted.

Too Late for Repentance?

9.

True repentance has as its constituent elements not only grief and hatred of sin,
but also an apprehension of the mercy of God in Christ.
It hates the sin, and not simply the penalty;
and it hates the sin most of all because it has discovered God's love.
— William Mackergo Taylor

When Berthe came to, she found herself lying on a polished floor, all alone.

Her eyes dimly focused on the ceiling above. A large circular painting caught her attention. In it, figures of men and women crouched within a grand tent. Their expressions of worry and distress echoed Berthe's own thoughts. Standing at the door of the tent looking in was a muscled man with golden helmet and breastplate.

The mural was a fanciful depiction of Alexander the Great before his captives, the family of King Darius. Elaborate raised mouldwork surrounded it, shining with gilding. Other paintings filled the rest of the ceiling.

She gazed at it all with hazy disquietude. *Where am I?* she thought. *I do not recognize…so opulent….* Her mind wandered back to the few hours of sleep in the church: *This…not a church; rather like (ah, but costlier than) a noble's house — Oh! The Queen! They are going to murder her!*

With that remembrance, all that had happened flooded into her mind. A new resolution was forming; *I will not side with these bloodthirsty wretches, these 'patriots,'* she thought. *From now on, I will do what is right….*

She sat shakily up, then saw that she was not alone. From somewhere ahead she heard a dull, confused roaring, then a thundering sound as if the mob was battering at some other door. But near her in a pool of blood lay Miomandre de Sainte-Marie, slashed and fractured. She cast a glance full of honor on him. *There was a true man,* she thought, and felt like weeping. *He died a noble death.*

She was standing up cautiously when his head moved. Her eyes widened. Dropping her basket, she darted forward. Though he had been grievously wounded and left for dead, he was still alive!

His eyes met hers, and she hastened to say, "I shall not hurt you —" She bent over him, already tearing a wide strip from the cleanest portion of her petticoat.

Blood was streaming from a deep wound on his brow. Berthe concentrated on it first. Taking the strip of cloth, she lifted his head slightly to pass it underneath, then bound it tightly. Her efforts were unskilled yet gentle. She was tearing off more of her petticoat when he spoke faintly.

"I must join my regiment."

With Berthe's help he managed to get up on his hands and knees, but no further. The sweat on his ashen, bleeding brow showed the agony the simplest movement cost him, but not a sound escaped his lips.

Inch by inch, the soldier began to crawl towards the faint noise up ahead. Berthe tried to assist him, but that only added to his pain. Seeing this, she picked up her basket, accompanying him slowly.

As the noise ahead grew louder, he spoke. "You must not come with me," he said painfully, with labored breath. "Too much danger. Leave me."

Berthe protested. "No, no, Monsieur!"

"If you insist," he said, with a pale face, "go — find the Bodyguards —"

With a nod, Berthe quickened her steps towards the tumult ahead. She came upon the hindmost ranks of the foaming mob before she realized it, and almost fell among them. They were all pressing forward, the foremost women beating on a closed door. From within the portal came a hubbub of a different sort — to Berthe, it sounded as if the Bodyguards (for so she guessed were the occupants) were piling chairs and furniture against it.

But why did these women, after striking down M. de Sainte-Marie, not burst into the Queen's room? Berthe wondered. *Were they somehow distracted by his brave stand? Or by something else?* She felt truly grateful that the mob had turned to seek other prey.

She asked a wraith-like woman, "Are the Bodyguards in there?"

"We chased them in," the woman laughed savagely. "The door will not hold long; then we will taste of their blood!"

Berthe shuddered involuntarily, but as her eyes sought the door, she was forced to acknowledge the truth of the woman's remark. *Oh, can nothing be done to save the soldiers? Could not they act like brave M. Miomandre?*

she thought. *But now to get back to him — yet how shall he reach his comrades? The mob will finish their work....*

Women, laden with plunder, were coming into the large chamber. It took her some time to press through them and slip back down the hallway towards where she had left M. Miomandre. She kept glancing back to make sure she was not followed. Indeed, several of the women had noticed her go, and one called out with a hoarse cackle, "We've taken care of the carryables — there's nowt left for you!" But to Berthe's relief, the hag turned away and paid her no further attention.

Lengthening her steps, Berthe almost tripped on her trailing petticoat. Setting down her basket, she paused long enough to tear off the strip completely.

When she reached the place where Miomandre had been, he was nowhere in sight. Her heart grew cold. *What has happened? Where has he gone? Have they taken him? But where?*

A rough gust of women's voices burst from the adjacent hall, coming closer. Berthe fled. She hurried down another hallway, turned several corners, then back-tracked to another branching hall and stepped quickly down it. Its gilded, richly decorated walls and expensive furnishings were an incongruous setting for a bloodthirsty, wolf-faced mob.

Several more frantic windings seemed equally fruitless. Then her eager green eyes flashed upon movement at the end of one corridor. An open door — two soldiers, half-dragging another. The prone figure was bloody, and as she neared she knew it: M. de Sainte-Marie. Her heart gave a leap of gladness. These were his friends — he would be safe! She redoubled her pace, but as she did so they looked up. One started; the other gave an inarticulate cry. Heaving Miomandre the rest of the way in, he slammed the door shut.

They think I am one of the mob, Berthe thought bitterly. *They will not believe my bare word.* Checking her pace, she stood irresolute. *What should I do? Which way leads out? Will I be seized as one of the mob?...I wonder — can I set out for Paris?* A wave of tiredness swept over her. Her legs trembled, and her aching arms protested.

She turned down the hall and doggedly retraced her steps. She had almost reached the swarming riffraff, still trying to break in to the Bodyguards, when above the cries and *thud-crack* against the door she heard the measured quick-march of many feet. A host of shrill yells and angry shrieks erupted — sounds of an altercation. The noise of the strife swelled — then started to fade away.

Berthe peeked around the corner and saw a great mass of soldiers swarming where the rabble had been minutes before. One man was shouting through the still-closed portal, "We are the *Centre Grenadiers*, the old *Gardes Francaises*! Open to us, Messieurs of the *Garde-du-Corps*; we have not forgotten how you saved us at Fontenoy!"

These were the men, Berthe thought wryly, *who marched out from Paris, saying their aim was to exterminate the* Garde-du-Corps, *and forcing LaFayette to lead them! Now, they are their deliverers….* She was not given long to ponder the changeableness of human nature. Even as the door opened and comrade embraced comrade in joyful relief, the officer began ordering the *Centre Grenadiers* to clear the palace of the mob.

Berthe knew not what to do. A detachment was already starting down the hall towards her. One voice reached her, "T'will be a pleasure to clear out these hoydens!"

"Here is one," another shouted, catching sight of Berthe.

"Truly, I am not," she cried, shrinking against the wall. She felt their eyes studying her muddy, torn clothing and knew they would not believe her.

"Out with you!" cried their officer. Firmly but gently, seeing her despairing face, they expelled Berthe, still helplessly protesting, into the multitude which seethed and screeched in the court outside the palace. She heard the door close and the bolts slide to.

Berthe stood silent for some minutes. The open ground was filled with women and men, all disappointed of prey but still eager for spoils and blood. A steady marching line in the distance heralded the arrival of LaFayette with troops, and behind in the palace could be heard the steady progress of the *Centre Grenadiers*, ousting the rioters.

Nearby a woman was carrying something atop a long pike. Berthe glanced up, then wished she hadn't. Atop the pike was the bloody head of one of the sentries who had been slain at the door. A moment later, another pike appeared, with the head of his companion. Women danced and sang jubilantly around them.

Berthe had had enough. She pushed her way through the crowd blindly. All she wanted was to get away from these brutal, horrid women. She was fleeing—where, she no longer cared.

As she left the cobbled courtyard and stepped ankle-deep in the wet grass, a magnificent riderless horse thundered past, the ground trembling under his feet. Startled, she looked to where he had come. A hundred yards off, a scruffy, ill-favored man was picking himself sulkily off the turf. Behind him, other horses from the Royal Stud dashed about.

Even as Berthe watched, several kicked up their heels, and a few other rascally would-be riders flew up, to land with a thud. Bucking and cavorting, the horses disappeared over the grass. Berthe half-smiled—it was the nearest to a smile she had felt in a long time. *They thought they would take some horses from His Majesty's stud, did they not?* she thought. *The harebrained oafs! Serves them right!*

She stumbled on, then her better sense awoke and she realized she was foolish to wander aimlessly. *The best thing would be to get some rest—just a few hours—then walk home.*

An empty shed loomed—in sight of the palace and the mob, but not too close. She shambled, swaying, to it, and sank onto the earthen floor, prying her fingers from their hold. Even in her tiredness she remembered to draw her basket close and throw the end of her soiled skirt over it.

In minutes she was fast asleep, heedless of the rabble which swarmed and shrilled outside of the palace, demanding that their fourth clause be complied with—that of having the King and Queen come to live in Paris.

~*~*~

The knock was muffled.

"Come in," answered a soft female voice.

A coachman stepped quietly to the great canopied bed. Propped up by pillows lay Madame Susanne la Motte. Her face was flushed and feverish, but her eyes were bright and clear. He bowed; once to her, and once to Elisabeth, who was sitting beside the bed.

"Any news, Gilles?" the marquise asked.

"None, Madame." Seeing how his mistress' face fell, he hastened to add, "We have been out since early this morning, Madame—but none of us have seen her. I myself, Madame, saw a likely-looking wench—she had reddish hair, at least—but she said her name was Cecile Laurent, and was a—" his voice lowered, embarrassed, "—a lady of the night."

"Oh, I had so hoped we could find her," Madame la Motte said, disappointment written on her face. "I thank you, Gilles, for your faithful efforts. We have received news that the King has agreed to live in Paris—I want you out watching for her as the procession passes."

"Yes, Madame. Any other orders?"

"Send Jules up."

He bowed respectfully and left the room. Madame la Motte sat up, beckoning to her daughter. "My writing desk, Elisabeth—I must send to Felicienne."

Elisabeth's small fingers soon brought the carved rosewood "desk." It had a slanted top for writing on, the compartment beneath holding quills, ink, wax, seal, and paper in neat wood partitions. Madame la Motte took it quickly and began to write.

> *My dear Felicienne,*   *late morning October 6th 1789*
> *I am Hurried to get this to you excuse my not giving full Particulars. My men have been out Search'g for Berthe with no sign but I Believe She is still here. The News is that the King (may God protect him!) has givn in to the Mob and will leave for Paris with them at One o' clock. I Fear he will be virtually a Prisoner there. The Mob almost Murdered the Queen and evn with LaFayette's troops are still very powerful I fear for the results of Giving in to their Wishes. It will make them more Impudent and Defiant.*
>
> *Francis may have Told you Already but the National Constituent Assembly has declared they are Moving to Paris with the King. 'Twill be very Pleasant for you, I know.*
>
> *I expect Berthe will be with the procession so She may be home this Evening. I pray that such will be the case. Do let me Know. I have a Fever from my Wetting — I hope She is not ill.*
> *Yours, as always,*
> *Susanne la Motte*

~*~*~

Berthe slept soundly for some hours, but was roused by a growing rumble. Sunlight streamed through a crack in the rough boards near her head. Her empty stomach felt hollow. Every bone seemed to ache, and she still felt desperately tired. Outside echoed the tread of many feet and hoarse cries of jubilation. She realized a vast multitude was swarming past her retreat. Rising stiffly, she picked up her precious, heavy basket and peered out through the crack in the door.

Wild women streamed past, emblazoned with tricolor ribbons and bearing pikes, shouting and hurrahing. One young, brazen woman, with a great swath of tricolor — white, red, and blue — wrapped round her wrinkled bodice as a sash, cried vehemently, "To Paris! Behold your success, ye conquering women!"

Hearing this, Berthe slipped from the shed. *If they are going to Paris, I will accompany them. 'Twill afford a sort of protection on the journey….*

She looked along the line and realized she could not see its beginning. Far in the distance, lifted up by a ridge of earth, she saw the National troops and artillery. Swarming behind and among them were the scum of Paris and Versailles, on foot or mounted on cannons or carts. Closer to her in the long line were several hackney coaches, loaded with jubilant, uncouth figures, bread on their pikes. Rumbling along were fifty cart-loads of wheat for the people of Paris, taken from the Versailles storehouses.

On either side, pressing in on the unwieldy column, were dense swarms of people from the country round. Berthe slopped through the mud with the exultant others. No joy was in her heart—it felt as heavy as the basket of gold *louis* she was carrying.

"You wear no tricolor," muttered a woman, giving Berthe a suspicious glance. "A filthy Royalist, hey?"

Berthe ducked back from the unfriendly eyes directed towards her and managed to retire further in the line. She still did not feel safe, so as they passed a grimy cluster of outlying dwellings she ducked out of line and into a doorway, feeling in her pockets for any ribbon. Unlike the march to Versailles, there was no constraint on her leaving the line now—no one cared a whit now to keep up the appearance of being protesting housewives.

With sluggish but steadfast purpose the procession streamed on, splashing and slipping in the thick mud of the road. Before her plodded a miserable group of the *Garde-du Corps*, the Bodyguards—they looked not only beaten but utterly shamed as they passed by hanging their heads. The press was so thick after them that Berthe was shoved against the building. Berthe's hand came out of her pockets for the fifth time with only some green ribbon. She shrugged with some relief—*I do not want to wear their accursed colors, anyway*. Stepping out, she joined the column once more.

Ahead she could just barely see the gilt coach of the King. She craned her neck to see behind—an outstretched train of carriages, buzzing floods of rabble, and silent divisions of marching soldiers met her eyes. She could not see the end of the column—it has been estimated at twenty thousand.

Exulting women pressed around the Royal carriage. Shrilling shouting a rough song, they directed suggestive gestures towards the King's carriage. "Courage friends!" the women sang, pointing derisively with their rough weapons. "We shall not want bread now; we are bringing you the Baker, the Bakeress, and Baker's Boy!"

Berthe tripped and half-fell in the sticky mud. A rough cart laden with Amazons was creeping by. Berthe cast a longing glance upward, and a thin girl saw her.

"There is room here," the young woman said, extending a frail hand.

The cart lurched and slowed over a pothole. Berthe, seizing the sideboard, exerted all her strength and managed to pull herself into it. She slumped against the low side, bone-weary.

A mile, then two, crawled by, seemingly begrudging any forward progress. The afternoon sun was speedily dropping towards the horizon, as if to shut out the disgraceful sight. Berthe put her head in her hands and wished for Paris—wished for Charlot's round face, Olivie's dancing smiles, her mistresses' gentle commands—for even the presumptuous Virginie.

The gold in the basket pressing down on her lap made her worse than miserable. *Not only did I plan to run away, but—but I took their money—I stole—to pay for these kind of doings!* she moaned inwardly. *Stole it, from my master! From my good—and kind—and wise—* Her shoulders shook with fierce sobs, but not a sound escaped her lips. *Oh, woe is me! What can I do? I can't go back….*

Denis wanted this money, he wanted it; but I shall not give it to him. She remembered his distracted words of love and how his eyes riveted on the basket in their nocturnal interview. *Did—did he care for me at all? Was it only a ruse?*

Hours passed, and darkness closed around the slow-moving procession. One cannot cry forever. For the last part of the jolting, weary ride Berthe sat silent and very still, looking forward into the blackness. She felt as though nothing worse could ever happen. There was only a tired, leaden resignation. *I must return this; I see it now. They will dismiss me, of course….It is but right….after what I have done….If only I could just go to some quiet place and die!—but not before I give back the gold….I must—I must give the gold back…the gold….* Her dull despair felt a shade lighter with that resolution.

After another hour a smear of light could be seen shining up into the cloudy heavens above—Paris, almost every house illuminated with rejoicing.

The light grew larger. Paris loomed ahead. Throngs of shouting people swarmed round the columns, lighting the way with torches and impeding the already-slow progress.

There was a long pause at the barriers—these had been renewed and manned by LaFayette as part of his efforts to quell insurrection. The delay was a long oration which Mayor Bailly delivered to the King. At last, they were moving again.

239

As they crept under the arching city gate and began to pass through the flushed, triumphant double line of people lining the streets, a dark-haired, lean man shook his fist at the King's coach, shouting imprecations. Though the man only vaguely looked like Denis, Berthe's numbed, fatalistic mood snapped awake with a sense of terror. *He will be looking for me – will know I am gone, will guess I was with the marchers –* Berthe had hardly prayed before, but now she bowed her head, hands clenching the basket till they turned white; *Oh, if only I can complete my last duty – return this gold – if he sees me, he will get it, he will....after, I care not, but – oh, he cannot get it! Oh – help,* mon Dieu! *Only this once!*

She slipped down lower in the cart, crouching behind several women. Half-standing and waving their weapons victoriously, they made a fair screen. She was still afraid of being spotted, and crushed her once-dapper hat deep over her head until its large brim hung limply over her eyes.

The equally-spaced *lanternes* shed their greasy light on besotted, shouting humanity and flared on the King and Queen whom they had conquered. Berthe shuddered at the vile ruffians and degraded women who seemed to have crept out of foul holes to revel in bestial glee. She thought she saw Denis' keen face, and ducked still lower, keeping her eyes down. Surely he would be searching for her.

A chill took her, and it was more than ten minutes before she gathered the courage to glance timidly up. She knew his power over her, and trembled with relief when she saw only unfamiliar faces. He was nowhere in sight.

It was nearing ten o' clock when the whole procession wound as much of itself as it could into the square in front of its destination, the *Hotel-de-Ville.*

Berthe slid off the cart. As the King and Queen entered the Town Hall with the Mayor, she began to shove her way through the packed mass of exultant spectators. She cared not to hear what the King would say: her one consuming thought now was to return the gold to the De Coquiel di le Merciers. About what would happen afterwards she dared not think.

The streets for blocks round swarmed with ragged, rejoicing people. Many times Berthe was brought to a breathless halt for several minutes before she could find a gap in the crowd and hasten forward. She pressed on. Tottering with fatigue, she was now constantly slipping on the wet, muddy cobbles.

At last she turned with a great sigh into the De Coquiel di le Merciers' wide avenue. Usually empty at this late hour, several people were about. From a brightly-lit house just ahead, a liveried manservant stepped out, clutching a message. He walked briskly down the street towards Berthe, muttering something under his breath about the weather and the lateness of the hour. Nearing Berthe, he glanced at her, almost passed by, then checked himself and came back to her side.

Berthe would normally have been mortified to be seen in such a dirty, shabby state, but she was past caring. She merely looked dully at him as he said,

"Berthe Durand! They have been searching for you — where, prithee, have you been?" He courteously offered his arm and Berthe took it, taking care to keep her basket away from him and under the sagging shelter of her stained white shawl.

"Versailles," she answered shortly.

"Ah — with the 'march of the women!' A grand and glorious victory you have won for us!" he said.

"Nothing grand *or* glorious about it," Berthe snapped.

They were almost at her master's house. As Berthe shot a fearful glance down the street, her eye caught a familiar figure in an alley. *Denis!* she thought in terror. At that instant he saw her, and rushed rapidly across. In a moment he would be beside her, reaching for the basket....

In Berthe's panic, her reflexes took over. Grasping her conductor's arm more firmly, she threw herself backwards. He was caught utterly off guard and swung round between her and Denis, throwing his arms out. She took to her heels, darting down the alley to the servant's door. Behind her she heard a collision and a volley of curses — then a lean figure with long black hair sprinted around the corner after her.

Berthe uttered a shriek, fumbling with the door handle. Too late she realized that it would be locked. The house was dark — a sign that everyone was asleep. Despair wrenched her very soul. All was lost.

Ça Ira — It'll be Fine

10.

If you have sinned, do not lie down without repentance;
for the want of repentance after one has sinned
makes the heart yet harder and harder.
— John Bunyan

D esperately Berthe twisted the brass door knob. Denis was racing up to her. His eyes shone in the faint lamplight. He was already reaching for the basket. With another scream, Berthe tugged at the knob. She was now sure it was locked and her case hopeless.

At that instant the door flew open in her nervous grasp. Berthe shot in. The door shut with a *crack* and was bolted as quickly behind her. By the light of a candle, she saw the placid face of Marcel Martin.

"We were told to keep watch for you," he said in his quiet way. "Though we did not expect you to come so urgently."

"Denis," Berthe gasped, leaning against the wall. Marcel stood watching her intently.

A candle flared in the passageway, and Madame Felicienne appeared. "My dear Berthe, you made it home! We have been so distressed for you! — Marcel, she is fainting with tiredness: help me take her to her room."

Berthe submitted to being led upstairs and sank on her bed, half-sitting against the headboard. Felicienne sent Marcel for hot water, then turned to her. Berthe had hardly noticed her mistress' expression in the dark passageway, but now she warily studied her face. It was quiet and loving, full of tenderness. Berthe knew she deserved none of it, and shrank away as her mistress approached.

"Let me help you into some clean, dry things, Berthe," she said, "then you must rest."

Berthe pushed away the fair, gentle hands that were beginning to unfasten her shawl. With the last remnant of her will, she sat up. "You must not treat me so, Madame —" she said stiffly, her green eyes brimming,

242

"—take this, and send me away." She lifted the basket she still gripped tightly.

"You are overwrought, Berthe," Felicienne said. Then, as Berthe's trembling arms still held out the basket, she reached out and took it. It dipped suddenly—she had not expected such weight.

Berthe was sobbing now. "Send me away," she choked, "I did it— Denis told me to—your gold—stole it—supposed to meet Denis—I was caught by the mob—" She lifted a tear-streaked face. "I know I did wickedly—I am so sorry now for what I have done! Madame, but it is too horrible; send me away—" In Berthe's mind flashed a picture of Denis' face as the door closed. She burst out, "Denis will make me pay…"

Marcel appeared with a maid and hot water, but Felicienne signed them to wait outside. He closed the door.

"My dear Berthe," she said, "you are repentant for what you have done. You have my full forgiveness." She smiled. "Come, let me help you into your nightgown."

Berthe covered her face with her hands. "You are too good—too good," she murmured between her fingers. She shrank from letting her mistress perform the menial task of helping her undress: "Madame, do not serve me!" But her mistress continued, and Berthe was too exhausted to protest further. She sat in a daze, taking in everything: the loving care in her mistresses' movements, the unthinking humility. If she had had any strength left, Berthe would have cried. As it was, she always said afterwards that she learned more about loving, selfless service in those few minutes than in all of her life.

As Felicienne finished tying Berthe's nightgown and turned back the coverlets, the whole story came out. Berthe told of her rebellious attitude, her support of the "patriot" cause (all of which was hardly a surprise to Felicienne), how Denis had poisoned her thoughts, then how she had begun to doubt—how her eyes had been opened and she had begun to despise the cause she once espoused.

"Madame la Motte is an angel," Berthe said.

"She is a lovely Christian woman," the marquise replied.

"She was an angel to me," Berthe said simply. Her eyes met Felicienne's green ones with a flash of bewildered passion. "I cannot understand—how *can* you forgive me?"

Felicienne pulled the covers up and tucked her in. "'Be ye courteous one to another, and tender hearted, freely forgiving one another, even as God for Christ's sake, freely forgave you,'" she quoted. "I have been forgiven so much by my Lord—shall I not forgive you, my dear, repentant Berthe?" Her face glowed as she continued, "I have been asking God to open your eyes, Berthe—He has answered my prayer!" She smiled down into the weary face on the pillow. "Now, try to get some rest. Sleep as long as you need."

Out in the hall, Felicienne told the story to Marcel.

What a Providential occurrence, she marveled to herself. *This would have been such a blow! For quite some time, Francis has been collecting all the money he could spare, meaning to send the coins overseas, but has been so occupied of late.... It traveled so far, and with such a company of ruffians! Praise God for guarding it, and also for changing Berthe's heart!* In her bedroom the marquise de Coquiel di le Mercier knelt and poured out her thanks to her Heavenly Father.

~*~*~

Fall whirled past, crammed with vague rumors and alarms. However, as a whole, the lower classes of Paris were satisfied at the accomplishment of their women and seemed content to rest on their laurels.

Others found the "march of the women," as it was called, a disturbing omen. Immediately after, Mounier, the Constituent Assembly's president, pled indisposition and fled the country. At the same time hordes of other deputies, mainly Royalists, left the Assembly also. Amazingly, by late Fall *one-third* of the Assembly had retired to their estates or gone overseas. The remaining members preferred to straddle the fence between pro-king and pro-revolution.

For weeks after the march of the women, Berthe shrank from leaving the house—and her fears were justified by reports from the servants. Many had glimpsed Denis' lean figure lurking in nearby alleys, watching the house. One kitchen wench out on business was stopped by him and bribed to carry a small note to Berthe—but brought the missive straight to her mistress. Felicienne passed it to Berthe, but the latter, shivering, refused to read it. She tore it to fine shreds and tossed them into the fire. Then Berthe wrote an icy note, telling Denis she had repented of their "wicked scheme" and "desired never to see his deceiving face again." The kitchen girl delivered it to Denis. Alternately brooding and raging, he kept up his surveillance for several more weeks. He tried to send another note, but it was returned unopened. At last, bitter with the failure of his scheme, he gave up the fruitless watch.

The financial crisis of France grew in intensity. Tallyrand, the irreligious Bishop of Atun, proposed that the government seize all land belonging to the clergy. In early November, the Constituent Assembly made this a law. The seized land was used to back a release of currency called *assignats*. In six months, those *assignats* were exhausted. More and more were printed with nothing to back them, setting the stage for rocketing inflation and later collapse.

The upheaval for the clergy did not stop there. The long-growing atheism of the French was finally exploding into action. By February 1790, the Assembly abolished all monastic vows and dissolved all religious orders.

By mid-Spring 1790, clubs were arising in swarms. The Breton Club already had a large popular presence. It was now meeting in the newly-empty monastery of the Jacobins, from which it would later receive the name "Jacobin Club." It seemed as if every Parisian was joining or forming clubs. Swaggering, Radical Danton was a towering figure in the Cordeliers Club, a rabid offshoot of the Jacobins. The club's motto: "*Liberté, égalité, fraternité.*" On the other side of the coin was the conservative spur of the Jacobins, to which LaFayette belonged; these called themselves the "Club of 1789, Friends of the Monarchic Constitution:" later, they were dubbed the Feuillans Club, after the convent where they met.

Despite the activity, the period from Winter 1789 to Summer 1790 was a peaceful lull compared to the previous two years, and a welcome one for many. Madame la Motte had quickly recovered from the effects of the forced Amazonian march—from her beaming health, one could hardly tell it had taken place. And Berthe was a changed woman—Denis, grinding his teeth, would have said it was for the worse, but most of her acquaintances knew it was for the better.

It was now July 12, 1790. Adele's willowy figure emerged from a darkened room of the Du Chemin's home, her face quiet and sad. For while Madame la Motte had recovered her health, Madame du Chemin, never in robust health, had begun to fail. *She is no better today,* Adele thought sadly, passing a gilt-framed painting in the hall. Madame du Chemin's weak heart had taken a turn for the worse in January. Despite care and rest, she was sinking. Adele felt her eyes fill as she thought of Madame du Chemin's serene inner felicity. *An example she is—never complaining, always focused on Christ....* Adele thought of her own daily temptations to be selfish, and resolved with God's help to live more like this dear, suffering saint.

As she paced quietly down the ornate hall her mind went back to old times, when the Du Chemins had stayed with them and Madame du Chemin had become like an aunt. Adele, hazel eyes dreamy, remembered the lovely talks in the "folly" at their chateau.

In the entranceway, the Du Chemin's doorman bowed profoundly, opening the door for her. She stepped through with a grateful smile. The outside sun was pleasant, the summer air warm on her uplifted face.

Seeing Adele, her coachman leapt off his seat. With a flourish he held the coach door open. Adele wondered at the change that had come over the servants in seven months. ...*I think it is due to Berthe. Ever since the march of the women, she has been different. Her new attitude has affected many of the servants for good.*

She was about to step into the coach when a striking bay horse reined up behind her carriage and a tall figure swung lightly off its back. "Adele! What an unexpected pleasure!"

"I am delighted to see you, Tristan!" Adele's eyes met his with a shared sparkle of pleasure.

Handing his reins to a lackey in one swift movement, he advanced towards her, pulling off his riding gloves. His sword swung gallantly at his side as he removed his hat and bowed.

"I was in to see your mother," Adele said softly.

"She makes no progress," he answered, his eyes on her face.

"I know," Adele's eyes filled, and she turned her head away towards the street beyond. Both of them remembered the doctor's words: "I do not expect her to live more than a few months, marquis."

Several urchins came running down the street with roistering shouts and cat-calls. A troop of girls followed, bedecked with fluttering blue, white, and red ribbons and waving green boughs. A motley group of citizens came after with shouldered shovels, singing in hoarse, unmelodious voices:

> "*Ah ! ça ira, ça ira, ça ira*
> The people on this day repeat over and over,
> *Ah ! It'll be fine, It'll be fine, It'll be fine*
> In spite of the mutineers everything shall succeed.
> Our enemies, confounded, stay petrified
> And we shall sing Alleluia
> *Ah ! It'll be fine, It'll be fine, It'll be fine...*"

Adele drew her eyes from the dancing maidens and zealous marchers frowning toward her carriage, and looked at Tristan. "That song is quite in vogue."

"Even more so at the diggings for the Fete de la Federation, Adele," he answered. "I was just there; I fancy these are proceeding thither. It is the song *du jour*—everyone and his brother is singing it as he wields his shovel or barrow, digging the tiered seats and arena for this upcoming event of national rejoicing."

"Will it be finished in time, you think?"

"Yes; there are something like a hundred thousand volunteers working on it. It should be done by the fourteenth—two days away."

"I suppose you will be there?" Adele asked. "Father has arranged for us to sit with the De Lobels; I believe the Du Sauchoys will also attend with us."

"It depends on my mother's health," he answered gravely.

"Father desires us to attend this event in our nation's history. I understand that many throughout France pin their hopes of national unity and peace upon it."

"Why they think that a grand display and a simultaneous swearing of fealty to the nation will bring in everlasting felicity is beyond me," Tristan remarked wryly. "But I must not detain you. I am glad we met. *Au revoir*, Adele!" He stepped with her to the carriage to hand her in.

"*Au revoir*, Tristan." Adele returned his warm smile.

Her coach had to proceed slowly behind the marchers, and she listened to the singing:

> "According to the precepts of the Gospel
> Of the lawmaker everything shall be accomplished
> The one who puts on airs shall be brought down
> The one who is humble shall be elevated
> The true catechism shall instruct us
> And the awful fanaticism shall be snuffed out.
> At being obedient to Law
> Every Frenchman shall train."

By 'the Gospel of the lawmaker' and 'the true catechism' they mean the Constituent Assembly and the Constitution it is writing, Adele thought. *But— from what Father tells us—there is no hope there....Even if they could create a constitution, the people could not be held to follow it....If there is no inner change—no new heart, which only Christ can give—no amount of outer sanctions will suffice.*

"Ah ! It'll be fine, It'll be fine, It'll be fine

Pierrette and Margot sing the guinguette
Let us rejoice, good times will come!
The French people used to keep silent,
The aristocrat says 'Mea culpa!'
The clergy regrets its wealth,
The state, with justice, will get it.
Thanks to the careful LaFayette,
Everyone will calm down."

'The clergy regrets its wealth...' that's praise for the assignats, the money created by forcibly taking the clergy's land, Adele commented inwardly. *Oh, I wish LaFayette had half the power they ascribe to him! The people idolize him – but only follow him if it pleases them: look at how the troops forced him to take them to Versailles during the march of women last October....He has tried hard by censorship and other powers to dampen the flames of rebellion, but....*

"Ah! *It'll be fine, It'll be fine, It'll be fine*
By the torches of the august assembly,
Ah ! It'll be fine, It'll be fine, It'll be fine
An armed people will always take care of themselves.
We'll know right from wrong,
The citizen will support the Good."

Adele's eyebrows raised in marveling scorn. *"We'll know right from wrong"? Just by the laws of the Assembly and our own brains? Dear, dear! It is the heritage, the natural development of the Enlightenment, of the ideas of Locke, Voltaire, Rousseau....Ah yes, by a few laws we shall totally fix the problem of sinful hearts that mankind has borne since Adam's Fall!*

"Ah ! *It'll be fine, It'll be fine, It'll be fine*
When the aristocrat shall protest,
The good citizen will laugh in his face,
Without troubling his soul,
And will always be the stronger.
Small ones and great ones all have the soul of a soldier,
During war none shall betray.
With heart all good French people will fight,
If he sees something fishy he shall speak with courage.
LaFayette says "come if you will!"
Without fear for fire or flame,

The French always shall win!"

The marching column ended their song with great vigor, shaking their shovels in the air. Adele's carriage turned off on a cross-street and soon pulled up in front of her dwelling. The coachman assisted her to alight, and Marcel, now the official doorkeeper, swung open the front door as she traipsed up the stone steps. He looked sharp and important in his livery—a green jacket with white facings—an impression which contrasted with his lackadaisical air.

His serious face did not change expression but his eyes brightened as he saw Adele. "The parlor is quite full, Madame Adele," he bowed.

"It is wonderful that Mother's salons are becoming more and more popular," she answered. "Where is Honore?"

"He went out—" Marcel shrugged. "I am not sure where. Mayhap to the Constituent Assembly to observe, or the fencing-master's. Your mother requested that I tell you she desires your presence in the salon."

"I shall be there." With a smile Adele hastened upstairs. Because of her mother's salons, Adele had taken up some of her mother's calls and visits of charity.

Salons were daily afternoon gatherings whose popularity usually depended upon the abilities of the hostess, also called the *salonnière*. They afforded opportunities for men and women to discuss events of the day, gossip, network, and listen to and talk about new books, plays, and the like. With her husband's encouragement, Madame de Coquiel di le Mercier had begun a salon because of its potential for influence.

Adele's room was brimming with muted sunlight. Several stray beams pierced through the lacy curtains, highlighting a fresh bouquet on her dressing table. *Olivie again,* Adele thought lovingly. *She almost always has a few fresh blooms there when I come home from calls....my darling, thoughtful sister!* Looking in the mirror, she adjusted her dress and freshened up. A large creamy rose from the bouquet provided the finishing touch for her masses of dark hair.

She was crossing the patterned wood floor of the entryway when Marcel ushered in a slight, sandy-haired gentleman in his mid-thirties. Seeing Adele, the man bowed.

Adele curtsied in return, with reserved pleasantness. She had seen the man before at salons but had never been introduced, so it was not for her to speak.

As a manservant opened the parlor door for them, Adele gestured for the visitor to go first.

249

"Pray enter before me, Madame," he said. His French was impeccable, but something about his quick, alert manner revealed he was a foreigner. In fact, he was the American Minister to France, having been appointed to the post soon after his superior, Thomas Jefferson, returned to America.

"I thank you, Monsieur," Adele answered. With another curtsey, she entered the parlor. The clear sunlight shone in the tall front windows and glittered on the jewelry and gold braid of the gathered elite. Adele seated herself near her mother.

The American Minister followed. After formal greetings had been exchanged, one woman spoke.

"Pray, what news do you bring, Monsieur Short?" the plump woman asked, shaking out the ruffle of her brilliant green dress.

"Does my face indeed speak for me?" he queried in return.

"Indeed, dear sir—you must learn the French manner," she rejoined.

"Which means, cover your life with an impenetrable veil of insouciance," a lady with a gold fan cut in, with veiled disdain. "*Some* of us find the American frankness a pleasant foil to such. Do tell your news, Monsieur Short."

The minister bowed to the last lady and said, "I appreciate your good opinions, Madame. As for my news: the Assembly has passed the bill on the Civil Constitution of the Clergy."

There was an interested rustle, and several comments.

"*Bon!*" said the lady in the green dress.

"'Twas expected," another put in.

"Many have fought it," the lady with the gold fan mentioned. "*I* consider it to have grave problems."

"What are the salient qualities, Monsieur Short?" Felicienne spoke. Adele looked at her admiringly. Her mother was easily the most beautiful there, and so poised and graceful. Adele breathed a silent prayer that some day she might be as gracious and able as her mother.

M. William Short smiled at Felicienne, the sun accentuating his handsome countenance and the almost reddish curls of his hair. "Marquise, it comes down to this: the clergy members are now employees of the state, elected as government officials are elected, with set pay rates. France now has a government-run church."

With murmurs of disapproval, the group scattered among the chairs, discussing the issue. M. Short took a seat across from Felicienne, saying, "It is a distinct pleasure to be here, Madame."

"I consider myself honored that you would grace my salon with your presence," Felicienne's green eyes were genial and sincere.

"I saw this young lady in the entrance; would you be so considerate as to introduce me?" he asked, motioning to Adele.

"Agreeably, Monsieur Short; this is my daughter, Adele Helene."

"Your daughter: I should have known! She has your lissome grace and beauty."

Mme. de Stahl, a prominent salon hostess of the time, would have hungrily listened to such praise and sought for more. But Felicienne said simply, "Thank you. Did you see my husband at the Assembly, Monsieur?"

"Yes, marquise; he stood against the measure nobly, but there were too many in favor."

"I hear you differ from your mentor Jefferson in some ways as to this French revolution," she said.

"I owe him very much," he replied, "and indeed feel as if he were my foster-father, marquise; but yes, my opinions on the revolution in this country do diverge somewhat from his. He has a disadvantage, Madame, in that he is not here to experience first-hand what goes on."

"Methinks he would remain in support of it even were he here," Felicienne answered.

"Perhaps, marquise," M. Short conceded. "I myself do not share all of your distrust; however, I have seen enough to conclude that something has gone far wrong. It is not like our American war at all. It is not the 'glorious revolution' visualized."

The warm sunlight streamed in unabated; around them talk was bandied back and forth, light billows punctuated by sharp sallies. Staring unseeing at the twining colors of her fan, Adele mulled over the American minister's words.

Playing with Fire

11.

This their way is their folly: yet their posterity approve their sayings.
— *Psalm 49:13*

J uly 14th, 1790 — the anniversary of the conquering of the Bastille. To echo properly the feelings of Paris, the sun should have shone brightly from a cloudless blue dome, and invisible breezes should have danced, clean and clear, across the panorama of a faultless summer's day. But such was not the case.

Girding on his sword belt before his many-paned window, Tristan noted the heavy, lugubrious clouds blanketing Paris. The streets seethed with activity — carriages crept past, impeded by the motley throngs. All were dressed in their best. Several wiry street gamins darted through the crowd; rings of dirt around newly-white features showed they had scrubbed their faces at some pump. From coarse butcher to merchant, all the men wore tricolor ribbons, pleated and sewn into cockades. The women, be they a wisp of a milliner's apprentice or a brawny fish-wife, were liberally bedizened with red, white, and blue ribbons. "The colors of Paris with that of the King — should they even include his colors?" Tristan muttered.

Crossing the high-ceilinged room he picked up a pair of cream-colored gloves and cast a glance in the mirror. With his free hand he re-settled the collar of his brownish-red outer jacket; it was unbuttoned, showing his embroidered gold-tan waistcoat. White stockings slid smoothly into brown shoes with metal buckles. After adjusting his intricately-knotted white cravat he drew on his gloves, picked up a round-brimmed hat, and stepped out.

In the maroon-papered hall, he paused. Thinking of the crowded streets, he decided against riding. Outside his mother's door, he met his square-shouldered father.

"She is resting," his father put a finger to his lips. "I shall be staying with her. She looks forward to hearing your report when you come back."

"Thank you, Father. It may be late afternoon."

"I know. *Au revoir*, son!"

"*Au revoir.*"

In the bustling street, a thin mist was falling, imparting an unpleasant damp to streets and clothing. The breeze was brisk and chill, though it was July. He settled his hat more firmly on his dark head.

Because of the crowds, it was longer than Tristan expected before the green rectangle of the Champ de Mars stretched before him. The banked seating surrounding the oval center area was crammed with onlookers. Some three hundred thousand people were there.

It was a brilliant scene. The many-colored dresses and hats of the women impressed the eye like a giant, dazzling bouquet. In the central cleared space stood rank upon rank of the National Guard. Dotted among their ordered ranks were eighty-three banners, each for one of the new divisions (*departements*) in which the Assembly had divided France. The old "province" lines had been altered and redrawn. By that one stroke the Assembly broke down centuries-old district ties and loyalties.

Tristan passed the *Ecole Militaire*, a long two-story stone building southeast of the swarming *Champ de Mars*. He slipped through the crowd and down the earthen steps; the onlookers giving place politely to his tall good looks and genuine good breeding.

Looking for the De Coquiel di le Merciers, he made his way up and down the newly-terraced ground, and at last caught sight of Honore's towering dark head of hair. Next to Honore a white hat with deep rose colored ribbons turned—Adele. On her other side, bending close to talk to her, was Sebastien du Sauchoy, dapper in a long striped blue jacket. On his other side the scintillating Stephanie, covered with tri-colored ribbons, chatted with dark Gaston de la Roche.

The mist turned to light drizzle as Tristan approached. Honore caught sight of him and waved him over.

"There is a seat here for you, Tristan," Olivie cried from beside her brother.

Before seating himself beside Olivie, he bowed to the adults— Monsieur and Madame de Lobel, M. du Sauchoy, and M. de Coquiel di le Mercier. The latter two were talking in low voices, obviously here to observe and not to acclaim, in contrast to the tricolor-flaunting De Lobels.

The Fete de la Federation, by Isidore-Stanislas Helman

Still standing, Tristan looked around. To his right was a pavilion, its golden pillars surmounted by a blue-and-white peaked awning and hung with gold-tasseled red flounces. It was for the King, who would enter from the great building stretching behind them and bordering the Seine river. In front and below, the tiers of earthen steps overran with people. In the center of the parade ground rose a dais for the speakers, while on the opposite side rose a stone arch with three curved openings. Below, several divisions were marching and forming, led by LaFayette on a prancing white charger. Despite the rain, the fete was proceeding as planned.

As Tristan wheeled toward his friends, Adele turned from Sebastien and looked up with a delighted smile, tilting her head and hat to keep the sprinkling rain out of her face. "What think you of the National Guard?" she asked, gesturing to the soldiers in the oval below.

"There must be a full ten thousand!" Tristan answered.

"At least fourteen thousand," Honore said. "Each unit of France's National Guard sent two men."

"That means—seven thousand units of the National Guard," fourteen-year-old Olivie marveled. "All in just one year!"

Tristan knotted his brow. "It is not miraculous if one heeds the rumors," he said. "There have been hints (and we know they are true) that the 'great fear' last year was engineered to bring about a nationwide National Guard. The mounted riders spreading 'Brigand' panic were directed by plotters whose goal was to have the alarmed cities create National Guard units."

"They did their job well," Gaston said, leaning past Stephanie. "A good strategy, well carried out."

"Names, Gaston?" Stephanie queried playfully. But he was already parrying questions from Tristan and Honore about the means and aims.

With a pout, she turned showily to Sebastien, her blue eyes brightening. "I am *so gratified* that you came, Sebastien."

His face lit up. "It is always my pleasure to gain even a glimpse of your bewitching face, Stephanie," he responded in a low voice, drawing back slightly with her from the others.

Gaston was leaning across them, saying, "…lawful? Why, anything is lawful, to gain a good end. *Quin veut la fin veut les moyens*—the end justifies the means."

With a glance of gladness at Sebastien's preoccupation and one of trouble at her cousin's coquetry, Adele sought Honore's face. "You sit here?" she murmured, barely moving her lips.

He smiled his understanding. Adele stood up, he slid over into her place, and she sat down beside Olivie, who squeezed her arm, a twinkle in her eye.

Honore was already answering Gaston, "As you use a common saying, I shall respond with another: *Quie seme le vent recolte la tempete*—he who sows the wind reaps the storm."

Gaston's handsome face darkened and he was about to speak when a great shout rose around them. "LaFayette! LaFayette!"

They turned their attention toward the oval arena. Slender, martial LaFayette had dismounted and was ascending the steps of the central platform. Blown by the breeze, his voice came clearly to the group:

"We swear forever to be faithful to the Nation, to the Law and to the King, to uphold with all our might the Constitution as decided by the National Assembly and accepted by the King, and to protect according to the laws the safety of people and properties, transit of grains and food within the kingdom, the public contributions under whatever forms they might exist, and to stay united with all the French with the indestructible bounds of brotherhood."

His young son, Georges Washington de LaFayette, stood near. Drawing his small sword, he saluted.

"He is eleven," Olivie whispered to Adele. "Charlot and I talked with him when Mother called on Madame de LaFayette yesterday. He has a man's heart already."

As the LaFayettes moved off, the president of the Constituent Assembly stood to take the oath, and Gaston turned to Stephanie.

Stephanie was at his side instantly, looking up into his face with her marvelous blue eyes. Gaston had caught nothing of her flirtation with Sebastien.

Sebastien, looking somewhat crestfallen, turned toward Adele — and found Honore.

The leaden sky dripped dismally, and the grand Fete continued on.

~*~*~

The city was still convulsed with festivities four days later. The LaFayettes and a few others feasted the public, their sumptuous tables groaning with food.

"There will be illuminations and a public ball at the *Champs-Elysees* tonight, dearest," Francis looked across the family circle at his wife.

"Yes, I have heard the illuminations will be quite splendid," she answered.

"It would give me pleasure to take you, the fairest woman in Paris," he smiled. "Will you, dearest?"

She blushed becomingly. "With delight, Francis. Let us bring the two oldest — 'twill be a treat for them as well."

Wending its way through jubilant streets, their carriage passed the Tuileries. Thinking of the imprisoned Royal Family, Adele peered through the darkness at its ornate exterior. Honore caught her eye and said, "It is a velvet glove that holds them — but methinks there is a steel hand underneath the velvet." Adele turned her eyes away.

Their carriage rolled to a gentle halt past the open square called the Place Louis XV. As Adele took Honore's hand to step out, she gasped with admiration and wonder. Every tree was alight with hundreds of small, flickering oil lamps, as if covered in fireflies. The sun had set, but a last pink cloud streaked the horizon under the first stars. Out here in the open, the breeze was invigorating.

Down the double line of trees lining the avenue promenaded both glittering aristocrats and the gaudy populace. In the grassy areas whirled hundreds upon hundreds of dancers, rich and poor alike, to lively strains of music.

Francis offered his arm to his wife and she placed her hand in it. Smiling at each other, they strolled off under the scintillating trees. Adele slipped her hand on her elder brother's arm and they followed several paces behind.

The moving, laughing figures in the darkness, the sweet night air, and her mother and father's obvious enjoyment of this rare time together, all combined to fill Adele with a feeling of bliss. They reached the end of the promenade and were turning round the second time before she spoke to Honore.

"Is not this lovely?" she breathed.

He glanced down at her uplifted face. "Certainly a relaxing change from the tedious round of social engagements."

"I do not want to be a murmurer, like the Israelites;" Adele said softly. "However, the round of salons, dinner parties, and balls gets awfully monotonous after awhile…"

"I concur," her brother answered. The little tree-lights showed his handsome, wry grin. "And they seem never-ending….At our estate we had parties, but they were the spice of an active life —"

" —not the focus of all existence," Adele finished his sentence. "Nevertheless, they are part of our duty here."

They were walking close under the trees, the trunks rising like dark pillars on their right. Overhead the branches were a network of black lace against the blue-black firmament, and the lights mingled with the stars.

A statuesque figure passing from the opposite direction glanced at them and paused in his stride for an instant. A moment later Adele heard rapid steps from behind, and Jules Durand appeared. The spangled light shone on his finely chiseled face, disheveled golden hair, and sensitive blue eyes. He bowed deeply to Adele.

"This glorious evening has increased in radiance ten-fold at the sight of your face, Madame Adele," he said gallantly. With less warmth he added, "Would you introduce me to your companion?"

"Surely, Monsieur Durand," Adele answered. "Honore, this is Jules Durand. M. Durand, this is my brother, Honore Rene-Luc de Coquiel di le Mercier."

Jules' face abruptly lightened, and after bowing to Honore, he turned to Adele. "May I have the pleasure of dancing with you, Madame Adele?"

"I prefer to stroll under the trees, but thank you," she smiled.

Jules did not answer, but moved to Adele's free side and walked on with them.

"The Water-jousting on the river two days agone was enjoyable to watch," Honore mentioned. His immaculate, tailored garments were a stark contrast to Jules' fashionable slovenliness, but Honore seemed not to notice the difference — his voice was friendly.

"So they say—I was called off on business, and missed it," Jules said. "Were you there, Adele?"

"Honore found places for us on a bridge—we had a marvelous view of the sport," she answered.

"Then I am doubly sorry to have missed it," Jules responded, with a bow in her direction.

"What think you of these grand rejoicings, M. Jules?" Adele asked. "Many think this is the crowning achievement, the *finis*, of this revolution."

"I believe they are wrong," Jules said with a short laugh. "Should we be satisfied—*are* we satisfied—with what we have gained? I warrant me the populace will long for new freedoms within a few months."

"So you feel that more needs to be accomplished," Honore remarked.

"We have not achieved half of what is needed," Jules said. "These accursed—" He suddenly cut himself short and glanced at Adele with some confusion, thinking to himself, *She is an aristocrat!...But why, why does she—do they—seem different to me? Why do I like being with them?*

Up ahead, their parent's *tête-à-tête* was interrupted by a strikingly handsome gentleman.

"My dear Madame Felicienne," Philip de la Noye bowed, "This is a rare and precious pleasance!" Half-turning to Francis, he said, "I am sure you enjoy this respite from the Assembly's grind, marquis."

"Is it ever a pleasure to leave one's family circle?" Francis answered.

"Not if one has such a radiantly beautiful wife," De la Noye replied, with a look at Felicienne.

Behind them, Honore, Adele, and Jules approached.

"Who is that gentleman?" Jules queried.

"Which one?"

"The one in the green satin, speaking with your parents—"

Adele peered into the gloom, then recognized the Roman nose and dark good looks. "'Tis the marquis Philip Emilie de la Noye."

Jules stiffened. His eyes grew frosty and distant. Abruptly he motioned to a group of musicians on the lawn, plying their string instruments with zeal. "Have you been on the lawn yet?"

Adele and Honore exchanged quick glances. "No; we might as well," Honore shrugged. "What think you, Adele?"

"It might be a pleasant change to stroll there," she replied.

They spoke casually, but both noticed Jules' sudden change of manner. Sauntering over the closely-cropped grass, Adele wondered. *Jules does not seem to mind speaking with us, and we are aristocrats....Then why this marked aversion? Has he met De la Noye before? Or...it it something else?*

~*~*~

Walking home from the Assembly the next evening, Francis peered over his shorthand notes.

"Hail, *marquis!*" cried a beefy voice.

He looked up and saw Etienne du Sauchoy, mounted on a superb chestnut.

"Ah! Du Sauchoy! But you have not heard—the title 'marquis' is forbidden now."

"I have heard well enough," the other answered, his beefy face lowering. "Take away our titles and privileges? Faugh!"

"I am sorry as well, Du Sauchoy," Francis answered. "It goes against the grain to begin calling everyone 'Citizen.'"

Du Sauchoy's face lightened. "At least *you* do not approve of the new regulations—every blasted deputy I have seen so far has praised them!" he growled.

"If it makes you feel better, quite a coalition voted against the bill—but we were too few to prevent its passing," Francis replied. He made a face. "The new law *is* quite comprehensive..." He looked down at his notes and read aloud; passing servants, street arabs, and workmen gathered to hear:

"1. The National Assembly decrees that hereditary nobility is forever abolished. Consequently, the titles of Prince, Duke, Count, Marquis, Viscount, Vidame, Baron, Knight, Lord, Squire, Noble, and all other similar titles shall neither be accepted by, nor bestowed upon, anyone whomsoever.

2. A citizen may assume only the real name of his family. No one may wear livery or have them worn, nor may anyone have a coat of arms. Incense shall be burned in churches only to honor the Divinity, and shall not be offered to any person.

3. The titles of Your Royal Highness and Your Royal Highnesses shall not be bestowed upon any group or individual, nor shall the titles of Excellency, Highness, Eminence, Grace, etc."

"Monstrous!" muttered Du Sauchoy. Leaning from his saddle, he spoke in a low, passionate voice to Francis; "These jealous, greedy levelers—they are bent on destroying us—may they be confounded and destroyed!"

Straightening, Du Sauchoy prominently displayed a riding crop engraved with his family arms. A growl went up from several workingmen nearby. They had heard the decree against livery and coat of arms.

A rough Brigand darted out a grimy hand, snatching the crop from Du Sauchoy's meaty gloved fingers. Startled, Du Sauchoy's powerful chestnut reared to its full height, scattering the nearest onlookers. With a sharp movement the Brigand broke Du Sauchoy's riding crop over his knee and tossed the fragments into the street. Du Sauchoy's face turned purple with rage, but he masterfully reined in his steed.

"If I were you, I would not make a fuss here, Etienne," Francis remarked quietly. "You could easily be mauled."

"You are right," Du Sauchoy hissed. "A curse on them all!" He gathered the reins. Casting a last furious glance at the gathering sans-culottes ("without-breeches")[1], he rode off.

As Francis turned and started again down the street, the mangled riding crop caught his downcast eyes. The coat of arms glittered up from the mud. *A fitting symbol of what is occurring,* he thought. *The people seeks to break us and trample us in the mud.*

As Francis neared his house he saw the family carriage out front. A scowling manservant with a brush was painting out the coat of arms on the door.

Francis paused and watched for a moment. It felt like every sweep of the brush obscured forever a part of his life. He knew it would never be the same. With a sigh, he ascended the steps.

~*~*~

"Did you not hear—tonight is the servant's holiday, Denis," De la Noye said, shifting in the padded chair. "Finish that, and be off."

Denis paused from straightening papers in the handsome *escritoire.* "Yes, Master."

De la Noye leaned in his seat and studied Denis' back. *I wonder....* he thought to himself. *But no, he has been quite faithful....* His mind went back to the dicey days in December when Thomas de Mahy, marquis de Favras, had been caught in a Royalist plot—a conspiracy in which De la Noye had been intimately concerned. According to reports, the plot involved encircling Paris with thirty thousand troops, rescuing the Royal family from the Tuileries, and assassinating the city's three main liberal leaders—Necker, Bailly, and LaFayette.

Thomas could have put many in danger, De la Noye recalled. *But he did not talk; even during the harrowing two months' trial –* He remembered how Denis had spent hours watching the trial and even tried to arrange a bold rescue when Favras was finally sentenced to death. *If only LaFayette and his troops had not foiled our plans to rescue him from gaol....*

Denis left the room, bowing deferentially. As he closed the door, the marquis' thoughts went back to his doubts. *But someone has been leaking information...and if my dunderheaded clerk had not muddled the accounts, I am positive they would have revealed that I have been quietly losing sums of money....Who is it? Which one of the servants?* His usually smooth brow wrinkled with irritation.

Far down the hall, he heard Denis' footsteps retreating, then the unmistakable soft thud of the servant's door. Denis had gone out.

The twilight deepened. More than an hour later, Philip looked at the grandfather clock, rose, and stepped into the echoing hallway. The house was silent. The lamps made luminous pools on the polished floor. Between the tapers an evening dimness was settling—the sun had gone down.

Good – all the servants are out. He lengthened his strides and checked the main rooms to be sure. All were empty. Out of the corner of his eye, he thought he saw movement—but as he turned, came face to face with a mirror.

A knock rattled the side door, and he moved quickly to answer, his steps light and strides long. In the darkness of the street stood a bulky figure enveloped in a cape.

"Enter," De la Noye said softly. The visitor moved past him into the hall, obviously used to the house.

De la Noye stopped to fasten the door. When he reached his study his visitor was already there, his cloak pushed back to reveal an ugly, pockmarked face resting awkwardly on a stout neck. The difference between tall, perfectly-proportioned De la Noye and this squat, seamed creature was striking—but appearance can be deceptive. The visitor was Mirabeau, the lion who could move the Assembly at will with his sonorous voice; the hero of the people.

"Welcome, Citizen Riquetti; pray be seated," De la Noye gestured to a chair. Noiseless as a cat, he slid over to the door. Flinging it sharply open, he looked quickly out. All seemed still; there was no one in sight. Satisfied, he turned back into the room.

261

"The servants are all gone but it always pays to be on guard and make sure no one has lingered," he remarked. "Could I offer you a glass of wine?"

"I thank you," Mirabeau answered. "I gladly accept, Citizen de la Noye." He shifted his unwieldy bulk in the chair, extending his hand for the bulbous wine glass.

"To your health!" De la Noye raised his glass. "May you live long and succeed in your plans!" He took a sip of the amber liquid and chuckled. "The King and Queen are fortunate to have you to aid them—the Assembly cowers at the sound of your voice."

Mirabeau gave a half-smile, his face gruff. "But rumors of my leanings towards the King are getting out somehow," he said. "If they continue, my influence with the populace will plummet."

"I shall find the leak and deal with it, never fear. We can play this game, Citizen," De la Noye answered with swashbuckling assurance, "and if Fortune smiles, we may succeed!"

"I drink to Her health," Mirabeau replied. "If we do succeed—"

"—what power will be ours!" De la Noye's keen blue eyes glittered. He set his glass down on the polished wood side table. "But now to business…"

Outside in the gloomy hallway, Denis crouched, his ear near the keyhole.

More Secrets and New Duties

12.

Go as far as you can see;
when you get there you'll be able to see farther.
— Thomas Carlyle

T hrough the keyhole, Denis could hear his master and Mirabeau. Then there was a sudden soft noise.

One leap in Denis' stocking feet carried him across the few feet of hall and into an open door beyond. He noiselessly but quickly shut the door and stood in the darkness, listening.

In the split second after Denis closed the door, he heard a sharp *whoosh* as the study door flew open. *Just in time,* Denis thought. There was a sharp pause, then his master's voice: "'Twas making doubly sure."

A throaty voice answered. "'Tis wise, Citizen de la Noye. I commend your caution."

Their voices began again, hushed as before. Several minutes passed, and then with a muffled rustle and the click of an opening door, Mirabeau's voice came louder: "*Adieu* for now, Citizen; I shall know how to thank you when you arrange my audience with the Queen."

"*Adieu!*" De la Noye answered. "You may rely on me…"

The voices faded down the hallway. Denis remained unmoving, pressed inside the dark closet. After tense minutes he heard his master's quick, light steps. They paused as if in indecision, then entered the door opposite Denis' closet. Denis passed a hand through his dark hair, but it was a quarter of an hour before he dared leave the stuffy room.

Carrying his shoes, Denis slipped hastily down the hallway to the servant's door. Hastily buckling his shoes, Denis shoved his hat down farther on his long locks and entered the alley. He sauntered out of the fashionable section and found his way through a labyrinth of back streets. Above, a narrow slit of gloaming sky brooded over the shabby buildings.

At last, a sputtering *lanterne* illuminated a creaking signboard tacked over the doorway of a vile-looking tavern. Under years worth of grime, the outline of a fox could just be ascertained. With a quick glance round, Denis plunged into the shrunken entry. The atmosphere was thick with smoke. Guttering candles shed an oily light into the haze, picking out the unwashed floor and smoke-stained walls. The place was crowded — squalid, uncouth figures sniggered and squabbled over glasses of cheap, unholy wine. Though he was not in livery, Denis' carefully-tailored garments and knee-breeches were in sharp variance to the patched, coarse long pants of most in this unsavory hovel. Even now the common people had begun to call themselves *Sans-culottes* — because in contrast to the wealthy, they wore full-length pants.

A group of bleary-eyed Brigands near the entrance were shouting the chorus of *Ca Ira*, brandishing their sticks to the music. One, more drunk than the rest, threw a wine glass at Denis, shouting, "Death to the aristocrat!" It struck the low beam above Denis' head and shivered into pointed fragments at his feet.

"*Aristocrat?* — you ninnyhammer!" cried one of the Brigands. "'Tis Denis!"

The inebriated fellow blinked several times, then remnants of sense crept back into his flushed face and he cowered in his seat. "*Un million pardonne*, Citizen!"

Denis waved a brusque hand and continued threading his way among the tiny tables. At the counter he thrust a hand in his pocket and slapped a pile of coins on the weathered wood.

"Drinks for all," he told the greasy, pot-bellied landlord as the latter bowed subserviently.

As men around the room voiced their thanks, Denis turned with a careless nod and made his way to the foulest, darkest corner. At a weathered table sat two men. Denis pulled back a rickety chair and sat down next to a small, shrewish man with darting eyes.

The other, across from Denis, was also short. His limbs seemed twisted, and his square face had been described as "hideous." His eyes were mere slits in blistering red skin, and foul locks of uncut hair fell about his shoulders. His painful skin disease could mayhap be traced to a sinful lifestyle.

Denis addressed himself directly to this man. "You are out of the sewers tonight, Citizen Marat."

"Yes; but all my rendezvous must be short, due to the patrols of LaFayette — curse him! To be hounded to London — then to return, only to hide in the sewers! But if I did not..."

"I should think there are quite a few who would willingly cut your throat," nervously commented the third man.

"Quite a few; quite a few! My writing infuriates the dogs in high places," said Marat. "But I shall continue! The people must be stirred so that we may drink the blood of our persecutors!" He pounded a fist on the table, making their wineglasses rock. Lowering his voice and leaning across, he fixed Denis with his small eyes. "Have you anything to report today, Denis?"

"Indeed I do." Denis scooted back a little to avoid the strong smells rising from Marat's unwashed, diseased body. "My master—who is, as you know, a Royalist under his patriotic front—met secretly with our 'great patriot' *Mirabeau* this evening."

Marat's eyes glittered.

The shrewish man stifled a gasp. *"Ma foi!"* he muttered incredulously, *"Mirabeau?* Not him—the glorious champion of the people!"

Denis nodded. "Yes, Mirabeau—the honorable Gabriel Riquetti."

"But what of the meeting?" Marat asked eagerly.

"Mirabeau desires my master to put him in touch with the Queen," Denis confided. "He said…"

~*~*~

Peering into a garden through the chinks between the tall buildings on all sides, the sun sent a few last beams across a book. Adele's girlish figure bent over it. As she turned the page, a long golden-brown ringlet fell down, shading her face.

"From the high mount of God, whence light and shade
Spring both, the face of brightest Heav'n had changed
To grateful twilight."

The words seemed wafted on the wind; only her moving lips betrayed that it was she who had spoken. She gazed up into the sky and remained still, her eyes feasting on the slowly-gathering colors of sky and clouds.

"Madame Adele, your presence is requested in the parlor." The housemaid Virginie curtseyed as she spoke.

Adele glanced up. "Thank you, Virginie." Noting her page number, Adele closed the book and rose. The maid stood aside to let her pass.

Soon all of the family and "Grandpapa de Duret" were in the parlor. Berthe and Marcel stood nearby.

"Is it family devotions, Papa?" Olivie curtsied, seating herself rigidly.

"No, little one." He smiled at them all. "I have some things to tell you, children. There is much to prepare for." Beside him sat Felicienne, four-year-old Paulette playing with a toy at her side. "First of all, as to the new laws regarding titles and names—I desire us to comply with them to the best of our ability. Thus, we will sign ourselves as the Le Merciers. Even our friend LaFayette is now the Sieur Motier. It is an indignity, but not a great one compared—" he broke off.

"The situation in France is very unstable," he continued after a short pause. "Yet I deem it my duty to stay here as long as I have any influence for good. However, there may come a time when we must leave." He glanced round at the surprised faces. "This must be kept a secret—it would be very dangerous if others knew that we are considering flight to England. I do not want to leave France—nay, I feel it is incumbent upon me to labor here as long as I can. But, children," he forced his voice to sound brighter, "in case we must go to England, your mother and I wish you all to be ready for such an event. Honore, Adele, Olivie—you have already learned English to varying degrees, but I desire you to study more. You younger ones—Charlot and Paulette—your mother will begin teaching you. I know you will apply yourselves."

"Yes sir!" Eight-year-old Charles cried, jumping up. "I already know a song in English, Papa—I remember the sailors singing it in Le-Havre-de-Grace—" Knitting his brows in concentration, he launched into song:

"Farewell and adieu to you, Spanish Ladies,
Farewell and adieu to you, ladies of Spain;
For we've received orders for to sail for old England,
But we hope in a short time to see you again.
We will—"

Charlot broke off, pressing his lips together as he tried to remember what came next. His family struggled to conceal their amusement—how droll it was to see a small, aristocratic French boy singing a shanty the muscular English sailors shouted as they worked. In his concentration, Charles did not notice their concealed merriment. Suddenly, with a rush of relief, he continued in his clear voice:

266

"We will rant and we'll roar like true British sailors,
We'll rant and we'll roar all on the salt sea.
Until we strike soundings in the channel of old England;
From Ushant to Scilly is thirty five leagues."

"But I do not know what the words mean," Charles added apologetically. "Can you start teaching me now, Mama?"

"Me too, Mama! Me, too!" echoed Paulette, clapping her hands at Charles' excitement.

Their father's face lit with pleasure. "There is no need to start this very moment," he said, putting a hand on Charles' shoulder, "but I thank you for your willingness, my son." He smiled into Charlot's eager, boyish face and added in a lower tone, "I am very proud of you, Charlot."

Adele gazed at the childlike enthusiasm shining in Charles' blue eyes, a warm glow in her heart. *So willing and eager to please – Lord, help me....There is a verse – our Lord Christ said: 'Except ye be converted, and become as little children, ye shall not enter into the kingdome of heaven....'* Her father was speaking again, and Adele leaned forward to listen.

"Daughters, if we went to England, some things would be different. We would have the same large staff of servants. I desire you to increase your abilities in the housekeeping domain and even in cooking. I wish you to be capable no matter where circumstances may lead."

"Yes, Father – 'twill be fun!" Olivie bubbled, and Adele spoke quietly; "I shall do my best, Papa."

"This is a great secret, children – we will prepare, but must not say anything of this," their father cautioned.

"We will not, Papa – not a word," Adele and Honore said in the same breath.

"Not to anybody," said Charlot.

"Never ever – our very own secret," Olivie said firmly.

~*~*~

The summer sun burned hot, and the air was oppressively still. Two couples sat inside the open French doors of the La Motte's new Paris dwelling. In light silk gowns, the ladies plied their gold fans vigorously.

Felicienne le Mercier directed hers to send some air in Francis' direction. On her other side was Susanne la Motte with her husband. A bead of sweat trickled down "Citizen la Motte's" high forehead. "'Twas cooler in Versailles," he mentioned.

"Being crowded in by houses does make an unpleasant difference. Oh for the breeze in Versailles!" Susanne la Motte replied. Even the heat could not dull the bright expression of her dark blue eyes. "But remember, Arnoul, that this is where we must be: near the King and Queen."

He smiled at her. "Yes, Susanne. I am grateful that you and the girls are healthy and able to bear the heat."

"Speaking of health and the countryside, Felicienne," Susanne turned, "did I hear you speak of visiting your estates?"

Felicienne fingered the long ends of the purplish-blue scarf round her tiny waist, glancing at her husband. "We *had* thought of it."

Francis added, "The sea air and cooler temperatures would be good, especially for the younger children. They could stretch their young limbs outdoors—altogether, 'twoud be a healthful change from this sweltering, fetid city. We considered it; however...." his clear hazel eyes looked out into the garden beyond.

At the farthest end of the garden stood a small apple tree, its topmost branches rustling gently. On a cool stone bench under its dappled green shade sat Elisabeth la Motte and Adele, heads bent together over their embroidery. Their golden and blue gowns brought the sky and sun into the garden's verdant bosom.

Francis drew his eyes from the restful scene. "Felicienne's salons are well attended, and we, who are staying here out of duty, would hate to relinquish anything which might influence others for good. That is what has finally decided us—albeit reluctantly."

"I am sorry, Francis; however, I fully understand," Arnoul nodded sympathetically.

"But—do not give up the idea, if that is all that hinders," Susanne protested. She also was gazing, albeit with eagerness, into the garden. "I think the solution sits right there." She motioned with her fan. "Adele is mature and capable for her age. Why not leave her in charge of the household and salon? I will be nearby if she needs aid, and can serve as a second hostess at your salon."

"Susanne was a very successful *salonnière* in Versailles," Arnoul added.

Felicienne's eyes lighted with the idea, and Susanne pressed home her advantage. "Do let her try. You can always come back early if need be. Then the younger ones will get the fresh air they need..."

"You are too kind," Francis said. "It certainly is tempting."

"It hardly involves any extra kindness on my part," Susanne smiled. "Adele is quite capable; you will see. Felicienne, your example and precept have given her the best preparation in the world."

"We shall think over all the aspects—I thank you for your suggestion and offer," Francis said.

~*~*~

Thus, two weeks later, the early August sun beat down on the Le Mercier's departing carriage. On the house steps stood Adele, Honore, and Grandpapa de Duret, with Marcel and Berthe waving from behind. Francis had said his goodbyes the previous night, as the Assembly was in session.

Charles and Paulette waved madly, pressing their faces to the coach windows, while glimpses of Olivie and their mother could be seen behind them.

The coach lumbered on, wending its way among the few pedestrians. Adele watched until tall buildings swallowed up the glittering speck. She wiped away a tear with a scented handkerchief. *How I shall miss them….* Then her jaw tightened decisively; she had learned from Grandpapa de Duret not to waste time in self-pity. Tucking away her handkerchief, she turned to Berthe.

"Let us get ready to visit Mme. du Chemin," she said, with only the slightest quiver in her voice, "as usual."

"Yes ma'am. 'Tis such a blessing her health has improved some," Berthe said, following her into the house.

"It would have been harder for Mother to leave if Mme. du Chemin had been doing poorly, as she was last month," Adele answered.

Honore gathered his hat and gloves and crossed the foyer—he was going to the *maitre d'armes.*

"May your time with the fencing master be profitable," Adele said. "Tristan says you are almost a match for the master himself."

He turned with a grin. "Tristan's the one to beat," he replied. "As for my part—well, I hope to give the master a hot morning of it."

A knock echoed through the foyer mere minutes later, as Adele descended the stairs in hat and gloves. She hastened to the parlor as Marcel answered the front door. Adele noted his especially-long face—*He already misses the little ones! At least he will have Honore.*

Entering, Marcel presented a card. "He asked to see the mistress of the house," he said as she took it from his fingers, "so I told him I would see if she was available." He smiled.

Adele looked up from the card, smiling too. "I am not used to being addressed by that title, Marcel," she said, "let alone performing the duties of that office." Then she rose. "But tell M. Diesbach that I will be pleased to see him."

Berthe glided in, accoutered for their outing, and sat down in a corner chair, pulling out some embroidery. Adele remembered Berthe's amazed tears when her mother told Berthe that she was leaving her to be Adele's chaperone. It touched Berthe's heart to realize they trusted her so much. *And she is worthy of trust,* Adele thought. *She is a changed woman — a 'new creature,' as the Bible says.*

The door opened, revealing blond, mustached Hans Diesbach. He was wearing his uniform—a red epauletted jacket, navy waistcoat, and white straps in an "X" across the front. His knee-breeches were creamy white. He put his tall bearskin hat under one arm and bowed. "It is a delight to see you, Madame Adele—you are looking very well."

Adele smiled to herself—*If he had only been here a few minutes ago, when I was red-eyed, crying over their departure!*

"We are honored to have you visit, M. Diesbach! Pray be seated." When he had taken a blue satin-covered chair, she continued, "Could you be so good as to tell me your errand?"

"Certainly. I was bringing letters for your father—reports from soldiers in other parts of France." He handed her the packet. "You have doubtless heard of the disturbances among the troops."

"Yes; I was intrigued by General Bouille's bravery." Adele laid her fan in her lap. "Is it true he stood alone against the rebellious regiment of Salm, in Metz?"

"Practically alone," Hans answered.

"Do tell the tale," Adele urged.

"The regiment of Salm, like many others of His Majesty's troops, suffers from quite an arrears of pay. You may have heard, Madame Adele, that they blame this on their officers—a convenient scape-goat in these times, since to be an officer one must be an aristocrat. It is the fashion to say, 'We are not paid because our aristocrat officers line their pockets instead.' But really, much of the backwardness in payment is due to the terrible financial state of France. Stewing over the issue, the German regiment of Salm demanded that General Bouille give them their arrears— some forty-four thousand livres, I believe. He tried to pacify them, but could give no promise of payment. When they saw this, the whole regiment—several thousand—shouldered their muskets and marched off! Their aim: to seize the colors and military chest from the Colonel's house!

"Drawing their swords, General Bouille and their officers ran pell-mell—" Hans' pale eyes gleamed with the tramp of war and admiration for the brave, "—and managed to reach the Colonel's dwelling just before the seething regiment arrived. Panting, Bouille and the officers stationed themselves on the outer staircase to defend the house. The mutinous troops of Salm surrounded them, a crowded, angry mass—but none dared as yet to move against Bouille's grim figure, highlighted against the stone steps. He sent off a quick messenger for help: 'Bring the Dragoon Regiment!'"

Hans' voice dropped lower. "The Dragoon officers mounted and commanded their troops to follow; but their men would not. They too were infected with rebellion's miasma. So Bouille would get no help—he had to face the regiment of Salm by himself. What were the odds? Thousands, against a mere handful. But Bouille stood manfully firm—how it disconcerted his soldiers! Who would be the first to fire on their own General? So there they stood, in the hot sun—thousands of troops, the rascality of the town egging them on—and one unyielding brave man, facing them dauntlessly."

He continued, "Since the mutinous soldiers, had not fired when their blood was up, in the end they could not get up the nerve to attack—and when the Mayor came and promised to lend money to pay some of their arrears, they disbanded and shame-facedly went to their barracks."

Adele's eyes were glowing. "Think you that this is the end of it?"

"Unfortunately—no," Hans said. "The regiments at Nanci are stirring seditiously, incited by the Breton club there; everywhere the fabric of discipline weakens. Officers by the score are emigrating—they realize the ship called the French Army is going down. Indeed, when obedience and respect towards officers departs, can an army exist?" He put a hand to his light mustache, his face brooding.

"I see you are wearing the Royalist officers' 'badge,' Citizen Diesbach," Adele commented.

"What? Oh, yes," he smiled. "My mustache. Many of us *Gardes Suisses* are wearing them nowadays." His face grew grave again, and he shook his head. "I wonder if we are the last faithful soldiers the King has."

"Surely it cannot be as dire as that," Adele said. But his face did not lighten as he bade her farewell.

From the parlor window Adele watched his erect figure striding down the street. Then, allowing herself no time for moping, she turned. "Now, Berthe, duty calls: on to the Du Chemins!"

~*~*~

The very air crackled with tension as Francis entered the *Menage* on a late Wednesday afternoon a few days later. The *Menage* was an old riding school near the Tuileries—the Constituent Assembly now met there. But Francis hardly noticed the looming pressure in the atmosphere; it was commonplace. Split into factions, all fighting and grabbing as they pressed on in the noble goal of making the Constitution, the deputies' inner antagonisms had broken into open hostility.

Salle Menage, Anonymous

Pausing in the center of the *Menage*, Francis scanned the room. It was long and narrow, with a high, arched ceiling and large square windows in rows near the roof. Inside the rectangle nestled an oval of tiered seats for the deputies. On the second story were galleries for spectators, with sections for the public and for friends of the deputies. Straight across from Francis, on his level, was the raised podium for the president and secretaries of the Assembly. To the right of the president sat the Royalists, while moderates took the long section of seats around the room. Where the seats curved back to the president's left sat "the Left" — Robespierre, Danton, and their "Thirty."

Francis remembered how the Royalist Faussigny had impetuously dashed into the center of the hall, crying, "There is but one way of dealing with it, and that is to fall sword in hand on those gentry there!" With a sweep of his frantic hands he had motioned to "the Thirty." But he had been pacified, and nothing had come of his frustrated hysteria.

Francis noted the dagger-like glances and hissings exchanged by deputies of opposite sides as they swirled past him to their seats. Nearby stood Abbe Maury in the black vestments of the clergy. A rustic fellow obviously straight from the country pressed through the crowd to the abbe. He grasped Abbe Maury's hand in a vise-like grip, pouring out tearful thanks for the abbe's strong Royalist stance. Shaking his white-wigged head, Maury answered with gruff wit, "*Hélas, Monsieur*, all that I do here is as good as simply *nothing*." Francis passed on, but the words seemed too close to truth to forget easily.

More deputies were striving to reach their seats—the session would re-convene soon. The galleries above were filling rapidly. Francis was caught in the crowd. A richly-embroidered pale blue suit caught his eye; he turned and smiled at the youthful Duke de Castries, a Royalist or *Black*—so-called because of the black cockades some sported. At the same moment Francis spotted an opening in the moving men ahead. He bowed, motioning for the Duke to go first. "*S'il vous plaît aller premièrement, Monsieur.*"

The Duke bowed in return. "No, no, M. le Mercier; if you would please to pass first."

Without warning, a few yards ahead, one of the simmering quarrels boiled over. Francis did not hear what had been said, but there was no doubt of who had said it—a hunchbacked Royalist deputy called Lautrec, noted for his acerbity of tongue. He was sneering up at Charles Lameth, one of the radical Thirty.

"Monsieur—" Lameth ground his teeth, glaring down at the hunchback, "—if you were a man to be fought with!"

"I am one!" cried a youthful voice. The duc de Castries leapt before Lameth, eyes flashing. He had jumped to the defense of his Royalist comrade.

"*Tout a l'heure*—On the instant, then!" cried Lameth.[1]

The young Duke turned calmly to Francis. "If you would please to act as my second…"

273

"If it must be so," Francis replied. He moved forward gravely to speak to the man who had accepted the duty of being Lameth's second.

Within minutes, the duel was settled. It would take place after the session in the *Bois-de-Boulogne* park. The parties went to their seats, and the session began as usual, but Francis couldn't rid himself of a feeling of foreboding. Duels were often fatal.... He shook himself mentally and concentrated on the droning speaker in the center of the room.

Dueling with Swords and Words

13.

Solitude is strength; to depend on the presence of the crowd is weakness.
The man who needs a mob to nerve him is much more alone than he imagines.
— Paul Brunton

T hat very evening, as Adele oversaw the dusting and airing of the
guest bedroom for the first time, her father was proceeding with
several other gentlemen across an open lawn in the *Bois-de-*
Boulogne. The grassy sward stretched level and verdant before them. At a
distance rose the hedges and flower beds of the structured gardens. The
small, serrated leaves of mulberry trees whispered overhead — King Henri
of Navarre had planted 15,000 there. It was a beautiful setting, but no one
noted its tranquil radiance.

Sober-faced, Francis took the swords and compared them. Then
with a wordless bow, he handed them to Lameth's second. How this
brought back the days of his youth; the duels he had seconded and
fought — he remembered the duel he had almost fought with Philip de la
Noye...and the years he and Denis had practiced together. Under Francis'
tutors because the youths were always together, Denis too had developed
into an adept swordsman....

The duc de Castries was stripping off his pale silk jacket and
waistcoat with deft, casual gestures. His opponent Lameth struggled
awkwardly with his coat, but at last shook it off. Taking Castries' blue coat,
Francis gave him his sword.

Together, Castries and Lameth moved into the golden clearing. A
butterfly fluttered past unnoticed, highlighted for a silvery instant by the
low sun. The duelists stood perfectly still: right feet advanced, poised for
immediate engagement. It would have been a pretty picture had it not been
for the deadliness of the game.

The signal was given: like lightning, the two swords darted
forward. Their metallic clash rang through the peaceful glade, tingling

men's blood. Back and forth in this terrible dance moved the two—their seconds watching each thrust and flourish with deepest attention.

Francis dimly noticed scattered groups of gathering onlookers. He paid them no heed, except to motion them to stay out of the circle. His eyes fixed on Castries' youthful, pliant figure, he was praying inwardly.

They seemed equally matched—the twin smallswords flashed and re-flashed. Beyond them, the flushed sun sent up red streamers against the glowing sky. On the grassy space beneath the trees, nothing seemed to move save the two central figures and their lightning swords. Quinte and quarte, stoccado and passado—ever alert, blocking the opponent's thrusts, springing forward and leaping back—these two knew their work.

Castries parried high, then whipped his sword round Lameth's almost too fast to see—but Lameth was quicker. He blocked Castries' stroke with his sword and iron wrist.

Seconds later, their swords clashed low. Lameth, feinting to the right, darted left—and his weapon rang on the whirlwind blade of his adversary. Castries pressed his advantage and drove Lameth back several paces, Lameth parrying frantically. Then Lameth regained control and stopped his backward rush, holding his sword nearly vertical as he moved the tip to block Castries' assault.

Suddenly Lameth lunged forward with his full weight, intending to transfix Castries and be done with it. But Castries was on his guard— lightly, he danced aside. Lameth's impetus carried him forward. He fell to the grass, his face twisted. Castries stepped back a pace. The seconds darted forward.

Lameth was already sitting up, clutching his arm. Blood flowed down his white sleeve, dripping on the close-cropped grass. In his lunge, Lameth had slit his own arm on Castries' sword point! The doctor was kneeling on the grass, wrapping the long, ugly gash.

The injured man in capable hands, Francis walked over to the duc de Castries. With quiet ease, satisfaction on his flushed face, the young man put on his pale blue coat.

"*Félicitations*," Francis said, pressing his hand.

"*Merci*." Castries flung an insouciant hand towards the encircling onlookers. A sibilant hiss came on the still air towards them; several of the coarser populace gestured angrily. "They do not seem well pleased," Castries observed carelessly. "Their god Lameth is defeated by a 'cursed Royalist.'"

Francis liked not the crowd's mood. "Come back this way, Castries," he said. "Lameth declares his honor is satisfied. Let us leave.

There is no use in tempting the people's loving-kindness by walking into their arms."

Castries smiled grimly. "I agree."

~*~*~

A solitary streetlamp burned fitfully in a narrow side-street. Almost opposite the lamp was De la Noye's servants' entrance. The far-distant bells of a church tolled once, then again, and again—ten times.

In an otherwise-empty street nearby, hats drawn low, paced two figures, talking in earnest, low voices. Both were lean, the golden-haired youth slightly taller than his black-haired companion. 'Twas Denis and Jules.

Denis stroked his chin thoughtfully. "...as for that, I have my doubts; my master may suspect..." His voice trailed off, and he muttered to himself, "I have my own troubles—barely have two *deniers* to rub together..."

A whip cracked. On a broad avenue hidden from view, a clatter of carriage wheels and the dull *thud-thud* of horse hooves on the packed earthen street revealed that a post-chaise had started up. Every so often the even, quick *thud-thud* would change to a *thud*-clang-*thud-thud* as a shod hoof glanced against a scattered cobblestone. With creaking joists and rattling wheels, it turned the corner and came down the thin street towards Denis and Jules.

The two pressed against a wall—'twould not be wise to risk getting run over. No doubt it was some aristocrat leaving De la Noye's, and would dash by in a thunder of hooves and wheels, rousing the echoes. A moment more, and it would be past...

But that moment did not come. Suddenly an extra-sharp clang of hoof and cobble rang out. One of the oncoming horses stumbled, checking its pace. It neighed—a ringing, clarion cry. The coachman hauled back on the reins and the other horse fell back on its haunches. The coach slid to a halt in front of Denis and Jules, swaying and creaking on its metal suspension bars.

The light made an uneven pool, illuminating the panic-stricken horses on one side and Denis and Jules on the other. Peering down, the coachman shouted, "Comrade Moreau! Help me hold these beasts for a minute, will you? This blasted street—always knew this would happen here—those jutting cobbles—the workers are too occupied with rabble-rousing..."

Frowning, Denis turned to send Jules away. But the coachman was shouting again—"Help me, would you? And you, young man—I think we've lost a shoe—"

Jules sprang forward. Denis, elevating his eyebrows, took the head of the nearest horse.

As Jules passed the coach door in search of the thrown horseshoe, the dark, handsome face of Philip de la Noye appeared in the opening. "What's—" De la Noye's question clogged in his throat as the lamplight flashed on Jules' fair face. *That aquiline nose, blue eyes, broad forehead and small, firm chin....*

Jules stared back. An imprecation trembling on his lips, he turned haughtily. Biting his lip to keep back his suppressed passion, he strode past Denis without a flicker of recognition and disappeared into the darkness.

Denis smiled with inward approbation; *Jules is nobody's fool. He acted as if he didn't know me;* but he still wondered how much his employer had seen—or guessed.

Inside the carriage, Citizen de la Noye again leaned back against the cushions, his face thoughtful. *That was* her *son with Denis!...Denis has preformed his duties faithfully—but I* have *suspected him....I must be on the alert.* His brow was still knitted when the carriage moved slowly off again through the gloomy streets.

~*~*~

The news of the Lameth-Castries duel spread fast. The lowest gutter-snipes talked it over, cursing Castries over their grimy wine-cups. Who cared to mention that 'twas a proper duel—evil rumors about the Royalists had already been circulating: "They have hired assassins to kill our champions;" "The papers say twelve *Spadassins* arrived from Switzerland...our patriots shall be forced into duels and dispatched one by one!..." The reports grew as they were repeated and poured into eager ears....

Two days after the duel, the populace reached boiling point. Angry talk bubbled up and spilled over into vehement action. The focus of the attack: the Hôtel Castries, the duc de Castries' palatial Paris dwelling.

Gaston's dark, lion-like head rose above the riffraff shouting before the Hôtel and swarming in the streets. Beside him were stooped Anton Petit and stocky, golden-haired Leuren Andre Lobel. An odd trio.

Gaston was eminently in control. "Look here—'twould be best to pass as honest townsfolk enraged by the unjust duel." His powerful eyes identified several leaders gathering near.

"Quite right," one grunted, a powerfully-built man in coarse brown garments. He turned to the milling mob and raised his voice to a bellow. "Advance and attack—but no plunder! He shall be hanged who steals a nail!"

With an animal cry the horde broke loose, viciously hacking at doors and windows.

"My friends and I shall stay at the door to make sure the orders are carried out," Gaston said. They stood aside as the mob rushed into the house over the door's broken shards. Leuren found himself on one side of the door with Anton, Gaston on the opposite side.

Several minutes passed. The commotion from inside increased.

Windows creaked open above; looking up, Andre was just in time to duck under a windowsill and avoid a shower of items streaming out of the upstairs windows. A set of fine china hovered in the air long enough for him to trace its intricate design and gold leaf edges—then the plates and dishes shattered against the cobbles. Thick, rich red folds of fabric cascaded by—Leuren realized they were bed-curtains. A mirror followed suit, adding glass shards to the rubble of clothing, desks, paintings, gold and silver bowls and plates, statues, chiffoniers....Leuren stared in disbelief at the increasing piles of beautiful, costly things, so wantonly destroyed.

"See the spoils of the rich!" Anton thrust forward his long neck, awkwardly waving his arms about. "We are better than they, for we disdain and refuse to profit from such gewgaws..." He was in full cry now; Leuren knew from experience that Anton would run on much longer. A man came out: as Anton paused to inspect his pockets, Leuren took advantage of the diversion to move over beside Gaston.

"This is what the people think of the Royalists, eh?" he mentioned.

"Yes," Gaston grinned. "Mayhap the Royalists will think twice before challenging one of 'the Thirty.'"

The heaps of broken goods in the street before them increased; a steady stream of expensive items flew out the windows and smashed against the stones below.

"A very satisfying revenge," smirked Gaston.

~*~*~

A hot breeze whispered through the half-open study window. A bluebottle buzzed back and forth tediously against the upper half of the sun-stained window pane. Philip de la Noye studied some papers once again, then struck the bell on his desk.

A dark-coated servant appeared, bowing.

"Tell Denis I wish him," De la Noye said.

As Denis entered, his master looked up, bronzed face impassive. "There you are, Denis." He remained seated, looking up at the standing Denis with calm concentration. "Denis."

"Yes, master?"

"The time has come to speak plainly. Despite my goodwill on your behalf, you have been unfaithful to me—have acted as a low-born spy and thief. Here is your dismissal."

"Master—what?—someone has tried to poison you against me; I am guiltless—" Denis did a masterful job of feigning innocent consternation, but De la Noye was not fooled.

"You have been spying on my visits with Citizen Riquetti and feeding the information to newspaper editors like Marat," his master said coolly. "You have pretended to serve me, while fraternizing with and aiding those who are against me. You have stolen various sums of money. If it were not for some hazy irregularities in the books, I would prosecute. You may bluster, but I have gathered proof enough to indelibly convince me that you are a thief, a liar, an utter miscreant, and a wholly unscrupulous and degraded villain. I am dismissing you; take your things and go." His voice had not grown louder, but it was crystal clear and firm, his face coldly contemptuous.

"So you have no concrete proof." Denis' voice was triumphant, though his eyes shifted around the room. "I shall take leave of your service with pleasure, you accursed Royalist! I know about your doings! I have contacts among the populace; you will rue this, you scoundrel! I despise you, you—*aristocrat!*"

He turned and was gone.

Philip rose and took a sip from a glass on the side table. *How I wish I could have had him arrested! If it hadn't been for the carelessness of that new stripling, Martin, who helps with my books, I would have had evidence enough....* He took a deep breath. *Ah well*—Mieux vaut tard que jamais—*Late is worth more than never. He was useful, in his way...even after I suspected his perfidy—for then he unknowingly served as a channel to pass misleading information to those rascally newspapermen....* He smirked at the remembrance.

~*~*~

Adele looked over the parlor once more. Yes, all was in place—the gilded frames dusted, curtains drawn back, chairs arranged....She wished Grandpapa de Duret could be there, but he was visiting Madame du

Chemin. Madame la Motte entered, casting an approving glance over the room. "It looks perfect, Adele," she said. "The visitors will soon arrive…"

It was the first salon since her mother had left, and Adele tried to ignore the butterflies in her stomach. *Father God, please cause this to go well; help me to fulfill my duties as a hostess, so as to not disappoint my parents' confidence….* She thought back to the influence of her mother's salon, and felt inadequate to continue such a positive impact.

There was a knock on the door—and for the next half-hour, Adele was so busy greeting guests and keeping conversation flowing that she had no time to think of butterflies. Then, as things evened out, she noted the conversation lagging.

"What an event at the Hotel Castries, yesterday." She dropped the words neatly into the moment of silence.

"Alas! Terrible, indeed—what is the world coming to?" remarked an elderly woman in a peach-colored satin dress. "Always such a pleasant young gentleman, too…"

"If Lameth chooses to get into a duel, his victor should not be punished," opined a thin woman, fingering her long necklace. *"These people!"*

"Irreparable damage, they say," added another. "It is too close for comfort—who knows which of our houses they might pick next?"

"Ruined, all the treasures of his house," a short man piped up, twisting his gold-headed cane. "Who cares if it was not stolen by those wretches—it was destroyed. Even the priceless painting by…"

The discussion continued, but Adele's attention was claimed by a quiet voice at her side: Sebastien du Sauchoy. "Have you heard of Marat's latest, sweet Adele?" he asked, proffering a newspaper. Across the top was written in coarse type, *"L'Ami du Peuple"* (Friend of the People). He added, "I brought it thinking it might be helpful for you in your new duties as *salonnière.*"

"I thank you for your thoughtfulness," Adele said sincerely.

He leaned forward and pointed to a paragraph. "Citizen Marat says here, in his usual scathing manner, that he knows the solution to France's troubles."

"Really."

He smiled cynically. "Quite a simple solution—all we must do is to erect eight hundred gibbets, and hang Mirabeau—pardon me, 'Citizen Riquetti'—on the first. Then we should fill the others with leading Royalists."

Adele's eyes narrowed. "An atrocious idea—as if a massacre will solve our national problems!" she answered. "But why Mirabeau on the first—why Mirabeau at all? He is the darling of the people, their savior-god!"

"Quite true—the people did place their hopes in Mirabeau," Sebastien said. "I do not know the full reason for this shift of opinion, but I have a shrewd guess. Adele, have you not also heard whisperings of a possible liaison between the royalty and Mirabeau? Even in the Assembly, he has deftly and unobtrusively been eroding away the sand beneath the feet of the Thirty."

"Interesting— now that you point it out, I do recollect such maneuvers of his," Adele said. "Thank you again, Sebastien. It is very kind of you." She knew he would understand that she needed to turn her attention back to the gathered assembly.

"Citoyenne Maurepas, you were not at the premiere of Etienne Mehul's opera, *n'est-ce pas?*" The speaker was a florid woman in a russet gown.

"I was otherwise engaged," Madame Maurepas replied. "His first opera, was it not?"

"Yes; *'Euphrosine, ou Le Tyran Corrige,'*" remarked a stout gentleman, taking a pinch of snuff.

"'Tis set in Provence at the time of the Crusades," the woman in the peach dress informed them. "The tyrant Coradin is the guardian of three orphaned maidens. Euphrosine, one of his charges, decides to persuade Coradin to marry her so she can reform his character. But the Countess of Arles, jealous of Euphrosine, turns Coradin against her, encouraging him to give her poison. The doctor warns Euphrosine about the plot against her life and she merely pretends to die of the poison. Believing he has killed Euphrosine, Coradin is suddenly seized with remorse; he asks the doctor to prepare more poison so he can commit suicide. At this point Euphrosine enters, alive and well, and forgives Coradin, who then agrees to marry her."

"Antoine Trial was at his best," the russet-gown lady enthused. "His reedy voice was *perfect* for the part of Caron, the jailor."

"Ah, we've seen him before," another woman said. "But the death scene, where Euphrosine pretends to die of the poison—ah! Jeanne-Charlotte Saint-Aubin played that part so well, a woman in the next box fainted!"

"She was riveting," opined a gentleman in green satin. "Notwithstanding, I could sympathize with Coradin best."

"How so?" queried the stout man.

"At the end, distraught at having killed Euphrosine (so he thinks), he commands poison to be brought with the design of ending his life," the man leaned forward, pessimistic eyes prominent. "That is all that is left some of us, now—a quick and noble death by our own hands."

Adele listened, torn with different emotions. *What will happen to the popularity of Mother's salon if I offend these, my elders, or create a stir?...But Father doesn't approve of suicide....And the purpose of this salon is to be a light in the darkness....*She wrestled inwardly, lips pressed together. *It is so tempting to say nothing....to let it pass....*

The next comment decided her.

"There may be something to what you say," said a slender man with a scholarly face. "As Pliny the Elder said, 'Amid the sufferings of life on earth, suicide is God's best gift to man.'"

Adele sat up a little straighter. Looking gravely (but with beating heart) at the last speaker, she spoke softly, "Then let me also quote from antiquity: Augustine of Hippo."

All heads turned in her direction—the sight of so many combined faces, and her worry about displeasing them, made her stomach churn. With an effort, she remembered the Bible's stance against suicide and her obligation to stand up for truth. Reaching for a book nearby, she quickly riffled through the pages and found the paragraph, grateful for Grandpapa de Duret's teaching. Then she spoke, "Augustine says, '...it is not lawful to take the law into our own hands and slay even a guilty person, whose death no public sentence has warranted. Then certainly he who kills himself is a homicide, and *so much the guiltier of his own death as he was more innocent of that offence for which he doomed himself to die.*'" Her faltering voice gained strength, and she spoke the last lines with quiet aplomb.

"Quoting from Augustine—well, *really*," tittered one of the ladies. "As if *that* proves anything."

"*I* would not criticize; to each his own," sighed another, languidly toying with her fan.

Adele's heart sank. Had her words no effect? Or had she just made herself a mark of ridicule?

The scholarly man was staring ruminatively at Adele. Then he spoke, "*Véritablement*, my ladies, I would hesitate to criticize her source; and even Virgil says,

> *'Fácilis descensus Averni:*
> *noctes atque dies patet atri ianua Ditis;*

> *sed revocare gradium superasque evadere ad auras.*
> *hoc opus, hic labor est.'*
> Translated, *'It is easy to go down into Hell;*
> *Night and day, the gates of dark Death stand wide;*
> *But to climb back again, to retrace one's steps to the upper air —*
> *There's the rub, the task.'"*

Rubbing his hands slowly together, he regarded the assembled elite with a cogitative glance. Adele cast a grateful glance in his direction.

"But who cares about what those old philosophers said," protested the lady in the russet gown. "The opera was so *romantic*—he reaches, full of anguish and remorse, for the poison...then—oh joy!—Euphrosine enters—she is alive! What a climax!"

"But what if—as would be more probable in real life—Euphrosine had not entered in time?" Adele asked.

"I suppose his suicide would have been for nothing," remarked one lady, looking thoughtful. Her hands lay clasped on the plum-colored silk of her dress.

Another flicked her fan impatiently. "Then he would have died nobly." Anger tinged her cheeks.

A young lady in a green dress spoke up. "Well, I have tickets to see the opera in the *Comédie-Française* this evening—but I will see it in a different light." Her eyes caught Adele's with heartening agreement.

From beside Adele, Sebastien spoke, changing the subject subtly. "I hear the 'Jealousy Duet' in act two is particularly interesting musically."

Thanking him with a smile, Adele launched off his words. "Citoyenne, what was your opinion of it?" She looked particularly at the lady in the russet gown, who prided herself on knowing all about music.

Mollified, the lady answered, "It really *is* quite dramatic—for the duet, the music oscillates between two pitches a third apart. This builds a looming, almost fierce tension underneath the vocalists' melody."

Another woman piped in, "During the other scenes when jealously appears, the theme reoccurs in the melody line—'tis a simple but effective musical device."

"Composing is quite its own art," mentioned the stout man, "as my friend..."

The conversation switched completely over to composing and music technicalities. Adele cast a quick glance around the room. The tension had slipped away.

Now that the confrontation was over, Adele felt weak—but encouraged. She had done it—had stood up for the truth—and the results had not been as drastic as she had feared. She would see some repercussions—some of the ladies present would, if their looks were any indication, eschew her salon for several weeks. But there were several thoughtful faces, like the scholarly gentleman and green-gowned young lady, and Adele took heart. Silently, she poured out thanks to her Heavenly Father.

~*~*~

Several days later, Adele lifted her head from a foolscap sheet covered in her mother's delicate script. "This morning is devoted to the kitchen," she smiled at the assembled servants. "Virginie, you will air the guest room—I will oversee the kitchen work."

A quarter of an hour later found the kitchen staff scrubbing and polishing. Adele was going over a wooden counter with a linen rag and sudsy water. A large apron covered her crisp white muslin dress, and her piled hair was tied up attractively with a green ribbon. The maids had tried to keep her from doing anything, but Adele was mindful of her father's words.

The hall door opened silently and Marcel appeared. "A gentleman to see you, Madame Adele." Amusement twitched the corner of his mouth.

Adele took the printed card: "Gaston Xavier la Roche."

Hurriedly taking off her apron and wiping her hands, she glanced into the mirror. "Tell him I shall receive him in the parlor." Marcel started staidly towards the front door while Adele slipped into the parlor.

Gaston's dark gray coat accented his gray eyes, and he acted as if he was highly conscious of the fact. "My dear *Citoyenne* le Mercier," he bowed deeply, "I missed your fair face at the De Lobel's last fete. You must not do that, for all the young men were asking after you—especially Sebastien."

Adele marveled at the incongruousness of his polite, aristocratic speech and his insubordinate attitude and styles. But she had no doubt he could drop the high-class act and speech at a moment's notice—and usually did.

"I had a previous appointment with Madame Ducroix," she answered dispassionately.

"That ancient crone?" Gaston laughed. "Don't tell me you enjoy *her* company more than the young men at the Lobel's! *I* know what a lovely young woman would prefer!"

Adele felt her cheeks grow hot. She wished wholeheartedly that Gaston would not act so overly-familiar. She was about to reply coolly when they overheard a knock at the front door, and Gaston was on to another topic. "Your doorman is such a dull blockhead!"

"Marcel?" Adele's eyebrows made two arches. "I do not understand you."

"Such an obtuse creature," Gaston said.

"He has been faithful—he is an orphan; his father was our servitor," Adele said. *He is quite intelligent and capable under his* laissez-faire *appearance,* she thought. Words defending Marcel leapt to her lips but something held them back. Instead, she merely said, "I am sorry if he is an annoyance to you."

"Annoyance—*non!*" Gaston smiled. "His stupidity does not annoy *me.* I had thought his carelessness might annoy *you.* But I suppose loyalty...."

After more conversation, Gaston mentioned the purpose of his visit. "I desire to locate Stephanie. She was not at her residence, and I went to the *Palais-Royal*—but she wasn't there either, so I thought she might be here."

"*Non*; she is not here," Adele said. "I am so sorry you have wasted your time."

"Not wasted—not when—"

Adele did not exactly interrupt, but she spoke as he paused, searching for gallant words. "I think you may find her at Madame Lefebvre's salon. Blessings on your search."

"I thank you exceedingly, Adele. *Chaque nuage a un revêtement d'argent*—Every cloud has a silver lining—and you were the silver of this cloud. *Adieu!*"

With a deep bow and brilliant smile, Gaston swaggered out, a fashion plate for the scruffy "patriot" look. Adele wondered at her cousin's infatuation. He was very handsome, yes—but to Adele it was obvious that his good looks were mere gold gilding over a plaster statue. Her thoughts were cut short by Marcel's entrance.

"A messenger for Château le Mercier arrived while you were occupied," he said. "I sent him to the kitchen to refresh himself. He had letters for you."

Adele's eyes lit with pleasure. "Thank you, Marcel." She took the folded sheets, feeling the raised lumps of sealing wax. *One from Mother, and one from Olivie....* She held them in her hands, oblivious of Marcel, engrossed in the pleasant task of deciding which to open first. At last, she chose Olivie's. In her sister's looping, careful handwriting she read:

My dear sister   *September fourth 1790*
    We miss You I am sure You miss us too. I wish You culd be ~~Heer~~ Here there is so Much to doo we go Riding Walking Visiting Evry Day. Mama says we Culd have gone Riding evn in Paris She is writing to the du Chemins I will Enjoin Her to tell Tristan to take You Riding so you can too. The air wuld do You good.

    How is Evrything tell me how Papa is Doing I am glad You are There to be with Papa.

    Charlot just Walk'd by singing a Sailor Song. Hee is Verry ~~concentraated~~ concentrated on Lerning English and is Lerning fast. he Begs the menservants daily to take him to Le Havre de Grace where the ships are I think he now Knows all the sea shanties that were Evr Composed.

    Evryone sends their love and kisses Write soon I miss you awfully.
    Ever loving
    Olivie

A Knife in the Dark

14.

...Adorn'd
With what all Earth or Heaven could bestow
To make her amiable: On she came,
Led by her Heavn'ly Maker, though unseen,
And guided by his voice...
Grace was in all her steps, Heav'n in her Eye,
In every gesture dignity and love.
— Milton

*T*he lamplighters emerged from their grimy hovels and marched on their way through the gray streets. The sun lay on the horizon, his golden beams still holding the stars in abeyance. In front of the Le Mercier's, several carriages waited their turn to discharge their occupants. Inside, the wide parlor rapidly filled.

In a new green-striped gown, Adele glided among the opulently-attired guests, talking with one here and another there. This was the first dinner party she had hosted, and Madame la Motte had been unable to attend, but Adele's pleasant face gave no indication of her feelings of insufficiency. She had spent an earnest half-hour before the party praying for strength and ability — her cares were resting on her Heavenly Father.

Her father stood among the guests — she flashed him a smile as she passed. Being informed by a maid that dinner was ready, she gave the signal and the company broke into pairs, gentlemen escorting ladies. Adele led the way on the arm of a tottering old marquis.

The dining room was ablaze with candlelight. It gleamed on the silver and reflected off the large mirrors and gilt wallpaper. The dark wood chairs and rich wine-colored tablecloth were a perfect foil, accentuating the scintillating brilliance of walls and table settings.

After sitting down at the long table, each guest dipped into pocket or reticule and brought out a piece of bread, placing it on the damask tablecloth beside their plate. The bread shortage was so severe that even aristocrats felt it. Each now brought their own bread to dinner parties, since 'twould be impossible for a hostess to procure enough. And a meal without bread? *Jamais!*

From the head of the table, Francis looked along the conversing guests till his gaze rested on Adele at the other end. She was listening with interest to an elderly marquis and the American Minister William Short, throwing in a question or comment every so often.

Francis remembered the pleased remark a dowager made earlier that evening: "Your daughter is a wise woman, Sieur le Mercier."

"*Oui*; but how so?" he had replied.

"She takes an interest in her elders, not in flirting with the youths. She has the respect and commendation of many."

Francis had an inkling of his daughter's valiant efforts to fill her mother's place, and knew the pains that went into each of Adele's society duties. His heart swelled with loving admiration, and he breathed a prayer of gratefulness.

The guests near him were discussing Necker's dismissal. Necker's attempts to solve the financial crisis had come to naught, and the Queen had been averse to him all along. The King had replaced him.

William Short left the dinner party thinking of the recent doings of the *Comite des Recherches* (Committee of Research) which he had heard from his youthful hostess and those sitting near. This committee, with its seemingly-limitless powers, arrested and searched people's effects with impunity, under the excuse that it was preventing treason and (Royalist) plots. *Of all the self-important, witch-hunting committees....* he mused.

Reaching his lodgings, he took a candle up the dark stairs. *I must write to Gouvernor Morris in London; 'tis overdue....* Placing the candle in a convenient holder, he opened his desk and sat down. The light fluttered against the walls, pooling on the smooth desk. Sharpening a quill, he dipped it in an inkpot and began to write in strong, flowing script.

Paris, September 12th, 1790.
Dear Sir,
...The present feature of affairs here is such, as confirms your friends in the opinion they had conceived of your judgment in such matters. I see often some of them, who say you not only predicted what was to happen, but how; they wish to consult you now, that you might tell them when the bankruptcy will arrive, and whether there will be a civil war, and what will be the event of it. There is no danger in talking of you in this manner as you are not here, but if you were within the jurisdiction of the Comite des Recherches, *I should be afraid of their making*

you a nocturnal visit. These visits have lately become fashionable; one of the most remarkable is one which has just taken place. A washerman found a letter in the dirty pockets of one of his fair customers, which had the appearance to him, as he did not know how to read, of a counter-revolution; by means of the district this came to the knowledge of the Comite des Recherches. The lady in question was called before them late at night, and underwent an interrogatory of some hours. Her papers were examined, but nothing found. The Comite des Recherches made their report to the Assembly, informed them, as a proof of their vigilance and zeal, that they had passed the whole night without sleeping, were applauded by the Assembly, and the female was ordered not to leave Paris. And all this is considered as the sure and certain road to the establishment of a free government, and particularly to the securing of personal liberty.

There is a plan for paper money now before the Assembly. The Assembly is divided in their opinion, and so are the commercial towns; but the people who fill the galleries, and who surround the Assembly-house often in crowds, seem to be unanimous in favor of it. Mirabeau undertakes to prove that it is not paper money. It is true that it is a paper, which you may force your creditor to receive, and which is to have all the legal proper ties of money, but still he swears and so do many others, that it is not paper money, because it has land for its pledge. Some insist on calling it papier-terre, and the idea was near passing. It has been lately decided, that the final vote shall not be taken on it before the 17th.... You will readily believe, that a government like this will not adopt the harsh business of forcing taxes, so long as they can make use of that gentle means of striking paper to satisfy their demands....

An opinion begins now to prevail here, that the Assembly are not very desirous of putting an end to their session. You know they have determined that their powers continue until the constitution is finished. You know also, that they are inviolable for criminal matters, though not for debts (by their decrees.) You know that they concentrate in their hands all the powers of government and exercise them daily. To an impartial person this certainly presents the idea of a very aristocratical and tyrannical body. It is observable that public inquiry begins to examine more attentively the nature of their powers; so that if they make no further progress in the constitution, than they have done for some time, it would not be at all surprising if public opinion should soon be as much against, as it has been for them.

You will have heard of M. Necker's retreat from the helm. It produced no effect either on the public mind or public funds. The Assembly received intelligence yesterday of his being stopped on his way to Switzerland by a municipality, although he had a passport from the King and from the mayor of Paris....The Assembly have directed their President to write to the municipality to give him his liberty. Some members were for voting their thanks to the municipality.

We have intelligence here from New York as late as the 20th of July. You have probably later. ...I will thank you, if you have any farther or later information of the proceedings of Congress, to inform me of them. Be assured of the sentiments of attachment with which I am yours, &c.
William Short [1]

Folding the letter, he reached for his seal and sealing wax. A watchman passed in the lightless street underneath his window. The steady tramp of his feet and his sleepy cry, "All's well," seemed incongruous. All was not well in Paris.

~*~*~

With long strides, Jules hastened down the faded street. His objective — Denis' dwelling.

Since Denis had been fired by De la Noye, Jules had seen him only a few times, in low haunts and coarse taverns. In the latter he was up to his usual game of playing the generous comrade; paying for drinks all round, giving "patriotic" speeches, helping the down-and-out with easy cash. Denis was viewed with hearty goodwill by the dissolute wretches which swarmed such places.

How can he afford such? He has not found new employment, according to my knowledge. Mayhap he tucked away savings. Jules turned into a narrower street, pushing past some playing urchins to the dingy house where Denis had rooms. *I must talk over with him Mother's new plot against that cursed De la Noye....* He opened the shrunken door. Taking hold of the banister, he started up the narrow, creaking stairs. At the second-floor landing he stopped in front of Denis' door and knocked sharply. The echoes of his knock came back to him: there was no sound from within.

Shuffling footsteps approached up the stairway, and Jules turned to see a large, dumpy woman ascending. From her air of self-command and the keys jangling from her capacious waistband, he gathered she was the landlady.

"Looking for someone?" she wheezed.

"Yes — Citizen Moreau, who lodges here — when will he be in?" Jules inquired.

"In? I wish I knew when he'd be in, the knave!" she burst out. "I'd like to get my hands on that rascal," she grated, folding her ample arms. "Skipped out last week, without paying a *sou* — three month's rent all unpaid!" Her sharp eyes drilled through him. "And you know him?" She took a step closer. "Where is he?"

Jules' eyes grew wide. "I am sorry, Mademoiselle," he said, backing up—she might try to collect her delinquent rent from him! "I, too, am looking for him. I hope you will be repaid," he added, edging towards the head of the stairs. "*Il n'y a que les montagnes qui ne se rencontrent jamais*— There are only mountains that never meet. You will doubtless come across him one of these days, Mademoiselle, and will be paid." He added as a final disclaimer, "Who knows where he is."

Though somewhat mollified by Jules' polite manner, the woman still bridled with indignation. Jules made his escape as quickly as possible.

He set off down the street, thinking hard. *So I was right—he could not afford such lavish expenditures....Why would he spend money like that? Denis is a deep cove....*

~*~*~

Clenching her fair hands and frowning into space, Stephanie stared dully at her mirror. Footsteps sounded in the hall beyond—she tensed. *If Mother comes in, I will scream!* she thought bitterly. The relations between mother and daughter had deteriorated, fomented by Stephanie's rebellious attitude and her refusal to help oversee household duties. Her mother was learning now—only too late—the results of her permissive "let them do what they wish" child-raising. The footsteps passed, and Stephanie relaxed into preoccupied brooding.

The scene at last night's ball reoccurred for the hundredth time....

She could see herself arriving a little early (to surprise Gaston), glowing and happy, searching through the gathered throng for him. Then (so painful to remember!) her eyes had lighted upon him—and noticed the simpering young woman clinging to his arm. In that frozen instant, it was etched in Stephanie's memory—the bold admiration in Gaston's eyes as he looked down at the girl, the young woman's brazen, inviting flirtations, their close proximity....

She had broken recollections of Gaston quickly leaving the girl and hastening toward her with his flashing, irresistible smile....The fervency of his greeting had left nothing to be desired and he had danced with her all the rest of the night, but....

She remembered how she announced her departure, then waited in the shadows—to see Gaston hovering over the girl and escorting the jade to her carriage!

Stephanie's lovely face twisted in utter wretchedness. *Does he care for me? Or....* His ravishing gray eyes and Apollo-like smile seemed to rise before her, and she gave a cry as if in pain. "Oh, I *must* have him," she moaned, hiding her face in her hands.

She remembered the attempts of the girl throughout the evening to attract Gaston, and flamed with anger. *My Gaston....'Tis all that horrid girl's fault...the shameless hussy! That Jezebel!* In her heat she forgot her own flirtations with Sebastien and others. Then she cried again, weeping, but still wholly enamored.

At last, she rose with a miserable face. "I must go to that awful Madame Maurepas' for tea....must smile and act pleased...." she grumbled.

Listlessly, she touched up her hair, powdered the flushed spots on her cheeks, and drew on her gloves. Romance and flirtation were the cornerstones of her pleasure—she had nothing greater to base her life upon. And now a cloud had come over her sun.

~*~*~

Stephanie entered Madame Maurepas' gilded drawing room with a false, brilliant smile. She curtseyed lightly to her hostess, then caught sight of Adele. Adele glanced up with pleasure, replying warmly to Stephanie's salutation and making room at her side.

"Do tell me all about what you have been doing, Adele," Stephanie bubbled, in her brightest manner. She hoped Adele would do most of the talking. She was horribly empty, and felt she could barely keep up her pretence of sparkling gaiety.

"I suppose I have been rather occupied," Adele mused. "Hosting Mama's salon, and arranging dinner parties for Papa's friends...and then fetes, teas, and other functions to attend, and calls to repay; mama's charities, too...." Her tone of voice revealed she was not trying to show off; rather, recalling them for herself.

"What a list!" Stephanie managed an arch smile. "How you have time for anything else—"

"Oh, I do have other tasks." Adele missed her cousin's gibe. "There is much to do at home—overseeing the maids' work, making sure Papa and Grandpapa de Duret have what they need—have I told you my latest victory? I finally persuaded Virginie to let me change the beds myself!" Her eyes lit up with the memory.

"Adele! This is *beaucoup trop* [far too much]!" Stephanie protested. "And you act as if you are enjoying yourself! It seems an insufferable bother!"

"It would be hard if one could not find joy in any thing," Adele answered. "At first I was not sure I would," she said frankly. "I never took on so much before—the responsibility of our house was on my shoulders; my parents relied on me. I can tell you, it made—still makes—me nervous; but—" She paused abruptly. Her cousinly eyes noticed Stephanie's dull listlessness. "I am afraid I am boring you."

"No, no—go on," Stephanie urged.

"Well, to answer your question—my tasks *have* become pleasurable to me. Have you ever felt the joy of knowing that everything is in perfect order—and you helped make it so?"

Stephanie cocked her head attractively as she puzzled over her cousin's words. *What makes her anxious — what disquiets her — is that she might not represent her parents well!* She could hardly make head or tail of such a statement; it stood in bewildering contrast to her own self-focused existence. She managed a noncommittal smile in reply to Adele's last question.

Stephanie did not see the envious glances of several other young ladies—begrudgingly, they studied her flawless, enchanting beauty, her gorgeous smiles, her stunning blue eyes. Many of them remembered, jealously, her handsome partner of last night's ball. How beautiful and happy she had looked! What a magnificent *beau* she had! Wholeheartedly, they wished they could be her…. But:

> *If inward griefs were written upon the brow,*
> *how many would be pitied who are now envied!*

There was a rustle near the door and Sebastien du Sauchoy entered, bowing dutifully. Several young ladies tried to catch his eye, but he made a beeline for the cousins.

Adele was explaining the results of a recent culinary experiment to Stephanie, and did not notice Sebastien until he addressed her.

"My dear Adele," he said, "will you grant me the felicity of sitting beside you?"

"If you desire," she returned.

"You look more beautiful every day, dearest Adele."

Adele noticed he had almost ignored Stephanie—*Why? And why are his eyes warmer than usual?* Then she noticed Stephanie's piqued expression. Light broke through the clouds. *Jealousy! He desires to make her jealous—she's been ignoring him and obsessed with Gaston!* The realization came as a relief. When not trying to make Stephanie green-eyed by paying extra attention to Adele, Sebastien had been a pleasant companion, if a trifle fawning — Adele gratefully remembered his assistance during the tricky discussion about the opera Euphrosine.

After a few exchanges, Adele caught sight of an elderly lady across the room and recalled that she needed to pay her respects. "I am sorry, but I have to excuse myself," she said to Sebastien. "I must ask Madame Ducroix a question. I am sure Stephanie can make up for my absence — will you, dear?" she finished, turning to her cousin.

Adele's eyes were sincere and shadow-free. Stephanie felt like catching her hand and asking, "Tell me your secret!" but when her ruby lips parted what came out was, "Surely, dear Adele."

Adele moved across to Madame Ducroix, and Stephanie turned an artfully composed face to Sebastien. "We have not talked in a long while — much, much too long," she said effusively. "What have you been occupied with, Sebastien?"

His face lit up. "Yours is the face I most have wished to see, dear Stephanie."

Stephanie's face was bright, but inside she felt hollow. She wondered to herself why compliments had palled — she remembered the thrill she used to receive from flattery; now more and more was needed to affect her at all. She turned the full glory of her eyes on Sebastien, stimulating further words of adoring praise.

Inwardly, though, her heart still twined with foolish adoration round a youth named Gaston.

~*~*~

Sturdy M. du Chemin shifted a nondescript package in his hands as he spoke to a servant. The opulent entrance-hall was vacant save their two figures, standing under a massive, gilt-framed landscape painting.

The servant's ruddy, rounded face and conservative, carefully-tended clothes gave the correct impression: a dependable retainer, though somewhat given to the wine-cup.

"As usual, the money from the recent collection of the estate's rent-dues arrived this afternoon, Auguste," M. du Chemin said. He handed the man the unexceptional paper-wrapped bundle, tied with twine. "Give this to my banker — the normal address. You should just have time to make it there and back before dark."

"Yes, Monsieur," Auguste bowed.

Auguste moved with a brisk step past the few pedestrians. As he spied a tavern ahead, he became conscious of a desire for a quiet glass. *Just a few minutes — it would not delay me long.* This was not surprising, for he had stopped for a glass there enough to make a habit. He never became inebriated—he was too conscientious a servant—he merely added a few minutes to his errands. He glanced at the sun setting above the housetops. *I really should deliver this money first; then, perhaps....*

Just opposite the tavern he recognized a middle-aged man, also in the well-kept, sensible clothing appropriate to trusted servants of the noblesse.

"Auguste!" the other hailed, altering his course. "You certainly have time for a glass." He added with a comradely grin, "'Tis inarguably destiny which decreed that we meet here."

"Only one—then I must be on my way," Auguste said. In minutes the two friends were chatting over their glasses, sharing gossip and commenting on "the state of affairs."

It was perhaps only twenty minutes later that Auguste and his friend emerged into the gathering dusk and turned their separate ways.

Glancing at the fast-deepening darkness, Auguste lengthened his strides with consternation. There was now hardly anyone in the streets, which were shrouded in that twilight murkiness just before the lamps are lit. He pressed on, his footsteps unnaturally loud in the fast-closing stillness, his package tucked firmly inside his coat.

Suddenly—so suddenly he had no time even to cry out—he felt the sharp point of a blade in his back, and a business-like voice said, "Halt! Hand me the money—over your shoulder."

There was no arguing with that crisp, commanding tone, nor the knife boring into his back. Auguste complied, fumbling in his coat pocket for the bundle.

He felt his hand lighten as the package was taken—the knife-point was removed, and Auguste looked round. The robber had vanished.

With too-late activity (but undoubted bravery), Auguste darted off in the direction he supposed the thief had gone, but with no results. He blundered through several dark winding streets, tripping on the uneven ground, but saw no one.

At last, with great chagrin and mortification, he turned his steps back toward his master's. Over and over again he berated himself, "If only I had not stopped for that glass! I have failed Master—however shall I tell him of my negligence—That thief! If I but had him for a minute, I would....Oh, if only I had not...."

Thus he chastised himself until he reached the Du Chemins to relate his tale.

Defend the Poor

15.

Defend the poor and fatherless: do justice to the afflicted and needy.
Deliver the poor and needy: rid them out of the hand of the wicked.
— Psalm 82:3,4

*O*livie dear,   *October 29, 1790*

Adele paused to sharpen her quill, staring off in thought before dipping it in the heavy inkwell. Early-morning light flooded the parlor as she kept an eye on the maids' housekeeping.

How are You all. I think of You Often and wonder how You are Doing.
Grandpapa de Duret has been Busy of late not Only instrcting me But Also spending Much Time at Mme. du Chemin's Bedside. Shee has Tak'n a turn for the Worse we pray daily for Her. Keep her in your Prayers the Doctor is Verry Gloomy when hee speaks of Her.
Have you been Workn'g on your Housekeeping? It has become a Delight to me and I hope to you. I must tell you my Latest — Cook has shew'd me how to make Soup! I made Soupe Aux Haricots Verts myself yesterday Papa & Grandpapa deDuret Admired it, not knowing I had made it.

Marcel entered. "Tristan du Chemin," he announced.

"Show him in," she answered.

As he disappeared, she spoke with a smile to the two maids, "You may go now; I will call you back. Thank you." They slipped out with their dusting rags, and Adele rose.

Tristan entered with a bow. "My apologies for interrupting your letter-writing," he said, glancing at the open missive. "My errand is not long."

"You are always welcome," Adele replied. "I was writing to Olivie."

"If you would, mention my regards to your family."

"It would be a pleasure," Adele answered.

"I came to see Honore—is he in?" There was suppressed excitement in Tristan's manner.

"I think so—let me send Marcel." Adele struck a bell, and when Marcel appeared, sent him on the errand. "Do sit down, while you wait," she told Tristan. "It may be a few minutes."

Tristan seated himself with his peculiar light grace. "I was talking to Elisabeth la Motte yesterday, when they visited Mother; she said to tell you there might be a few newcomers to your salon today. She met some spinsters in the Park who were very interested."

"Elisabeth is always thinking of others," Adele said. "Trust her to use a chance meeting to recommend Mother's salon."

"She is 'as busy as a bee' assisting others," Tristan answered.

Adele smiled again. It was so enjoyable to be at ease with a young man. Tristan was like a brother—not full of flattery or flirtation, just his own congenial self. "I have wanted to arrange a respite for her—finally she will be able to come to tea next day-week."

Tristan slapped his thigh. "That reminds me! Your mother suggested in her last letter that I take you and perhaps Elisabeth riding outside the city—extra studies prevented it at the time, and now Mother has had a relapse—I am very sorry, Adele!" He looked pained. "She mentioned how nice it would be for you to get out of this close city for once."

"Never mind," Adele smiled. "I have had pressing duties, as well."

The door opened behind Tristan, and Honore entered. Tristan rose, greeting him heartily. Adele gathered her writing instruments and curtsied, preparing to leave.

"Oh—do stay, Adele," Tristan said. "I would like you both to hear this news."

"News? What has happened?" Honore placed his hand on Tristan's shoulder.

Adele caught her breath. "Your mother?" With one movement, she set the quill and letter on the table, her eyes on his face.

Tristan's face lightened. "No, nothing like that. This does not concern her health, though it is declining." His tone shifted. "Last night, our quarterly rent-roll came in, and Father sent Auguste (as usual) to deposit the money at the banker's. He was delayed, drinking with a friend. Then, in a dark, empty street near the banker's, he was accosted—the first thing he knew was a knife poking his back and a voice saying, 'Hand me the money—over your shoulder.' He did so—then the man disappeared."

"So the money is gone!" Honore's grasp tightened. "That villain, whoever he is—!"

"Oh, I am so sorry," Adele said.

"Father has other revenue—the loss hurts, but that is all," Tristan replied.

"If *only* Auguste had not stopped to drink!" Adele lamented.

"He blames himself greatly," Tristan said, "He is quite cut up. But Father and I think he may have been robbed even if he had not delayed so—the thief seemed to have been lying in wait, as if he knew Auguste was coming. Indeed, he deposits quarterly."

"Robberies are becoming more frequent in this unsettled state of affairs," Honore said.

"True," Tristan said, with a grimace—but Adele's hazel eyes sparked.

"Berthe told me of a robbery just a week or so ago," she said. "I do not remember the details—let me call her."

Berthe appeared in a moment, curtseying. "Madame Adele?"

"Berthe, you were telling me of a robbery at the bakeshop—do tell the story."

"It was two weeks ago, Madame," Berthe began, wondering a little. "Henri the baker was cursing and grumbling when I went to get bread—worrying about how he would buy grain for the next week's baking. I asked what was the trouble, and he said he had been robbed! When he was taking the week's earnings home the evening before, he was accosted from behind; a knife was put to his back, and he was ordered to hand over the money. He never caught sight of the thief." She added, "'Twas an awful blow—with the rising prices of grain and the mob's demands that bread be sold cheaply, the bakers have been hard pressed. He was near despair."

Something in Berthe's manner attracted Adele's attention. "You aided him, Berthe—didn't you?"

"Oh, well," Berthe blushed, "Yes, I gave him a sum; I have a little stash."

Adele smiled. "You do so many good works among the destitute. You can always ask us to help, Berthe."

During Berthe's tale, Tristan's face had tightened with keen determination. He seemed hardly to notice this little interlude, for he spoke directly to Honore. "Something must be done. The larceny we experienced was nothing; a bother, nothing more. But tales like these—to steal from the poor!" Into his countenance crept the resolute look Adele had seen before:

the memory of their search for the passage came to her mind. He spoke decisively. "Honore, we must act on behalf of these needy people!"

"I agree." Honore's green eyes were full of answering purpose. "The *gendarmerie* can do nothing in these matters—they merely act as guards, making arrests only when there is strong evidence."

"But here, the evidence must be gathered," Tristan said, "and, Lord willing, we shall gather it."

"We may not succeed," Honore said, "but we at least owe it to these poor people to try to uncover these thieves. They are not our tenants, but Father says our duty as aristocrats is to protect and provide justice for the poor."

"Yes," Tristan replied. "I suppose the first step is to gather news of more thefts, and perhaps also patrol the streets...." The grandfather clock chimed the hour, and Tristan glanced at its face. "We must talk more of this later."

"Give my love to your mother; tell her I have no appointments tomorrow afternoon and will visit her," Adele said. She looked at him and Honore, her eyes shining. "And may God prosper your search!"

"*Au revoir*, Adele!" he smiled. "Honore, unless Mother is worse I shall see you at the *salle d'armes* tomorrow."

Tristan left with another bow, and Honore, after pacing up and down the room, also departed. Calling back the maids, Adele addressed herself to her letter once more. *I must finish this—I have calls to make in a half-hour,* she thought.

Tristan just came in Hee says to convey his regards. Hee bore the news that their manservant was Robbed last Eve there is no clue as to the Thief. How horrid!

The Troops are all rebellious Mirabeau has Ev'n said that the Only Thing to Do now is Abolish the present French Army And Remake a totally-new Army.

The people of Paris now call Themselvs Sansculottes—"without breeches"—It is rather Amusing that they think So Much of the fact that they Wear long pants and Aristocrats wear knee-Breeches.

Sunday I saw Elisabeth and Christelle they send their greetings I am including a Pressed flower from Christelle.

Give a Kiss to Paulette for me and tell Charlot I heard a new Song the other day I will teach it to Him when you come to Paris—that is a month from now Oh I miss you all!

Yours truly
Adele

~*~*~

Below the towering carved façades of expensive houses, Honore patted his antsy bay and swung into the saddle. He and Tristan had settled on calling at hostelries and boarding-houses to learn about other robberies. Landlords at such places might be in touch with such matters. Because Tristan's ailing mother took up much time, Honore would start the search.

Tristan and Honore were products of their times—with one exception. They both felt the emptiness of the accepted aristocratic life. Many fluffy, flirtatious girls and insipid, pleasure-seeking youths were coddled in a shallow, self-focused world—but as Christian young men, Honore and Tristan had been trained to live meaningful, unselfish lives. The callousness of the higher classes towards the people's needs, and their wretched condition, stirred their blood and made them long to help the oppressed. They felt that the present rebellion, although wrong, did not negate the need for true reform. Thus, the news of the thefts stimulated Honore and Tristan to action.

Honore held his bright bay to a walk as it tossed its sculpted head impatiently, eager to go at a faster pace. Honore laid a soothing gloved hand on its black mane.

"Quiet, Roland," he murmured. "I know you want to run."

The horse quieted under the calm pressure of Honore's hand and firm seat. A few minutes later, though, Roland stretched his head, "feeling" the bit and cocking his ears impertinently back at his rider. He had caught the scent of grass; though it was only a walled garden. The enforced quarters of the city and his fiery energy made him restive, though he was tractable enough under Honore's generalship.

Several minutes later, Honore pulled up in front of a hostelry. Swinging down from his horse, he was swarmed by a horde of stunted, gaunt street gamins, each vying to gain a few deniers by holding his horse. Honore's glance sifted the group, and he selected a half-grown but wiry youth in gray rags. Handing him the reins, he entered the building.

The edifice gave the impression of having fallen upon hard times, and this sensation was increased by the dingy gloom of the entry.

A bustling man with greased hair hastened forward. "Are you looking for a room, Monsieur? I have one just right for you—spacious, clean, new sheets on the bed, fair water provided—"

Honore held up a hand. "I am provided for in that respect, Citizen, but I thank you. I have come to inquire. Have you heard of any robberies of late—perhaps one of your lodgers has been accosted?"

The man passed a hand through his stringy hair. "Let me see...I recollect one boarder—but that was a month agone...."

"A month is recent enough for me," Honore said.

"Let me see...." the landlord rubbed his hands together ruminatively, cracking his knuckles with slow relish. "He was a foreign-looking fellow—I cannot seem to remember his business....Ah, I remember now—all those colors of cloth; he said that fine linens required...."

"How was he robbed?" Honore flicked his riding whip impatiently at a buzzing fly.

"Ah, yes—the robbery. I do believe he said he was coming back late one evening from the other side of the city, where he had been trying to sell his goods—someone came up behind him in the *Rue Martin* and ordered him to hand over his money. I do believe it was rather a shock...and he was in rather a bind afterwards; he told me he could no longer pay for his room....I have not seen him since, Monsieur. It was regrettable because he was one of my few boarders who were lodging for an extended time—and you know the trouble of folk just passing through...."

"No other thefts, then?" Honore asked.

"No, I do not think so, Monsieur; but I would not know, for many of my tenants only stay a few days. As I said...."

Honore had listened, eyes narrowed, and now made a gesture of farewell. "I thank you for your help, Citizen." He pressed some coins in the man's hand. "Keep on the alert for other thefts; you can contact me at—"

An explosive neigh echoed in the street outside.

Honore glanced out the small windows, but they were thick with grime. Springing to the door, he wrenched it open. The boarding-house keeper merely gaped after him—he did not know, as Honore did, that Honore's horse had been especially spirited that morning.

Several insolent youths in disordered sans-culotte-patriot fashion were gathered a little distance away. Even as Honore watched, one stooped. The next second, a mud-ball snapped against Roland's flank. As Roland's ears went back and his hind foot arced, Honore could hear the rascals' coarse laughter and cries of "Aristocrat's horse!"

Another mud-ball followed and Roland half-reared, piercing the air with a sizzling neigh. Honore's eyes went to the beggar-youth he had paid to mind Roland. Grimly, he hung on Roland's reigns, even while the horse reared and lunged angrily. Honore took the steps in one leap. He had seen the terrified helplessness, mingled with resolve, in the boy's haggard eyes.

"Here—Here; calm down, Roland—there, good boy," Honore said, grasping Roland's bridle. "*Merci, mon garcon,*" he said to the waif.

Honore's resolute action and manly bearing seemed to nonplus the bullies. With parting jeers, they faded off down another street. The horse also calmed, feeling his master's strong hands through the reins.

His free hand stroking the horse's neck, Honore turned toward the street gamin. "I am most grateful to you for holding him tight, *mon garcon.* Those rascals were trying to annoy him, *n'est-ce pas?*"

"Yes, Monsieur." The fright slowly began to fade from the boy's eyes. "They are bullies."

Honore smiled wryly. *I doubt not these ruffians feel they are true "patriots," seeking to annoy the aristocrats—but they oppress the needy as badly as the "oppressors" they revolt against. Ah—c'est la vie!*

Roland stirred, and Honore looked up at him, speaking softly. Then he spoke to the boy. "Take this as payment and reward."

The tattered boy stared in amazement at the coins in his hand, then up towards Honore.

"I am on the lookout for thieves," Honore said, swinging up into the saddle. "I would appreciate your aid, if you hear any clues. Go to the *rue Villeneuve* and ask for the Le Merciers' house." He smiled. "Thank you again!"

As Honore rode off, the boy followed him with his eyes, then started with sudden new vigor to an eatery a few doors away, the light of a soon-to-be-quenched hunger in his wan countenance.

Though Roland had ceased to flick his tail and his ears had regained their natural position, he was still fractious. Honore turned him towards the *Champs-Elysees*, which at that time was surrounded by open stretches of parkland—not large expanses, but enough to release some of Roland's excess energy. *I should have given his legs a stretch earlier, but how was I to know those rapscallions would come along and bait him?*

He let out the reins a bit and Roland surged across an empty meadow. Honore was still musing over the robberies—and thinking half-humorously of the landlord—when he checked Roland's pace some minutes later and drew him at a walk back under the avenue's double line of trees.

Having been allowed his head, Roland settled down. Honore called at quite a few more hostelries, but with no success. Some landlords looked suspiciously at the aristocrat youth and would not give information, while others knew of no recent thefts. Realizing he should head home for tea, Honore was directing Roland back when he came upon a little lodging-place he hadn't noticed before.

Dismounting, he turned Roland over to a stout boy who hurried up. He entered a plain, empty room. A dusty table and chair rested against one wall, while an open door lent a glimpse of a hall and narrow staircase. A muffled bumping overhead suggested that someone, at least, occupied the premises. Honore rapped sharply on the doorframe.

The bumping stopped for a moment, then continued more faintly, while the stairs creaked. A lean woman appeared, adjusting a frilled mobcap. "Many pardons, Monsieur; I was engaged in helping one of my tenants—" she cut short, as if not sure how to finish. "I was occupied with a lodger, monsieur—but can I help you?"

"I was interested to know if you have heard of any robberies of late—sometime in the last few months?" Honore asked pleasantly.

The woman started. "Why—that was why I was upstairs, helping Louise turn out her things!" she exclaimed, gazing at Honore incredulously. "The woman claims she was robbed, as she cannot find the sock in which, she says, she stored her little hoard."

"You think she may not have been robbed, Citoyenne?"

"No, not that—but you gave me a start, you did, asking about it," the woman said.

"I am seeking to unearth some thieves—perhaps just one—who have been making depredations of late," Honore said.

"Let me bring Louise down—she will be glad, that she will, to tell you all about it." She hurried up the stairs.

In a few moments a small, shrewish old woman was standing before Honore and speaking with bewildering rapidity. "Yes, it was stolen—and it was all my savings—no, I do not have any suggestion as to who did it—if I did, do you think I would be standing here, jabbering to you! Now listen, Monsieur, this was my little pile, and I always kept it in a sock—I kept the sock well-darned, see, so no coins would sneak out—and do I go out much? Oh no, I am always in my room; ask her." This with a vigorous nod to the landlady standing in the doorway behind. Without a pause, the little woman rattled on, "As I said, I am always in, but last night I had an engagement—and the low-living scoundrel (whoever he is) must have snuck in then, because I was gone and am never gone any other time and so…"

Honore listened with admirable patience (he was gaining that art from his inquiries) as the woman talked on. Realizing no further information could be obtained here, he waited till she paused for breath.

Bowing politely, he gave her some money to tide her over and made his escape, thanking them for their time.

The landlady and her voluble tenant had been using their eyes as well as their tongues. After his visit, every little thing about the mysterious young aristocrat—his manner, words, and attire—served as eager fodder for discussion.

As for Honore, he made his way home with many thoughts, not the least of which was the reflection that perhaps this was an impossible task. But he set his chin and remembered their decision. And the words of a Psalm came to mind:

> *Doe right to the poore and fatherlesse: doe justice to the poore and needie.*
> *Deliver the poore and needie: save them from the hand of the wicked.*

A Lowly Flower-Seller

16.

All circumstances taken together, the French revolution is the most astonishing that has hitherto happened in the world. The most [staggering] things are brought about, in many instances by means the most absurd and ridiculous, and apparently by the most contemptible instruments. Everything seems out of nature in this strange chaos of levity and ferocity, and of all sorts of crimes jumbled together with all sorts of follies. In viewing this monstrous tragicomic scene, the most opposite passions necessarily succeed and sometimes mix with each other in the mind: alternate contempt and indignation, alternate laughter and tears, alternate scorn and horror.
— Edmund Burke, November 1790

N ovember 1790. As the last two guests lingered in the entranceway with Adele, she could hardly restrain her brimming excitement. The afternoon's salon had gone well — more attendees than ever — and the Civil Constitution of the Clergy proved a thought-provoking topic. But Adele was not thinking of the salon. Her mother and siblings were coming back from Le Havre de Grace!

"Do present my respects to Felicienne and the others, Adele." Her grandfather shifted his hat in his hands. "Tell your mother I will come by tomorrow afternoon to see her."

"I will certainly do so, Grandpapa des Cou," Adele smiled.

"By the by, Adele, you have become an accomplished *salonnière*," he said meditatively. "Of course I do not agree with some of your opinions, but attending your salon has been intriguing and worthwhile. Almost you persuade me to your views…"

Adele blushed. "God has been gracious; a very present help in trouble."

Her grandfather stared for a second, then shrugged. "So, it has been difficult? But you have risen admirably to the occasion," he returned. "*Adieu*, Adele; *Adieu*, Sebastien." Bowing, he left before she had time to reply.

Sebastien spoke as her grandfather left. "I, too, have enjoyed your salons, Adele. I am quite persuaded by your charmingly and logically-expressed views."

"They are not my views alone," Adele blushed, "they are my father's as well. You know we do not hold purely Royalist views."

"Yes, I have noticed that your father differs with my father and other strict Royalists on certain issues," Sebastien said, "but I appreciate his balance. He is against the rebellious revolution, but realizes that reform is needed. The hidebound Royalists seem to forget that reforms are desperately needed. And yet even the constitutional monarchists like LaFayette are mistaken in some ways—they view this rebellion as good up to a point, unmeaningly excusing the murder and excess that has taken place."

"Well put, Sebastien. I think my family could be called anti-*revolutionary*, but not anti-*progressive*, Royalists." Smiling at him, she said, "I have appreciated your aid in the salons; thank you."

"I have but added a phrase or two—nothing to mention," Sebastien said, but he looked pleased. "You downplay your own talents too much, dear Adele," Sebastien bowed over her hand, "I was confident in your success from the first. Your salon has borne much fruit. I shall see your fair face again soon, I hope."

"Good-bye, Sebastien, and thank you," Adele replied.

As soon as he was gone, Adele fairly rushed upstairs to her mother's room. A chambermaid was tucking in fresh bed sheets. Tall wood bedposts soared up above their heads, supporting the rich blue canopy. Adele ran a finger on the bureau, checking for dust.

In the next room, Virginie was industriously scrubbing windows. In a neat, folded stack on a velvet chair were the bedclothes. Adele picked the top one off and started making Charlot's bed.

Instructing the cook, airing and arranging the bedrooms, and overseeing the setting of the table kept Adele occupied until the first shadows of evening began to fall.

She was giving the rooms a last look-through when she heard through an open window a large coach clatter to a halt, the horses' last hoof-beats ringing in the still air. Adele scurried to the landing—looking down into the entrance hall, she saw Marcel opening the door. "Grandpapa de Duret" and Honore, who had been waiting restlessly on chairs in the entryway, were outside in a moment.

Adele reached the bottom of the stairs as Paulette bounced into the house. Her little face beamed when she caught sight of her big sister. Adele scooped her up without ceremony, pressing her close.

The next minutes were joyous cacophony—a delighted swirl of glowing faces, so dear and precious. Adele heard snatches of Olivie's rapturous account of rides in the country, at the same time greeting her mother's smile and trying to look at the shell Charles was showing her—"I found it when I was listening to the sailors, Adele," Charles said seriously. Olivie's lapdog Leon raced in circles underfoot, barking.

Adele realized they'd all changed subtly: Olivie's cheeks had a new healthful bloom, Charles a lithe, bronzed look, and Paulette was taller in just three months. Their mother had a radiant glow, as well. The country air and climate had been beneficial for all.

Olivie's voice broke in, "...so the priests in all the villages around us became '*not*-priests!'"

"Because of the Civil Constitution of the Clergy?" Adele smiled—at this moment, anything made her smile.

"Yes," her mother answered. "Scores of priests returned to the laity rather than take the oath. They—rightly, I think—refused to place themselves under government control."

"I agree, Mother," Adele said. "We had a worthwhile discussion at the salon—Grandpapa de Duret was a helpful ally." She smiled at M. de Duret, who was playing with Paulette nearby.

"How has everything fared, daughter?" her mother asked, drawing close.

"Quite well—" Adele broke off. "But excuse me—I must see about the soufflés—" With quite a housewifely air, Adele hastened down the hall.

Her mother gazed lovingly after.

~*~*~

A cellist bowed artfully, compressing his lips in concentration. The queue of his wig jerked with his movements, the tune characterized by energetic rhythm and arching, graceful melody. Shining gowns and embroidered coats swirled round him—'twas another large fete.

A handsome man excused himself from the bright chatter and edged casually over to a red-faced gentleman near the cellist.

"Breval, is it not?" he queried.

"I believe so, De la Noye," Du Sauchoy replied brusquely.

"His latest works for cello are very popular," Philip de la Noye said. "And his operas—" his voice transitioned quietly from chitchat to a more serious topic; "—what think you of His Majesty's captivity, Du Sauchoy?"

Du Sauchoy's beefy face deepened in hue. "Something *must* be done."

De la Noye lowered his voice. "Come—this potted plant is a rare specimen..."

Du Sauchoy looked at him levelly under thick brows, moving into the nook with equal nonchalance.

Philip de la Noye posed insouciantly, but his quite tone was crisp. "What should be done, in your opinion?" His clear blue eyes were penetrating.

"Save the King—if we can." Etienne du Sauchoy's eyes were wary but interested.

"Are you truly devoted to Their Majesties, devoted enough to risk something for them?"

"He may be weak, but he is the King. Besides, if something does not happen soon, I shall lose everything," Du Sauchoy replied bitterly. "Of course I am willing. But what can be done?" Their soft voices were covered by the rich tones of the cello.

De la Noye studied him for a moment more. "I know several," he said meaningly, "who feel as you do. I need not tell you of the risks."

"I am certainly interested—if this is not an accursed trap and there is a fair chance of success," Du Sauchoy answered.

"There is," De la Noye said. "The King has given his approval. If you would join in this venture, go to the "White Unicorn" next day-week at half-past nine in the evening. A man will be waiting for you—he will have a red handkerchief."

"I shall be there," Du Sauchoy promised crisply.

With a bow, De la Noye melted into the crowd. Only several paces away, his eyes caught a ruby-gowned, slim figure. He pressed forward with a cry of admiration and pleasure.

Toying absently with her ruby sash, Felicienne le Mercier spoke with blonde Stephanie de Lobel. A moment later Philip de la Noye was bowing before them. "My dear Felicienne," he said, "your holiday in the country has only increased your irresistible charms..."

Stephanie curtseyed farewell to her aunt and slipped off, her blue eyes searching through the throng. Outwardly very animated and bright, the blond girl paused under a large overhead chandelier; it shone on her smooth arms and neck and danced in her eyes. Inwardly, however, she was tense with conflicting emotions—this would be the first time she would see

Gaston since that devastating party. She headed purposefully toward a group of young people.

Moving towards the dance floor on a young man's arm several minutes later, she heard a manly, cocksure voice from behind. "My dearest Stephanie—"

That voice! Her back tightened and a rush of memories swelled up.

"Ah, it is you," she said distantly. But while her voice and eyes were detached, she displayed her charms to their fullest extent as she turned.

He bent over her white hand. *"My dear,* may I have this dance?"

"I have this one," her escort broke in, glaring.

Gaston eyed the fellow with equal cheer, then focused again on Stephanie. "Then may I have the next?"

"That is taken; Sebastien asked me," she replied aloofly. "I am engaged three sets deep." Coolly, she turned with her escort and joined the other dancers.

Taken aback but quickly hiding his feelings, Gaston pressed his lips together, staring after her bewitching figure. *That girl at the last party!* he realized. *As if a fellow cannot have some fun....but Stephanie....I must win her back....*

Sebastien would not give up his claim to the next dance, and Gaston again had to wait. But when the music ended he hastened forward and showily took Stephanie before her next partner, a pale, wishy-washy youth, could claim her.

Stephanie's glacial attitude began to melt under his forward gallantry—and his rapturous grey eyes and whispers of assurance that she was the only one he cared for completed the conquest. By the time the dance was over she was as warm as ever.

However, something had changed, though she did not notice it then. A bit of trust—that precious part of any relationship—had slipped through the cracks.

~*~*~

Using a gold-headed cane, Grandpapa de Duret stumped down the street. Twisted clouds filled the benumbed blue sky, gliding slowly westward. A bracing December wind tossed pamphlets and tugged greedily at people's hats.

Shoving his *chapeau* more firmly on his head, he leaned into the stiff breeze. Up ahead, a woman in a tattered blue dress announced her wares in a nasal sing-song, a spindly arm thrown over her basket of flowers to shelter them from the blast. Her feet were almost bare, and the dull, listless look in her hollow face spoke of hunger and weariness.

A large man in a long red coat pushed past, throwing a scornful glance at the blooms she held out for his inspection. More passersby hurried by her, seeking shelter from the wind.

De Duret's eyes took in her need and despair. He stopped, holding his hat on against an especially fierce gust. "How much, Citoyenne?"

"Five *deniers*," she replied, uncovering her basket. The brightly-colored red and pink petals tossed in the wind.

"I will take two." Reaching into the worn basket he selected two small clumps, transferring them to the hand holding his cane. Pressing money into the woman's worn palm, he made his way down the street with a new briskness. Glancing hastily over his shoulder, he turned into a side street.

The woman uncurled her hand to slip the money in her faded reticule — and stopped, staring at the coins in astonishment. *He has overpaid me!* "Sieur —" Clutching the coins, she gazed open-mouthed down the street. Her benefactor was nowhere in sight.

The woman hastened after. Others trudged by, some holding their hats, but there was no sign of a stout elderly gentleman in a green coat. Giving up her search at last, she paused against the rough boards of a shop. Sobs shook her frail body — tears of gratefulness and hope, as she thought of her famished little ones at home.

As for "Citizen de Duret," only a few more blocks took him to a bookseller's. The book-shaped sign over the gaily-painted door screeched in the wind. The small-paned windows were crammed with books of all shapes, sizes, and colors — a bibliophile's paradise. But M. de Duret was not there today to browse. Minutes later he exited, tucking a parcel under his arm.

As he pushed open the door of the adjacent café, two elderly men in wigs looked up from a corner table. One was thin, dressed in embroidered orange satin, while his green-garbed companion was short and round-faced.

"*Bonsoir*, De Duret!" the thin man's pointed face broke into a smile. "You are a little later than usual."

"My apologies," Grandpapa de Duret bowed. "And how does the day find yourselves?"

"As good as can be, considering France's woes," replied the man in green. Seeing the carmine blooms, he chuckled, "Flowers! Surely they are a gift for Antoine and I."

"No, no," De Duret smiled, sitting down at the table. "I bought them for the flower-seller's sake. The poor wench!" The other two nodded sympathetically.

"What is that package—a book?" queried the thin gentleman, taking a pinch of snuff.

"Yes; 'tis the latest—<u>Réflexions sur la Révolution de France</u> [Reflections on the Revolution in France], by M. Edmund Burke."

"I have read it." The short man nodded his bewigged head. "'Twas very astute and well-written—for an Englishman. I heartily agreed with his points."

"I read a friend's copy," De Duret said, "and am buying this one for myself. The bookseller, M. Pierre-Gaëton Dupont, told me this book is in great demand—two thousand five hundred copies sold the first day, and they are preparing a second printing."

"That is good."

"It is certainly encouraging," the short man said thoughtfully. "Though Burke is across the sea, methinks he has a clearer view of Paris than many here. His stance against *this* revolution is especially noteworthy considering his support of the American Revolution."

"That commends him further to me," opined the rangy gentleman. "He does not hate change for its own sake. He praised the Americans for protecting society and staying under authority while saying 'no' to a tyrannous King who was breaking his own laws. However, he sees the problems with our revolution—how the masses are rebelliously overturning all society and wantonly throwing off restraints."

"I agree: he *is* even-keeled," De Duret flipped through the first pages. "He loves liberty, and does not jealously wish to keep it from other nations, but, he says, he cannot rise up in ecstatic praise when someone claims 'liberty' without first discovering what they mean by liberty, and how they have achieved it. He continues, '*Abstractedly speaking, government, as well as liberty, is good; yet could I, in common sense, ten years ago, have felicitated France on her enjoyment of a government (for she then had a government) without inquiry what the nature of that government was, or how it was administered? Can I now congratulate the same nation upon its freedom? Is it because liberty in the abstract may be classed amongst the blessings of mankind, that I am seriously to felicitate a madman, who has escaped from the protecting restraint and wholesome darkness of his cell, on his restoration to the enjoyment of light and liberty? Am I to congratulate a highwayman and murderer who has broke prison upon the recovery of his natural rights?*'"

"An apt allegory," the thin man said. "I have not yet read the book."

"Hear this," the short man said, his finger on the page, "He says that *without a proper distribution and manifestation* of government, armies, revenue, morality, religion, property rights, peace, order, and social manners, '*liberty is not a benefit while it lasts, and is not likely to continue long.*'"

There was a murmur of approval. De Duret mentioned, "'Twas well said that we do not need to destroy all social and governmental order to gain liberty. The oppression and terrible conditions of the poor *did* need to be addressed — but we could have done so without an uprising; we could have lawfully made recourse to our ancient constitution, instead of throwing it out and attempting to craft a new one." Taking up the book again, he read, "'...*You might have repaired those walls [of your old constitution]; you might have built on those old foundations. Your constitution was suspended before it was perfected, but you had the elements of a constitution....*

"'*You had all these advantages in your ancient states, but you chose to act as if you had never been molded into civil society and had everything to begin anew. You began ill, because you began by despising everything that belonged to you....*'"

"That is so." The slender man took a snuff-box from his orange coat. "I must certainly purchase a copy for myself — this M. Burke sagaciously evaluates our situation."

"I agree — and yet I wish he had spoken of the peasants' plight, and ways their lot should be alleviated — I feel some of his sentimentality about the former state of France is misplaced." M. de Duret's words went unheeded, for the stout man was leaning over and turning the pages, his round face absorbed.

"*Here* he gives a moving account of what has happened in our country," the short man said, starting to read: "'*They have seen the French rebel against a mild and lawful monarch with more fury, outrage, and insult than ever any people has been known to rise against the most illegal usurper or the most sanguinary tyrant....This was unnatural. The rest is in order. They have found their punishment in their success: laws overturned; tribunals subverted; industry without vigor; commerce expiring; the revenue unpaid, yet the people impoverished; a church pillaged, and a state not relieved; civil and military anarchy made the constitution of the kingdom; everything human and divine sacrificed to the idol of public credit, and national bankruptcy the consequence; and, to crown all, the paper securities of new, precarious, tottering power, the discredited paper securities of impoverished fraud and beggared rapine, held out as a currency for the support of an empire....'"*

"Read on!" cried the thin man, with a burning face.

"He says, *'Were all these dreadful things necessary? Were they the inevitable results of the desperate struggle of determined patriots, compelled to wade through blood and tumult to the quiet shore of a tranquil and prosperous liberty? No! nothing like it. The fresh ruins of France, which shock our feelings wherever we can turn our eyes, are not the devastation of civil war; they are the sad but instructive monuments of rash and ignorant counsel in time of profound peace. They are the display of inconsiderate and presumptuous, because unresisted and irresistible, authority.'"*

"*Bonsoir*, Citizens," a voice spoke from above. The three (bending close over the book in their interest), looked up simultaneously into a square, aristocratic face. "What is this intense study?" M. du Chemin smiled.

De Duret smiled back. "<u>Reflections on the Revolution in France</u>, by M. Burke. You have read it?"

"Most certainly; and with much agreement," Du Chemin remarked.

"Listen to this quote here:" the stout gentleman said, "'...*with* [France], *we have seen an infancy still more feeble growing by moments into a strength to heap mountains upon mountains and to wage war with heaven itself.'"*

"LaFayette and many others feel that the revolution is ended; that it has accomplished its aims, that things are quieting down," Du Chemin remarked. "But M. Burke explodes such wishful thinking. Anarchy and turmoil are around the corner, he predicts." He shook his head. "I pray this book will open the eyes of France."

"Amen," M. de Duret said, and the other two voiced their assent. Then he asked, "How is your good lady?"

"The doctor does not expect her to live a fortnight." There was pain in Du Chemin's strong voice.

"I am very grieved to hear it," De Duret answered, his eyes moist. "I shall keep her — and you — in my prayers, Christophe."

"I thank you most sincerely. And now I must return to her bedside. *Adieu*, gentlemen!" The wind swung the door shut after Du Chemin with a quivering crack.

The small gentleman in green, who had been thumbing through the book, pointed with a stubby finger; "Here it is! M. Burke warns of the danger of a military coup d'etat: '...*armies have hitherto yielded a very precarious and uncertain obedience to any senate, or popular authority; and they will least of all yield it to an assembly...of two years.... In the weakness of one kind of authority, and in the fluctuation of all, the officers of an army will remain for some time mutinous and full of faction, until some popular general, who understands the art of conciliating the soldiery, and who possesses the true spirit of command, shall draw the eyes of all men upon himself. Armies will obey him on his personal account, [and he shall become] the master of your whole republic.'"*

"That may not happen soon; especially with LaFayette as head of the National Guard: he would not stoop to such," the tall man commented. "The patriots may laugh at these words now....Yet if another man with less character than LaFayette takes charge of the army, we could face a situation like M. Burke predicts. I only hope his words are not prophetic!" But they were, for only a few short years later a reeling France turned to a military dictator—Napoleon.

"His critics say he condemns this revolution too harshly, but one sees his wisdom and moderation *here*," M. de Duret flipped to the end of the book. "He writes, *'But am I so unreasonable as to see nothing at all that deserves commendation in the indefatigable labors of this Assembly? I do not deny that, among an infinite number of acts of violence and folly, some good may have been done. They who destroy everything certainly will remove some grievance. They who make everything new have a chance that they may establish something beneficial....[Some say] that the same things could not have been accomplished without...such a revolution. Most assuredly they might, because almost every one of the regulations made by them...[was] voluntarily made at the meeting of the [Estates General by the King]....The improvements of the National Assembly are superficial, their errors fundamental.'"*

He looked up from the page, seeing his companion's sober agreement.

The busy café life circulated around them; several young rowdies laughed loudly at some "patriot" joke and brandished their sticks. "Long live Robespierre and the Thirty!" one cried. From various tables, people nodded approval, and several raised their wineglasses.

Grandpapa de Duret sighed. "I fear that although M. Burke's words will influence foreign opinion, they will not effectively wake up those who need it most—the French people."

The Angel of Death

17.

Verily I say unto thee, To day shalt thou be with Me in paradise.
— Jesus, Luke 23:43b

I t was evening, and very dark. An expensive coach pulled up in a quiet street. Above, a pale charger with an elongated horn gleamed with fresh paint — "The White Unicorn."

Etienne du Sauchoy spoke quietly to a servant before stepping out of his coach. "Follow at a distance on foot — do not let yourself be seen."

"Yes, Monsieur." The short man, a trusted servant, buttoned his dark jacket tightly across his midriff.

While Du Sauchoy exited pompously, the stubby servant slid inconspicuously out the other door and sheltered in a black alley opposite.

After perhaps twenty minutes, Du Sauchoy emerged from the tavern with a slender man in neat dark clothes. The two started briskly down the street. His servant slunk out of the shadows and pussyfooted after, keeping a distance.

A short walk took them to the side door of an ornate dwelling. At the slender man's coded knock, it opened quickly, and they stepped inside, the door closing directly. The shadowing servant settled down behind some barrels, keeping his eyes on the house.

Following his escort through a dim hall, Etienne du Sauchoy kept all his senses alert. *He was obviously directed to prove me before bringing me here,* Etienne recalled the keen questioning at the tavern.

The man stopped short and drew to the side. Opening a door, he motioned Du Sauchoy to enter. Light from within spilled out into the passageway.

Philip de la Noye rose and came forward, while three others stood. The room brimmed with sophisticated embellishment — from intricate ceiling moldings to busily-patterned rugs.

After preliminary greetings, Etienne voiced his concern. "I should hope this is not the entire cabal."

"Most assuredly not," a stout gentleman said. "But some are so highly placed that they must not appear until each new member has been properly scrutinized and approved."

Du Sauchoy bowed. "Of course."

A tall, gaunt gentleman fixed piercing eyes on Du Sauchoy. "You must swear allegiance…"

When the gentlemen were satisfied of his trustworthiness, the talk turned to the plot itself.

"Almost everything has been arranged," De la Noye put in; "the passes to the King's presence, the carriages….His Majesty has been approached, and is favorable. There are only a few more loose ends to tie up, and then we must await a favorable opportunity."

"Despite the people's vigilant 'jailor's' watch over the King, we shall succeed," the other man rubbed his hands. "What we need you to do, Du Sauchoy, is…"

The candles flickered over the five mens' bedizened garments, highlighting the forest green of one man, Du Sauchoy's yellow waistcoat, and the sage green and royal blue jackets of the other two—while the multi-faceted and complex designs of the furniture and walls competed for attention. Their showy finery formed a strange contrast to the desperate, dangerous plan they had sworn to. These men were not decorative peacocks.

~*~*~

Skyward, above the splintered tops of buildings, the stars were blurred and distant in the frosty winter sky. Honore, Tristan, and Marcel paced the narrow street below, heavy coats drawn against the cold. The struggling moonlight picked out the gleam of scabbards poking out underneath their long wool jackets.

It was not uncommon in Paris for young men to be out in the evening streets—coming home from parties, strolling the wide avenues, just loitering. But for this vigilant and methodical trio, such rambles meant looking for clues to robberies and protecting the populace.

They were in the depths of a crime-ridden district; the few passersby shot menacing glances at them, but the trio were unfazed. At eighteen, they were men now. Each was

…in the very May-morn of his youth,
Ripe for exploits and mighty enterprises.

317

After another long street, Honore steered into a deep doorway. "A few minutes' breather from this wind." A solitary streetlamp flickered fitfully at a dismal corner far ahead.

Partially sheltered, Marcel and Tristan rubbed gloved hands together, while Honore stamped his cold feet.

"Nothing suspicious as of yet," Honore rubbed his hands as well.

"Go over the list again, in summary," Tristan's brow wrinkled.

"There was the 'foreign fellow,' the boarder; he was suddenly accosted from behind with a knife," Honore began, running over a mental index. "Then the garrulous woman whose money was stolen from her room. There was your Auguste, who had a knife to his back—and also the baker, who had a similar experience. We have heard of quite a few other thefts, but no details were known. All were within this radius, this large area."

Tristan said nothing for a moment or two, eyes half-closed in concentration. Abruptly, he looked up. In the darkness they could just see each other's faces. "Do you not see a pattern?" he queried, his eyes glowing. "The robberies seem varied—we have discussed the difficulty in tracing so many thieves. But yet—as you spoke, Honore, I realized there is a thread of similarity between some of them."

"Yes?" Honore said.

"You mean," Marcel spoke quietly, "the sudden, knife-in-back kind?"

"Yes," Tristan replied. "We discussed once that they may point to the work of one man. They seem to have a time sequence, and the thief somehow obtains previous information—he is lying in wait for his victim. We at least could follow up on that trail."

"While tracking that thief, we may come upon clues to the others," Honore said. "I think you have hit upon something, Tristan!"

"What is the chronological order?" mused Tristan. "First would be the foreign boarder—"

"—September 30th or so," Honore finished his sentence. "Next of the knife-in-back robberies was the baker, on October 15th, and then Auguste was robbed on October 28th."

"Roughly two weeks apart," Tristan's eyes gleamed.

"As of yet, we have heard of no November knife-in-back robberies," Honore mentioned, "but does that not also point to one thief, perhaps, who is satiated for the present with the money from Auguste?"

"It is at least feasible," Tristan replied. "Let us keep our ears and eyes open! We may yet find clues to the other robberies—but this will narrow our first searches."

The three were crowded in a dark doorway, speaking in hushed whispers. Unconscious of their presence, a well-muffled, solitary figure hurried past, keeping to the middle of the street. When the man was no longer in sight, they stirred from the sheltering doorway.

"We had better separate to patrol now." Honore glanced round. "Where did that fellow go, just now?"

"Turned right on the next cross-street," Marcel said briefly.

"That is my direction," Tristan said. "I will go after him; not that he is suspicious, but he looked in rather a hurry."

"We shall be down flanking streets, as usual," Honore said. "You know how to summon us."

With shared nods, they parted. Tristan turned down the street the man had taken, eyes straining through the blackness. The man was nowhere in sight, though he could easily be just beyond the short range of vision.

As Tristan walked on, his body alert, his thoughts traveled to his mother. Mme. du Chemin was fading fast; each day brought her closer to eternity's brink. Tristan had thought of desisting in their search to spend all his time and energies with her, but his mother had gently dissuaded him. "You are trying to aid and defend these poor people," she had said, "and that is a noble cause, my son—do not give up such work for my sake." Still, Tristan spent much time with his mother, only planning outings such as this when his father would be there to sit with her.

The street was long. Short, miserable alleys connected to nearby backstreets. Between the scarce, scattered flickers of light, the tenebrous dark pressed down with heavy silence.

Unexpectedly, a scream pierced the air up ahead.

Tristan started at a dead run, loosening his sword in its sheath. Neighbors in dingy nightshirts were already opening doors and poking bleary faces out, but Tristan's attention focused on a few figures in the center of the street. He felt, but did not turn round to see, Honore, then moments later Marcel, come panting up.

In the center of the cobbles stood a gnarled man in a nightcap. He was directing a small lantern on a wasted young woman in a thin cloak, half-supported by a slight man—"The man we were following earlier!" Tristan whispered in Honore's ear.

The slender young man was speaking to the young woman as the three approached; "...when you were so delayed, Julie, I went after you."

"We were kept late, working on an outfit for a marquise." Her voice was weak and exhausted.

"Curse them!" The older man spoke in a cracked voice, his lantern providing the scene's only light. A woman peered from a window a few stories up, candle in hand, but her light only illuminated her gaunt, peevish face and the hanging strings of her gathered nightcap.

"Good that your lover came up then," piped in a frowsty woman. "Thefts happen all the time 'round here, and with those cursed employers keeping working-people late, they are fair game in these dark streets...."

"Is the young woman unharmed?" queried Honore. "We have been seeking information as to several thefts in this area."

Heads turned in his direction, and the babble of voices stilled.

"'Tis some cursed aristocrats," a rough voice said. "No need for *them* in our affairs."

"That's right," other voices chimed in. "They're the cause of our troubles." Several moved further away into the darkness; the knot of people began to break up.

"We are not here to pry," Tristan said. "We were passing by, and hearing this young woman's scream, came to aid her. We may be able to help—were you robbed, Citoyenne? How did it happen?" He turned to the girl, since the others were unresponsive.

She answered shyly, "No, Monsieur. A man tried to steal my wages, but Claude came up—"

The slight man who still supported her with an arm said, "Come, Julie—one can never trust 'gentlemen.' No need to tell *them*." Shooting a suspicious glance at the three, he melted into the blackness with the girl.

Doors creaked shut and windows scraped closed. The three were left alone, standing on the hard, cold cobbles, the stars in the dark firmament above them. Honore and Tristan exchanged glances of dismay.

"Of all the—" Honore cut himself short, shaking his head.

"*Ridiculous!* When all we were assaying to do was *help* them," Tristan replied in a low voice.

They moved off on their patrol—there seemed nothing more to say.

When they gathered at their designated corner, Tristan said, "What really hinders us most is the difficulty in obtaining information. You and I, Honore, have spent much time—and yet have heard only a few of the many stories. And what do mere stories give us, when we have not a vital link to the thieves' dens and hangouts?"

"I agree," Honore said, "but we must press on. Mayhap some will not be as aloof and close-mouthed."

"We certainly must continue our quest—especially on this thread of similar larcenies." Tristan's face was set.

~*~*~

The folds of night closed hard upon the city two weeks later. It was the last day of the year 1790.

The Du Chemin's abode was filled with the strange subdued bustle of a house on which rests the shadow of death. The doctor passed in and out; the extra maids hired to care for Mme. du Chemin went back and forth noiselessly from kitchen to sickroom.

In her bedroom, only a few candles pierced the gloom of night. Madame du Chemin lay quietly, her face ashen. She had been sinking all day. Her eyes were closed, her face almost bloodless. At her bedside her husband held her hand, with Tristan seated nearby, his eyes on her wasted countenance.

A little distance away, Felicienne le Mercier sat ready to give comfort or assistance. She could see the unmistakable signs of death in the paling face and faint, labored breathing.

The room was very still, save for the tick-tick of the clock and the slight breaths of the sufferer. It was a few minutes before midnight.

There was movement from the bed; Madame du Chemin's hand pressed her husband's. Her eyes opened and lips moved faintly. Her husband leaned forward: Tristan and Felicienne slipped softly to the bedside. They caught her faint words, which seemed addressed to her husband: "…France needs staunch men….God bless and—comfort you— He will give you peace….He has blessed us richly, my love."

Madame du Chemin's dying eyes sought Tristan. "May God protect you," she whispered, "fight for Him, my son—my son."

There was a pause, as her strength ebbed. The others pressed close, with that heartbreaking love and breathless waiting that comes at the very end—the desire to catch every last word, every last look.

"He is faithful," she said, rousing herself. "He is coming—for me!" Her countenance lighted with a glory altogether unearthly—and she was gone.

There was hushed silence before the doctor pronounced her dead. A wondering awe lingered in his usually stolid features—"She saw Him," he muttered. "She was so joyous!"

And so passed her soul with the old year, from darkness to light. A new year had dawned upon the world—a new life upon her. She was now in Heaven, where

God shall wipe away all tears from their eyes;
and there shall be no more death, neither sorrow, nor crying,
neither shall there be any more pain:
for the former things are passed away.
...And there shall be no more curse:
but the throne of God and of the Lamb shall be in it;
and His servants shall serve Him:
And they shall see His face; and His name shall be in their foreheads.
And there shall be no night there;
and they need no candle, neither light of the sun;
for the Lord God giveth them light:
and they shall reign for ever and ever.

~*~*~

Dong, dong, dong, dong, dong... Half-asleep, Adele counted the strokes of the distant bell. Twelve. *The beginning of the new year,* she thought drowsily. *Oh, how is Madame du Chemin...Lord, be with her!* She shifted in bed, turning onto her side.

She had spent all day, and most of the night before, watching at Mme. du Chemin's bedside. Earlier in the evening her mother sent her home to rest—but despite Adele's attempts, sleep would not come. She was too tired—too full of sorrow—to sleep.

But she *was* exhausted. After hearing the bells announce midnight, a peace settled over her. Thought slowly ebbed into dreamless quiet, and the moon peeked in the curtained panes onto her slumbering countenance.

Adele slept deeply and woke when the sun was high. It was an abrupt waking. Olivie burst into the room with a rending cry: "Adele, Madame du Chemin!"

Startled, Adele sat bolt upright, blinking her eyes. "What did you say?" Her sleep-blurred eyes focused on Olivie's distressed face. It told the news more eloquently than words.

"She is dead?" Adele asked, though she knew the answer.

"Yes; last night, Mother says—at midnight—she told me," Olivie sobbed, sitting stiffly on the edge of Adele's bed, one arm twined about the nearest bedpost. Drawing close, Adele slipped a white-sleeved arm around

Olivie's shoulders. The ruffles at the wrist of her chemise spilled over onto Olivie's stiff sage satin gown.

At first Adele felt only heart-wrenching remorse that she had not been there. Olivie cried softly, her head pillowed on Adele's shoulder, but Adele's heart felt frozen into silence. But suddenly, like a crashing wave, Adele's first, stunned response was tossed aside like a cockleshell by the torrent of sorrow that swept in. *I will never again hear her dear voice or see her coming through the parlor....* Madame du Chemin was gone from this earth—gone forever. Adele felt tears running down her cheeks; fumbling for a handkerchief, she realized she was in her nightgown—there was no dangling reticule. A tear dropped on Olivie's arm, and Olivie glanced up.

"Here—use mine." Slipping from Adele's grasp, Olivie pressed a damp ball into Adele's hand and left the room, presumably to get another. Left alone, Adele ignored the sodden linen square with its fine tatted edging. Throwing herself in a most unladylike gesture across the bed, she buried her tear-streaked face in the pillows.

Five minutes later, Olivie silently looked in. Seeing Adele lying across the bed, she drew the door shut softly and went downstairs to cry in her mother's arms.

Some time later Adele rose, drained. Her listless fingers selected a midnight blue gown from the tall wardrobe. Slowly she did the laces and pins, her fingers stumbling over the fastenings. At last the dress was on. Rummaging among her ribbons, she abstractedly pulled one out. She was tying the blue-black ribbon around her waist when a flood of memories cascaded over her. She gazed at the ribbon with filling eyes. *'Twas a gift from Madame du Chemin, when they first visited us, so many years ago....* Blinded by tears, she sank on a stool, clutching the ribbon.

But her keen grief was not despairing. It was deep, but not fatalistic. It cut sore, but there was an element of calmness, of peace, of— yes, *joy* underneath it all. Adele could not explain it, except to repeat the words of her Lord:

Verily I say unto thee, To day shalt thou be with me in paradise.

"She is with Him," she whispered, "and she is content. She will have no more pain, and—she will be waiting to welcome us Home when our time comes." With a few more tears, Adele tied the ribbon around her waist and reached for her Bible. Laying it open on the table beside a curving vase of flowers, she read:

So when this corruptible hath put on incorruption,
and this mortall hath put on immortalitie,
then shalbe brought to passe the saying that is written,
Death is swallowed up into victorie.
O death where is thy sting? O grave where is thy victorie?
The sting of death is sinne: and ye strength of sinne is the Lawe.
But thankes be unto God,
which hath given us victorie through our Lord Jesus Christ.

He has given her the victory, Adele mused, light breaking through her tears. *Death is swallowed up in victory, for her.*

Adele did not realize in the present moment of grief, but her sadness over Mme. du Chemin was completely different from her wild sorrow for her *gouvernante* Marie. Both deaths were equally sad: the difference was that now Adele was a Christian. *Now* she knew where the dead one had gone — *now* she had assurance of seeing Mme. du Chemin again someday.

The sting of Death was gone — forever — because the Lord Jesus had suffered and conquered Death once and for all.

Vogue la Galère — Keep Rowing

18.

My Saviour, mid life's varying scene
Be Thou my stay;
Guide me, through each perplexing path,
To perfect day.
In weakness and in sin I stand;
Still faith can clasp Thy mighty hand,
And follow at Thy dear command.
— Elizabeth Godwin

*I*n a rich green room, a fire burned dully. Its flames illuminated Francis and LaFayette, both standing, their faces pale against the room's shadowed affluence. An ornate grandfather clock showed half-past ten in the evening.

Laying some papers on the table, Francis seated himself. Dipping a quill pen into a silver-chased inkpot, he made a note on one page. "Thank you for bringing that to my attention. I will certainly make note of it in tomorrow's Assembly session."

"My apologies for the late notice; I called earlier, but you were out," LaFayette replied.

"I am sorry you were inconvenienced; I was attending Madame du Chemin's funeral," Francis said quietly.

"I heard the news — my condolences go with you," Gilbert answered.

"I thank you, marquis," Francis replied.

"I am the *Sieur Motier* now," LaFayette smiled.

"These new names; 'tis hard to change the habit of years, Gilbert," Francis answered, his eyes gaining a twinkle. "But pray be seated; may I call the servants for some light refreshments?"

"No, but thank you, Francis. I shall not tarry long." LaFayette sat down on a velvet chair opposite, putting his fingers together.

There was a pause as Francis rose and put the papers away. Then LaFayette spoke, "I know not where you stand on this matter, Francis, but I know I can trust you—and I feel I must speak to someone of my concerns." He took a breath. "Those Royalists—I am afraid they shall be the ruin of France."

Francis looked at him keenly. "Why so? You yourself are loyal to their Majesties."

"I am; that is why I fear the actions of the rabid Royalists," Gilbert's brow furrowed. "Between the violent sans-culottes on the one hand and they on the other...." He looked straight at Francis. "I have been endeavoring to bring the revolution to a peaceful close; hoping to usher in a constitutional monarchy—a balance of power between the King and Constitution. You know how I have worked to pacify things. But these Royalist plots to rescue the King from the Tuileries stir and alarm the people, bringing their excitement to a boil again, after all my efforts."

"I can see how you are between a 'rock and a hard place,'" Francis said. "Have you considered that perhaps your task is impossible?"

"Sometimes," LaFayette said, "but I press on for our country's sake."

"The demagoge's intoxication of power, already tasted by the downtrodden populace makes a potent *aperitif*. The Royalists who pursue the ends you deplore—rescuing the King from Paris, then returning with an army to crush the insurrectionists—may have fixed on the only solution to this tangled web," Francis said. "Besides, how can we expect your commendable goal of an orderly constitutional monarchy to result from anarchy, riot, and murder?"

LaFayette stared thoughtfully into the fire, and Francis said no more. The flames flickered and danced—surging upward and collapsing upon themselves, like the brave but chimerical dreams of so many throughout history.

"I cannot see things as you do," LaFayette answered at last. "I believe we can bring things to a peaceful conclusion. As I have written to General Washington, 'Our revolution is getting on as well as it can, with a nation that has swallowed liberty at once, and is still liable to mistake licentiousness for freedom.'" He looked across the table. "Yet there is much to conquer. I covet your prayers."

"You already have them," Francis said. "I honor you for fighting like a man and standing for your principles. *Vogue la galère*—Let the galley keep rowing; keep on, whatever may happen."

~*~*~

The air was foul, close, and bitter—the narrow street no more than an overgrown alley. Broken pinnacles of tenements creaked on either side. Tucked at the foot of one was a low eatery, poking bleary lights into the darkness. But Jules was used to such places—he swaggered into the greasy depths of the tavern without a pause.

The seamed, dirty faces turned up upon his entrance seemed unprepossessing, but Jules recognized several underground leaders—"movers and shakers"—of the revolution. He tucked his knotted stick under the arm of his coarse jacket. Pushing through the crowded tables, he was almost to the bar when a man stood up.

"Jules—do you not recognize me?" the man queried.

In an instant, Jules took in the thin figure with its long black hair and familiar scar. "Denis Moreau!"

"The same," Denis smiled crookedly. He drew an arm over Jules' shoulder. "Come, join me. It has been months! I was almost beginning to think the old proverb wasn't true—*Il n'y a que les montagnes qui ne se rencontrent jamais*—There are only mountains that never meet."

With something like a start, Jules remembered using that phrase when speaking to Denis' irate landlady. "I did try to look you up," he said, "but met instead your imposing landlady."

"She was rather less than pleased, I take it. I was broke—she can thank her stars that I left, instead of staying and making her bill longer," Denis chuckled dryly. "Ah, well—it is good to see you again, Comrade Jules." With an expansive motion to the *garçon de comptoir*, he cried, "A drink for this Citizen!"

The bartender nodded obsequiously, looking towards Jules. Jules gave his order. Before the man turned away to get it, Denis carelessly tossed some coins on the oily counter. He raised his voice. "Drinks for all, Comrade." A roar of approval emanated from the packed room—many rose and slapped Denis on the back.

"You're a true friend, Citizen Moreau!" cried a man with a hungry face, and others shared his opinion. Denis bowed grandly and turned back to Jules.

"You have found employment, Denis?" Jules queried, his eye on the pile of coins.

"*Non*—at least, not what I would call real work," Denis said lightly. "Have you ever heard the saying, '*Nécessité est mère d'invention*—Necessity is the mother of invention?'" He grinned suddenly. "My time is quite taken up by 'important revolutionary duties.'"

327

Jules' drink arrived, and Denis half-turned to speak to the landlord/bartender. Jules sat back in his chair, sipping his wine abstractedly and watching the swirl of activity. It seemed to center on their table. An editor of one of the most reactionary papers casually dropped into an empty chair. Denis greeted him familiarly; when the man glanced at Jules, Denis said, "I will vouch for him; he is a true patriot."

The man nodded, satisfied, and hunched across the table, talking in a voluble undertone to Denis. Jules let them talk — his mind was turning over several things. *Denis is not employed — or so he said…yet he has plenty of money. How in the world….*

His thoughts were broken by the departure of the newspaper editor and the arrival of three Brigands of the worst sort. They hung about the table, cracking coarse jokes with Denis and filling the air with swaggering *gasconade*. They seemed people of importance, at least here — Jules noted how many eyes surreptitiously were turned their direction.

At last, Jules rose to leave — his mother would worry if he was out too late. Besides, he somehow felt an uneasy dislike for the present company.

"We need to meet somewhere, man, and catch up on things; there's too much activity here," Denis said. "I have an idea on how to teach a lesson to that scoundrel…." he trailed off with a wink.

Though the nearby braggadocios had no clue to whom Denis referred, they snickered as if they understood — and Jules knew that Denis was even more influential than he had guessed.

"Yes we do." Pushing the hair out of his eyes, Jules said, "What about at my mother's, tomorrow afternoon?"

"Done, Comrade," Denis cried. With a final slap on the back, he waved a hand as Jules rose and threaded his way to the door. Curious glances were thrown after Jules. Who was this young man whom Citizen Moreau delighted to honor?

~*~*~

The strong wind blustered against Grandpapa de Duret as, leaning on Marcel's arm, he made his way to his usual fortnightly meeting with his two elderly friends, Antoine and Charles. They often met at home, but today they met again at their favorite tavern.

Marcel's aid was called for because of a startling event the day before. "Grandpapa de Duret" had been bringing food to a famishing family. As he left, a group of roughs had surrounded him. De Duret's cane was an old family heirloom, and as such still bore his heraldic arms on the head. The Brigands caught sight of it, and with a yell thronged the old man menacingly. Snatching the cane, they broke it to pieces. Then, turning on De Duret, they buffeted him about. When the woman of the house came out, protesting volubly, it took the Brigands back a bit. And when a passing carriage stopped and the sturdy occupant and coachmen seemed inclined to meddle, they slunk off with curses. Providentially, the man in the carriage was a casual acquaintance of M. de Duret's—else he might have passed by, not being inclined to involve himself in a fracas with the easily-stirred populace.

Now, escorted by Marcel, De Duret was turning down a side street when he was halted by a cry. Marcel turned sharply. A thin flower seller was running down the street, her eyes fixed on De Duret.

Curtseying, she looked up, tears beginning to trickle down her wan cheeks. "Monsieur—here you are, at last—oh, how I have watched for you, to thank you, Monsieur—your kind gift allowed me to buy bread for my—my children..."

Marcel looked at the woman uncomprehendingly, but De Duret instantly recognized her: the flower-seller he had purposefully overpaid months before!

"I do not need thanks, Mademoiselle," he said kindly. "Give thanks to God, the giver of all. I am glad to hear it blessed you."

"Oh, Sieur, if you only knew—they were starving; indeed, the littlest I thought would die! My husband has no work; I earn the barest pittance, not enough to buy the food they so needed. But your gift, Sieur, was enough to pull them through—they are so much stronger now!"

"I am Citizen de Duret; what is your name, and where do you live?" De Duret asked.

"In the Rue Jezin, opposite Simon the butcher's," she replied. "My name is Margot Thomas. Oh, good sir—Heaven's blessings be upon you for your good deeds! If I ever can be of help to you—if I can do anything for you—to pay you back, good sir!" Her dirty face was streaked white by tears. She looked so frail and worn that Marcel could not help thinking that however great her desire, there would never be a way she could aid them.

Grandpapa de Duret rested a hand on her flower basket. "Now that I know where you live, Margot, perhaps you would not be amiss to my visiting you and your family?"

She gave him a timid glance, half-incredulous, half-glad. "Oh, Sieur—that would be a great honor!"

"I will call soon, then," Grandpapa de Duret smiled. "Au revoir, Mademoiselle!"

"Good-bye, Monsieur—thank you, thank you!"

As they walked away, Marcel wondered at the vigorous pace De Duret set—he pulled Marcel around the corner and darted into the tavern door. But the reason became apparent a moment later. Through the leaded glass panes, Marcel spotted Margot, looking eagerly from side to side. New tears were on her cheeks, and he caught a silver glint in her clenched hand.

Grandpapa de Duret is up to his old tricks; he must have slipped her money when his hand was on the basket, Marcel surmised. He smiled at the abashed, quiet way in which De Duret succored the needy—never seeking outward praise, trying to do his alms "in secret" as much as possible.

Like many things in this life, there was no outward sign of the good they would reap because of De Duret's kindness. But somehow the woman's tear-streaked, grateful face stuck in Marcel's mind, even as he leaned at ease behind De Duret's chair.

BOOK THE THIRD

Lost Gambles

The King's Last Chance

1.

But, Mousie, thou art no thy lane [you are not alone]
In proving foresight may be vain:
The best laid schemes o' mice an' men
Gang aft a-gley, [oft go awry]
An' lea'e us nought but grief an' pain,
For promised joy.
— Robert Burns

*A*ll was still and soundless in a hidden by-way—but deceptively so. Tucked in a walled yard opening onto the alley sat a company of horsemen, accoutered for travel. The faint moonshine picked out the cold gleam of their weapons.

One of the horsemen, the marquis du Sauchoy, spoke in an undertone. "D'Inisdal is on his way to inform the King that all is ready for instant departure—he shall soon be back." He tucked his coat closer against the cold.

"A mere formality—the King has never withdrawn his approval," nodded another. Even under the shadow of his hat, his handsome face was unmistakable—'twas Philip de la Noye.

Another leaned forward with suppressed excitement. "The guards have been bribed, the carriages prepared—we will be his armed escort. All is set—we shall succeed!"

"Shhh!" another warned. They fell quiet, looking intently in the direction of the Tuileries, though buildings blocked it from view.

Winter wind lashed the Tuileries' ornately carved facade. The night gathered strength; it was yet ten o' clock. Inside, genial candles illumined four figures around a small table, cards in hand.

The light revealed the King's affable, weak features; the Queen looked lovely, tho' a bit worn. A rotund man and plain, large-nosed woman completed the quartet—the King's younger brother Louis Stanislas

Xavier XVIIII, and his wife Marie Josephine. They resided at the nearby Luxembourg palace.

Other than the faint slap of the cards as they were laid down, the room was silent. The ornate cherubs on the wall seemed to watch the foursome with interest.

A discreet knock broke the quiet. The chief Usher, Campan, entered with low obeisance. "I bear a message for Your Majesty."

"Speak on," said the King, looking up from his cards.

"I bring a message from the Comte D'Inisdal; he waits in the outer antechamber," Campan said. "He bade me tell you that tonight's National Guard captain is won over; post-horses are ready all the way; and there is a party of armed and determined Noblesse waiting to escort you; if you will consent, before midnight, to flee."

The King's eyes turned back to his cards. He switched the position of one in his hand. Campan waited expectantly for an answer, but there was only an acute silence.

The Queen broke the stillness, her face strained. "Did your Majesty hear what Campan said?"

"Yes, I heard," the King answered. He laid down a card, and the game continued on — the others casting quick glances at his face.

"'Twas a pretty couplet, that of Campan's," his brother hinted, after several heavy minutes dragged by.

His Majesty the King played on, disregarding the remark. The others played their cards in turn — but tension charged the air. His brother & sister-in-law were in a difficult situation themselves — most probably Louis Stanislas had wished a thousand times before now that he had fled with their brother Charles after the Bastille fell in 1789. Now it was 1791 and it was a sticky business to even think of escape, let alone attempt one.

The game continued, Campan waited; at last the Queen mentioned, "After all, one must say something to Campan."

"Tell M. D'Inisdal," the King spoke at last, "that the King cannot *consent* to be forced away."

Exiting with with a bow, Campan proceeding with trembling step to report to D'Inisdal in the outer antechamber.

"I see!" cried the comte D'Inisdal. "We have the risk; we are to have all the blame if it fails."

He angrily stormed out — and (though the King knew it not) the last hope of fleeing Paris was gone forever.[1] The King encouraged these many plots, but never had the courage or decisiveness to carry them out — until one fateful day in June, when it was too late.

~*~*~

The armed aristocrats waited impatiently in the cold street for D'Inisdal. The only sound was the occasional stomp of a restless horse hoof.

At last D'Inisdal appeared, in a towering passion. Brusquely he related the failure of their plot—"all because our King is so weak, pusillanimous, vacillating..."

The plotters—who had risked their lives and honor in this venture—grumbled among themselves.

"'Tis true, what Mirabeau said," one spoke bitterly, "'The Queen is the only *man* whom the King has about him.'"

Du Sauchoy chewed his lip. Uncharacteristically, he did not spew out curses, like the others; but he was deeply disappointed.

"Complaining will do no good; we are in needless risk here," De la Noye's face was clouded.

The others saw the wisdom of his remark, and quickly rode off in separate directions. Thus the grand plot, so near fruition, dissipated into the formless night.

Though she had heard her husband's words, the queen seemed to place hope in the hint he gave that he would be happy to be "forced" away, "without" his consent. In her shadowed room in the Tuileries, the queen stood packing her jewels for a rendezvous that would never take place.

~*~*~

One-two-three-four, one-two-three-four, sang the horses' hooves, dancing over the wide tan meadows near Versailles. Adele's outing took place after all—though it had expanded to include the La Motte young ladies, and also Sebastien du Sauchoy; for Adele had said, "He is rather down; Stephanie has been so keen on Gaston of late..."

The breeze swooped playfully about Adele, filling her with joy and making her glad she had secured her hat firmly. She glanced down at her beautiful red riding outfit—impeccably-tailored jacket with gold buttons, matching gathered skirt which, being shorter than usual, showed her stylish black riding boots....The other girls were accoutered similarly: Olivie and Elisabeth in two different shades of blue with silver highlights, Christelle in orange.

Adele rode lightly and well. The turf stretched before them. As they gave their horses more rein, the jouncing trot suddenly released into a smooth, rhythmic canter. Adele felt like she was flying on a roiling gray cloud. The turmoil and strife of aristocratic dagger, maundering King, and sans-culotte *Lanterne* seemed far, far away.

Over the wintry grasses they flew, minding not the brisk air. Adele saw small signs of winter's end everywhere. A small flock of fat-bodied birds darted across the sky; all that were left from the excessive hunting by the peasants, since they were now allowed to hunt anywhere. Adele found her eyes following the wheeling pigeons.

Honore motioned casually to a glint of metal under Sebastien's open, close-fitting jacket. "If I may ask, what do you have there?"

"A poniard," Sebastien answered. "I had it made by a metalworker we know; it took him some time, as there were many other aristocrats wanting daggers of this type."

"'Patriot' rumor has it that the sudden surge of aristocrat interest in daggers is part of some evil oligarchic plot to assassinate 'the Thirty' and other prominent sans-culottes," Tristan said. "I, of course, do not believe it—but would be curious to know your opinion."

"All lies or distortions," Sebastien scowled. "Can we not carry weapons for our own protection, and for the King's?"

"That is why I wear this sword," Tristan touched the ornate hilt.

"And I," Honore echoed.

"A dagger is easier to conceal," Sebastien mentioned off-handedly. "Besides, swords are seen as symbols of the aristocracy, and thus viewed with hostility."

Honore's and Tristan's eyes met in a flash. They needed no words to tell each other, "That's just what we need!"

"Where did you say you had yours made?" Honore asked Sebastien.

"The metalworker's at the northwest corner of the *Place de Greve,*" Sebastien said. "I am sure he could make you one, if you desire."

"Thank you very much; I will certainly call there," Honore smiled meaningfully at Tristan.

"What think you, Sebastien," Adele asked, "of the youths who brag and openly sing Royalist couplets in cafes?"

"*Outré*—a trifle too *outré,*" Sebastien said, looking at her. "What good does it do? It merely inflames the people further against us."

"They are inflamed, certainly; the masters of the mob are waiting impatiently for some excuse to riot," Tristan said.

The scattered clumps of naked forests spread and changed; through an opening in the brown tree trunks ahead, the cropped, tan grass ran gently down to the banks of a stream. The party separated a little, riding up close to the dimpled, leaden waters. The shadows of the overhanging trees were a little too chill for this time of year; the sun, though pale, was welcome.

Adele drew her mount near the verge of the stream and peered into the crystalline depths, enjoying the rippling sound of the water over the stones and drooping grasses. Along the stream and in a half-circle round, the skeleton trees rose, with an exposed, lace-like beauty quite different from the lush green of summer. One hoary branch drooped near Adele, its tiny purplish leaf-nodules heralding spring; she reached up and snapped off a small twig, tucking it in her red jacket for a memento.

"It is so delightful to ride once more," Elisabeth said.

"Simply euphoric," Adele agreed, as they drew their horses reluctantly away from the cool water and set off again.

"How felicitous to ride like this—between innumerable fetes and accompanying calls, we have been much occupied," Elisabeth added.

"Father has been very busy—the Assembly is full of business, continuing to work on the Constitution, setting up new courts...." Adele said.

"A Citizen Robespierre was appointed the 'Public Accuser' for the new 'Courts of Judicature,'" Elisabeth said. "I remember that he is a leading member of 'the Thirty.' Do you know aught of him?"

"He is such a prim, precise little man that he seems ill-fitted to be a revolutionist," Adele said, "but Father deems him more dangerous than even massive, lion-like Danton."

A gust of dancing breeze dashed over them, its chillness invigorating. "Oh—the air is lovely!" Adele rhapsodized. Patting her steed's neck with a gloved hand, she fell mute, her eyes drinking in the gray tree-lined hills. The faintest promise of green lightened their summits. *What will this new year be like?* she wondered.

Elisabeth followed her gaze, saying nothing—she had one of those rare qualities found in good friends; the ability to just be silent, without the awkward need to be constantly conversing. When she sensed that their pause had run its course, Elisabeth remarked, "The seasons stay the same—but how we mortals boil and change against their cyclical backdrop!"

Adele looked quickly at her. "Just what I was thinking—how did you know?"

Elisabeth's blue eyes twinkled. "Practice," she laughed. "We have talked often enough, Madame Adele."

The afternoon was summed up by a lovely tea, at which Mme. la Motte presided like a good fairy, enjoying herself as much as anyone else.

Day of Poniards

2.

"The spirit of France waxes ever more acrid, feversick: towards the final outburst of dissolution and delirium. Suspicion rules all minds: contending parties cannot now commingle; stand separated sheer asunder, eyeing one another, in most aguish mood, of cold terror or hot rage."
– Carlyle, writing of Spring 1791

February 28, 1791. Letting the door slam, Leuren Andre de Lobel sauntered off down the blustery street. With casual indifference he passed the usual trinket-hawkers, nodding once to a grimy workman. Knots of jaded ruffians, servants hurrying on their errands...it was a typical day.

"There you are—at last!" Gaston cried, seizing his arm. "There is good work for patriots today—come, Andre!"

"Anton—Anton Petit?" Andre was jolted from his ennui.

"He's already there," said Gaston.

Andre followed, gasping questions—he eventually sorted out that there *was going to be* a rising among the dregs of the city, mainly in the Saint-Antoine district.

"Those staid burghers of the Paris Parlement, in the Hotel-de-Ville—they've decided to repair the castle of Vincennes," Gaston said, tossing sentences over his shoulder in fragments. "Sent out workmen this morning—*They* say it is because the other prisons are full—say they need more space. Need more space for who? For the true patriots? But we shall put a stop to their plans!"

They hurried on, dodging carriages and lumbering carts. At last, around them loomed the wretched five-story tenements of Saint-Antoine. The dirty streets were packed with rowdy people; lank Anton Petit gestured with a long arm to the disheveled unemployed men, assertive Brigands, and squirrelly street urchins.

A wizened, dark-faced man addressed the masses in shrill tones. "Comrades, why should they repair the battlements of Vincennes? This

338

symbol of oppression must be torn down! Was not Mirabeau imprisoned once here? Its very walls speak of the crushing power of the aristocrats! We conquered the Bastille—shall we not conquer this lesser fortress?"

Gaston plunged into the crowd as its wolfish cry of agreement was still ringing in everyone's ears. He began haranguing a different part of the herd. His handsome, passionate face and fierce energy did much to stir the fainthearted. As for the coarser, bolder sort—impatient of words, they rushed headlong through the streets towards the castle of Vincennes.

At length the ten towers and crenellated walls came into sight, ringed by their moat. Busy workmen lifted stones into place on the walls, while others pounded away with hammers. In the street, other workmen repaired the low moat coping.

The water checked the mob's first-comers. The dutiful workmen stared uneasily as the angry throng poured in greater and greater numbers around the castle, waving rude improvised weapons. The workmen on the mob's side of the moat were especially frightened. With menacing voices, the crowd chanted, "Raze it! Raze it! Tear it down!"

The workmen remonstrated, telling again and again that they had been instructed by the Paris parlement to repair the building, and that it was for the good of the people....

"Less talk, more action," muttered Gaston. He raised his voice. "Friends—shall we not act?" With a gigantic gesture, he wrenched a sledgehammer from a workman on their side of the moat.

The crowd roared its approval. Some seized and opened the outer gate; others forced down the drawbridge. The whooping rabblement rushed over it, forced open the gate, and dashed into fortress.

Andre kept close to Gaston. They felt the dull *thunk-thunk* of the drawbridge underfoot, then the smooth stones of the courtyard. Gaston led the way to the iron window-stanchions—with the sledgehammers, these were wrenched out and broken into lengths, then passed to the crowd for use as crowbars. In the building, armed with one of the makeshift crowbars, Andre found a sort of entertainment in prying open doors, smashing furniture, and tossing the fragments out the windows. The noise of others applying their crowbars to walls and tiles, punctuated by shouts of evil merriment, resounded throughout the castle. The workmen had long since fled, carrying their woeful tale to the *Hotel-de-Ville*.

~*~*~

A highly-agitated gentleman rushed into the Du Sauchoy's parlor. Sebastien and his father had been sitting in silence; his father making notes in a handheld social calendar, Sebastien alternately perusing a newspaper and staring absently into the fire.

The gentleman was obviously upset—he had scurried in without waiting to be announced. For an aristocrat who loved ceremony, this neglect was astounding in itself. "The sans-culottes are aroused!" he cried, eyes bulging. "They are attacking Vincennes, and the King shall be their next target!" Panting, he hurried on, "I have talked with D'Espremenil, Chevalier de Court, and others—we have agreed we must use our Tickets of Entry and rally round the King!" His hands clenched and unclenched spasmodically. "I must go and tell others—*au revoir!*" With a perfunctory bob, he hurtled out, a bundle of nervous fears.

Etienne du Sauchoy rose steadily, stuffing his engagement-book into a pocket. "I shall be back, Sebastien," he said, "unless things go wrong for us."

Sebastien sat in stunned silence, then thought, *I will ask to go with Father.* He remembered longingly Honore and Tristan's close relationships with their fathers. But as he moved after his father, the cook stepped in. With a scraping curtsey to the youth, she inquired after the meal.

Despite his calmness, Du Sauchoy moved swiftly. By the time Sebastien brushed past the cook, his father was at the door in black coat and riding-boots, a poinard's knobbed hilt just visible from an inner jacket pocket. Sebastien hurried after, but his father had already stepped into the carriage and ordered the driver to proceed with all speed to the Tuileries.

~*~*~

Meanwhile, in the *Ménage* (close to the Tuileries), the National Assembly rocked with a furious verbal tempest. The debate centered on a proposed law against emigration.

Jean de Lobel scowled from his seat among "the Thirty." The Breton club (to which he belonged) had created this law against the émigrés and was determined to pass it, but were facing stiff opposition from the Right. For not only did the Royalists have friends among the émigrés, but they knew that they themselves might have to flee France someday.

The Thirty's clout and vocal power had been dauntingly vast, but the Royalists had risen with passionate, fiery resistance. The verbal battle had been going on for days with no diminution; indeed, it seemed hotter than ever.

A Royalist was standing, shouting "aristocratic cant" against the law, waving his arms hysterically, but influencing no one. When the man ended, Jean de Lobel started to his feet, eyes blazing, but a nearby deputy was already bawling approval of the bill and cursing the emigrating aristocrats.

Then, Mirabeau advanced to the speaker's place with his shambling gait. Jean marked the unhealthy flush in his great seamed face, the weakness in his movements. *He looks ill! He is wearing himself out with his labors – and his* amours. *'Twill be a good thing for us....*

Though his body was wracked, Mirabeau's voice had lost none of its people-swaying power. "I swear beforehand that I will not obey such a law," he roared. His bulging eyes darted unspeakable scorn on "the Thirty." His voice rushed on — soothing, scathing, cajoling, commanding — working its magical influence once again.

"Silence," he cried, concluding his speech. "Silence, the thirty voices!"

The rumbling echoes of that last sentence died slowly into nothing; "the Thirty" sat silent. They had been stilled by the power of one man;

...and the Law is once more as Mirabeau would have it.

~*~*~

Even as the Assembly's debate peaked, LaFayette, on his white charger, arrived at the castle of Vincennes' fast-tumbling walls. Blue-coated National Guard soldiers (the Saint-Antoine Battalion, led by Citizen Santerre) had already assembled there, but they merely stood watching the destructive mob.

Andre and Anton were outside, prying at a wall with improvised picks. Andre was leaning against it to mop his brow, feeling this was harder work than he was used to — and thus he was one of the first to notice LaFayette's arrival. The National Guard regiment had caused some alarm when they arrived a bit before; but since they did not hinder, the attack on the castle stones continued.

"Hoo — here's the Sieur Motier, come to tell us what to do!" Andre cried.

"That's the spirit," Gaston chuckled approvingly.

Looking up, the mob found any tremors stilled when they saw the Sieur Motier (LaFayette) riding up alone — no troops with him. Hooting and jeering, the swarming masses showered him with mocking, coarse bravado. A foul, unwashed man seized LaFayette's boot, trying to unhorse him. The rabble feared not the General. They knew their own regiment of National Guards would not side with him against them.

Ostensibly working hard, Gaston slid along the wall to the corner. Andre followed, puzzled. Wielding his sledgehammer, Gaston murmured, "Now we can slip out of sight if needful."

Andre followed suit, using his crowbar once more, but answered back, "There is nothing he can do."

"If so, we are doing as good work here as there," Gaston replied. "But when a man has a face shining with brave resolve like that, 'tis wise to not let oneself be singled out for special notice."

Hearing Gaston's words, Anton stopped work to motion with his hands. "A face like his is merely the face of a proud aristocrat," he said. "It is all proven in the veritable study of physiognomy. That particular nose, for instance, is the mark of a scheming tyrant, as is illustrated so clearly by the fact that one can see that same nose on the faces of oppressors such as…"

The work of destruction went on, the people screeching their defiance or laughing harshly at LaFayette's commands to desist. Not content with vocal opposition, some advanced to attack the General. Turning in the saddle to Santerre, LaFayette soberly ordered the National Guard captain to command his men to fire on the contumacious rabble.

Captain Santerre looked smoothly back at his general and responded in a voice loud enough to be heard even by Andre, "These are the men that took the Bastille." That was his last word; and his troops' settled faces showed their rebellion. Andre felt relieved, though he knew he had seen a terrible thing—military disobedience.

LaFayette turned to the magistrates of Vincennes. Andre could tell that the weak-kneed magistrates were not going to back the general, either. They protested that they could not give him any warrant of arrestment, or provide him any support at all.

Spurring his horse some paces forward, LaFayette addressed the mob in clear, ringing tones. If the troops and officials would not enforce law and order, he would do it alone—or perish in the attempt.

Gaston had been prying at a particularly obstinate stone. But as the General spoke, more and more rioters desisted, turning uneasy, sullenly resentful faces towards La Fayette. Gaston motioned to Andre. "Best stop at present; I don't like the look of things; no need to draw attention by being among the last workers."

They laid their tools down, realizing that Anton was finishing his soliloquy—he apparently thought they had been listening; "…and so by the test of historical comparison, as described by M. Lavater, one can confidently state that the Sieur Motier embodies the finished features of a cowardly, oppressive, and worthless member of the oligarchy..."

"His new study — physiognomy," Gaston muttered in Andre's ear. "But what a mistaken analysis! If only LaFayette *was* cowardly and worthless — Look!"

Advancing a few more paces, LaFayette pointed out several ringleaders. His gestures were commanding — and he was obeyed. The men were pushed forward and held — held sulkily, but still held — by nearby members of the rabble.

With adamantine resolve and unwearied patience, LaFayette accomplished his task. The demolition was stopped and the mob dispersed; he arrested some dozen of the most prominent and left the square with his prisoners — victorious, by the sole force of his will, over the sans-culottes.

Gaston, Anton, and Andre slipped away around the corner and into the maze of streets. Like the other scattering masses, they were filled with two main emotions: resentment and bafflement. Their victory over this "small Bastille" had been thwarted; torn from their grasp by one man.

~*~*~

Jules and Denis watched these developments from the shadows. As the would-be conquerors slunk off, foiled, Denis came to life. "Now's our chance — we will have a victory yet, Jules. LaFayette cannot be in two places at once." His black eyes flashed. "You know what to do. Meet at the north-west corner of the palace."

They glided off in separate directions. Jules fastened onto a departing Brigand and began to talk in a low, earnest voice. "Surely, comrade, you know there is work to do still."

The man glanced narrowly at Jules, trying to look knowing.

"The Royalists are gathering at the Tuileries," Jules said. "They plan to steal away with the King."

The man's face grew red. "Not if I — if *we* —" his swinging arm gestured to the scattered figures slinking into alleys and byways, "have anything to say about it!" Raising his voice, he called, "Comrades! The aristocrats mean to help the King escape! Our enemy Austria stands waiting to welcome our traitorous Sovereign and declare war on our country! To the Tuileries — we shall foil their schemes!"

Jules could hear agitated voices down a nearby street — Denis was having success as well.

"To the Tuileries!" rustled through the streets. Though some, too disheartened, slunk on to their hovels, many surged towards the Tuileries, spurred by an angry desire to vindicate themselves. At the head of an increasing mob, Jules ran through the cobbled streets. Strangely, he felt no elation, though he did not waver as he led them on. When they reached the Tuileries, he joined Denis at the appointed corner. They shared silent grins of success. The Tuileries stood black against the lurid sunset, its lighted windows shining in the fast-growing darkness.

~*~*~

Inside the Tuileries (the King's residence), M. du Sauchoy paced restlessly up and down an ornate anteroom. The palace was crowded with black-coated aristocrats: some talking in low tones, others brooding nervously alone.

Using secret tickets of entry, they had all gathered some hours before, when alerted of the mob's attack on Vincennes. As the hours wore on, the suspense grew more intolerable.

The sun was setting in the porcelain blue sky, casting long, yellow-red shafts of light in the windows. As the orange glow diffused and danced, reflecting off gold and silver wallpaper, it made the cimmerian aristocrats look like black silhouettes. Their simplified shapes created an interesting picture, Du Sauchoy noted. Each figure looked somehow sinister and fantastical when painted only in ebon profile. His friend there, he had always known to be tall—but when seen as a living shadow, he looked absurdly thin, almost gaunt—and he'd never noticed how ridiculously the man tied his cravat.... His attention shifted to another figure, whose stout form, now divested from personhood by the odd light, looked like a ball with legs.... And how farcically those tufts of hair stuck from that balding man's head—*He surely should have stuck to wearing a wig,* Du Sauchoy told himself.

One of the human contours was moving towards him—Du Sauchoy recognized a husky aristocrat from a family he personally despised. He had no wish for empty salutations. He turned, breaking the fancies he'd been toying with—wondering at himself, for he was not usually imaginative. *It must be the strain of this cursed waiting,* he excused himself, feeling a little ashamed. He paced down the room. One of the King's guards (a *Centre Grenadier*) glowered beneath his helmet at the gathered aristocrats, his eyes full of suspicion.

Continuing on, Du Sauchoy saw a short fellow-Royalist arriving, and bowed with polite cordiality. The man responded, uneasily fingering the knob of his gold-headed cane.

"A bad business, this. Any fresh reports of the riot?" Du Sauchoy asked.

"I heard a rumor as I was coming through the streets: LaFayette has quelled the disturbance," the other answered.

"That is good—very good, if it is true," Du Sauchoy said, relieved.

"Yes." The man tiptoed to whisper in Du Sauchoy's ear, "I am worried about these *Centre Grenadiers*. They suspect us—rumor has it that we engineered this Vincennes outbreak to distract Paris so that we can spirit away the King."

The little man sank down on his heels, but a moment later was stretching up to hiss into Du Sauchoy's ear again. "I fear they are stirring up a pot of trouble....The *Centre Grenadiers* are all 'patriots,' and thus hate us—they resent our special passes; and the foul newspapers spread foolish lies, saying we have been plotting all along to help the King escape! I heard the guards saying a moment ago that such was obviously our plan, since some of us are wearing riding-boots, as if for travel!"

A suggestion of a smile flitted over Du Sauchoy's face at the man's heated denial of former plots to rescue the King. But glancing at the hostile guards, he felt his mirth vanish. He took two more turns about the room, noticing other Royalists were also casting edgy glances at the *Centre Grenadiers*.

A few *Grenadiers* gathered in a corner, whispering and pointing at the aristocrats. Suddenly one guard stepped forward, reaching for a gentleman named Chevalier de Court.

"Hold, Monsieur!" the guard cried.

Chevalier de Court walked off, ignoring the summons, but the other guards seized him. By now, the eyes of the whole room were fixed on the disturbance. More guards entered, and Du Sauchoy and the other Royalists watched as the *Centre Grenadiers* held De Court. A guard pulled a wooden bludgeon out of De Court's left *lapelle*.

"Ah! As we said—a dagger!" the soldiers hissed. "No doubt to slay the Patriots!"

Another turned towards the watching Royalists. "What of them?" he gestured. "Have they daggers too?"

The Royalists recoiled backwards *en masse*, as if to leave by a back-hallway or stairs; but the *Centre Grenadiers* were everywhere. Seizing those nearest, they began searching them. The incensed hubbub increased when, one after another, they found a weapon on each aristocrat—whether a pistol, sword-cane, or poniard. The *Grenadiers* threw each onto an ever-increasing pile, their rage escalating.

What was the crime of having a weapon? None. But the *Grenadiers* had been swayed by the paranoid press.

Du Sauchoy was farther back, but his height gave him an advantage. Above the dismayed Royalists in front, he saw an unbelievable sight. Several of the Grenadiers opened the door to the stairs and flung the Chevalier de Court bodily down. From the thuds and sharp yells, Du Sauchoy perceived that the sentries were aiding De Court's downward progress with blows and kicks. He could hardly believe his eyes and ears.

Others were equally stunned—but the Grenadiers continued on, searching man after man and shoving them down the stairs, to run the gauntlet of abuse and blows. *Atrocious! What will the King say? He will surely put a stop to this!* Du Sauchoy thought, incensed and dumbstruck. He was not long in finding out.

The din reached the King, for he stuck his flabby face around the door leading to his inner sanctuary. "I command you all to give up your weapons." Then he shut the door on the sound of his loyal supporters' distress-cries.

Du Sauchoy, face flushed with anger at his sovereign, drew forth his poniard and threw it to the tiled floor. It clattered helplessly. He glanced out the window—dusk had fallen.

"We came to protect him—and this is how he treats us!" scowled a Royalist several paces ahead.

"He desires to avoid bloodshed," another frowned even as he tried to excuse their King.

"'Avoid bloodshed!'" shrilled the other. "He shall find this brings more bloodshed, this emasculated, namby-pamby course of conciliation to rebels!"

The Grenadiers, faces alight with fierce merriment, reached for the man as he spoke, and began dragging him toward the staircase's dark, open mouth.

~*~*~

As they reached the bottom of the stairs, the hapless aristocrats were thrust impertinently into the outside courtyard, where a huge throng of sans-culottes had gathered. They greeted the black-garbed men with rough words, gibes, and rude violence.

In the twilight, Jules stood with Denis among the crowd they had gathered and galvanized. Though both had orchestrated this, their faces were very different. Jules watched with mixed emotions. Even he felt this was a disgraceful scene—like hitting a man when he is already down. Denis' face, however, expressed great satisfaction as the waiting crowd chaffed the already bruised and rumpled aristocrats as they landed at the bottom of the stairs and tried to make their escape.

There was a noise on the outskirts—Jules turned to see a glimmering white horse, and knew the rider instantly. LaFayette!—returning victorious from the castle of Vincennes.

LaFayette pressed his horse though the multitude. His expression at this new disturbance was not pleased. By brief questioning, he discovered that this new outburst was "due" to "made to order" poniards found on some Royalists. The suspicious guards and people asserted that this was "proof" of underhanded aristocratic plotting against the people.

Poor LaFayette! In his mind, the path to a free France lay in a moderate Constitutional Monarchy, but the overhanging cliffs of the Royalists on one side and the rabble on the other threatened to destroy it all.

Even as LaFayette learned what was going on, a figure in black ran desperately through the crowd, chased by several active sans-culottes. LaFayette spurred forward. Reaching the hapless aristocrat, he waved the pursuers back, then began berating the man sharply. The noise of the crowd prevented Jules from hearing most of LaFayette's tirade, but the last words were clear: "…and you would go ahead and bungle everything!"

Turning from the man he rescued, LaFayette pressed his horse forward to extricate the other unfortunate Royalists, emerging from the staircase quite the worse for wear.

A man scurried up near Jules and pressed into the swarming mass. Jules recognized Pétion, a radical member of "the Thirty" and recently lauded by the populace.

A few minutes later Pétion came back, dragging a besmirched aristocrat—D'Espremenil, the man who some three years ago had been the hero of the Paris parlement. As they passed him, Jules' caught D'Espremenil's bitter words of warning to Pétion: "And I too, Monsieur, have been carried on the people's shoulders."

Fickle as the wind, as a woman's mood—how difficult it is to please an emotion-driven populace!

So ended the last day of February—in which Constitutionalism stood victorious (for the moment) over sans-culottes and Royalists.

LaFayette had conquered the mob which was attacking Vincennes, and even though the rabble had rallied and harassed the aristocrats, LaFayette had also put an end to their Royalist-baiting. LaFayette wrote of it to General George Washington:

"The rage of parties, even among the patriots, is gone as far as it is possible, short of bloodshed.... I myself am exposed to the envy and attacks of all parties, for this simple reason, that, whoever acts or means wrong, finds me an insuperable obstacle ; and there appears a kind of phenomenon in my situation ; all parties against me, and a national popularity which, in spite of every effort, has been unshakable. A proof of this I had lately, when disobeyed by the guard, and unsupported by the administrative powers who had sent me, unnoticed by the National Assembly, who had taken fright. The King I do not mention, as he could do but little in the affair, and yet the little he did was against me. Given up to all the madness of license, faction, and popular rage, I stood alone in defence of the law, and turned the tide up into the Constitutional channel."

Jules is Enlisted

3.

I carry in my heart the death-dirge of the French Monarchy:
the dead remains of it will now be the spoil of factions.
— some of the last words of Mirabeau

T he breeze still had a nip; the warm Spring sun was welcome as it
beat down on the elaborately-carved stone façade of the *Palais-Royal*
and spilled into its lively courtyard.

Honore shifted position on the café seat and cast his eyes on the
paper in his hands. He was here to look for any clues, and had been
scanning the area from behind his paper. *I must at least make a pretence of
reading,* he thought wryly. *The account of Mirabeau's illness contains nothing I
have not heard – everyone knows that he is sinking.*

Picking up another paper, he read: "*L'Ami du Roi* (Friend of the
King), 22 March 1791." An article caught his attention, and he read with
real absorption:

FRANCE IN DIVISION

Authorities who condemn the oath demanded of the clergy:	*Partisans of the oath demanded of the clergy:*
The pope and the cardinals	Mirabeau
Thirty bishops in the National Assembly	Two bishops of the National Assembly
Ninety-six other French bishops	Three or four other French bishops
The greater part of the priests from the city of Paris	Fifteen or sixteen priests from the city of Paris, out of fifty-two
All the cathedral and collegiate chapters	Some apostate monks
The Sorbonne, the greater part of the University of Paris, the provincial universities	Academics of the current philosophies
Fifty thousand priests or vicars	Seven to eight thousand priests or vicars—ambitious, troublesome, fanatical, ignorant
All the Catholic churches of Europe, foreign nations, even the Protestants	The emissaries of the Jacobin Club, the propaganda missionaries
Three-quarters of the city of Paris	The Palais-Royal, the hired public
The right wing of the National Assembly, or the élite of the defenders of religion and of the throne	The left wing, and the monstrous assembly of the principal enemies of the Church and of the monarchy, Jews, Protestants, Deists
All the papers, friends of order and truth	All the newspapers in the pay of the factions, such as the execrable rage of Desmoulins, Brissot, Marat, etc.
All good Frenchmen who love their country, their religion and the happiness of their brothers	All the brigands who burn chateaux, pillage mansions, set up their gallows; all the scoundrels who have bathed France in blood, and yet still breathe, thanks to the impunity of their frightful instigators.
All worthy and virtuous citizens	All the libertines, cheats, Jews, and Protestants
The will of our good king	The most detestable tyranny, which has taken his place, and exercises in his name a most frightful despotism.

Honore looked thoughtfully at the cream-colored sheet, asking himself the question he always did when reading such papers: *How much of this is true? Quite a bit of it,* he answered himself. The garter of his knee-breeches itched, and he leaned over to scratch the place.

A scruffy man jostled past, with a murmured hiss of "Aristocrat!"

Honore's head went up, but all he saw was a departing coat-back and a pair of long brown pants. He shook his head. *How will I ever gather any information when the people I am trying to help are so antagonistic?*

His green eyes moved among the busy expanse, alert to any suspicious figures. There was a plethora of rude clubs and pikes—stuck carelessly in waistbands or protruding beneath loose coats. He recalled the furor caused a week ago when, alarmed by the spread of violence, the Municipality banned the lowest classes from carrying arms. Honore had reason to remember the fire-storm of indignation which swept Paris; he and Tristan had been patrolling that evening. The populace forsook sleep that night—every man and woman were out in the streets— even usually-deserted byways rustled with many footsteps and the clamor of choleric voices. Cowed by the outburst, the next morning the city government pasted new placards—annulling the arms ban. Now, everyone who wished carried a weapon of some kind.

He caught sight of his cousin Leuren moving nonchalantly with Gaston de la Roche through the crowd. No one was paying *them* the slightest attention. *They blend in, attired as commoners,* Honore contemplated. His mind seized an idea, and he followed them more intently with his eyes as they ambled towards the cafe.

As Honore watched, an equally-unkempt youth in dull brown jacket and scuffed full-length pants lounged toward them, a sheaf of papers under his arm and one held high in the air. Brown hair stuck loosely out from under his cap, patriot-fashion. The newsboy accosted Gaston, trying to sell him a paper. Gaston took a paper carelessly and gave the youth a coin. The young man slouched towards Leuren, who shook his head and passed the paper-seller without a second glance.

As the newsboy moved on through the crowd, Honore's thoughts returned to Leuren and Gaston. *They pass as 'patriots,' which they are—but why? Because of their clothes and mannerisms....Why—why should not Tristan and I adopt the same idea? If we dressed like sans-culottes....* He had risen to his feet in his excitement, mechanically stuffing his paper in a pocket. It was time to meet Tristan at their rendezvous. *I must tell him my idea!*

~*~*~

Their rendezvous was the small back room of a wineshop which fronted the green *Champs Elysees.* A few street musicians—two violins, a bass viol, and a recorder—sent up a festive tune at the corner, and Honore threw a *livre* in their bowl as he hurried past. Pushing open the wineshop door, he moved decorously through the whitewashed room to a private room he and Tristan had reserved. Turning the knob, Honore stepped into it, closing the door after him.

He stopped short in utter astonishment.

There, seated casually in a chair, slouched hat shading his face, was the newspaper-seller from the *Palais-Royal!* Honore stood stock-still. *Why would anyone else be in this room – Tristan and I reserved it! And why this scruffy sans-culotte, of all people?*

Honore found words at last. "What are you doing here, you tatterdemalion? This room is engaged —"

The seated newsboy looked up with swaggering rebelliousness, exposing a handsome face, though begrimed, with intent brown eyes. He rose; as he did so, his loose, slouching manner fell away, and he stood as tall and straight as a noble. His head, which had been thrust forward, was now held high; shoulders squared themselves; his shifty eyes became direct, taking on the look of serious merriment that Honore knew so well.

"Tristan!" Honore exclaimed, staring incredulously.

Tristan broke into one of his radiant grins. "Took you in, did I not?"

"But — you never told me, you — you rascal!" Honore cried, shaking his friend's shoulder.

"I wanted to see if my disguise was good enough," Tristan said.

"It sure was," Honore admitted. "It took me in; Gaston and Leuren, as well." Then he said, "And I was all excited about my grand idea..."

"What idea?" Tristan asked, pushing some of his hair back — "Grand bother, having one's hair loose," he muttered.

"I had the brilliant and *novel* idea that we could disguise ourselves, and rushed here to tell you," Honore said facetiously.

"It still is a marvelous idea," Tristan said, "but not necessarily an original one." They both laughed.

"But how did you think of this?" Honore asked.

"It was some weeks after my mother's death," Tristan replied. "I was standing by my window, looking out into the street and remembering how Mother always encouraged our efforts. I realized the only way we could gain information was disguise — to look like the people. Your mother loaned me Marcel for hours and hours, and...here I am." He smiled.

Tristan's mind flashed back to that day.... He remembered Marcel's voice saying, "Imagine yourself not as lord of a manor, but as beaten scum. But don't cower, or you won't pass as a Brigand." Marcel's slow smile had spread across his face as he added, "Think of Gaston — he *could* walk like a gentleman, but instead walks like a groom carrying two pails."

Then Marcel had gone to buy secondhand clothes, and Tristan had returned to the window to stare intently into the street, trying to copy what he'd seen....The cocky head toss two gutter boys made to each other absorbed him for ten minutes. Over and over again he reminded himself,

Let everything go slack. Such was his training that his muscles kept unconsciously straightening his posture. After many failed attempts, and not a few chuckles at himself, he'd been moving toward the door in a fair rendition of a lumbering sans-culotte—awkward and loose in his movements, but with a certain swagger—when Marcel came back. Tristan had continued forward, still in his "Brigand" manner—Marcel stopped and watched him intently, drawing the door closed.

"If any young aristocrat has a chance, I believe you do," Marcel said at last. "Though..." he went on to point out some discrepancies in manner, his mouth sometimes twisting with inner mirth. Tristan knew why Marcel was amused: the contrast was great between the usual Tristan — perfectly-dressed, square-shouldered—and Tristan's ragged garments, loose hair, and slovenly movements now. But he had sensed Marcel's admiration, too—"Not many aristocrats would sacrifice their pride to do something like this," Marcel commented. *Marcel was such a help; his observant eyes don't miss a single detail....* But Honore was speaking, and Tristan snapped back to the present.

"The clothes are masterly," Honore said, "but that's not it. You were *moving* like a sans-culotte!"

"Marcel has been very patient with me," Tristan said. "It has taken weeks of hard practice. Even now, he tells me there are aristocratic tricks of voice and manner that I have not eradicated."

"You must have natural aptitude for acting," Honore said. "I doubt I could pass for a Brigand even if I practiced—the posture lessons drilled into me in toddler-hood have an iron grip on my backbone."

Tristan smiled and changed the subject. "By the way, Honore, I uncovered another 'knife-in-back' robbery the other day, when out practicing my disguise."

"Yes?" Honore leaned forward, his hand on a carved chair-back.

"A butcher told me the usual story, with a twist; he was still at work in the evening when he received a distraught message from his brother, in dire straits, asking him to bring money as collateral, or else he would be ruined. The butcher closed up shop, went upstairs to his dwelling, took out his small savings, and hastened to his brother's assistance. He was hurrying along the streets when accosted from behind and deprived of his money. The brother was indeed in financial difficulty, but had not sent such a message."

Honore's brow knotted. "This is the first successful one we have heard of since the robbery of your father's servant. I suppose the thief ran through your father's money and now must recourse again to his sinful trade."

"And," Tristan said, "the butcher's robbery occurred almost four weeks ago. Perhaps the thief will act again soon—we need to be especially on the alert!"

Honore nodded vigorously. "Yes—and your disguise will aid us."

~*~*~

"Now, Jerome, why cannot I try?"

The afternoon sun cascaded into the Le Mercier's small garden, catching the flowers and turning them into bright jewels amidst a living green. The early April breeze waltzed by, filling the air with the sweet and spicy scents of the flowers. Adele's crisp blue gown made a portrait worthy of a painter against such flourishing abundance. Her pearly blue overskirt came down in front and was bunched in the back, balanced by the frothy white kerchief at the neckline.

Her attention was focused on the gardener, an elderly man kneeling at a flower bed. He got stiffly to his feet, brushing the soil off his knees, and addressed her. "No, Madame Adele, if you please."

"I truly desire to learn," Adele said.

"I do not think an applicable knowledge of gardening befits a lady," he answered dubiously. "If you would like, now, I can consult with you as to what flowers should be planted. Begging your pardon, Madame, but a lady never actually gets in the dirt."

"Have you never thought that perhaps even a high-born lady may have to, some day soon?" Adele queried, looking at him with large hazel eyes.

"Saints preserve us!" he ejaculated. "I pray not, my lady!"

Adele smiled. "I shall not 'get in the dirt,' if it so horrifies you; but I desire you to teach me about gardening," she temporized. "Tell me when to plant, and what the plants need; show me the best way to harvest seeds, and how to propagate."

The old man still looked at her mistrustfully, thinking of the old ways and of the haughty dames who scorned the thought of manual labor. At last he said, "If you truly wish it, Madame Adele."

"Yes, I do—and thank you, Jerome," Adele's eyes danced as if at some great victory—like her cousin Stephanie's eyes the week before, when the belle of a party. Carrying on her advantage, she pressed on, "Now, explain to me what you were doing just then, and why."

The gardener turned his weathered, wrinkled face with another incredulous glance at her. *So beautiful and ladylike, yet unconventional and resolute—like her lady mother,* he thought. Then he slowly got down on his knees again and reached for his pruning knife. Adele leaned over, intent.

"Adele?" a manly voice spoke from behind.

As she straightened and turned, her face broke into a smile—it was Honore and Tristan. "It is a pleasure to see you both!"

Tristan answered, bowing, "It is always a delight, Adele."

"News?" Adele asked.

"You know that Mirabeau has been sinking; all Paris has waited for the last few days with hushed foreboding," Tristan said.

"Yes; we heard that the streets near his house are jammed with people waiting for updates on his condition," Adele said.

"There shall be no more updates," Tristan said. "He passed away a few hours ago."

"What a man—living a debauched and vile life;" Adele said, "stirring up the populace, then in these last months struggling for the King…." She shook her piled curls with true remorse.

"The question now is if anyone will be able to restrain 'the Thirty' and the sans-culottes," Honore said. "Mirabeau's oratory and magnetic influence did much—but I see no other man."

"He referred to that in his last words," Tristan nodded. "He said, 'I carry in my heart the death-dirge of the French Monarchy: the dead remains of it will now be the spoil of factions.' He held things back, for a time." He grimaced. "How lamentable that France should owe anything to such a degenerate wretch; that a nefarious adulterer should have been the one to check the radicals! The Lord uses even the wicked to accomplish His purposes."

Gathering up his few implements, the gardener passed them with relief, bowing. He would not have to teach gardening to his youthful Madame—at least not today.

Adele seated herself on the nearby stone bench, Honore and Tristan on chairs. The leafy bower of a small tree hovered just overhead, casting gracious shade across the small patch of grass. Nearby, a climbing rose thrust its dark green foliage and deep pink blooms toward the sun.

"We desired your assistance, Adele," Honore said. "You know we are on the track of these robberies. We have been patrolling the streets at night, as well as continuing to ask at various hostelries. Tristan has gone in disguise various times, seeking further information; the populace shies from aristocrats, even those attempting to help them. The Press has seen to that."

Adele nodded.

"The difficulty is in gaining clues and reliable information," Tristan said. "If only we could contact an honest person from the lower class! That would be an immense aid."

Adele drew her brows together. "Let me think...." Then her eyes lit up. "What about Jules Durand?"

"Jules Durand?" Tristan looked blank.

"You remember Jules, Honore," Adele smiled. "You met him the evening of the great outdoor ball in the *Champ Elysees*, after the Fete de la Federation—"

"Ah—the blond fellow dressed like a Brigand?" Honore said. "Yes, I remember."

"He is ardently in favor of the revolution," Adele said, "but for all that I believe he *might* be willing to aid you."

"I remember he showed an open dislike to the marquis de la Noye," Honore said. "However, he certainly did not seem antagonistic to Adele and me, though he knew we were also conservative aristocrats."

"I cannot see *anyone* being antagonistic to Adele," Tristan smiled. Adele blushed hotly, half-laughing in protest, and turned her attention to one of the drooping roses; but she looked up as Tristan continued, "Yes, he would be worth approaching. Do you know how we can contact him, Adele?"

"He often attends the De Lobels' fetes; they invite patriots from the lower classes. In fact, they are having a party tonight—that is why I thought of him." There was a movement at the doors of the house, and Adele paused.

A manservant approached across the pavement with a bow. "Madame Felicienne wished me to inform you that she received a message from the De Lobels, saying that because of the death of Mirabeau, all parties are suspended. Their fete will necessarily be postponed until next day-week."

"Thank you," Honore replied. With another bow, the man retreated, closing the house doors.

"Well! I suppose we shall have to wait until next day-week," Adele said, arranging her skirt.

"If you would present him to us then, you would be of great assistance," Tristan smiled.

"I will certainly do so," Adele said. "I surely hope he will agree to cooperate."

A subdued, moaning rustle passed through the streets; the populace mourning "their Mirabeau." Despite his recent support of the King, he had somehow remained enshrined by the people as their deliverer.

From King to commoner, France bewailed the passing of a man who—powerful, debauched, scheming, vile, but eloquent—had endeavored to direct their stormy kingdom. There would not be another Mirabeau; unchecked, and prodded by equally unscrupulous men, France rushed madly towards ultimate chaos.

~*~*~

Adele moved around a group of chattering young ladies in tightly-corseted, low-necked silk gowns. Coming face to face with Tristan, she greeted him with a look. "No, he is not here—yet," she spoke quietly, in answer to the question in his eyes. "Stephanie told me he was invited; she thought he would be here…"

"*Certes!*" Tristan answered *sotto voce*, looking down at her. "I hope she is right."

Watching this colloquy out of the corners of their eyes, the nearby knot of girls cast envious glances at Adele. Some may have wondered why she, rather than they, was receiving such attention; her perfectly tailored dress was a modest contrast to theirs. Her curving corset defined her slender waist, but her neckline was much higher than theirs, and was filled in—not merely shadowed—by the white scarf across her shoulders. Her attitude also was very different; instead of flirting with Tristan, she treated him with sisterly unaffectedness.

"He may arrive late," Adele finished softly; "I shall hope so." With a curtsy, she passed on; and Tristan was instantly waylaid by the nearby young ladies, all smiles, fluttering their fans artfully. He cast a sighing glance after Adele's retreating figure, then turned manfully to contend with the clamoring coquettes.

Adele strolled on through the crowded ballroom, keeping an eye out for Jules. *O Lord, please enable him to come!* However, the minutes passed with no sign of him.

Half an hour later, as the dancing began, Adele sadly paced along the outskirts of the crowd towards where Honore stood, near a large painting on the other side of the room.

Passing the open doors leading into the ballroom, she suddenly froze. There, in the entry, was Jules! There was no mistaking that stylishly disheveled outline nor that statuesque face. She cast a quick, triumphant glance across to Honore.

Jules noticed Adele immediately and bowed low, saluting her in the flowery style of the day. "My dear Madame Adele, can I believe this felicitous chance—you being the first person I encounter? I have been pining for a sight of your comely face..."

"I was looking for you as well, M. Durand," Adele replied.

He looked at her with some surprise. From the lips of any other girl, such words would have been expected: but from Adele?

"You were looking for me?" he asked. "I feel quite complimented, Adele."

She blushed, but looked directly at him. "I know you are a 'patriot,' M. Durand, and thus despise the aristocrats; but I feel you are also honest and desire to defend the poor against *any* oppressors."

"Certainly, Madame Adele," Jules said. "No matter who the oppressors are, they must be brought to account."

Her face lightened. Drawing him out of the crowding wallflowers and elderly, she said, "Then I know of a worthy cause that would benefit from your aid."

"Any cause that *you* believe is worthy—" he began gallantly, but she gently cut him short.

"I should hope that you would be involved in a cause on its own merits, not out of changeable deference to anyone else," she said serenely. "Would you let me present you to my brother and another, who are heading this undertaking?"

"Surely, Madame Adele." Jules followed her, wondering anew at her genuine inner loveliness, the unsullied light in her eyes. Jules could not understand yet that her character was due to her Christianity; he knew nothing of the inner freedom Christ brings. But he saw, and wondered— wondered especially how this intriguing young woman could be an aristocrat, one of that high-born brood that he hated.

His contemplations ended as they reached a far corner. Candles in the nearby sconces lit up two tall, faultlessly-dressed youths. Jules recognized Honore as Adele introduced them, "You have met before: Honore, this is Jules Durand; Jules, this is my brother, Honore le Mercier." Adele motioned towards the other youth; "Tristan, this is Jules Durand. Jules, this is Tristan du Chemin." They bowed.

Normally people with such impeccably genteel gestures grated on Jules. However, these two had a straightforward interest that disarmed most of his usual hostility. In fact, Jules found himself inexplicably *liking* them—a feeling he tried to resist.

"Some cases of theft came to our attention four or five months ago," Adele said, looking at Jules with her clear hazel eyes, "in our district. The victims (most of them poor already), were brought to extreme straits. My brother and Tristan have been endeavoring to track down these thieves, but it is difficult to gather information."

"We wondered, Jules, if you would be willing to aid us," Honore said. "You have the contacts we do not have; you are not an aristocrat. So far, we have been much hindered in our quest to uncover these rapacious scoundrels. Yet we feel it is our duty to defend the needy from those preying on them."

Jules looked at them, waging an inner war. *They are* aristocrats—*why help them?—why help them in any way?* one part of him argued, while another part noted their sincere interest in the destitute. He thought of his aristocrat father's base behavior and his heart hardened; then he remembered these two were different, wanting to *help* the downtrodden, not *use* them....

He glanced away, torn. Among the glittering throng that swayed and waltzed about the room he noted several other aristocratic youths—and could not imagine them even halfway caring. And these two—they were endeavoring to do something! He remembered his mother's gentle teachings on doing right, helping the helpless, being honest....Something gigantic and nameless stirred in Jules' being—something that, once unloosed, would be difficult to reconfine. This venture stirred him more than rabble-rousing in the name of the oppressed. He looked at Honore again. "I will join you," Jules said decisively. "You may count on me."

Tristan smiled broadly. "Thank you, Jules!" Honore's delight was just as clear, and Adele radiated gratefulness.

Honore brought up the robberies they had unearthed and Tristan filled in with tales of their patrols. Neither referenced Tristan's successful disguise—they felt it would be better to tell Jules when he had proved his trustworthiness. Jules listened with interest, sensing their true concern for the poor, their sweet camaraderie, and wondering at it.

Time passed by unheeded—at length, they glanced round the room and noted the party was breaking up.

"We must decide on a good rendezvous point, Jules," Honore mentioned.

"It would not be wise to be seen together in the streets or cafes," Jules said. "You both are recognizable as aristocrats. I do not want my acquaintances to mistrust my zeal—I wholly support the revolution," he said, with a half-apologetic smile. "Perhaps the least suspicious way would be if I pass on what I learn to Madame Adele when we meet at parties and such. She can keep me informed on your progress and any new developments. If you need to contact me—the Le Merciers have bought hats from my mother's shop before."

"That sounds wise," Tristan said. "Thank you for your willingness to assist us, Jules!"

Jules looked as though he wanted to say something: paused, hesitated; then went out into the dark night.

No Trip to Saint Cloud!

4.

If Voltaire once in splenetic humor, asked his countrymen:
"But you, Gualches, *what have you invented?"*
they can now answer: "The Art of Insurrection."
— Thomas Carlyle

L euren Andre de Lobel stood before his window, brow furrowed and lips pursed in concentration. He was dressed for the street—tattered, purposefully-sloppy jacket and long pants—but still he continued his listening vigil, refraining from going out.

Three days before, the King announced his intention of traveling to Saint Cloud today—Easter Monday. His Majesty was suffering from congestion, he said, and desired to enjoy a few days in the lovely Spring weather. With utmost suspicion, the populace scowled on this proposed journey. "This is just a pretence," many voices hissed; "His Majesty will not stop at Saint Cloud, but flee on to Austria!" Feeling Paris' vast opposition, LaFayette sent for a division of the National Guard.

LaFayette described the state of things to his beloved General (now President) Washington: *"But we are not in that state of tranquillity...; the refugees hovering about the frontiers; intrigues in most of the despotic and aristocratic Cabinets; our regular army divided into Tory officers and undisciplined soldiers; licentiousness among the people not easily repressed; the capital, that gives the ton to the empire, tossed about by anti-revolutionary or factious parties; the Assembly fatigued by hard labor, and very unmanageable."*

It was past midday on the eighteenth of April, and Leuren was worried. *Did I miss the signal — perhaps during the midday meal?* Biting his lip, he rested a sturdy arm on the sill.

His eyes lit up. *The signal!* Faint but unmistakable upon the breeze came the clamor and clangor of bells—the bells of the Church of Saint-Roch.

Opening the door a crack, he slid out into the hall. Past his grandfather's room, he glanced behind—and stumbled into a small half-circle table. Jerking his head round, he recovered his balance, but the table swayed, and a book on it plunged to the floor. Leuren stooped to pick it up; placing it on the table, he glanced about and hurried off.

Once outside, he mopped his brow with relief. *Whew! At least Mother did not see me.* His mother had been nettled by his rebellious behavior, and especially had objected to his "gadding about." If she had heard him leaving, there would have been a row and he would have been delayed.

The streets were bustling; many others also hurried in the direction of the bell. Before ten minutes had elapsed, Andre, panting from his haste, had entered the square on the Tuileries' eastern side. He scanned the crowd for Gaston. Over the people's heads he saw the Royal carriage drawn up, its eight gleaming horses tossing their heads in readiness to start. At last he spotted Gaston near their meeting-place. He looked impatient, ready to leave their rendezvous any moment and join the throng around the carriage: Andre pushed roughly through the crowd.

From atop his white horse, LaFayette harangued the people, his aides-de-camp eyeing the crowd tensely. The General adjured the throng to disperse, enjoining them to put no hindrance to the King's proposed outing.

"*Taisez-vous*," rumbled the people in reply, "the King shall not go."

Andre reached Gaston. "There you are!—this way!" Gaston cried impatiently. The two shoved through the sea of sans-culottes towards the Royal carriage, reaching the horses' heads just after the King and Queen entered it.

A whip cracked overhead. The coachmen urged the horses to start.

"Don't let them go!" someone shouted. Nearby "patriots" grasped the horses' bridles, holding them back. Andre clutched the nearest leather bridle strap tightly. The horse rolled its dark eyes, laying its ears back wickedly. Suddenly, it erupted upwards, rearing despite its traces. The other men holding it let go, dropping to the ground in terror, but Andre, mouth open, hung on as the horse hovered in the air, thrashing wildly. His desire to be a "good revolutionist" and gain Gaston's approbation prevailed over his fear. Suddenly, the horse's front legs hit the ground with a tremendous jolt, but still Andre clenched the bridle, gritting his teeth. Other unwashed sans-culottes squeezed forward, patting Andre on the back with rough praise and helping him hold the horse. It meant much to him. Andre's rebellion made him especially dependant on the approval of his comrades in crime.

Let no man be bold enough to say,
Thus, and no farther shall my passion stray:
The first crime, past, compels us into more,
And guilt grows fate, that was but choice, before.

The horse still flicked its ears dangerously, but seemed cowed by its fruitless effort. LaFayette addressed the mob in impassioned tones, commanding it to allow their Majesties to proceed. Andre set his face; a roar of protest swelled from the crowd. In vain LaFayette expostulated. Attempting to aid, chief usher Campan was seized, shoved about, and forced to flee.

The *Centre Grenadiers* drew up, but they were useless to LaFayette. They spoke rebelliously to the General, threatening to shoot the King's mounted guards "if they hurt a hair of the people's heads."

The coachman again commanded the horses to move: but the screaming swarm clutched the bridles and blocked the way. The din was so loud that no words of command or remonstrance could be heard; LaFayette's voice was drowned in the tempest.

Riding to the carriage window, LaFayette offered to open the way, with cannon if necessary, if His Majesty would just give the word. The King hesitated, as usual; his Royalist friends urged concession and conciliation. All around, the human squall thundered and bellowed.

So the impasse stood—or rather, *boiled*—for almost two hours. Caught up in the ballistic excitement, Andre scarcely noted the passing of time until he tried to shift his grasp of the bridle. Then his stiffened hands refused to unclench. He was peeling each finger away singly, wincing at the tingling pain (for his hands had fallen asleep) when, among the deafening cacophony of shouts, he became aware of a change.

A rabid, ringing cry of victory—Andre glanced towards the carriage and yelled in hoarse triumph. The King and Queen were exiting; they had given up their journey to Saint Cloud!

The populace had won—again. But the King's annoyed countenance showed that this defeat, for once, had stirred up his inmost being. It would spur him towards the thing which he had toyed with and refused before—*escape*.

~*~*~

Some two weeks later, the candles flickered fretfully in the De Lobel's dining room.

"Where is Leuren?" Grandpapa des Cou asked, noting his empty chair.

"With Gaston, I have no doubt," Madame Juliette de Lobel replied acidly, "scheming up trouble somehow."

"Gaston does not stir up trouble!" Stephanie replied hotly, glancing up from her sullen study of a table-knife. "He is a patriot, bringing about the freedom of France!"

Her mother arched her eyebrows. "There are patriots, and 'patriots.'"

Stephanie's blue eyes flamed. She opened her scarlet lips in anger—but her grandfather was speaking again. She contented herself with shooting daggers at her mother with her eyes.

"Leuren is always out nowadays," Des Cou fretted. "The other day, he woke me from a nap by the most awful clatter in the hall. And evening after evening he tromps by in the wee hours just as I have fallen asleep—you must take him in hand, Juliette."

"He is an ungrateful, wretched boy," Juliette said. "If I have told Jean once, I have told him a thousand times that Leuren is a man now, and Jean must control him." She glanced waspishly at her husband's empty seat—Jean was staying late at his favorite haunt, the Breton club.

Leaving this pleasant family scene and traveling over Paris' darkening rooftops, one could spy a great concourse of people in the *Palais-Royal*. Disapproving of the governmental acquisition of the clergy, the Pope had excommunicated Talleyrand, its avid supporter—and the people of Paris were protesting.

Jules, fashionably disheveled as ever, moved lightly through the crowd. In the center of the courtyard rose two paper-and-lath figures—one the King's friend Royou, and the other instantly identifiable by robes and tiara as Pope Pius the Sixth. Piled beneath these mock figures were "condemned" issues of the *Ami-du-Roi*—fuel for the funeral pyre. The people's faces were distorted with evil glee; though they looked as if it would have pleased them more to burn the *real* Pope and Royou.

Jules glimpsed something out of the corner of his eye, and turned just in time to see a black-coated man whisk a deft hand out of another's pocket. The victim seemed oblivious, but Jules was off in a flash, deftly winding his way through the crowd after the thief.

A loafing, threadbare youth in a patched brown coat and tan pants stirred lazily at about the same time, sauntering in the same general direction. Jules noted him through a break in the crowd, but gave no further notice. Jules' attention was fixed on the pickpocket.

Perhaps with a vague sense of pursuit, the thief slipped out under the spiked gates of the *Palais-Royal* and darted across the street, disappearing in the crowds. Jules had to hurry, dodging strolling groups and the gathering *canaille*. Behind him a great blaze of light shot up, accompanied by extended hurrahs—the images of the Pope and Royou were alight, the greedy flames licking up paper and wood with red-orange relish.

When he again caught sight of the thief, dodging into a deserted backstreet, Jules received a distinct surprise. Between himself and the shadowy thief was someone else—*on the same trail?* The pickpocket darted past a lone streetlamp, glancing back into the darkness. Moments later, when the robber was no longer looking back, the second figure slid past the *lanterne*, disappearing at once into the shadows beyond. The second figure had only been illumined an instant, but Jules recognized it. *The loafer in the brown coat!*

Jules hurried past the lamp's revealing rays after follower and followed. *Perhaps he, too, saw the theft?* Jules wondered. *But why would such a lounger give a fig? He looked the type with no scruples about such work.*

The darkness deepened: had Jules looked up, he would have seen stars winking through the city's smoky haze. It took all his energies merely to keep the second figure in sight, let alone the first, the robber. All at once, peering ahead at a bedimmed lamppost, Jules realized that the thief had not passed it. *He must have gone off down another side-street.* Jules looked dubiously at the various openings nearby. *Which one did he choose?* He dashed down several tortuous little byways with no result. Despite his familiarity with most of Paris' backstreets, this part of the city was strange to him. At last he turned disappointed steps back to the *Palais-Royal*.

The second figure—the one trailing the pickpocket—had disappeared also.

~*~*~

Midnight was long gone when Jules slipped with relief out of the *Palais-Royal's* feral crush and into dark streets that, though not empty, seemed pools of silence compared to that ebullient courtyard. His shoulders hung with discouraged fatigue, and yet the events of the evening still stirred his brain. Home—and sleep—didn't appeal to him in his present state of mind. When he saw up ahead, lithe against the stars, the muscled shapes of mounted men, his old haunt, Goriot Stables, drew him unaccountably.

Their evening dress faultless, the two riders swung down onto the cobbles. One made a jesting remark, and the other's youthful lips curled with a sneering laugh.

"Ho—groom," the first shouted. He was scarcely older than Jules, and yet the contrast couldn't have been sharper between this perfumed dandy, raised in shallowly-gilded drawing-rooms to be arrogant and self-assertive and sure of his social rights, and Jules, raised in the streets to be bitter and shrewd, fiercely resentful, trying to seize such rights for himself. The only thing they shared was a certain mental cynicism, a hopelessly atheistic view that the spiritual things were bosh and all there was to life was the physical.

"What's taking him so long?" the other exclaimed, daintily flicking something from his spotless breeches. "Hostler!"

Jules slipped forward, his face magically blank. "I'll take them, Citizen." His hands slid over the reins, gathering them up and making room for the second pair. The horses bumped him gently, snorting and tossing their heads, impatient for their stalls and feed.

One youth flicked him a contemptuous coin before turning with his companion. "Take good care of them, you scum." Their fancy shoes clicked across the cobbles, and they were gone to their silken sheets and airy rooms, heedless of the feelings of low-born *canaille*.

Flaming inwardly, Jules led the horses into the smelly stable and to the farthest corner stall, which was empty.

"Ah, Jules, you again," rumbled the stout, sweating proprietor, hustling from an inner room. "Why people keep such ungodly hours is beyond me—and me having to stay up to please them, whether I will or no! But 'tis past midnight, and now that those two fine gentlemen—" he looked lovingly at the two steeds, "—are back, I shall roll upstairs to bed. Jacques shall take care of any more comers." He nodded acidly to his groom, a grimy wisp of a man snoring in a huddled heap in a straw-filled corner. "Drunk, as usual, the waster. Ah, well, I can never seem to fire him. Make yourself at home, my boy; if the mother is angry at you, you're more'n welcome to spend the night, as you've done before." He winked, then a yawn engulfed him. Opening a door at the back, he stumbled up the narrow stairs.

His footsteps grew fainter and disappeared, Jacques' snoring continued loud, irregular and unmusical, and Jules leaned with tired leisure against the slats of the stall and monotonously rubbed down the red-brown neck of the bay horse. It leaned ever so slightly toward him as he stroked a favorite spot, tilting its head with pleasure, and Jules felt

366

himself drowsily and slowly beginning to feel right with all the world, even though it contained such dissolute wasters as Jacques and such enigmas as seedy loungers who followed pickpockets. He leaned against the horse's warm body, still stroking the beautiful curve of its neck.

A low mutter of voices, which must have been going on for some time, roused him some time later from what must have been a doze. But Jules had not been brought up in Paris for nothing, and he remained perfectly still, listening.

"...and since we know you're a good comrade, Jacques, and keep your tongue as well as the best of them, you'll get a share if it comes off, if only you keep up your end. You're sure this is the best horse?"

"Belle's the fastest of all he's got." Jacques' voice was distinct. "I'd back her, anytime. Remember the d'Arcy robbery? I told Marc to use her. He got clean away—never even suspected."

"Yeah, but that was when they were gone, and all," a third voice spoke. "This'll be close work—we'll only have an hour or less before somebody's going to find out that They are missing. And then—boy, the hornets will be all over!"

"Mayhap, if the chances are so slim, I shouldn't let you use Belle," Jacques said. "If you get caught they'll trace me through the horse..."

"It's all planned out; nothing'll go wrong," the first man urged. "We'll take care of the old lady for good if she happens to be there. And don't worry—you'll get your fair share of the jewels."

The third man spoke, his oily voice evil. "Besides, Jacques, if you don't let us borrow her, maybe we'll drop some hints to the police about the *Cerise* affair, huh?"

"Shush, man!" hissed the now-frightened Jacques. "Some things are best buried under a hundred fathoms of blue water! I'll have Belle at the corner beside the confectioner's in *rue Dubois* at 12 o'clock tomorrow night, without fail."

"That's as well; now you're thinking sensible, my good Jacques," the third man laughed. "*Au 'voir* 'til 12, then."

Feet shuffled across the rutted floor and the two visitors were gone, but Jules stayed frozen long in one place, thinking but not daring to move.

The first beams of the sun were feebly stretching their arms when Jules was finally certain that Jacques was asleep again and he could safely slip out without detection into the lemon-colored streets.

~*~*~

The De Lobels' next party would be a fortnight later, and Jules fretted at the delay. He was almost contemplating taking the risk of searching for Honore or Tristan at some public place when he remembered a salon open to patriots where he had seen Adele once or twice.

Mayhap — there is a chance she will be there, he told himself, impatient to tell the three of the mysterious tracker he had seen while following the pickpocket—and of this planned robbery. He'd reconnoitered the spot in the early-morning half-light before going home, and found it was the home of an elderly aristocratic lady who, though not rich, clung to her ancestral jewels with a kind of foolish but high-spirited pride, keeping them in her bedroom when they would be much safer in a vault. A few questions unearthed tales of an emerald necklace, several diamonds with and without settings, a ruby ring of fabled splendor... *I've got to let the Le Merciers know, somehow...*

He dressed carefully, in that compromise between shabby sans-culotte style and spiffy aristocratic neatness which he affected when going about in higher society. His loose blond hair was combed; he wore knee-breeches, and put a flower in his buttonhole. With a final glance into the shard of a mirror propped against the dresser top, he stepped into the front room.

His mother was making some adjustment to the headdress of one of the pasty wax ladies. Hearing his steps, she turned with her usual careworn expression. "Jules—would you purchase some ribbon for me?" She held out a scrap of silk. "The usual shop; buy a yard of satin ribbon an inch wide, in this color. He closes early this afternoon—four o'clock—and I must have it. I must needs trim a hat before six tonight."

Jules took the silk with ill grace; *This errand will cut in upon my time at the salon.* But his mother's face took on the worn, pleading look he knew so well, and he nodded. "I will."

"There is no other way for me to get it, Jules—I have appointments all afternoon." She looked wistfully at his irritated face. He waved it off, trying to smooth his features.

"It is nothing—I shall get it for you, Mother."

I will go to the salon first. If Adele is there right away, good — if not, I can stay until...say, a quarter to four. Then I will leave to pick up the ribbon.

He entered the fashionable salon with a bow to the plump, tightly-laced *salonnière*. A searching glance round showed, to his disappointment, that Adele was not there. He found a seat affording a view of the whole room and involved himself in the conversation, keeping an alert eye towards the entry.

He tried to stop dwelling on the fact that she might not come at all. This was made worse by the constant under-running current of his thoughts: *Two weeks — two weeks, if you do not see her today; two weeks to wait....*

The gargoyle-footed grandfather clock ticked away with great relish; its seeming pleasure at the passing of time grated on Jules. He scrupulously avoided its sly glances, but it still boxed his ear methodically. *Almost time to leave, and she is not here!* Jules bit the inside of his lip. Shifting in the padded seat, he tried to listen to the conversation. *Tick-tick, tick, tick,* came that chuckling little voice. *"Ha-ha, ha, ha."*

~*~*~

Meanwhile, the elderly gardener and Adele knelt in the vibrant green grass of their pocket garden. Above, the afternoon sky rose on invisible pillars, while across it glided great white chariots — the clouds.

Dark head bent to one side, Adele intently watched the gardener's movements. Thrusting a small shovel in the rich brown earth, he set the dirt to one side and picked up a rooted seedling.

"I leave about this much space between rosemary plants, Madame Adele," he gestured with the hand holding the plant, "they fill out quickly and crowd other plants if not given room."

"I see, Jerome," Adele answered. Time moved leisurely as she watched, asked questions, and listened. "Hurry" seemed a word belonging to another planet.

A cloud drifted across the sun; its gargantuan shadow sliding with vast slowness over neighboring houses and into the garden. After a pause, it seemed to gather itself up, moving with equal sluggishness over other dwellings, letting the sunlight spill in once more.

Adele reached for the shovel, beginning to say, "Could I try, but once?" when from the house skipped five-year-old Paulette, her white ruffled dress fluttering in the breeze. Clutching Adele's skirt with her chubby arms, she laid her head on the turquoise blue silk. Adele caressed the little girl's shoulder, meeting the lifted hazel eyes with a warm glance.

"Is this 'portant, 'dele?" Paulette queried.

"Why, what do you mean, darling?" Adele asked.

"You told me yest'day you would be busy with 'portant things this aft'noon," Paulette answered, her big eyes full of a child's innocent, adorable seriousness. *"Can* you play?"

369

"No; I am sorry, Paulette dear," Adele bent to kiss the round cheek. "I thank you for reminding me. This *is* important," she continued, glancing at the gardening, "but the truly important thing is a salon I must go to this afternoon—'tis part of helping Honore and Tristan." She glanced at the ornate sundial. "Oh, no—the salon is almost over!"

Adele thanked Jerome sincerely, then with a final kiss for Paulette and a whispered "Maybe we can play tomorrow morning," she hastened into the house to freshen up.

Shortly thereafter, Adele stepped with unstudied grace into the salon's entryway. A bowing footman opened the parlor door. Adele's first act was to greet the hostess (a distant relative), so Adele did not see Jules. But he noticed her, with a great surge of gratefulness. He had just been standing up to leave!

Adele turned from saluting the *salonnière* to find Jules bowing at her side. "My dear Madame Adele! If you would have the courtesy…"

Smiling, Adele replied by taking the seat offered. With another bow, Jules seated himself beside her. The seats were well-picked—to Adele's right was a very deaf elderly lady, while a potted palm provided a handy gap between Jules and the chattering woman on his left.

"This is a blessing indeed," Jules' voice revealed his relief.

"I am very sorry you were waiting for me, "Adele said. "Indeed, I could have arrived earlier had I remembered."

"No matter now," Jules answered. "I have two pieces of news, but first, the most urgent. I discovered that thieves plan to steal old Madame d'Arcy's jewels around 12 o'clock tonight."

Adele's eyes grew wide. "Tonight, at midnight? She lives in the *rue Dubois* near the confectioner's, does she not?"

"Yes, that is she. Tell Honore and Tristan that I shall be there, in the shadows, but would crave their help—I gather that this gang plans to have one take the jewels out of Paris beyond reach of a search, while the others melt into Paris' underworld."

"I shall tell Honore and Tristan as soon as I can," Adele promised. "They will be thrilled to have something concrete to try to thwart! They will be there too, I am sure." She smiled. "Thank you so much, Jules! What a horrible thing if you had not found out about this—the old lady could easily be slain by those wretches! You have already been such a helpful ally."

"It was nothing, Adele; I merely happened to be there," Jules said, but he flushed with pleasure. "I seemed compelled to drop in on the stables, even at that late hour."

"The second bit of news?" Adele queried.

"It is this. You heard of the mocking *Auto-da-fe* which took place two nights ago—burning the Pope in effigy?"

Adele gave a short nod. "Yes."

"I spotted a pickpocket there," Jules went on, still in a lowered voice. "I began to follow him—but found that *another* person was trailing the thief as well!" He cast a puzzled glance at Adele. "I know not why. He was an unremarkable sans-culotte—I noticed not much besides brown hair."

Adele pursed her lips to keep from smiling, but her eyes twinkled. She recognized the story—only she had heard it from the perspective of number two in that line of three. She was glad that Honore and Tristan, in their last discussion, had said there was nothing preventing telling Jules of Tristan's disguise. He had proved himself.

Jules studied Adele's countenance, wondering at her suppressed amusement.

"I know who that second figure was," she said. "Tristan—"

"No, this person was definitely a commoner, Adele," Jules said.

"All the same," she continued, "it was Tristan—in disguise. He has been practicing for several months now."

Jules gazed at her, his expression changing from puzzlement to astonishment. He cast back in his mind, trying to remember the youth's appearance more distinctly. *The hair is the same color, and the handsome, chiseled chin—what I remember of it—is the same type as Tristan's....If shoulders and head had been erect, and he'd not slouched and swaggered....*

"Tristan!" he said at last, as if much was explained. Then, eagerly, "Did he manage to stay with the thief?"

"No;" Adele said, "though he tailed him a bit farther after he lost sight of you. Then the pickpocket vanished in a dark stretch, and could not be found."

Jules glanced at the clock, realizing with chagrin that he must leave. "We must devise a better method for getting in touch, for if you had not come today, there would have been a fortnight's delay."

"Yes," Adele nodded. "I shall mention it to Tristan and Honore."

"Thank you, Madame Adele." He glanced at the clock again. "I must be on my way; I shall see you at the De Lobel's in two weeks."

"Honore and Tristan said to tell you to keep up your work. They shall continue patrolling; we have not heard of a knife-in-back robbery for two months, and they suspect one could occur any time. I shall tell them of your news, and they shall be in the *rue Dubois* well before midnight tonight."

Nodding briefly, Jules rose to leave. He stooped down again to say, with that wonder again creeping into his voice, "Tell Tristan his disguise was *marvelous*."

He left, his head still spinning. *That* was dedication—to practice so! And all for the helpless: those who could not and would not repay! There was nothing to be gained from such efforts—and yet these aristocrat youths were investing time and effort to protect their district. Jules shook his head in incomprehension.

Mayhem at the *Champ de Mars*

5.

Confound their politics,
Frustrate their knavish tricks.
– Henry Carey

O n June 20th, the King escaped from the Tuileries!
After immeasurable messages to the arming émigrés in Coblenz, Austria, and reams of ciphered correspondence to General Bouille (who commanded part of the French army at Montmédy), at last the King took the plunge — too late.

The King's brother and his wife also fled that Monday evening (June 20th), by a different route. What diverse fates the two parties had! The Royal coach was fatally slow: it traveled at three miles per hour even with fresh installments of post-horses. It was also eye-catching — a brand-new *Berline* drawn by eleven horses, with three yellow-coated courier/bodyguards. The King's brother chose an unremarkable coach and escaped successfully; why didn't the King do the same? Perhaps, even though he stooped to disguising himself as a valet, the Kingly head could not brook the idea of looking *too* menial.

Even these missteps might not have been fatal: but Providence was against them, and small events began snowballing. Small events: such as villagers quarrelling with soldiers loitering in their town (secretly deployed to escort their Majesties), which forced the commander to withdraw them. They marched off as slowly as they dared, in a vain attempt to let the Royal coach catch up.

Small circumstances: like that of a postmaster being outside in the wee hours to watch a carriage draw up, noting that the valet's face looked strangely familiar; calling for a piece of money and realizing that the "valet's" face was the same as the one on the coin — then spurring his horse after their departed carriage.

Small turns of Fate: even after the King and Queen were seized by outraged villagers, brave captain Deslons and his hundred drew up outside the town and could doubtless have stormed it and rescued the Royal family; but when Deslons offered to "cut the King out, if he would but order it," the King answered, "I have no orders to give." By that, the King forever closed his last slim possibility of escape.

Then, it was too late. Alas! They were a mere sixteen leagues (some 40 miles) from safety—actually, a mere few miles, for nearby were loyal French troops sent by General Bouille to escort them! Alas! For while the King and Queen sat dumbly, their plans shattered, the King's brother and sister-in-law arrived safely in Flanders. Had their positions been reversed—if the King's escape had been successful—what a difference that would have made in French history! A difference so vast—so uncertain— that we cannot begin to guess its outlines.

The King's Capture, Anonymous

In the meantime, the city of Paris was in the most uncontrollable state of nerves. The news of the King's flight broke with a thunderclap on Tuesday morning, the 21st. Those of the *Cote Droit*, the Royalists, feared for their lives, while secretly rejoicing at the King's escape.

"The Thirty" were also on edge, taken wholly by surprise and fearing that the King would reach General Bouille and coalesce with the émigrés' army. *Then* those armies, aided no doubt by the Austrians, would descend upon Paris to quell the revolutionists! Dapper Robespierre was even heard to croak in terror, "We [he and the other radicals] will all be hung within forty-eight hours!"

Disturbed as the deputies were, they were calm and controlled compared to the vast populace. Doubt, rumor, conjecture—the worst fears held sway. The people did not know what to do or where to turn. Messengers raced throughout all France, relaying the quaking alarm.

But by the next day, things had quieted somewhat. The National Assembly declared itself in permanent session; it continued on with the day's business as if nothing unusual had occurred. The people, taking the hint, began to think, in an amazed fashion, that the sky had not fallen; that they were quite as well—perhaps even better off—without a King: that, in fact, they did not need one after all! They were Frenchmen; they were Parisians; and they could care less (or so some said) about the King.

Then came the news that the King had been captured by a zealous postmaster in the small hamlet of Varennes! The Royalists grew gloomy and bit their lips—the sans-culottes and "the Thirty" gloated with fierce satisfaction.

It was a warm, melancholy Saturday three days later when the King was brought back to Paris. A placard in Saint-Antoine blared in large letters, "Whosoever insults Louis shall be caned, whosoever applauds him shall be hanged." No longer addressed as "the King;" merely "Louis!"

Vast concords of people stood, hats on, eyes fixed on the occupants of the *Berline* as the horses drew it heavily by. Slowly, slowly it crept past rank upon rank of sullen, silent sans-culottes. Very different from the wild, victorious reception when the King was brought from Versailles two years before—and yet that "welcome," though fiercely exultant, was better than this. This voiceless scornfulness boded ill.

Weary and terrified, their position utterly uncertain, the King and Queen entered Paris—never to quit its hemming walls again.

~*~*~

But now that they had the King, what would they do with him?

That was the question that seethed and stormed in the dens of vice as surely as in the National Assembly's *Ménage*. To the French people, they were now dealing with a King who had committed treason against his people—who had allied himself with foreign powers. From the King's view, he had merely attempted to escape imprisonment in Paris and reach the loyal segment of his army—he had planned to come back to Paris and suppress the rebellion. But no one cared about what the King thought. The populace was firmly fixed in their opinion: Treason!

The National Assembly set itself to decide what should be done with the King. Almost three weeks later, the debate in the *Salle Ménage* rose in vehement surges, seemingly no nearer a decision on that important topic than before, at least to an untrained eye. But Francis de Coquiel di le Mercier was well accustomed to such scenes, and he saw a break in the clouds. Despite their bluster, the Thirty were being overpowered.

Francis viewed the small signs of impending victory without elation. He passed a hand over his lined brow. It was not the fact that the King would be reinstated that troubled him—he was glad for that. It was the way it was being done that troubled him.

Because of the widespread conviction that the King had committed treason by fleeing, the Royalists seized on a fabrication. They argued that the King was not to blame; that he had been forcibly spirited away, *against his will*. Now this was a lie, and most of the Royalists knew it: the King had engineered his flight. But they said it so long and with such vigor that they beat down the naysayers. At last, Francis perceived that they would carry the day and force a vote to reinstate the King. But the Right's duplicity bore heavily on Francis. He had abstained from even slightly supporting, by word or look, the false statements; though he had spoken with great earnestness in favor of not deposing the King.

Jean de Lobel noticed Francis' carefulness, and his estimation of his brother-in-law grew. But as the tide turned and Jean saw the Thirty losing the battle, a great bitterness grew in his heart. His soul had stirred when the King had been brought back a prisoner—Jean had visions of an ever-expanding, ever-soaring France, freed from the shackles of authority. He envisioned himself as one of the coterie then free to rule France. But with the Royalists' success, Jean saw his dreams totter. His heart grew blacker with hate towards the Right; in his words, they were "maliciously seeking to suppress liberty."

Even before the vote was tallied verifying the Royalist's win, Jean drew aside with several others. They would meet at the Jacobin club (the former Breton Club) once the session ended, and scheme as to the best way to turn this defeat around.

The session concluded, with the Royalists victorious and exultant. Jean, sullenly pushing through the delegates, found himself beside Francis, also attempting to leave. Jean drew away angrily, casting a bitter glance. Was not Francis a Royalist—one of those who had stifled their glorious plans? Quickly, Jean stepped through a gap ahead.

Francis saw Jean's look, and his face grew sad. His lips moved and he stepped forward as if to speak, but Jean was gone.

~*~*~

Two days later, "the Thirty" and Jean de Lobel struck back. Sunday morning, a scroll lay on the elevated wooden framework of the "Altar of the Fatherland"—the place where the Fete de la Federation had been celebrated.

The scroll contained a petition protesting the National Assembly's decision. From the dawn's first rays, great, choleric throngs pressed forward to sign it. Many were illiterate and could only make an "X" for their name. Seething with excitement and anger, they presented a very menacing aspect indeed.

Francis le Mercier had been detained, taking counsel with LaFayette. His family had gone ahead to the Du Chemin's for their small Protestant church gathering. Because he was late, Francis took a short cut, passing the Fete de la Federation ground. His heart went out to the revolutionists, so zealous and misled—who rejected the Truth and were following their own desires, self-deluded and deluding, tearing down deep heaven upon their heads....

O Jerusalem, Jerusalem, thou that killest the prophets,
and stonest them which are sent unto thee,
how often would I have gathered thy children together,
even as a hen gathereth her chickens under her wings, and ye would not!
Behold, your house is left unto you desolate.

~*~*~

Jules pressed through the crowd that afternoon, his bosom stirring with indignation at the Assembly's decree. Joining the line, he waited impatiently for his turn to sign the scroll. Thousands had already signed; twenty thousand inflamed people swarmed the great amphitheatre. Many did not seem content to merely sign a protest against their King.

Silhouetted against the dull sky stood a coarse sans-culotte, laboriously scratching his name. Suddenly his leg jerked. Bending, he peered down at the floor of the platform. *Was that a screw poking out of the boards?*

"Hasten, you," called an impatient woman, shoving forward. "What is detaining you, blockhead?—The boards are sound enough for me." There was a laugh round, for she was a large woman.

377

"A gimlet!" he said, motioning incredulously. The point of a hand-drill was rapidly disappearing.

"What? Treason, perhaps!"

Eager arms tore away the boards. A howl rose from the crowd as two men were hauled from under the platform! Everyone pressed upon them, demanding answers. The two men stared stupidly around; one had a wooden leg, and the other held the fatal drill. A bag of provisions was also found underneath the platform—but no gunpowder, though the easily-excitable populace had already begun to voice that suspicion. Questioning only drew out that the two were there out of mere curiosity, and had been boring a hole to see. "A likely excuse! They are spies for LaFayette!" many hissed.

Clearly seeing the lack of evidence—*These two befuddled ninnies could not be spies!*—Jules spoke for putting them in a guardhouse. Others—the more peaceable—agreed. They managed to push through the naysayers and reach a temporary gaol; with more difficulty they secured the two inside. Once they were safely locked up, Jules headed back to the signing, but many still flocked around the guardhouse with implacable vengeance.

Jules was standing atop the wooden structure, just putting quill to paper, when he looked across the heads of the crowd and saw a great disturbance around the guardhouse. "Spies! They are spies for LaFayette!" A great shout welled from the depths of the throng—the people were growing wild; wild for blood.

Jules had consented to the hanging of Foulon. But recent events had begun to change him, though he did not know it. Without signing, he bounded down the steps, pressing madly in the direction of the hurricane that had the two simpletons in its grasp.

"Calm down, man; we cannot all have the pleasure of personally stringing them up, you know."

Jules turned sharply and beheld Denis' lean, cynical face. Jules made an impatient gesture, a feeling of revulsion welling up inside.

"Look; they are already up," Denis said. "*La Lanterne* makes justice easy!"

"But—they may have been innocent!" Jules said.

"Two fewer busybodies," Denis shrugged. "You are not growing Royalist, I hope," he sneered.

"I am a true patriot," Jules answered, stung at the imputation. His mind stirred with early remembrances of the Ten Commandments, taught by his mother, and he almost added, "However, not a murderer." A moment later he chastised himself for such an unpatriotic thought.

The great swelling satisfaction of the mob at the deaths of the "spies" surged around them; Jules saw calloused delight on an old crone's withered face and felt somehow sick.

"Have you signed, comrade?" Denis asked.

"No," Jules said shortly. "Not yet."

"Say, comrade, I need to talk to you about De la Noye," Denis said. "I have a plan: let us meet at a tavern later this evening for a *tête-à-tête.*"

"Sure. The *Tigre National?*" Jules mentioned a well-frequented public-house.

Denis made a face. "No, no. How about some small, quiet place — the Red Fox?"

Jules threw him a questioning glance, and Denis explained with an ill-contented voice, "A few jobs of mine have fallen through of late — I am rather low on funds. 'Twould not do, you see, to dispel my image of a generous comrade by not paying for drinks all round." His face brightened a bit. "An up-coming opportunity, however, should bolster my coffers."

There was an almost imperceptible quiver in Denis' shoulders; he was laughing inwardly. Jules eyed him critically, liking him less and less. He had no time to wonder at his revulsion — to wonder why he now drew away from the man he had admired and aided for so long. He struggled against it.

"The Red Fox, then," Jules answered. "In an hour or two, perhaps?"

"I am needed here; let's meet at dusk — a little after seven 'o clock, comrade?"

"Yes, that is fine," Jules answered.

Jules wondered that he had never noticed how unpleasant Denis' smile was. There was something wolfish about it. He tried to shake off the feeling. Yet instead of joining Denis in line, to sign the petition, he turned away through the inflamed crowd.

~*~*~

The news of the hangings spread through the streets. Having now stepped over the line to murder, the heaving thousands became even more belligerent. As the hours wore on, the disturbance merely increased, at an alarming rate. Bailly, the Mayor of Paris, was at last forced to declare martial law — the situation was getting out of hand.

Jules had climbed the tiers of amphitheatre seats and was looking down on the crowd. Abruptly, the rattle of drums thundered from a street entering the square. The drums grew louder and more insistent. There, flapping in the darkening blue sky, flew a blood-red flag.

Everyone knew what that meant—martial law had been declared. Beneath it marched LaFayette and his troops. He had brought dependable National Guards this time—their faces meant business. In a clear, loud voice, LaFayette commanded the agitated throng to disperse.

Jules' hatred flared at the sight of the red flag and official uniforms—but all the same he shrunk from the wild sans-culottes who had in cold blood hung the two simpletons.

The crowd surged towards the soldiers with rebellious shouts, ignoring LaFayette's repeated, merciful commands to disperse. Jules spotted Denis near the front row. Several in the crowd bent quickly—when they straightened, paving-stones arced through the air. Others pelted the soldiers with mud, stones, and refuse, howling their defiance. From his elevated position Jules could see Denis' lean face contorted with fiendish fury.

Things had reached a head. The soldiers stood firm, rifles on the ready, enduring the barrage of stones and projectiles. Once more, LaFayette commanded the crowd to disperse and desist. They answered with increased vituperation and missiles.

With a stern face, he turned and gave a sharp command. A sheet of fire blazed in the early dusk, followed instantly by rumbling gun reverberations, whining bullets, and cries of pain. The whole front of the crowd broke up, fleeing, before the soldiers, leaving some twelve rioters dead upon the cobbles.

Looking under the feet of the silent, advancing soldiers, Jules paused long enough to assure himself that Denis was not among the slain. Then he clambered down and snuck off quickly towards the Red Fox.

It was not far. Jules took a seat in a shadowed corner. Resting an elbow on the rough table, he shaded his face with his hand. A storm of emotions rose and broke in his breast. *Why wasn't I there in the front line, resisting the soldiers?* Then the thought broke in, *But the soldiers, being attacked, were not wrong to fire....Yet—are not "the people" right? Are not their wishes the best ones? What kept me back, kept me from signing, from joining the patriot's armed resistance?...Was it the—the murder (can I call it that?) of the two simpletons?* He shuddered.

He couldn't order his thoughts logically as emotions crashed round him—horror at the bleeding "patriots" on the ground; the remembrance of Denis' sneering taunt that he was perhaps "growing Royalist;" thoughts of Honore and Tristan's work, tinged with deep disappointment and a sense of futility — *I overheard that plot at the stables, and we kept watch for several long nights outside Madame d'Arcy's — but all for nothing! Something must have upset the gang's plans — mayhap they saw us, but it could've been something else, too... We did catch sight of Jacques and the mare the first night, but he seemed as puzzled as us that no one came...* He hung his head in discouragement, but even so his emotions stirred him with a confused, renewed revulsion towards Denis....

A voice spoke from above him — a cool, cynical voice he knew well. "Are you perhaps mourning my loss?"

Jules lowered his hand as Denis slid into the seat opposite. "Two glasses," Denis said aside, to the waiter.

"No; I saw you were not among the fallen," Jules replied.

"That was surely comradely of you, my dear Jules. Here, take a glass — yes, 'tis strong, but 'twill do you good after such a scene. I suppose you are stewing because of the massacre?"

Jules took a long draught of the heady wine. "Yes, but —" Jules knew not how he would finish, but Denis, with a keen glance at the youth's turbulent face, deemed it time to break in.

"Those bloodthirsty soldiers," Denis hissed, "led by that despicable LaFayette! We must revenge these martyrs — martyrs for the cause of freedom!" He took a sip from his glass. "We shall need every patriot voice to encourage the populace — the cause of freedom will need you, Jules; this bloody affair is already driving the patriot leaders undercover. Curse LaFayette! He has been a stumbling-block in our way, time and time again! Curse the proud aristocrats who oppress us!" Then he shifted subtly, keeping a sharp watch on Jules' emotions. "Now about De la Noye; he is one who must be brought down. I had an idea..."

Draining his glass, Jules' face lit up — the mention of De la Noye swung his feelings again towards Denis. "Yes, tell me of your new plan. I *desire —*" Jules clenched his hand passionately, "I *shall* break his proud front!"

Darkness closed round outside — scared, scattered *sans-culottes* slunk by in the shadows, utterly cowed. But in the artificially-lighted tavern called The Red Fox, huddled eagerly over a rough deal table, two figures talked earnestly long into the night.

It was a relief to Jules to slide back into his former hate and rebelliousness. It had been so much harder to struggle against it all. The Le Merciers and their glowing ideals seemed far away now.

But the manmade candlelight was an apt picture of his release; for it was not the life-giving light of the day — he was only slipping back into bondage. A trap is usually easy to get into; it is only when one tries to get out that one realizes one is ensnared.

The Thief

6.

...thy work shall be rewarded, saith the LORD;
and they shall come again from the land of the enemy.
— Jeremiah 31:16b

*A*ugust, 1791. Large and still, the moon brooded over the vast, torturous labyrinth of Paris streets. The air was close and heavy. These were the last days of summer.

Adele lay sleepless on her canopied bed. Though the second-story windows were open, her curtains hung sullenly, moved by no breeze. The heat was oppressive. She found her mind reverting to the recipe she had tried that evening—a sauce for asparagus. One line ran through her brain:

...make a sauce with good fresh butter, a little vinegar, salt, and nutmeg, and an egg yolk to bind the sauce; take care that it doesn't curdle...

'Take care that it doesn't curdle' — That was the tricky part, she thought sleepily, *...it did curdle the first time; but next time I added the ingredients more slowly....'Take care that it doesn't curdle'...that it doesn't curdle...that it—doesn't....* She was drifting off when the doorknob rattled slightly, starting her from the threshold of sleep. Eyes closed, Adele wondered drowsily who was there. Her arm lay outside the thin coverlet, and a small hand touched it. Opening her eyes, Adele turned on her side; out of the darkness emerged Paulette's wide-eyed round face.

"'Dele?" she lisped.

"Paulette—what are you doing here, out of bed?" Adele sleepily raised herself on one elbow. The moonlight sneaking palely into the room highlighted her nightgown's graceful folds and gathering ribbons.

"I was scared, 'Dele," Paulette whispered.

"Berthe—" Adele began. Berthe normally cared for Paulette at night. It was unthought-of for parents, much less other siblings, to do so. Having a nurse to care for the young ones was essential in any upper-class household. Though Adele's parents allowed their children much freer interaction than most aristocratic households, there were many things they did not even think to question.

"I wanted *you*, 'Dele." Paulette held out her chubby arms to be taken up into the bed. Her pleading, trusting look melted any further resistance on Adele's part. Scooping up the little white-gowned figure, she cuddled her close.

"You were scared, Paulette?"

"Yes."

"Did you repeat your verses?"

"No, 'Dele."

"Here, I will go back with you to your room, and we will repeat your verses together," Adele said.

They traversed the dark hall hand in hand, Adele looking lovingly at the little feet pattering along the parquet floor. In Paulette's room, she tucked the covers up to Paulette's smooth little neck and kissed the cheek that shone white in the moonlight. A feeling welled up in her that such a delightful task should never be given to a nurse—that she would be happy to miss sleep for the pleasure of caring for her little siblings.

"Repeat after me, darling: 'The Lorde is my shepherd, I shall not want.'"

"The Lorde," whispered Paulette, "is my shepherd, I shall not want."

"He maketh me to rest in greene pasture, and leadeth me by the still waters…"

Paulette's little voice murmured the time-worn words after her.

"The Lord bless you, darling; sleep soundly," Adele said at last. Casting one last glance at the chubby face on the small pillow, she slipped out.

The house had been utterly silent, but even as she entered the hall she heard booted feet, and a moment later the glow of a candle shimmered along the floor. A few seconds more and Honore came into sight, fully dressed. He had been out on patrol.

"Any news?" Adele whispered as he drew near.

"No; nothing," he whispered back. The candlelight illumined his tired face. "Since the *Champ-de-Mars* fracas the rabble-rousers are lying low; for weeks hardly anyone has been in the streets."

"It seems fruitless—but press on, Honore," Adele said, though her own heart sank with the seeming futility of the task.

Honore looked down at her dispirited countenance. "One good thing, Adele—crime has decreased in the neighboring boroughs, mayhap because our patrols. Rumor has it that youthful vigilantes are on the lookout."

Adele smiled. "What is the verse Father so often quotes? '...let us not be weary in well doing: for in due season we shall reap, if we faint not.'"

"Amen," Honore responded. "May He be glorified. *Bon soir,* Adele."

"*Bon soir.*"

~*~*~

Telling her mother the next morning about her unexpected nighttime visitor, Adele smiled lovingly over the silver candlesticks at Paulette's pixie face, finishing her account with, "May I care for her in the nighttime, Mother?"

Felicienne's green eyes were thoughtful. "Your father and I have considered it. However, I can see nothing against your taking over such duties, Adele—indeed, it would perhaps be helpful preparation, as your father desires."

When the idea was presented to him, Francis approved warmly. "I know not why we never thought of it, dearest," he said to Felicienne as they sat together in the library. His hand rested on the legal tome he had been perusing.

"Do not chastise yourself; everyone has a nurse for the young," Felicienne said. "I know I always felt an innate longing to take more part in caring for the little ones, but it simply is not done."

"Tell Adele she may certainly care for Paulette. I believe it will be a good thing, and helpful if we go to England."

So it was settled, to Adele and Paulette's great delight, although Stephanie, when she heard of it, tossed her golden curls incredulously. "You shall soon tire of it," she stated.

"I may—in fact, I am sure that sometimes I shall become weary of the task," Adele replied. "But all good undertakings have times of dullness, when one learns character by pressing forward in the face of difficulties. With the Lord's help, I shall be learning the patience a mother needs."

"Not a mother of your rank," Stephanie replied. "How you can do such things is beyond me, Adele. Babies *can* be cute, but they are *such* a nuisance most times—rumpling one's dress, always needing attention, crying, waking at awkward hours; most of all, interfering with parties—I shall certainly hire a nurse, if *I* ever have children."

385

"If your hoped-for societal changes come to pass, even women of our rank will have to care for their own children," Adele said.

Shrugging an elegant shoulder, Stephanie changed the subject. "Mother is so silly about Gaston," she said. "Of course, arranged marriages are the norm—but it is so stuffy and *cold-blooded* for parents to use their children's marriages to make studied alliances with other families based on social weight, political influence, and wealth! *Faugh!*"

"I agree with you that it is *deplorable* when parents think selfishly—not for the good of their children, but for themselves alone. 'Tis truly awful. But that is not always the case, Stephanie," Adele smiled. "You know that though theirs was an arranged marriage—she but 15, he 17—General and Madame LaFayette loved each other. Many parents do consider the wishes of their children."

"Oh, *I know*," Stephanie pouted, "but *my* parents—" She arched her brows scornfully. Continually fretting against their safeguard, Stephanie sought in countless ways to influence her parents in the direction of her latest "gallant."

"I think they desire your best," Adele said. "I know that my parents would not choose a husband for me without my consent—Stephanie, they love me and seek the best for me."

"I am glad you have such faith in them," Stephanie said. "I might; but really, my parents just need to see how right I am about Gaston. And another thing—I don't see anything wrong with enjoying the moment and flirting with as many as I can. Everyone does it."

"I know—dalliance is so common it is hardly noticed," Adele said. "But as a Christian, my goal is to be an obedient daughter, to remain unentangled, to keep my heart pure for my future husband." She flashed a radiant smile at Stephanie. "Our desire for love, for companionship, is given by God; but there is a proper time and place for it—and I think it will be all the more rich and sweet if we wait than if we snatch it off the tree now."

"Maybe," Stephanie conceded, "but this is different. I know Gaston and I are meant for each other." Then she was off on another topic—Adele felt her words had fallen on deaf ears. "Oh, *do* come to the opera with Mother and me tomorrow! Will you?" Stephanie queried. "Gaston will attend us, and Sebastien said he would come. You must set yourself free from your sober round of cooking and housekeeping, Adele, at least once—come be carefree and enjoy yourself!"

"Do you really think I do not enjoy myself?" Adele met her cousin's flashing blue eyes fully with her sweet hazel ones.

And Stephanie could not shake the conviction that Adele had more joy and fulfillment than her own shallow pleasures provided. Without answering Adele's question, she prattled on about the opera, interspersed with bits of gossip, speculating as to who would be there and with whom — filling her emptiness with the fleeting spice of rumor and flirtation. Stephanie seemed happy — but Adele noted the vapidity lurking in her beautiful blue eyes.

Adele's heart ached for her cousin. *It may fulfill now — though I doubt it truly does — but later — !*

~*~*~

The curtain of evening was drawing slowly across the sky above the old gray city of Paris. Tristan, Honore, and Marcel turned from richer thoroughfares into crowded, miserable arteries. A lamplighter trudging ahead of them was the only person in sight.

"Things are still quiet," Tristan mentioned. "The fracas between LaFayette and the sans-culottes has had a repressive influence."

"*Certes*," Honore replied, "and no hint of our knife-in-back robber for a while now — could he have moved his operations, perhaps?"

"I do not know," Tristan admitted. "There certainly is a temptation to be discouraged. But I have this hunch —" he set his jaw steadfastly, "I feel we should keep trying — keep patrolling and making inquiries. At the least, the overall rate of crime has decreased here."

They had reached their usual corner for starting on their separate patrols. Without a word, they slipped off into the streets, each apart but within hailing distance.

Honore moved softly down the center of his chosen street, eyes alert beneath his dark felt hat. At times his foot struck against a loose cobble or stepped on refuse, while his nose was assaulted with the varied smells endemic to over-crowding and poor sanitation. In the dark, his ears told him more than his eyes. They picked up many now-familiar sounds: the faint shouts of drunken roisterers, a baby's shrill, muffled wailing, the ever-present indistinct hum of a large city....

Presently, however, he picked up the *pad-pad* of footsteps somewhere behind. He drew aside as quietly as he could, but stepped into a gutter and fought to keep from falling. Regaining his balance, he pressed against a dark, mean doorway.

A man walked hastily by, staying scrupulously in the center of the street, away from doorways and gaping byways. He seemed ill at ease. Honore stepped quietly out after him (avoiding the crater that tripped him earlier) and followed at a cautious distance. It was so dark he only had a general impression of someone stout, walking at a brisk pace. Honore had much to do to remain unobserved—he sensed rather than saw that the man kept glancing round, as if fearing an assault.

The darkness grew deeper, the avenue narrowed. Honore increased his pace, drawing nearer to keep the man in sight. Though intent on following unobserved, he had no hopes that anything would come of this—how many countless times before had he trailed someone for miles, only to have naught come of it!

His eyes caught an unexpected blur of movement ahead. His body sprang into action before he could even think. There, in front of him, was what he had dreamed about for so many months! A dark figure had darted behind the stout man, a gleam of metal in his hand.

The two figures struggled in darkness—the nearest streetlamp peered uselessly into the gloom some twenty yards away. The stout man was trying to turn, his right hand grasping or thrusting something away. But the attacker's strength was overcoming him—the gleaming knife moved slowly downwards even in the seconds it took for Honore to near. With a shrill whistle—the signal to Tristan and Marcel—Honore closed on the figures.

With a curse, the robber wrenched his arm from the stout man's grasp and turned to flee. In that very instant, his face—though still in darkness—was silhouetted against the greasy, distant patch of light.

"Denis!" Honore exclaimed in astonishment.

Half a second later, the lean figure of the thief disappeared in an inky, torturous alley. Heedless of danger, Honore bolted after him, drawing out a weighted cudgel. A moment later, in the pitch-dark alley, his left hand closed on the man's shoulder. It was a dead-end street—Denis was trapped.

Honore tensed. Knife fights were dangerous—and the dark increased the danger a thousand-fold. In that split second, his mind formed two plans—one if the man tried to flee, the other if he fought.

With a muffled exclamation, Denis twisted to face him. Honore released his hold instantaneously, leaping backwards to put as much space as possible between them. *Space* was so important—once one's attacker closed in, serious or fatal knife wounds were inevitable. Wishing desperately for more light, he peered through the gloom, holding his knotted stick in a position to parry blows or give them.

Providentially, the clouds parted and the moon illuminated Denis' on-rushing figure, his knife arm arched to strike. Lifting his cudgel, Honore struck Denis' raised arm, then spun to the side and backwards. Denis' momentum carried him past. Honore pivoted to face him once more, his bludgeon knocking away the knife aimed at his back.

He swung again, landing a good blow on Denis' left shoulder, but an instant later had to leap back to avoid a knife-thrust directed at his stomach. Honore had practiced much at the *salle 'd armes* and was a good swordsman, but this type of fighting was different. There were no long weapons to keep the other at a distance—here, one must move in close to attack. But his fencing skills were not useless—the long-practiced coolness and rapidity of movement were essential.

It was a strange feeling, fighting such a vengeful opponent and knowing he was a former servant. *Can this murderous assailant really be the valet who jested and talked with me since I was a toddler?* He could not see him distinctly now, but that one glimpse in the street had been enough.

Dimly, Honore sensed Denis' victim panting up to offer assistance, but he could not spare even a glance. He was too busy fighting—fighting a strong, ruthless foe.

Denis' knife flashed forward. Honore met it, bringing his cudgel down on his knife-wrist with all his force. The knife dropped to the ground. Honore kicked it among the shadows, but that slight movement made him unprepared for Denis' next move.

Denis made a cat-like leap forward, knocking Honore backwards. Honore staggered back against a wall.

Denis turned and ran: with a yell, his former victim plunged after him, catching his coat-tails. "I've got you, you scapegrace!" he cried. There was a sudden tussle, then Honore, still leaning against the wall from the force of the blow, saw Denis wriggle out of his coat, throwing it over his assailant's head. Denis was out of sight before Honore could assist the man, still struggling with the coat. The encounter had lasted only minutes.

"He is gone," Honore said, chagrined. He pulled the twining coat off the man. "Are you hurt?"

"No—and thanks to you," the other replied. His French was good, though he spoke with an English accent. "Come into the light, so I may see my preserver."

Once under the bleary *lanterne*, Honore had his first good look at the man. Under whitening hair, humorous, penetrating dark eyes and a straight nose gave him a bluff, hearty appearance. The man's clothes and manner clinched Honore's guess. *An Englishman.*

An honest man, close-buttoned to the chin,
Broadcloth without, and a warm heart within.

Pounding feet broke the dark stillness. With a look of alarm, the man turned toward the oncoming figures.

"It is only my friends," Honore assured him, as Marcel and Tristan panted up.

"Any friend of yours is quite welcome," the man smiled.

"What happened?" Tristan eagerly asked, instinctively greeting the man with a bow.

"I was walking along behind this man here," Honore answered, "when out of the shadows sprang a dark figure with a knife. Our English friend here was on the alert and managed to catch the thief's wrist and hold the knife back. When I arrived, the robber wrenched free and fled."

"My story tallies with yours," the Englishman said. "I am a merchant. I leave tomorrow, but had not filled up my allotted cargo. When I received a last-minute note from a merchant to view some just-acquired goods, I assented, though it was already growing dark. The note asked me to bring a substantial down-payment, so if I decided to buy we could square the deal immediately. However, when I arrived, the shop was closed. I could get no answer to my repeated knocks. It was growing dark, and I began to fear a ruse. I hurried through the streets, hoping to avoid footpads. Suddenly I glimpsed movement out of the corner of my eye, and—" here he chuckled, "well, I was not brought up in London for nothing! I was just in time to seize the man's knife hand. We struggled, but he was getting the upper hand when out of nowhere this youth sprang to my rescue. I am deeply indebted to you, young man. No doubt you saved my life," he said, shaking Honore's hand vigorously. "What did you exclaim, on seeing the thief?"

"'Denis,'" Honore announced.

"*Denis!*" Tristan cried. "Are you sure?"

Honore's brow furrowed. "That's the thing. I saw the outline his face distinctly for a split second. I could swear it was Denis—but it was just a silhouette."

"Outlines can be quite distinctive," Tristan said.

"Yes; but I fear 'twould not wholly convince a judge." To the Englishman, Honore explained, "Denis is my father's former valet. Did you glimpse the robber, Monsieur?"

"I saw nothing I could swear to," the Englishman said. "But if I may ask—from your speech I gather you are an aristocrat—how comes it that you were in the streets so opportunely?"

"Yes, I am of the *noblesse*, as is my friend Tristan—" Honore began, then paused, feeling the oddity of not being introduced. "We have not the honor of being introduced, Monsieur—"

"I suppose I *should* properly present myself," the man chuckled, his dark eyes twinkling under his tousled white hair. "Here is my card—"

He held out a small rectangle of paper, and the youths crowded round to read it. Inside a highly-ornate scroll-work frame were the words:

BARKER & BARKER
Fine Imported French Goods
THREADNEEDLE STREET, LONDON
Thaddaeus Barker, prop. public welcome

"I am Thaddaeus," the Englishman explained. "The other 'Barker' is my younger brother Archibald. He superintends our warehouse."

"It is a great pleasure to meet you, M. Barker," Honore said. "May I present to you my friend Tristan du Chemin and my manservant Marcel Martin. I am Honore de Coquiel di le Mercier."

"It is an even greater pleasure to me to meet you," M. Barker bowed. Then he looked at them with a smile. "It is rather dark, standing under this lamppost—let us adjourn to a more comfortable place; say, my lodging-house? I confess I am quite curious to hear your reasons for roaming the streets."

"I should have suggested it before—pray excuse my lapse in hospitality," Honore answered. "Do come to my abode—we can talk at length there."

They turned and set off together through the smelly, dark streets. But there was a light in their hearts that mere physical darkness could not dampen.

~*~*~

Jules went to the next party at the De Lobels with a strange reluctance. Since agreeing to aid Tristan and Honore several months ago, he had begun to look forward to their meetings. But somehow after the *Champ-de-Mars* "massacre," things had changed. He felt his long-slumbering conscience pricking him when he thought of his recent plotting with Denis—but he refused to heed it.

391

The room was brilliantly lit, brimming with light banter, satins, and sparkling jewels. Jules quickly engaged himself in conversation with a young lady, half-hoping that perhaps the Le Merciers were not there.

An hour passed, and the dancing began. Jules found a partner, and was soon among the whirl of dancers. He had not seen the Le Merciers, and a little part of him relaxed.

When the dance ended, the girl was claimed by another youth, and Jules found himself standing alone. Several couples separated, and suddenly he noticed two figures very close by. One was Adele, and the other Sebastien du Sauchoy. Jules heard their conversation clearly.

"Certainly you will give me just *one* dance, Adele," Sebastien was saying.

Adele's manner was quiet and cool. "No, but thank you, Sebastien."

A laughing girl swept by, clinging to a young man's arm, her beautiful face alight with artful coquetry. It was Stephanie. For a moment, the two girl's faces were juxtaposed—Stephanie's brilliant, selfish countenance, crowned with flirtatious eyes, and Adele's modest, gracious one, straightforward and pure. Stephanie normally looked strikingly beautiful and happy to Jules—but for that one moment, as her face was set beside Adele's, he received almost a shock. He glimpsed a vacant hungering and emptiness in it.

Stephanie passed on with her escort, but Jules stared after her. Since his evening with Denis, he had been "one" with rebellious "patriots" like Stephanie and Gaston, once more had enjoying the "sweetness" of revenge. But that one moment drew him back to the Le Merciers and Tristan.

He was bowing to Adele before he consciously knew he'd made a decision. "Madame Adele, how dulcet you look this evening."

Sebastien turned away, with a final glance at Adele.

She looked at Jules with one of her open, artless smiles. "Jules! I am pleased to see you!" Lowering her voice, she added, leading him to a private nook, "Honore had a breakthrough when patrolling a few nights ago—here, let him tell you himself."

When Honore finished his story, any further diffidence on Jules' part melted. He had listened with amazed wonder—and when Honore mentioned that the robber was Denis, things clicked in his brain.

"It all fits!" Jules said, dazed. "I did not tell you; but he mentioned when I saw him last that 'several jobs recently have not worked out, but I have one in the works,' or something like that. I noticed at the time his inward amusement, but could not guess why…"

With revulsion, Jules realized that it was due to Denis' coaching that he had plunged back into hatred and rabid patriotism's blindness to right and wrong. The honesty his mother had drilled into him recoiled at the thought of Denis as a ruthless thief; *Not a true patriot at all!* Jules was still a patriot. But helping the oppressed like these aristocrats—that was a truly patriotic cause.

In indecision the King lost his chance to escape, but Jules made his choice. He would never regret it.

Denis Swears Vengeance

7.

Zoese: *Perhaps. Thou wilt not aid me then?*
Aloinda: *I dare not.*
— The Cid of Seville

I t was late when Jules returned home from the De Lobel's *fete*.
Fumbling in the dark with the latch, he slipped inside. As the creaking
door shut, he was surprised by a glimmer of candlelight.

Seated on a rickety stool, his mother bent closely over a hat. A
candle guttered in the crude holder beside her. She looked up, her eyes
tired in her embittered, once-lovely face.

"Up so late, Mother?"

"This hat must be done by tomorrow early," she hunched once
more over it, her needle flashing unsteadily as she sewed on the feathers.

"A pest on it!" Jules said.

But his mother answered with unusual softness, "Claude, a
milliner friend, stopped by today. He said that if business does not pick up
soon, he will be penniless and forced to close. So many aristocrats have
fled — there are fewer and fewer to purchase our goods. I suppose I should
be thankful to have this increase in business. Many of my trade are in
difficulty, yet in the last year I have even been able to set aside a small
reserve." Sticking a pin between her lips, she held the hat out critically.
With a nod of approval, she rose. Crossing the room to put it away, she
noticed Jules' face.

"What is it, Jules? Do you have news of — of De la Noye? Is there
anything we can do *now* to foil him? This waiting — we must *do* something!"

"Nothing new with regards to the accursed De la Noye, Mother —
though I have heard something about one who aided us against him."

"Sit down and tell me, Jules — what is it?"

"I told you that I and others have been searching for the thief who
has been preying on many — especially poor tradesmen."

Camille nodded. "I remember."

394

"'Tis *Denis*, Mother—he is that robber!" Jules exclaimed. Camille gasped as Jules told her how Honore foiled the thief and discovered his identity.

Camille's face stiffened. "Is it certain?"

"I trust M. Honore to recognize him—and his word (though he is an aristocrat) is to be depended on, Mother. When he says it was Denis—it was Denis."

Camille said like one stunned, "Yes—yes, M. Honore is trustworthy." For a moment she was still, then she broke out, "Oh, *Denis*—that perfidious man! I care not if he helped us against De la Noye—you must renounce all friendship with him, my son. That lean-faced blackguard! Pretending to be an advocate of the people, and robbing them instead!" Her passionate mood broke, and she asked more quietly, "Your friends have put him in gaol?"

Jules shook his head moodily. "Alas—though they have Honore's testimony, they fear 'tis not enough to convince a judge. Denis will have compatriots to swear to any alibi he wishes."

Yet while he agreed with his mother, he felt long-built ties to the former valet. How many times had they been comrades in various ventures to "free" France! It is hard to snap a chain of shared experiences in a moment.

~*~*~

But it was different the next evening. Turning the grimy front windows to murky gold, the sun's last rays sent an orange light into Camille's small shop, touching a dusty bottle here and there with fire. The row of glass canisters in front of the pasty wax busts seemed filled with some elixir of flaming potency. Camille was giving Jules a list of assorted things to buy when the front door opened. Jules instantly stepped back as his mother moved towards the door with a shopkeeper's peculiar air.

However, it was no beribboned lady or plain-frocked maid. It was Denis himself.

"My respects to you, Mademoiselle Camille," he said, an unctuous smile on his lean face. "You look more beautiful than ever today—Fortune has been good to you."

Camille's cheeks *were* rich in color, but there was a look in her pale gray eyes that hinted at another explanation than happiness or health.

Denis continued on, slapping Jules on the back, "—and how is my comrade? 'S been too long—we've got some plans to carry out, eh, my lad?"

Jules stood still, his mind a whirl of emotions. He managed, "This is an unexpected visit, Denis."

"Ah, yes—but I'm rather in a bind—and I knew you, my true friend, would come to my aid," Denis grinned warmly at Camille. "Indeed, this is coming to the point rather rapidly, but—" he shrugged, "—we can get this over quickly, and then sit round for a good talk on De la Noye; I have some ideas on how to discommode that rascal. To be plain, I've run into hard luck—several jobs of mine have fallen through most abominably—and I need some money in this temporary hiatus. I knew that not only are you the soul of patriotism, my dear Camille, but you would help an old friend." His quick eyes must have noted his stiff reception, but his comradely manner did not change a whit.

As Denis spoke, leaning easily over the back of a chair, Jules' feelings finally narrowed and steadied. He was opening his mouth to answer when his mother's voice broke the momentary lull. It was very decided, but with a suspicious quiver.

"I am afraid your request is impossible," she said. "I enjoin you never to enter this house or speak to me again."

Denis straightened, a confused and injured look on his mobile face. "Now, Camille, surely you are too quick. What have I done to offend you? I, who have been a good friend, the faithful comrade of your son? I, a zealous patriot? I, who—"

Camille's withheld passions burst forth. "You recreant wretch! To pretend to be aiding the downtrodden, when you yourself prey upon them! You, a common footpad! And to pretend that you need money to carry yourself through a hard time between lawful employments, when it is only because your latest robberies failed!" Her breath came quick and fast; pale eyes flashed beneath her narrowed lashes. "I may be only a low milliner, but I know stealing is wrong!"

Denis' look of surprise was not feigned. "My dear, where did you hear such base, lying rumors?"

"They're not lies—you know as well as I do who interfered with your villainous robbery the other night; and his witness is trustworthy!" Camille hurled back.

Denis' lips had drawn tight, but he turned to Jules. "My comrade—"

Jules stepped back. "Hear what Mother says. Your mask has been torn, Denis—I renounce you as what you are: a common thief!"

Denis made a step towards Camille, as if to take her arm. She backed against the wall.

"For the love of your friendship—" he began, but was cut off by Camille.

"None of your winning ways, you thief!" she cried. "You shall never get a *denier* of my money, you—*Begone*, and never *darken* my door again!"

Denis' pale face blazed from the dark frame of his straggling locks. His scar shone lividly. Jules had never seen that face of vengeful hate turned toward himself before, and it chilled his blood.

"You shall repent of this someday, you false woman!" Denis cried. "I swear...I swear it by all things! There will come a day when you shall wish you had died rather than having spoken those words. And my vengeance that day shall be sweet!" His fiendish laugh echoed through the room, and he was gone.

Jules glanced round, almost dazed. The room seemed dark and cold—the sun had gone down even as they spoke. Then he saw his mother sway, and sprang forward to catch her.

"I am fine," she murmured, laying her head on his shoulder, "just—oh, what a viper—and we knew it not!" She raised her head, looking out into the ashen room. "I still hold firm to my words—I am glad that I did not give him money. I will have *nothing* to do with thieves! To think!— pretending to be a friend of the people, and robbing them! But, oh—" she shivered a little, " —I *fear* that man, Jules! Beware of him!"

~*~*~

Laughter, lights, and music welled in scintillating gusts from the evening fields of the *Champs Elysees,*

> *whilst twilight's curtain, spreading far,*
> *Was pinn-ed with a single star.*

Why the rejoicing? Why did all Paris meet with beaming face, and, stranger yet, hail the King's passing carriage with shouts of *"Vive le Roi!"*? Why dancing, feasting, and fireworks every night, these last days of September 1791?

Because on September 14, the King signed the completed Constitution! The Constituent Assembly, its sworn work (the Constitution) finished, was wrapping up its business prior to turning its duties over to an all-new governing body—the Legislative Assembly. And not only that, but LaFayette proclaimed a general amnesty for all past political offenders! France gave itself over to delirious joy.

Her small hand on her husband's arm, Felicienne le Mercier passed through the teeming throng in the *Champs Elysees*. Overhead shone many-colored lights, casting swaying luminescence on aristocrat and commoner alike. A few steps behind were Honore and Marcel. As they passed a long stone bench underneath the spreading trees, Felicienne recognized a woman in a ruffled, low-cut dress. "There's Juliette," she said to Francis. "I would go and speak with her."

Juliette greeted her sister warmly. "Felicienne! What a delight! Do come and sit; there is room for you and Francis..."

Francis handed his wife to the seat, bowing to his sister-in-law. "It would be a pleasure to join you both, but I must needs speak to M. Dupin —" he gestured to a blue-coated gentleman some way off. Honore also excused himself with a bow, but Marcel lounged against a nearby tree.

The sisters talked for some time. Around them shifted the ever-moving crowd of merrymakers; gathering in fluid groups and breaking away to promenade up and down the avenue. Felicienne saw many she recognized — deputies of the Constituent Assembly; the popular radical *salonnière* Madame Roland; and Madame de Stael, on the arm of M. Narbonne — she was scheming to make him the War Minister. Under teeming lights a little ahead, dancers swayed on the grassy sward.

Leaving the dancers, beautiful blond Stephanie flitted towards Juliette and Felicienne, at her side Gaston de la Roche. A middle-aged maidservant followed as chaperone.

Stephanie approached her aunt with a smile. "Where is Adele?"

"Adele sent her love, but said to say she was occupied this evening," Felicienne answered.

"She was here last night," Stephanie said, still clasping Gaston's brawny arm.

"She stayed home to tell Paulette a bedtime story," Felicienne replied.

"A bedtime story, more important than *this?*" Stephanie asked incredulously. But she evidently deemed it a rhetorical question, for she turned to Gaston and drew him away, her golden head near his dark one.

Juliette glared after them. "That girl!" she vented, her brows drawing together in a frown. "Entirely unmanageable; running around with that ultra-reactionary loose gallant....And now pressing us to 'arrange' a marriage! Nothing I say makes a jot of difference...."

"I am truly sorry," Felicienne said.

"She says she loves him, and says that's all that matters!" Juliette fumed. "As if her feelings...."

Felicienne waited, then said quietly, "But—dear sister, did you not teach your children that the heart is man's arbiter of right?"

Juliette turned her face a little away, her jaw set in a displeased line. A moment later she said petulantly, "*You* raised *your* children very unlike what is customary, too. Instead of being segregated from you and each other, as is the proper method, they have been very close. I don't know why you should reprove *my* childraising methods."

A sad look swept Felicienne's face. She opened her full ruby lips to answer, then paused, her eyes neither angry nor defensive—only compassionate. "Francis and I have made many mistakes with our children, I know," she said gently, "but being together as a family is one thing we do not regret."

Juliette said nothing, but the curve of her cheek and the corner of her eye (all Felicienne could see) were soft. Felicienne continued, "Why else does it say in the Scriptures: "And these wordes which I commaund thee this day, shalbe in thine heart. And thou shalt rehearse them continually unto thy children, and shalt talke of them when thou tariest in thine house, and as thou walkest by the way, and when thou liest downe, and when thou risest up:'? The custom among our class is to sequester the children by age with various maids, only being 'presented' to their parents once a day for five minutes. How does that go along with the Biblical injunction?"

"Oh, I am not in the mood for one of your theological discussions tonight," Juliette pushed back some of her curls. "Can you not have one conversation without mentioning that book?" But she looked bored and distracted, not truly annoyed.

Together, the sisters gazed on the scene; Francis finished his conversation and joined them. Before them danced and rejoiced the motley crowd—celebrating the beginning of a new and happy France, regenerated, rising on the ashes of the past to better things.

With a crack, a firework soared up, exploding into brilliance above the partying multitude. Following it with her eyes, Felicienne thought it an apt picture of the people's present happiness. It was a blazing spark which would go out ere long, leaving the darkness of discontent and rebellion even blacker than before.

She sighed, turning to Francis. "I am ready to go home, darling."

~*~*~

Her hand on Paulette's diaphanous curtains, Adele gazed out the window. Behind her slumbered Paulette, long lashes shading her chubby cheeks. One little hand rested outside the coverlet—moments before, Adele had been holding it.

The moon blazed into the room with her muted white light, and Adele thought it must be light enough to read. Sitting on a padded stool by the window, she picked up the book she had laid down.

Its smooth green cover reminded Adele of their short but enjoyable time with M. Barker, the Englishman Honore rescued—what talks they had had! The jolly Englishman had left for London soon after the attempted robbery, but promised to let them know when his business brought him again to Paris. He had given them this little book of English poems. Opening it, Adele's eyes fell on a poem written almost two hundred years before.

A DIVINE RAPTURE
by Francis Quarles

E'en like two little bank-dividing brooks,
That wash the pebbles with their wanton streams,
And having ranged and search'd a thousand nooks,
Met both at length in silver-breasted Thames,
Where in a greater current they conjoin:
So I my Best-beloved's am; so He is mine.

E'en so we met; and after long pursuit,
E'en so we joined; we both became entire;
No need for either to return a suit,
For I was flax, and He was flames of fire:
Our firm-united souls did more than twine;
So I my Best-beloved's am; so He is mine.

If all these glittering Monarchs, that command
The servile quarters of this earthly ball,
Should tender in exchange their shares of land,
I would not change my fortunes for them all:
Their wealth is but counter to my coin:
The world's but theirs; but my Beloved's mine.

The message of the poem—the delight of knowing Christ—resonated within Adele's heart. *How true it is,* she thought, *how blessed and satisfying it is to know Him! What a freedom and joy He brings!* The poet spoke from an overwhelming love for Christ, and it thrilled and inspired Adele—made her long for a closer companionship with her Savior.

Clasping her hands on the dainty green volume, her rich brown hair fell across her cheek as she bowed her head. "Lord," she whispered, "draw me closer to Thee! Help me to love you more, to find even more fulfillment in Thee. Thou art worthy to receive praise; give me more grace to seek Thee more…"

For He *satisfieth* the longing soule: and *filleth* the hungry soule with goodnesse.

~*~*~

It was the last session—the very last session. On one of the hard benches in the *Salle Ménage*, Francis thought of many things.

The deputies of the National Constituent Assembly had decreed that their places would be filled by a biennial parliament, titled the Legislative Assembly. Francis glanced up into the spectator's gallery where the seven hundred and forty-five elected members of the Legislative Assembly sat, ready to take up their duties the next morn. They were an inferior lot—mainly popular, middle-class revolutionaries. Francis' eyes scanned their faces, praying inwardly that God would change their hearts and cause them to do right. He suddenly stopped and looked again.

Yes, there was no mistaking that face. He had seen it every day of his life for thirty-five years—until two years ago, after the fall of the Bastille. Denis. *Denis! A member of the Legislative Assembly! Heaven forefend!*

Denis' liberal hand among the revolutionists had accomplished his desire. Triumph was written on his pale, lean face. After a moment, Denis' head turned in Francis' direction. Their eyes met. The scar across Denis' cheek whitened, but his eyes were full of victory. Francis gazed at him compassionately, praying that God would change or thwart his former valet. *At least now, if Honore and Tristan can prove the robberies, we shall know where to find him.*

Hearty applause broke their shared glance. The King had finished a speech full of platitudes about peace and future tranquility. "*Oui, oui!*" cried the deputies, applauding his innocuous and hopeful words.

At last, Thouret (president of the National Constituent Assembly) rose to conclude the session. All eyes turned towards him. In a strong, even tone he said, "The National Constituent Assembly declares that it has finished its mission and that its sittings are all ended."

It was a solemn moment. For a space, all was still, and then the silence was broken by the rustle of deputies gathering up papers and effects for the last time. When Robespierre and Pétion exited, they were swept up and carried on the shoulders of the elated crowd. It was a gala day for France—they had succeeded! *Or had they?*

Francis' labor was not done—there was much he still could do to influence events. But his grinding, nettlesome duties as a deputy were over. He had been "through fire and through water" attempting to do right, often standing up as a lone voice amidst extremist and reactionary factions. Through his mind flashed the forced summoning of the Estates-General, his election to it, Denis' underhanded efforts, the drawn-out struggle culminating in the Tennis Court oath and the King's acquiescence to the Third Estate, the taking of the Bastille, the March of Women, the fiery Assembly clashes between "the Thirty" and the Royalists, and more recently the unsuccessful flight of the King and the *Champ de Mars* massacre.... He had been a deputy through it all.

As he passed out the *Ménage's* stone doorway, he felt a burden lifted. Twenty-nine months of intense, agonizing toil and disappointment were over.

Heart Struggles

8.

We sigh for human love, from which
A whim or chance may sever,
And leave unsought the love of God,
Tho' God's love lasts forever.
— Effie Smith Ely

That evening, a delightful party was hosted by the Le Mercier's. Soon after Francis arrived home from that last session, the La Mottes arrived, followed by the Du Sauchoys, several families from church, and the Du Chemins. Adele smiled as Olivie and Christelle la Motte talked: she knew the will-effort involved in keeping down the girls' natural bubbly effusiveness and instead behaving "like grown-ups." But it was her father's relaxed face that gave Adele the most pleasure.

The sky quivered with color—a glimpse of the twining gold and purple clouds through the open French doors drew Adele into the garden. Then she noticed that others were there before her—Sebastien du Sauchoy, Elisabeth la Motte, Tristan du Chemin, and Honore were conversing on the tiled patio. Adele studied them, her hand resting on the doorframe.

Nearest, his back towards her as he talked to the others, was Sebastien, his handsome deep green jacket highlighting his impeccable dark brown hair. He had begun to attend church in the last months, and Adele wondered at his reasons. Also he had not been paying attention to Stephanie and her set, and was more conservative politically—Adele attributed it to Honore and Tristan's influence, and was glad.

Her eyes next fell on Elisabeth's exquisite cherry-colored silk dress. Black ringlets framed her deep blue eyes and dainty chin. But Adele noted most her radiant inward beauty. How often had Adele been encouraged and blessed by Elisabeth's deep and abiding love for Christ and for her parents!

Tristan was next, his clear, serious face intent. As Adele watched, his white teeth flashed in response to a comment of Sebastien's. Adele's pulse stirred with sincere admiration as she recalled his efforts to protect the populace, his godly manliness and devotion to the truth. She felt the same about Honore—her eyes grew warm as she gazed at him. How handsome Honore looked; his marvelous green eyes turned on the speaker, his every move speaking of unspotted manhood. Adele thanked God sincerely for such a brother, and for the amazing change in him since Grandpapa de Duret came.

As he talked, Sebastien half-turned, gesturing, and his eyes lighted on Adele. Breaking off his discourse, he advanced several steps. "Do join us, Adele," he bowed. "Your *ravissante* face was all that was lacking this glorious evening."

Adele blushed in protest, not deigning to answer, and with him joined the others.

"We were discussing the present state of affairs in France," Elisabeth told Adele. "My Father feels he can do no more. Keep it a secret, but he plans to emigrate. The King no longer desires his counsel—His Majesty is a mere puppet, creating such peace as we experience through being a nonentity."

"I feel more inclined than ever to take that stance," Sebastien said. "All efforts seem useless...."

Without thinking, Adele's eyes flashed to Tristan's, and his dark eyes answered hers. They were remembering the patrols.

"We should not give up if there is still duty to discharge," Honore began.

Adele felt a tug on her periwinkle skirt. Paulette, dressed, but with all her laces loose. "'dele? Can you—"

Adele stooped gracefully to her little sister's level. "Paulette—you were to be in bed!"

"Yes, 'dele," the little girl fidgeted, twining her chubby fingers and looking at the floor. "But—Berthe *was* helping, then she went 'way. I waited and waited, but she didn't come back...."

Taking Paulette's hand, Adele straightened up. "I must excuse myself, but I will return," she smiled to the others.

Putting five-year-old Paulette to bed did not take much time. On her way back to the parlor, Adele heard voices from the half-open library door. As she passed, she saw her father and M. du Sauchoy in close conversation. Seeing her, they instantly broke off, only beginning again when she was out of earshot. It seemed curious; she wondered as she walked on towards the parlor. However, any curiosity was swept into oblivion by the whirl of the party: chatting with several dowagers; trying to avoid Sebastien's compliments; talking and laughing with Honore, Elisabeth, and Tristan....

Once the last guest departed, Adele ascended the stairs with a full, happy heart. Through a crack in her curtain she saw the swarthy sky, the moon only a waning sliver. The burnished stars had been out for hours. By the candlelight, Adele undid her hair and carefully put away her gown. As she sat down on her bed, she heard a faint sound. A moment later, Paulette's little hand pushed the door open.

"You are supposed to be in bed, Paulette," Adele said.

"Yes, 'dele, but a noise woke me up," Paulette said. "I tried to put on my covers like you showed me; but I couldn't, 'dele."

"I will help you; I can show you again," Adele said.

The bed sheets *were* quite tangled. Adele straightened them out, tucked the sheets close around Paulette's little face, and listened to her verses. Even as Paulette finished, her eyelids drooped. As she fell asleep she put out her hand, reaching for Adele's.

Adele was still seated in the gloom holding her little sister's hand when she heard muted voices from the hallway.

"I do think....proper time soon...." came her mother's voice.

"Yes....have been praying about it...." answered her father. He said something else which was unintelligible.

They were speaking low; Adele only heard a few words here and there. She did not desire to eavesdrop, but her hand was captive in Paulette's. The next distinct phrase she heard was,

"...a good time, perhaps, to betroth Adele...." Her mother's voice grew quieter, but that phrase had been unmistakable.

Instantly, all Adele's senses were quivering. She was seventeen, a proper and accepted age for marriage—she felt a thrill.

"...feel very certain....he is the one...."

There was more murmurs which Adele could not catch, then her father's voice: "...M. du Sauchoy told me...."

"...Sebastien....indeed, a nice young man...."

Sebastien! Adele froze in shock. *He **was** extra-attentive this evening— indeed, he's been so for months!...And M. du Sauchoy and Father were closeted, obviously discussing something important—something I wasn't supposed to overhear....Betrothing Sebastien and I was what they were discussing!*

She recoiled from the thought, but even as she did so she remembered that her parents would not arrange a marriage without her consent. If she told them she did not want to marry Sebastien, they would call off the match.

But she desired to obey their wishes. She tried to reason with herself. *Sebastien is a nice young man; of late he has been changing and growing in maturity.... He is sincere and handsome – if my parents desire me to marry him, they are surely seeking my best,* she told herself. ***But...***

Suddenly, a veil was torn, and Adele saw her own heart. She slid to her knees, burying her face in her hands. "Oh, Lord, help me!" Horrified, she realized her affections had already been silently given away to someone else.

I have grown lax, she told herself bitterly. *I was so self-satisfied, so sure in not dancing, in the other things I was doing to shield my heart, that I grew unwatchful. And now – oh, I have given part of my heart away! Oh, Lord – my goal was to save myself for the man my parents arranged, to not become entangled, as others, who find they must rip their heart away from someone when their parents arrange their marriage! But oh, Heavenly Father – I have done it!....*

Before her mind's eye stood handsome, dark-haired Tristan du Chemin, a sparkle in his steady eye and a smile on his lips. *Oh, if only his father had asked – if it had only been – O Lord!* Adele broke into sobs, none the less passionate because they were quiet. She buried her face in the draped bedskirt.

A far-off church bell tolled the quarter-hours, but all else was quiet. The darkness folded around a white-robed girl, kneeling beside the bed of her little sister. At last Adele raised a tear-stained face, tightly clenching her hands in her lap. "O Lord – help me," she whispered. "*Help* me gain control of my heart....Now that I have seen this, help me to – to – oh, *help* me, Lord!"

It was the best thing she could do – turn to the Lord; for even

the rolling ocean rocked with storms
Sleeps in the hollow of His hand.

~*~*~

A week went by. The first fierceness of Adele's emotions ebbed, but the daily struggle revealed how entrenched her affections had become. How frequently her mind would wander out of habit to Tristan, thinking of him, admiring his manly qualities, longing to see him.... As the thoughts came, she endeavored to take each one and divert it, trying to think of something else. *It is not wrong to ever think of a young man,* she reminded herself, *it is just that at present the thought of him is too tempting for me, so I must eschew it altogether.* Swimming against a strong current, she was tempted to despair and give up.

When Sebastien called, it was difficult enough for Adele to act as friendly as before. When Tristan came by for a visit, Adele kept herself tightly reined and barely spoke. Afterwards, she realized she'd probably seemed cold and abrupt; *I must treat him as a brother — nothing more. Excessive shyness is as much a symbol of viewing him as a 'potential husband' as is flirtation. Lord, help me as I seek to do right!*

Something occurred at the end of the week which imbued her with hope and insight in her struggle. Unusually abstracted that morning, her father had, in his weary haste to get out on political errands, forgotten to say his usual goodbye to his wife. Adele, her mother, and Olivie had been invited for tea at the De Lobel's. Since the weather was warm for late Autumn, the tea things were set up in the garden. The breeze did have a nip to it, but the afternoon sun made it still pleasant outdoors.

After taking tea with their mothers, Stephanie and Olivie wandered off to explore the garden. Adele's eye was caught by a late-blooming rose. Seeking it out, she was soon hidden from view behind a hedge. The rose—a vibrant pink-and-white one—absorbed her for several minutes. Then she turned her attention to the nearby plantings, pondering their layout and remembering things her gardener told her about their care. She had started back down the path when she heard a new voice—a man's—at the table beyond the hedge, and paused to hear who it was.

Then a servant's voice said, "Madame Maurepas to see you, Madame Juliette."

"I shall be there," her aunt answered. Turning from the servant, she said brightly, "You must excuse me, Felicienne, and you, Philip, though you have just arrived; but I must attend to Mme. Maurepas, and shan't be able to dismiss her quickly—you know the type." She gave a little laugh, and her high-heeled shoes clicked across the paved patio and into the house.

Then the smooth, manly voice which had caught Adele's attention spoke. She recognized it as M. de la Noye's. "My dear Felicienne, I have hardly seen you at all for the last months, but I assure you that my thoughts have always been with you, my lady."

Her mother's voice answered, quiet and cool, "I am grateful for your consideration, Citizen la Noye."

"'Citizen la Noye!' —there was a time when you called me *Philip*— oh, cannot you do so again, my dear Felicienne?"

The voices had grown more distinct; Adele surmised that they had risen and were standing right on the other side of the hedge.

"Perhaps I did so long ago," Felicienne answered, "before I was married."

"I saw your husband this morning, rattling about the city," De la Noye remarked drily. "He has changed much—so worn and preoccupied, no longer the handsome, ardent youth you married. I wager this morn he neglected to kiss the beautiful face he possessively calls his own."

His voice changed and grew warm. "Surely, Felicienne, in such a case, you must admit to thinking a bit lovingly of me, the one who still loves you as he did then?"

"I must ask you not to touch me," Felicienne said, with quick command. Then she answered, "I am married, De la Noye—and even if I did have such sinful thoughts, it would be my duty to dispel and not harbor them. We are commanded, 'keep thy heart with all diligence.' Satan would like no better than to bring in 'innocent' flirtations and ruin the precious trust relationship between husband and wife. I must ask you never to speak of this again to me, De la Noye."

Her voice dropped, and she said in a tone rich with meaning, "If you knew how *much* I love Francis, and *how* he single-heartedly loves me in return, you would abstain from the topic *of your own accord.*"

There was a pause. Then her voice lightly asked, "What think you of the King's situation? I know you are in touch with the palace."

Adele stood stock-still, pondering her mother's words. *So...even in marriage, there is need for keeping one's heart!*

Up to this time, her ingrained trust in and obedience toward her parents had held fast against her wayward emotions—but now a new light of hope and purpose dawned. This time of struggle would strengthen her for marriage. Unconsciously twisting a leaf from the hedge in her fingers, she thought in wonder, *Lord, thank You for showing me this!*

~*~*~

It was October. The gold and orange trees generously spread out carpets of rich color. A brisk wind picked up several leaves. Crunching and swirling under the horses' hooves, they danced behind the Le Mercier's carriage, playing a final game of tag before their winter sleep.

As the carriage rattled along to Versailles, Adele snuggled further into her warm wrap, gazing out the small window. Bathed in the early evening light, the open countryside rolled in tan waves, broken up by clusters of weather-worn dwellings and the red and orange forests. It was beautiful, but Adele's thoughts lingered in a high-ceilinged room in Paris, where she and Stephanie had visited that afternoon.

Vividly, the scene lived again before her eyes. She had been seated on a red velvet sofa, while Stephanie dallied about in a cornflower blue gown, leaning on the back of the plush couch and looking down at Adele. Adele remembered how her cousin brought up the subject of Gaston, grumbling at her parent's opposition to the match.

"...but I can twist them round in time, I think," Stephanie crooked her eyebrows archly, a knowing look in her bright eyes.

"You ought to acquiesce to their wishes," Adele protested, turning to look up into her cousin's face. Laying her arm along the sofa back, she placed her hand on Stephanie's.

Tossing her head, Stephanie removed her hand from under Adele's.

Adele tried again. "But—what if they are trying to protect you—they know Gaston would make a bad husband for you or something—and you are disregarding that shield?"

"They simply don't understand," Stephanie said, coming halfway round the couch. She added, as if in unanswerable logic, "I *love* him, and he loves me."

Adele's heart throbbed for a moment with her own heart-struggles. She answered with a new light of experience in her eyes, "But cousin, love does not excuse all—does not make all right! You may love someone and yet that does not mean that they are the one for you, or—" thinking of her own case, "that it is the right time for that love."

Stephanie gazed intently down at Adele for a moment. Her lips parted, then she pursed them and studied Adele's bright, sincere face. Leaning over the end of the couch, she tucked back a stray lock of Adele's bronze hair. Coming round the sofa and sitting beside Adele, she slipped an arm round her waist. "I never can understand you, dearest," Stephanie said. "You say the *oddest* things, and in such *dreadful* earnest!"

"I *am* in earnest," Adele answered. "I am concerned for you, dear Stephanie. Oh, do please listen to your parent's cautions!"

Stephanie laughed, but it sounded a trifle forced. "I shall trust my heart—you will see that it all comes right in the end, dear coz!" She patted Adele's cheek and deftly switched the subject to fashion, what was "in" and what was "out." "...and can you believe, Mme. Fournier wore ostrich feathers in her hat—those are so *dépassé!* Oh, and have you heard...."

Shaking herself from her reverie, Adele sighed, and one sentence came back to her: "You may love someone and yet that does not mean that they are the one for you, or that it is the right time for that love."

Lord, You put those words in my mouth. I thank You for doing so! I see their wisdom and cherish their truth. Help me, Lord, to keep my heart, to protect it whole for my future husband. I shall see Tristan tonight — help me to act in a sisterly manner, and not 'make provision for the flesh.' And — Lord — may Thy will, not mine, be done through it all. Amen.

The horses slowed — they were entering Versailles. The rough, rocking motion of the high road was replaced by the more even jolting of cobbles. Adele was reminded of the reason for this visit: the state of affairs in France. After the Legislative Assembly's accession, things had slid from bad to worse. The deputies' boast — that they represented the downtrodden poor — was lame indeed. Except for Denis and a few others, the Legislative deputies were moneyed, middle-class *bourgeoisie*. Their policies were revolutionary, and though there were factions, there were no Royalists (as in the Constituent Assembly) to keep them in check. Therefore it was no surprise to Adele, though it brought sadness, that the La Mottes were secretly emigrating. The Le Merciers were on their way now to the La Motte's Versailles country-house, for a final farewell party.

But though it would be a final goodbye, they could not show it — for the La Motte's departure must be secret. The coach drew up in front of the stately entrance, and they were handed into the illuminated house by a footman. A gust of yellow leaves swept past, skittering along the stone steps under Adele's feet.

Wishing to savor the last golden moments together, Adele and Elisabeth retreated to the quiet library. Great, beautiful books lined the walls, and a many-branched gold candlestick shone on the green plush divan where the girls sat, reliving sweet memories and laughing at little drolleries from the past. It seemed that mere Time was too short to say all the things they wished to say.

Far too soon, Olivie and Christelle looked in to say that the Le Merciers would be leaving shortly. Because the public goodbyes must be formal and restrained, to not give suspicion of the La Motte's flight, Adele and Elisabeth said their real farewell in the library.

Adele took both of Elisabeth's hands in hers, and they gazed into each other's eyes, their grasp tightening. Adele's willowy figure, hazel eyes, medium brown hair, and warm coloring contrasted prettily with Elisabeth's petite figure, blue eyes, striking black tresses, and clear color.

The next few minutes were filled with last-minute words and half-tearful, half-smiling injunctions. Then Elisabeth exclaimed, "Oh — before we part — the Lord has been impressing a certain verse on me of late, and I must share it with you." She pulled a slip of foolscap out of her reticule. "It

410

reminds me that no matter what the future looks like, He is ruling over all, and will be with us."

Taking it, Adele read in her friend's curving handwriting:

> *For I knowe what I have devised for you, saith the Lorde:*
> *My thoughtes are to give you peace, and not trouble,*
> *and to give you an ende as you wishe and hope to have.*
> *Jeremiah 29:11*

The words went straight to Adele's heart. *Oh, Lord,* she prayed silently, clutching the paper, *how You love to encourage Your children! Thank You for reminding me again that Your thoughts are towards me for good, and that You have a wondrous plan for my future! There are struggles now, but You have a plan for them.*

Elisabeth saw a tear slip down her friend's cheek. "Do not be sad," she said. "The Lord gives us hope."

"Oh — it is not that," Adele said. "This verse is *indeed* a blessing to me. Thank you for sharing it — may I keep this paper?"

"Yes — oh, Adele, how I will miss you!"

Adele answered with a look more expressive than words. After a pause she said, "You will write, will you not?"

"Of course I will — though the mails are so unreliable between London and Paris at this time....God bless and protect you here, *dearest Adele!*"

"God bless you, *my friend* Elisabeth!"

Each were holding back tears for the other's sake. After a final embrace, Elisabeth broke away with a sob, saying, "We must be dry-eyed!" — and darted out. Adele sat down on the divan and put a hand over her eyes, her heart aching.

"Adele? Your father sent me to say the carriage is leaving now," a manly voice said. Adele looked up to see Tristan in the doorway. "I am truly sorry," Tristan said, compassion in his dark brown eyes. "I know how close you and Elisabeth are."

"I thank you," Adele said in a muffled voice. Avoiding his eyes, she hurriedly slipped past — she felt it would be too much for her recently-tamed heart to say more.

Her parents were bidding goodbye to various people in the crowded hall. Elisabeth was along the wall on one side, and after curtseying her thanks and farewells to the adults, Adele's foot hesitated one instant on the threshold. Her eye caught Elisabeth's for one last moment, bursting with a million unsaid things—and then she was on the illuminated entry steps, the carriage before her. She stepped in, the door shut, and the carriage whirled away through the midnight streets.

Leaning back among the cushions, she gave way to silent tears.

War?

9.

War? Will war save our country?
So say the counselors:
"Patriotism then surges,
All hearts together
Push forward in sacrifice,
Squabbles forgotten."
"War!" Says the King,
"Let us try the experiment" –
History reveals his hope
Ineffective and empty.
— Ianthe

*A*ugust 1791. Inspired by the "Rights of Man" and the Constituent Assembly's "equality" laws, the slaves in the French colony of Saint-Domingue (now Haiti) revolted. Scouring Saint-Domingue, they perpetrated murder, rapine, and terror. Though the whites there had seen signs of the outburst and had been preparing, 100,000 slaves on the loose was an overwhelming power. By early 1792, the slaves controlled a third of the island, and the country was a war zone. Before the uprising, Saint-Domingue produced sixty percent of the entire world's coffee and forty percent of its sugar. But now torn by war, the crops were not being cultivated or harvested—a serious blow to the mother-colony, France. The loss of that immense revenue dangerously strained the already-dying French economy. Sugar became scarce everywhere, even in Paris. The ideas of the Revolution were already producing fruit—bloodshed, dearth, and destruction.

In an attempt to keep their successors (the Legislative Assembly) from hasty law-making, the Constituent Assembly had decreed that no Bill could be passed until it had been printed and read aloud thrice, "unless the Assembly shall beforehand decree there is urgency." What a handy loophole! Impatient always, the Legislative Assembly merely decreed *"qu'il y a urgence"* before each bill, and impulsively piled bill upon bill.

413

But even when passed, not all bills became law—for several times the King vetoed legislation. Prominent among the bills thus canceled were two in particular. The first was against the priests who refused to swear the governmental oath. The second was a bill declaring all emigrants "suspect of conspiracy" and outlawing them if they did not return before New Year's Day. Both were struck down by the King, fueling the people's anger.

The emigrated aristocrats (some 15,000) gathered mainly in Coblenz, Austria. There they and foreign powers were amassing an army to rescue the King and bring France back to her senses. The Royalist newspapers in Paris said the army was four hundred thousand strong. Multiple schemes swirled among the émigrés. Several forged *assignats* (paper money) and sent the fake bills into France to further bloat and weaken the tottering monetary system.

Many scorned the émigrés as mere selfish intriguers. But really these noblemen, used to luxurious living, were sacrificing much. Many of them were willing to give their last *sou* and final ounce of strength for their country. The marquis de Vibraye, himself an émigré, wrote,

"*You have no idea of the discomfort suffered by these poor nobles since our departure from Worms and the patience, courage, and gaiety with which they have put up with it in the hope of doing something. There have been no complaints, no regrets; in truth it is a phenomenon which history will one day, I hope, record with respect.*

"*To give you an idea of the way we have been living since we've been in this country, I will just tell you that out of 1580 nobles, half have no sheets and have to sleep in their shirts and boots and the other half have two bundles of straw: those are the beds. And as many as 15 to 20 sleep together in a peasant bedroom, the floor of which often consists only of very damp earth.*"

Some retained their humor; for when the Assembly issued a proclamation "inviting" the King's brother to return to France within two months—*or else*—in a newspaper parody, he invited the Legislative Assembly "to return to common sense within two months."

Meanwhile, the King still sent ciphered messages to his brothers in Coblenz and plunged money into the abyss, trying to influence events. The historian Carlyle later alleged, "…the King's Government did likewise hire Hand-clappers, or *claqueurs*, persons to applaud. Subterranean Rivarol has Fifteen Hundred Men in King's pay, at the rate of some 10,000 pounds sterling per month; what he calls a 'staff of genius': Paragraph-writers, Placard Journalists; 'two hundred and eighty applauders, at three shillings per day': one of the strangest Staffs ever commanded by man. The muster-rolls and account-books of which still exist." The King was but trying in his

414

clumsy way to meet fire with fire; for the revolutionists were doing all that and more. Bribing Legislative Assembly deputies was one oft-used way — indeed, some took the King's money and then merrily went on their revolutionist way.

In the meantime, the Le Merciers and their friends had not been idle. In December 1791, Honore and Tristan journeyed to their families' estates, gathering rent-rolls and taking account. Following his father's instructions, Tristan quietly gathered assets to send overseas. Honore did the same. Their estates were fairly quiet, but in other parts of the country the Catholic peasantry were taking up arms against the Revolution. Marcel and Jules patrolled in Honore and Tristan's absence, but found no further clues, though word reached their ears of another (successful) knife-in-back robbery. Denis seemed extra-wary — would they ever gain the proof they needed?

Adele found the first few weeks of heart-struggle the hardest. Her parents had said nothing about a match, and she waited for them to approach her when they felt best. She planned to tell them she did not desire to marry Sebastien, but would do as they advised. As the winter progressed, she absorbed herself in serving at home and enjoying her siblings, and found her focus once more centering, her temptations to think immoderately of Tristan lessening. In fact, she gained a new level of contentment. The battle to control her heart had driven her even closer to the Lord — she had grown to love and trust Him in ways she had only glimpsed before. More and more, Adele exemplified the words the poet Cowper wrote some ten years before:

> *Sweet stream, that winds through yonder glade,*
> *Apt emblem of a virtuous maid —*
> *Silent and chaste she steals along,*
> *Far from the world's gay busy throng;*
> *With gentle yet prevailing force,*
> *Intent upon her destined course;*
> *Graceful and useful all she does,*
> *Blessing and blest where'er she goes;*
> *Pure-bosom'd as that watery glass,*
> *And Heaven reflected in her face.*

~*~*~

The last months of 1791 ebbed and passed in a swirl of foam. The new-born wave of 1792 crashed upon the eternal beach with hissing vehemence.

It was late January now; Winter still held Europe in its icy grip. Her hand on Honore's arm, Adele strolled among the *Palais-Royal's* arched arcades. Presently, Honore stopped at a pamphlet stall.

While he bought a few papers, Adele tucked her hands in her thick brown muff, her eyes sweeping the crowd. She was herself an object that might attract attention in her blue-striped gown, a rich cream-colored cape trimmed with nut-brown fur bringing out the brunette of her hair and eyes. A matching hat with blue ribbons completed her attire.

The snatches she could hear from the orators all harped on one theme. War: should France go to war with her threatening neighbors now, or wait and gather strength?

A stooped youth approached. His seedy, turned-up collar and flapping muffler-ends made him look like an ungainly stork. Adele recognized him as a friend of Gaston's, but could not remember his name. He saw her, took a step back, looked at her meditatively, then plunged forward, loose limbs awry. Adele covered a smile at his *gauche* manners.

"Citoyenne—you may remember me," he bowed clumsily. "I am Citizen Anton Petit—and my heart is ever at your service."

Adele pressed her lips together to keep them from smiling. She guessed he had picked up that last phrase from more-polished Gaston.

"Yes, Citizen Petit, I do remember you," she curtseyed, "though I must admit your name had escaped my memory."

"Surely you are not alone, Citoyenne—if you are, I would be much gratified to escort you home," Anton said, with an unnecessary gesture.

Adele motioned round at Honore, who was leaning an elbow on the counter, deep in conversation with a shopkeeper. "No, thank you; my brother is with me." To be polite, she mentioned, "Despite the weather, the fervor here is unabated."

"Not at all," Anton's face fired with rising zeal. "A little cold shall not chill the hearts of the patriots, Citoyenne! Send rain! Send wind! Send troops! We shall not be crushed—we shall press on and upward, casting the shackles of this dead civilization behind us and using their broken remains to climb still higher toward the full and glorious sun of Liberty!" He made an especially-large movement, and his outstretched arm narrowly missed knocking off Adele's hat. She put a hand up to protect it, but he continued oblivious, "There shall be sacrifices—but we shall make them! There shall be foul tongues of criticism—but we shall still them and prove them wrong! What nation shall then compare to France the illustrious, the free, the—"

Sebastien du Sauchoy pushed through the crowd, his faultless, fashionable attire standing out among the crowd's rough, dirty, and threadbare clothes. He bowed to Adele and Anton, looking askance at the latter.

Adele used his arrival to politely end Anton's impassioned tirade. "If you would excuse me," she said to Anton with a smile, "this gentleman is a friend...."

"Of course, Citoyenne; I shall hope to finish our discourse another time," Anton said. "I must needs speak to Gaston before tonight's meeting at the Jacobin Club." Bowing cumbrously, he went on his way.

Once Anton was out of earshot, Sebastien asked, "Who was that gawky boor?"

"A friend of Gaston's," Adele said, without derision.

"Humph!" Sebastien replied. "Of all the eccentric fanatics—"

"—he is more ludicrous and less dangerous than most," Adele finished his sentence charitably. "*Certes*, can you see anyone taking him seriously?" A moment later her smile faded and she said more seriously, "I am sure some do. But I think you know my meaning."

"I should hope I do," Sebastien bowed. "The more I cultivate your acquaintance, the more I admire your beautiful face and lovely heart, sweet Adele."

Adele flushed and looked away—Sebastien's compliments were difficult for her. "It is God's grace in me," she answered, looking into the swarming throng underneath the leaden sky. Several pamphlet-hawkers caught her attention, and she pointed them out to Sebastien. "See how each one lustily bawls the 'unique' merits of his particular paper."

"Indeed, they do, the rascals," Sebastien said. "Look at that one coming toward us in a fifty-year-old coat—"

As the bedraggled newsboy sauntered towards them, holding a paper high, Adele almost started in surprise. *Tristan!*

Tristan stopped before Adele and Sebastien, asking "the Citoyenne" to buy a paper. Adele glanced at him with blank eyes. With only slight fumbling, she retrieved a coin from her reticule and paid the newsboy. She was grateful for the discipline she had exercised in the past months—it helped now.

"Thanks, Citoyenne," the pretend newsboy mumbled, with the peculiar slip-shod pronunciation of the lower class. Touching his greasy cap, he shambled off, calling out his papers.

Tristan is hoping to catch sight of Denis here (where so many "patriots" gather) and track him home — then he and Honore can keep a watch on his flat and his movements, Adele thought.

"What a specimen of bedraggled humanity!" Sebastien laughed. "Those coarse accents can only have been bred in a gutter!"

"Who do you mean?" Honore asked, coming up.

"Oh, that tatterdemalion newspaper seller —" Sebastien pointed to the youth working his way though the crowd. "A genuine example of the degraded masses."

Honore's face shifted one whit, and Adele knew he had recognized the newsboy. "Ah," Honore remarked. "There do seem to be many rogues about."

Sebastien still stared off into the crowd. After a moment's pause, he spoke abruptly, "I suppose what these wretches really need is to turn from their hopeless atheism to the Lord."

"Indeed, the heart *must* change before society can," Honore agreed. "That should be our earnest prayer — for repentance and revival to sweep through this nation." He looked at Adele. "May I take you home now, Adele? — I have done my business here."

"Yes." Slipping a gloved hand from her fur muff, Adele bid farewell to Sebastien, then took Honore's arm.

"I shall count the hours until I see you again, dear Adele," Sebastien said as they left him.

"There is a party tomorrow night, I believe," she answered serenely.

As soon as they were well away, Adele squeezed Honore's arm with dancing eyes. He grinned back. *How grand and hilarious that Sebastien did not recognize Tristan!*

"Those coarse accents...can only have been bred in a gutter!" Honore whispered, his broad shoulders shaking with inward merriment.

"It is an understandable mistake; how masterful Tristan's disguise is!" Adele murmured back. Inwardly, her heart was light with gladness; for after those months of struggle, her heart was free, and she could now rejoice uninterestedly in Tristan's successes. Indeed, she breathed a prayer as she continued on down the street: *Lord, grant Tristan a wife who is perfect for him — one who is* worthy *of him.*

~*~*~

Jean de Lobel passed hastily through the former Jacobin monastery's arched stone cloisters. He was late — the session was already in progress. Greeting the doorkeepers, he entered the main room—the former nave of the church—and found a seat.

Entrance to the Jacobin Club, Anonymous

The building had given its name to the radical club that met in it— the Jacobin Club. The club was spreading indoctrinating tentacles across France—already there were three hundred "daughter societies," disseminating revolutionary ideas and discouraging conservative views. But the former monastery was the hub.

The issue on the table was the one troubling Paris the most at the moment—the question of war. Already rumors of alliances between Prussia, the émigrés, and Austria abounded—behind them, so Lady Rumor whispered, were several other countries, even the giant Russia.

A portly speaker was shouting in favor of war, while the audience applauded vigorously. Jean drew his brows together in a scowl. Jean was one of the few, like Robespierre, who felt that war was a useful tool for the Royalists. The speaker ended his tirade, mopping his brow with a red kerchief. Jean rose to his feet and started down the aisle.

But someone reached the podium first. A brown-haired young man with a strong, attractive face—Gaston de la Roche. Jean dropped into a vacant seat in the front, gazing up at the youthful speaker with a heavy frown. *It is that rascal Stephanie wants to marry,* he fumed.

He buried himself in some papers, refreshing himself on a few points he planned to address. But as the audience began applauding vigorously, Jean found his attention riveted by the speaker.

Gaston was using words of fire and yet logic against the proposed war. Jean was surprised and pleased by his passion and the notable influence he was having on the audience. He began to think, *Perhaps I have misjudged him.* Power over the masses—and on his side—appealed strongly to Jean. He himself was moved by Gaston's words, and even jotted down several lucid points.

As Gaston finished his discourse, the shouting, clapping audience swept forward. Taking him up on their shoulders, they carried him out in triumph.[1]

Jean's attitude toward Gaston had utterly changed in the last minutes. This sign of clout broke down any last barriers. Pressing, elbowing through the crush, he managed to get near him. With a glow of pride, Jean seized Gaston's arm and insisted on taking him to his own house. Gaston's father, a beefy, dusty man, fell in on the other side, and Leuren, unkempt and grinning, joined them. Jean shared in the glow of adulation.

The shouting crowd followed them all the way to the De Lobel's door, and even then required Gaston to wave and bow several times before they allowed him to disappear inside.

Friends and revolutionists stopped by all evening to commend Gaston; the whole house was in a state of merry elation. Leuren was more civil to his father than he had been in years: he hovered round, looking at Gaston with the eyes of a devotee.

Sometime later in the evening, Stephanie, looking her winsomest, drew her father into a sheltered alcove. Taking his waistcoat lapel, she directed his eyes with hers to where Gaston stood like a triumphant warrior, surrounded by a circle of admirers.

"Will you, *Papa?*" she purred, using the name she had called him as a little girl.

"Will I what?" he answered, affecting to misunderstand.

"You think Gaston is a very nice young man *now,*" she said, using her blue eyes to advantage.

"Yes; he certainly—he is an effective speaker," her father said. He glanced back over at Gaston. A dapper, bookish man in lavender silk was commending Gaston warmly. Robespierre's face even stretched into a smile as he complimented Gaston on his speech.

Jean turned to his daughter. "I shall talk to your mother and to his parents."

"Oh, Papa—you are wonderful," Stephanie gave him one of her most jubilant smiles. "Thank you—thank you!" She arched her brows playfully. "I shall hold you to your promise!" Then glancing round with affected demureness, she tip-toed and placed a kiss on his cheek before darting away.

Stephanie had gained her wish at last. But would it prove to be what she really desired?

~*~*~

In her sunlit room, Adele sat writing a letter. Despite the little fire which crackled and popped cheerily in a diminutive metal stove, her room was chilly. Most houses did not have fireplaces in every room, so cast-iron heaters were used instead.

Propping her pen in its stand, Adele pursed her lips, reading what she had just written.

My dear Elisabeth,   Paris, *March 21ˢᵗ, 1792*

Much has happened since you Wrote last. I reciev'd Your Latest yesterday by the hands of M. Barker. It gives me Pleasure to know that you are well there though it is Painful to think of the long miles Which separate Us. You said it was in some ways Difficult to fit in there Is it because of their manners perhaps or the Language? You were doing Fairly at English when you were Here. I would like to Know because then I can prepare myself if need Arises.

The country Parts of France have been Much disturb'd by fears such as you may ~~Rememmber~~ Remember happened three Years Ago. This time, as well as Fearing the Brigands, the people are terrified by NonExistent Austrians and Aristocrats; false tales of murder and Bloodshed seem to Send the peasants Off their Heads with fear.

Food too is scarce Evrywhere M. Baille made an Unconscious joke when he said: All goes well here, food is not to be had.

You have heard the King of Sweden was Assassinated? That has caus'd Political uncertainty here; an added Factor in the swirl of opinions Surrounding whether we should go to war or not.

Last week red woolen caps appear'd on several Revolutionists. They caught on like Wildfire now Everyone seems to be wearing this Badge of Revolution. They Supposedly are the True cap of Liberty first worn by the Phrygians. A Priest here was nearly Beaten to Death when he refus'd to wear one! Hee met a group of Rascals & upon his spirited Refusal to put one on they Assaulted him with their sticks. They would have Killed him too if some National Guardsmen had not Rescu'd him.

But Enough with Political News I know you want news of friends. Stephanie will be Betroth'd to Gaston next month Shee is happy Yet Pythagoras said It is a harder lot to be Slave to one's Passions than to Tyrants. I have found myself That is True.

We are all staying Occupied here I am working on some Gardening now that the Weather is warming. Charlot just Turned Ten and I Eighteen How time flies! Olivie says her dog Leon sends Greetings, and says to tell Christelle bonjour. Many Friends are Emigrating, however Papa and M. du Chemin feel they still are Call'd to stand by the King.

I am Send'g this by the Hand of M. Barker; may Heaven bless that Good man! He is Full of Feeling and Religion very Refresh'g after the usual Converse here. He waits below so I must close this Epistle but not without sincere Love and Affection to my dear friend. Adieu!

> *Yours,*
> *Adele*

Folding the letter, Adele dripped on hot wax, pressing it with a seal. She hastened downstairs. In the parlor, M. Barker was talking with Honore and her parents, and also another visitor—Captain Hans Diesbach.

"M. *le Capitaine!*" Adele stepped forward with pleasure. "It has been long since you have honored our house, though we have seen you several times at church meeting."

"Yes, indeed it has," he bowed. "Unfortunately I have been much occupied, but I have not forgotten my friends."

"Indeed, we knew you had not," Honore smiled.

The afternoon wore away; they hardly noted the passing of time. Enjoying in turn the genial Englishman and the straightforward Swiss captain, they forgot for a short space France's worsening political troubles.

At length, as evening shadows fell, M. Barker regretfully announced that he must leave. Handing him her letter, Adele thought tenderly of Elisabeth, wishing to see her more than ever. But the verse Elisabeth had shared with her steadied her heart and gave her comfort:

> *For I knowe what I have devised for you, saith the Lorde:*
> *My thoughtes are to give you peace, and not trouble,*
> *and to give you an ende as you wishe and hope to have.*

Two Betrothals

10.

Two lives, following different paths.
The culmination comes:
Does it satisfy?
To one, who looks to it for completeness
It brings disillusionment:
The other, already fulfilled, finds in it
Fullness of joy.
Only when complete in Christ
Will we find true joy on earth.
— Ianthe

S pring had come. At last, in early April, the day of Stephanie and Gaston's betrothal arrived. This was not their wedding (that would be in some months) but was a formal occasion in which the parents finalized the marriage agreement.

Entering, the De Lobel's, Adele's eyes grew bright with admiration. Entryway and parlor exploded with flowers, arranged in vases here, in garlands there....Contrasted by green swaths of foliage, yellow, red, white, and pink roses opened their petals with beautiful perfume. The De Lobels had spent money lavishly to make their daughter's betrothal the highlight of the social season. Adele had been to more extravagantly-decorated parties, but none as lovely as this.

Resplendent in a new mauve silk suit, her grandfather beamed all over as he greeted her. Was this not the gala day on which his first grandchild was betrothed? Adele knew he had not approved of Gaston, but had philosophically acquiesced to the impetuosity of youthful love.

"This is a momentous day, Adele," he said, taking her arm. "Have you seen Stephanie yet? You look beautiful yourself tonight, granddaughter. I am so pleased to see you: the deep coral-color of your dress becomes you well. Here, this rose will be perfect—hold it, and—" he stepped back to admire his work, "—there! The finishing touch to your costume! Now, come with me, and I shall have the prettiest belle here, excepting your cousin, of course..." He bubbled on, thoroughly enjoying the grand occasion. Perhaps it reminded him of the betrothals of his own daughters, or mayhap of his own betrothal so many years ago, to the grandmother Adele had never known.

Adele's aunt was also glowing, using the occasion to impress others and rise socially—but Adele knew, from the twist of her aunt's mouth, that Juliette still rankled at the way Stephanie had connived this match. Adele guessed rightly that her aunt and cousin had had a spat on the subject that very morning.

The signing of papers was soon over, and the fete proceeded with a flourish. Stephanie, radiant, looked more beautiful than ever. Even so, Adele looked at the gallant at her cousin's side and felt misgivings. Gaston had matured, yes, but by a strengthening of the worst elements in his character. The very look in his masterful, wanton eyes revealed he was one who followed his passions—and, Adele feared, with no scruples to bar his way.

But this was what Stephanie thought she wanted. An old French proverb came to mind—"*Comme on fait son lit, on se couche*—You've made your bed, now you must lie on it." There was nothing that could be changed now, unless by a miracle Stephanie could be persuaded to break the betrothal. Adele breathed a prayer that despite the inauspicious beginning, they would be happy. *Lord, help them both to find You, to turn from their rebellion and selfishness to Your plan for them....*

Even as Adele prayed, the two passed by in the crowd, Stephanie on Gaston's arm. Stephanie leaned over to Adele and whispered with a twinkle, "I told you I would manage to twist them round! And it is *quite* worth it, dear coz!"

Two verses wrote themselves in burning letters in Adele's mind:

Honour thy father & mother (which is the first commandement with promise) that it may be well with thee, and that thou mayst live long on earth.

The eye that mocketh his father and despiseth the instruction of his mother, let the ravens of the valley picke it out, and the young eagles eate it.

Instead of honoring her parents, Stephanie had despised their counsel, willfully going her own way in this and many other things. It boded ill.

Turning, Adele found M. du Sauchoy at her elbow. His fleshy face creased into a smile. "You are looking very well, Madame Adele."

"Thank you, M. du Sauchoy," Adele said gracefully. She always shied from the admiring way he looked at her. "I hope you are the same."

"Fair—fair," he remarked, shaking his graying head. "Between troubles at home and abroad (I am in close communication with friends in Coblenz), it's enough to try a man's heart."

"Very true," Adele smiled sympathetically.

"Do you know, the young man who marries you will have a treasure," he remarked. "I would be delighted to be the father of such a lucky young dog. I don't usually drop hints, but...." He trailed off meaningfully.

Adele felt he said it with satisfaction, and tensed inwardly, her cheeks flaming. But her reply was as sweet as ever: "That is very kind of you, M. du Sauchoy. I owe all to the training of my parents and the grace of God."

He chuckled again, in that assured way, and bowed once more. "If I may excuse myself, I see Citoyenne Motier, and must speak to her before she leaves," he motioned across the room to Madame LaFayette. "But here is someone who enjoys your company even more than I."

Adele felt the walls closing in on her—it was Sebastien! How *could* she speak to him normally after what his father had said? But Adele had reserves that she little dreamt of, built up by God during those months of inward battle.

"This is an auspicious occasion on which to meet, dear Adele," Sebastien bowed deeply to her.

"I do pray the best for both of them," Adele answered.

"Are you favored with the knowledge of when the marriage will take place?" he inquired, adding with a winning smile, "I should not even ask—you are favored in every other way."

Adele's color heightened, but she answered with sweet steadiness, "I believe the marriage will take place sometime this winter."

"Ah—thank you for illuminating me, dear Adele" His dark brown eyes smiled into hers.

"A small matter indeed," she said, avoiding his eyes and looking out into the gaily-decorated room.

The rich, sweet perfume of a rose wafted up from somewhere below. Glancing down at the rose her grandfather had given her, Adele saw that as she'd talked she'd unconsciously crushed the blossom to pieces in her tense fingers. Following her eyes, Sebastien noted the rose's crumpled state.

"Here, let me get another for you," he said gallantly, "that one is spoiled." Reaching onto a nearby mantelpiece, he took a heady yellow rose from one of the twining arrangements.

For some reason, Adele's mind flashed back to another time someone gave her a rose. When they left for Paris three years ago, Tristan had cut a bloom of her rose for her. A sweet memory—and it brought no pain. It had been a brotherly gesture—nothing more—and her heart warmed with the knowledge that she could still, by God's grace, treat Tristan in a sisterly way.

Sebastien handed her the bloom with a gallant bow. "Thank you. It is beautiful," Adele smiled. Taking the golden rose, she buried her nose in it, inhaling deeply. The rich, ambrosial scent almost brought tears to her eyes, reminding her of her own rosebush and beloved chateau. She almost forgot Sebastien, who stood studying her and the rose.

The murmuring of stringed instruments swelled, giving notice that the dancing was about to commence, and Adele's eyes were drawn to movement nearby.

Some paces off, her mother was seated on a divan with Grandpapa des Cou, and Francis approached, bowing deeply. "Yours is indeed the fairest face here," he smiled at his wife. "Will you grant me the pleasure of this dance, my love?"

Felicienne flushed, the crimson surge illuminating the warm, rich beauty of her dark hair, emerald eyes, and ruby lips. She gave him her hand. Placing it to his lips, he drew her toward the dancing-floor. Her parent's pure, single-hearted love for each other swelled Adele's bosom with love, trust, and admiration. *Lord, Thy will, not mine, be done. Yours, though sometimes seemingly harder, brings fuller joy at the last.*

Stephanie and Gaston whirled by. How grateful Adele was that she had not followed her cousin's path.

~*~*~

Though it was only afternoon, the towering wooden tenements cast foul shadows across the ill-paved street as Adele stepped light-footed around a pile of rotting refuse. With a final farewell to the worn young woman in the doorway, Grandpapa de Duret got into the coach after Adele.

"God bless you, Sieur!" the woman called, tears streaking her grimy face. She was the flower-seller he had met through his generosity the year before. "Thank you, oh, thank you!" A few frail children, clinging to her patched skirt, waved small white hands in farewell. Even her husband, a great draggled man, nodded his unwashed head in a friendly manner. He was one of Paris' thirty thousand unemployed.

Adele and Grandpapa de Duret were visiting various needy families, and this was the day's last stop. Grandpapa de Duret settled back among the cushions—he tired easily, and suffered from rheumatism these days. Squalid buildings flashed by through the coach windows, then they left the slum and moved through better streets.

Passing through the *Place de Greve* (the open space in front of the Town Hall), Adele glimpsed a strange new machine atop a platform, painted blood-red. Two tall upright posts and a shiny blade surmounted a seeming jumble of framework. The steel shone menacingly. The Guillotine!—the new government-approved method for executions. It had been used for the first time the day before, to put to death Nicolas Pelletier, a notorious highway-robber. He had assaulted a passerby in the rue Bourbon-Villeneuve and taken his wallet and several securities, but his victim's cry roused nearby authorities and he'd been caught.

Adele wondered if this would have any effect on Denis' robberies. Thousands had come to watch. *Did he, too, watch the execution with his impenitent eyes?* Many complained afterwards, "It was too swift and not entertaining enough." Adele shuddered. *If the people love blood and dying agonies so much, what does that bode for the future?*

The *Place de Greve* was crowded. Just a week before, at the King's request, the Legislative Assembly had voted on the question of war—and voted "yes." Flushed with patriotism, able-bodied men swarmed to enlist. Was not the cause doubly noble? They would be protecting their country from their historic enemies, the Austrians, *and* the "traitorous" *émigré* aristocrats!

At last, the carriage pulled up before their house, and Grandpapa de Duret eased his achy joints out while Adele collected her skirts and belongings. Basket in hand (it had held simples and nourishing food items for the needy), Adele went up the steps. The entry seemed especially cool and spacious after the stuffy carriage. Two virile figures were standing under a large oil painting; they looked up as she entered.

"Adele—well met!" Honore exclaimed, hasting forward. "I was just telling Tristan that you were out—"

Only a step behind him, Tristan said, "Simply consummate timing, Adele. Will you please join our meeting?"

Adele smiled back at him, noting

the majesty
That from a man's soul looks through his eager eyes.

How different he and Honore were from Sebastien! Though pleasant and affable, Sebastien did not have their depth of character. She stilled her heart with verses that had richly helped her:

...Thou hast holden me by my right hand.
Thou wilt guide me by Thy counsell, and afterward receive me to glory.
Whom have I in heaven but Thee? and I have desired none in the earth with Thee.
My flesh faileth and mine heart also:
but God is the strength of mine heart, and my portion for ever.

"Here—Marcel, find someone to take your post at the door, and join us in the library," Honore said. "Marcel will take your basket, Adele—"

"Thank you," she smiled at Marcel. "Take it to the kitchen—Virginie knows where it goes."

Adele seated herself on a divan between two bookcases, a low cherry-wood table before her. Tristan and Honore drew up padded armchairs—Marcel came in a moment later.

Tristan looked from one to the other. "Lately, I have been thinking and praying much about our search. It appears that we are making no headway in gaining proof against Denis. We can't seem to even locate his lodgings."

"Too true." Honore bit his lip. "He is more wary than ever. Yet *vogue la galère*—let the galley keep rowing. Let us not give up." Marcel nodded.

"I could not agree more," Tristan said. "However, as I was praying, I believe our Lord gave me an inspiration. *If I masquerade as merchant, and drop the right hints, Denis might rob me!*"

Adele could not stifle a gasp. Honore burst out, "It might work—but Tristan, 'tis too dangerous! What if—" he left his sentence hanging.

"I have considered the dangers," Tristan replied. "Yet—we must bring Denis to justice."

"Yes, but—oh, hang it all, Tristan, then I shall join you," Honore said. "Two foreign merchants, looking for good deals, and a little gullible...."

"No; it must be one alone," Tristan answered, with the air of one who has prayed and thought over every angle. "Denis would probably not take the bait were there two. Besides, it is easier for *one* to stay under cover, and you have not done much in disguise."

"But I will not let you go into peril, while I stay home like a poltroon!" Honore exclaimed, laying his hand on Tristan's. "If there is danger, I will share it with you, Tristan."

Marcel had been studying the table in silence, his solid face especially heavy. Now he looked up. "It must be one; and it cannot be you, Honore. However—we will have an important part to play. We shall need to be nearby, ready to leap out and seize Denis when he makes his appearance."

Tristan grinned. "Believe me, that will be a worthwhile task. Indeed, that is why I deem this venture not as hazardous as it sounds." He looked with manly affection at Honore's keen face. "Your desire to share the danger means much to me, my friend Honore."

"Have you mentioned this to your father? I shall ask mine," Honore said.

"Yes: he has given his approval," Tristan said, "though he told me to wait several weeks—saying we should allow ourselves enough time to make all the proper preparations."

Adele was careful, as usual, to guard her eyes—she knew from experience how easy it was for her heart to become entangled. But as the others talked, her spirits thrilled at the unfolding plan, yet with a sense of dread. She wished she could help in some way: of course, her prayers would be with them....

Even as she thought so, Tristan turned to her. "The latter area is where you can most aid us, if you would. What would a young merchant of my type—an Englishman—wear? All the fine details, I mean—"

"'Twould be best to buy clothes from a visiting Englishman," Adele mentioned. "It can be hard to duplicate the peculiar cut and finish of their garments. Alas that M. Barker is not here! But there is a young Englishman attending Mother's salons—I can talk to him."

"That would be advantageous," Tristan said. "I leave my costume in your hands, Adele."

"It would be advantageous to include Jules," Marcel said.

"Yes, let us certainly inform him," Tristan answered. "He may be of great assistance."

"Now, how should we set up your arrival?" Honore mused. "I suppose you could come in by boat, as if you'd sailed from England...."

"Yes, every detail...."

They talked on, absorbed, each adding insight and fresh ideas. They were devoting effort to a worthy cause—how different from the swarms of fashionable young people throughout Paris who were spending the afternoon in cards, idle gossip, and flirtation,

in wayward passions lost and vain pursuits.

~*~*~

Dusk had fallen, staining the sky with unrivalled pinks and deep purple-blues. Adele had brought a book into the garden, while Charles and Paulette "played house" on the small patch of grassy sward with a doll and some dishes. Charlot had buckled on a sword, playing both shopkeeper and "knight errant" as need arose.

Full of perfume, the cool evening air whispered a message of sweetness all its own. Neglecting her book, Adele watched Charles and Paulette, savoring their business-like expressions and humorous little mannerisms.

"Yes—the customary order." Cradling her "baby," Paulette nodded to Charles.

"Here is your package." Charles held out an imaginary parcel. "This is quite heavy, Citoyenne—let me carry it home for you, if you please."

He shouldered an invisible parcel, which now seemed to have reached a Herculean weight, and followed Paulette the few feet to the spot on the lawn which signaled her dwelling. He let the "parcel" down with a gasp. "There—that was heavy."

"Thank you, Citiz'n," Paulette said seriously. "Here is a *sou.*"

"Your fair face is payment enough, Madame," Charles answered gallantly.

"You learned that from S'bastien," Paulette giggled.

With a hot blush, Adele turned to her book.

"Adele?"

Adele looked up to see Berthe's kindly countenance. "Yes, Berthe?"

"Your mother requested your presence in the parlor," Berthe curtseyed.

"Thank you—I will be there." With a final loving glance at her younger siblings, Adele entered the house and moved decorously down the long paneled hall. *Probably a visitor,* she thought, *or Mother may want to discuss tomorrow's menu....*

Entering the cool parlor, Adele saw that it was empty save for her parents, seated in a corner near one of the tall windows. The curtains were drawn; lighted candles diffused the room with a warm glow. Curtseying to her parents, Adele stood waiting.

"Do sit down; there is a chair here." An unusually-deep smile rested on her mother's face. "There is something we would like to speak with you about, dear daughter."

Adele's father leaned forward, the light shining on his kindly, clear-cut features. "Your mother and I have been praying for quite some time about your betrothal," he said, "and we feel that the right time has arrived."

Adele's mind was instantly aflame with the sickening thought— *Sebastien!*

Her father continued, "We have watched this young man—he has grown in godliness and manhood, even in the last few months."

Oh, how will I tell them I do not care for Sebastien! Adele pressed her lips together.

"He is a godly, caring, manly youth. We feel you will be a wonderful complement to him, dear daughter," her mother said. "He is definitely the kind of man we would wish for a son-in-law."

The form of Adele's burning thoughts shifted imperceptibly: *How can I tell them!...*

"His father and I waited some months," her father explained, "because times are uncertain. But we have concluded that the state of affairs will merely worsen, and we firmly feel it is God's will to betroth you now."

Adele opened her lips to speak, but the next word stopped her short.

"Tristan—"

Adele's heart seemed to stop; her eyes looked like stars. *"Tristan?"* she breathed, hardly daring to hope.

Her mother's fond smile was singularly knowing. "Yes, Tristan Alain du Chemin."

Adele's eyes filled with tears—tears of awestruck happiness. *O Lord,* her heart sang, *thank You! Oh thank You!* After a moment, she looked up through her tears at her parents, and found them beaming at her.

"Then you give your consent to this betrothal?" her father smiled.

"Yes!—oh, yes!" Adele cried, with all the fervor of her soul.

She left the parlor almost dizzy with joy. Hastening upstairs, she knelt by her bed, her heart too full for words.

Adele: Two Girls. Two Paths. One Revolution.

After dying to it, her desire had come—and it was a tree of life.

*But seeke ye **first** the kingdome of God, and his righteousnesse,
and all these things shalbe added unto you.*

The End of a Trail?

11.

Is the world truly coming to an end? Men struggle on.
For some, 'tis the end of the chase —
Wait! Once more, he slips the noose;
But the death-throes of the nation will not stop for that.
— Ianthe

*A*dele woke the next morning with an overwhelming sense of ecstasy. She lay in bed, gazing up at her canopy and playing over again that beautifully-astounding meeting with her parents.

At length she rose to perform her morning toilette. Lacing her stays or pinning her hair, she often paused to savor the pure wondering delight which filled the air like the rarest perfume.

And to think I thought all that time it was Sebastien! she smiled into her mirror. *Mother explained what I overheard — M. du Sauchoy did ask about betrothing Sebastien and I that eve, but she and Father already had their eyes on Tristan....* She beamed at nothing in particular, then turned to the mirror once more to pin the last curl in place.

With a light patter of silk shoes, Olivie entered Adele's room, crimson roses spilling from her hands. *"Bon!"* she said. "My surmise was correct — you *are* wearing your white morning gown with the rich red sash! These will look charming in your hair, Adele."

"You are such a dear," Adele smiled fondly. "Thank you, Olivie."

Sixteen-year-old Olivie's ruffled dress swished as she drew close; it was pale blue muslin with a sprigged pattern of tiny flowers. A white rose adorned the upswept brown hair above her sweet, ingenuous face. Adele wondered who God planned to be the husband of her beautiful younger sister.

Olivie artfully securing the crimson blossoms in her hair. "There — now you look simply scrumptious, Adele — ready for our breakfast guests."

Adele turned, a question in her eyes. "Guests?"

"Late last night, Father sent a messenger asking the Du Chemins to breakfast," Olivie's eyes danced.

Adele flushed. "I did not hear—I must have been in my room."

Crooking her brows knowingly, Olivie studied her sister's blushing, joyful face. "I am so happy for you, Adele," she said—then flung her arms around Adele's neck. "Father told us—I am so happy for you and Tristan—oh, I have prayed...."

"Thank you, dear Olivie." Eyes moist, Adele added softly, "God gave me back my desire, after I laid it at His feet."

A rattle of carriage wheels in the street below was punctuated by a coachman's hoarse cry. With a final jar, the noise ceased under their window. Olivie unwound her arms and tripped fluently to the many-paned window. A glance sufficed.

"Yes, 'tis them." With a final glance at Adele's eloquent face, Olivie hastened decorously downstairs, her full skirts rustling musically.

There was extra vivacity in Adele's step, too—but as she neared the bottom of the staircase, a sudden shyness seized her. She hung back slightly behind the others, a delicious blush on her cheeks.

It seemed like the whole family was in the entryway. His usually-bland face embellished with a grin, Marcel swung open the door. M. du Chemin entered, his genial face beaming. Bowing to all, he advanced a step to meet Francis—but Adele's eyes were not on him.

Through the door stepped Tristan, his face radiant with a happiness Adele had not seen since before his mother's death. As etiquette demanded, he bowed to the adults—then his eyes searched for Adele. She dropped hers, shyly.

He only said one word; "Adele," but it told all. Her eyes met his and stayed there—and everything else grew indistinct in the face of their great joy.

~*~*~

The crowning event of May was their betrothal. Their wedding-day, the actual consummation, would be some months later—Winter was mentioned, but the date would be determined by affairs in France.

With lustrous eyes, Adele watched the formal betrothal papers being signed. It was still hard to believe she had a right to let her heart knit with the handsome young man who stood beside her. She glanced up, found his dark eyes studying hers, and let her eyes speak into his.

Among the many guests were M. du Sauchoy and Sebastien. As Adele and Tristan passed through the gaily-decorated room, Tristan's attention was claimed by an elderly dowager, and Sebastien bowed low before Adele.

"Your face is the light of the room, Adele," he said.

"The *Lord* is my light and my salvation," Adele quoted. "How fares it with you, Sebastien?"

Sebastien searched her face, then leaned forward, speaking in a guarded undertone. "This is a secret: I and my father leave tonight—for Coblenz."

"May God go with you," Adele replied. "I pray that you will serve Him there."

"'Tis my aim," he replied; then, plucking a rose from a silver chalice, he spoke with a rush; "I shall take this with me, in remembrance of the purest and fairest maiden I have known. Once I had hoped—" he broke off. "—But Tristan is worthy of you. May God be with you both—Farewell, dear Adele!" His lips were pale, but his eyes steady.

Adele looked at him with a compassion deepened by her own wondrous happiness. "Farewell, and Godspeed."

The elderly lady parted from Tristan, and he turned to Sebastien. "Farewell, Sebastien," he smiled. "May God go with you—and bless you with such a fiancée as I have been given."

Sebastien flushed, bowed, and with a final look turned away through the crowd, the rose in his hand.

Adele glanced up at Tristan, and her own cheeks colored at the look he gave her. "The Lord has been good to me, Adele—He has given me the desire of my heart." He mused, "It is strange, is it not, how the Lord gives us back our desires when we delight in Him."

"I, too, have found that to be true," Adele said, and blushed once more.

Stephanie was there, her blue eyes fixed on Adele and Tristan. The joy in their faces seemed to dazzle her. She turned away, a thought rising: *I twitted her for not enjoying young men—but her face now!—it looks.... How remarkable is the overflowing, unshadowed joy in her eyes!...Could—could she be happier now because she waited and 'kept her heart'?....*

To the Nuptial Bow'r
I led her blushing like the Morn: all Heav'n,
And happy Constellations on that hour
Shed their selectest influence; the Earth
Gave signs of gratulation, and each Hill;
Joyous the Birds; fresh Gales and gentle Airs

Adele: Two Girls. Two Paths. One Revolution.

Whisper'd it to the Woods, and from their wings
Flung Rose, flung Odors from the spicy Shrub,
Disporting, till the amorous Bird of Night
Sung Spousal, and bid haste the Ev'ning Star
On his Hill top, to light the bridal Lamp.

~*~*~

Midday, mid-June 1792. A small but goodly-sized vessel breasted a busy Parisian dock and hove to. Battered but still sea-worthy, her patched sails fluttered in the salty breeze. Her peeling figurehead gazed dully down on dock workers and merchants, the former making her fast, the latter waiting to board and haggle for the English goods aboard.

When the first onrush of merchants ceased, a slender young man stepped down the gangplank, looking uneasily about. Lounging fishermen and dockworkers regarded him with shrewd, jocose eyes. His powdered wig was so obviously English, and the way he clutched his trunk and cast little glances round—!

After hesitating a moment on the busy dock, he approached a portly idler with a red Phrygian cap and asked in halting French where suitable lodgings could be found, "near this address, if possible," he said, fumbling in a pocket. When it yielded some string, several Bank of England notes, and a dinted snuff-box, but not what he looked for, his expression became decidedly anxious. Setting his trunk down between his legs, he stuck a nervous hand in another pocket.

"Alack," he muttered to himself in English, "if—"

A moment later, his expression changed, and he held out a carefully-folded slip of paper. "Near this address, if you please," he repeated in rough French.

The lounger pushed his red cap back with a grimy finger. "You must read it for me."

The Englishman looked suitably chagrined, then slowly read off the street address. Leisurely blowing smoke from his lips, his informant directed him to a lodging-place in the *rue des Fils.*

Pressing an English bank-note in the man's outstretched palm, the Englishman picked up his trunk and set off in the direction indicated. His unconcealable greenness made the idle gawkers chuckle. What a fresh-caught Englishman, to be sure!

"He'd better take care of his purse," one rough fellow gibed.

"He knows it, too—look at him clutch his trunk," another said, his eyes on the fellow's retreating back.

~*~*~

War's first patriotic thrill had died away, and the atmosphere in the popular tavern the *Tigre National* was gloomy. At the end of April, the French armies had invaded the Austrian Netherlands, but now they were being beaten in engagement after engagement. Frenchmen everywhere were alarmed. A Royalist in Paris, M. Fougeret, wrote:

> "It is rumored that some of the army is in revolt against its leaders and ready to disband. Should such a misfortune occur, villages and small towns will be pillaged by bands of soldiers who will have no other means of existence.
> "Vital foodstuffs are rising to exorbitant prices. In Paris, meat costs 12 sous for households which buy a lot, but small households are having to pay 13 or 14 sous a pound and mutton is 18. Baker's assistants are demanding a pay raise, and all the workers are following their example. However unfortunate this may be where the other trades are concerned the consequences vis-à-vis the bakers are serious and it is feared that the price of bread will rise.
> "Policing and security are nonexistent. People commit robbery and murder in the middle of Paris as if they were in the depths of a forest, and after 9 o'clock in the evening the outlying areas are death-traps.
> "Wine, wood, vegetables, everything is going up in price and is becoming prohibitably expensive. Meanwhile, it's virtually impossible to get your hands on your income. The interest owing from state bonds is not being paid out. Bankruptcies are common and the interest rate on the assignats is getting higher every day.
> "...we have a few wretched troops still in a state of rebellion, undisciplined, apparently short of everything they need, and with entire regiments continually going over to the émigrés who must, because of this, have more than thirty thousand armed men."[1]

Swayed by rumors and "patriotically" distrusting their officers and generals, the French soldiers were almost useless. At Lille they panicked and fled upon seeing the enemy—then hanged their innocent general, Dillon, unjustly blaming him for the rout. The Austrians and allies pressed forward victorious—the three French generals (LaFayette, Rochambeau, and Luckner) were too busy keeping their own armies under control to effectively fight the enemy without.

The *Tigre National's habitués* were all good patriots, so instead of facing the truth (that the armys' troubles were largely due to revolutionary thinking), they laid the blame at the feet of the generals and officers, castigating them as aristocrats and traitors.

Such was the talk that simmered in the tavern that evening. At a table against the sooty wall, an awkward young Englishman motioned to a harried waiter. He had become almost a regular, coming in most evenings for almost a week. He had made sporadic attempts to talk with various patrons, but mainly sat drinking in self-conscious silence. When the waiter bobbed near, the Englishman ordered another glass of wine.

"You have already had quite a few, I wager," remarked a seedy little man in a red cap who sat at the same table. "You look a bit tipsy, Citizen."

"Not I," said the foreigner, in stilted French. The instant he spoke, his thickened voice revealed that indeed he'd had a couple of glasses too many.

The little man could've fancied that the Englishman's eyes darted for an instant toward a lean-faced man at the next table, but a moment later he seemed still focused groggily on the small man.

"'Just one for the road—'tis dark out, Citizen—dark, and it's a long walk to the *rue des Fils*, where I lodge." He seemed to fancy that the small man looked at him questioningly, for he went on gregariously, ""You're thinking the city's not safe, eh? Well, let me tell you, Citizen—" He took a gulp of wine. "I know it—I've read the papers! That's why—" He hunched forward, whispering loudly, "That's why, s'help me, I don't leave the money in my rooms. No, no," he said, looking as wise as an inebriated man can, "Comrade, I know better than to leave all my employer's money in my room! I know all about—all about your maids and valets and all, see?" He patted a pocket with sententious satisfaction. "Safe—safe w' me, Comrade," he nodded, then subsided into his chair, finishing his glass.

He seemed to doze off, then some fifteen minutes later, as the clock struck the hour, he staggered to his feet. "Better be on my way," he said, blinking and trying to orient himself. "Bit dark, eh?"

Hesitatingly, he made his way out. The door creaked shut behind him and his slow, uncertain steps faded into the black night.

It was a bustling place; hardly anyone noticed him leave. Even the small man he'd addressed was soon drinking again, absorbed in his own troubles. But one pair of dark eyes had followed his exit. For a moment the owner of those eyes looked more like a deadly tiger than the rampant one painted on the tavern's signboard.

~*~*~

Tristan shuffled slowly away from the *Tigre National*'s low doorway, pausing once to steady himself against a wall for the benefit of any watcher. He guessed someone *was* watching—certainly, Denis had been near enough to overhear his "inebriated" discourse.... He could only hope—and remain on guard while outwardly pretending befuddled helplessness.

He shuffled down the street—the night grew darker. Blundering into an especially-tenebrous alley, Tristan risked a quick look around. No one—not a soul—was in sight. *Oh, if he didn't hear—or worse, if he heard and didn't take the bait....* He bit his lip.

He shambled on, sometimes faster, sometimes slower. *Are Honore and the others nearby? They should know my route....well, it is no use, if Denis doesn't....* He felt the beginnings of despondency, but then grinned inwardly. *I've managed to pull this off so far!*

A moment later, his attuned ears, sharpened by many hours of patrols, caught a slight noise from behind. It was a cautious footfall. Of course, it could be Honore or one of the others, *but...* Unconsciously, his hand closed on the poniard in his pocket.

Some twenty yards further, he again heard a muffled step—this time, closer. Disciplining his muscles, he kept up his slightly-tipsy exterior, but inwardly everything tensed, ready to meet an ambuscade. His pulse was racing. *This might be it!*

There was a sudden movement from behind. Tristan whirled. With a single leap, twisting in mid-air, he faced his would-be attacker. As soon as he landed, Tristan took another quick step—backwards—his knife out and ready. He whistled shrilly.

For a second, Denis stood stunned by the lightning change in this green, inebriated foreigner.

A gush of lantern-light suddenly hit Denis' face. Several figures rushed out of the darkness. Leaping backwards with a curse, Denis was brought up short by a figure behind. He turned. The unseen someone struck the knife from his grasp. Denis gave an exclamation of rage. "*Jules!* You—"

His pale face set and determined, Jules set his boot on the knife. "Your dirty game is up, Denis," he said tersely, grabbing Denis' arm in a grip Denis himself had taught him.

The others closed in; dark-headed Marcel reached for Denis' other arm.

Denis' dark eyes blazed with hate, but he seemed to realize all was over; his shoulders slumped and he stopped resisting Jules' hold. Then, with a sudden lunge, he threw Jules off guard, breaking his grip and swinging him against Marcel. An instant later he was beyond the circle of light.

"After him!" As one, the four pelted down the dark street, the lantern swinging wildly and throwing jagged pools of light.

"To think—I let him fool me!" Jules said between his teeth.

The dark maw of a side street loomed—without speaking, Jules and Honore dashed down it, while the others continued on. But a moment later, there was another cross-street, then an alley, and more twisted back-streets—a labyrinth; and one in which, they were finally forced to admit, Denis had vanished.

"At least we have proof—enough to lay before the gendarmerie," Honore remarked as the dejected quartet trailed along the midnight street. "They will arrest him—if they see him."

"*If* they find him," Jules remarked morosely. "These days, there's little chance of that." He burst out, "Just say what you are thinking—berate me for letting him escape!"

"It could have happened to any of us," Tristan said. "What an artful trick! We do not blame you, Jules."

"No—'twas something we should have been prepared for—if I blame anyone, I blame myself, for not seizing him more quickly," Honore said.

Searching their faces in the uncertain flare of the lantern, the light of wonder began to creep over Jules' countenance.

~*~*~

After that night, Denis disappeared. He no longer appeared in the *Salle Menage* as a deputy; nor, as far as Jules could discover, the *Tigre National* or his other haunts. He had vanished among the six hundred thousand Parisians.

On the afternoon of June 20th, Honore was pacing his room, mulling over this impasse, when Marcel came in with a message. In Tristan's handwriting were the words:

Meet me at the place appointed. Bring weapon. — T

When in disguise, Tristan usually used this method to access Honore. Tucking a poniard in his belt, buttoning his jacket, and slipping on a dark hat, Honore hastened out. A few minutes sufficed to take him to where a young patriot lounged in a crooked, otherwise-deserted alley.

Honore took a long glance round, to make sure no one was near. Then a few long strides took him to his friend's side.

"Can I truly believe it—you desire to see me, and not Adele?" Honore teased. But as Tristan pushed his hat back, his tense expression dashed away Honore's smile.

"There's no time to waste," Tristan said. "Can you come, Honore?"

"Assuredly," Honore said. "What is in the wind?"

"A mob is gathering round the Tuileries. They started by planting a 'tree of liberty' in the Feulliant courtyard, but now they are protesting at the palace gates, demanding that the King cease his vetoes."

Honore nodded swiftly. He knew how the King's vetoes of the Assembly's most radical laws had angered the populace.

Tristan glanced at his shabby disguise, then at Honore's finery. "We cannot go together, but—we must protect the King, if possible; I fear they will break into the palace."

With a brief farewell he moved hastily off, his slouching strides those of a sans-culotte. After waiting a moment to put some distance between them, Honore hurried after, his steps those of a self-assured aristocrat.

Before the palace was even in sight, Honore was stopped by the vast throng. He tried another street, then, realizing all were similarly choked, began pushing his way through the mass of bodies.

He managed to get to the corner of the square, but there the press was so bad that even vigorous efforts availed nothing. Angry growls rose and unfriendly glances were cast his direction. He looked around. *If I can't get through, mayhap I can at least find a higher vantage-point!*

One of the opulent stone facades looked familiar—he smiled with victory. Squeezing through the press, he rapped on the door. A nervous footman opened it a mere crack, took his card, and re-locked it. But a minute later he opened it again and hastily beckoned Honore inside.

"This way, sir," he motioned, bowing.

As Honore entered the lavish green-and-gold parlor, a portly woman in an ochre gown rose, all a-flutter. Nearby, a slight young woman was seated at a tambor frame.

"It was so good of you to come, M. le Mercier," the woman cried. "Such a gallant action! What a terrible crowd there is outside, to be sure—think you that they will force their way into this house?"

"I should think not, Madame Fournier," Honore replied, as he bowed to them both. "Yet it was wise to bar the windows and doors on the first floor, as your menservants have done. Actually, I fear the mob is trying to break into the Tuileries. I came, endeavoring to aid His Majesty."

"Ah! The King!" Madame Fournier looked suitably dramatic. "But I shall leave you both—I know when I am not wanted," she simpered.

Honore's jaw tightened—it would never do to be stuck entertaining Madame Fournier's daughter! What of the King? And he remembered the like wiles with which Madame Fournier had recently married off another daughter. "Madame, in actuality I called to ask if I could use your upper-story windows to gain a better view of the disturbance."

"Ah—if that is the case—Anastasie, would you show M. le Mercier upstairs?"

With a flattering glance at Honore (which he totally missed), the girl rose. He followed her peach skirts up the staircase to a room overlooking the square.

With a polite, "If you would excuse me," Honore leaned eagerly against the windowsill. Hundreds upon hundreds of people swarmed the palace, pressing against the gates with crushing force. Their angry cries reached him even where he was. *At least the mob have not entered the palace yet!*

The National Guardsmen stared nervously through the quivering fence at the mob. Honore's quick eye noted several emblems raised on poles above the seething crowd, and he glanced at Anastasie Fournier. "Were you looking out when they first came by?"

Gazing at him with colorless but not unintelligent eyes, the girl's pale curls bobbed as she nodded. "Yes, M. le Mercier."

"Would you chance to know what those emblems are?" he asked.

"Yes, I saw them march by," she said eagerly. "One was a bull's heart transfixed with iron; written under it are the words, 'Aristocrat's heart.'" She shuddered. "The other—a pair of black silk knee-breeches. It says, *'Tremblez tyrans, voila les Sansculottes!'*"

Honore repeated the words. "Tremble tyrants, here are the without-breeches!" Even as he scanned the crowded square apprehensively, his habitual politeness made him ask Anastasie, "Your estate is in *Le Midi*, is it not?"

"Yes—more particularly, near Dijon," she replied.

"I hear there have been troubles there," Honore remarked.

"Have not there been risings 'most everywhere?" Anastasie said. "Yet as summer builds I long for the coolness of the countryside. Paris has its charms," here she glanced particularly at him, "but I tell Mother that it is no safer than Dijon."

"I think Paris may be more dangerous," Honore said soberly. "All France is aflame, yes — but I fear Paris may become a walled death-trap."

"May the Virgin preserve us!" Anastasie cried.

"I would say 'the Lord Christ,'" Honore said gently. "He alone can protect us — the Virgin Mary was only a human like us, with a sin nature, but Christ was—" He broke off with a half-suppressed exclamation of dismay. "They are breaking in! Oh, those craven soldiers!" A moment later he muttered, "Alas—mayhap they were not given an order to fire—but were I there—!"

Over the broken gates, an exultant multitude poured into the Tuileries courtyard — the soldiers fell back without firing a shot. An instant after, the main door of the palace splintered and caved in under the weight of the onrushing crowd. The unwashed, menacing mass poured into the palace.

I must go! Turning to Anastasie, Honore bid her good-day and thanked her as hastily as etiquette would permit, then, bursting with impatience, made his way downstairs. But the "stars in their courses" seemed to conspire against him — for Mme. Fournier met him as he stepped into the hall.

"Just in time for a bit of tea," she said. "M. le Mercier, surely you will not be so discourteous as to leave so soon — I insist on your staying for this crumb cake I ordered especially for you...."

Honore bowed, but even as he smiled gracefully he was edging towards the door.

"Remember—" Madame Fournier wagged a white finger, "you *promised* last time that you *would* stay for tea when you came next."

Honore pressed his lips together to hold back impatient exclamations. *Of all the—* he thought, then, *The King! And surely I must not become the third betrothal of the season! But — alas! — she did finagle that promise out of me last time! And I must keep my word....* Looking through the window at the hallooing, hurrying mob, he realized, *Several hundred must be in the palace already; there is nothing I can do to help at the moment. Maybe when the first rush subsides....*

Covering his vexation and impatience as best he could, he entered the soft ambiance of the parlor — the rich smell of freshly-baked cake and the thin, hot aroma of tea met him. Madame Fournier chatted pleasantly, her daughter pouring tea with thin but skillful fingers.

But Honore appreciated none of these amenities. He felt a helpless prisoner. What if even now the King was being massacred, while he sipped tea in this fair parlor?

BOOK THE FOURTH

Death Throes

They Were Faithful Unto Death

1.

The end draws nigh;
The night closes in.
Evil plans come to fruition —
That red is indeed blood,
The blood of the valiant and good.
— Ianthe

*B*eing disguised, Tristan fared better than Honore. As the flood-gates broke and the slogan-shouting mob poured into the Tuileries, he contrived to be in among the first rush.

Storming the Tuileries, by Pierre Gabriel Berthault

His hand on his concealed truncheon, he thought desperately, *If they attack the King, maybe somehow I can effect a diversion or defend him long enough for their Majesties to escape!*

Suddenly, the onrushing mob fell back upon itself. Standing calmly in front of them, with a few National Grenadiers, was the man himself. The King!

Tristan was poised for desperate action. Taken aback, the unwashed, ragged mass stared at their King, and he stared back at them.

"What do you want?" the King asked.

The front ranks recoiled, but those behind pushed forward with cries of, "Veto! Patriot Ministers! Veto!" They were angry at his vetoes and at his dismissal of his patriot cabinet. The King had had many fleeting groups of ministers in the last few years—his most recent one, composed of patriots, had been displeased at his vetoes and he had fired them. The people wanted him to call that ministry back.

"This is not the time, nor the proper channel to present such a petition," the King replied.

The King and the Mob, Unknown

Someone handed him a red cap of liberty. Setting it absently on his head, the King resumed staring at the weltering crowd, while they goggled back at him. It seemed neither side could really believe this was taking place.

After some time, the King said he was thirsty; a half-drunken sans-culotte handed him a bottle. After drinking, the King resumed his unsure review of the mob. They in turn gaped at him, still undecided on what to do now, face-to-face with their King.

Meanwhile, M. Diesbach had arrived from his barracks and met Honore outside the palace. Unable to enter because of the press, they waited apprehensively.

For three hours, the palace seethed with stagnant, staring sans-culottes. When Mayor Pétion finally arrived at seven o'clock, his flowery speeches persuaded the mob to leave; the great mass began to flow out of the palace.

"So it comes to naught, after all," Honore said, with relief. "The King is unharmed."

"For now," M. Diesbach replied. "But how easily could it have had a different result!" He shook his head as he surveyed the grimy, pinched faces passing by. "The palace is not safe—the end is near, Honore."

~*~*~

As soon as the news reached him, LaFayette left his army at the North border and hastened to Paris, arriving on the 28th of June. He pled with the Legislative Assembly to move against the Jacobins (the principal force behind the uprising). But the Legislative Assembly (many of them Jacobins themselves) received him coolly.

Seeing no aid from that quarter, he secretly gathered supporters at his Hôtel (his palatial dwelling), asking, "Can we not put down the Jacobins by force?" But his efforts were unsuccessful. The name LaFayette was not the talisman it once was, and the Jacobins had already crushed the more-conservative Feuilliant Club. Many that would have aided LaFayette were gone by now—either overseas or to Coblenz. After a fruitless week of trying, he was obliged to give up and return to his command—the Jacobins, working through the Legislative Assembly, were filing a suit against him, labeling him "traitorous." And that was a very dangerous label these days.

A month later, July 28th, the Duke of Brunswick (head of the Austrian coalition) issued a proclamation which spread virally through Paris. The manifesto promised that if the French Royal family was not harmed, then the Allies would neither loot nor harm French civilians. If acts of violence to the French Royal family were committed, however, the Allies would burn Paris to the ground.

The Duke's proclamation was intended to intimidate the revolutionaries and ensure the King's safety—but it accomplished the exact opposite. It provided the final fuel for the pyre the revolutionary leaders had been carefully building. Grinning mirthlessly, they tightened the net environing the King.

Staring into the street the next day, ten-year-old Charles was merely a dark shape against the hot sun's radiance. "Adele—look, there is another regiment," Charles turned a puzzled face.

Her white dress rustling musically Adele put down her embroidery and came to the window. "They look rough indeed." She pulled the curtain aside to see the uncouth, marching ranks.

Brandishing weapons, the soldiers burst into a vigorous song, their drum rattling. It was a song Adele and Charles would hear day and night in the remaining weeks.

"Arise, children of the Fatherland,
The day of glory has arrived!
Against us of the tyranny
The bloody banner is raised,
The bloody banner is raised,
Do you hear, in the countryside,
The roar of those ferocious soldiers?
They're coming right into your arms
To slit off the throats your sons and your companions!

To arms, citizens,
Form your battalions,
Let's march, let's march!
That a tainted blood
Water our furrows!

What does this horde of slaves,
Of traitors and conjured kings want?
For whom are these vile chains,
These long-prepared irons?
These long-prepared irons?
Frenchmen, for us, ah! What outrage
What fury it must arouse!
It is us they dare plan
To return to the old slavery!"

With bestial faces, the newly-arrived soldiers swung into the refrain:

"To arms, citizens,
Form your battalions,
Let's march, let's march!
That a tainted blood
Water our furrows!"

As Adele stared worriedly, Charles spoke. "Adele, didn't the King say they could not have troops around Paris?"

"He did," said a voice from behind. They both turned to see Tristan, hat in hand. With an especially-warm smile, he took Adele's hand, then turned to Charles. "The revolutionists circumvented the King's decree by saying the troops were gathering for the Fete de la Federation. Even though it is over, it is a handy excuse—and who dares to question why the troops have stayed?"

"So now there are soldiers to back up the Parisians if they move against the King," Adele said in a low voice.

"Yes." Tristan was equally grave. Motioning towards the marching, singing figures, he added, "The radical Barbaroux wrote to the southern city of Marseille, asking for 'six hundred men that know how to die.' Here they are—and their looks bode ill."

The Marseilles National Guard was a determined, alarming addition to the many troops gathered in Paris. One Parisian wrote of them:

"…these beastly [soldiers] spewed up by the Marseilles….One cannot imagine anything more horrifying than these 500 fanatics, three-quarters of them drunk, almost all wearing red bonnets, marching bare-armed and disheveled….They fraternized at all the drinking shops with groups as dangerous as themselves."

Charles still stared into the street, but Tristan drew Adele a little apart, to talk more quietly. After a few moments, she laughed at something Tristan said. Then her cheeks deepened, and she said, "Mayhap I should not laugh when—when France is approaching its end."

"Do laugh, dear Adele," Tristan said earnestly. "It does me good. Keep your merry heart, darling—it is better than medicine."

The following week seemed especially short. Events rushed on with cataclysmic force. The popular, vitriolic pamphleteer Marat wrote:

"Fear the reaction; your enemies will not spare you. You are lost forever if you do not lop off the rotten branches at the [local government levels]….I therefore propose that you kill one in every ten of the counterrevolutionary members of the municipality, the courts…and the Assembly….Hold the King, his wife, and his son as hostages until they can be tried, let him be shown four times every day to the

people....Warn him that if, within two weeks, the Austrians and the Prussians are closer than twenty leagues to our borders...he will lose his head."

~*~*~

The King's Sunday afternoon *Levée* (a formal gathering in which courtiers came to pay their respects) on August fifth, 1792 was more crowded than it had been in years.

The very air of Paris crackled with tension—just across the courtyard from the palace, in the *Salle Ménage*, the Legislative Assembly debated on whether they should depose the King. "Forfeiture must happen—depose the King and crown his young son, with the Assembly to direct him!" was the cry of the patriots.

Perhaps that was why the King's *Levée* was so well attended—the remaining aristocrats knew the end was near, and came to support him in this final hour. Silk and satin shimmered in dulcet hues, gold glittered amidst gauze and lace—perhaps for the last time.

Francis and Felicienne were there. She noted the sad cast of all faces, the traces of tears in the eyes of some. There was not much that could be done, now. But there was still a faint whisper of hope—an escape-plan was afoot, to carry Their Majesties to the Castle of Gaillon. Swiss Guards were stationed at Courbevoye in readiness—His Majesty seemed willing to attempt it. But that evening the King wrote, saying he would not go; "I have reason to believe the Insurrection is not so ripe as you suppose."

Ah! Fateful decision! Five days later, all the proof he needed would stare him in the face.

~*~*~

Things only grew more tense. The revolutionaries declared, "If the Legislative Assembly does not pronounce 'Forfeiture' by August 9th, we will depose the King ourselves!"

*Mob law is the most forcible expression of an abnormal public opinion;
it shows that society is rotten to the core.*

As the shades of evening fell on the 9th and the Legislative Assembly closed without deposing the King, two movements took place. Brisk sans-culottes of a knowing sort moved off rapidly to spread the news "no Forfeiture," while the few remaining Royalist aristocrats, garbed in black, strode hastily to the palace, ready to die for their King.

Francis, M. du Chemin, and Tristan arrived at the Tuileries together. The National Grenadier guarding the entry let them in on seeing their tickets of entry. As the door clicked shut, Francis turned back a moment, then shook his head and joined M. du Chemin. "The National Grenadiers will not stand for the King against the mob, I fear."

"Their commander Mandat says they will—and they might, with him to lead them," M. du Chemin answered, but his face, too, was especially grave. "You did not bring Honore, I see."

"If I fall, someone must take care of Felicienne and the children."

Tristan knew Francis' deep affection for his wife, and was sure their parting had been painful. They might be going to their deaths. Tristan thought of Adele. *What if I never see her again?*

The general audience chamber swarmed with determined-faced men in neatly-tailored black outfits, come to defend their King. Corridors and anterooms overflowed with seven hundred men—men who saw their duty and would do it. Men who stood for law and order, even though it was unpopular—who stood by a King, not because he was likeable or had given them favors, but because he was the appointed authority. Like the Marseille regiment, they too were men who knew how to die.

Commander Mandat had divided his squadrons, some on the Pont-Neuf, others near the Town Hall, to cut in half any mob coming from tumultuous Saint-Antoine. There were also a thousand red-coated Swiss Guards—faithful and wholly true.

The hours wore on, the darkness deepened. *It is a beautiful night,* Tristan thought, looking out a diamond window. *Oh to be strolling in the garden with my Adele, looking at these bright stars together! But here is war and rumor of war....*

All seemed still, but messengers bustled through the byways of Paris—the revolutionaries' long-laid plans were being deployed at last. Part of the scheme was to replace the Paris parlement with rabid patriots— at mini "town-hall" meetings in Paris' forty-eight sections, new delegates "with full powers" were chosen. Soon those one hundred and forty-four vigorous revolutionaries took their places as the new parlement—with full powers. And they used them. First, they boldly declared Paris in a state of insurrection, then called for Commandant Mandat, to inquire into his warlike preparations.

Tristan turned to look into the room. His father and Francis were conferring with several courtiers, among whom was M. de la Noye. An elderly man, bent with the blast of eighty winters, walked stiffly past. It was Maille, the Camp-Marshal of old. Though aged, he was here to defend his King with his last drop of blood.

Tristan recognized a familiar face under a Swiss Guards helmet. "M. Diesbach! It may sound strange, but I am sorry to see you here—I hoped you had been sent to Courbevoye with the detachment of Swiss Guards a few days agone." He wrung the captain's hand as one bidding farewell to a dear comrade.

"No; my regiment did not go," M. Diesbach replied. "Yet we are not defeated yet; *if* the King gives us full rein, we can hold this palace, I deem."

"'Tis a big *'if'*—he has never done so yet—but may it be so," Tristan replied. "May the Lord defend the right."

"Amen," Hans answered. "If we never meet again, Tristan, remember I died serving my King and my Lord. We shall meet again in Heaven."

Tristan's eyes grew moist as he wrung the captain's strong hand.

A clashing bell broke the hushed night murmurs. Even as its first peals shattered the silence, others joined in from all quarters of the city. The courtiers flocked to the open windows to listen—they knew that each new bell meant that section of the city was given over to the revolutionists.

"That is the bell of Saint-Roche—that deeper note," De la Noye said, coming up beside Tristan.

"I think I hear Saint Jacques'," Tristan answered.

More and more bells tolled. The whole city throbbed. Suddenly, Philip de la Noye stiffened. "That is the Town-Hall!" he cried.

Tristan listened—yes, he could pick out the bell of the Paris Town-Hall, pealing out that it, too, joined the insurrection. Marat himself pulled the tocsin. The bells rang on:

> *The same metal that rang storm, two hundred and twenty years ago;*
> *but by a Majesty's order then; on Saint Bartholomew's Eve!*

In each section of the city, the insurgents roiled and tossed, trying to get up the nerve to march on the Tuileries. Hearing that the neighboring borough would not stir, they would weaken; then receiving word that another section *was* advancing, would pour out into the street again... swayed back and forth by passions and fears.

The hours passed, weltering, full of rumors and alarms, all men in a fever-pitch of excitement. Unsuspecting, Commander Mandat went to the Town Hall at the parlement's third summons—to be astonished at a brand-new parlement. Questioning him coldly, they decreed that he be sent to prison for later trial. Sent outside, he was promptly massacred by the gathering crowd. The National Grenadiers — the soldiers guarding much of the palace and manning cannon at important defensive posts — were told they had a new commander, Santerre (a zealous patriot). Thus, in one blow, another of the King's defenses was cut from under his feet.

~*~*~

The night dragged on, but it could not last forever. After weary, tense hours, the distant sky began to lighten. It revealed a grim sight.

The tocsins had done their work. Relentlessly onward, like an angry sea, marched rows upon rows of armed men. The new-risen sun shone silver on their weapons. Bloodthirsty, rabid onlookers cheered them. A sea of men — a sea big enough to drown in.

In the Tuileries, the crowded halls came to life. Incongruous among rich paintings, opulent upholstery, and gilded statuary was the sight of men "looking to" their weapons. Red-jacketed Swiss checked the priming of their guns. Black-garbed aristocrats pulled out their weapons — blunderbusses, rapiers, bludgeons, poniards. Tristan even saw one checking the edge of a fire-shovel. Everyone was rigid. This was it — the long night of waiting was over, for good or ill.

Tristan loosened his sword in its sheath and tried not to think of Adele, steeling himself for the coming battle. *Lord, be with us all — and help the right!* When he looked up, he noted a sudden confusion among the aristocrats. The King was hunched over, hands on knees, as though he had just received a blow. And indeed he had — the cannoneers of the dead Mandat had just refused to fight for him. Losing heart, he turned to the Queen, saying, "*Marchons* — Let us walk."

With his family and sister Elizabeth, the King passed through the Royalists and Swiss Guards towards the *Salle Ménage*. By deciding to leave the Tuileries, he was giving up — putting himself under the protection and authority of the Legislative Assembly. For all purposes it was abdication, though he may not have seen it that way.

Tristan stared, almost unbelieving. *He's — he's just giving up!* The other aristocrats, who had risked much to defend him, gazed painfully after the King's retreating figure. He was leaving them!

But saddest of all, Tristan felt, were the faces of the Swiss Guards as the King and his family passed through the red line of those devoted men. *They have sworn to protect and serve him, and are still bound to that promise! By doing this, the King is leaving them to die at the hands of the mob!*

The Royal family passed on—the little dauphin kicking playfully at leaves strewn across the path. The royal family entered the *Salle Ménage* and disappeared from sight.

~*~*~

The King was safe now—but what about the faithful men who had come to die for him? As the screaming mob converged on the palace, the aristocratic courtiers realized their duty was ended. Swiftly the black-robed men, some disguising themselves, fled the beleaguered palace as best they could.

"Let us go to the *Salle Ménage,* to see what will be done with the King," M. du Chemin said.

Wanting to say goodbye to Hans Diesbach, Tristan searched for him, but the captain was elsewhere. With a tortured prayer for the captain on his lips, he followed his father and Francis. As a former deputy, Francis knew a back way, and they managed to find seats in one of the galleries.

A circle of angry steel now ringed the Tuileries. Who cared that the King was no longer there? The people lusted for blood, and were set on crushing the last faithful guards and taking the palace.

The Swiss Guards presented a manful, steadfast front to the demented, howling mob. The King may have left, but their duty was to guard his dwelling.

Comprised of National Guard battalions and the rabble of the city, the mob assaulted the Swiss Guards with hot words, pressing close, demanding the palace. The din grew louder and louder. But the mob did not plead long—they knew a swifter way to end disputes! Out came the sabers of the Marseilles and other regiments, while above their heads, the Marseilles cannon poured shot into the unwavering Swiss Guards.

They had been fired upon! Coolly, the Swiss shouldered their muskets and fired a crisp volley in reply. The foremost insurgents—those that were still living—fled in terror. Some ran all the way back to Saint-Antoine!

But only some fled. Countless more, maddened at the sight of blood, rushed forward, their yells of fiendish hate rising even above the roar of their muskets. Bullet after bullet sung death as it sped towards the Swiss.

The Swiss were firing in rolling volleys now, desperately trying to keep back the enraged multitude. The mob was a vast and terrible sea, beating with horrible power upon the thin red line of Swiss. But still the brave, disciplined Swiss stood firm.

The issue looked doubtful. However, one of the greatest military geniuses of all time was there. Napoleon Bonaparte later said that if the Swiss had had a commander, they would have won. But they had no commander—and worse than that, they had an imbecilic, unsound King. For across the battling sea came a scribbled note from His Majesty, commanding his faithful Swiss Guards to cease firing. By doing so, the King sentenced all of those devoted thousand to death.

Obedient to the last, the Swiss ceased firing. Yelling horribly, the frenzied mob rushed upon them, shooting, stabbing, slaying.

One ranked party of Swiss rushed down the *Rue de l'Echelle*, but was utterly massacred. A larger column dashed towards the *Champs Elysees*—hoping, perhaps, to reach their Swiss brethren in Courbevoye. Broken up into fragments, fighting in little knots from street to street—one by one, they were overwhelmed and killed.

Only one or two managed to dart into houses, to be hidden by kind-hearted people. J. B. Good, a Lieutenant in the Swiss Guards, was one of the few who managed to hide:

"To my brothers and sisters whom I dearly love till death. I begin to write this sorrowful tale without knowing whether you will ever receive these lines, which your death-pursued brother sends to you. The chances are small, and the danger unspeakably great, but perhaps I will be able to gain some comfort by describing my painful situation and what I have gone through today.... At 8 o'clock this morning, I was on guard duty at the king's treasury...when word came that many people had gathered at the Place du Carrousel and that they were awaiting the inhabitants of Faubourgh St-Antoine who were planning to storm the palace and raze it to the ground. Only one Regiment of the Swiss Guard was there, but I was not at first afraid, because I hoped that the National Guard would prevent the mob from destroying the Swiss. But a few minutes later came word that the Swiss had opened fire on the mob and that the battle had been joined. I could not at first believe this. But soon we heard cannon-fire. Each of us now stirred uneasily and walked about quaking. Soon it was confirmed....Some good friends came by and urged me and my six soldiers to hide ourselves, and then I really began to be afraid. I quickly went to my rooms and took my soldiers with me. Fortunately there were some civilian clothes there, and I immediately put them on. I said to the soldiers that they should stay in the room and try not to be seen. I cannot describe how bad our situation was. We stayed in my room. My wife was our contact, bringing us all the news in our prison, and almost all of it was horrible! The first time my wife came back crying, and said that the people were already parading through the streets with the hats and guns taken from the Swiss.... A little later one of my friendly protectors came in and said that the streets were filled with dead Swiss and some people were carrying about on spears

the hearts which had been cut out of these men. Indeed, whenever someone passed our house with an arm or leg or another piece of the murdered Swiss Guards, I heard people cry out, 'Bravo, bravo.' — a sound which pierced every bone of my body....So often as I would hear that cry outside, I could not help but cry aloud in my room: 'My God, there goes another piece of one of my brothers and fellow-countrymen.' You can't possibly know how my heart was beating. I was beside myself with pity, fear, terror and fury. What should I do; what should I try; what will happen to me?"

The writer was one of a handful that escaped. The majority perished, fighting hand-to-hand to the last.

The National Guard seized fifty and were marching them as prisoners to the Town Hall—but the ferocious people tore them from their guards and massacred every one. What a terrible day for France!

Hans Diesbach knew that every way but one meant instant death. He led some of his men in a wild dash for the *Salle Ménage*, where the Legislative Assembly met. There, imprisonment doubtless awaited; but perhaps not massacre. There, they were taken and locked in a crowded cell, to await death another day.

But they were among the few—the very few—that escaped death that day. While patriots shouted and danced for joy, the streets ran red with the blood of almost a thousand Swiss Guards.

They were faithful unto death.

Outfoxing a Fox

2.

Grain by grain,
Second by second,
Time runs out of the glass —
Ah, the weight of a single
Moment!
Destinies hang
In the balance.
— Ianthe

"*A*ll passports are denied; the city barriers are almost always closed. Five hundred have been arrested for 'treasonous activities'—meaning, standing against the Revolution...." M. du Chemin trailed off, shaking his honest head. "The Jacobins and other revolutionary leaders have not been idle, these fifteen days since the fatal Tenth."

There was a pause—those in the Le Mercier's glowing parlor were remembering how the Jacobins had seized power in the few short days since the taking of the Tuileries. The Legislative Assembly immediately suspended the King's powers, and incarcerated the Royal family in the Temple. At the beck of Robespierre, Marat, and Danton, the Legislative Assembly appointed a six-man council to rule France, also setting up a new Criminal Tribunal to try the "crimes and conspiracies" of the Tenth ("the Tenth" referred to August 10th, when the King left the Tuileries and the Swiss Guards were massacred). Ironically, the Tribunal's blind witch-hunt punished those whose only "crime" was being true to the old France, while it ignored the real murders of the Swiss Guards.

The new Minister of Justice was fiery Danton—a man who would show no pity to the men who defended their King. A "Committee of Vigilance" sprang up "to guard the people against treasonous plotters"—its head bitter, vengeful Marat. Under his instigation, the number of arrests exploded: none knew who would next be singled out as "anti-patriotic."

The revolutionaries were the *real* ones committing treason, as they stamped out those loyal to France.

Attempting to bribe LaFayette into co-operation, messengers were sent offering him an executive position. He refused, arresting them as "agents of a faction which has unlawfully seized power." But other messengers were sent out—and he knew an order for his own arrest would follow. Realizing he could do no more for his country, he fled on the 18th, with several officers. They were aiming for neutral Holland, but the Austrians captured them, as enemy soldiers, and threw them in prison.

Of their friend Hans Diesbach, the Le Merciers could gain no news. With sorrow, they assumed he had perished in the massacre.

Francis glanced round—the heavy door was closed. "Lord willing, we shall leave tomorrow afternoon. I believe the Lord is directing us to depart as soon as we can."

A perfect storm of glances flew around the room. They had all known that their escape attempt was imminent, but tomorrow—!

"Because of your role in the National Assembly, you are surely a target for arrest," M. de Chemin agreed. "Is there any way Tristan and I can assist you?"

"One thing would facilitate matters greatly," Francis said. "The barriers are our first major difficulty. Could Tristan check the western barrier and let us know when—and if—it is open? When—if—we receive a positive report, we will drive to a concealed spot near the western gate. There, Adele, Olivie, and Honore, disguised as sans-culottes, will slip out and go through the gates on foot. Felicienne, Berthe, and the two younger children will be dressed as if they were going out for an afternoon pleasaunce—with Grandpapa de Duret and I disguised as their coachmen. Beyond the city, we will pause to pick up Honore, Olivie, and Adele, and then—haste to Le Havre de Grace as fast as our relays of post-horses can take us."

"It is a bold and clever plan," M. du Chemin said. "May God enable you to succeed!"

"And you, Christophe?" Francis gazed at M. du Chemin's sturdy face. "You are more than welcome to come with us."

M. du Chemin shook his head. "I cannot bring myself to leave yet; though I know every day increases the danger. I feel I must still attempt to aid the King."

Francis nodded without speaking. At last he said, "You will be in our most fervent prayers."

"To avoid drawing undue attention to you," M. du Chemin said, "we will not come tomorrow to say good-bye—this will be our last meeting."

Adele's stricken eyes flew to Tristan's. It had been hard enough to think that they would part—perhaps forever—but to know that it must be tonight—! While her emotions tumbled, she knew M. du Chemin was right. *It is safest for both families this way.*

But if so, she had something… She rose with a hasty curtsey. Her mother looked up and said, "You may go to the garden if you wish, children. The servants have departed for the evening."

As they left the parlor, Olivie caught Adele's arm. "You are coming with us to the garden, are you not?"

"Yes—I will be there in a moment." Adele hastened up the staircase.

In the muted twilight of her room, Adele pushed a lever on her bureau and a small drawer sprung open. Pulling out a small hand-sewn silk bag, she loosened the drawstring and peeped inside. A smooth, silky-brown lock of her hair was inside, tied with a slip of rose-colored ribbon. She had snipped it to give to Tristan at their parting.

Her heart rose, but she reminded herself, *I must not waste a moment.* With light feet she hurried to the garden.

Night was settling fast—final racks of indigo clouds rested on the western horizon, only a few shades darker than the sky. Pinpricks of crystalline light heralded the first stars. If one shut out the never-ceasing hum and rattle of Paris, it could almost have been a serene evening at their chateau….

> *How lovely are the portals of the night,*
> *When stars come out to watch the daylight die.*

Discussing the escape in eager whispers, Olivie, Charles, and Paulette gathered on a stone seat. Honore and Tristan stood apart on the grassy sward, talking earnestly. As Adele approached, Honore wrung Tristan's hand and moved to join the others.

Tristan turned to Adele as she joined him. They said nothing at first, but their eyes spoke more eloquently than words.

At last, Adele laid her lock of hair on Tristan's palm. "Take this, as a remembrance," she said. "Fare thee well, Tristan, and may our God bless and keep you."

"Thank you, dearest." Tristan tucked it in a hidden coat-pocket. "I shall keep it with me always." Then, reaching into another pocket, he drew out a velvet bag. "Once, years ago, I cut a rose for you from your garden," he said in a low voice. "Do you remember?"

Adele's eyes were bright and deep. "Yes," she said, and felt as if she had loosed a great secret.

Tristan bent his dark eyes on her with a rich expression. "Last December, when Honore and I visited chateau le Mercier, I plucked this, in remembrance of that day and in hope for the future." Out of the sachet he drew a dried rose; the scent wafted up sweetly.

Adele knew it was from her own rosebush. "Oh..." she breathed.

"May I give it to you now, Adele, in remembrance of old times and as a token for the future?"

Adele could barely find voice, but her face answered him. Then she said, "*Yes*—a token for now and forever."

Time flew much too swiftly. Except for the few scattered lanterns, it was dark indeed outside when their parents came to the French doors. Francis was speaking. "...in England I shall go directly to M. Barker—he told me that his younger brother Archibald, who aids him in business, can direct me to a suitable domicile."

"That is well." M. du Chemin stepped out onto the patio. "I am afraid to say we must go, Tristan." His voice was regretful. "We must not stay, so we do not arouse suspicions."

They crowded round to say good-bye to Tristan and M. du Chemin, each in their own sincere fashion—Paulette throwing little arms about their necks; Olivie curtseying with half-girlish, half-woman earnestness; Charles, bowing while his lip quivered—Honore wringing Tristan's hand.

"God preserve you and bring you safely to us in the end, my brother in arms!" Honore's face showed his emotion.

In the entrance-hall Tristan turned his dark eyes on Adele. "Farewell, my Adele. Whatever happens, know that the Lord works in all things for good. If I die—be consoled that I died serving Him. If the Lord spares me, I shall come and take you as my bride, no matter how many leagues of God's earth separate us." His voice stopped short with a strong man's pain. "I commend you to Him, my Adele." He broke off. Turning abruptly, he followed his father out the door.

Adele stood as a statue, her eyes fastened on him. Only when the front door clicked shut did she stir. Her eyes filled with tears; she half-stumbled up the stairs.

A dark feeling of despair swept over her as she knelt in her shadowed room, her head and arms pillowed on her gilded chair. The storm of anguish swept and lashed over her. In broken, disjointed phrases, she prayed for help and strength.

At last she raised her dark head and whispered, "Lord—I give Tristan to You—You can care for him much better than I. Months ago, when despairing of betrothal to him I gave him to You, You gave him back to me..." Pressing her lips together she looked upward with resolute, tear-streaked eyes. "Lord—I leave him in Thy hands. Thy will—not mine—be done."

~*~*~

Late afternoon of the following day was warm; the fitful breeze did not cool the baking heat. Gaston strode with casual ostentation along the street.

A passing carter stopped and stared, then clapped Gaston on the back. "One of the heroes of the Tenth!" he cried. "I saw you there, leading the charge against the palace, Citizen!" Several street gamins and laborers cheered.

With a final swagger, Gaston mounted the De Lobel's two steps and rapped on the door. The answering doorman told him, "Madame Stephanie is in the garden; if the Citizen pleases I shall inform her." A bell tinkled, and the man said hastily, "If the Citizen will wait in the parlor, I shall attend to his errand in a moment." He bowed and was gone.

As a privileged visitor, Gaston decided to not wait for the servant. He headed assuredly down the hall.

In the back garden, he glimpsed Stephanie's low-necked, ravishing blue gown through the arching green foliage. Coming round an intervening hedge, he quickly noted her unusual stillness. She did not look up as he approached, and her hands were clenched tightly in her lap.

"Stephanie darling..."

She looked up. Her golden lashes were wet with tears, and there were suspicious streaks on her colored cheeks. Gaston's heart smote him— had she somehow found out about his latest "harmless" dalliance—?

"What is wrong, dearest?" he queried, raising her.

"N-nothing," she answered, shaking her head—but she kept her eyes shaded by her hat brim.

"You were crying. No secrets, Stephanie."

"A tear or two," she admitted, "but really—" Taking his arm, she looked up at him winningly, "—really, it was a mere nothing. And now that you are here, my brave Gaston, the shadow has flown. My darling! My life!" She gazed up at him with affected infatuation. "You told me of the magnificent assault on the Tuileries, and the final victory—did you know that Mother's friend Claire Lacombe was there fighting among the men? What will they do with his inanity the King, now that he is safely imprisoned in the Temple?"

With relief (*She doesn't know about Marianne!*) Gaston told her the news of the day, his mind elsewhere. His suspicious eye noted a small book lying on the stone bench, and caught the words, "Holy Bible." *Stephanie wouldn't be reading that….But….and crying, too* — non!*…However, Adele might have given her a Bible…as a parting gift, perhaps? And…she would cry if those cousins of hers were leaving!* Hurriedly concluding his update, he bid Stephanie a hasty adieu and turned rapid steps to a certain tavern.

Stephanie remained in the garden, wondering. *Gaston came, only to leave….Why did he depart so abruptly?* Her eyes fell on the Bible. Fear leapt in her heart. *Did he see that? Could he suspect? No, but if….Surely he is not off to arrest them! He wouldn't; they are my cousins….* she thought, then, *He would…his sense of duty….*

Stephanie was nearer praying than she had ever been in her life. *Let him succeed in all else…but just this once…just this once, may his plans be foiled! They — they will be caught if he spreads the alarm!* She buried her face in her hands, tears of helpless frustration seeping through her fingers. Yet Gaston's caresses were still fresh. Emotionally, she clung to him, repeating, *This is only overzealousness on his part…but, O God — if there is one — let them escape!*

Meanwhile, Gaston's booted feet spurned the pavement with two friends. They were marching straight for the Le Mercier's.

~*~*~

"There—that looks about right," Adele stepped back, surveying Olivie's hair with a critical eye.

"We have not had word from Tristan, have we?" Olivie asked, twisting to look at Adele.

"No—not yet. Oh, I *do* hope we can pass as peasant-girls…"

"Our dresses and hair look the part well enough, Adele."

"Yes—the errands of charity have aided us; but our skin is much too pale and delicate…and our voices and mannerisms could easily betray us…" Adele's brow crinkled.

"We have done all we could," Olivie philosophized. "We must leave it in God's hands, Adele." Rising, she picked up a worn basket.

466

Adele's worried face broke into a smile. "Thank you for the reminder, Olivie."

"You have done the same for me many times before," Olivie smiled back. "There—was that the door? Perhaps 'tis the message from Tristan—I shall leave you to your final preparations, Adele." With a curtsey, she was gone.

Adele moved quickly around the room, putting important last items in her open valise. Half a minute later, Marcel entered. Seeing the paper in his hand, she rushed to him.

"Tristan says that the barrier at the western gate has just opened—but he knows not for how long. He bids us hasten." With a bow, Marcel disappeared to tell the others.

Adele turned swiftly to her open valise.

They were grateful the barriers were open—not knowing of the imminent danger which hurried toward them with implacable strides.

~*~*~

Less than fifteen minutes later, Marcel appeared again at Adele's door. "The carriage should be here any moment." He started downstairs to take up his post in the entrance hall; Adele turned the key of her small valise and followed after.

Marcel had barely regained the front door when the wood pulsated with three sharp knocks. Marcel sluggishly opened the door, seemingly stifling a yawn. His eyes were dull, his movements languid, as usual.

Three men stood on the steps. Marcel recognized Gaston and stooped Anton Petit, but the third—a stocky, older man—was unfamiliar.

Gaston took a half-step forward, extending his card with casual grace. "My companions and I are calling upon Citizen or Citoyenne le Mercier."

Marcel took the card slowly, as he had done so many times before, looking at it woodenly and then back up at them. "What names shall I announce?" he asked, spacing the words listlessly.

"My companions are Anton Petit and Hugues Roux," Gaston said impatiently.

Marcel bowed, deadpan. "I shall inquire."

While he was gone, Gaston turned and gazed unseeing into the street beyond. A few errand boys scuttled past, and a laborer trudged heavily by, shoulders bowed. A carriage passed slowly and turned into the side street beside the Le Mercier's. A gaunt dog darted down the street, his tail between his legs and a morsel of scavenged food between his teeth.

Anton pulled out a handkerchief to wipe sweat from his brow. The heat from this late warm spell seemed to stagnate and bake between the high houses.

Gaston hissed, "If they have already left—!"

"The doorman certainly did not think so," Hugues said. "Have you ever seen such an indolent fellow? If his master and family had fled, do you think he would be standing there gawking at us? Especially so unconcerned? Ah—here he is again—"

"My mistress will see you in the parlor," Marcel said unemotionally.

As the three followed him, Gaston's face fell. "But I truly thought—" he muttered under his breath.

Felicienne rose to meet them as Marcel closed the parlor door. She looked as calm and at ease as ever, her buttercup yellow gown almost glowing. "This is an unexpected call," she smiled graciously at Gaston. "Will you be pleased to introduce your friends? I do believe…"

~*~*~

When Gaston knocked, Adele was halfway down the staircase. At the knock, she fled lightly back upstairs. If anyone saw her in her peasant clothes all would be lost! Darting into her room, she pressed against the wall near the half-closed door, trying to hear what was going on below. *Who are the visitors?* Her heart was thudding against her ribs.

Heeled shoes moved quickly across the tiled entryway, and she heard the parlor door click shut. Then she could hear nothing but vague murmurs.

Only moments later, Marcel appeared breathless at the top of the stairs and bounded silently to her door. "Your mother is in the parlor with Gaston and his friends! If you haste, you can get to the kitchen while they are detained."

"Thank you, Marcel. Farewell, and may God bless you!"

As softly as she could, Adele slipped down the staircase, past the closed parlor door, and down the interminable hall. At any moment she expected to hear the parlor door open…. She let out her breath in a gasp of heartfelt relief when the kitchen door closed behind her.

Berthe, Charles and Paulette stood near the sink, dressed is everyday attire. Near them were her father and Grandpapa de Duret; Adele smiled. *Father and Grandpapa de Duret look so funny as coachmen! But I think they'll pass—hardly anyone pays attention to coachmen….* Honore and

Olivie were, like Adele, dressed as commoners—Honore had even smeared grime on his face. All had been overseen by Tristan and Marcel.

They were ready—but would the plan work? In tense, nervous silence they stood waiting, waiting for Felicienne's visit with Gaston to end, hoping—and praying—that he would not suspect anything....

Adele noticed fear in Paulette's big eyes. She put an arm around her.

"Children," Francis' voice was calm and reassuring, "when your mother comes, we will leave immediately. Grandpapa de Duret and I will go out first and take our places—the coachman is a friend, and will leave on foot. Then Adele, Honore, and Olivie, you slip out into the carriage. Your mother, Berthe, and the two younger ones will follow together."

Light footsteps rushed down the hall; Felicienne appeared in the doorway. "They're gone," she said, looking at Francis. "But I think they suspect, and may watch the house."

"Let us go, children," Francis said. "May God grant us safety and success!"

~*~*~

When, after refusing Marcel's offer of some refreshment, the three visitors exited the Le Merciers, Gaston paused on the steps, half-turning to his companions. "I still think—I still suspect they are trying to escape."

Hugues Roux grunted. "You're a good patriot, Gaston, but I think you have chased a wild goose this time." He laughed roughly, and Gaston flushed. "You said yourself that you were only going on a hunch." Taking Gaston's arm, he steered him toward the street. "Young ladies have a myriad of reasons to cry—mayhap she'd read a doleful book, or perhaps a favorite pet died..."

Gaston shook his head.

"Hugues said," Anton began, "that a warrant for the Le Merciers is in the works—that it will no doubt be here an hour hence."

Hugues nodded. "Our fellow patriot Denis set the warrant in motion."

"Moreau?" Gaston queried.

"Yes, Denis Moreau," Hugues said. "He's been lying low for one reason or another, but appeared at the Town Hall a day agone to get a warrant drawn up for the Le Merciers' arrest—seditious Royalists, he said." He added only to himself under his breath, "The lady did not seem so poisonous—very beautiful and gracious, though she knew we were patriots—but duty before pleasure, I always say!"

During this digression, Anton had been waiting impatiently, making spasmodic attempts to interrupt, and now he burst in. "Here is my idea. As citizens, it is our duty and calling—and a noble one, too—especially in times of great crisis, to lend willing arms and—ah—bodies to the State. It is then that the prompt and firm action of the individual patriot holds back the arm of Fate and steps in to turn the course of events towards Liberty, Equality, and Fraternity." He made a broad flourish as if holding up a torch, and continued with an uplifted face, "When the hand of the government is slowed, a few men may stand valiantly in the breech and accomplish great feats, bringing about the most—ah—salubrious..."

"Come to the point, man!" exclaimed Hugues, stomping a foot on the lowest step.

"I am getting there," Anton replied with dignity. "These aristocrats, the Le Merciers, may or may not be planning to flee, but we may as well make sure. Why do we not watch the house to see that they do not leave before the warrant comes? The cause of liberty, fraternity, and—"

"An admirable idea," Hugues interrupted. "Around the corner there is a side door—Gaston, you take that. I shall station myself at this corner, and Anton, you take that other one."

Striding to the cross-street, Gaston stationed himself against a nearby house. He little knew that if he had reached the corner scant seconds before, he would have seen the Le Merciers step into a waiting carriage, pull away from the side door, and begin to rattle down the street.

The birds had already flown.

~*~*~

Bumping along atop their curtained carriage, Francis chose thinly-populated streets. They passed a shattered statue of King Louis—on the 13th, the roaring, rejoicing populace had torn down all symbols of their former monarchs. At last, the carriage drew near a quiet corner close to the western gate. It barely paused, then rumbled on—but three young peasants were now trodding on foot in the same direction: towards the hopefully-open barrier.

Adele remembered Tristan's instructions to let her shoulders droop and not carry her head erect. Her clumsy, uncomfortable shoes made it easier to shuffle and not walk with confidence. Holding market baskets, she and Olivie stayed together, while Honore moved on ahead to make their group less large. Even so, it seemed to Adele that the passersby looked at them suspiciously; she steeled herself to keep from looking fearful and furtive.

The little streets seemed endless. But at last the great barrier gates loomed ahead. Their carriage was stopping at the pillared barrier building. For minutes that seemed like hours, it paused as the guards spoke to the occupants. Adele held her breath, tense with prayer—then it was waved on.

There was rather a crowd of people at the gate—though the barrier was now open, it might shut at any time. Guards stood ominously scanning, and sometimes searching, the outgoing throng. Adele's grasp tightened on her basket handle.

As Adele and Olivie drew near the gate, three young gallants detoured to accost them. "Look what we have here," one said, his eyes insolent.

"These surely are fair wenches to be but country-bred," one remarked. "My beauties, how goes it with you today?" He bowed deeply, sweeping the ground with his hat.

Adele tilted her head down, shading her face with her loose country hat, and kept walking forward. Moving closer to Adele, Olivie's cheeks grew bright, but she too ignored the rowdies. *Oh, please don't turn around, Honore,* Adele thought. *They will discern you are no sans-culotte, and we'll all be caught!*

"Let me take your basket, Citoyenne." Another laid loutish hands on Adele's basket, bending his dark-haired head to glimpse her face.

Adele had not spoken, fearing her speech would betray her, but now with a toss of her head she hoped was peasant-like, she retained her basket. "Please leave me alone."

She sensed movement out of the corner of her eye; oh, no!— another sans-culotte youth was swaggering up!

"Citizens, have you heard the latest intelligence?" a familiar voice asked. "The Austrians have moved; there's work to be done and rewards for good patriots—But *faugh!* this heat works up a thirst; let me buy drinks round. Here, leave these fair wenches and I will tell you more." *Tristan, in disguise!* Adele's heart leaped, but she forced herself to glance at him with no recognition.

"Aw, we didn't mean any harm," drawled the black-haired youth, but he released Adele's arm.

"A drink sounds mighty good to me—a curse on this warm sun!" another said. "I'll come with you, Citizen."

"What have those foul foreigners done now?" another queried.

In the one second her eyes met Tristan's, Adele read his message: *Move on.* She and Olivie hurried towards the gates. Tristan's casual conversation with the rowdies soon ended, and to Adele's relief the gallants' voices faded away in the opposite direction.

The tall dome of the barrier gate rose threateningly above them. *Oh, Lord,* please *help us to pass unsuspected,* Adele prayed. *Please....*

Denis' Revenge

3.

"Yes, persist, O infatuated Sansculottes of France! Revolt against constituted Authorities; hunt out your rightful Seigneurs, who at bottom so loved you, and readily shed their blood for you, — in country's battles as at Rossbach and elsewhere; and, even in preserving game, were preserving you, could ye but have understood it: hunt them out, as if they were wild wolves; set fire to their Chateaus and Chartiers as to wolf-dens; and what then? Why, then turn every man his hand against his fellow!
— Carlyle

T he domed gateway arched ponderously overhead, like a monolithic creation from some early and elephantine period of architecture. The hot sun made the pallid air stifling. The massive guard held the power to ruin their escape....

Adele hoped her shuffling steps did not betray her anxiety; though the arm on her basket looked light, in reality every fiber was tense.

The guard, having seen their *rencontre* with the sans-culotte youths, assumed they were peasant-girls on their way home from market. He nodded them through without a glance. They were under the arch—they were through it! With huge inwards sighs of relief, they slowly plodded along the high road leading out of the great and cursed city of Paris. Ahead stretched the rambling suburbs.

Mingled with a few other walkers ahead, Honore was strolling along, seemingly without a care in the world. It did the girls good to see him.

Adele glimpsed Tristan lounging across the street. He had caught up with them. What a temptation it was to glance his direction—to share one last look!—but that would be dangerous indeed. Even the slightest suspicion of a connection between them could be fatal to him later. Controlling her eyes, she concentrated on the road before her.

Almost half a mile from the walls, Honore disappeared down a little side-street beside the appointed tavern. As casually as possible, Adele and Olivie followed. There was their coach—they repressed the impulse to run. Adele paused, as if tired, to make sure no one else was in sight.

No one was. Quickly, the girls covered the last few yards and stepped in. The door jarred shut, the head coachman (their father) snapped the whip; with a "hup!" the horses set themselves against the harness. They were in motion, the wheels turning, turning over the free soil, farther every minute from the danger behind....

But Adele was not thinking of this. Twisting round, she peered through a crack in the curtains and stared back at a motionless sans-culotte leaning against the tavern wall. Tristan was watching them—even as she looked, he placed his hand on his coat where her lock of hair was hidden.... Adele's eyes blurred with tears. *Lord, will I ever see him again?*

~*~*~

Restive, Gaston shifted against the wall, cursing the warmth—hardly any breeze made it into the narrow side street. The afternoon sun was torrid. Filling with late-afternoon traffic, the mainstreet's buzz of voices and feet reached Gaston's post.

Abruptly, stocky Hugues appeared, beckoning to Gaston. "The warrant for their arrest is here—the officers have come."

Following Hugues into the main street, Gaston saw that the foot traffic had stopped. A little crowd was already gathering in front of the Le Mercier's house, crying, "Down with the traitors! Down with the aristocrats!" Some poured into the side street, eager eyes fastened on the servant's door. No one would escape that way.

With satisfaction, Gaston pushed forward with Hugues for a better view. The officers were hammering against it: minutes passed, and the crowd grew louder.

Then, with an almost laughable calmness, the front door of the Le Mercier's opened and Marcel's sleepy face looked out.

"We have come to arrest Citizen and Citoyenne—" the head officer began, but his words were drowned by an impatient howl from the quickly-gathering crowd. There was a forward rush. The officers were pushed into the house by the mere weight of bodies as the waiting mass dashed in, seeking plunder.

"I should like to see the faces of those oppressors of the people when they are caught," Anton began, with a large movement of his bony hands. "The mixture of fear, of chagrin, of impotent rage, which their countenances shall express will be as food to the patriot heart..."

Hugues Roux made an impatient gesture, hissing, "Be quiet, man!" Perhaps he was thinking of the fair lady he had met, for he said in an undertone to himself, "Duty before pleasure—though I wish *she* were exempted. But, as Marat says, we *must* be strong and pitiless against the foes of our nation." He set his chin, newly-stern.

Gaston's eyes were fixed on the doorway. "They should have been dragged out by now."

As the stream of ingoing sans-culottes ebbed, the three companions pushed into the echoing entrance hall. Pressing through the chaotic mass of squabbling "patriots" they looked for the officers. A man was hacking at a great oil-painting, while two others were trying to shift a cupboard, as if there might be a trap-door behind it.

"Were they found?" Gaston stopped to question a greasy man with a great bundle of expensive garments under his arm.

"Nar," the man grunted before pushing past. "Nobbut in the house but that simpleton."

Gaston gave an exclamation. "*Ma foi!* It cannot be! No one has left the house since—since..."

But the man was already out of hearing. Catching sight of one of the officers descending the staircase, they shoved impatiently towards him.

"Were they—they cannot have escaped!" Gaston darted forward to the blue-coated officer. "Citoyenne le Mercier was here when we visited, and we have watched the house ever since—" His face was a study of baffled rage.

"Be that as it may, Citizen," the officer replied, "there was no one in this house when we entered save the doorkeeper, who, between ourselves, seems lacking..." He touched a forefinger to his temple significantly. "Indeed I think we shall get little of use out of him."

"You will detain him?" Anton asked.

"My warrant does not cover him, and as he seems as incapable of treachery as a babe just born, I see no reason to do so," the officer answered, "but if you insist, Citizen, we shall detain him for a day or two, perhaps. We will certainly keep an eye on the house—the Le Merciers may be on a mere outing and will return."

"But—" Gaston still seemed thunderstruck, "they must be here! Did you search?"

Several grimy men and women were pushing past, their arms full of booty. Hearing Gaston's words, one ill-savored woman looked up. A dainty blue hat with cream-colored feathers was shoved atop her ragged hair. "They are gone of a surety, Citizen," she cackled. "Their jewels are gone—curse them! We tore the furniture apart upstairs, and nary a bauble did we get for our pains." The officer moved off on pressing business—he wasn't paid to listen to hags; he had a duty to do.

Hugues Roux had stood a little apart, his face creased. "That carriage!"

"Which carriage?" Gaston demanded.

"The one that passed by and turned down the side street before we went in to see the Citoyenne! What if—what if they managed to enter it and leave before you reached the corner, Gaston!"

"Well—but I was there right away," Gaston said.

"We talked a few minutes first," Hugues replied. "It would be cutting it awfully close—but that lady may have discerned that we suspected them."

"They have given us the slip!" Anton said. "Alas for the cause of liberty! Curse the treacherous, cunning, aristocrats! Was it not so in the case of…" Measuring his sentences and waving his hands, Anton continued on, but the others were not listening.

"We must send a messenger after them, with the warrant—" Hugues said crisply, " —a well-mounted rider could catch them, I ween."

"That is what we must do!" A new light fired Gaston's eyes.

It took several minutes to get the attention of an officer, but when he heard their idea he said briskly, "We shall have to return to the *Hotel-de-Ville* for authorization and to get a messenger."

What with one thing and another, and the movements of the doorman Marcel (who disappeared, had to be looked for, and was finally found in the debris of the cellar inanely wrangling with a drunken fellow, endeavoring, so he said, to get a glass of wine for the officers), it was quite a while before they set off for the *Hotel-de-Ville*. There, to Gaston's increasing impatience, things took even more time, but at last all was arranged, and a mounted messenger rode out of the western gate (the only gate open that afternoon). Watching his diminishing figure fade into the twilight, Gaston clenched his fists, grumbling about the lost time, but Hugues and Anton were sanguine.

"A carriage can only go so fast," Hugues said. "He will overhaul them on the road out of Paris, I ween."

~*~*~

In the dark firmament, the bright stars seemed closer than in the smog of Paris, but most of the occupants of the carriage were too tired to care. It was almost midnight on the next day. They had been jolting on and on for thirty-four hours; the uncertainty made it seem like years. Every minute a fast messenger might catch up with them....Indeed, it was a mystery why he had not. They thanked God for the relays of horses (arranged by Honore earlier), and journeyed on.

At last, the carriage drew to a shuddering halt. The younger ones woke. Peering out, Adele could see nothing at first, then dimly perceived a bristly rectangle blotting out the stars. Was it, could it be, the familiar shape of their hedge?

A dim figure quietly opened the carriage door. "We have arrived," Francis whispered.

Stretching weary, stiff limbs, the travelers fumbled in the dark and made their way awkwardly into the blackness. Adele's foot had gone to sleep; she winced at the tingling pain. The almost-full moon provided a ghostly illumination for eyes used to darkness.

A stubby, well-dressed man emerged from a gap in the hedge, followed by two coachmen. Bowing to Francis, he greeted him in warm, subdued tones. "Praise our Lady that you are here, Monsieur! I have been in great anxiety ever since your message came. And you, my lady—it is a great joy to see you, Madame. Nothing has changed—I am to proceed to Le Midi with this carriage ('twoud be far enough away to throw off any pursuers)?"

"Yes, Benoit," Francis replied. "I thank you. If 'twas found nearby, this carriage would give us away."

"Marie-Louise should be here soon," the steward, Benoit, said. "As you instructed, she has taken care of food arrangements."

Benoit and the coachmen hauled the luggage out rapidly, piling it on the other side of the hedge. Halfway through this operation, a bent, skirted figure drew near, curtseying. "Praise be to God! Oh, my mistress..." her cracked, quiet voice lost itself in tears. It was Marie-Louise, the elderly peasant-woman who had called the ladies "the sunshine" when they had visited her those many years before....the one who with her ailing husband Marc had warned them of the coming storm....a faithful, devoted former servant.

"I am sorry it must be dark, Monsieur," Benoit apologized, "but if one of the servants looked out and saw a lantern....How I would like to welcome you as in the old days!"

"It must be so," Francis replied. "Farewell, and God bless you, Benoit!"

With a final bow, Benoit stepped into the carriage, and his two coachmen started the horses. Francis turned. "We are ready now, Marie-Louise—lead the way."

They crossed the dark lawn as silently as possible, keeping close to hedges and trees. Marie-Louise's bent old figure was barely-discernable as she led the way. Felicienne and Francis were together, while Berthe held Paulette's hand; Adele and Olivie kept close to Charles. Carrying a piece of luggage, Honore helped Grandpapa de Duret. The older man had been much fatigued by their long journey.

A dark figure loomed up, and Adele started. *A statue,* she realized, with weak relief!

They stumbled on through the darkness. At last, another trimmed silhouette rose against the stars—the hedges around their garden! Also near towered the beautiful carved stone façade of their chateau. Adele's heart grew warm at the very sight.

But they would not be going to the chateau. That would be the height of madness—the first place that would be searched. Instead, they crept through the hedge to the marble folly, and Marie-Louise stooped to the dark earth. Laying down his bundle, Honore pressed forward to aid her.

Then he disappeared into the black ground. Adele knew where he had gone—down the steps of the secret passage—but still it was an eerie sight. Her mother followed with Paulette, then Olivie; then Adele stepped downwards into the pitch blackness and felt firm stone beneath her feet. She felt her way down the steps, then paused with the others at the bottom, her hand against the rough wall.

Francis and Marie-Louise followed. Only after the trapdoor was closed did they risk a light. With her tinderbox, Marie-Louise coaxed a flame, applying it to the unlit lantern. The light seemed bright at first, since their eyes were used to darkness. Adele noted the tired lines on her parent's faces, the general grubbiness of all. A delicious feeling of rest and safety flooded her tired body. Resisting the urge to lean against the wall and close her eyes, she followed the others slowly down the hallway.

Charles' usual high spirits revived at the sight of the tunnel, and he frisked back and forth, whispering delighted sentences to himself as he recognized things discovered three years before. "...I waited as guard....There's the door, ahead, where naughty Denis hid his disguises!....And we found it, this tunnel, all by ourselves!..."

Marie-Louise's lantern shot out into the wide chamber. Setting down his load, Francis turned to his family. "Lord willing, we will hide here until the 29th. Marcel arranged for the sloop *Clemence* to take us aboard secretly and smuggle us to England. Let us thank God for his mercies, and for preserving us thus far."

As her father prayed, his rich voice filled with deep gratitude, Adele felt her heart grow still with peace. Their Lord would be faithful in all things, no matter what happened—even if all failed and death came, she knew she could trust Him and bless His Name.

~*~*~

Jules trudged homeward. Shadows lay thick upon the cobbled street, and the last twisted clouds of sunset expired in slow motion behind him. Mind racing, he pondered the swift takeover of the government. In the confused, mad days since the Tenth of August (this was the 27th), a few strong men had seized power before most people even knew what was happening.

Two main factors aided the power-hungry plotters—the abdication of the King (which caused a vacuum of power in the government), and the alarming turn of the war. The Austrians and their allies were taking city after city in France, moving inexorably toward Paris itself. In the ensuing panic, totalitarian, freedom-seizing measures that would have otherwise been looked at askance were welcomed, as long as they bore the excuse of solving these problems.

Jules was glad now that he had been distancing himself from the extreme revolutionaries. The horrible massacre of the Swiss Guards on the Tenth still made him shudder. The day after, at the ravished Tuileries, he had been sickened by the piles of dead Swiss and the fiendish men and women who gawked and sneered over their dead bodies. He knew in his heart that this was a terrible wrong.

Knitting his handsome brow, Jules ducked into his low doorway. *Odd – 'tis locked.* He rummaged in a pocket and pulled out a key. *Mother has been out more than ever recently – and at odd hours,* he mused, stepping into the dark, empty house.

He had been in the disheveled kitchen for only a few minutes, however, when the creak of the front door and his mother's steps announced her. She looked very weary, but smiled at seeing her son.

"Out late, Mother—whence?" Jules asked, as she slumped onto a rickety stool. "You have tired yourself." Being with the Le Merciers had softened his attitude towards his mother.

Her brows drew together. "It is for a worthy cause, a worthy cause. I would not mind spending myself utterly to attain my end." Raising a cracked cup to her lips, she laughed shortly, her eyes glittering. "Philip de la Noye is still in Paris; I suspect he will try to escape soon." She gritted her teeth. "Once gone, my vengeance will never reach him! Other aristocrats have disguised themselves and fled. But I am watching his house—let him disguise himself as he may, I shall discover him!—and if I give the alarm, all in the area have been alerted and will aid me in arresting him!"

Jules' face grew equally taut. At the thought of De la Noye's escaping, his undercurrent of hatred, never far from the surface, broke out again. "You cannot do the task alone. I will aid you, Mother!"

Her face turned tenderly toward him; it seemed utterly out of place, considering their vengeful topic. "Thank you, Jules, my son. I knew you have been much occupied, so I refrained from asking for your assistance—but you will be of great aid." The light of the candle stub flickered against the grimy walls as she outlined her relentless plan. Though De la Noye did not know it, the lines of a snare were drawing closer round him.

~*~*~

The next evening, the 28th, Jules was stationed in the dark shadow where De la Noye's house stuck out beyond its smaller neighbor. He had an unobstructed view of De la Noye's side-servant's door, while he himself was utterly concealed. Across the street, his mother was hidden. They had been taking turns watching the house, but the attacks against the *noblesse* had increased, and Camille guessed De la Noye would try to escape very soon. She wanted to be there when he was arrested, "to see his face and let him know that it was I," she had said.

The streets—even at night—were busier of late. Over the course of the evening, Jules noted several other lounging figures in unobtrusive recesses—he knew his mother had alerted several others. There were not enough passersby to excite suspicion, but enough to detain De la Noye should he make his appearance. It was a chilly Autumn night—Jules tucked his cloak closer round, peering at the door to his right.

Almost without noise, it opened a crack and a cloaked figure slid into the dark street. With admirable nonchalance, it paused to lock the door, as a servant would, before starting off. The man's hat was down, with a cravat round his chin against the cool night air—Jules could see nothing to distinguish the man's face.

The man passed near the *lanterne* where Camille was stationed. Jules leaned forward tensely.

Abruptly, a sharp cry rent the air. "An aristocrat! In disguise!" His mother's voice! Jules sprang forward.

With a curse, the man lengthened his strides—but to no avail. A passing butcher darted at him; already an angry little crowd was gathering.

"'Tis one of them in league with the Austrians—one of those aristocrats!" a hoarse voice shouted, and the increasing crowd howled again.

"Seize him—take him to gaol!" several voices screeched.

Jules pressed to the front, to make sure De la Noye was safely secured. And he was—several unwashed laborers were fighting over the privilege of holding him. Jules caught a glimpse of De la Noye's face—as cool, handsome, and disdainful as ever, though surrounded by wild, cursing, bloodthirsty men.

With the horrible, unreal suddenness of a nightmare, a black-haired man shouted, pointing straight at Jules, "His son! Do not let this aristocrat's son escape!"

Before Jules knew what was happening—before he had noticed anything except the astonishing fact that the speaker was Denis Moreau—the crowd turned furious hands on him. Seized roughly, he was dragged to the center of the mob, where De le Noye was. There was a piercing scream from the outskirts of the crowd. Jules found his voice.

"I am a patriot!" he cried. "I was assisting in the capture of this aristocrat! It is a mistake, Citizens!"

Denis' clear, loud voice cut in, and his fiendish joy chilled Jules' blood. Denis was having his vengeance, as he had sworn, and was finding it sweet. "Look at them! Two peas in a pod! Is there any doubt that he is this cursed aristocrat's son, my noble Citizens?"

The crowd turned gaping, cruel faces on the two. Illuminated by the nearby orange lantern, the resemblance between father and son was unmistakable. Jules' chiseled face, piercing blue eyes, and firm chin were almost duplicates of De la Noye's. But for the fact that Jules' hair was blond and De la Noye's brown, there seemed no difference except age. A chorus of agreement surged from the crowd—there was no doubt in their minds. And even if there had been, the crowd would not have been denied another victim.

"To the gaol!" they shouted, dragging their prisoners forward.

Camille was beside herself. Her poised knife of vengeance had been plunged into her own bosom. She threw herself on the nearest members of the crowd, crying, begging....

At the last moment, Denis turned towards her with a half-bow, an evil grin on his lean face. "You should have loaned that money to me, Citoyenne," he hissed in her ear; then was gone, leading the group through the broken darkness toward the prison.

Jules heard his mother somewhere, screaming and pleading for him—and dully knew her words were having no effect. A great darkness closed round him. This was the end—he knew he would never see the light of day again. Had he not been recently contemplating the mock trials and speedy executions since the Tenth?

Jules' heart swelled with fresh hatred—hatred towards his father, hatred towards Denis, hopelessness and rank anger. Nothing could turn the minds of the mob now.

A Midnight Chase

4.

"All citizens must stay indoors and refrain from going out into the streets," a herald bellowed, passing down the sunny afternoon street with measured, important tread. A bill-sticker scurried from corner to corner, pasting up the proclamation.

It was now the 29th of August. As the herald passed, the occupants of a tavern looked out with degrees of interest varying from apathetic boredom to interested wonder.

"Shouldn't be surprised if the authorities are finally moving against the aristocrats who still foul and endanger the city." A coarse man tipped his chair back and drained his glass.

"Yah," his companion grunted. "Last night our new Minister of Justice Danton passed a decree, authorizing city officials to search any house for weapons or horses—the war-need being so desperate, you know—and to arrest any suspicious persons or suspected traitors."

"We know what *that* means," the other chuckled hoarsely, holding out his cup for a refill. "Any cursed aristocrats that *they* don't like." He laughed again.

"*I* say, good riddance," a small man craned his skinny neck to look at the others. "Think of it—there are still some sixteen thousand aristocrats in this city! They could attack us from within, while the Austrians come against us from without!"

A seemingly-careless Brigand youth in a moldy corner glanced down at the worn table to conceal the alarm he knew was in his eyes. Tristan (for it was he) found himself thinking of his father, at home and

483

unsuspecting. *Oh, if there was only some way I could warn him....* There was no way he could leave by the front door. The others heard the command to stay indoors—they would prevent him. *I must find a way....*

He glanced at the back recesses of the tavern—*what about the back kitchen door?* But as he started getting up to dart out, the brawny cook emerged from the smoky depths and leaned carelessly in the open doorway. "I say, Martin, what's this about no one going about..." the cook began lazily. There would be no getting past the cook's bulky figure.

Tristan glanced at the street-door again. *What if I make a dash?* But even as he thought of it, several guardsmen tramped by, leaving one to guard the street. Tristan was trapped. He clenched his fists under the table in an agony of helplessness. *O Lord, protect Father! O Lord....*

~*~*~

All afternoon the city sat as if paralyzed or dead. Time stood still. For once, the never-ending buzz and movement of Paris ceased. Only the leaden tramp of soldiers echoed in the silent streets.

The soldiers were busy. Some blockaded each street, some froze the ports to prevent escape by boat, others guarded the closed city barriers. Many others aided City officials in the sinister work of searching suspected houses and hauling new victims off to the already-full prisons. The city was forebodingly hushed; as if it shut its eyes to the doings of those hours.

For Tristan, the hours crawled by in agony. Several times clusters of soldiers marched past in the golden street outside the darkened tavern, their blue uniforms crisp and somehow unreal. Once, Tristan glimpsed the pale, proud face of an arrested man in the center of such a group—'twas an aristocrat Tristan had met several times at brilliant salons. Tristan remained still by the force of his will. *I can do him no good....I must not be captured—I must aid Father!*

It was late evening when life began to slowly resume. As soon as was natural, Tristan slipped out and made his way with breathless haste—but outward nonchalance—through quiet streets towards his house. *Has Father been taken?*

But he never reached it. In a fever of inward anxiety, he was about to turn into the street in front of his dwelling when a hand grasped his arm. He whirled. *Marcel!*

"Fancy meeting you here, Citizen," Marcel drawled. Then hardly moving his lips, he breathed, "Come with me."

Tristan knew Marcel well. With as careless a voice as he could, he replied, "And you, as well, Citizen! How about a friendly glass—there's a tavern a few streets down."

"By all means," Marcel grinned back. Releasing Tristan's arm, he turned with him away from the Du Chemin's.

In his heart, Tristan knew why Marcel had intercepted him, but he shrank from the thought. Detouring into a deserted alley, he turned to his companion. "Tell me the worst." Tristan's voice was steady, but his face pale.

"Your father was arrested a few hours ago," Marcel said. "I know not who denounced your family. They left soldiers at the house to arrest you when you returned, so I decided to 'arrest' you myself."

"Thank you, Marcel." Tristan's heart was dull and heavy, and he totally missed Marcel's attempt at humor. His face tightened as he gazed unseeing up the dingy alley. His mind swarmed with the impossibility of getting anyone out of the heavily-guarded prisons, and yet he was determined to try, come what may. His dear father, completely innocent of criminal subversion...in prison, and no doubt one of those that would be executed for political "crimes!" His heart grew sick, and he pressed his lips together.

There was a long pause. It was Marcel who spoke first, his long face impassive. "We cannot stand here forever," he said, the irony of his tone seeking to galvanize Tristan. "Some one will come by eventually, even down the least-frequented alley." His eyes flashed into Tristan's. "Besides, we must find a place to commence operations."

Tristan shook himself. "What about seeing if we can lodge with Jules? Or he might know of a simple room for let."

"Yes, let us waste no time. I know the way," Marcel replied.

Melting into the fast-darkening shadows, they headed cautiously (to avoid patrols) for Camille Durand's dingy milliner's shop.

~*~*~

Crouched on the rude stone floor, Jules Durand pillowed his head and arms on his knees. Since entering this thick-walled cell the evening before, he had given up all hope. He had sat like this, locked in his own world of misery, all the weary hours, heedless of the talk and movement around him.

He and De la Noye had been thrust into a large but overcrowded cell-room. But all the prisons were overladen: what with priests who would not swear to the Civil Constitution of Clergy, the few remaining Swiss

Guards, and those—aristocrat and otherwise—arrested on political pretences.

There were mainly the latter in Jules' cell. The chatter of those who had become acquainted grated on his nerves, and he sank still deeper into himself. Out in the streets, Jules was a quick-witted, cool-handed sans-culotte if ever there was one. But shut in like this! There was nothing he could do. *This is the end,* he repeated bitterly.

De la Noye did not huddle morosely, like Jules, but he also kept aloof from the talk and banter. Back and forth, back and forth he paced, his handsome dark face a mask. But he too, like Jules, knew it was the beginning of the end—and he cursed inwardly.

Heavy steps echoed in the hallway without, and several of their cellmates began a running fire of guesses.

"I think they shall stop here," one said. "I am getting hungry."

"Faugh! 'Tis too early for that," another answered. "Besides, by the sound, there's too many feet for that."

"I guess it is—"

With grinding bolts, the cell door screeched open. One guard stood stiffly at the door, while other guards herded in half-a-dozen new prisoners.

"Hey—we're too crowded already," one of the older prisoners cracked at the guards. "I shall lodge a complaint with—with—"

"You shut your trap—or else! All the prisons are just as full," a squat guard snapped back, but another keeper laughed raucously.

"Sure, lodge your complaint," he sneered. "Then mayhap Danton will solve the problem by giving *you* over to Madame Guillotine!" He shoved the last prisoner—an elderly man—into the room, and left.

The babble of voices rose again, as the prisoners talked with the newcomers, endeavoring to gain news. What was going on in the great city just outside their barred window? Why so many new prisoners, and all at once? Was it a wholesale roundup?

Jules did not glance up—he could not care less who came and went. Then a hand was laid on his arm. Head still bent, Jules shook it off with a growl, but a man's voice said, "Jules—I am indeed sorry to meet you here." The voice was M. du Chemin's!

Jules looked up wildly into the square face bent over him. "You here!" he gasped. "And Tristan? Is he taken?" In the many months of searching for thieves he had become close to Honore and Tristan. He had grown to admire their manliness, their character, the *something else* that they had which he did not fully understand....

"I know not." Pain flashed across M. du Chemin's face. He added in a passionate whisper, as if Tristan could hear him, "Oh, my son, do not go back home! They are waiting there!"

With dull, throbbing agony, Jules realized they would probably never know if—or where—Tristan was imprisoned. "I am sorry, sir, about—Tristan—oh, sir, he and Honore were true comrades!" He wanted to add the words, "I wish I could be as true a man as they!" but instead heard himself saying, "And you, sir—I fear we shall all be killed!"

"It is in the Lord's hands," M. du Chemin answered. "I have done my duty, and if it is my Lord's will, I do not fear death. 'Though He slay me, yet will I trust in Him.'" Jules stared uncomprehendingly. M. du Chemin knelt stiffly on the floor beside Jules. "How came you to be here, Jules? Why would *you* be arrested?"

Jules' story poured out, his vehement anger rising to the surface in a flood. M. du Chemin listened, his square face thoughtful.

"I hate them both—I *hate* them!" Jules hissed, his pale face flushed and eyes glittering. "And now to be shut up here waiting only to be dragged out and killed..." he trailed off.

M. du Chemin studied Jules' face for one long moment. When he finally spoke, Jules expected the older man to say words of condolence or understanding, but instead Du Chemin, his eyes prayerful, asked a question. "I noticed you wondered at my peace earlier. Jules, do you desire to be freed from the terrors of death and what lies beyond?"

Jules stared, but answered readily enough, "Surely; if it were possible."

"This peace I have is because of my trust in the Lord, Who saved me, giving His own blood for me," M. du Chemin said. "I was a damned sinner, but the Lord Christ came to earth to die a terrible death and take mankind's sins upon Himself. If we believe on His name, we will be saved—our sins will be washed away and we will be freed from sin's chains. Trust in Him, Jules. It is human and natural to hate," Du Chemin said gently. "But, Jules, it will bring spiritual destruction to you. The Lord God can help you gain freedom by letting go of your hate and bitterness and forgiving those who have done you wrong. Your bitterness is keeping you from the kingdom of God."

Pacing past, De la Noye's legs swished by. Jules' hate and wrath surged up tumultuously, and the emotions were sweet. "Forgive Denis—forgive my father?" he croaked. "Never!" Turning his back on M. du Chemin, he gave himself over to bitter thoughts.

But the conversation had stirred him. Thoughts of the Le Mercier came unbidden— *They escaped the city four days ago— I hope they were successful....If they were caught, though, they would— they would—* Jules knew somehow that, when death stared them in the face, the Le Merciers, like this Christian man beside him, would have a different reaction than he or De la Noye or....

But the thought of De la Noye steeled his heart. *And Denis, too! I cannot— I will not— Those cursed, dastardly, despicable brutes....* It gave him a sort of twisted pleasure to think of dying, hating them with all his soul to his last breath....

~*~*~

The candlelight flickered from the stone walls as Adele packed the last items in her valise, snapping it shut. She glanced round the dark underground chamber that had served as home for the last few days, and tried not to think of the beautiful, airy, light-filled rooms in their chateau. *Yet I am truly grateful for this comfortless place— it has sheltered us in our time of need. Mere hours after our arrival here, a mounted messenger arrived with arrest warrants for all of us! He is searching Le Havre high and low....* She remembered Marie-Louise's words: "Happily, no one had any news to give," Marie-Louise had chuckled, shaking her grey head. "Naught but Marc and I know. But the officer is staying in your chateau— the boor!— to keep an eye out for you, so he says."

Marie-Louise had also told them that the Catholic peasants in La Vendee (a region in France), were rising up in armed revolt against the atheistic revolutionaries, trying to protect their lords and their religion. It was a forlorn, martyr's cause— in the end, the ill-armed peasants would be overwhelmed, hunted down and massacred by the revolutionaries— but they were fighting as men for their wives and children and religion.

It was time to depart. The Le Mercier's were ready to leave— Marie-Louise had arranged to bring a cart to a little-used lane nearby. It would take them to the ship; the *Clemence* would anchor in a small, secluded bay tonight.

A light flared in the dark passageway, and Adele glanced up to see Honore's set face.

"What is the look-out above?" Francis asked.

"Not good," Honore replied. "That messenger has decided to live it up since he has not found us— he and some rough cohorts are partying in the garden. They have been carousing for some hours, and who know when they will retire?"

"Not near the folly, perhaps? — could we still slip out there?" Felicienne asked. She did not mention what they all were thinking — they had to reach the *Clemence* by a certain time. The ship could only linger so long, and then she must slip away to England, with or without her unauthorized passengers.

"Let us wait a quarter of an hour," Francis said, "then check again — mayhap the revelers will have gone inside."

He bowed his head, and Adele knew he was silently — fervently — praying. She was praying herself. *O Lord, enable us to escape – O Lord…*

The fifteen minutes seemed like years. Marie-Louise, waiting with the market cart, would be growing anxious even at this small delay. At last Francis and Honore disappeared down the dark passage. They returned with grim faces.

"They are all over the garden," Francis reported. "But every moment is precious, and the *Clemence* is our last hope — who knows if she or another ship will have another chance to take us off? Perhaps never. We must attempt it." He put an arm around Paulette's little shoulder. "First, let us pray." They gathered close.

"Almighty Father," Francis prayed, "be with us now, our strength and shield, our defender in times of trouble. Hide us under the shadow of Your wings from these men who seek our lives, and if it is Your will enable us to reach the *Clemence,* and England, safely — that we may serve You there. I pray this in Your Son's Name, Amen."

The tense knot in Adele's stomach was still there, but she felt a new calm and comfort. Her mother blew out the few candles, leaving them in darkness except for Honore's dark lantern. Carrying the bundles assigned to them, they crept down the rocky passageway.

When they reached the stone steps leading to the trapdoor, Honore tightly closed his lantern, plunging them into dense blackness. Then he climbed to the top of the stairs and quietly slid the secret door's catch. A widening square of midnight-blue sky opened above. Honore's dark shoulders obscured the view for a moment, then his black silhouette crouched above the hole. He scooped up his luggage, motioned for them to follow, and slid to the right, out of view.

Felicienne followed almost as silently, her hands busy with her full skirts and bundle. Adele saw against the dark sky the darker shape of Olivie, then Berthe with Paulette and Charles…. It was Adele's turn.

Half-climbing, half-lifting herself out of the hole, she realized how real the danger was. To her left, just beyond the marble folly, a bonfire shot a great glow of light over the garden. She glimpsed sprawling, moving figures, hearing their uncouth songs and laughter. Some reeled along the walkways with brazen maids. *They are so awfully close — what if....* She refused to think of it. Kneeling down, she pushed through the hedge which ran round the garden, holding her breath as the branches rustled and crackled. The noise seemed loud enough to wake the dead.... In a moment, however, she was with Honore and the others beyond the hedge.

Barely breathing, they wondered anxiously what was taking Francis and Grandpapa de Duret so long. Honore was just about to go back — Adele was remembering how Grandpapa de Duret had been having trouble with his knees lately — when suddenly there was a shout. The hedge bulged and broke; Francis burst through, an arm around Grandpapa de Duret.

"They've seen us — fly!" he panted, half-supporting the older man as he hurried into the darkness.

Adele slowed long enough to make sure Berthe had Paulette, then her feet winged their way over the smooth turf with the others, as enraged shouts erupted from behind them. Almost carrying Grandpapa de Duret, her father was guiding his family across the coverless silver lawn towards the dark fingers of ornate woods to the left.

Behind was a confused cacophony of light and noise. Adele risked a glance back and was happily surprised to see the first pursuers were just starting from the broken gap of the hedge. She blessed the inebriation which had slowed their enemies. *Even now they could catch us!* She bit her lip in panic. *We are cumbered with baggage and little ones....*

They were running through the artfully-spaced trees now: Adele felt a stitch beginning in her side. She had not run since she was a little girl, and felt horribly out of practice. Stray wisps of hair lashed her face. As she turned her head to shake them out of her eyes she saw their pursuers, lanterns flashing erratically. Even as she looked, one tumbled on a hassock and lay prone, shouting drunkenly for his comrades: his lantern had gone out. Another, puffing unsteadily, stopped to help him, and Adele's heart grew light with desperate hope. *If it comes to a fight, the odds are more even now....*

But an instant later her thoughts grew dark. *The horses! They will have them out of the stables by now. Then all is truly lost!*

They ran on through the forest, their breath catching in their throats, their weary legs half-tripping over uneven ground and underbrush. Above, the trees made dark, monstrous shapes — the forest grew thicker around them. Their pursuers were hidden by the brush, though they were still blundering through the bracken — Adele could hear their shouts. Her skirt caught on a clump of brambles, and she was forced to stop, panting, to wrench it free. The pounding of her heart sounded like pursuing hoofbeats....

Rending, her skirt came free, and she was running again, her breath tearing her throat, her legs aching. She wondered dimly how much longer she could keep going.

Abruptly, a small dirt road glimmered ahead through the forest, and she saw a most lovely sight—the homely cart of Marie-Louise! Adele clambered aboard with the others, her legs weak and trembly. Her father, his brow wet with sweat despite the night's chill, helped Grandpapa de Duret up, and leapt aboard.

"Saints be praised—I have been mightily worried!" Marie-Louise exclaimed. She had already flicked the reins; the jug-headed horse was clop-clopping down the narrow road at a surprisingly brisk pace.

As they pulled rough potato sacks partly over themselves, ready to hide under them if the cart was challenged, Honore whispered to Adele, "If they have not sent out riders, we may make it yet."

"They will *surely* think of the horses," Adele answered softly.

"We can pray that they are too befuddled—or else, take the wrong road," he answered. "The Paris messenger will not know of this little-used path, and our servants are not used to the drink he was plying them with— I pray they will be too inebriated to remember it..." his voice died away. Adele glanced at his face and saw he was praying.

Over the creaking of the cart as it jolted over ruts, the *thud-thud-thud* of the horse's feet, and murmuring of the wheels, Adele found herself straining anxiously for sounds of pursuit. On and on they went, the stars very clear in the chill sky. Skirting the city of Le Havre, the rutted track would past sleeping cottages into the deeper forest. Somewhere ahead lay the coastline—somewhere behind were their pursuers.

Her head on Adele's lap, Paulette was asleep by the time they saw the glitter of water beyond the trees. The cart stopped. Stiff and cramped, they clambered out, Adele helping sleepy Paulette. Advancing out of the woods onto the shore, Honore gave a low whistle. Almost immediately there was an answering whistle from across the water. Her parents turned quickly to Marie-Louise.

"God bless you, Marie-Louise; we can never thank you enough!" Felicienne said.

"It is naught, Madame Felicienne—only what is due," the old woman replied. "It gives me joy to fulfill my duty towards my liege lords. Marc and I will be true to old times till the last."

"You must haste to be away—you cannot let anyone connect you with us," Francis warned. "Even now pursuers may be near." As Marie-Louise nodded and the horse started off, he placed a bag on the seat. She made a quick movement as if to give it back, but he shook his head.

"God bless you and keep you forever!" she cried, her voice cracking. Then she disappeared through the trees—she would take little-known trails back to Le Havre.

Bundle in hand, Adele stepped through the last fringe of dark woods and onto the silvery beach, her shoes sinking in the sand. Moored within the hidden cove lay a dark bulk with white sails: the *Clemence!* While she watched, a dark spot—a large rowboat—detached itself from the ship and scudded along the grey water towards them. The Le Merciers stood together on the shore awaiting the ship's boat, a small, bedraggled group.

The boat ground against the sandy bank. As soon as they were in, and the sailors bent to their oars. Moments later, Adele was being hastily hauled aboard the *Clemence*, and the anchor-chain was rattling up.

Francis—the last—was just climbing over the rail when horsemen galloped, shouting, onto the beach they had just left. Their pursuers had caught up at last! Some of them plunged girth-deep into the ocean, waving their weapons in impotent rage—but they were too late. Smoothly but rapidly, the *Clemence* slid out to sea.

Adele stood at the rail, Paulette's hand in hers, gazing at the dim blue shore. It was the shore of her beloved France…would she ever see it again?

A moment later, Paulette's little voice broke the hush and murmur of the waves. "You crying, 'dele? We 'scaped the bad men."

"Yes, thanks be to God," Adele replied, but she kept her tear-dimmed eyes on the shadowy line until it blended with the darkness of the night.

Freedom in Prison

5.

Ev'n the darkest night
Is encircl'd with stars.
— Ianthe

As the Le Merciers tore through the midnight woods in their life-and-death race, Marcel and Tristan arrived at Camille Durand's shop, hoping to find Jules. The night was dark and still around them as they knocked on the flimsy door.

After a tense wait, a feeble step was heard on the wooden flooring inside, and the door opened a crack. Peering out, Camille recognized Marcel (he had often accompanied the ladies when they went to her shop for hats).

"Come in." The candle she held illumined her ashen face. Closing the door after them, she asked with wrenching apathy, "What is your errand."

"We called to see Jules," Tristan answered. "You look weary, and I would not bother you — do you know when he may be home, Citoyenne? We can call later."

"He shall never come home!" Camille cried. She buried her face in her thin hands and gave way to a flood of tears.

"No! What has happened?"

Bit by bit, punctuated by heart-rending sobs, her story came out. Wildly she bemoaned ever trying to capture De la Noye; she cursed Denis, then seemed to slip into the distant past, crying, "My baby! My little, helpless, golden-haired boy! And no one to have pity — no one...."

Tristan and Marcel tried to comfort, but their words seemed to have little effect on the distraught woman. Lodging with her would not be safe — what if Denis lurked near, ready to rub salt in her wounds?

"We will try to find out where Jules is imprisoned," Tristan told her as they left — though even if they knew his cell there would be no way to get him out. He slipped a small bound book into her hands before stepping out into the street with Marcel. It was a Bible—how he prayed she would read it.

Blessed be God, even the Father of our Lord Jesus Christ, the Father of mercies, and the God of all comfort, Which comforteth us in all our tribulation, that we may be able to comfort them which are in any affliction by the comfort wherewith we our selves are comforted of God.

The two youths slid into the shadows, thinking of Denis. They were well away before they paused to talk. "Where to now—do you have any ideas?" Tristan asked softly, lounging "carelessly" against a wall.

"I've been asking myself that," Marcel whispered, his brow smooth and seemingly carefree. "Inns invite questions—we'd be open to scrutiny and suspicion; we'd better count them out. However, there is a woman who sincerely offered to do anything in her power to aid Grandpapa de Duret or anyone dear to him....She is a flower-seller—we could ask her for lodging."

"Lead on—if you trust her, I do," Tristan replied. Without wasting words, they sauntered off down the narrow, dark street. It was late.

Patrols of soldiers roamed the streets, but happily their boots betrayed them. Tristan and Marcel managed to be hidden in a dark alley or down another street when soldiers passed. It was very late when they finally reached the dingy tenement where Margot Thomas lived. They wound their way up the creaking staircase, finally reaching her flimsy door. Before knocking, they bowed their heads.

"Lord God, please work in everything," Tristan whispered. "We need a miracle to help Jules and Father. Be guiding even in this visit, and protect us... In Jesus' Name, Amen." He knocked.

Margot answered the door tentatively, but upon recognizing Marcel her face lit up and she beckoned them in. Fastening the door, she drew up two tipsy stools and urged them to sit.

"Is there any news of M. de Duret or the Le Merciers?" she asked Marcel eagerly. "I went by their house on my rounds, and it looked shut up—they are not arrested, I pray!"

"We hope not," Marcel answered, "Lord willing, if they weren't caught, they were to embark for England this evening. I pray they were successful."

"Oh, I have been praying, too!" Margot pushed brown wisps of hair from her face. "But tell me your errand—" she caught their shared glances, and said with indubitable sincerity, "You may safely trust me with your lives — I would do *anything* to aid friends of M. de Duret. The children are asleep."

Marcel explained, introducing Tristan. Margot's pale eyes grew wide when she heard Tristan was an aristocrat.

"But, sieur — how can that be? I would not have known you from a Brigand!" she exclaimed. "Yes, I have an empty garret; if you desire — though I know it is not what you are accustomed to — you are welcome to lodge there. My cousin, who stayed there, departed a week agone."

"That would be wonderful — thank you, Margot!" Tristan replied. "We will pay you for the risk you are running."

"What of your husband, Margot?" Marcel asked.

"He has a job now, as a jailor in the *Salpêtrière* — 'tis not the sort of work he wanted, but it is feeding the little ones," Margot replied. "With the deplorable increase of prisoners, more guards were needed, so he was hired; making the proverb true: *A quelque chose malheur est bon* — every cloud has a silver lining. But though he is a gaoler, you need not fear him. He remembers M. de Duret's kindnesses, and like myself would do anything to repay him."

The latch rattled, and Margot rose to unfasten the crude bolt. "It is Robert." A powerful man somewhat under middle age shouldered into the room, pausing as his eyes lit upon the visitors. Though outwardly rugged and forbidding, he greeted Marcel with provincial warmth. "And any friend of yours is welcome, though I know not your errand," he added, motioning to Tristan.

Margot rapidly explained, and Robert slapped his thigh with wonder. "*Ma foi! You* an aristocrat? What a joke on those bloodthirsty rascals — " his laugh rumbled through the cottage, " — I wager they pass you in the street and nod approvingly! Ha, ha!"

"Well, I am glad you are on our side," Tristan glanced at Robert's massive thew and sinews. "I would not like to meet you in a fight."

"You haven't reached your full strength, I reckon," the man grinned.

"Marcel and I are but twenty years old."

The talk turned to M. du Chemin and Jules, and Tristan described both as well as he could. Robert promised to see if they were in the *Salpêtrière*, but warned the odds were that they were in another of the half-a-dozen gaols. "Even if they are in the *Salpêtrière*, there may not be a way to communicate with them. But I will try, and may God aid me." Then he slapped his thigh again. "Stay — I know a faithful gaoler in the *Abbaye* — he is so sickened by the job that he would willingly aid you. Let me get him—I know where he will be taking his customary glass."

Robert returned, dwarfed by a massive companion, whom he introduced as Pierre Laurent. Pierre's bullet-shaped head rose above wide shoulders, and his manner was rough yet sincere. Listening intently as Tristan retold their story, Pierre's eyes narrowed thoughtfully as they described M. du Chemin, Jules, and De la Noye.

"I shall do my best," he said when they finished. "I didn't balk when we had real criminals to guard, but...a nasty business, this! I would do anything to cheat those ruffians out of their prey, I would!"

"So you wish to rescue this De la Noye, too?" Robert queried.

"De la Noye?" Tristan seemed startled. "Oh—I only mentioned him because Jules was arrested with him." He looked across at Marcel.

"M. de la Noye seems to keep popping up wherever we turn," Marcel's placid face twitched with a smile. "There is no love lost between him and Jules, for sure."

Tristan grinned faintly. "Yet he has been imprisoned unjustly—and he *was* an old friend of Mme. le Mercier. If we find opportunity to save him as well, I think we should attempt it."

The youths were shown up to the garret, but Tristan slept little. His mind was racing: full of piercing concern and grief for his father, wishes that Jules was not jailed (*He would have been of great aid*, he thought), prayers for Jules and his distraught mother, fervent hopes that the Le Merciers were safely out of the fickle, man-eating quicksand of France....

~*~*~

Two days later, Jules rose from his crouched position and went over to the window, pressing against the bars and resting his arms on the embrasure. His thoughts were legion, and he wanted fresh air to sort them out.

"Look," the self-appointed wit of their cell remarked, "he stood up! The novelty of it! Not huddled in a corner, like he's been for days—something astonishing must have happened!"

Jules paid little heed to the man's jibe. Since M. du Chemin had arrived and spoken to him two days before, he had thought and struggled much. Though he had rejected M. du Chemin's words and clung to his hate with fierce passion, he had not been able to keep his thoughts from what the older man said. His mind wandered to Honore and Tristan, envying their peace and happiness....

Without a word, M. du Chemin had placed a small book beside Jules the day before. Jules realized it was a journal-book, full of writing—pages and pages in a clear, curving hand. Many Protestants of the time copied out large sections of the Bible by hand, but Jules did not know that. His curiosity as to what a man like Du Chemin would write overcame his apathy of hate. The first thing he read was,

"The Holy Gospel of Jesus Christ, according to Matthew"

This must be part of the Bible I've heard them mention, he thought, half-closing it; but the temptation to read what his friends had talked about was too strong. He opened it again. *I will read for ten minutes or so, just to see what it's like.*

He was surprised, all at once, to find it had grown too dim to read. Looking up to see who blocked the window, he found, to his astonishment, that it was evening. He had become so absorbed in the book that he had lost track of time. He sat still in the fast-growing darkness, wondering, doubting, feeling drawn towards this man called Jesus.... He did not sleep well that night, as usual, but for the first time it was not because he was full of inexorable, choking hate.

Now it was the next morning, and Jules leaned against the window, pondering these things. He did not know it, but God was drawing him—as Jesus says in the book of John,

No man can come to Mee, except the Father, which hath sent Mee, drawe him: and I will raise him up at the last day.

Jules' hatred had grown dim and unimportant beside the Living words of the book he held. He longed to know more of this amazing, loving Man—this Son of God who healed and served and walked among the people. He thought of God's greatness and holiness, and how he had wronged the loving Creator of the Universe. A breeze rippled the pages, and his eyes fell upon the words,

And He stretched forth His hand toward His disciples, and said, Beholde My mother and My brethren. For whosoever shall doe My Fathers will which is in heaven, the same is My brother and sister and mother.

Jules glanced over his shoulder at sturdy M. du Chemin. *He—he and Tristan and the Le Merciers...they are good; they are doing what is right, doing the will of God,* he thought, drooping against the barred window. *And yet they do not trust in their works; but only, they say, in the blood of the Lord Christ....*

They are good – and I am not, he thought despairingly. *I have not even done good works or been religious, as they have...* He bowed his head even lower, cataloging the things he had done wrong in his twenty-one years of life. *There is no hope for me. Even the things I did, helping Honore and Tristan against thieves, will not atone for – for....* For more than a quarter of an hour, Jules stood pinioned with despair and grief.

He cudgeled his brain to bring back fragments of things they had tried to share with him. Broken memories of the Ten Commandments (taught to him as a child by his mother) swirled before his mind, and stronger still came scenes and sentences from the Book he had just been reading. *Hell,* he shuddered, *that is where I am going, and soon....*

Words M. du Chemin spoke on that first afternoon in the prison (two days ago? He could hardly believe it: it seemed like years) came to mind. "My peace is not due to myself, but to my trust in my Lord, who saved me, giving His own blood for me. Trust in Him..."

Jules knotted his brow. *He would not have said that if...if <u>I</u> could not be....* He turned to the crucifixion of Jesus, his heart bleeding as he read the horrible narrative. *Sold – betrayed by a friend!* his heart cried. *Given a false trial, whipped, then crucified...oh....* Suddenly, his eyes fastened upon a scene:

And one of the evill doers, which were hanged, railed on him, saying, If thou be that Christ, save thy selfe and us. But the other answered, and rebuked him, saying, Fearest thou not God, seeing thou art in the same condemnation? We are in deede righteously here: for we receive things worthy of that we have done: but this man hath done nothing amisse. And he sayd unto Jesus, Lorde, remember me, when thou commest into thy kingdome. Then Jesus said unto him, Verely I say unto thee, to day shalt thou be with me in Paradise.

That man...he was evil...if he could be saved, could be forgiven by Jesus... A new light – that of wild, unbelieving hope – broke in Jules' eyes. *O Lord Jesus,* his heart adjured passionately, *remember me when Thou comest into Thy kingdom!*

At that instant, new life began in Jules – something more than joy flooded his being. With an exclamation of happiness, he turned and found M. du Chemin close by, praying.

"I have found Him!" Jules cried. "And – I am free!"

~*~*~

The air nipped at Tristan's shabby clothes as he swaggered down a thoroughfare. The streets were crowded and bustling—he was jostled often—but the people were not happy. Feverish anxiety lined many faces, desperate resentment others. Were not the Austrians advancing, while within the city (so Rumor said) the aristocrats plotted the people's utter destruction?

Presently, Tristan turned into a broad street. Nailed against the building fronts in gaudy colors were sign after sign—a boot, a red board rudely shaped like a piece of meat, wooden scissors.... Years before in Paris, hanging signboards became so large that they obstructed light and traffic, so a law had been passed ordering all signs to be fastened flat to the buildings.

Just past an apothecaries' mortar-and-pestle signboard, Tristan saw his destination and turned in a door underneath a vaguely-painted white bird. He wound his way past the rough tables and their rougher occupants to where the barman/landlord stood wiping his hands on a slip of dishrag.

"I reserved your back room, Comrade," Tristan reminded, tucking several coins into the man's palm.

"It is ready for you, Citizen—the fire has been lit and all should be in order," the bartender answered. Motioning with his rag, he opened the door of a cozy little room. Though not the cleanest, a fire danced in one corner, while over a small circular table, a lit lantern hung cheerily from weathered beams.

"Thank you, this will do well," Tristan nodded nonchalantly, slouching to a seat facing the door. The man stayed, twisting the cloth, until Tristan said, "That will do; I shall call if I need you, Citizen."

Bobbing, the man left, closing the door after him. Tristan remained motionless, sunk down in his chair, hands thrust deep in pockets, until the doorknob moved again some ten minutes later.

A bluff, white-haired Englishman followed the bartender into the room and bowed to Tristan, who rose.

"I hope you did not have long to wait," the Englishman said courteously, in good French.

"But ten minutes," Tristan replied. "Pray be seated."

The other referred to a paper from his pocket. "Your firm sent a note asking if I would meet an agent here, on business matters. I assume you are their agent?"

"Yes, Monsieur Barkay—*Barker*—you must excuse my pronunciation," Tristan answered. "May I order you anything?"

"No, but I thank you," said M. Barker.

Tristan half-turned to the bartender. "Then we do not need your services, Citizen—we will call if we do. Thank you." When the door was firmly closed, Tristan looked straight at M. Barker. "I trust you are a man who can take surprises, Monsieur?"

M. Barker looked at him, puzzled. "I suppose my nerves are as good as any other man; but I do not see how the question pertains—" his voice died away, and he stared wide-eyed.

In one movement Tristan sat up, pushed his hair back, straightened his shoulders, tightened the loose muscles of his face—even his eyes changed. "You recognize me, Monsieur Barker?" Tristan asked; but it was a rhetorical question.

"Tristan du Chemin! As I live!" M. Barker exclaimed. "You and your friends rescued me from that robber! And how I had hoped you were safely away! When I came but a week ago, I was glad to find the Le Mercier's house empty and nothing but rumors of their mysterious escape. Business prevented me from going to your house until the 30th (yesterday, the day after that terrible afternoon of arrests) and then I prayed that you too had fled and not been arrested. Where is your father? And did the Le Merciers get away, or were they...."

"It is a long story, full of Providential timing," Tristan answered, "but they made their escape on the 25th, and should have left for England by now. As for my father—" he paused only for a second before saying, "—he was arrested."

M. Barker's face showed his sorrow. "Oh, these people...." He glanced keenly at Tristan. "I know it sounds mad—the prisons are so securely guarded and all that—but can't anything be done? Have you any ideas?"

"Naught that show any promise of success, but we must attempt," Tristan replied. "The Lord has connected Marcel and I—" ("Ah, I am glad you have him with you," Barker interjected) "—with two jailors. Just this morning, the one who works in *l'Abbaye* discovered that my father and a friend, Jules, are imprisoned there, but Pierre (our jailor friend) says that at present it is too risky to pass even a note to them."

"Never say die, Tristan," M. Barker replied. "I shall add my wits to yours, and we will pray the Lord to open the 'gates of Babylon' for us. If He works a miracle, the next great difficulty would be to get you out of France—every way of escape is straitly blocked and guarded...."

He put a hand to his head, but a moment later he looked up, his eyes almost merry. "*Heavens!* And I was fretting about it just this morning…." Shaking his head, he leaned eagerly across the table. "Tristan, when I came here, I expected to buy some weighty goods, and brought seven Englishmen to help lade boxes. Five deserted me for the grand excitement of Paris. I have had to hire laborers here, and it has been quite a task to keep them up to their work. But I still have the English workers' exit papers; and I see now what a Providence it was that they left! You and Marcel—and your father, if we can save him—can try to get to England with me using their papers! You all know English, and surely can pass muster if you dress in English clothes and don't speak much…."

Though they had no new idea for his father's rescue, Tristan left with a lighter heart. One of his myriad of pressing cares had already been arranged by his Heavenly Father.

~*~*~

All day long, prison guards had been tramping up and down the Abbaye's stone corridors, shifting prisoners, trying to make room for newcomers. At last, a little knot of rough, hefty jailors entered the cell in which Jules, Du Chemin, and De la Noye were incarcerated with many others.

One of the guards, a giant of a man, remarked to his fellows, "This room must needs have some prisoners removed—awful crowded."

Another, a squat fellow with a seamed face, cackled, "It won't be packed for long, Comrade—or my name's not Canax!"

The third, whose beetling brows were a graying black, spoke to the first, ignoring Canax's macabre jest. "I bethink me of that little unused garret—we could at least put several in there, Comrade Pierre."

"The *violon*—ah, certainly," Pierre answered. "I had forgotten it, since 'tis hardly ever used. I shall choose a few out; Comrade Canax, you fill the water and check the window bars while Bernard guards the door."

Turning his long, heavy face towards the prisoners, Pierre took several lumbering steps into the room. Leaning against the wall near him was golden-haired Jules, and Pierre motioned to the youth. "You are to come with me." With an expressive face, Jules turned to an older man nearby, as if to say farewell. Seemingly moved, Pierre motioned the other man to come as well.

"Oh, you're too softhearted, Comrade Laurent," Canax hissed derisively, passing to check the barred window.

Seemingly stung by the remark, Pierre waved a hurried, negligent hand toward a dark-haired aristocrat standing haughtily against the opposite wall. Then, without a further glance at his three charges, he walked back to Bernard. "These'll do, Comrade." Canax took up the rear of the procession.

Once the cell door was bolted again, Canax hastened off on another errand, and Bernard and Pierre started down the opposite hallway with their charges. They went on and on into the labyrinth of the old prison, down uneven stone hallways, mounting several sets of short staircases, going upward to the third story of the building, down a seeming-deserted hallway, and at last stopping in a dead-end hall. Pulling out his great ring of keys Pierre finally separated out a puny, unexceptional key and tried it in the small door.

The hinges were rusty and creaked dismally, but it opened upon a tiny, dusty, and deserted room with a very high ceiling. Pierre had brought a bucket of water and set it inside, thus finishing the requirements needed to make the place habitable in the eyes of the government. Then the three prisoners were herded inside. Hinges complaining loudly, the thin door thudded shut. Bernard and Pierre's heavy steps faded into the distance.

The three unlikely cellmates looked at each other, and De la Noye stepped to the other side of the room. He would have gone to the window, but there was no window. In truth, Philip Emilie de la Noye did not know exactly what to make of the present situation. He had been completely astonished the day before when Jules had approached him saying that he had forgiven him (De la Noye) for what he had done to Camille and himself, and asking his pardon and forgiveness for plotting against him and encouraging Denis to do the same. Truly, there was a new light, a *rest* in Jules' face, which before had been so hard and hopeless—but De la Noye, a proud man, had drawn away from his son's plea.

De la Noye had built his whole life around being a debonair, self-assured, masterful man-of-the-world. Forgiveness was a weak word in his mind. Besides, he doubted Jules' sincerity: *What is he trying to gain out of this sudden change? — suspiciously swift, if you ask me.* He knew not the life-changing rapidity with which Christ can enter and unchain a soul.

God had brought Jules to the point of desperation where He could speak to him—but De la Noye was not there. Still, self-confident, he believed that when brought before the judges he might be able to talk his way out by sheer force of character, eloquence, and mayhap a bribe or two. He had not yet played his last card and found it wanting.

The Fiendish Days of September

6.

I tell you naught for comfort,
Yea, naught for your desire,
Save that the sky grows darker yet,
And the sea rises higher.

Night shall be thrice night over you,
And heaven an iron cope.
Do you have joy without a cause,
Yea, faith without a hope?
– G. K. Chesterton

T hat evening—the first of September—a grim, despairing quintet gathered in Margot and Robert's small front room. Pierre Laurent's account of how he put their friends in the garret-room had raised a tenuous hope, but then Marcel's report of his news-gathering forays sent their hopes plummeting lower than before.

"...everything is primed for an outburst," Marcel finished. "The slightest spark will set off a grand explosion. The people believe the ridiculous rumors that the aristocrats will burst out of the prisons, rescue the King, and join the Austrian armies in leveling Paris. We know how impossible that is—but it is believed, terrifying the populace and driving them to desperate madness."

"They cry in the streets, 'Fraternity or death!'," Tristan added, "but what they are saying is, 'Be my brother or I will kill thee.'"

"The breaking point is near, and we know what that means." Marcel stared at the whitewashed wall, his face pale. "Bloodshed and massacre."

The others nodded without speaking. They, too, had felt the same as they had gone about the streets on their various outings. It seemed there was no more to say.

Tristan's jaw tensed. "If only we had more time—!"

"Yes," Robert said. "Time might afford the opportunity we need."

Pierre nodded agreement. "Though it seems hopeless, we should be ready to act. Mayhap a miracle will light our way. If violence breaks out, you two wait in the alley behind the *Abbaye* — I will then endeavor to slip out and give you updates."

"It is the best we can do," said Tristan. "Marcel and I will be there."

Robert turned to his wife. She sat knitting furiously, her lips tight together as if she feared she might cry. "Margot, we men have no rescue ideas other than impossible ones — has your woman's wit anything to add?"

She looked up with brimming eyes, shaking her head. "I have thought and thought and prayed and prayed until my head is dizzy — and I can think of nothing. Besides, if these bold youths cannot think of anything, what hope is there for me?"

"We must be ready for anything," Tristan said. "And we must keep beseeching the Lord for wisdom — He may miraculously give us an opening."

"Yes, a moment's chance may give us an opportunity," Marcel agreed.

Margot burst out, "It is such a hopeless venture — I see you agree by your faces — do not sacrifice yourselves for naught! Do not risk your lives, young sirs..." Her voice broke, and the tears she had been holding back came coursing down her cheeks, shaking her with sobs. "If there was a chance — yes — but....no — you will be captured and killed!"

~*~*~

The very next day, the spark fell on dry timber. On the wings of the wind came the terrifying news: Verdun had fallen to the Prussians! It was one of the cities holding back the enemy armies from advancing on Paris — and now it had given way! The people's fears could not be contained. "The Prussians will march straight upon us! They will be here in a day or two!"

Vast multitudes rushed to enlist; all the church bells rang wildly; the alarm-gun was fired again and again. Building and tossing in every corner, the mass hysteria mounted — until, reaching full boil, it dashed hissing out of the pot, running down in scalding streams.... It was the second of September 1792, a date which would be burned with a searing iron into the ledger of world history.

No one now knows how much was instigated by revolutionary leaders. Were scum hired to begin the massacre or not? True indeed it was that there were many men in Paris who needed not the promise of money

504

to commit works of bloodshed. Fingers point through the ages at Danton and Marat—Danton, whose fiery voice shook the Assembly-hall that afternoon; "Legislators! It is not the alarm-cannon that ye hear: it is the *pas-de-charge* against our enemies. To conquer them, to hurl them back, what do we require? To dare, and again to dare, and without end to dare!" Those who heard his passionate words shouted in acclaim, fired up to do and dare—even if it meant bloodshed.

The killing began a little past three o'clock. Some twenty priests (who had refused to swear the Civil oath) were being moved from the Townhall to the *Abbaye*. Gaston, Anton, and Leuren were among those pushing and shouting "Priests of Beelzebub" round the six carriages, cursing the priests and accusing them of bringing about the present troubles.... Several of the crowd, bolder and angrier than the rest, leapt on the carriage steps to have a better vantage-point to hurl insults. The guards remained impassive—perhaps they agreed with the crowd. A priest tried to pull up the carriage-blind, but a "patriot" struck it down. At last, provoked, one priest smacked a grabbing Brigand with a cane, trying to make the man let go.

With a howl, the swarm descended upon the carriages. His truncheon out, Gaston rushed forward; Leuren followed, drawing out a poinard. But Leuren had no chance to use it—half-a-hundred hands were already at work among the carriages, dragging out the priests and butchering them even as they cried for mercy.

Leuren emerged from the melee with a new face. He had participated in murder. His eyes sought Gaston's.

"It's begun!" Gaston hissed. "Now for more daring, my countrymen! Our country—*la patrie*—is in danger!"

Leuren never knew exactly how it was arranged, but soon an improvised judge and jury sat in the main room of the *Abbaye*, "trying" the prisoners. Similar "Courts of Justice" (or as historian Carlyle calls them, "Courts of Revenge and Wild-Justice") sprang up in each of the other prisons—*La Force, Châtelet, Conciergerie, Bicêtre,* and *Salpêtrière*—too simultaneous to be coincidental.

A prisoner, Jourgniac Saint-Meard, wrote in his diary:

"*Sunday: At half-past two, we prisoners saw three carriages pass by attended by a crowd of frantic men and women. They went on to the Abbaye cloister, which had been converted into a prison for the clergy. A moment after, we heard that the mob had just butchered all the ecclesiastics who, they said, had been put into the fold. — Nearly 4 o'clock: The piercing cries of a man whom they were hacking to pieces with sabers drew us to the turret window of our prison, where we saw a mangled corpse on the ground opposite the door. Another was butchered in the same manner a moment afterwards. — Near seven o'clock: We saw two men enter our cell with drawn swords in their bloody hands. A turnkey showed the way with a flambeau, and pointed out to them the bed of the unfortunate Swiss soldier, Reding. At this frightful moment, I was clasping his hand, and endeavoring to console him. One of the assassins was going to lift him up, but the poor Swiss stopped him, by saying in a dying tone of voice, 'I am not afraid of death; pray, sir, let me be killed here.' He was, however, borne away on the men's shoulders, carried into the street, and there murdered."*

It was a dark hour for France, the end result of France's godless philosophies. One which led to four days of atrocious massacre!

September Massacres, Anonymous

~*~*~

Through their barred window, Hans Diesbach and the remaining Swiss Guards heard a vast tumult and shouting, cries and dying screams. They knew not all that was transpiring, but knew their turn would no doubt be soon — that they would join the hapless prisoners being fed to the mob.

Hans took the back of an envelope out of his now-bedraggled uniform pocket. For a moment he stood motionless, eyes closed in prayer;

then took up a quill and small vial of ink (given to him by a doomed prisoner some weeks ago) and wrote a few short words—a prayer and a pean.

The key rattled in their door. The guard, his sleeve and sword all bloody, commanded them to come out. Hans set the paper on the windowsill, then followed his comrades. It lay there, alone and unread, the prayer and resolution of his noble heart:

> *It is as a soldier I despair,*
> *But the Christian keeps his faith.*
> *Lord, I answer Your call without fear.*

The "trial" the Swiss Guards faced downstairs was very succinct. The "jury" asked a few terse questions, then as abruptly declared them: "Guilty." The "judge" rapped out their sentence: "Let them be conducted to *La Force.*" Cruel, deceiving words! For they mean the prisoners will be tossed into the living wrath outside!

The soldiers, knowing what awaited them, clung to one another, their faces ghastly with fear: "Mercy, Messieurs, ah, mercy!" they cried.

Out of the cowering blue group stepped one soldier—Hans Diesbach. A martial nobleness hallowed his solemn face. "I go first," he said calmly, "since it must be so; adieu!" Dashing his hat sharply behind him, he cried to the butchers, "Which way? Show it me then."

The blood-stained, uncouth men opened the folding gate, announcing him to the multitude.

He stood a moment, a noble and heart-wrenching sight—then plunged forth bravely among the bloodthirsty pikes. The people—men and women both—howled with satisfaction, striking again and again— and his soul went to be with his Lord, a martyr indeed.[1]

~*~*~

One gentleman, Nicolas-Edme de la Bretonne, later wrote this eyewitness account of the massacre:

"*I arose, distressed by the horror. The night had not refreshed me at all, rather it had caused my blood to boil. . . . I go out and listen. I follow groups of people running to see the 'disasters' — their word for it. Passing in front of the* Conciergerie, *I see a killer who I'm told is a sailor from Marseilles. His wrist is swollen from use. I pass by. Dead bodies are piled high in front of the* Châtelet. *I start to flee, but I follow the people instead. I come to the* rue St.-Antoine, *at the end of the* rue des Ballets, *just as a poor wretch came through the gate. He had* seen how they killed his predecessor, but instead of stopping in amazement, he took to his heels to escape. A man who was not one of the killers, just one of those unthinking machines who are so common, stopped him with a pike in the stomach. The poor soul was caught by his pursuers and slaughtered. The man with the pike coldly said to us, 'Well, I didn't know they wanted to kill him. . . .'

"There had been a pause in the murders. Something was going on inside. . . . I told myself that it was over at last. Finally, I saw a woman appear, as white as a sheet, being helped by a turnkey. They said to her harshly: "Shout 'Vive la nation!'" "No! No!" she said. They made her climb up on a pile of corpses. One of the killers grabbed the turnkey and pushed him away. "Oh!" exclaimed the ill-fated woman, "do not harm him!" They repeated that she must shout "Vive la nation!" With disdain, she refused. Then one of the killers grabbed her... She fell, and was finished off by the others. Never could I have imagined such horror. I wanted to run, but my legs gave way. I fainted. When I came to, I saw the bloody head. Someone told me they were going to wash it, curl its hair, stick it on the end of a pike, and carry it past the windows of the Temple. What pointless cruelty!"

C Massacres des 2, 3, 4, 5 et 6 Septembre
1792

September Massacres, Anonymous

As they waited in the alley behind the *Abbaye*, the long, horrible hours passed like torture for Tristan and Marcel. Again and again they restrained themselves from springing out, as passing sans-culottes callously joked of the butchery they'd done or displayed "souvenirs" — pieces of dripping aristocrat flesh. Only the knowledge that action would ruin any chance to free M. du Chemin and Jules kept Marcel and Tristan silent, but their faces were set and fists tight. When Pierre had stepped out, white-faced with horror, he promised to let them know if their friends were brought down. Though it was doubtful that Tristan and Marcel could rescue them, they were resolved to give their lives bravely.

So many were killed that their butchers wearied, their implacable blades dulled and needed to be re-sharpened — but there were always more killers to replace those whose sword-arms grew tired. The massacre continued, hour after terrible hour. The Duc de Villelume-Sombreuil recounted his mother's terrible experience:

"My mother [who had been arrested on 10 August 1792 along with her father, the Count of Sombreuil, and her two brothers] did not like to talk about the events of this frightful and horrifying September day….[As they were being led out by the mob, the man walking in front of them], the comte de St.-Mart, was suddenly pierced through the breast by a lance and fell dead. She immediately threw herself upon her father, to protect him from a similar blow and as they tried to drag her off…received three wounds. In the scuffle, her hair (which was very long) came loose, and she pulled it around her father to protect him. Finally, bleeding from her wounds, she succeeded in calming the people who admired her fighting courage. One of them grabbed up a glass, caught up some of the blood which was still spurting out of the body of M. de St.-Mart, mixed it with some wine and said that if she would drink a toast to the health of the nation, they would spare her father.

"Without gagging, she drank it down, and was immediately hoisted up and carried around the room in triumph. Since that time, my mother could never bear to wear her hair long; she had her head shaven clean. Likewise, she could never bring a glass of red wine to her lips. Indeed, for a long time, even a glimpse of wine produced painful recollections. [Her father and two brothers were subsequently guillotined, but although imprisoned until 1795, she herself was freed and subsequently married the duc de Villelume. She died in 1823]."

With the coming of night, Marcel and Tristan's hearts grew more and more despairing. Maybe Pierre could not get word to them, and Jules and M. du Chemin already been taken before the tribunal and killed!

Near midnight, several singing, shouting Brigands swaggered by. One carried a lantern; its flashing orange-yellow light made their figures even more hideous than daylight. Coagulating blood plastered their shirts to their bodies, and their weapons were gory.

"I am as weary as a hodman that has been beating plaster!" one exclaimed. "We had work, didn't we, comrades?"

"Work to my liking," another laughed brutally.

Tristan bowed his head in desperate prayer.

~*~*~

An intimation of the slaughter even reached M. du Chemin, Jules, and De la Noye's small garret-cell. At first, they knew not what the confused hubbub of shouts and cries meant, though they knew it meant evil. After some time, from words caught from jailors venturing up to cells on the same level, they gathered that the prisoners were being massacred.

As the bloody afternoon and night at last gave way to equally-chaotic morning, De la Noye grew more and more tense, though he tried to conceal it behind his usual careless mask. Yet he was also drawn to the son he had never met before, and stared furtively at times at Jules' handsome, steady face. Jules and Du Chemin were often praying together, but De la Noye divided his time in fits of pacing and listening at the door.

He was thus the first to distinguish a different sound—great thudding noises. "What is that?" he whispered, pressing his ear against the door. The other two drew near.

The noises grew louder: their very door trembled. They were a series of heavy blows; something was thudding against a wooden cell door down the hall. Short, angry bursts of conversation wafted their way:

"...cursed aristocrats!" one of the guards swore, "...this blasted door...."

"...barricaded....here, give a hand here...shoulders to the lock....Go!" another cried.

As the three understood the words, De la Noye's face took on a look they had never seen before. "Some prisoners have barricaded themselves in," he said dully, "it is worse than we thought. All is lost." Finally, De la Noye realized that he, the suave aristocrat lord, was no longer in charge of his own destiny. He was helpless before the fate pressing relentlessly towards him.

There was a huge crash from the hall, accompanied by splintering wood.

"*None of that!*" came a guard's voice, with the sharp sound of a blow.

"—you only gave yourself a few extra minutes before the end, see?" another cackled hideously.

There was a rush of feet, then the air quivered with shrieks, curses, and vital blows. At last, the sounds died away into throbbing silence, and the guards' sullen feet faded down the hall. The blockaded prisoners had been butchered in their cell.

Jules' eyes flew to the trapdoor in the high ceiling above their heads—and his thoughts darted back to its discovery, soon after they were thrust in the cell. "Here's a trapdoor; let's investigate," he had said. "If we make a ladder—one of you on the back of the other, and I'll climb on the shoulders of the second..."

Du Chemin had braced himself on the floor, and De la Noye (with aloof disdain) stood on his back and lent his shoulders to Jules. Jules recalled how, after a struggle, he'd managed to push open the ceiling trapdoor. Hauling himself up, he'd stuck his head in, then climbed down, his face pleased. "One could fit up there, certainly."

"Then one could perhaps hide from the jailors?" Du Chemin had asked, his face interested.

"Yes; but only one," Jules had answered at the time, "it takes a ladder of two to get anyone high enough to reach, and then there is no room for more."

There the matter had rested—until now. "The trap-door!" Jules exclaimed. "Here, M. de la Noye—it shall be you."

De la Noye looked at him, his eyes burning strangely. "I see not your meaning," he said stiffly.

"You are the only one of us who has something to fear when Death comes," Jules said. "M. du Chemin and I know we are going to be with our Lord; if *you* die, you have no hope." Suddenly Jules cried out passionately, "Father—" (he had never used the name before) "—Father, oh go up! Perhaps if you are spared the Lord will bring you to Himself!" He drew near as he spoke, laying a persuasive hand on De la Noye's arm.

De la Noye straightened and looked at Jules—with a different look this time. There was no mistaking Jules' sincerity now—his hatred had truly been changed to love; a love willing to sacrifice itself. Something broke at the thought. De la Noye stared—then bowed his head and began to weep.

Broken at last—weaponless; cast to earth;
Victorious foes crowd forward with glee,
Wolfishly crying for his life and blood;
Now he has naught but Me.

Torn to vain wreckage by the foe-man's blast,
His advantages (looks, might, all from Me,
The One he rejected) can aid no more;
Now he has naught but Me.

Clear-seeing Despair sets him free at last

From pride's tyranny; while his body
Is still bound in the waiting-hole of Death:
Finally, he has naught but Me.

But he has Me. He has Me! His last gods,
Finally exposed as illusions, flee —
Greedy sans-culotte Death draws swiftly nigh;
But at last — he has Me.

De la Noye's pride was finally shattered. He sobbed like a child. At last he lifted a new face and said simply, "My son; M. du Chemin — please pray for me, that the Lord will yet receive me despite all the wrong I have done."

~*~*~

Midday on the 4th, Camille Durand could bear the strain no longer. Wrapping a threadbare shawl round her shoulders, she proceeded with trembling step toward the *Abbaye.*

In the harrowing hours since the massacre began (two days before), Camille was driven back to the religious remembrances of her youth. Broken prayers came to her lips — she groped in the shadowy dark for God, praying to the Virgin and to the Saints. Her former deeds tormented her now, and she bewailed her sins, promising candles…. How much she would have given now to never have arrested De la Noye — for then, her son — her only son — would not be in prison, facing a violent death….

She could have cried aloud in her inner torment, but she drew her hat down and hid her feelings as best as she could. At one street corner, a crowd was gathering round a newly-pasted City placard, and Camille drew near. It was an official circular, posted by Paris' Committee of Public Safety, and it read:

A part of the ferocious conspirators detained in the Prisons have been put to death by the People; and we cannot doubt but the whole Nation, driven to the edge of ruin by such endless series of treasons, will make haste to adopt this means of public salvation; and all Frenchmen will cry as the men of Paris: We go to fight the enemy; but we will not leave robbers behind us, to butcher our wives and children.

Under these words were affixed Marat's signature, "Friend of the People," and seven others. Camille hastened away, astonished. She remembered how she had once praised such men… had once believed they

512

were patriots standing up bravely for the downtrodden... *This glorious Revolution,* she thought bitterly, *is merely a* coup d'etat! *How wrong I was, thinking they were for Liberty, that they were freeing us from tyranny!*

Not every government leader actively encouraged the massacre, but those few who expostulated had no power—M. Roland (a member of the King's former "Patriot Ministry") wrote indignant messages, but they fell on deaf ears. The Mayor of Paris, Pétion, went farther—he actually went to the prisons and pleaded with the mob. But as soon as his back was turned, the bloodshed went on as before. The Legislative Assembly sent a little deputation to protest, but the delegates were received coldly and finally forced to retire—making this feeble excuse to the Assembly, "It was dark, and we could see but little."

Many government officials simply turned a blind eye, or, like Danton, said nothing but supported the bloodshed. They were partisans of the Revolution—most of them had risen to their positions because of their radical opinions. Why would they have done anything to stop it? Besides, if they opposed the slaughter, they might seem disloyal and in need of similar measures.

There was a great crowd in front of *l'Abbaye.* Camille shrank back at the blood-stained clothes and weapons, the fiendish, bestial faces... but near the gate to the prison, a man in a little black wig and puce-colored coat was haranguing the crowd. Camille saw his tri-color scarf and knew he was a city official, Jacques Billaud (general counsel of the Paris Commune). *Perhaps he is here to stop the murders!* Camille pressed through the crowd, her eyes on him. But suddenly she stopped and turned deathly pale.

"Brave Citizens," Billaud addressed red-stained butchers, "you are extirpating the Enemies of Liberty; you are at your duty. A grateful Commune and Country wish to recompense you adequately; but cannot, for you know its want of funds. Whoever shall have *worked—*" (here he grinned horribly) "*—in a Prison shall receive a draft of one *louis,* payable by our cashier. *Continue your work.*" [2]

The mob's shout of assent quailed Camille's heart. As Billaud left, he came in her direction, and through the gap thus made in the crowd Camille saw a horrible sight. Piled in heaps around the doorway of the *Abbaye,* right where Billaud had stood moments before, were mangled corpses, disfigured and ghastly. Camille staggered back with a half-stifled cry of horror. Her foot caught in the gutter and she fell backwards against a nearby wall, half-fainting.

But the instant she put down her hands, she thrust herself up again, for she had landed in a pool of wetness. She looked down at her hands. They were covered in blood. She bit her lips to keep back a scream. A stream of human blood ran in the gutter at her feet.

Camille, already at the zenith of horror, would have fainted straightway except for one thing—as she swayed back against the wooden wall, her eyes caught sight of a lean, dark-haired man among the murderers, gory sword in hand. His face and figure were caked with blood, but she knew him—*Denis!*

Fear kept her from fainting. She tottered away, even as the screams of new victims rent the air behind her. She no longer had any hope of seeing her son—for all she knew, he might already be lying in that dreadful heap of dead....

Her heart was broken, her dreams shattered, and the darkness of the world closed about her with ferocious malignity. In her distress, Camille found herself calling not upon painted images—the Virgin and the Saints—but on the God whom Berthe had found.

Camille had always resisted Berthe's pleas to leave the religion of her youth, but this horror was beyond the aid of her statues and saints. Only a God such as Berthe's could help her now.

The Past is Blotted Out

7.

Did I ever hold back?
Ah! One word, one look from you
Would have melted me even then —
Forgive? Aye, the past is blotted out
By your embrace!
— Ianthe

T he nightmarish hours passed on, their tune the victims' agonized screams and the killers' brutal shouts. For the three in the garret, the tramp of guards removing prisoners from other cells came at heart-stopping intervals.

The afternoon was red and old when De la Noye's quick ear heard rapid, booted feet marching their direction. Walking below the open trapdoor, he looked up. "I believe they have taken everyone else in this hall. It is our turn at last, my son. Be ready; we shall try to lure them beneath! Don't leap till they are close."

Jules was pale but determined. "I am ready, Father."

Once the light of the Gospel flooded his soul, Philip de la Noye was a changed man. Tears on his face, he had asked Jules for forgiveness, giving his own in return. Then the three had discussed the trapdoor. De la Noye suggested that Jules hide in it. M. du Chemin's square face grew thoughtful. "Perhaps," he said, "perhaps we could use it to defend ourselves. If two of us stood under it and the guards approach to take us, a third could leap from above, throwing them off guard and giving us at least a chance to fight for our lives." Though desperate, it seemed the only plan. Jules had said, "If we overpower the guards, we can make a dash for escape. I know it is hopeless, but…"

Now they would see…. Christophe du Chemin craned his stiff neck to look up at Jules, speaking rapidly as the guards' footsteps came closer, "Wait till they are immediately under, if possible, before you leap.

515

May God grant us success! If we fail we will die like men and shall be with our Lord, eternally blessed."

De la Noye nodded. He felt the plan to be hopeless, too, but in his eyes was a new peace—a peace beyond human understanding. A key grated noisily in the rusty lock. It was the end—but how De la Noye's heart swelled with the joy of knowing Christ! He shook his head at his hopeless, prideful folly and the horrors of Hell awaiting him before. *Lord, You have been merciful to me, a sinner.*

With a shriek, the door flew open.

Three men burst in—the short jailor named Canax and two blood-caked sans-culottes, one with a sword strapped to his body. The killers rushed under the trap-door, grabbing for De la Noye and Du Chemin, while the squat jailor stood back a pace, gloating. "Good work, Gilles and Thibaut! Soft-hearted Pierre took a fancy to you prisoners, I deem, and put you up here, thinking you'd escape notice," the jailor cackled, "but I—Hey! Where is the young—"

Gilles, the burlier of the sans-culottes, was reaching for Du Chemin's silk sleeve, grating, "Come with us, you cursed aristocrat!"

Jules jumped directly on him. Yelling in astonishment and pain, Gilles crumpled to the ground. But even as he fell he seized Jules' arm, holding him close while his other hand sought the bloody dagger in his belt.

"How now! What's this?" his companion Thibaut shouted, unstrapping his sword to face De la Noye, while the jailor grappled with M. du Chemin.

While rummaging in the tiny barren attic earlier, Jules had found a stick of wood and had given it to his father. Now De la Noye raised it, parrying the thrusts of his sword-wielding opponent. As Jules wrestled with Gilles, trying to hold back the man's knife-arm, he noticed that at each sword-thrust, De la Noye's stick splintered, being cut smaller and smaller....Now it was a mere stump; now it was gone. Thibaut lunged forward, success in his hands....

Desperately, Jules twisted, rolling over and over with his combatant, trying to knock his father's assailant off balance with their writhing bodies....They were between the men's legs now. Suddenly Gilles dropped his knife and gripped Jules hard, stopping their roll. "Run him through, Thibaut!" he called. "I've got him fast!"

"With pleasure, Comrade Gilles," Thibaut sneered, stepping close. He aimed a cautionary thrust at De la Noye that sent him staggering against the wall to avoid it.

Jules struggled, to no avail, in Gilles' iron grip. Thibaut's blade darted forward like a snake—closer, closer.... *At least we made a go of it, and did not die tamely,* Jules thought.

"No!" With a cry, De la Noye threw himself before the descending blade.

Before Jules even scrambled to his feet, he knew his father was dead. De la Noye's falling body broke Gilles' hold on Jules, and Jules surged upwards with burning passion, leaping at the swordsman, heedless of his own life. Taken totally by surprise, Thibaut crashed heavily backward, losing his sword in a wild effort to save himself. His head hit the stone wall with a loud crack, and he crumpled and did not move.

Jules swayed to his feet. But burly Gilles had crawled from under De la Noye's body and had the sword now. Out of the corner of his eye, Jules saw M. du Chemin thrashing about, gripping the stout jailor's weapon-hand, obviously weakening—but he could do nothing to help. Hopelessly, he dodged away from Gilles' sword. *It's all over.*

One sound sparked a tiny flicker of hope and at the same time extinguished it utterly. Heavy boots clattered down the hall towards their cell. *More butchers! Lord, I commend my soul to You!*

The swordsman lunged. Jules twisted to the side and slipped. As he fell, his shoulderblades tensed for the coming sword-thrust.

But it never came. Instead, the killer crumpled on top of him. Astonished, Jules twisted upwards—and met the eyes of Marcel Martin!

Wiping his bloody sword, Marcel extended a hand. "Jules? Are you hurt?"

Jules could only stare. He saw a sturdy jailor (Pierre) pluck M. du Chemin's assailant off him and hurl him across the room. He lay still. "He was a bad one," Pierre muttered simply. Then he spoke to M. du Chemin; "You are wounded, monsieur."

Tristan was leaning over De la Noye.

"He is dead," Jules choked. "He died to save me." He knelt beside Tristan, dry-eyed with shock. "My own father..."

Tenderly, he closed his father's eyes. As he crossed De la Noye's arms, a paper crackled. *The letter he wrote this afternoon, and told me to deliver if he could not!* Jules remembered. His hand shook, but he could read the name on the outside: "Camille." As Jules tucked it inside his blouse, a hand was laid on his shoulder.

"We must hustle, lads," the jailor Pierre boomed. "Others may be along any minute."

"He would not wish you to risk your life by lingering," Tristan's compassionate eyes were fixed on Jules' face. "Besides, you have a commission...." he nodded towards the letter.

"Yes." Jules seemed to awaken. He noticed that Marcel had bound M. du Chemin's bleeding arm and exchanged his embroidered silk coat for a rough sans-culotte disguise.

"Come, Jules; we can do nothing for him. He died nobly, trusting in our Lord Christ," M. du Chemin put his hand on Jules' arm.

"We must swagger carelessly in the corridors; some of the killers have been helping the guards bring out prisoners, so mayhap no one will notice us—at least, that is our only hope," Tristan said hurriedly.

Marcel handed the blood-stained weapons of their attackers to Jules and Du Chemin ("Swing them about!" he directed), then nodded to Tristan.

"Let's go—and may God aid the right!" Tristan said.

They hurried into the hall. Though he knew the need for haste, Jules cast one long, last tear-dimmed look at his father's body. More noble than ever in life, Philip Emile de la Noye lay there, his handsome face forever still. *Lord, help me to always remember his sacrifice, and live my life in accordance,* Jules prayed, his heart broken for the father he had known only too late.

Massive Pierre led the way down the stone corridor, pausing to listen at the downward-leading stairs. Apparently satisfied, he started down, the others in a loose group behind. It seemed counter-intuitive to stomp along—but they must appear as careless Brigands, roaming the prison for fresh victims.

Booted feet echoed from one of the branching corridors, and Pierre turned abruptly down a side-hall. The low roof increased the oppressive atmosphere. After a minute of breathless anxiety (but outward insouciance), they turned down a new hall. The shouts and cries from the street were louder now.

Presently a dark, gaping hole at the end of the hall showed a stairway; they quickened their pace. But a moment later, the head and shoulders of a brawny man emerged up the stairs. Others tramped up after him. There was nothing else to do but go forward and chance it. Repressing the impulse to turn and run, they sauntered down the hall.

"You've got quite a troop, Comrade," the first man, a jailor, addressed Pierre. The three Brigands behind him were splashed with clotting blood, looking a lot like rumpled and bloody Jules and M. du Chemin. "Taking a group of loyal helpers as I am, eh?"

"What would you expect, Comrade?" His big body slouching, Pierre gave no appearance of haste or concern. "But most of the upper cells are empty now."

"Eh? Well, there are several on this floor," the other replied. "'So long!" He passed by with the Brigands, and Pierre's group tromped loudly down the stairs.

As they reached the bottom, Pierre led them away from the noise of the tribunal and instead took a crooked little stone corridor. It dead-ended at last: a small, heavily-barred portal blocked further progress. In a moment Pierre had his keys out and was sticking one in the lock. It did not fit. The tension mounted. Pierre pawed hastily at his key-ring.

"Out in the street, we will split in two groups. Marcel, you take Jules," Tristan whispered. "We'll meet at Camille's."

The jailor tried another key—this time, it turned. With a quietness belied by his size, he slid the door open, motioning "hurry!" There was no time to express their deep gratefulness. Marcel and Jules darted into the street, followed almost instantaneously by Tristan and his father. They had hardly gone five paces when the door closed and locked behind them. They were in the back alley of the *Abbaye*—where Tristan and Marcel had waited in agonized suspense those many, many hours. Marcel and Jules turned to the right; Tristan and M. du Chemin sauntered rapidly to the left.

They were soon forced to slow their pace: M. du Chemin was weak from loss of blood. Tristan and Marcel had agreed that, if they *could* rescue them, they would stop to rest and eat at Camille's. Then, when darkness cleared the streets, they would travel the farther, more-dangerous stretch to Margot's. Tristan realized that his father's exhaustion was another reason for the necessity of a stop at Camille's.

People sauntered through the streets, but not many gave a second glance to a stalwart sans-culotte youth with a sword strapped across his body—booty, no doubt—and a shuffling middle-aged man in dirty, bloodstained clothes. Du Chemin's tiredness did much to break down his aristocrat ways and make him walk like a commoner.

Tristan prayed that Marcel and Jules were faring equally well—and yet he knew it would take just one passerby to ruin everything. Their flight was not over—it was just beginning. But his heart filled with intoxicating joy—they were out of that hellish place! He was with his father once more: now, whatever came, they would face it together.

~*~*~

In darkling space down dropt the red sun, slain,

With all his banners drooping. Far and wide
Spread desolation's vast and blackening tide.

There was a brief lull in the steady egress of victims. Denis' eyes narrowed as he dispassionately viewed the huddled mounds of corpses. Denis' face was working—but not with any shadow of remorse or tender feelings. Anyone would have shuddered at his keen, hateful look—he meant evil towards someone.

His dark eyes flicked over to a prison guard leaning against the *Abbaye* entrance. A severed hand rested on the blood-red cobbles in Denis' path—he kicked it unceremoniously aside and splashed through the pools of blood to the guard.

"Comrade," Denis addressed the guard, "Have you noticed if a blond sans-culotte youth—Jules Durand—or an aquiline-nosed, fetching aristocrat—Philip de la Noye—have passed through?"

"*Ma foi!* It's enough to remember my own name!" the guard laughed. Then his eyes met Denis', and he sobered. "I cannot be certain, but I should think not, Citizen. I would have noticed De la Noye—accursedly handsome and proud, is he not?"

Denis nodded abruptly, then sank his chin on his chest. "I am sure they have not been brought out," he muttered to himself, clenching his fist. Strapping on his bloody sword ("borrowed" from some Royalist's), he turned again to the guard.

"They are still in there—" he jerked a thumb upwards at the building, "—I believe they have been overlooked. They must be brought to justice, Comrade."

"Surely," the guard answered. "Your zeal is commendable, Citizen. Come, we will find them."

Pressing through the door, they entered the main room, where the "Court of Justice" presided. The "President," or head judge, was a grey-coated man with a sword at his side. He stood leaning his hands on a table and addressing a frail elderly prisoner—the prisoner none other than old Marshall Maillé, who had gone to defend the King on the Tenth. Ten men were near the President, some seated, others lounging against the walls, others laying on the benches in exhaustion. An elderly turnkey and two men in bloody shirts stood at the door into the prison.

Denis and the guard with him paused, waiting for the "trial" to end. Two National Guards, one drunk, were presenting an appeal from the Section of Croix Rouge in favor of Maillé.

Coldly, the Head Judge answered, "They are useless, these appeals for traitors."

"It is frightful; your judgment is a murder!" exclaimed old Marshal Maillé.

"My hands are washed of it; take M. Maillé away," the President answered.

With brutish countenances, the guards drove the frail elderly man into the street, where he was cut down.

Careless of the old man's brutal demise, Denis and the gaoler were already questioning the turnkey as to the whereabouts of prisoners Jules Durand and Philip de la Noye.

Wrinkling his forehead, the turnkey fiddled his key-ring between pudgy fingers. "I cannot recall..." his voice faded, then he said, "Ask Bernard or Pierre; they did much of the shifting of prisoners a few days agone."

As Denis and his companion entered the bowels of the prison, a brown-haired, nervous prisoner was already facing the grim Tribunal.

As the two searched the corridors for Bernard, they met groups of uncouth men hauling fresh prisoners. At last, turning another corner, the gaoler exclaimed with satisfaction. "Bernard!"

The grizzle-headed jailor turned, accompanied by two blood-stained patriots. "Ah—Comrade—what is the news?"

"This Citizen desires to make sure that two guilty prisoners stand before the tribunal," Denis' gaoler companion replied. "Would you know where a Jules Durand or that proud dark-haired Philip de la Noye were placed?"

Bernard rubbed his stubbly chin reflexively. "The first name has no meaning to me, but I remember we moved that suave nobleman....now where....ah! That was it! He and two others were relocated to that little unused garret-room—I warrant me that it was overlooked. Yes, he and two others were taken there."

"Thank you, Citizen!" Denis' face lit up. He turned to his companion. "Can you lead me there?"

Bernard answered. "I can take him; if you, Comrade take these."

"Sure, Bernard. Thanks, Comrade."

While the others tramped off, Denis and Bernard wound through more passages, moving upward to the second floor, then the third. At last, the gaoler stopped at a small door in a remote corner. Denis eagerly watched the man fit a key into the keyhole.

Protesting, the door swung open. They both gasped. Huddled about the room were four bodies.

"What—!" Darting forward, Denis stooped over the first body, while Bernard bent over another.

"This one's all laid out like for a funeral—it's one of the prisoners we put in here," Bernard's voice was puzzled.

Denis glanced over. "De la Noye!" he hissed. "These sans-culottes are as dead as doornails, too."

"Here's Canax, a fellow-jailor," Bernard said. "Where are the two other prisoners?"

A movement answered him—the huddled jailor moaned and stirred. Denis sprang to the corner bucket and splashed water on the man's face.

Finally the man was in a condition to talk, though he still cradled his head in his hands as if he was afraid it would fall off or blow up. His mumbled tale was short and easily told—the prisoners had fought back—"young man dropped from somewhere"—Thibaut had killed De la Noye—and just when he and Gilles were about to kill the two remaining prisoners, he was seized and flew through the air—he remembered no more.

"You don't know who came and attacked you?" Bernard asked.

"No," Canax muttered. "Just when I was about to run that middle-aged fellow through..." He subsided in pain.

Bernard queried further, but Denis retreated into his own thoughts. *They must have somehow sneaked out! It is just possible—these corridors have been busy with people other than the jailors....If so, where would they go? Jules would go to his mother...or would he?* He spoke to Bernard. "I thank you for your aid, Comrade Bernard. I think I know where at least one of these vile escapees has fled. I will bring him back to be punished, if he is there." Denis' malevolent face was full of an intense purpose that was hardly ever thwarted. *I shall get them, never fail.*

"I wish you success," Bernard said mechanically. Even as he helped Canax up, Benard remembered Canax's reputation for cruelty and for a moment was almost glad the blonde youth had escaped. Then, "coming to his senses," he told himself sternly, *No doubt this Citizen is right in pressing for their deaths.* Supporting Canax, Bernard lingered, re-locking the door of the death-scene. Denis' feet were already hasting down the stairs.

Entering the extemporaneous "Court of Justice" once more, Denis noted that the prisoner standing before the judges was the same one whose trial was beginning when he went upstairs. *A longer trial than usual.* He paused, for the President was speaking.

"I see nothing to suspect this man: I am for granting him his liberty. Is this your vote?" the "President" finished, turning towards the judges.

"*Oui, oui*, it is just," they replied.

The men outside, who moments before had been waiting fiendishly hack the prisoner to pieces, joined the rough rejoicing at this reprieve. As the man exited, his would-be killers received him with embraces and hysterical cries of joy. How strange—but stranger still their inhuman delight as they massacred the next prisoners! An English eyewitness, Earl Gower, saw another instance of acquittal:

"*To be convinced of what I could not believe, I made a visit to the prison of the Abbaye about seven o'clock on Monday evening, for the slaughter had not ceased. . . .Two of the Municipality were then in the prison with some of the mob distributing their justice. Those they found guilty were seemingly released, but only to be precipitated by the door on a number of piques, and then among the savage cries of vive la nation, to be hacked to pieces by those that had swords and were ready to receive them. After this their dead bodies were dragged by the arms or legs...[and] laid up in heaps till carts could carry them away. The kennel was swimming with blood, and a bloody track was traced from the prison to the Abbaye door where they had dragged these unfortunate people.*

"*I was fortunate enough to be present when five men were acquitted. Such a circumstance, a by-stander told me, had not happened in the operations of the horrid tribunal; and these inconsistent murderers seemed nearly as much pleased at the acquittal of a prisoner as they were at his condemnation. The same congratulations attended the others that were acquitted and the same those that were condemned. Nothing can exceed the inconsistency of these people.*"

Denis' face darkened, however, at this acquittal, and he shouldered his way out into the gory street, turning rapid steps towards Camille's. If Jules was at his mother's, Denis would capture him. *What an exquisite torture it shall be, to snatch him away again when Camille has just received him back as from the dead! Mayhap I will include her in the arrest, as well.*

~*~*~

Tristan and his father approached Camille's tiny hovel with great relief. M. du Chemin was exhausted, and the chances of recognition in the streets were nerve-wracking. Though, if Tristan had known the implacable Denis was already on their track, he would have risked all to press on and put as many crooked streets as possible between themselves and this deceptively-safe resting spot. But he did not know—and he hailed the sight of Camille's with gratefulness.

Tristan recognized a familiar duo entering the far end of the road. Otherwise, the streets were deserted. He stepped quickly up to Camille's door and knocked.

Camille opened cautiously, her face wan and hopeless beyond words. She drew aside to let Tristan and his scrubby, tottering companion enter.

"What news?" she whispered, the horror of her terrible visit to the prison still prominent in her pale grey eyes.

"Marcel will be here in a moment," Tristan replied. "This is my father—we were able to rescue him from those butchers. And—"

Camille turned towards M. du Chemin, who had sunk upon a stool. "I have some bread, and I will get some water."

As she was in the kitchen, muffled bumps heralding her haste, Marcel and Jules slipped in the front door.

"My mother?" Jules asked.

"She is in the kitchen," Tristan replied. "Step back a bit, into the corner—we must try to break things to her gently."

The shadows already lay thick in the shop. With six-story tenements crowding on all sides, twilight came to the street-level long before it came to the upper reaches. Marcel and Tristan held a whispered consultation, their faces joyful that they had succeeded so far, but tense with the still-present danger.

"I shall go outside as lookout. In an hour or two, it will be dark enough to leave for Margot's," Tristan said quietly.

The kitchen door opened and Camille stepped out, bearing a loaf on a wooden trencher. She handed it to M. du Chemin.

"Madame, we were able to rescue someone else," Tristan began.

Turning sharply, Camille looked up to see her son Jules standing before her. With a cry, she threw herself into his arms, broken exclamations tumbling from her lips amid sobs of joy.

At last Jules said, "Mother, I am only here because someone gave his life for mine."

Camille's eyes filled with amazed gratitude. "Who? Who, my son? Ah, I shall be grateful to him forever!"

In answer, Jules pulled the letter from his pocket. "He wrote this to you before he died." Seeing the handwriting, Camille gave a cry, as if in pain. Her hands shook as she opened it and read:

My dear Camille,

It is too late for me to tell you with my lips what I would; but, indeed, it took these dire straits for God to break me and turn my sinful heart to Him. I do not expect that you will forgive the great wrong I did you, but mayhap once I am dead you may, in some later year, think of me with a little kindness.

I beseech you, Camille, on my knees. I did wrong. Nothing can change the past, but I ask that you would forgive me for the original wrong and for my selfish, hardhearted actions afterwards. How God has rived my heart in these last few hours as I think of my many sins.

It amazes me to think that the Lord Christ has forgiven me, but I know for a certainty that He has. All has been paid in full. Through His innocent sacrifice, I, a vile sinner, am now prepared to meet Death — and the Righteous Judge who will try us all at the end of time.

And indeed my time on earth is short. I must draw this letter to a close. I commend our son to you — I pray that he will escape the murderers. He is all a father could wish for — a son in whom, all too late, I rejoice. But it was my pride that kept me from knowing him earlier; I lay all the blame on myself.

Adieu, Camille — I pray that you will find my Saviour. Mayhap I will meet you once more in Heaven when the tears of this world are past.

Your repentant
Philip Emile de la Noye

Pillowing her head on her son's shoulder, Camille shook with sobs. "Oh, Philip," she moaned, "Philip! I forgive you! You have atoned for any wrong you did me — you have given me a priceless gift; our son. Oh Philip, I always loved you!"

A Final Duel

8.

Tel est pris qui croyait prendere —
It's the biter bit;
He is taken who thought he could take.
— French proverb

*T*ristan ensconced himself in a caliginous nook a little distance from Camille's door. Twilight was falling, but it was not yet dark enough to make a dash to Margot's, so Tristan was standing guard. Neither he nor Marcel felt secure at Camille's, knowing Denis' keen, vengeful mind. But they hoped he would be preoccupied with the massacres. It might be hours before the garret-room was checked — perhaps not until the wholesale murders ended and usual prison routine resumed.

Tristan let his body relax completely against the corner while keeping every sense alert and ready. With a faint rumble, a cart lumbered down a nearby street…closer, the wail of a fretful baby….

Used to seeing in the far darker gloom of night, his eyes picked out a swift shape scuttling around the street-corner into the ragged shadow of a tenement. Tristan focused on a lighter spot ahead, and was rewarded with another glimpse as the figure slipped into the next shadow. Was it edging towards Camille's? *Perhaps it's an escaped prisoner or aristocrat trying to hide,* Tristan thought, but didn't believe it. This man was an adept — Tristan almost missed his dashes from cover to cover. Growing in his mind were the letters of one name: *Denis.*

Almost opposite Camille's, the secretive figure ducked into a pocket of shadow and remained there, hidden. But Tristan had glimpsed the lean face. It *was* Denis.

The shades of Camille's shop were drawn; no view could be had of those inside. Tristan wondered what Denis' next move would be. He had not long to wait. After tense minutes, in which (he did not doubt) Denis was studying the house for clues, Denis went to a tenement-door directly across from Camille's. His knocking echoed ominously in the otherwise quiet street.

After a moment's delay a weary half-grown girl appeared, bouncing a sobbing baby. Tristan could not hear, but saw by Denis' face that he'd gained the information he wanted. He slipped a piece of money in the girl's hand, and turned, a sneer of triumph on his face. *Unless he is stopped, all is lost!* Tristan realized. With rapid steps, Denis started off down the street.

With a casualness he did not feel, Tristan left his hiding place and sauntered after him. *Can I somehow warn Marcel, then lure Denis down a side street so they could make a dash for it? No doubt he has confederates close by….I could throw a pebble against Camille's window — but no, Denis might hear that and then the game will be up!* He lengthened his steps after Denis — *I have to catch him before he brings reinforcements!*

Denis was turning into a small cross-alley when Tristan got close enough to call. "Hail, Citizen," he said affably. *"Nouvelles?"*

Denis turned with almost a start. But his voice was just as *dégagé* as he answered, "News? Of the grandest sort, Citizen! Justice is proceeding right fine at the prisons. Have you been there?"

"Of a certainty," Tristan replied. They had paused in the alley. His mind was working with desperate rapidity.

"So've I," Denis' face was full of grim laughter. "You can see that by my clothes." Then he grew confidential. "You look a rising revolutionary, Citizen, and I have work of the most patriotic stamp to accomplish. Some escaped prisoners, aristocrats, are in a house on that street — " Tristan's dry eyes followed his pointing finger, " — and I'm going around the corner to get some patriots to help arrest them. Will you come along to aid me?"

Though Denis' eyes were still full of rough friendliness, there was a certain firm tension of his chin which told Tristan that Denis was determined to have him come: *Perhaps he suspects me….*

"And yet you shall not do so, Denis — stand on guard!" Tristan's voice rang in the stillness, and his sword flashed in the waning light.

Denis' eyes shifted, but that was his only indication of surprise. Wrenching his clotted sword from its scabbard, he stared strangely at Tristan. An instant later he lunged viciously forward: Tristan leapt nimbly out of the way, parrying the thrust with a vigorous side-stroke.

Now recognition flashed into Denis' eyes. Something about the battle carriage of his opponent, the way he squared his shoulders…. *"Tristan!"* he cried fiercely. "Curse you!" He swept his sword round in a mighty blow—and it was again blocked by the steady, darting steel of Tristan's blade.

"I shall conquer this time!" Denis' face contorted with deadly hate. "Finish you, and then your friends!"

Denis soon controlled his first furious passion, resuming his usual cool, calculating deadliness. Thrust and parry, keeping a firm, deft wrist, leaping lightly forwards and backwards as occasion dictated....

The weathered grey giants of tenements towered over them, staring down with impassive, blind eyes at the two small, dark figures darting and thrusting against the pale cobbles. It was unusual that there were no human eyes to see—but all Paris was jarred out of its usual business during these bloody days. The world was blind to the duel—but life and death hung in the balance nonetheless.

On and on they fought, Tristan's unsullied sword and Denis' besmeared one meeting again and again with clashes to wake the echoes. Tristan's mind concentrated on one fact: *I must conquer! Denis must not summon others! He must be stopped!*

All at once, with a clever twist, Denis' sword danced round Tristan's. Belatedly, Tristan leapt back. A searing pain stabbed his upper arm. *First blood,* he thought grimly.

But there was no time to even glance at his wound, though he felt warm blood trickling down his sleeve. His eyes were on Denis: Tristan's blade responded almost quicker than thought as he saw the turn Denis' sword took for each new stroke.

He knew now why Denis had that scar on his cheek—he was an excellent swordsman. Tristan had no time for anything but a few disjointed, fervent petitions to God—he was fighting with every nerve and fibre, fighting for his life.

Adele's face came to mind, and he gritted his teeth. He *had* to win! He had to! Calling up every trick he had ever learned, his sword flashed desperately. Purple sunset clouds closed in overhead. *Oh Lord, help me, Lord!*

After minutes of strenuous conflict, Tristan noted Denis' ragged breath, milliseconds-slower defenses. *He is tiring!* Denis had been butchering people for hours, and his sword-arm was showing the strain. Tristan's blade felt the difference, and he pressed forward in a desperate offensive.

But Tristan, too, was failing—he felt a creeping weakness as his arm bled on. Gritting his teeth, he ignored it, dealing stroke after stroke, thrust after parry. Ever so slightly, Denis' defense was yielding....

Denis' face grew dark, and he rallied, driving Tristan back with intense, violent blows. He was the heavier and more hardened. He knew, as Tristan did, that if he could hold till Tristan weakened from blood loss....

Parrying a looping thrust, Tristan feinted high, then whipped his sword under Denis' still-upraised blade and lunged deeply forward. As Denis vaulted back, his foot slipped on the blood-dabbled road. Tristan's sword-hilt thudded home, and Denis fell backwards on the cobbles. He glared up for one instant, then his face crumpled into the staring look of the dead.

His chest heaving, Tristan pulled out his sword, wiping it mechanically. Staring down at the motionless figure, many things flashed through his mind: their youthful spying on Denis in Le Havre; Denis using Berthe to rob the Le Merciers; how she had repented after being forced to accompany the 'March of Women;' the countless hours of search for the 'knife-in-back' robber; discovering that Denis was the thief; Denis' disappearance, then reappearance to wreak vengeance on Jules and Camille...and now the end.

"Justice is done," he said soberly, dragging Denis' body to a dark corner. The movement set his left arm throbbing, reminding him of his wound. Tearing off a portion of Denis' jacket-skirt, he tied it tightly round his arm. He would have to attend to it properly later—but Time was the most precious thing now. They must be on their way to Margot's as soon as possible. Denis might have told someone else about Camille's.

Sheathing his sword, he started briskly down the street. Despite a ringing, vapid sensation in his head, his heart sang with a Psalm:

Blessed be the Lorde my strength, which teacheth mine hands to fight, and my fingers to battlle. He is my goodnes and my fortresse, my towre and my deliverer, my shield, and in Him I trust...

~*~*~

Four days—from Sunday the 2nd to Thursday the 6th. Four days of massacre—massacre which still brings horror to the human heart after two hundred years. But all things must end at last. On the 6th the killings finally drew to a close. When all was done, one-half of Paris' prisoners were dead. The number of those murdered: one thousand eighty-nine to one thousand four hundred.

One thousand and several hundred human souls! The cries of the men, women, yea, even children still ring in our ears.

529

Yet was not this the same France—the same Paris—that two hundred and twenty years before, on Saint Bartholomew's Day, murdered an estimated 10,000 to 20,000 Huguenots on the queen of France's orders? Those Huguenots not slain fled, leaving France without salt and light. When God is thrown out and a false god erected, His commandments are cast by the wayside.

Woodenly, the government of Paris moved on to the next item of business—the disposing of the dead bodies. Carters were paid to load and haul the mangled remains, vast featureless holes were dug, large quantities of quick-lime purchased, buriers employed...as if it was all part of a day's work. The Septemberers, *Septembriseurs*, as the killers were called, were each paid punctually by the City for the "work" they had done. In fact, city records referred to the killers as:

"*...workers employed in preserving the salubrity of the air in the Prisons, and persons who presided over these dangerous operations.*"

Driven and tossed by her godless philosophies, spurning God and following her heart as the arbiter of Right and Wrong, her conscience calloused by impenitence, France marched on towards the Terror.

This was only a foretaste. The bloodthirsty reign of *La Guillotine* was yet to begin.

~*~*~

The pale sun approached its zenith, and an autumn wind lashed the crooked streets, fingering loose boards and hinges as it passed. Sashes quivered in sympathy, adding their complaints to the whining of tiles and joists.

A small, incongruous group gathered in a cramped, gaunt tenement. The walls were notoriously thin, but the wind covered their talk. A little three-legged brazier huddled against one wall, adding a stunted warmth to the chilly room. Disguised as English stevedores, Tristan, his father, and Marcel were bidding goodbye to their friends.

"Last night when we talked," M. du Chemin looked at Jules and Camille, "you had some plans. Have you come to a conclusion? I am sore grieved to think of leaving you both here—I wish with all my heart we could take you with us."

The bitter lines that had marred Camille's face were gone. She looked younger; something like the beauty of former days rested on her face—though there was a new and lasting sorrow there, too. "Jules and I cannot pass as English," she said. "Now that Denis is dead, my house is most likely safe. We shall stay there."

"We should be as secure at home as anywhere in this accursed city," Jules said grimly. "Our neighbors know Mother and I are patriots. When it is safe, we would like to move somewhere else—perhaps near Father's estate, or mayhap to England. France has no beauty for us now."

"I pray that you will be safe." The fire's orange glow pulsed across M. du Chemin's wide face. "May you prosper wherever you go. It would give me great delight to meet in England some fair day in the future." A bell throbbed outside above the noise of the wind. "We must bid adieu," he said reluctantly.

Jules bid farewell to Marcel and Tristan with emotion, saying hoarsely, "How much I owe you, Comrades! If Adele had not brought us together...and what grand times we had, patrolling! Your example then helped soften my heart—and you rescued me...." He wrung their hands. "May you escape safely!"

"I wish with all my heart you were coming with us, but you are right to assist your mother. May God prosper and protect you, whatever betide," Tristan answered. "Adieu, *my comrade!*"

Her eyes filled with tears, Camille was speaking with M. du Chemin. Turning from his friends, Jules spoke to him as well. "To you, sir, I owe my salvation—a more precious thing than even life itself."

"No, my son in Christ; you owe your salvation to our Lord. May His Name be glorified!" Du Chemin replied reverently. "May the Lord strengthen you in His narrow path! Keep the New Testament I gave you, and read it often."

Margot and Robert had slipped out a few minutes before to make sure the passage was clear. She came back in now.

"No one in sight, Monsieur," she whispered, her hand on the knob.

"Oh, God *bless* you, sieurs—and may you never want for anything!" Camille cried, her face streaked with tears.

Just before Margot opened the door, M. du Chemin paused once more, raising his hand in a gesture of blessing.

"I will leave you with these words from Psalm twenty: '*The Lorde heare thee in the day of trouble: the name of the God of Jaakob defend thee: Send thee helpe from the Sanctuarie, and strengthen thee out of Zion. ...And graunt thee according to thine heart, and fulfill all thy purpose: That we may rejoyce in thy salvation, and set up the banner in the Name of our God, when the Lord shall performe all thy petitions. ...Now know I that the Lord will helpe his anointed, and will heare him from his Sanctuarie, by the mightie helpe of his right hand. Some*

trust in chariots, & some in horses: but we will remember the Name of the Lord our God. They are brought downe and fallen, but we are risen, and stand upright.'"
With a final wave, the three left the room after Margot.

Once more, farewell!
And if we meet hereafter, we shall meet
In happier climes, and on a safer shore.

Down the creaking, empty passageways, all doors were closed. They met no one until they came upon Robert in the little hall at the back door. "God bless you, sieurs," he said.

"God be with you, Robert, and your family," M. du Chemin replied. "Words can never express our gratitude to you and Pierre."

Half-opening the door, Robert scanned the street. "All clear, sir."

Holding their hats against the wind, Tristan and Marcel stepped into the gusty street. Placing something in Margot's hands, M. du Chemin strode after them. Scraps of garbage and paper flew past, alternately tumbling along the street and sailing erratically in the air. Lord willing, this was their last view of Paris—but would their impersonations hold? *Qui vivra verra*—Time would tell.

Margot and Robert stood watching them go. Presently she said in a muted voice, "Robert—do you remember the place in the Book where I read about entertaining angels unawares?" Robert was illiterate, and Margot had to read aloud from the Bible De Duret had given them almost a year before.

"Yes, I think," Robert answered, his eyes on the three as they turned a final corner and disappeared from sight.

"I—I believe we have been entertaining angels, Robert—we need not worry that you quit your job as a jailor." Her voice was drowned in tears. A heavy bag clinked musically in her frail hands.

~*~*~

At the quays, a long and narrow yawl was a scene of bustling activity. Sailors and dockworkers scurried up and down the gangplank, carrying aboard last-minute items. The stout captain stood on deck, barking orders to his small crew. In Rouen, many miles closer to the sea, goods would be transferred from smallish boats like this to larger craft and taken the rest of the way down the Seine and across the ocean channel.

Anonymous

At the foot of the gangplank stood an official, smart in tricolor uniform. A guardsman stood stolidly beside him. They were there to prevent any contraband or aristocrats from escaping—the city was a sealed death-trap.

Five Englishmen were carrying various-sized bundles from a pile on the dock to stow them aboard the vessel. One of the group, a middle-aged man, seemed not as strong as a usual dockworker, and another, a handsome youth, covertly favored his left arm when lifting and carrying. Directing the operation was a white-haired Englishman with a hearty face. At last, all packed neatly aboard, he spoke to his men in English. "We must present our papers."

They followed him down the gangplank, drawing up in front of the official. The latter scrutinized them suspiciously.

Pulling a sheaf of papers from his pocket, the bluff-faced leader spoke in French, bowing to the official, "Citizen, my name is Thaddaeus Barker, and I and these my men—Joshua Crump, Reuben Cook, Harold Smith, William Jameson, and George Miller—are slated to sail on this ship. Here are our papers."

The official took the papers, but instead of perusing them, he keenly scanned the six men. The atmosphere was electric—*What is the official thinking?* He was eyeing them with deep distrust. At last he said, "I am not sure these passes are valid. Due to the escape of so many foul,

533

traitorous aristocrats, my superior must be advised." With a stiff bow, he walked off, leaving the guardsman to block the gangplank.

I hope the passes hold, Barker thought, a crease of worry on his usually-jolly face. *They've never called another official before! Things change so rapidly in this accursed city that a proper pass one day becomes useless the next.*

Despite the wind, the air grew suddenly stifling and close. *Will we be refused permission to leave? Will we be recognized?* The hunt for aristocrats tightened every day…hardly any managed to escape from the city, though a myriad of disguises were tried.

Though outwardly casual, inside they were tense with worry. A bead of sweat rolled down M. du Chemin's face—or rather, "Reuben Cook's." As he pulled his hat down across his eyes, his companions knew he was praying. They were too.

The End of this Tale, and the Beginning of Another

9.

Be still my soul: thy best, thy heavenly Friend
Thro' thorny ways leads to a joyful end.
Be still my soul: when change and tears are past,
All safe and blessed we shall meet at last.
— Katharina von Schlegel

Quietly, Adele passed through their gilded English residence. It lay among the pastoral south-east suburbs of London. Through the open library doors she saw Olivie and Paulette, a children's book open on their laps. Adele paused to listen.

"When Tommy has a mind to ride," Olivie read aloud, bending her head close to Paulette's, "he pulls a little bridle out of his pocket, whips it upon honest Jowler—"

"Look—Olivie, do you see? Jowler is a dog—he rides a dog!" interjected Paulette, giggling.

"Yes, a dog; how amusing," Olivie twinkled, then resumed her reading: "—and away he gallops tantwivy. As he rides through the town he frequently stops at the doors to know how the good children do within, and if they are good and learn their books, he leaves an apple, and away he gallops again tantwivy tantwivy."

"Tantwivy, tantwivy," Paulette relished the word. "*Tantwivy, tantwivy...*"

Down the hall, Adele saw the butler opening the front door. Honore stood on the stone steps just without, bidding farewell to several mounted young Englishmen, sons of neighboring gentry. His voice reached Adele. "You are most welcome to enter and partake of afternoon tea."

"I would accept your offer most gladly, were it not that we have an engagement elsewhere," one replied.

"Give our most humble respects to your lovely sisters, and convey to them that we shall most certainly take up your offer another time," the other said. "It was a pleasure to ride with you, M. le Mercier."

"I must claim the same pleasure," Honore replied courteously.

Raising their hats in answer to Honore's bow, the youths touched their gleaming steeds and set off at a lively pace down the graveled path.

Once they turned into the road, Honore entered the house. Adele saw the shadow on his face, and heard his half-audible words: "Oh, for my Roland, and a good gallop with Tristan!" He drew in his breath sharply. "Ah! Lord! How fares it with *Tristan?* And *Marcel?* Protect them, Lord!"

Adele's heart echoed his pained cry. Before she was betrothed to Tristan, she had learned that doing the little duties of each day, being faithful in the small responsibilities, was the best method to keep from giving way. The lesson stood her in good stead now, in these heart-wrenching days of waiting. And there was so much to learn—strange customs, the idioms of the language, and more. Elisabeth la Motte and her family lived in Lewisham; it was a comfort to have another French family within driving distance.

In the parlor, her father and Charles were discussing an arithmetic problem. Grandpapa de Duret sat in a deep armchair nearby, reading a hefty tome. Near the open windows, framed by the glowing Autumn landscape, her mother sat tatting on a low divan. Adele went to her and curtsied.

"Yes, Adele?" her mother looked up with a sweet smile.

"Mother, I had a question about the dinner tonight—" That was far as she got, for with a clatter of hooves, a middle-aged rider appeared on the drive outside. Adele glimpsed his face through the window. "The younger M. Barker!"

Her father said, "He may bring news—perhaps even a letter from Paris?"

Adele wished she could keep her heart from fluttering spasmodically. Outwardly decorous, she seated herself with a white face beside her mother. The news that there was a visitor flew swiftly through the house—before he entered, Honore, Olivie, and Paulette had gathered in the parlor.

The young people rose, curtseying or bowing, as M. Archibald Barker came in. Archibald was a younger version of his brother Thaddaeus—his face less wrinkled but equally genial, his brown hair merely tinged with gray. He bent his keen, dark eyes on Felicienne.

"This letter was brought in this morning, Madame," he said, presenting it with a bow, "and as I know how precious news is at this present state, I brought it round at once."

"My most sincere thanks, M. Barker," Felicienne said. "Though I am afraid you have gone out of your way to do this kindness. Would you have the courtesy to stay for tea?"

"You are most thoughtful, Madame—but I must be off," he bowed again. "With my brother Thaddaeus still on his Paris trip (though, Lord willing, he will arrive soon), my presence is of some use at the shop. Besides, Madame, I would leave you alone to peruse your letter. I pray that it bears good news—all that is coming from France has been dire enough of late. All ears are ringing with—" He cut himself short, as if he had been about to mention the massacres and then thought better of it. "God's benison on you all." With a final bow, he took his leave. A moment later they heard his horse's hooves crunching the gravel.

"A good and worthy man—so like his brother," Francis said.

Adele saw the curling writing on the cover of the packet--unmistakably her aunt's.

"Charles, would you please take Paulette out," Felicienne smiled. "We will tell you the tidings later." As the younger ones left the room, she slit the seal with a letter-opener that shook slightly. Then, spreading the foolscap on her lap, she read aloud,

5 September 1792
My sister Felicienne,
   I take up my pen with great distress—but we were always friends, Felicienne, and I have no one else to pour out the thoughts that wrack my brain and heart. I tried to speak to Jean, but he only quotes proverbs such as "Aux grands maux les grands remedes" [Desperate times call for desperate measures] and "On ne fait pas d'omelette sans casser des œufs [You can't make an omelet without breaking eggs]." As for Stephanie, I have long left off looking to her *for any sympathy. She and Gaston have quarreled sharply, I think; at least I suppose so because she is now flirting madly with another Brigand rascal, despite the fact that she is still betrothed. Leuren is incorrigible, and thick as thieves with Gaston. He is hardly at home nowadays, which is more bearable than his insolent presence and coarse talk. I feel sure that he was involved in the killings, but I am afraid to ask him and confirm my worst fears. Yes, it was murder; the mock trials were a complete farce. Oh—sister! Have pity on your little sister! Everything is calculated to wring my heart to the utmost—I am beside myself. But I am prattling*

on to put off the tale of horrors — I must apply myself to telling of these ghastly events.

We are under the knife of Robespierre and Marat; they are doing all they can to stir the people up and turn them against the National Assembly and the council of ministers. They have set up a star chamber, they have a little army which they bribe with what they found or stole from the Tuileries and elsewhere, or with what Danton gives them — he being the secret leader of this horde.

9 September. My friend Danton controls everything; Robespierre is his puppet. Marat holds his torch and his dagger: this wild tribune reigns — at the moment we are merely oppressed, but waiting for the time when we become his victims.

If you knew the awful details of the killing expeditions! Women...torn to pieces by these tigers, guts cut out and worn as ribbons, human flesh eaten dripping with blood!...

You know my enthusiasm for the Revolution: well, I am ashamed of it! Its reputation is tarnished by these scoundrels, it is becoming hideous! In a week from now...who knows what will have happened? It is degrading to stay here, but it is forbidden to leave Paris; we are being shut in so that we can have our throats cut at their convenience. Adieu: if it is too late for us, save the rest of France from the crimes of these madmen.[1]

I know nothing of the Du Chemins, save that arresting officers visited their house on the 29th and since then more than half of the prisoners have been killed. Our butler said he saw a youth among the heaps of the slain that looked like Tristan. Give Adele my condolences. Our old friend De la Noye is also murdered. And the pure Princess Lamballe! I will not ruin your sleep by describing the atrocities wreaked upon her body by those fiends.

Ah! Woe is me! I wish I had even a piece of your serenity, sister — I am sore vexed, and prey to a thousand horrors.

Adieu, your unhappy sister
Juliette

~*~*~

With new feelings, Jules traversed the streets as evening fell over grand, terrible Paris. Paris was no longer, as he'd viewed it in his misguided radicalism, a soaring, thriving place of progress. Neither would evenings in the streets be "hunting" expeditions for the thief anymore — Denis was dead.

Though he still had a mission to do good. Through the influence of patriot friends, he had been given a post as clerk in a village — this was his last night in Paris, he hoped. Not only did he aim, as a Christian, to finally support his mother, but he aspired to somehow be able to save some wretches from the Revolution's pitiless grasp.

Paris' hustle and bustle had resumed shortly after the four days of butchery, but it would never be the same. The elite's carriages were immured in stables now; only a brave few still went about on affairs or to quiet salons or dinners, but for the most part the brilliant, oft-passing carriages were no more. Gone were the gay *fetes* and balls of the aristocrats: the ten thousand still in the city made themselves as scarce as possible.

A half-grown urchin scampered by, calling out a raffish greeting to a friend. A bent old woman shrunk out of the way as a group of wild Brigands swaggered down the avenue. One was bragging to his companions of his part in the massacres, while they, in turn, spoke of what they'd done. The streets were more dangerous — and yes, that was possible. Now the most barbarous showed themselves boldly. Robbery, assault, murder....

Past the rowdies, Jules recognized the De Lobel's glowing abode. They were patriots, and in favor — for the present. Nearing, he paused, remembering old times. A party was going on — the *fetes* of the patriots had multiplied since the massacre. *How often I attended festive events there....*

The door opened, sending a gush of light, music, and laughter into the darkening street. Jules thought of the people he used to meet there — *Adele, Honore, Tristan....Was it only a year ago that I joined their venture to search for thieves? So many weary, fruitless night patrols....Then, Denis, my "friend," the thief!* His thoughts went to Tristan. *Did he and his father get safely away? The searches for aristocrats are so thorough — how could they have evaded them?...They could easily be in prison now...I've heard nothing from them....* He shuddered.

He envied not the swank patriots whose dark shapes he could see dancing and gossiping through the lighted windows. He knew their emptiness; the selfishness, disappointment and bitterness environing their lives; the sincere misled patriotism of some, who were led about on a ring by devilish leaders — he knew, because he once had fallen prey to similar snares. And he shivered — not because of the cold. *France is now the victim of such demons!*

His mind went to a verse he had read that morn:

Therefore will I send a fire upon Moab, and it shall devoure the palaces of Kerioth, and Moab shall die with tumult, with shouting, and with the sound of a trumpet.

France is dying that way; tumult, shouting.... he thought sadly. *Mayhap she will not utterly perish, but she is feeling the firstfruits of destruction....When will this all end? – and how?* Jules turned and made off down the street, deep in thought and prayer. Though darkness was over and around him, pierced by only a few bold stars, he had an inner peace of heart.

In contrast, Stephanie swirled, dazzling, in a blaze of candlelight.

And yet even as she waltzed through the press, her hand on a handsome youth's shoulder, his eyes looking boldly in her face, Stephanie felt a twinge of—was it regret? Surely it was only old memories. Her thoughts went back to her cousin Adele, of the many times they had met in this room, the parties they had attended. Perhaps it was because Stephanie had so eagerly accepted this particular dance, and Adele would have modestly refused. An image arose, almost clearer than life: Adele and Tristan at their betrothal. The pure joy in their eyes....

Suddenly, Stephanie felt a surge of conscience-pang. Deep down inside, she knew she should be faithful to her betrothed—though, to be sure, not many in Paris followed such a precept. Words came to her mind, burning words of bitterest truth, telling of the enchainment, rather than freedom, of her many flirtations:

> *Where will this end?*
> *Each draught of this forbidden joy – this joy*
> *Which yet is pain, is sadness, is despair –*
> *Inflames the thirst for more.*

Looking across the room, she saw Gaston's gray eyes upon her. It was flattering to think of how jealous he must be.... The murmured, ardent compliments of Alain, her present escort, sounded sweet to her ears....

Glancing coquettishly up into his green eyes, she threw her former thoughts to the wind. But there was disillusionment in her beautiful blue eyes—their sparkle was hard. She had chosen her path, though its pleasures did not truly satisfy. Yet still there floated back that wisp of remembrance....

The dance ending, Alain led Stephanie off the floor. She was clinging to his arm and laughing kittenishly up into his face when she became aware of Gaston, standing very near.

"I shall relieve you, Citizen," Gaston said coldly, his eyes fixed masterfully upon Alain.

Stephanie felt Alain stiffen. Murmuring farewell, he disappeared into the crowd.

Nothing could have chilled Stephanie more. *Alain is so bold and spirited!* She could hardly believe her eyes—then cold realization dawned. *Was it not Gaston who attempted to arrest my cousins, and has dragged many others to gaol? He's been wielding such leverage since the massacres....And his boastings of midnight meetings with Robespierre and others! Even Father isn't in with them like that....That is why Alain wouldn't stand up to him, and gave me up without protest! Gaston is a power! If one is not in the "inner circle," an accusation from a "favorite" will get one arrested—and execution is an easy step away....* She shuddered.

"Cold, Stephanie?" Gaston queried drily. "I have not known you so silent, darling."

Stephanie rallied with her best smile. "Perhaps it is because your company is so enchanting, Gaston."

"You know, dearest, you must speak to your father about arranging our marriage. I have waited long, *chérie.*" His eyes were fixed on hers with passionate clarity, but she doubted him now.

She had always known that her family was of a higher station—more landed, *more moneyed*—than Gaston's; but never, during those enraptured months, had she given it a second thought. But now she wondered... *Is <u>that</u> why he is so keen on marrying me? But now, what can I do to stop it, without bringing danger to myself?*

"It is not winter yet; you know that was the time mentioned," she answered.

"Why wait, my little Stephanie?" he asked. "I grow impatient to have you as my own."

Stephanie felt a chill with Gaston's eyes upon her. *So this is the game I have to play,* she thought. *Well, I'm not exactly unskilled when it comes to intrigue....*

Following the "freedom" of her emotions had led to bondage. More of a slave than ever, Stephanie embarked upon perilous toadying to those in power—*no matter what* her feelings. It was a world partly of her own making—she had unthinkingly forged some of the fetters, and countenanced the iron bars of the government which now beset her round...

Yet despite her awakened suspicion of Gaston, and the new dread filling her soul, her vanity was tickled by the idea of being married to a man of such influence. *And he is so handsome, too—I'll marry him, but 'twill be utterly to my advantage,* she thought. *With that new prominence, mayhap I too will be a power....*

She did not know that in two short years Gaston would, as a roving agent for Robespierre's Committee of Public Safety, personally send two hundred people to the guillotine.

~*~*~

Drawing a shawl about the shoulders of her long white dress, Adele stepped out of the house. Its deep rosy hues set off the classical beauty of her dark lips, hazel eyes, and wealth of brown ringlets. But there was a beauty beyond mere outward attractiveness on her face—that which comes from "charity out of a pure heart,...a good conscience, and faith unfeigned."

She traversed the richly-scented garden with Berthe and Olivie; it was time for their usual stroll. Berthe opened the little back-garden gate, and Adele's favorite walking-path wound ahead through trees, finally cresting a high green forested hill called Shuttershill.

...on top of [Shuttershill] you see a vast prospect....some lands clothed with trees, others with grass and flowers, gardens, orchards, with all sorts of herbage and tillage, with severall little towns all by the river, Erith, Leigh, Woolwich etc., quite up to London, Greenwich, Deptford, Black Wall, the Thames twisting and turning it self up and down bearing severall vessells and men of warre on it.

Berthe and Olivie strolled on ahead, but Adele soon fell behind. Since her aunt's letter, she had needed time to grieve. She had so hoped that somehow M. du Chemin and Tristan would have escaped Paris before the arrests on the 29th. She had tried to keep from thinking that her betrothed might have been killed in the massacres.... But now her aunt's letter had destroyed all such wishful thinking. Things were so much worse than she had imagined. M. du Chemin had been a staunch Royalist, and those cruel judges and blood-intoxicated populace would not show pity to either him or his son...

They had reached the top of the hill. Berthe and Olivie had gone on to Severndroog Castle, a large folly erected eight years before by Lady James of Eltham in honor of her gallant husband Sir William James.

Resting her hands on a stone wall beside the path, Adele gazed at the panorama spread before her. It was beautiful indeed—but her heart was miles away.

Through arch and court the sweet wind wandering goes;
Round each high tower the rooks in airy flight
Circle and wheel, all bathed in amber light;
Low at my feet the winding river flows;
Valley and town, entranced in deep repose...

Recalling the bitter hopelessness of her aunt's letter, she remembered with deep gratefulness how God used Grandpapa de Duret and the Du Chemins to bring herself and her family to the Lord. *What would I do without Him? How could I bear this wrenching uncertainty, this horrific news?* she wondered. *Oh, Lord, You are my Rock and my fortress! I fly to You in this time of great trial!*

As she thought of Tristan, tears blurred the landscape. *He would fight to the last for his father — but one man can do naught against a mob of bloodthirsty killers!...He died nobly....* While the thought brought pride, it also brought heartrending pain. "Oh, Lord—" she began, then her voice was lost in overwhelming emotion.

She drew forth a velvet sachet from a ribbon round her neck, loosening the drawstring. The dried rose's wafted scent evoked indelible memories, both sweet and heart-breaking. Blazoned into her memory were Tristan's words as he gave her that rose: "May I give it to you now, Adele, in remembrance of old times and as a token for the future?"

In remembrance of the past, yes, Adele's heart cried, *but there shall never be future memories together!* Pulling out a handkerchief, more of his parting words came to mind: "Whatever happens, know that the Lord works in all things for good. If I die — be consoled that I died serving Him."

Adele stood motionless, her heart overflowing with grief. At last, she whispered, "Oh, Lord, I gave him to You—I give him to You again. If he is dead, You—You know best; You have taken him to Yourself. But—O Lord!—if he is alive, spare him, if it be Your will!" She remained motionless, her whole soul and body praying with wholehearted intensity, her unseeing eyes turned toward the valley spread below.

There was a step on the gravel path, but Adele did not turn round; Berthe and Olivie must be coming back. She hoped they would pass by.

Then an unforgettable voice spoke. It said one word, but that word was richer than all the treasure-houses in the world.

"*Adele.*"

Adele turned, and the world faded into nothingness as she gazed into her beloved's eyes.

543

The Lord had answered her prayer—and all was very good.

For as a young man marrieth a virgin, so shall thy sons marry thee:
and as the bridegroom rejoiceth over the bride, so shall thy God rejoice over thee.

THE END

* * *

Historical Epilogue

The September massacres were only the beginning. The Terror, which would claim 30,000 to 40,000 victims (many of them the very ones who started it), was still to come. Of that period a moderate deputy wrote:

"The Terror began on 31 May 1793 and ended on 9 Thermidor, 27 July 1794. Of that terrible period we should say, as the Chancellor L'Hospital said of the Saint Bartholomew's Day massacre: 'Excidat illa dies' [Let that day be forever erased].

In a despotic state the leader, the courtiers, certain classes and certain individuals at least, are safe from the terror they inspire. They are the gods who launch the thunderbolts without fear of being struck down by them. In France under the reign of the Terror no one was spared, it hung above every head and struck impartially, arbitrary and swift as the blade of Death. The Convention as well as the people supplied their share of its victims.

Nothing could have been less systematic than the Terror: its development, despite its rapidity, was only gradual; people were drawn into it little by little, and followed it without knowing where they were going; they went on advancing because they dared not turn back, and there was no visible way out....the people...sought in [their] own midst obscure victims to nourish the Terror, just as slaves, who, having broken their chains and wiped out their tyrants and their liberators, then massacre one another, drunk with blood and blinded by their own victories."
— memoir of Thibaudeau

Acknowledgements

* * *

What is a book? A (hopefully inspired) collection of scenes, guided by an author. What influences an author and their unique "take" on life? Only God fully knows. Here are a few of the influences I am grateful for:

My first thanks go to my Lord and Savior, Jesus Christ. Without Him, I would be in as hopeless an eternal condition as the most ungodly aristocrat or murderous sans-culotte.

Many thanks to my dear Mom, who edited and edited and re-edited, endured my questions and long monologues, motivated me, and gave such helpful advice…

And to my Dad and my siblings, who let me use the computer for hours on end, supported me, and unconsciously modeled many of the good qualities which found their way into this book.

Karen Spangler offered inspiration and tireless, lucid editing (a task not for the faint-hearted!). Many thanks also to Melissa Merritt! :)

I am also grateful for all the original source material and books that assisted my research. In particular, I want to mention *The French Revolution: A History*, by Thomas Carlyle; *The Days of the French Revolution*, by Christopher Hibbert; and *Voices of the French Revolution*, edited by Richard Cobb and Colin Jones.

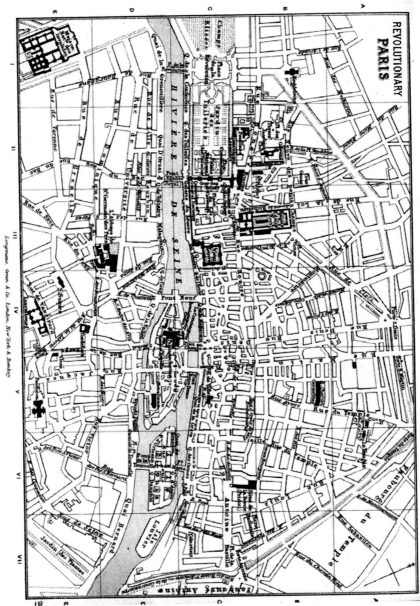

A CONTEMPORARY MAP OF PARIS

References and Footnotes

BOOK THE FIRST

The Storm Gathers Strength

Chapter 1
"Storming her world with sorrow's wind…" – Shakespeare, "A Lover's Complaint"
Chapter 2
"Ask what is human life…" – Cowper
1. This story, and the one about the Huguenot baby, are true.
"witching twilight…" – Ianthe
Chapter 3
"My grace is sufficient for thee…" – II Cor. 12:9, Geneva Bible
"Now the bright morning Star,…" – Milton
"She was not fair…" – Longfellow, "Hyperion"
Chapter 4
1. This is an actual pamphlet from 1789
Chapter 6
"Because that when they knewe God…" – Romans 1:21,22, Geneva
Chapter 8
"thunders of applause for every sentiment…" – Carlyle, "The French Revolution"
Chapter 9
"How blest the man who keeps…" Psalm 1, Geneva Psalter
1. this scene, and that answer, actually took place.
Chapter 10
"O fools (said I) thus to prefer dark night…" – Henry Vaughan, 1621-1695

BOOK THE SECOND

Explosion

Chapter 1
1. Desmoulins' words are factual
"A Psalme of David. The Lord is my light…" selections from Psalm 27, Geneva Bible
Chapter 2
"Thou shalt not follow a multitude to do evil…" – Exodus 23:2a
Chapter 3
"King Marsile layed at Sarrague…" – The Song of Roland, from the 12th century (translated by Charles Kenneth Scott-Moncrieff)
Chapter 4
1. But for changed names, this letter is real.
2. This note is real.
3. This letter is real
Chapter 6
"O Richard! O my king!…" – from "Richard the Lion-Hearted," an opera by Andre-Ernest-Modeste Gretry
Chapter 8
"Long live Henry IV…" – called "Henri Quatre," composed anonymously around 1590
Chapter 10
"Ah ! ça ira, ça ira, ça ira…" – first heard in May 1790. Authorship unknown.
Chapter 11

1. *the common people were calling themselves "sans-culottes," meaning "without knee-breeches," because they wore full-length pants as opposed to the knee-breeches of the aristocrats*
Chapter 12
"From the high mount of God, whence light..." – John Milton, "Paradise Lost," Book V
"Farewell and adieu to you, Spanish Ladies..." – English sea chanty, authorship unknown
1. *the words of Abbe Maury and the duel challenge scene are factual*
Chapter 14
1. *This letter is real*
"If inward griefs were written upon the brow..." – Metastisio, "Giuseppi Riconsciuto"
Chapter 15
"Doe right to the poore and fatherlesse:..." – Psalms 82:3-4
Chapter 17
"...in the very May-morn of his youth..." – Shakespeare, "Henry V"
"God shall wipe away all tears from their eyes..." – Revelation 21:4, 22:3-5
"Verily I say unto thee, To day shalt thou be with me in paradise." – Luke 23:43
"So when this corruptible hath put on incorruption..." – I Cor. 15:54-57

BOOK THE THIRD
Lost Gambles
Chapter 1
1. *this scene is reported as true in Carlyle's masterful book on the French Revolution*
Chapter 2
"...and the Law is once more as Mirabeau..." – Carlyle, "The French Revolution," p. 356
Chapter 4
"Let no man be bold enough to say..." – Aaron Hill, "Athelwold"
Chapter 5
"O Jerusalem, Jerusalem, thou that killest the prophets..." – Matthew 23:37-38
Chapter 6
"The Lorde is my shepherd..." – Psalm 23, Geneva Bible
"An honest man, close-buttoned to the chin..." – Cowper
Chapter 7
"whilst twilight's curtain, spreading far..." – MacDonald Clarke, "Death in Disguise"
"For He satisfieth the longing soule..." – Ps. 107:9
Chapter 8
"the rolling ocean rocked with storms," – Caleb Winchester
Chapter 9
"Sweet stream, that winds through yonder glade..." – Cowper
1. *Gaston, and this speech, are based on a true 16-year-old youth, Marc-Antoine Jullien. In 1793, Robespierre made Marc-Antoine a roving agent for the Committee of Public Safety, and he reveled in the work of crushing moderates who rose against the Revolution, personally overseeing the guillotining of 200 people.*
"For I knowe what I have devised for you..." – Jeremiah 29:11, Geneva Bible
Chapter 10
"Honour thy father & mother..." – Eph, 6:2,3
"The eye that mocketh his father..." – Pr. 30:17
"the majesty/ That from a man's soul..." – William Morris
"...Thou hast holden me by my right hand..." – Psalm 73:23b-26
"In wayward passions lost and vain pursuits." – Thomson, "The Seasons: Summer"
"But seeke ye first the kingdome of God..." – Matthew 6:33
Chapter 11
"To the Nuptial Bow'r..." – Milton, "Paradise Lost," Book VIII

1. this letter is real

BOOK THE FOURTH
Death Struggles
Chapter 1
"Arise, children of the Fatherland..." – *"La Marseillaise," written and composed in 1792 by Claude Joseph Rouget de Lisle*

"Mob law is the most forcible expression..." – *Timothy Thomas Fortune*

"The same metal that rang storm..." – *Carlyle, "The French Revolution," p. 488*
Chapter 2
"How lovely are the portals of the night..." – *Thomas Cole, "Twilight"*
Chapter 5
"Blessed be God, even the Father of our Lord Jesus..." – *Cor. 1:3-4, Geneva*

"No man can come to Mee, except the Father..." – *John 6:44*

"And He stretched forth His hand..." – *Matthew 12:49-50, Geneva*

"And one of the evill doers, which were*..."* – *Luke 23:39-43, Geneva*
Chapter 6
1. A true account of the death of a brave unknown Swiss Guardsman

"Broken at last – weaponless; cast to earth;..." – *Ianthe*

"Brave Citizens, you are extirpating..." quoted by Carlyle, "The French Revolution"

2. The circular & Billaud's words are factual
Chapter 7
"In darkling space down dropt the red sun..." – *Julia C. Dorr, 1825-1913*
Chapter 8
"Blessed be the Lorde my strength..." – *Psalm 144:1-2, Geneva*

"...workers employed in preserving the salubrity of the air..." – *Carlyle, "The French Revolution," p. 540*

"Once more, farewell!..." – *Addison, "Cato"*
Chapter 9
"When Tommy has a mind to ride..." – *Goldsmith, "Tommy Trip's History of Beasts and Birds," a children's book of the period*

1. The four paragraphs above this symbol are taken verbatim from a letter written by Madame Roland. She, like Juliette, supported the Revolution until the Sept. Massacres opened her eyes.

"Therefore will I send a fire upon Moab..." – *Amos 2:2*

"Where will this end?..." – *Laughton Osborn, "The Cid of Seville"*

"...on top of [Shuttershill] you see a vast prospect..." – *Celia Fiennes, diary entry, 1697*

"Through arch and court the sweet wind wandering goes..." – *Julia C. Dorr*

"For as a young man marrieth a virgin..." – *Isaiah 62:5*

Note: "Ianthe" is a penname of Elisha Wahlquist

CPSIA information can be obtained
at www.ICGtesting.com
Printed in the USA
FSOW02n1719160116
15576FS